PENGUIN BOOKS

Damage

Born to two hippies in a small town in Maine, Caitlin Wahrer left the state for college but returned to attend law school and practise law, where she worked on cases involving some of the broad issues she writes about in *Damage*. She lives in southern Maine with her husband.

Damage is her debut novel.

532 887 85 2

Damage

CAITLIN WAHRER

Penguin
Random House
UK

PENGUIN BOOKS

UK | USA | Canada | Ireland | Australia
India | New Zealand | South Africa

Penguin Books is part of the Penguin Random House group of companies
whose addresses can be found at global.penguinrandomhouse.com

Penguin
Random House
UK

First published in the US by Pamela Dorman Books/Viking 2021
First published in the UK by Michael Joseph 2021
Published in Penguin Books 2022
001

Text design by Cassandra Garruzzo
Printed and bound in Great Britain by Clays Ltd, Elcograf S.p.A.

The authorized representative in the EEA is Penguin Random House Ireland,
Morrison Chambers, 32 Nassau Street, Dublin D02 YH68

A CIP catalogue record for this book is available from the British Library

ISBN: 978–1–405–94601–8

www.greenpenguin.co.uk

MIX
Paper from
responsible sources
FSC® C018179

Penguin Random House is committed to a
sustainable future for our business, our readers
and our planet. This book is made from Forest
Stewardship Council® certified paper.

For Ben

I.

MONSTERS

—⊳

I have known monsters and I have known men.
I have stood in their long shadows, propped
them up with my own two hands, reached
for their inscrutable faces in the dark. They
are harder to set apart than you know.
Than you will ever know.

CLAIRE C. HOLLAND, *I Am Not Your Final Girl*

1

The dying detective's house was a tall, dark blue thing with chipping trim and shutters. It loomed against the bright sky, set back from the snowbank lining the street. The house was dusted with last night's powder, but the black *23* tacked above the front door was brushed clean. There was room in the narrow driveway, but she parked on the street.

Julia Hall shifted in her seat to expose the pocket of her heavy winter coat. She crammed her hand deep inside until her fingers scraped the edges of the folded paper. As she pulled the note free, she willed it to say anything but the address she'd located—anything that would let her drive on, maybe never to find the house. There, on the crumpled sheet, she'd written *23 Maple Drive, Cape Elizabeth*, and here it was.

"Just go," she said aloud, then looked sideways at the house. Windows abutted the front door, and each appeared empty with the blinds drawn. At least he hadn't seen her talking to herself, then.

The wind blew the door from Julia's hand as she climbed out of her SUV. This winter had been bitterly cold. As she aged she found the winter a little less pleasant to weather each year. She pulled her hat tighter over her ears, then turned back to the car. Without thinking, she slammed

3

the door hard. She winced as the sound rocked down the neighborhood street. She hadn't done that in years—she was thinking of her old Subaru, the one that demanded a rougher touch. The one she'd had three years ago, back when she had occasion to talk to the man waiting for her inside that house.

In spite of last night's flurry, the front walk was freshly shoveled. Had he done that for her? The path and steps to the porch were layered in salt, and she focused on the sound as she crunched her way up to his door. She shook out her hands and rang the bell. Before the chime had subsided inside, the door swung open.

"Julia," said the figure in the doorway. "How are you, dear?"

She was certainly better than he was, wasn't she? Because the man standing before her was Detective Rice, or at least the husk of him. His once towering frame seemed to have caved in on itself like a rotting flower stem. His face was sallow, and he had deep bags under his eyes. A Red Sox cap pushed down on his ears, obscuring what appeared to be a completely bald skull.

"I'm good, Detective Rice. I'm good."

They shook hands awkwardly, as he had leaned in as though to hug her.

"Well, would you like to come in?"

Every day since you called me, I've thrown up my breakfast was what she wanted to say. Instead, she smiled and lied. "Yes, of course."

"And please, you can just call me John," he said as he wobbled backward to make room for her to step inside. He seemed to have aged ten years in the last three, maybe from the cancer. Not that she was doing much better. For most of her life, Julia had looked young for her age. Somewhere in the past few years, that stopped. She looked thirty-nine now.

As Julia pulled off her boots, she surveyed Detective Rice's mudroom, a little voice in her head pointing out how strange it was to be in *Detective Rice's mudroom*. The bench she sat on was sturdy, practical. A few

4

pairs each of work boots and dress shoes butted up against the base. The bench was flanked by a bucket of salt on her right, and a wet shovel leaned against the wall. To her left was the only curious feature: a petite shelf crammed with gardening books. She never would have guessed him to be a gardener when she met him all that time ago. It suggested an earthiness that she had missed.

"I don't know if I can," she said as she stood. "I think you'll always be 'Detective Rice' to me."

He grinned at her and shrugged.

She followed him down a narrow hallway lined with family photos and religious artifacts: there were various portraits of a younger Detective Rice and his deceased wife, Julia assumed, and three children; a crucifix and a dried palm; a picture of a grandchild, probably, next to a picture of Jesus.

Detective Rice said something muffled as he led her down the hallway. "What?"

He turned and faced her over his shoulder. "Was just saying you got a new car."

"Oh, yeah." She pointed her thumb behind her. "Guess I've upgraded since I last saw you."

She studied the change in his height. He was still a tall man, she thought as she followed him, but his illness had stolen several inches.

"I was thinking we'd sit in here."

He motioned to the first room they came upon. It was decidedly a *sitting room*: something that Julia only ever saw in the homes of older people. Like others she had seen, Detective Rice's had a buttoned-up air to it, despite its obvious purpose for hosting company. The room was staged around two big recliners with a small table between them.

Detective Rice motioned for Julia to sit in the chair on the right as he continued down the hallway.

She waited a few seconds, then poked her head out into the hall.

5

Another doorway on the right. Kitchen at the end. She listened but heard nothing.

She turned back into the sitting room. *Deep breath*, she thought, and inhaled.

She moved toward the picture window across the room. It looked out on Maple Drive and a big house across the street. A steady chill radiated from the pane, and Julia touched a trembling finger to the glass. There were few things as bleak as Maine in February.

The cold months were hard; always had been. Every year, Julia was faced with the reality of Maine's autumn and winter, neither of which ever matched the nostalgia-tinged versions that lived in her head. The snow usually started in December, lasted through April. And after *that* winter—after the winter she last laid eyes on Detective Rice—winters carried some kind of existential melancholy that had to be shoveled away with the snow.

"Endless, isn't it?"

She started when she heard his voice behind her.

He was in the doorway again, smiling at her. In his hands he held two mugs.

He was just getting coffee. She breathed out, probably with obvious relief.

He motioned to the chair again, and this time she sat. She accepted a mug and watched him settle into his own seat. The scent that met her nostrils was not coffee, in fact, but tea. She tasted it and found it heavily sweetened. That was a surprise.

"How are your children?" Detective Rice asked as he sipped at his drink.

"They're good, thanks."

"How old are they now?"

"Uh, ten and eight."

"You'll never be ready for them to grow up."

6

There was something about him that made it easy to forget he had children of his own. Grown children; grandchildren, judging by the pictures in the hallway. It wasn't his personality that made her forget—it was his profession. There was something about him being *a detective* that made her forget that he existed outside of that.

Julia nodded and waited for him to ask her how Tony was.

"I suppose you were surprised to hear from me last week."

That answers that, she thought. Something about his passing over her husband felt like a personal slight, especially given everything that had happened, and she felt herself suppressing a frown.

She *had* been surprised on Thursday, when she picked up her cell at the end of a long morning in court to find a single voice mail waiting for her. It was the mark of an easy day if she only had one missed call by noon. She shouted goodbye to the marshal at the door and pressed Play as she strode from the courthouse. The voice that had croaked out of her phone halted her midstep; it was slow but unmistakable. A voice she had come to dread. Years ago she had worked herself into a state of near panic any time the phone rang or her voice mail blinked, for fear that his voice would be on the other end.

"I was surprised to hear from you," Julia said. "And very sorry to hear that you were sick, too." She leaned toward him slightly, realizing she hadn't mentioned it since they spoke on the phone last week and he asked her to come to his home.

"What's your . . . prognosis?" There was no comfortable word, not that she could think of.

"Well, it's not too hot," he said in a voice like he was discussing the chance of another flurry. "My doc thinks my 'quality of life' is going to get pretty bad over the next couple months, and it might all go pretty quick after that."

Julia could hear the quotes around "quality of life," and she pictured Detective Rice sitting in his doctor's office in a dressing gown, saying,

"'Quality of life'? What the fuck does that mean? Just tell me when I'm gonna die."

She smiled at him warmly. "I'm glad to see that you're still able to be at home."

"Oh, well, we'll see."

They each took a sip.

"Well," he said, and laughed lightly. He shrugged.

Was he nervous?

"I appreciate you coming up," he said. "Like I said, I wanted to talk to you before, well . . ." He shrugged at himself.

"While you still have that 'quality of life.'"

Detective Rice laughed, let out a wheezing cough, and reached behind his chair. There was the squeaking sound of an ungreased wheel, and he pulled a portable oxygen tank around to his side. He held the mask up to his face and breathed, holding up a *One minute* finger to her.

Jesus Christ, I better not make him laugh again.

He began to put the mask away.

"Why don't you keep that on," Julia said. "I really don't—"

"No," Detective Rice said firmly. "Thank you, but no."

The mask in its place on the tank, Detective Rice sat himself back up. The wind whistled at the window. "I wasn't sure you'd come, after everything. But I needed to talk to you. Well, to say some things to you. And I think you have some things to say to me, too."

Julia had to push herself to hold his gaze. His eyes were watery pink, and hers wanted nothing to do with them.

"I really wasn't sure you'd come," he said again. "But you always were too nice to say no to anyone."

The sick ache in her stomach intensified. What was she supposed to say to that?

He didn't expect a response, it seemed, because he spoke again. "So. Back to the beginning?"

2

The first time John Rice saw Julia Hall, she was standing in her kitchen, barefoot, washing a pile of dishes in the sink.

Rice was about twenty hours into the investigation at the time. Until that moment, it had been twenty hours of ugliness. Nothing but the kind of evil only man knows how to execute.

He'd seen the victim, a young man named Nick Hall, at the hospital the night before. He hesitated to think of him as a man at all. Nick was twenty years old, yes, but he should have been on the last legs of his boyhood. Instead, there was a look in his eye like he'd never feel young again.

Rice didn't want to overwhelm Nick by interviewing him that first night, when he'd already given statements to a nurse and an officer. Rice just wanted to introduce himself as the lead detective on Nick's case and ask him to write out a statement. It always felt a little callous to ask victims to write it out, ask them to relive the crime so soon. It was for the best, though, for everyone. Made Rice's case stronger; made the victim's memory better. Not to mention, the beginning of the case was usually the easy part. Most of the time, the victim hadn't grasped what had happened yet. The mind was in shock, the body in survival mode, and there was little to no affect. Nick had been like this: surprised, a bit confused, but mostly flat. Better for him to relive it now.

And he had. Before coming over to the house, Rice had picked up Nick's two-page statement at the hospital. Nick's older brother, Tony, was there again. He'd been there the night before, too, and now he had the baggy undereyes of someone who'd tried to sleep in a hospital chair. Tony stepped out of the room and handed Rice the statement. Told him Nick was sleeping. Rice said he'd come back later.

Rice found Tony Hall's house without trouble. It was a pretty little thing in the rolling outskirts of Orange, unassuming after a drive past some of the other houses in town. Rice's sister-in-law lived in Orange, too, but closer to the town center. Like many towns in southern Maine, probably like many towns everywhere, it was like two different places entirely depending on where you stood. Town center was where the wealthier inhabitants of Orange collected, either crammed into cul-de-sacs in large, cookie-cutter houses (Rice's sister-in-law included), or in Maine's version of mini-mansions on sizable plots of land (these were the very, *very* wealthy). The greater part of Orange, though, was farmland. Little of it was active. The Hall address was there, two plots down from a giant, ramshackle place overrun with geese, complete with a barn the earth seemed to be taking back. The Hall house, by comparison, was small, old but well-kept, and charming, at least what he could see from the road. The driveway was full, so he parked on the street.

Rice climbed the steps of the open porch to reach the front door. He could hear voices talking over the doorbell, then the solid inner door swung open and Rice faced a short, spry-looking woman with salt-and-pepper hair. She looked his own age, late fifties, maybe.

She opened the outer door and said, "Hello?"

Rice introduced himself, and she immediately nodded soberly and said that her son, Tony, was still at the hospital with his brother.

"I'm not Nick's mom," she said. "Just Tony's."

"Yes," Rice said. "Tony explained this morning. I just came from the hospital. I'm actually here to see Julia, if she's available."

Even three steps inside, the house held certain markers of wealth not enjoyed by many of the families Rice encountered on the job. The floors were gleaming hardwood running down to tiles in the kitchen, and the hall was framed in a rich dark trim. The space immediately evoked a feeling of safety and an impression that this was a deeply *functional* family. As the thought revealed itself, Rice felt heat on his ears. He realized quickly he'd made certain assumptions about what the Hall family would be like, based on little information. The address in farm country, the brothers with different mothers. The total absence of Nick's parents at the hospital at a time like this. The consequence of the mandatory "sensitivity training" the station had done back in the spring was not that his biases disappeared—it was simply that he noticed them more often and felt like an asshole for it.

The short hallway opened into the kitchen, where a younger woman stood at the sink. The October sunlight spilled in through a window just in front of her, making her white blouse glow and illuminating hair that should have been just brown but seemed to contain strands of yellow and red in the light. She looked almost ethereal, except that she was frowning and rinsing a dish.

"Sorry," she said. "Sorry, I'm just . . ." She turned off the faucet and set a glass casserole dish on the crowded drying rack. "There. I heard you come in, but I just *had* to finish that."

She grabbed a dish towel off the stove and wiped her hands quickly before offering one to the detective. Her hand was damp and warm, and she said, "I'm Julia."

"John Rice," he answered. "Detective with the Salisbury Police Department."

There was a muffled thud upstairs, like feet hitting the ground.

"Shall I finish the dishes or go upstairs?" Tony's mother asked from the hallway.

"Yeah, if you could keep them distracted while we talk," Julia said.

"On it."

"Thanks, Cynthia," Julia called toward the hallway as her mother-in-law ascended the stairs.

"The kids are happy to have their gram over," Julia said as she pointed at the ceiling. "They don't really understand what's going on."

Julia looked young, so Rice guessed the kids were, too. "How old are they?"

"Chloe's seven and Sebastian's five. We told them their uncle is sick so their dad will be busy taking care of him, but . . ." She shrugged. Now, talking about her children, Julia looked bewildered. "They're too young to understand, and I think that's for the best."

"Sure is," Rice said.

"How can I help?" Julia asked as she passed Rice a mug of coffee in the cool morning air on the porch.

Rice had suggested they speak outside, out of the children's earshot, and Julia agreed. The two settled into side-by-side Adirondack chairs padded with nautical-looking cushions, and Rice set his mug down on the small table between them. The smell of his steaming coffee mingled with the citronella candle on the table. Acid on acid.

"Well," he said, "Nick was still asleep when I went over this morning, and your husband looked like he hadn't slept at all, so I thought I'd give them a couple more hours' breathing room before I put 'em through the wringer again. Tony said you could give me a family history for my notes."

Her face washed with relief. "Oh, *that* I can do."

Rice pulled a small pad and pen from his windbreaker. He would have to get into what she knew about Nick, but he'd ease her in first.

"Do you care where I start?" Julia asked.

He shook his head. He was glad for the excuse to stare at her while she spoke. Meeting Tony, who was undeniably handsome, Rice had expected an equally striking wife. And Julia Hall was pretty, yes, but there was a plainness to her that was hard to name, now that she'd moved out of the morning light. Her face was round and without significant definition; as she spoke, her features were the same from all angles. It gave her an air of straightforward honesty—what you saw was what you got. It also made her look younger than she likely was. Rice might have guessed she was thirty were it not for the fine wrinkles she already bore: crow's-feet at her eyes and lines hugging the sides of her mouth. This woman was a smiler and a laugher.

"So Tony's parents are Cynthia"—Julia pointed backward at the house, indicating the woman inside—"and Ron. They were married for a while before they had Tony. Ron is—" She paused. "Ron had a really tough upbringing himself and wasn't the steadiest dad. Ron and Cynthia were together until Tony turned seven."

She was choosing her words like a politician, or maybe a lawyer. Either job would be ugly on her.

"Ron wasn't, like, abusive or anything. Or maybe, well . . ." She paused again.

Rice held up his pen at eye level. "How about I put this down for a minute and you relax about Ron?"

Julia laughed and brought her hand to her face as if to hide behind it.

"Just a little background on the family dynamic can be helpful." He didn't always make a point to ask about a victim's family but regularly enough. More often in a case like this, where the victim's life would be turned inside out by the defense, looking for blameworthy material.

"I get it," Julia said. "I've worked with just about every family dynamic possible."

"What do you do?"

"I work in policy now, but I used to be a defense attorney—all juvenile and criminal cases."

Rice shifted to pull his right leg over his left. "Then you *do* understand."

She nodded. "And honestly, Ron would fit right in with maybe the middle of the pack, you know? He's an alcoholic—he has been Tony's whole life—and it was easier for Ron to mostly just fade out of the picture after he and Cynthia separated. Cynthia is so warm and loving; Tony got really lucky there. Nick didn't get so lucky with his mom."

"So Nick's side of this."

"Right," she said. "So Ron is their dad, and Tony was seventeen when Nick was born, so he was, like, maybe fifteen or sixteen when Ron and Jeannie got together."

"So what's Jeannie's deal?"

"She's an addict, too, and she gets a little . . ." Julia waved her hand over her head. The word *manic* came to Rice's mind.

"Do they know what happened?"

Julia shook her head. "They don't even know he's there. He doesn't want to tell them."

Her voice faded out, and she shrugged. Her face sank into that frown Rice saw all the time when people tried to hold back their tears in front of him.

"He's gonna be fine, Julia. It'll take a while, but Nick will be fine." Rice pulled a packet of tissues from his pocket.

"Nick is just awesome," she said as she accepted a tissue. "Tony loves him so much. Honestly, he made Tony the man he is, you know? Who knows what he would have been like if he hadn't had that little baby."

"What do you mean?"

14

Julia shook her head. "Cynthia says Nick being born softened him. When he was a teenager he was kind of a macho tough guy, and *so* angry at Ron, and kind of the world I think. And you've seen what he looks like, he has *handsome jerk* written all over him."

Rice snorted and concurred. Not only was Tony Hall fit, but he had magazine looks. The kind of face that made you dislike him, just for having what you didn't. Rice wondered what Julia would have thought of him when he was her husband's age. Rice had mild acne scarring on his cheeks that persisted to this day, but when he was younger the pockmarks made him look tough. That's what his wife had told him, at least.

"But Nick just melted his heart," Julia said, dabbing the tissue at her eyes. "Tony grew up to be warm and emotional and a good communicator, which is probably super cliché to say about your husband." She laughed. "But whatever, I know I'm lucky. And I know I have Cynthia to thank for some of that, but I really think it was mostly because of Nick. You probably won't ever meet the real Nick. He's funny, wickedly funny, and charming and just, like, sincere. But now, I don't know."

Behind them, Rice heard the kids come bouncing down the staircase he'd seen inside the house. Seconds later, he heard Tony's mother trailing behind them. The noise faded down the hall and into the kitchen.

Rice's hand returned the tissues to his pocket and reappeared with a small, silver tape recorder. "I know this is hard," he said, "but I need to ask you some questions about yesterday."

"Okay," Julia said with an exhale. "Nick didn't call us until after dinner."

3

That Saturday evening had been ordinary. Tony and Julia had been sitting on the front porch, watching the sky go pink. Their neighbors had spread a golden blanket of hay over the field across the street, and the view from the porch was like an oil painting. And then the phone rang.

As Tony sat in the waiting room, he tried to remember the caller's specific words. She said her name, Dr. Lamba, maybe. She was calling from York County Medical Center.

At that point, his first thought was of his father. *He's finally killed himself driving drunk*, Tony thought. *Please, please say he didn't hurt anyone else.* But the doctor wasn't calling about Ron. She was calling about Nick.

"Your brother's been hurt," she'd said on the phone. That was as specific as she had been.

Tony had asked if it was a car accident.

"No," she'd said. "Can you come see him now?"

Tony had gotten to him as fast as he could—he'd rushed out of the house, sped down the highway, jogged through the parking lot, only to be halted in the lobby. The energy that had pounded through him earlier was still trapped inside him, buzzing, buzzing.

He pulled his phone out of his pocket. Texted Julia,

ETA?

She was at home with the kids, waiting on his mother. He would feel better when she got here, he told himself. Or once they let him back to see Nick. But *would* he feel better then?

"Your brother has been hurt." The strange words had played over and over in his head as he sped to the hospital. Vague, yet grave. The doctor had given him nothing, besides that it wasn't a car accident. What, then? Alcohol poisoning? A bar fight? Neither sounded like Nick, but things could get a little wild in college. Oh, Jesus, not a school shooting. He would have heard something on the radio on his drive. Still, there in the waiting room, he pulled out his phone and opened the browser. "University of Maine Salisbury news." Nothing. "Salisbury Maine news." Nothing.

What else had the doctor said on the phone? Something about Nick's age. She'd asked how old he was. When Tony said Nick was twenty, she said something about him having a fake ID on him, so she'd wanted to be sure. Said Nick didn't want her to call his parents, and she wouldn't have to. He only wanted Tony.

"Mr. Hall?" An older woman in a white coat stood in the doorway. He launched from his seat and met her with a handshake. She said she was Dr. Lamba from the phone, her voice low and confident. He was relieved to detect no message of condolences in her kind, dark brown eyes. Nick could be fine.

Tony followed Dr. Lamba down a long hallway as she explained that Nick had come in earlier that day, late morning.

"And as I said on the phone, he only wanted us to call you."

As she talked, Tony found himself fixated on the scrunchy in her silver hair. It was velvety black and sat at the nape of her neck. They were approaching a new set of double doors. Above them read BEHAVIORAL HEALTH UNIT.

"Wait." Tony's eyes hung on the letters as they walked under them. "Nick's in here?"

Inside the double doors was a small room surrounded by chicken-wired glass and a heavy door leading into the unit. Dr. Lamba motioned for them to sit in two small black chairs to the right of the room.

Dr. Lamba put her hand on Tony's forearm and said, "Your brother was sexually assaulted last night."

Tony stared at her.

"Whoever did this to him beat him up pretty badly, so I wanted to prepare you for that. We've—"

"Wait. Stop. Stop."

Dr. Lamba paused.

Tony shook his head. "No. No, no one would do that to him, that doesn't—that makes no sense." As he heard the words he'd said, a strangely detached voice in his mind whispered, *No, you make no sense.*

"I'm so sorry, Mr. Hall," Dr. Lamba said.

He buried his face in his hands. "Please, no."

He felt her hand on his shoulder now. "The emergency department treated Nick's injuries, and the good news is that he could go home now if he wanted. But the other good news is that he took my advice and admitted himself to our mental health unit, to give himself a couple of nights here."

Through his hands, Tony said, "Could you stop saying *good news*?"

"Yes." The hand rubbed his shoulder in a circular motion.

Someone did this. The simplicity struck him like a blow. Tony lifted his face from his hands. "Where's the fuck who did this?"

"Nick has already spoken to a police officer." Dr. Lamba met his eyes again and held them as she said, "Please, focus on your brother right now. He needs you. Don't focus on this other person, that's what the police are for. Focus on Nick."

⟀

Nick's face was ruined.

It was the first thought Tony had when he saw him. Nick was lying on top of the covers of his hospital bed, like he was watching TV at a hotel. But his face was all wrong—the shapes of it were off, just a fraction: his lip was split and swollen, an eyebrow was cut. He had bruises on a cheek, his forehead, his chin, like he'd fallen down a flight of stairs.

"Nick?"

Nick smiled at Tony and then winced, licked the scab on his lip.

Tony's voice went watery. "What the fuck?"

"I'm fine," Nick said, and smiled reassuringly.

Tony pointed at Nick's chest. "Can I?"

Nick raised his arms.

As Tony crouched to hug Nick, his vision blurred with tears. He wriggled his hands under Nick's back and laid his head against his brother's. When he pulled away, there were tears on Nick's cheek. They were Tony's—Nick's eyes were dry.

"Sorry," Tony said.

"For what?"

For crying on you, he thought. *For being weird when you're saying you're fine. For taking so long to get back to your room. For whatever happened.*

Instead, Tony said nothing. He turned to pull a chair to the bedside and saw that Dr. Lamba had closed the door behind Tony. The two were alone.

Tony said, "So . . . ," but he was lost in a barrage of thoughts. Should he ask what happened, with what words, did he want to know, was he being selfish, *how* could this have happened, was that the wrong thing to ask.

"Where's Julia?" Nick's simple question nudged out all the others.

"Home with the kids. My mom's heading there, and then she'll come here as soon as she can."

"Julia'll come here tonight?"

"Yeah, if you want—*only* if you want."

"Yeah, of course, I almost asked for her instead of you to begin with."

Tony rolled his eyes. "Oh, *okay*."

"She wouldn't have cried," Nick said with a grin, then winced again. He brought a finger to the slit in his lip. Whispered, "Shit."

Tony watched his little brother. They must have misunderstood him. This wasn't someone who'd been *sexually assaulted*. Clearly he'd gotten his ass kicked. Maybe he made a pass at the wrong guy and the homophobic fuck beat him up, that was possible. Or he could have been mugged. But not that—not what the doctor said. Their banter was unfazed. They might as well have been play-squabbling over a game, like when Nick was a kid and Tony used to pretend he was losing to him at checkers. And Nick was calm—*so* calm. He must have told someone he was assaulted, and they took it the wrong way. That had to be it. Nick seemed—

A knock at the door cut off the thought. A deep voice said, "Sorry to bother you." It came from the large man standing in the doorway. He was in plain clothes, but it might as well have been a T-shirt reading "I'm a cop" under his windbreaker instead of the white button-down, no tie.

"I'm Detective John Rice," he said, stepping into the room. "I'm from the Salisbury Police Department. I think Officer Merlo said I'd be stopping by?"

Nick adjusted himself to sit higher in bed. "Yeah, hi."

Tony felt the tension of that first silence swell back into the room.

Detective Rice made his way to the opposite bedside in two steps. He had to be six six, maybe even taller. His face was weatherworn and wrinkled; Tony guessed he was in his early sixties. The giant drew two business cards from his windbreaker and handed one to each of them.

The detective shook Nick's hand like Nick was joining the police force. "Well, nice to meet you, Nick." He turned to Tony. "Are you the brother?"

"Yeah." Tony stood to shake his hand. "Tony."

"Nice to meet you." The detective turned his face and shifted back to Nick. "I'm not here to stay, just dropping off these victim impact forms."

"What are these?" Tony reached over his brother to take the sheets. They were forms with a few spots at the top for details like NAME, DOB, DATE OF CRIME and then blank-lined space.

The detective pointed at the sheets. "Nick gave a statement to Officer Merlo, and he already saw a SANE nurse, so—"

"A sane nurse?"

"Sorry," Detective Rice said with a cough. "A sexual assault nurse examiner, over in the emergency department."

Tony glanced at Nick. Nick was looking down, twisting his hands together in his sheets.

"Oh, right," Tony said dumbly.

"The SANE nurse usually gets a pretty good statement, so I want to let you rest. But I need to come back tomorrow. That okay, Nick?"

"Yeah," Nick said.

"Why do you need to come back?" Tony flipped through the sheets; they were all the same.

"To interview him. It's important in a case like this that I get a thorough, consistent statement as close in time to the event as possible. The sooner you talk about it, Nick, the better your recall will be later, and it'll help me do my job. For tonight, I need you to fill out a statement of everything you remember that happened, starting at the beginning of your day on Friday. It was Friday, yesterday, right?"

"That it happened?" Nick asked.

"Yeah."

"Yeah it was last night, late last night. So I just write all of my day?"

"Well, you don't have to get too into the weeds with stuff before dinnertime, I'd say. And I can ask you for more details tomorrow if I need to. I'll collect them"—he pointed at the sheets—"sometime tomorrow morning and review them before we talk. Can you get it on paper sometime tonight?"

Tony looked down at his brother again. For the first time since he'd arrived, Nick looked like he was close to crying.

"Yup."

"Attaboy. Tony, if you could just step out with me and confirm some contact info?"

Tony nodded.

"I'll see you tomorrow, Nick."

Tony and the detective stepped out into the unit lobby. Tony shut the door behind him as he went. "Is that written statement really necessary, Detective, because I don't think—"

"Listen," Detective Rice interrupted. "I understand that this is a difficult time, I really do, but I promise you I don't ask rape victims to do anything that isn't totally necessary."

Tony winced at *rape victims*. It felt sharp, hearing those words in the place of Nick's name. Like the detective had hurt him on purpose to back him down.

"We're building a case," Detective Rice said. "You have to remember that. Best-case scenario is we catch the guy who did this, but catching him means nothing if we don't have evidence to prosecute. Nick's story is part of the evidence."

"Can I—" Tony's voice cracked; he was about to cry in front of this man. He widened his eyes so the tears wouldn't spill out over his lids. He exhaled sharply and tried again. "Can I help him fill out the statement?"

"It's better if he writes it down himself. A lot of the time, cases like this turn on whose side of the story is more believable. Won't do us any good if you write out his statement for him. But you can sit with him while he does it."

Tony answered the detective's questions about names, numbers, addresses of the Hall family, but all the while *rape victim*, *rape victim*, *rape victim* repeated on a loop somewhere behind his ears.

The detective departed, and Tony stepped back into the room. From his bed, Nick frowned at him. "Why did you shut the door?"

A hot, damp cloth of a headache crept from his temples, spreading over his skull and down his neck. "I just did."

"Why?" Nick fired the word so fast it was clear he hadn't even listened to Tony's response.

"Nick . . ." He stopped. There were no words. "I'm sorry, I'm not trying to baby you, I just wanted to ask him if you really had to fill out those forms tonight."

"So you *did* baby me, because it's literally writing words on paper, and I said I would do it."

"Jesus, Nick, is it so bad that I would try to baby you today?" Tony's voice had almost climbed to a shout.

The brothers stared at each other.

"So, what?" Tony said. "I'm supposed to pretend everything's fine?"

"I *am* fine," Nick said.

Tony shook his head. Looked down at the sheets in his hand. Looked at the words *VICTIM IMPACT STATEMENT*.

Nick stared at him. Said nothing.

"I don't know how to ask you what happened."

4

NICK HALL, 2015

This is what happened.

On the first Friday of October, Nick Hall got a text message from the boy he liked.

In the middle of an Economics 101 lecture, Nick edged his phone from his pocket to check his notifications. The screen listed the names ELLE, MOM, and CHRIS. As his eyes registered the final name, a rush of butterflies pummeled his throat. No question: a text from Chris was worth the risk of getting caught with his phone out in class.

Nick pulled the phone free and balanced it on his thigh, quickly flicking past the other messages.

Chris G:

Hey

That was it. No punctuation, no response to Nick's last text, no effort. But at least he had texted. And *hey* was kind of sexy, Nick thought, in the right voice. Chris would have said it in the right voice in person: the kind of *hey* that had an ellipsis after it. The text was only twenty minutes old. Nick couldn't respond yet; *too desperate*. Unless responding now would show Chris that Nick didn't play games and wasn't afraid to go after what he wanted. Yeah, Nick thought, maybe he *should* respond now. He glanced up. His professor was lecturing right at him. He grinned sheepishly and shoved his phone back into his pocket.

$\sim$

As a junior in good standing at the University of Maine Salisbury, Nick had the privilege of living in a shithole off campus as opposed to a dorm on campus. A single management company owned a number of houses on Spring Street, which generations of students had long dubbed Frat Row. Although UMS had no official Greek life, house parties were frequent occurrences on the street. Nick and three friends had rented the yellow house on Frat Row for their junior year. Their freedom from the tyranny of dorm life came at the price of sticky doors, a damp basement carpet, and tiny closets.

As evening fell on the first Friday of October, Nick stood in front of one such closet, considering his reflection in the cheap mirror hanging on the door. He was wearing fitted blue jeans and a short-sleeved button-down with little polka dots. Add his dark navy kicks and gray utility jacket, and this was his latest feel-good outfit. He'd worn it to dinner a couple of weeks ago, and Tony and Julia had both gushed about how good he looked. And they'd been right . . . so why did it look like shit tonight? He crossed his bedroom to his dresser, crouched down to open his T-shirt drawer. Ran his fingers over the soft cotton band tees on the left side of the drawer, contemplating a cooler look. Chris had that effortless I-don't-give-a-fuck thing going on all the time. It was the sum total of Chris's short Afro, his nose ring, his perfectly worn jeans, his attitude he wore like an aura. Nick had taken one look at himself and realized that he looked like he gave a fuck, very much so, and that was bad. He pulled out his well-worn Springsteen tee: it was faded white with his *Born in the*

U.S.A. album cover on the front. Just looking at it Nick could hear a crackling hiss, the pop of a needle, and then "Dancing in the Dark" was grooving out of his dad's record player. He was eight again; his dad was buzzed and pulling his giggling mother around the living room. They'd been fighting, but the Boss could cut through their bullshit better than anyone. It didn't matter what his mother had threatened (calling the cops, getting a divorce, "taking Nicky to my mother's and you'll never see him again"), and it didn't matter what his father had broken (a plate, a beer bottle, the window in the back door once). All Ron Hall had to do was drop the needle on that ancient record player and they made right up.

The music and any reminder of it infused him with a mixture of nostalgia, homesickness, and something like regret. It was the perfect shirt to take his look from *eager* to *brooding*.

As Nick reached for his top button, his bedroom door creaked open slowly. Mary Jo, one of his roommates, appeared in the doorway.

"You decent?"

"Not that it mattered."

She grinned. "Just tryna sneak a peekatha deek."

"Ew, get out!" He whipped the T-shirt at her, and she caught it with a shriek.

"If you still want a ride, Eric is picking me up in like ten or fifteen."

Nick grabbed his phone off the dresser. Three hours after Nick responded to the "Hey" text, Chris had suggested that they "meet for a drink."

Chris was a senior, twenty-two, and tired of house parties. Chris went out to bars. Nick wouldn't turn twenty-one until March of next year, so he was relegated to using a fake if he wanted to even get in to most bars, let alone get a drink.

Nick had responded:

Jimmy's?

26

Salisbury was located tantalizingly close to Ogunquit, which housed some of the best bars and clubs in southern Maine. Or so Nick had heard. All the places he'd tried to get into in Ogunquit had turned him away after one look at his fake ID. Jimmy's Pub, on the other hand, had let him in twice. Jimmy's was near campus in Salisbury; pretty divey, but it had everything you could want: dim lighting, cheap drinks, and a small, sticky dance floor. Chris hadn't responded yet, but what else was new?

"I dunno if I need a ride after all," Nick said to Mary Jo with a wave of his phone.

"Fuck Chris, okay? He's jerked you around long enough. Why don't you meet me and Eric after dinner? *We'll* go to Jimmy's with you!"

Nick's phone vibrated in his hand. He looked down to see Chris had responded.

It read:

Interesting choice. 10?

Nick couldn't help but grin. Mary Jo was right—Chris did like to jerk him around—but right now, Nick didn't care.

"As much as I'd love to third-wheel it," Nick said, "looks like I've got a date."

Mary Jo rolled her eyes. "What did he say?"

"He thinks I'm interesting, and he's meeting me at ten."

"Ten? TEN? It's barely past seven and you've been texting all day and he wants to meet you at ten. He's a *jerk*, Nick; he's not even pretending this isn't a hookup."

Elle's head appeared in the doorway behind Mary Jo. "I wasn't eavesdropping," their roommate began, "but if I had been"—she pushed her way around Mary Jo—"I would have an idea for you." She plopped herself onto Nick's unmade bed and brushed a hand through her glossy black hair. "*We* go to Jimmy's, have a couple drinks, maybe a shot, just get a buzz on but no more." She gestured *Stop* with her hand. "When Chris shows up sometime after ten—you know he'll be late—I'll leave you alone and you can tell him off!"

"I'm not telling Chris off," Nick groaned. "You're wrong about him. I mean you're right, but you're wrong. It's so good when we're together."

"But he makes you feel like shit when you're apart," Mary Jo replied.

She was right. They were all right. Even Johnny, their other roommate and a man of few words, once said of Chris: "Seems like an ass."

Mary Jo and Elle stared at him expectantly.

"Fine! God. A couple drinks to give me the balls to tell him to shape up or get lost."

Elle squealed and clapped like a child.

"Now get out while I change!"

—⁓—

It was 10:38 and not a word from Chris.

Nick had made good on Elle's suggestion that he have a couple of drinks: three since they arrived just after nine, though the first was a shot of tequila. Nick wasn't exactly in the mood to rip shots, but Elle had been so sweet to come with him, and Elle was all about shots.

The first hour had zipped by. Elle had ordered them into a booth across from the bar, and she made Nick sit with his back to the door, reasoning she'd have his full attention that way. Elle was the perfect friend to keep him out of his own head, and they lightly gossiped about their roommates and other mutual friends to pass the time. When Nick pressed his phone screen and it read 9:59, he steeled himself to his plan. He would tell Chris how he felt. They'd been doing this on-and-off thing—Nick was always on; it was Chris who was wobbly—since the end of last year. He was crazy about Chris, so why didn't they just do this thing already, for real?

At 10:03, every creak of the door behind Nick rocked him with a wave of adrenaline that crashed each time he craned his head and it wasn't Chris. At 10:16, he started to feel angry.

I'm a catch, he thought, *a goddamn catch, so he needs to act like it or cut me loose. No, or* I'll *cut* him *loose.*

By 10:38, Nick had looked at his phone maybe forty times. No text, no Chris. He contemplated telling Chris not to bother coming . . . but texting him anything at all would betray how much he cared.

"Okay," Elle said loudly, slapping her palms on the sticky table. "I'm calling it. I'm going to the bathroom, then we're doing another shot and dancing. And if he shows up at all, I'll kick him in the balls and we'll leave."

Nick smiled but couldn't muster a laugh. God, he was pathetic. Why did Chris keep doing this to him? And why was Nick letting him? "Just go, I'm fine."

Elle scooched her way out of the booth, then stood over him. "Two more tequila shots," she said, then turned away.

As Nick approached the bar, he knew the night would end one of two ways. If he was lucky, he and Elle would close down Jimmy's, drinking and dancing until staff started putting the stools up on the bar. If he was lucky, the night would be a surprise hit. More likely, though, was the second outcome: Nick would take the shot, half-heartedly dance with Elle for a song or two, then steal away into the bathroom to stare at himself in the mirror. He would watch his features grow pronounced and strange under the influence of the cheap tequila and poor lighting, and he would try to discern what it was about him that was so easy to reject.

The bartender deposited the two shots in front of Nick.

"Is one of those for me?"

Nick turned toward the voice to his left. The voice's owner was settling onto a barstool. Nick hadn't seen the man come in—he'd been watching the door for Chris, and he couldn't have missed a face like this. The man was uncomfortably handsome. He wore his hair longer on the top, so a dark curl drooped over his pale forehead. Light blue eyes, high cheekbones, a dusting of facial hair. *Ho-ly shit.* It might have been the lighting, or the first three drinks, but this might be the best-looking guy who'd ever talked to Nick.

"Uh," Nick breathed. The man waited with a sly grin. *Elle will understand if I give away her shot, especially to a guy who looks like this. Actually, she'll take credit, since she sent me up here in the first place.*

"Yeah," Nick said. "Yeah, I always buy shots for guys *way* out of my league, just tryna level the playing field."

The man laughed, and Nick swelled with pride. How he had managed to put *any* words together was beyond him. He slid one glass toward the handsome stranger.

"You sure *she* won't mind?" The man nodded in the direction of the bathroom. He must have seen Elle.

"Nah," Nick said. "She probably won't even make it back to the booth—she'll be out there dancing with some girl she met in the bathroom."

The man moved the shot glass in a tight circle on the bar. "So you two have an understanding."

"Oh, yeah," Nick said. What the man meant, Nick wasn't sure, but he kept his voice confident. He felt smart, cool—the opposite of how Chris made him feel. How was that possible when he was talking to a guy who looked like he was fresh off a modeling gig?

"I'm Josh," the man said, and lifted the glass.

"Nick," he responded. He threw his head back and felt the cheap tequila wash down his throat; it tasted like burnt rubbing alcohol.

"Whew!" Josh exclaimed, looking at Nick as though he'd poisoned him. "That might be the worst tequila I've *ever* had. You must be a poor college student to drink that shit." Josh leaned forward and pulled his wallet from his snug back pocket. "Next round's on me."

As he watched the handsome stranger flag the bartender, Nick realized he'd been wrong. There was a third possible outcome tonight.

Sunlight beamed onto Nick's throbbing face. He began to roll himself over, and his brain swirled in his skull. Nick held still for a moment, trying to ease the sensation, but instead it spread. The pain seemed to pulse down his neck, shoulders, abdomen . . . *Oh. Oh my God.* Nick shifted and felt a hot ache deep inside him. No. *No.*

In his ear, Josh's voice from last night: "You like that?"

No, *STOP*, he thought, *I'm fine, I'm fine.* He sat up, head pounding, and the pain stabbed beneath his belly. *You like that? STOP.*

He was alone. It was a motel room, small and beige and stinking of cigarettes.

He pulled back the thin comforter. Blood. There was blood on the sheets beneath his thighs.

"Oh my God." His voice was a whisper.

Was Josh still there? He listened. Heard nothing.

"Hello?"

Still nothing.

"Okay," he whispered. "You're okay."

What if Josh came back?

A thought in his head, distinct from the voice that needed to whisper: *You need to get up. You need to leave.*

Nick swung his legs out of the bed and felt a sharp, stabbing pain as he stood; he heard himself whimper, and he felt like a child. The sensation dulled into an aching burn, and the pain in his head announced itself again.

Keep moving, the voice said, *you need to leave.*

There were his clothes on the floor—he grabbed his jeans and pulled them on, leaving his underwear on the carpet. Shit, he'd get blood on his jeans. How would he get blood out of his jeans? He pulled on his T-shirt inside out and snatched up his jacket. Nick could feel his wallet in the back pocket of his pants, but where was his phone? He fumbled for it in

31

his jacket—the pockets were empty. He got down on his hands and knees, and his brain pounded on his skull, screaming at him not to tip so far forward. There it was, under the bed. *Grab it and go.* Nick reached, closing his hand on the soft leather.

There was a sound at the door behind him, and he yelped, bringing his head straight up and cracking it on the bed frame.

"Housekeeping," a soft voice announced.

Nick pushed himself out from under the bed and onto his feet. *Cover the blood.* He pulled the comforter up, turned as the door opened. The thin woman in black startled and said, "Oh, sorry, hon, they said you checked out."

"Sorry," Nick said.

She moved out of his way as he passed through the door.

"Honey," she said, "you forgot something."

He turned to see her pointing at his briefs on the floor. A woman he didn't know was staring at his underwear. Asking him to pick it up. Assuming—correctly—that he didn't have any on.

"Sorry," he said again as he grabbed them and folded them into his jacket.

Nick stepped into the chilled morning air and immediately spotted a cab parked under the MOTEL 4 DELUXE sign on the driveway to Route 1. Jacket clutched in his hand, Nick ran down the stairs and across the lot. His mind was still caught on the housekeeper. That poor woman. She'd see the blood. She'd have to strip the bed. Or would she—what would she do when she saw blood on the sheets?

The driver rolled down the front passenger window as Nick approached. Shit. He'd spent the last of his cash at Jimmy's.

Nick gripped the window. "Do you take cards?"

"Uhhh, yeah, I'll have to call it in, but I can take a card." Cabdrivers almost always registered annoyance at this question, but this man seemed worried. "Get in, kid."

Nick sat himself gingerly in the back seat. The blood. The blood might soak through his pants, stain the seat. He sat on a hand.

"You okay, kid?" The heavy man turned to face him. He was middle-aged and wore a newsboy cap.

"What?"

"Who did that to you?"

Nick felt himself flush deeply but said nothing.

"Your face," the man said.

Nick looked above the man at the rearview mirror. His reflection was wrong. His lip was split and there was blood crusted above his eyebrow. *Give your address.* "Eleven Spring Street," he said. "Please."

The driver looked at him for a beat longer and sighed. "All right."

Would the housekeeper call the police when she saw the blood? Did the motel have his name? *Check your phone.* Nick pulled out his phone. The screen was loaded with texts. Chris had texted twice, apologizing just after midnight for getting "caught up," and asking, this morning, if he could make it up to Nick. At 10:59 last night, Elle had started a group message with their roommates announcing:

NICK GETTIN IT AT JIMMYS.

This was followed by a poor-quality photo of Nick sitting at the bar with Josh and a dozen messages from Mary Jo and Elle, and one from Johnny this morning asking,

Wait, what did I miss last night?

Nick's mouth flooded with saliva.

"Pull over," he groaned. The driver obeyed, and Nick opened the door and leaned out. The fresh, dry air washed over him and the urge to vomit was suppressed. He took a couple of deep breaths. *Stop thinking about it.*

He sat back against the seat, shut the door. "Sorry."

"It's fine," the driver said. "Rough night?"

Nick was silent, and the man drove on.

When they reached the house, the cabbie took his card and called it in. Handed it back.

"You should put something cold on that face."

Whether Nick said "Thank you" aloud or just thought it, he wasn't sure.

He got out and stood on the sidewalk in front of the house, legs locked. Maybe no one would be home to keep asking questions. But then he would be alone. *There's no right thing to hope for*, the voice in his head said neutrally. *You'll just have to go inside.*

As he stepped into the entry, he heard Elle's voice carry down the hall from the kitchen. "Nick, is that you?"

"Uh, yeah," he answered, horrified to find that tears had sprung up at the sound of her voice. It was like something inside him had disconnected at the motel, and her question—*Nick, is that you*—had snapped the piece back into place.

"What happened last night?" Elle asked gleefully as she burst into the hallway. Her face fell. "What happened to your face?"

A sob burst from his mouth.

"Nick, oh my God. Nick, what happened? What did he do to you? What did he do?"

They sank to the floor together, Elle holding the sides of his face.

"Johnny! Johnny!" Elle's voice sounded strained and hysterical.

In a rush of chaos, Johnny crashed halfway down the stairs, ran back up, and came pounding down with his car keys. Elle and Johnny yelled nonsense at each other as they lifted Nick by the armpits back to his feet. He knew they were taking him to the hospital.

II.

MESS

—→

This mess was yours,
Now your mess is mine.

VANCE JOY, "MESS IS MINE"

5

JULIA HALL, 2019

I t took me a while to see just how badly Nick's rape had hurt your family."

Julia winced at the word. Three years gone and the sound of it still scratched at her ears. Detective Rice seemed not to notice that it had bothered her.

"Nick and your husband's family were a little rough around the edges, but what you and Tony had, that was solid."

She shifted a bit in her chair.

"Did you see it coming from the beginning? I certainly didn't."

"See what coming?"

"How bad it would get."

Julia shook her head. No, she had not.

The detective held her eye for a moment, then looked down into his mug. "Now, I always sympathized with victim's families. It's a natural response to being around people going through something tragic, one, and two, it made people talk to me more, and tell me more, see? Made me better at my job."

Julia nodded, a small frown forming.

"But in your case, well, I crossed a line. I sympathized a little more than I should have, with everything that was going on, and it made me unprofessional."

Julia stared at him intently now. She'd played out endless scenarios in preparation for this day, but this featured in none of them. *Where is he going with this?* She felt herself cock her head as he went on.

"The way it all ended, with me and your family and the Ray Walker situation, I mean. I've never felt good about it."

The skin on her neck prickled at Raymond Walker's name. She had known she would hear it today, and she'd heard it a thousand times before, but she still couldn't suppress her reaction to hearing it spoken. She shifted her weight and crossed her right leg over her left. A feeling was stirring in the pit of her stomach: an emotion so palpable it nearly felt alive and separate from her—some nagging, gnawing monster she had finally lulled to sleep years ago. At Detective Rice's phone call last week, the monster had cracked an eye open. Now, with a raised head, its tail swished in anticipation.

She raised her mug to her lips and sipped.

6

Rice sat in his car looking over his notes and Nick Hall's written statement. A cold cup of Dunkin' sat in his cup holder, nearly full to the brim. It was Sunday, late morning. He'd gone to interview Julia Hall, read Nick's written statement, checked in with the evidence technician who'd processed the motel room, talked to the Assistant District Attorney. He'd done what he could to give Nick a couple of hours of sleep, but Rice needed to conduct a recorded interview before too much more time lapsed.

He flipped through the notes he'd taken when he spoke to Officer Merlo and the nurses the day before. So far things were looking pretty good—no obvious inconsistencies or eyebrow raisers in Nick's story. Sex cases often turned into a battle of he-said-she-said, or assailant-said-victim-said, in this case. A defendant would pick apart the various records of the victim's statements (to police, doctors, anyone) looking for inconsistencies. It wasn't always an effective technique, but on the right facts or with the right defense attorney, it could work to force a crap plea deal, a weak sentence, even convince a jury to acquit. But then, none of this mattered at all if Rice didn't have a defendant; he didn't even have a suspect.

The kid was consistent on a number of important points across the statements: Nick had a total of five drinks himself that night; he was confident he could identify his rapist, "Josh," if he had the chance to see him again; Josh had two drinks that Nick saw; and Nick remembered being hit over the head just after they entered the room at the Motel 4 Deluxe. Nick said the rest was gone, until he woke up Saturday morning beat up and knowing he'd been sexually assaulted.

Nick's memory lapse was a problem. Rice had already discussed it with the Assistant District Attorney who would be handling the case. She asked Rice to circle back to it during his interview of Nick. Make sure he couldn't remember anything at all about what happened in that motel room.

And he'd been drinking—drunk victims always complicated these cases. People would question Nick's ability to remember what the assailant looked like; question whether he'd consented on account of lowered inhibitions. But if they could find "Josh," the fact that the prick had beaten Nick up so badly should make it easy enough to prove that this wasn't a consensual situation. No one consented to having their face beat up during sex, did they? The choking—that was a sexual thing for some people, and Nick had been choked. But the SANE nurse had told Rice that her exam of Nick's body would support a case of nonconsent. And they had physical evidence, bloody bedsheets. Thankfully, the cleaning woman at the motel had taken one look at the sheets and told management, so the room had been largely preserved.

A sedan pulled into the space next to him. It was Lisa Johnson, from a local victim advocacy center. He'd been glad to hear from Merlo last night that it was Lisa assigned to the case. All the advocates were good, but he'd worked with Lisa before, and she was a favorite of his. He held up his hand to her and shuffled his papers back into the manila envelope marked *N.H. 10/2/15*.

"You're late," Rice said as he shut his door.

Lisa looked at him wide-eyed and then down at her phone. "I am two minutes early."

"Yeah but I was fifteen," he said with a grin.

Lisa rolled her eyes at him and smiled wide. "You are bad, always trying to make me think *I* am bad!"

Rice led Lisa to Nick's room in the BHU. She hadn't seen Nick since he'd come over from the ER the evening before. Nick and his brother were watching TV with the door open. Facing the doorway together, there was a strong resemblance in the brow, mouth, and shoulder spread of these two men, and Rice imagined he could picture what their father might look like as well. Lisa greeted Nick and introduced herself to Tony.

Tony was convinced to step out easily enough, leaving the professionals alone with Nick.

"Cleaner this way" was all Rice had to say. Since his wife was a defense lawyer, maybe Tony understood why. Somehow Rice couldn't see sweet-faced Julia cross-examining a victim about whether they were too embarrassed to tell the truth about a sex crime in front of a family member, though, so maybe not.

Nick had been lounging on top of his bed in sweats and a T-shirt. He switched off the TV and sat back against the pillows, suddenly looking pale.

"Sorry to have to ask you to talk about this again, Nick," Rice said as he pulled a chair toward the bedside. "This should be the last of the interviews for a while."

"It's okay," Nick said quietly.

"I just need to get a complete statement from you while your memory's still good; it might fade with time, so we should get the details down now."

Nick nodded.

Rice pulled out his recorder and set it on his chair's thin armrest. If they'd been able to do this at the station the interview would have been video recorded, but with the kid in the BHU for the next couple of days, Rice didn't want to wait.

Rice had Nick tell his story, starting with when he woke up Friday morning. Nick filled in the details of that day that had so far gone undiscussed: breakfast at home, a class called Business English, homework and lunch back at his apartment, Economics 101 class, then home again for the rest of the afternoon and early evening.

When Nick got into the part Rice already knew, he was consistent with his written statement and the shorter version he'd told Merlo when he first got to the hospital. Nick had planned to meet a guy named Chris Gosling at Jimmy's Pub. His roommate Elle Nguyen had gone to the bar with him, and Chris had never shown up. Instead, Nick met Josh. After some time at the bar, they took a cab to the Motel 4 Deluxe, where Josh was staying. They stepped into the motel room, and Nick felt a blow to the back of his head. Fade to black until morning.

"Okay," Rice breathed as he shifted to cross his legs. "Thank you, Nick. Do you need anything before I ask you some questions about your story?"

"Bathroom break? Water?" Lisa spoke for the first time in about twenty minutes.

"No." The kid wanted this over with, that was for sure.

"Okay," Rice said as he flipped back in his notes. "First, let's go back to the bar with Josh. He never gave you a last name?"

Nick shook his head.

"Could you say yes or no out loud?" Rice pointed to the tape recorder.

"Sorry, no. No last name. Just Josh."

"Can you remember anything he said about himself?"

Nick was quiet for a while and said, "He didn't really talk about himself, but he seemed, like, kind of rich, maybe like a business guy or something."

"How long were you together at the bar?"

"Well, if I could use my phone I could give you more specifics."

"By all means!" This was good news. Anything with a timestamp would be helpful.

Nick produced a black smartphone from under his bed covers. These kids were never more than six inches from their devices; it was probably going to give them all cancer by fifty.

"First off, I know it wasn't eleven yet when I went up to the bar to get two shots for me and Elle. I had been looking at my phone a lot waiting to see if Chris was gonna show up. He was supposed to be there at ten. It was sometime after ten thirty but not eleven yet."

"Good," Rice quietly prompted.

"And Josh started talking to me within, like, a minute of me being at the bar. He might have been just getting there, but I'm not sure on that. And we were still talking at eleven forty-two, since Elle told me she sent this right when she took it." He turned his phone toward Rice to reveal a photo of two men at a bar.

"Hold up, is this you and him?"

"Yeah," Nick said, an unspoken *Duh?* hovering in the drawn-out *h*.

Rice took the phone in his hand. "You have a *photo* of him."

"Yeah, I told that to the cop last night. He said you guys would get it from me."

For fuck's sake. Rice was going to chew out Merlo the second he saw that moron back at the station. What if something had happened to the photo? What if the kid hadn't brought it up again?

"Can you email me this picture right this second?"

Nick raised his eyebrows in surprise. "Yeah, sure."

Rice's heart rate began to come back down when the email from Nick loaded on his phone. He forwarded it to the admin with the directive:

PRINT.

When he looked up, Lisa was looking at him with wide eyes and a tight smile.

"Well, okay," Rice breathed. "So we have a picture."

"Yeah, it's a little dark and far away, but he's the one facing the camera more, and I'm the one turned away. Elle took it from over near the dance floor."

Rice studied the photo more carefully. The lighting wasn't great, but the figures were clear: two men at a bar, one facing the camera, the other turned away. Rice zoomed in on the face. Josh, if that was his real name, looked like Nick had described him: Caucasian with dark features; older than Nick.

"So, sometime between ten thirty and eleven you meet, and at eleven forty-two you're still at the bar, and he didn't tell you where he lived, what he did?"

"No." Nick looked crestfallen.

"Nick, I'm not blaming you. My point is, well, did he have you talking about yourself?"

Nick nodded. "He wanted to know all about me."

Rice took a long look at Nick's face. His cuts looked uglier today, darker, and his bruising was worse. There were purple lines on the left side of his neck now. Nick only remembered one blow to the head, but he'd been hit multiple times and choked. A man didn't just unleash on a stranger like this once without having done something like it before. And he'd probably do it again.

Nick had said earlier that Josh asked if Elle would mind Nick talking to him. Nick seemed to think Josh meant to ask if Nick's friend would be angry to be ditched for a hookup. Rice had other suspicions. This Josh— he thought Elle was a beard, a fake girlfriend. And he'd asked Nick if he'd "done this" before. Maybe he didn't mean going home with a stranger. Maybe he meant sex with a man.

Josh thought Nick was in the closet. Maybe he'd done this before, to men who didn't want to out themselves by reporting the assault.

"Do you need a break?" Lisa asked softly.

Nick shook his head.

"He just bought you the one drink?"

Nick's eyes shifted from Lisa back to Rice. "Yeah."

Rice glanced down at his notepad. "So you had a shot of tequila when you got there around nine, two whiskey ginger ales between nine and ten thirty, another shot of tequila, this time sitting at the bar with the man, and then he ordered you an old-fashioned?"

"Yeah."

"So if you met him around ten thirty or eleven, how fast did you have that last drink?"

"I dunno. I was kind of milking it, because it was disgusting."

Rice and Lisa both laughed.

Nick smiled. "I'd never had one before. But I drank the whole thing. I wanted to look like, you know. Like I drank real drinks."

"You finished it before you left?"

"Yeah."

"When was that?"

Nick looked back at his phone. "At twelve seventeen Elle texts the group chat that I just left with him."

Rice triple-circled Elle Nguyen's name on his notepad. Megan O'Malley, another detective in his office, was interviewing Nguyen, along with the other roommate who'd driven Nick to the hospital. A Johnny Maserati. Ridiculous name. Rice would call O'Malley from the car and follow up.

"Would you say you were drunk?"

"Is it bad if I was?"

Yes, Rice thought. "I'm just trying to understand how you were feeling when you left."

45

Nick nodded slowly. "Drunk. Not, like, sloppy."

"Okay."

"More just . . . tipsy, I guess."

"But you didn't black out, or brown out, or anything?"

"No," Nick said. "No, I remember everything until he hit me."

It was helpful to know what Nick could remember from earlier in the night, but, in Rice's view, it didn't mean the alcohol hadn't contributed to the memory lapse he was suffering. Maybe the blow to the head caused an injury that combined with the effects of the alcohol. If they could get enough to hand the case over to the DA's office, the state would need to find an expert.

"Okay," Rice said. "Who asked who to leave?"

"He asked me. And he asked me if I'd ever had a one-night stand before."

"He did?"

"Yeah." Nick looked to his side like he was remembering. "He asked if I'd 'done this' before. But I think he meant hooked up with someone I didn't know."

Or, maybe he was asking if Nick had ever had sex with a man before. This "Josh," he was carefully choosing who he brought back to his room.

"Okay," Rice said. "So you left at twelve seventeen, and you cabbed to the Motel 4 Deluxe?"

"Right. He paid for the cab with cash. That reminds me, though, I did ask him about Motel 4, because seriously? And he said something about his company paying for it and they're all about the bottom line. Like that was why he was in such a shitty motel."

"So he made it seem like he was from out of town?"

Nick nodded. Rice pointed to the recorder, and Nick said, "Sorry, yes."

"Did you ask him about why he was in town?"

"He just said business." Nick paused and flushed. "He said he didn't

46

really want to talk business tonight." The kid's eyes began to well up as he shrugged.

Lisa passed him a box of tissues, whispering, "This was not your fault."

Once, a couple of years ago during an interview of a rape victim, the victim advocate had said something like that when the victim started crying. Afterward, Rice had told the advocate, a petite, quiet woman, that she really shouldn't say things like that during the recorded interviews—didn't want a defense attorney calling them biased or saying they were reinforcing the victim's version of events. The woman had looked at him incredulously and seemed to swell in size as she said, "I understand that you're building your case, Detective, but once this is over for you, it's not over for her, so if I see a survivor struggling with feelings of guilt, I'm going to tell her it's not her fault." Rice had been floored, and he never complained about anything a victim advocate did again.

Nick wiped his eyes, blew his nose, and looked back to Rice. He wanted to keep going. Tough kid.

"Can you walk me through entering the room one more time? Go slower."

"There's not much slower to go. We went up to the door, Josh already had a key card. He opened the door; we went in. I shut the door, then I felt him hit me on the head." Nick shrugged. "That's all I remember."

"What was happening as you walked up to the room? Anything between you two?"

"I was going there to hook up with him, if that's what you mean."

"No, well, I mean were you holding hands, talking, uh, kissing, anything?" Rice hoped his hesitance had gone unnoticed. He knew people were gay, it was a thing, it was fine, none of his business, but he had a hard time asking the more intimate questions.

"We had started making out during the cab ride," Nick said, "and he

47

took my hand as we walked to the room." He paused. "We kissed outside the door before we went in. It was . . . I thought we were, like, really compatible, I guess I'm saying. I don't know why he . . ." Nick shrugged and took a sharp breath.

"What, ah, was the plan when you got inside?"

Nick looked confused. "Plan?"

"What had you wanted to do with him?"

Nick dropped his gaze to the tissue in his lap. "Just hook up, I guess."

"But what does that mean, for you?"

Nick's eyes hardened. "I didn't have a plan," he said. "I was gonna take it one thing at a time. I didn't know I needed a plan."

"I don't mean to say you did, I just had to ask." Rice's neck flushed with itchy heat. "I'm not blaming you."

Nick looked up at him. "I know."

"You see what he used to hit you?"

Nick shook his head. "I was looking the other way. And it was still dark in the room. It happened so fast."

"And that's it? You don't remember anything else?"

"I don't know what else you want."

"I want to find this guy, and when we find him I want to nail him. It could be your word against his. If you remember stuff later, that's fine, but it always looks a little . . ."

Nick dropped his gaze back to his lap.

"The sooner you give us information, the more believable it looks. Does that make sense?"

Nick stared at his lap and nodded, pulling the tissue to moist shreds.

"So nothing else?"

Nick shook his head.

"Did you, ah, clean yourself up at all at the motel?"

"I just got dressed and left."

"Okay," Rice said. The evidence tech had found a dirty towel in the

48

bathroom. If Nick hadn't used it, maybe Josh had. If they were lucky, it would give them his DNA.

Rice asked Nick a few questions about the morning after, then turned off his recorder. Before he left, he had Nick hand off his phone and sign a consent form so they could pull the data off it, and another for his medical records.

"Thanks for your time, Nick. I know this was hard."

Nick shrugged like it had been nothing, but his eyes were tired.

Rice stuck his head out into the hallway. A nurse told him Tony's wife had shown up and they'd gone to the cafeteria.

"I'll stop by the caf on my way out," Rice said to Nick. "Send them back to you."

"I will wait with you," Lisa said.

Nick looked spent, but if he didn't want her there, he was too polite to say so.

7

When Detective Rice left, Nick and Lisa were quiet for a moment. Nick understood now why people called it "giving" a statement. With his words, he'd given away his energy. He lay back into the pillows behind him, staring down at the loaner T-shirt and sweatpants Dr. Lamba had given him. His eyelids felt heavy.

"Okay," Lisa said. "I will only ask once, but I must: How are you feeling?"

Coming from anyone else, the question would have bothered him. Might have even enraged him. But from Lisa, it was genuine. She knew he wasn't okay, and she didn't expect him to pretend he was. At the same time, she didn't look at him like everyone else did, like his life was over. To Lisa, all of this—police interviews and hospital beds and *rape*—was just something that happened sometimes.

Nick liked Lisa. He wanted to give her the truth, but he searched and felt nothing. "I don't know," he said.

Lisa said nothing, prompting him to try again.

"I keep saying I'm fine. I almost *do* feel fine. Like nothing." In his lap, Nick rolled the pieces of shredded tissue into a ball. During the nurse's exam in the ER, he'd felt like he wasn't there. It wasn't his body she was peering into. Wasn't him she was photographing, naked in a bright room. "Why do I feel so little?"

"Your body, your mind, they are protecting you. It is your way of easing into the knowledge of what happened. There is nothing wrong with you."

That was good. Nothing wrong with him.

That was the other thing he liked about Lisa. Not once did he see in her eyes what he had seen so many times in the past two days: second-hand shame at the sight of a man who was raped. He'd seen it in the cop's eyes, and the detective's. He'd seen it when they got to the ER, at the front desk. The woman asked why they were there.

"I think I was sexually assaulted," Nick said.

Her face had been surprised. Her eyes had flicked to Elle and back to Nick. "You were sexually assaulted?" she asked. Implicit was the question: *Did you mean to say that* she *was?*

To Lisa, nothing was wrong with Nick.

"The next part will be bad, right?" The day before, Lisa and the nurses had given Nick pamphlets and a folder of information specially made for rape survivors. Eventually, the deep freeze he felt now would thaw. Instead of his normal self, though, those pages said he might be depressed, guilty, sleepless, suicidal.

"Maybe," Lisa said. "It is truly a bit different for everyone. Dr. Lamba told me you will be seeing Jeff Thibeault when you leave."

The therapist. "Yeah," Nick said.

"Jeff is a wonderful man." Lisa's broad face spread into a pleasant smile, like she knew Jeff well. "I think you will like him. And if you don't, you find someone else. You choose who is on your team. You decide."

Nick nodded. That would feel good: to be in control. He hadn't felt in control since—well, since he left the bar with Josh. Elle and Johnny had taken him to the hospital. He remembered them talking over his head, Elle saying they had to go to the hospital, Johnny asking if they should go to the police instead.

"He's hurt," Elle kept saying. "He's hurt."

When he saw Elle in the apartment, a dam had broken in him and he'd cried too hard to talk. Too hard to say, *Yes, take me to the hospital; no, don't call the police.* Elle called 9-1-1 in the car on the way. And then suddenly, the tears stopped. He could speak again, but she'd already called the police, already told them Nick's name, the hospital they were driving to. So Nick grew calm again. He grew calm, and he made a plan.

"Your brother loves you very much," Lisa said.

Nick nodded. "Yeah."

Tony being so upset had been the worst moment so far, worse than every humiliation he'd felt seeing the housekeeper and knowing she would find his blood on the sheets; worse than the two-hour exam; worse than talking to the nurse, and the officer, and the detective, one after another. Nick had felt pain, actual pain in his chest, when they released themselves from that first hug and he saw that Tony had been crying.

"How old is your brother?"

"Uh, twenty plus seventeen is thirty-seven."

"Seventeen years apart!"

Nick gave his normal two-word explanation: "Different moms."

Lisa cocked her head. "Where is your mom now?"

"She's, ah, not good with this kind of thing." How could he explain? It wasn't worth the effort. "She gets upset. It would be hard."

Lisa nodded. Her eyes were curious, but she didn't pry.

"Tony takes care of me fine," Nick said, but he was underselling it. Tony was more than fine at taking care of Nick; he'd been doing it Nick's whole life. They weren't like any of the other sets of siblings Nick knew. They didn't fight. They were never in competition for food, toys, attention, anything like that. They hadn't grown up together: Tony had grown up without Nick. Tony was an adult in every memory Nick had of him. He was almost like an extra parent. He remembered Tony buying him things—ice cream cones and action figures. He remembered Tony taking him to the playground by Nick's house. He remembered them playing games, so many games, but not as equals. He'd always been the kid, and Tony the cool guy Nick wanted to be.

Lisa shifted in her seat. "Do you have questions for me, while I'm here?"

"What are the chances they'll find him?"

Lisa shook her head. "I don't know."

For some reason, ever since Nick had made it safely into the cab outside the motel on Saturday morning, it hadn't occurred to him that he might see Josh again. Even after the examination, the swabs, the questions, the photo he told the cop he had. He knew Elle had called the police. The police were there to solve crimes—solving crimes meant finding the bad guy.

They had a shitty photo of Josh. If his name even *was* Josh. They had whatever they got from Nick's body yesterday. So maybe they had Josh's DNA, but maybe not. Maybe they wouldn't find him. Maybe, after some time, the police would give up, and maybe one day Nick would wake up and he wouldn't remember any of it.

8

It turned out, the taste of hospital food changed depending on why you were at the hospital in the first place. This obvious truth had not occurred to Tony the first two times he ate at a hospital: first, after Julia had given birth to Chloe, and again after Sebastian. On neither occasion had the food been *good* by any stretch of the word. But anything, anything at all, would have tasted fine on those days. Damp sandwiches, weak coffee, packaged pudding cups. They had all sated his need to eat something, anything, so he could get back to his new baby, his wife, their excitement.

Today, he'd have rather fasted. When Julia showed up to see Nick, the detective was interviewing him, so she started in on Tony, nagging him to eat something. *Nagging* wasn't fair—she knew how upset he was. Knew he wouldn't have eaten. So they'd gone to the cafeteria, and Tony had selected the blandest thing available: ham and cheese on white bread. With every bite he took, the soft bread stuck to the roof of his mouth. Eating felt wrong, so wrong that he felt the tickle of his gag reflex kicking in.

They sat together in silence, Tony working at his sandwich, Julia sipping coffee.

When Tony looked up, Detective Rice was walking across the cafeteria.

"We're all set," the detective said. "Thanks for stepping out for so long."

Tony nodded. The bite he'd just taken was at the back of his mouth, resisting descent.

"It was no problem," Julia said for him. "It gave me the chance to make him eat something."

"What'd you get?"

Tony took a sip from his Styrofoam cup. The coffee took the lump of sandwich with it. "Ham," Tony said.

"I've had it." Rice nodded. "Not great."

Julia laughed. Tony cleared his throat, pushed the plate forward on the table.

"Hey, Nick did great today. One of the hard parts is behind him now."

Tony nodded. Good to have it over. The detective had been in there with him for hours.

"How long until the sexual assault kit comes back?" Julia asked. Tony wondered if she'd told the detective that she used to be a defense attorney. She knew more than most people did about the world Nick was stepping into. He grabbed her hand and squeezed it, grateful to have her.

"No promises," Rice said, "but probably about a month."

"Oh," she said. "I thought it would take longer."

Tony was surprised. A month sounded like a long time to wait.

"No," Rice said. "Not usually. Our crime lab normally turns them around pretty quick. Since Nick's willing to prosecute and we don't know who did it, we've already sent the kit up to Augusta." He hesitated. There was something he wasn't saying. "We don't know if the kit will be much use, you know?"

In his peripheral vision, Tony saw Julia nod.

Tony didn't know what that meant. Before he could ask for explanation, the detective spoke. "But, hey, Nick gave me a lead."

Tony's stomach fluttered. "He did?"

Rice nodded. "Yeah, I mean, no guarantees. But he has a photo of the guy."

"Oh my God," Julia said. They shared a glance. There was excitement in her eyes. A photo. A photo was good.

"So now," Rice said, "we share the bastard's face. See if anyone knows him."

When Detective Rice left, he took their silence with him.

Julia turned her body toward Tony. "Did you know there was a photo?"

"No," he said.

"Me neither. That's huge."

"What did he mean about the kit not being useful?"

"Oh," Julia said. She set down her coffee. "I think he means that there might not be DNA in the kit. The hope is that they got the guy's DNA. From Nick."

"I get it," Tony said. That was enough. He didn't want to think about that. "So if that takes a month . . ."

"I know," she said. "It's all going to take a long time."

"If they find him, what comes next?"

Julia picked up her coffee again. "I guess it depends. They might arrest him right away, might wait until they indict him, with a grand jury. I don't know how they make their decisions—I think every department does it their own way. I never had a sex case in Salisbury."

Tony frowned. "A sex case?"

"Oh." She winced. "That's what people called them. Sometimes. I mean a sexual assault case." She paused. "I'm sorry."

Tony turned his eyes back to his sandwich. It stung, to hear her say something like that. The words felt callous and gross.

"It's just shorthand for a case that involves a sex crime," she said. "I know what happened to Nick wasn't sex."

When Julia had been a defense attorney, she talked about a lot of her cases in broad strokes, but he couldn't remember her talking about any that involved sexual assault.

"So you've had one before in the towns you covered?"

"Nothing specifically like this," she said.

"But sexual assault cases?"

She hesitated. "Yes."

She hadn't talked about those cases at home. Maybe she'd been ashamed. He'd never thought about it before, but the thought of Julia defending rapists . . . it was off-putting, to say the least.

Not that she'd had much choice over the cases she got. That wasn't how it worked. She had been a court-appointed lawyer, paid by the state to defend people who were poor enough to qualify for a free lawyer. Mostly she talked about her juvenile clients—teenagers who'd been charged with crimes—but he knew she defended adult criminals, too. Then there were the parents in the child protection cases . . . parents who'd abused or neglected their kids so much that the state had stepped in. He knew she helped those people, but he couldn't understand how she could face them, why she would do that kind of work. So, she didn't talk about it. She and Tony got along best when they both pretended it wasn't part of her job.

Maybe she hadn't been ashamed to defend rapists. Maybe she just hadn't trusted Tony not to judge her for it.

And maybe she'd been right. That she could look those people in the eye and treat them like they were anyone else, regardless of what they were accused of . . . he might have judged her for it before. Might have judged her just now, in his mind a moment ago. But he was lucky, he realized. So lucky to have a wife who was calm in the face of darkness.

"How bad is it going to be?" he asked.

"For Nick?"

Tony nodded.

She looked at him like she was weighing how much truth he could handle. "Honestly," she said, "I think it's gonna suck."

9

The house was ready for Nick's arrival. Seb was all set up to sleep in Chloe's bedroom. There were fresh sheets on Seb's bed for Nick. Tony and Julia had even picked up some of Nick's favorite snacks on the way to the hospital. All that was left was to sit through a discharge meeting with Ron and Jeannie.

Whenever someone left the structure and safety of hospitalization, it was important to have a meeting where the patient and his people made a plan for what would come next. Julia had been to discharge meetings before, but always as someone's attorney. Nick's meeting felt different.

It was happening in a small conference room in the behavioral health unit. As they all sat around the sterile table, Dr. Lamba told the Halls about Nick's treatment plan going forward.

"We've connected him with a therapist about ten minutes from campus," she said. "It'll be easy for him to get a ride there when he eventually moves home."

Jeannie turned to her son with wide eyes. "You'll stay with us first?"

"Don't he have school?" Ron's question caught Julia off guard. Until that moment, he'd looked like he was on another planet, staring at the center of the table with glassy eyes. The subtext of his question was clear:

he didn't want his son coming home with them. Judging by the bready smell of beer wafting off him, he wasn't handling the news of Nick's assault well.

"My professors said I can take some time," Nick said. "I'm gonna figure it out as I go."

"Mummy can drive you to school," Jeannie said with a hint of baby voice.

Julia looked to Dr. Lamba, hoping she would deliver the news that Nick had already decided to come stay in Orange.

"Tony's house is much closer to the school and his new therapist," Dr. Lamba said.

And unlike your house, Julia thought, *it's emotionally stable.*

Jeannie turned to Julia. "But you have the kids."

"They're excited for their uncle Nick to stay with us," Julia said.

"So you knew."

Julia felt herself flushing. "Yesterday we talked—"

"Right," Jeannie said. "Yesterday. See, we didn't know yesterday." She motioned to herself and Ron. "We get a little meeting on his way out the door of the *hospital*. Been here since Saturday, we get the call Monday." She turned to Dr. Lamba now. "And I know, 'he's an adult, he makes his own decisions,' but did it occur to you that he is still a child mentally?"

Tony cut in. "What are you even *talking* about?"

"Not even old enough to drink," Jeannie said. "Not an adult in the eyes of the law."

"He is, though," said Dr. Lamba. Her face was calm, but a hardness had edged into her voice.

"You're all sitting here," Jeannie said, "pretending we're a little team, thinking we're too stupid to notice you've all been making the decisions for him without us."

"I'm making the decisions." Nick spoke so loudly that Julia started.

Jeannie shut her mouth.

Nick looked at his mother with a miserable frown. Even on the third day of seeing him with those bruises, his appearance was jarring. It was what her imagination did with the markings. Fists had pummeled his face. Hands had squeezed his throat.

Nick lowered his voice. "I'm making the decisions, and I didn't want to tell you yet. It was too much."

Jeannie's eyes spilled. She dug a tissue from her purse.

Under his breath, Ron said, "Who do you think put that idea in his head?"

Julia knew Tony would take the bait, but she put a hand on his thigh anyway, hopeful he'd let it slide.

"Seriously?"

"You show up on your high horse like you always do, tell him he don't need us—"

"You *wish* I told him; he knows he doesn't need you."

"Stop it, Tony!" Nick groaned and pushed his chair back. "I can't fucking breathe in here." He turned to Dr. Lamba. "Do we have to do this?"

"No," she said, "if it's not going to be helpful."

The room had fallen quiet, and with any other group Julia might have thought people were considering whether they could all behave and finish the meeting. But not with this crew. She knew the classic Jeannie exit was brewing.

"Fine," Jeannie said. "We'll go, then." She pushed her chair back and stood. "Cut right out of his life like you all wanted, until he's strong enough to think for himself." Tears streamed down her face as she moved to the door.

"I'll never forgive you," she said, maybe to all of them. "I'll never forget this as long as I live. No matter how hard you try to pretend it didn't go down like this, I will never forget, never forgive."

Jeannie opened the door and left.

Ron paused in the doorway and said loudly, "Typical," then followed her out.

No one spoke for a moment.

"And *that* is why I made you call Tony," Nick said to Dr. Lamba. He meant it to be punchy, and everyone laughed tightly, but Julia felt like crying.

Nick deserved better. He deserved to be cocooned in love, told nothing was his fault, promised he'd be kept safe. Instead, he had Ron and Jeannie.

And Tony. He had Tony, too.

10

The descent had been swift after his retirement. Nearly overnight, John Rice became an old man, all dressed up and no place to go, just waiting for the young people to arrive—his daughter, his grandkids, and today it had been Julia. He had wandered the house he'd already cleaned, sweater tucked in, belt resting on the bones of his hips, straightening picture frames and waiting for the sound of her car.

When he saw her walking up the front path, he felt ugly and self-conscious, angry, hopeful, so many things. He welcomed her in like he'd pictured doing a million times, but he never came close to setting their meeting until a couple of weeks ago. It took that last appointment with his doctor to force himself to pick up the phone and try her old cell number. The Lord must have known how badly he needed to speak to Julia before his time came, because her number was unchanged. Now that she was here, it was hard to know where to begin.

When he had breakfast with his friends or called his daughter, he could cut to the chase of what he wanted to get at. This would be different: Julia wouldn't want to talk about where he was heading. He would have to force her along, almost like an interrogation. He would have to show her, on his own, that talk was her only option.

"The way it all ended, with me and your family and the Ray Walker situation, I mean. I've never felt good about it."

She sat in the recliner beside him, sipping at her tea in silence.

"I guess I should have known it would be a complicated case. Sexual assault cases have their unique challenges."

She nodded but kept her eyes on the floor in front of her.

"But it had felt so straightforward at the beginning. I couldn't believe how fast we found him."

In the week following Nick's attack, Rice and Megan O'Malley, another detective from the department, interviewed the motel staff. Collected the bloody bedsheets and a towel from the bathroom. Tracked down the woman who rented the room; she'd been paid to do it by a handsome man who approached her where she'd been panhandling near the motel. They interviewed the bartender at Jimmy's and a few customers who'd been there that night. Jimmy's was cash only, so there was no record of a name, and no one knew the man who'd called himself Josh— the man Rice now knew to be Raymond Walker.

That first week, O'Malley hit the books and made a couple of calls to try to figure out what kind of rapist they were looking for. Since Nick was beaten up so badly, O'Malley thought they were probably looking for one of two types of rapists: one driven by anger, or one driven by sadism. If their suspect was driven by rage, he'd likely have a criminal history and be known for outbursts. If he was a sadist, well, there were two types, but given the damage to Nick's body, he was probably the *overt* type—the type who tried to cause his victim pain. Ditto the criminal history, and probably low intelligence. These were imperfect generalizations, but they were a start.

All that said, they knew Nick's assailant was likely to be a guy who flew under the radar. A man whose charisma would blind people to his less-attractive characteristics.

When they did find Walker, the looks and the charm were apparent. At the time, Rice and O'Malley didn't know how far off they were on the rest.

11

The first few days with Nick in the house were long ones.

On Monday after the discharge meeting, they brought Nick to his apartment in Salisbury so he could pack up some clothes. Julia put on a CD in the car, and they drove without speaking, listening to Alicia Keys. They reached Orange and drove through the town center, past the historic manors and the elementary school. Past the two rival gas stations, the library, the park. Past the housing developments creeping into the country. They carried Nick out to the farmland, where their house sat on the edge of a field their neighbor owned.

The kids had been excited for a long-term sleepover with their uncle, but the uncle who arrived that Monday was not his usual playful self, and they quickly grew indifferent to his presence.

On Tuesday, Nick borrowed Julia's car and went to his first counseling session. He returned to the house raw and edgy, sniping at Tony and crying abruptly without warning. To his credit, he reserved these small outbursts for when the kids were outside or upstairs.

The next two days, Nick seemed like a ghost, drifting in and out of rooms, either unsure of how to interact with the family or too tired to bother. Although Julia worked from home, she had a home office, so at least she was out of his way during the daytime.

Her workspace was at the end of the hallway on the second floor with the bedrooms. Each morning, after Tony had left for his office in Portland and the kids had been delivered to the school bus, Julia took the stairs to the second floor and paused on the landing to listen. Nick had slept late each morning, once into the afternoon. After her daily check on Nick, she made her way down the hall to her tiny study, closing the door as quietly as she could.

The room had once been a large, mostly useless closet on the second floor of the house. Five years ago, Julia had returned from the movies with her best friend, Margot, to find that the outing had been a ruse: while she'd been gone, Tony had converted the closet into an office for her. At the time, she was pregnant with Seb, Chloe's stuff was everywhere, and Julia was trying—and failing—to do her new job in policy from home. In a single, frantic afternoon, Tony had emptied the closet, painted the walls lavender, and assembled bookshelves and a standing desk with an adjustable stool. He was covered in sweat when she got home from the movies.

Some days when Julia opened the office door, she swore she could smell the fresh paint again, and for a second she was transported back to that day. A day she had been exceedingly grateful to have a husband who had never met a problem he wouldn't try to fix. In truth, it was not always her favorite trait of Tony's.

On Friday, late morning, she was standing in the open doorway of the study, mind adrift in the history of the room, when she heard Seb's door creak open behind her. She turned and saw that Nick had gone down the hall toward the bathroom.

"Hey, good morning!"

Nick startled violently, spun to face her.

"Oh, jeez, I'm sorry." Julia stepped into the hallway.

His face ran white, but he brought a hand to his chest in relief. "It's fine," he said.

67

"I'm so sorry."

"Really," he said, before she'd finished saying the word. He smiled and rubbed at the back of his head. "Mind if I shower?"

"No, of course not."

He started to turn away, then pivoted back. "And I have counseling today."

"I know," she said. Julia could feel her cheeks growing warm, her body continuing to register what she'd done. She'd spooked him, yelling out like that. He was probably extra sensitive to things like loud noises right now. He'd suffered a trauma, and she should have known better. *Stupid.* "You can take my car again. I don't need it back until two."

Nick nodded.

She stood in the hallway for a while after he closed the bathroom door. It was invasive, she knew that, but she was listening for sounds of crying. There was nothing, and then the shower came on.

She went back to her study and closed the door.

—⌒—

A bit after two, Julia opened that door to a silent house. She called out and heard nothing. Wandered the house. The driveway was empty. She called Nick's cell, but he didn't answer.

Therapy could have run long. Nick might just be taking time to himself. He kept saying he was fine but she knew he wasn't. There was no way he could be. He was trying so hard to act normal for them. She wished he would stop—just let it out. No good would come from hiding how he was feeling, not from his family.

She should have been relieved to be alone—free to bang around without worrying about startling Nick or wondering what he was thinking.

She only felt uneasy.

12

Jeff's office was on a back road in Wells. The road was Route Something, Nick couldn't remember. He'd just followed the GPS both times he'd driven here. It was a road that snaked through the woods; the kind of road that invited you to roll down the windows, turn up the radio, and floor it. Nick had not done this on either drive to see Jeff. He came down the front steps of the building and thought absently that it was fall. The air, the leaves, the sky—everything was crisp in the fall. The world around him was sharp, and his edges had melted.

He took a deep breath, hoped the clean air would ease his headache. Talk therapy was supposed to help him "get through this." That's what Dr. Lamba had told him, and Jeff had repeated it. So far, the only thing he was sure it did for him was give him a throbbing headache, as if a vise were clamped at the base of his skull. He brought his hand to the spot where the pain was the worst, then his fingers climbed higher until they found the scab.

He'd found it in the shower, on Tuesday morning. In a way, it was the simplest of his physical injuries to focus on. It was a far subtler reminder than the private, intrusive ache that had finally faded away sometime that week. It had nothing on the stomach-wrecking course of antibiotics the hospital had prescribed him to fight off potential STDs, or the bruises on his face and neck that announced to anyone who saw them that he was a *victim*. The cuts and splits on his face were nebulous—they could have been from a bar fight or a drunken fall in the street—but the fingerlike bruising on his neck was damning. He had been choked . . . dominated. *Victimized*.

So the scab was nothing, but he still couldn't keep his hands off it. He found it while he was washing his hair: it was a crusty bump, near the top-back part of his scalp. He'd fingered it curiously through shampoo suds and inspected it a second time with slick, conditioned hands. As he rinsed his hair, Nick rubbed the scab until he felt it crumble away. *There*. That was better.

The next morning, he awoke in his nephew's bed to find that the bump had returned. It was softer and tender to the touch. He flicked at it with his middle finger until he felt it scrape clean. It stung that time, but at least it was gone. Just a day ago, *again* he'd caught himself searching for the scab at the back of his head.

The urge to pick at it while he sat in Jeff's office today had been brutal. He'd wedged his fingers beneath the edges of his thighs and tried to focus on Jeff's face.

Jeff was as Dr. Lamba said he would be. He was kind of old, older than Nick's dad, and had a deep, relaxing voice. He laughed and smiled a lot. He seemed smart but not in an in-your-face way.

"I'm a survivor of childhood sexual abuse," Jeff said in their first session, earlier that week. He said it without shame, like he might have said anything about himself. He had said it, Nick was sure, to make Nick feel less embarrassed about what had happened. Nick had not pointed out how different they were: Jeff had been a child. Nick had not.

Another thing that both Jeff and Dr. Lamba had said was that therapy would help Nick "own" his "story."

"Why would I want to *own* this?" Nick had asked Dr. Lamba over the weekend.

She'd tilted her head. "Because it's yours."

"What if I'm not ready?"

"Jeff won't ask you to talk about it much, not at first. You'll do it over time, and slowly, you'll practice talking about it. Eventually, you can decide what to do with the story."

This had been a strange way to put it, he thought now as he stepped into the parking lot below Jeff's office and checked his phone. He had a missed call and a voice mail, and even though he hadn't saved the number, he recognized it. Detective Rice had called him while he was in therapy. It was funny that the therapists thought Nick could process the story on his own terms. That was bullshit.

He scratched at his head until he felt the scab lift off under his fingernail. He flicked it onto the pavement, then he called Detective Rice back.

"We'd like you to come into the station," the detective said. "We have a photo lineup for you to view."

—⟶

The police station was not what Nick had expected. He'd imagined his first sight would be something like a city precinct on a TV show: a bullpen of desks, maybe a cell where some town drunk would be sleeping off a bad night. The door to Salisbury's police station, instead, opened to a simple lobby. Sterile walls, linoleum tiles like a school. A white-haired woman sat across the room behind a desk and a thick pane of glass. She asked cheerily how she could help him. Nick introduced himself, and she called Detective Rice on the phone.

After a minute or so, Nick heard a door slam across the empty lobby. A petite, dark-skinned woman stepped from the doorway. She was really quite pretty, with long eyelashes and a bright smile. She was an officer—she wasn't in uniform, but it was clear from her posture and stride.

"I'm Detective O'Malley."

Nick shook her extended hand. "Nick."

"I wanted to take the opportunity to meet you," she said. "I've been working with Detective Rice on your case. Your friend Elle might have mentioned me."

Elle hadn't. They hadn't talked at all yet. Elle had texted Nick a few times, checking on him, but he hadn't responded. There was nothing to say.

"Let's go up and look at some photos."

He followed her up a narrow stairwell and down a hall to a small room where a heavyset man in uniform was waiting. Detective O'Malley waited in the hallway, and Nick stepped into the room. On the table was a closed manila folder.

The cop smiled and said, "Hi, Nick."

Nick returned the greeting.

The man introduced himself and handed Nick a sheet of paper. "These are instructions for the photo array," he said, and waved at the folder on the table. "Please take your time and read them."

When Nick finished reading, he lowered the sheet. The cop told him he could open the folder and look at the photos. "Leave it like that as you open it," he said, indicating how the folder was laid horizontally on the table. "So that the top of the folder blocks my view."

Taped in the folder was a grid of photos of men's faces. Two down, three across—six in all. They weren't mug shots; they looked more like headshots than anything. Each photo had a numbered label in the corner.

There, at the bottom left of the grid, was Josh. The photo was like a magnet; Nick's gaze fell on it almost instantly. No stubble in this picture, but the light eyes, the high cheekbones, even the single dark curl on his forehead.

"Call me Josh," this man had said to him, nearly in a drawl, the name had spilled so slowly from his mouth.

Bile rose in Nick's throat. His picture looked like a business portrait. He looked important. Nick could feel the cop staring at him.

"He's here," Nick said, and his voice sounded sad. Was he sad?

"Which one, Nick?"

The moment was so surreal that something in Nick's mind detached and spoke, separate from himself. It was an indifferent voice, pointing out a simple truth. *This will be the moment you will always identify as the one from which there was no turning back. Not the report. Not the forms. Not the interviews. This moment.* Nick turned and looked behind him, expecting to see the detective in the doorway, but the door was closed. Nick turned back to the table.

"Him," Nick said, and he placed a finger on the hollow of Josh's throat. "Number four."

"Where do you recognize him from?"

Nick lifted his finger from the photo. "That night. At the bar."

"Can you be more specific?"

Nick looked up at the cop. His fleshy face was relaxed, but his bright eyes were trained on Nick's. This man—the police—they needed him to say it. To say it *again*, to *another* person. The more people he told, the bigger it got, and the further it slipped from him.

"He's the man who assaulted me."

"How confident are you?"

The officer's eyebrows jumped and fell so quickly Nick might have missed it if he'd blinked. It wasn't a real question. This was a script. The officer knew what Nick would say. There was only one acceptable answer.

Nick looked down at the photo. "Positive."

13

Say what you will about its part in the decline of American culture, but social media was a beautiful thing from a law-enforcement perspective. It could show you who knew who, what people called themselves, where they were at a specific point in time. People would post incriminating photos and statements that could be screenshotted and placed in a file long after a post was deleted. Rice would never get sick of seeing what social media could do for them next. Just now, it had delivered him a rape suspect.

O'Malley had put the photo of Josh and Nick at the bar on the station's Facebook and Twitter accounts and asked people to share it. In the post, she called Josh "a witness to a crime." He and O'Malley had talked over the wording of the post for a while in advance. What they knew of Nick's assailant was that he was calculating, charming, and violent. To them, he smelled like a serial rapist. He was handsome, white, possibly well-off. Most of this added up to a guy who people probably didn't see as a monster. Maybe he seemed a little *off*; on the flipside, it was even possible he was well-liked. It was doubtful people saw him as the kind of guy who could be a rapist. If someone who actually knew Josh saw the photo of him with the caption "suspect in a rape case," they'd think, *That couldn't be Josh, even if it does look just like him.* But "a witness"? *Yeah,* they'd think, *that could be Josh in the photo.* And that morning, Rice walked into the station and learned it had done the trick.

The evening before, a woman called the tip line and said that the man in the photo on Facebook looked like her coworker, Raymond Walker. "What did he witness?" the coworker probably asked.

His own life go up in smoke, if Rice had anything to say about it.

An officer had hopped online and found a work headshot of Raymond Walker. Compared it to the photo at the bar. Things looked good.

When Rice got in that day, he called in Nick Hall for a double-blind photo array. Nick identified Walker's headshot.

Rice plugged all of this into the warrant he was drafting at his computer.

When he was done, he emailed a draft to the Assistant District Attorney for her comments. Then he called Raymond Walker's office.

Walker played dumb when he came on the line. Rice had identified himself to the secretary, so Walker was already on the defensive. Rice introduced himself politely, addressed him as "Mr. Walker."

Ray's response to Rice's credentials was: "All right?"

"Your name's come up in an active investigation."

"Oh, that's surprising."

Rice couldn't help but smile. You'd think someone who was actually surprised to find himself on the phone with a detective would ask *What kind of investigation?* But Walker already knew that. "Is it?"

Annoyance edged into Walker's voice. "Yes, it is."

"I'd like you to come in and answer some questions today."

A beat, and Walker said, "That might not be possible, I usually work late."

"So do I, Mr. Walker." Rice paused. "How about you swing by whenever you're off work tonight. Maybe we can clear all this up."

"I'm not sure I should do that," Walker said. "It's nothing personal, but without knowing why you want to talk to me . . ."

"'Course it's your call," Rice said. "This would just be your chance to give us your side of the story, before we have to go further."

There was a pause, and Walker said, "I'll be in around six."

Rice caught O'Malley's eye across the bullpen. Gave her a thumbs-up. "See you then."

14

Far off beyond the fields, the leaves were starting to turn. Sprays of red and orange dusted Julia's view from the road as she walked the kids home from the bus stop. Most of the trees would explode into their fall colors in a week or so, and there would be bare limbs all around before October was up. It wouldn't be long before the soft, springy plants in the garden were stiff and gray. The only way to survive what was coming was to harden and wait.

They were halfway back to the house—Seb chattering about school, Chloe whining about the walk—when Julia heard a car approaching behind them. She turned to see her own car coming down the long country road.

When Julia announced that it seemed Uncle Nick was coming to pick them up, Chloe squealed. They paused on the side of the road to wait for him.

Nick pulled up and apologized for being late.

"It's fine," Julia said. It really was—it was beautiful outside, and the kids had been dressed for the temperature—and she was too relieved to see him to care. Something about him going radio silent had unsettled her.

77

Julia loaded the kids into their seats and climbed up front with Nick. His face was drained of color, and he acknowledged her with nothing more than a flick of his eyes.

"Uncle Nick, where were you?"

Nick glanced up at the rearview to look at Seb. "I had to go to counseling."

"Why do you need counseling?" This time it was Chloe.

Before Nick could speak, Julia gave Chloe the party line. "It's to help him feel better after his accident."

Seb chimed in. "Did Grammy Hall do counseling after *her* accident?" That was a new one, apparently about Tony's mom's car accident the year before. Julia glanced at Nick apologetically. Kids had a way of pulling at the threads you most wanted to leave untouched.

"Sometimes getting in an accident is very scary," Julia said. "And so it helps to go to counseling to talk about it and feel better. So you feel less scared."

They pulled into the driveway as Chloe said, "Uncle Nick, are you scared?"

Nick put the car in park.

Julia spoke. "Kids, why don't you—"

Nick put his hand on her shoulder.

"Yes," he said, and he turned to face his niece. "Yes, I am scared."

He was right to tell them the truth, but it frightened Julia to hear him say it. It was part of a greater truth Chloe and Seb hadn't learned yet: there are things that can't be fixed. Maybe part of what Chloe was trying to understand was why Nick would need help from some other source, from outside their house. With her perfect life, Chloe had no reason to know that there were some things her parents could not make better.

15

Rice barely made it back to the station before six. While he'd been at the courthouse, O'Malley had set up the small conference room for their interview with Walker. Minutes after Rice arrived, the secretary called back to the bullpen, said Walker was there. Rice sent Merlo down to bring Walker to the conference room while O'Malley double-checked that the camera and mic were working.

They switched up their routine on occasion, but generally, Rice played good cop to O'Malley's bad. Counterintuitive on first thought, maybe, to have the female officer not playing the good cop, but the reasoning was simple: one detective was there to apply pressure, and the other was there to look like a lifeline. Most of their suspects were white men like Walker, and white men were more apt to believe that Rice could cut them a deal for cooperation. Rice had sex, age, and color on O'Malley. Wasn't right— just the way it was. So they used their differences to their advantage. And for her part, O'Malley enjoyed getting to treat a guy like Walker like she thought he was a guilty piece of shit.

They let Walker sit in the room for eight minutes before they joined him. They would watch the video later to see how many times he checked the clock behind him, fiddled with his phone, got up to look into the hallway. For now they waited in the bullpen. Rice slid a couple of unrelated printouts into the file to bulk it up.

Rice went in first. Walker had sat in the chair nearest the door, leaving one seat opposite him and one beside him.

"Mr. Walker," Rice said as he stretched out a hand. "I'm Detective John Rice, and this is my colleague Detective Megan O'Malley."

As she often did when they worked a suspect together, O'Malley posted herself in the doorway without a handshake or a word. She leaned against the doorframe and crossed her arms.

"Raymond Walker," the man said, "but you already knew that."

Rice laid the folder down on the table and took the seat across from Walker. "Sorry if we kept you waiting."

Walker smiled. Even under the fluorescents he was good-looking. "I'm sure you were busy," Walker said.

"Very," O'Malley said.

Walker looked sideways at her and then back at Rice. "Am I in some kind of trouble?"

The annoyance from the phone was gone. He was back in control of himself.

"You tell us," O'Malley said.

Rice held up a hand at O'Malley in an unspoken gesture that said, *Quiet*. "Well," Rice said, "we're trying to figure that out."

Walker's face shifted to that of a brownnosing child trying to please a schoolteacher. "How can I help?"

"Do you know why you're here, Mr. Walker?"

"Not a clue."

Rice pulled a photo from the file and slid it to Walker. "Do you recognize this man?"

Walker studied the picture. His eyes were narrowed ever so slightly, like he was working out what to say. It was a sweet picture of Nick Hall;

Rice had asked Tony for a recent photo for the file, and Tony had emailed him one from the past summer. Nick was bare-armed and grinning, his wet curls plastered to his forehead. He looked like he'd just climbed out of the lake behind him and pulled on a tank top. In the photo, Nick looked like he was on the cusp of manhood but still a boy in many ways. Rice would use the word *man* this evening, with Walker. It had occurred to Rice earlier that he could use his own biases to his advantage.

Walker spoke. "What's this about?"

"It's a simple question," O'Malley said. "Do you recognize him or not?"

Walker kept his eyes on Rice and smiled apologetically. "I think I have a right to know why I'm here."

"You're only here if you want to be," Rice said. "You're free to leave any time. Let me ask you this—if I told you this man says he knows you, how would you explain that?"

Walker dropped his gaze to the photo again. He was stalling—was he smart enough to know he was trapped with any answer? An admission that he knew Nick was further evidence that Nick had correctly identified him; a denial was evidence that he was a liar, since they had the photo at the bar to prove that the two had met. Anything feigning uncertainty and Rice would ask him if he always forgot the people he slept with. Then Rice would throw him the lifeline of consent—yeah they'd slept together, but it was consensual, right? And then they had him, because someone knocked out cold wasn't consenting to anything.

Rice started in. "Let me tell you what I think. I think you two had a sexual encounter."

"That what you're calling 'rape' these days?" O'Malley said.

Walker looked sideways at her, then back to Rice.

"And you know what my colleague thinks," Rice said, gesturing to O'Malley. "She believes him." Rice tapped the photo with a finger. "Maybe I should, too. But I don't like to leap to conclusions, especially not about what goes on behind closed doors between two adults."

O'Malley thudded her fist against the doorframe behind her. "Would you cut the boys'-club-consent bullshit?"

"Why don't you take a walk," Rice said.

O'Malley looked long at Walker, then slipped from the room. Rice got up and made a show of gently shutting the door. He sat back down in his seat and leaned toward Walker confidentially.

"O'Malley can get a little emotional about these cases. I think it's hard for her, as a woman. Don't get me wrong," he said with a wave, "she's an excellent detective. But there's a reason they give me the lead on cases like this."

"It's not right to just blindly believe whatever someone tells you because you have some chip on your shoulder."

"I know; I'm sorry about her."

"I've never hurt anyone in my life, Detective. Believe me."

"I do, to be honest. Not like this was some pretty little girl you could throw around." Rice chuckled as he spoke, and Walker smiled with relief. "He's a grown man," Rice said.

Walker nodded.

"Just help me understand what's going on here," Rice said. "Give me something to run up the chain."

"We never—" Walker stopped, like his tongue had snagged on a word.

"You two never what?"

Walker's gaze sharpened with defiance. He smiled with half his mouth. "That was good," he said quietly. "That was really something. Huh. I'm all done."

Rice wasn't ready to concede. "So we agree you knew him."

But it was too late. Walker's chair was already scraping back on the linoleum. "Goodbye, Detective."

Walker pulled open the door to the hallway. There was O'Malley, a thin stack of paper in her hands.

"Warrants," she said.

Rice had talked it over with the Assistant District Attorney and decided to secure the warrants for Walker's arrest and a DNA sample before the interview. He'd bombed over to the courthouse late that afternoon, gotten back just in time to interview Walker himself.

O'Malley circled a finger in the air. "Turn around, Mr. Walker. I'm placing you under arrest. We'll do your saliva at the jail."

16

TONY HALL, 2015

As Nick talked to the detective, Tony studied his face. Tony knew Nick had gone to the police station earlier that day and had identified a picture of Josh. It was him—Nick was sure of it. Julia had told Tony all of this; when Tony got home, Nick didn't feel like talking about it. Now, standing in the hallway with the phone against his ear, Nick's face looked like he was getting bad news. He murmured "Okay" every now and then but said nothing more.

Nick hung up.

Finally, Tony said, "Well?"

"They found him," Nick said. "They arrested him."

Tony's first thought was a selfish one: *Thank God; I might actually sleep tonight.* Tony's attention had been divided since that first call from the hospital. It didn't matter if he was at work, eating breakfast with the kids, or trying to sleep: his worry for Nick was ever present. But now, it was over. They had him.

Julia moved to Tony's side and asked what the detective had said.

"Something about bail," Nick said. "He needs $100,000 to get out."

Julia looked at Tony with wide eyes. "Wow. That's great."

"But there'll be a hearing on Monday, and it could get lowered. If he gets out, he won't be allowed to talk to me."

Bail. Right. It wasn't over. Now there would be court. Tony turned to Julia. She would know what came next.

"Are they gonna indict him?" she asked.

"I think he said something about that."

"Okay," Julia said. "Do you want me to call him back and ask?"

Nick shook his head. "He said someone would call me and I'd get to have a meeting or something."

"Oh, with the ADA?"

"What?"

"The prosecutor," she said.

"I think so." Nick's eyelids were drooping like he was exhausted.

"Sorry," she said. "I'm sure he just hit you with a lot of information."

"It's okay. I think they'll tell me more at the meeting."

"I'll go with you," Tony said.

"Okay," Nick said. He sounded annoyed.

"If you want."

Nick shrugged. "I'm gonna go to bed."

"Wait," Tony said. "Did he tell you the guy's name?"

Nick looked upward. "Yeah . . . I can't remember now. It's not Josh. Something with an R."

———

Raymond Walker. That was the man's name. It was on the paper's website the next day. Nick's name was absent.

Now, the man in the dim photo from the bar with the pale skin and dark hair had a name. Tony hadn't realized it before, but until that moment, the man in the photo had been a monster. He hadn't been a real person to Tony—he'd been nothing but the evil act. A name transformed him: Raymond Walker had an identity. He had a life. Tony had to know what it was.

He started by searching Walker's name.

Raymond Walker was a salesman at a company in Portsmouth, New Hampshire, where he sold waterworks products around New England. Under his photo on the company website, his brief bio read that he lived in southern Maine.

Raymond Walker lived in Salisbury, like Nick, according to a White-pages website.

Raymond Walker had graduated from the College of New England in 1998, making him thirty-eight, give or take. Thirty-fucking-eight, to Nick's twenty.

Raymond Walker had a private Facebook page. That was worse than him having none. All Tony could see was a profile picture: it was Walker flexing in a sleeveless shirt in front of a gym, grinning like a snake.

What Tony did not find was evidence of who he knew this man to be. There was no entry on a sex-offender registry, no other court cases, no news articles about prior victims.

Deep in the pages of a Google search, Tony found the 1997 obituary of one George R. Walker, who was survived by his wife, Darlene, and his son, Raymond. To say he found the obituary was a slight exaggeration—he found a link that was described as containing this obituary, but the link did not work. All he could do was read the description. It taunted him. An obituary might have divulged more personal information about Raymond's history, if it was even the same Raymond.

Now he searched the name Darlene Walker, and her Facebook page appeared. That morning, she had posted a long block of text on her page. In it, she wrote that her son had been arrested on "nothing more than a story, of which his side is completely different." She called Nick's accusation "the made-up story of a boy who went willingly."

Something surged in Tony as he read the words, and his chest boiled. "You fucking bitch," he hissed at his phone. People had shared the post and written comments—people who were friends with the Walkers, clearly. Lots of shocked and angry emojis on behalf of Walker and his mother.

"Unbelievable," one man had written.

A woman wrote: "Ray is such a good guy, have faith Darlene."

"I know," someone added. "Did the cops ask literally anyone who knows Ray? Because they either have the wrong guy or the other guy's lying."

One comment nearly stopped Tony's heart: "Does anyone know the accuser's name?" There was no response to that one.

To the rest of the world, Ray Walker was a good person until proven otherwise. He had a job, a house, a gym, a mother who loved him. Tony, Nick, Julia, the detectives—they could see what he really was. They had seen the sickness inside of him. When would everyone else see it, too?

Julia was working in her study that weekend. She often worked a bit on the weekends—she always felt she was behind. On the weekends, the kids were largely Tony's responsibility. Now, he stuck them in front of the television and knocked on her office door.

"What comes next?"

"Hmm?" She was standing at her desk, typing something.

"What comes next in Nick's court case?"

"Oh. It sounds like they'll get an indictment." The question must have been apparent on his face, because she explained herself. "The prosecutor will present evidence to the grand jury. Nick will have to testify."

"What will it be like?"

"I've never been to one. The defendant and the defense attorney don't go. Nick will have to tell *me* what it's like," she said with a laugh. Then she grew serious again. "He'll have to tell his story under oath. There will be people in there—the people sitting on the grand jury, the prosecutor, some kind of court reporter. The point is for the prosecutor to prove she has enough evidence to bring the charges against him. The real point, I think any prosecutor will admit, is to test the case. See how the evidence looks so far. She might even want to see how Nick does testifying."

Tony thought for a moment. "I'm glad he doesn't remember."

Julia cocked her head like she was considering this.

"Don't you think?" he asked.

"I think it's bad he doesn't remember."

"Why?"

"It gives the defendant free rein to make up whatever he wants."

"I thought his lawyer would have to stop him."

Julia looked confused. "Where did you get that?"

"You," he said. "You told me once you couldn't let clients lie."

"If I knew they were lying."

"Anyone would know he's lying."

She shook her head. "Not just if you *think* your client's lying. You have to know—like if he tells his lawyer 'I raped him,' the lawyer can't let him testify and say 'he consented.' But I doubt he'll tell his lawyer the truth."

"Did you have clients lie to you?"

"Yeah," she said apologetically. "I'm sure I did."

Julia had only been a defense attorney for four years, but in that time she represented all kinds of people. Most of them normal people, maybe even good people who'd made bad choices. But she'd represented some bad people, too. A wife-beating professor. A teenage drug dealer. A long line of parents who abused and neglected their kids.

And apparently there had been rapists. Tony just didn't know anything about them.

The thought of her defending someone like Raymond Walker made him sick to his stomach.

"I'll let you get back to work," he said quietly, and he closed the door on her.

17

A week after Josh—or Raymond—was arrested, Tony drove Nick to a meeting at the District Attorney's office. It was around the back of a courthouse where the case would happen. That was all Nick really understood: *the case would happen*. But what that meant—what would actually happen—he didn't know. He felt clueless about what he had started.

The District Attorney's office reminded Nick of the police station; it actually seemed more secure than the station had. The woman at the front desk sat behind a thick layer of glass to their right and she had to buzz them into the building through a locked door.

She brought them down a hallway to a room where two women were waiting.

"Can I get either of you a drink: coffee, a soda?"

"You have Coke?" Nick asked.

"You got it."

Meanwhile, the women in the room stood up, and the older one reached out her hand to Nick.

"Nick, it's nice to meet you." Her handshake was firm, and Nick tightened his grasp. "I'm Linda Davis, your prosecutor." She was striking, with red lipstick and jet-black hair. Nick wondered immediately if it was dyed.

The younger woman had a softer handshake. "Sherie," she said. "I'm your advocate." She smiled, revealing a gap between her front teeth.

"And you must be Tony," Linda said, turning to him.

They all sat down around the table as the woman from the front desk returned with Nick's drink.

"How are you doing?" Linda asked.

Nick popped the tab. "I'm okay."

"You in therapy?"

Nick nodded as Tony said, "He is."

Sherie was staring at Nick. She was probably looking at the yellow bruises on his cheek and neck. They were fading but still noticeable, at least if you knew to look.

"Really," Nick said. "I'm doing fine."

"Well, that's great," Linda said. "We wanted to go over the court process with you, answer any questions you might have so far."

"And I'm your girl when you have questions later," Sherie said, "because you will." She pushed two business cards across the table. Nick and Tony each took one. Beneath her name were the words *VICTIM WITNESS ADVOCATE*. "My job is to help you understand what's going on and to be there for court. And I can help you advocate for yourself."

"Are you a lawyer?" Tony asked.

"No," she said. "I'm just there to support Nick. But I work with Linda—we're always in touch—so when Nick has questions he can call me." She turned to Nick.

Sherie's voice went apologetic. "It's going to be a lot of information all at once, but then it's gonna be slow. It normally takes a long time for a case to end."

At the same time, Nick and Tony asked, "How long?"

"It can take a year," Linda said.

A year. The word was small, but it held a lifetime: Christmas. His twenty-first birthday. The summer. Next school year, his senior year. *This* might still be the center of his life?

"That's ridiculous," Tony said.

"I know," Linda said. "But this is a high-priority case," Linda continued, "so I'll do everything I can to make sure it goes before the grand jury in November. But the court gives the defendant time to hire a lawyer, do an investigation, get an expert. There's a lot that goes into a case like this."

An investigation? What was there for Josh—Raymond—to investigate?

Linda went on. "A month or two after we get an indictment, we'll have a court date where the defense attorney and I talk about the case and try to come up with a deal."

Right. Plea deals.

"So it could be over then," Tony said.

"It could be over then," Sherie said, "but you should know it usually isn't."

"I thought most cases ended in plea deals," Tony said. "My wife's a lawyer."

"Many do," Linda said. "But cases involving sexual assault go to trial more often than others. Plea deals are still common, just not *as* common. But if we can get a conviction and a sentence we like, we absolutely want to avoid you having to testify."

Nick had felt Sherie's eyes on his face again when Linda said the words *sexual assault*. She was looking for a reaction from Nick.

"Is that something you're willing to do, Nick?"

He turned to Linda. "What?"

"Are you willing to testify?"

"Oh, yeah," he said.

"It's important for me to know if you don't want to."

Nick was confused. Obviously he didn't *want* to. "Don't I have to?"

"Well, if you want a trial, yes. I can't have a trial without you. But it's your choice. If you don't want to testify, I'll do what I can to get him to plead to something. I just need to know where you're at."

This was confusing. Nick didn't know what to say.

"Your name will stay private," Sherie said.

"Is it private now?" Tony asked.

"Yes," Linda said. "I filed a motion. That's why the criminal complaint calls him 'John Doe.'"

Nick didn't know anything about that.

"I didn't know you could do that," Tony said.

"We have to have a reason," Linda said. "It depends on the case. I wanted to maintain *some* privacy for Nick." She turned and began addressing him. "Your case is open to the public, which means reporters or anyone else can come watch the court dates. They just don't learn your name, so it shouldn't get published anywhere."

"I know it's still a huge invasion to have to testify about this," Sherie said. "There's no judgment if you don't want to. You've been so brave to even report this."

"It's not a big deal," Nick said. They were acting like testifying would kill him. He didn't want to, obviously, but he could do it.

Linda was studying him. "It's your choice, Nick. Just tell me if there comes a time when I *need* to settle the case. I won't go to trial if you aren't testifying."

"It's fine," he said. "I'll do it."

"Okay," Linda said. "Let's hope he'll take a deal and we'll avoid that.

But even if it does settle, it normally happens a lot later on, closer to trial."

"Okay," Nick said.

"A year," Tony said again. He glanced at Nick.

There was an in-breath of silence, like everyone was expecting Nick to say something. He didn't know what else to give them.

18

A *year.* The words kept repeating as they walked down the hall, out of the DA's office. They might be doing this *a year* from now. Tony looked over at Nick.

Nick was wearing Tony's clothes. He'd brought a pair of jeans from his apartment, but that morning before they left for the meeting, Nick had grown anxious about his outfit.

Tony thought Nick looked good when they met in the hallway upstairs.

Nick grimaced. "I look like I'm not taking this seriously." He gestured down at his cotton-and-denim ensemble.

"You look great," Tony said. He'd taken the day off work to go with him.

"I should have brought something nicer," Nick said.

Tony tried to understand. "Are you worried they won't respect you?"

"Do you think we have time to stop somewhere?"

Tony looked at his watch. No chance. "What size are you?"

"Thirty-two/thirty-two."

Tony smiled. "You got Dad's waist. Hold on."

Tony went to his bedroom closet and dug for a pair of pants he was sure hadn't gone to Goodwill yet. He'd had Ron Hall's waist once, too, but those days were gone. With parenthood came dad weight, and no

94

amount of ab work seemed capable of scraping off the last of his new inches. He found the tan pants hanging in the far back of the closet. He selected his smallest dress shirt and a tie, just in case.

When Tony came out of the bathroom a few minutes later, Nick was opening the door to Seb's room. His tie hung open on his collar.

"Can you tie this?"

Tony stepped up to his little brother. He wasn't so little anymore— Tony's shirt was snug on his shoulders. He'd seen Nick in his hand-me-downs many times over the years, but never in clothes from Tony's adulthood. The juxtaposition of this moment against his five-year-old son's bedroom made his chest feel tight.

He grasped the tie and began. Tony brought the knot up close to Nick's throat; Nick gasped, stepping back as Tony let go.

"I'm sorry," Tony said, overlapping Nick's rushed "It's fine."

Nick brought his hands up to the tie, fumbled at the knot.

"I can get it," Tony said.

"Let me," Nick said. He worked at the knot, his eyes welling, and finally it came loose.

He handed the tie back to Tony.

"Just give me a minute," Nick said, and closed the door.

That was the thing. Sometimes Nick seemed fine. Looked like his old self. And Tony would forget what had happened. In that outfit, Nick looked like a man, but to Tony he was a kid again.

Tony held the door as they left the DA's office. "I'm proud of you."

"For what?"

"Being so brave," Tony said. "You could be like 'this isn't fair' and not do anything. It wasn't your fault, but you're still doing something."

Nick groaned loudly. "Would you stop saying that?"

"Saying what?"

"That I'm brave; it wasn't my fault. Do you know how many people have said that to me?"

"We're saying it because it's true."

"But it doesn't matter." Nick tilted his head back and drained the last of his Coke.

"It *does* matter," Tony said. "It wasn't your fault, Nick."

Just off the walkway, there was a large, covered trash can with RETURNABLES written on the side, and Nick walked to it.

"You're not helping," Nick said as he lifted the lid.

"Okay, so how can I help?"

Nick tossed in the can and turned to face Tony. "How about you let me speak for myself?"

"What?"

Nick pointed at the building. "You couldn't have talked over me more if you were trying."

"You *weren't* talking! Someone had to."

"I didn't have the chance."

"Fine. I'll sit there in silence next time."

"Great. Now tell me I'm not a victim." There was something in his voice that sounded like a taunt. Like he didn't expect Tony to say it.

"You're not," Tony said.

"Then stop acting like I am."

Tony didn't know what to say.

Okay, he was babying him. But what was he supposed to do? Pretend it hadn't happened? When Tony did that, he did stupid shit like hand Nick a tie after he'd been choked by a guy. Nick *was* a victim, something awful had happened to him. Was it such a big deal, that he had been a victim? Just in that one moment?

"It was just a single moment," Tony said. "I wish I'd been there."

"God*damn* it." As Nick spoke, he pushed the trash can beside him, tipping it over and spewing cans onto the lawn.

"Nick!"

"You think *you* would have stopped him."

"I would have *killed* him."

"Shut up, Tony, just shut up!" The vein in Nick's forehead was bulging. He kicked a can at his feet and crouched down, sat in the grass.

Nick groaned, angry and raw, and buried his face in his hands.

Tony stood for a moment, shocked at Nick's display. He'd never seen Nick get angry like that before.

Above Nick, he could see a pale face in the window, looking out at them from the DA's office.

He walked to Nick's side and stooped down, pushing handfuls of cans and bottles into the trash can. Then he righted the bin and offered Nick his hand. They walked to the car in silence.

⌐

They were almost home when Tony apologized.

Nick had been staring out the window, maybe watching the fields roll by, maybe stewing. He turned to Tony. "For what?"

"I should have just shut up when you said I wasn't helping. I'm acting like I think I understand, and I don't."

Nick nodded. "I know you just want to make it better."

Tony said nothing. He wanted to tell Nick he was right—tell Nick it was killing him not to be able to just undo what had happened. Frustrating him beyond explanation that he couldn't understand what Nick was feeling. He and Nick had always understood each other. Yeah, Nick was gay and he wasn't—there were pieces there that Tony could never truly *get*. But on a base level, they understood each other like no one else did. It was pretty simple: they'd had the same dad. Heard the same slurs, felt the same cuff to the ear, been told—in Ron Hall's varied but persistent ways—that they were worthless. So they understood each other. They even had a simple message in code. When Nick was little, Tony would take his hand and squeeze it three times: *I love you*, it meant. Nick would return four squeezes: *I love you, too.*

To feel so clueless about this tragedy, so separate from Nick, made Tony's chest ache.

But he didn't say any of that. He seemed to be getting everything wrong. And all of that might just make Nick worry about how this was affecting Tony when he should be worrying about himself.

"I'm sorry, too," Nick said. "I don't know why I flipped out like that."

"It's okay." Tony paused. "It's okay, and that's all I'm gonna say."

"Ha," Nick said. "Thank God."

⟶

That weekend, Nick moved back to his apartment.

19

J ulia had always fought against the addition of a second television. "One in the living room is *plenty*," she used to say to Tony every six months or so when he would mention how nice it would be to watch a movie in bed, or how he wished he could keep an eye on the game as they made dinner. When Chloe was born and Julia started nursing her, however, she quickly changed her mind about the TV in the bedroom. She and Tony had made a deal that he would pick up a small one at Target, and it would move out of their bedroom and into the kitchen whenever Julia stopped breastfeeding the baby. It sat on a small table in the corner beside the hamper and entertained them with episodes of *Lost*, *CSI*, and Tony's secret favorite, *The Bachelor*. Then one day Chloe was done breastfeeding, but Julia said nothing, and eventually Seb was born, so the TV stayed. Tony had the luxury of a TV in his bedroom for four years before Julia finally moved it one day while he was at the office. He had feigned devastation when he came home to find it in the kitchen, collapsing on the floor to the giggling glee of his children.

This was how, three years after that, Julia came to be packing lunches for the kids with the television on a local news program the morning that Raymond Walker made bail. She was shaking baby carrots into plastic baggies when she heard the words behind her: "A man from Salisbury who is accused of sexual assault posted $100,000 surety bail today." Julia spun toward the television and moved closer.

One of two local anchors looked grave as she spoke. "Local business-man Raymond Walker was arrested for gross sexual assault for an alleged incident on October second of this year. The victim is a twenty-year-old male from the York County area. *His* name is private in the court records at this time."

Julia's heart pounded in her ears, and she exhaled hard at this line.

"This morning, Mr. Walker was released after filing proof of a $100,000 bail lien on his home in Salisbury. The State plans to seek an indictment of Mr. Walker next month."

Julia heard heavy feet on the stairs. She unclenched her damp palms from the counter's edge and switched off the television before Tony could see.

—⌒—

That evening, Julia left the TV off when she started dinner.

All day she had resisted the urge to call Detective Rice and ask him how Raymond Walker had been allowed to post bail at all. If she'd known the prosecutor she would have called her to talk about it, but their paths had never crossed during Julia's brief time in practice. Detective Rice was the only person on Nick's case she felt any real connection to. But there would be nothing for him to say to her. Of course Walker had made bail. Unfairly, it was only the poor who had to wait out their case from a jail cell. Walker had offered up his house as collateral for his continued at-tendance in court. There was nothing abnormal about it, really. Under other circumstances, Julia would have acknowledged that it was a good thing: a defendant was supposed to be innocent until proven guilty. There was supposed to be a balance: the government couldn't punish you without proving that you'd done something wrong. In theory, the public could be protected by bail conditions while the defendant awaited trial. But now that this was happening to her family, suddenly the whole concept of due process seemed dangerous.

She knew there were bail conditions in effect now; she had texted Nick earlier that day to see how he was. When he didn't answer, she called and he picked up. Nick promised her he was okay, not that she fully believed him. In the weeks he'd lived with them, she never felt he was showing how he truly felt about the situation. But yes, he should at least be safe. Walker would not be allowed to speak to Nick, let alone come near him, but court orders did not always prevent violence. And what if he ran away? What if he disappeared, leaving Nick frightened? Leaving Walker free to hurt other men?

Tony got home while she was chopping root vegetables to roast. He had barely stepped both feet in the kitchen when Chloe came running in, followed closely by Seb. Both were hollering "Dadaaaaaa" as though they were missiles screaming by.

Julia set the knife on the cutting board and turned to Tony with a grimace.

"Enough, beasts!" he shouted. "Let me kiss your mother!"

Tony waded over to Julia, one child on each leg, and kissed her hello.

She looked at her ridiculous, precious family and breathed deeply. *This is perfect. Be happy.*

⌒

After the kids were asleep, Julia and Tony stood on opposite sides of their room, undressing for bed. As Julia pulled off her earrings at the dresser, she contemplated whether she should tell Tony about Walker. He'd been in a good mood all evening, and now he stood behind her, humming. There was no way he knew. Was it patronizing to hide it from him? She'd saved him from one day of ruminating on Nick and Walker. Selfishly, she wanted to spread some of the bad news to someone else and to relieve herself of the guilt of keeping this secret from him. But she could carry this for him—the burden of knowing that the man who assaulted Nick was free again, for now. *Christ, listen to yourself. Not telling your husband something that's public news makes you some kind of martyr? Get over yourself.*

She turned to face him. "Ray Walker made bail this morning."

Tony finished pulling his shirt off. His hair was a pile of static; he looked electrocuted.

"Oh, honey." Julia laughed and moved toward him. "Your—"

"He made bail," he cut in, leaning away from her hand.

"It was on the news earlier. He had to put up his house; it's not like he's going anywhere."

"That's not . . . he—" Tony fumbled for words. "Have you talked to Nick? Does he know?"

"Yeah, I texted him earlier to make sure."

"But not me."

Julia waved her hand at him. "I thought you'd get upset, and I was right." She heard herself sound defensive, but Tony seemed unfazed by her tone.

He was looking out their window, fists clenched, a tight frown clamped on.

"Honey," Julia said. "Nick knows, and he's okay."

"He should come here, tonight, just to be safe."

Julia shook her head. "He doesn't want that. There's a no-contact order; that man can't talk to Nick or go anywhere near him. He doesn't know where Nick lives." She had closed the distance between them and smoothed down his wild hair. "Nick is gonna be fine."

Tony hung his head.

"I've had some of these same thoughts," she said. "I have. But I talked to him, and he's actually good. He's happy to be back at school, hanging with his roommates. He just wants to get back to normal. We have to let him have that." Her voice went to a whisper. "Okay?"

Tony nodded.

She kissed him deeply and guided him to their bed.

20

NICK HALL, 2015

When Nick moved back to his apartment, the scab came with him. That weekend, he realized it had been two weeks since it happened—two weeks since that night—and still the small wound hadn't healed. He resolved to leave it alone.

The first couple of days he was restless, quick to tune out his professors' voices in class. His mind was a tangle of thoughts: Why had he left with Ray? Why was he living like this? What had he expected? And his fingers were on the scab, rubbing, flicking, but each time he realized—*goddamn it, I'm picking at it again*—he sat on his hands to stop himself.

On Wednesday morning, he awoke to a text from his sister-in-law: Hi honey. Hope you're hanging in there. Just thought I'd give you a heads up that RW posted bail, better to hear it from me than the news. If you need anything we're here for you. His hand reached back, and his fingers dove beneath his hair; this time, when the sting alerted him to what he was doing, he scratched harder. As he pulled the loosed scab through his hair, a couple of strands came with the skin. Maybe if he pulled out some of the hairs, the wound would breathe and heal faster; if it would just heal, he would stop picking at it. He pinched his fingers around a couple strands and pulled; his scalp stretched and released the roots, which came free with a painfully satisfying pop. Nick looked down at his hand. The nail of his index finger was rimmed in light red blood, and a small tuft of his own hair was pinched between his fingers.

Oh my God. I just pulled out my hair.

It had all happened so fast. Nick crept from his bed to his door and listened. He didn't hear any of his housemates outside, so he opened the door and scuttled across the hall to the bathroom. Mary Jo's hand mirror was in the cabinet where Nick remembered it would be; he leaned toward the mirror over the sink, using the hand mirror to inspect the back of his head. There was nothing—wait, yes, there was something. "Oh shit, *shit*, what did I do?" Nick hissed aloud. The pristine landscape of his dark hair was marred by a pock of white scalp and red wound.

His phone was ringing in the bedroom. He hurried back across the empty hall to his room. Julia was calling him.

Was he okay, she wanted to know.

Yes, he told her.

Had he seen her text, she asked.

Yes, he had, he said. He was fine—good, actually. Nice to be getting back to normal. He wasn't even thinking about Josh. Raymond.

Okay, she told him. Her voice was light, and she believed him. She didn't know him well enough, apparently. She couldn't hear the strain in his voice.

The rest of the week, he wore a Red Sox cap his dad had given him years ago. It wasn't his style, but he'd kept it out of sentimentality—a good day with Dad. It came in handy now, not that anyone seemed to notice the little patch of skin when he did remove the cap. The rest of that week, Nick occasionally found himself touching the spot, rubbing at it mindlessly, but he resisted damaging the area further.

But then Ray gave a public statement.

It happened on the last Sunday of October, a miserable bookend to the worst month of his life. Somewhere in the early-morning hours of that day, Nick had finally shut his laptop and gone to sleep. He awoke bleary-eyed and disoriented, unsure of where he was. The room was bright with sunlight. There was his bedside clock: it read 11:27. There was a knocking behind him, and he realized he was in his bedroom and someone was at his door.

"Yeah," he croaked, his vocal cords coated with sleep.

"Can I come in?" The voice was dulled by the door, but he recognized it was Elle.

"Yeah."

He rolled toward the door as Elle pushed it open. She took two reserved steps into the room. "Are you just waking up?"

"Yeah." Things had been awkward between them since the morning after it happened. He didn't blame her for any of it, but he knew she blamed herself. She kept apologizing. Was painfully careful around him. It made Nick tired.

"You haven't been on your phone?"

Nick rolled back and reached for his phone on his bedside table.

"Hold on," Elle said as she came toward him.

Nick's screen overflowed with notifications.

"What's going on?" Nick felt immediate despair.

"Um, that guy, Ray, he sent, like, a statement into all the newspapers."

Nick had missed calls and texts from Tony and Julia, Tony's mother, friends, even Chris. He hadn't spoken to Chris since he stood Nick up that night. He opened the message.

I'm so sorry.

Nick looked up at Elle. "What did Ray say?"

Elle looked like she was going to cry. "Um, basically that you two went home together and you were, uh, basically that it was all, like, consensual and you . . . Well, he said it in a weird way, but he made it sound like you wanted him to do what he did."

Nick shook his head, trying to process Elle's gibberish.

"Like rough sex. Like you wanted him to be rough. And now you're lying."

Disbelief rolled upward from deep in his stomach. At first Nick couldn't speak: he felt his mouth hang open in a horrified smile. No one would believe that . . . would they?

Inexplicably, his first question was, "Which newspaper?"

"All of them. Or, I don't know." Her voice cracked. "Like, the Maine papers."

Nick sat up higher in bed. "Wait, does he name me?"

Elle's eyes filled with tears. "He said you went to school here."

Nick looked back at his phone. Chris knew it was Nick.

"Do people know it's me?"

Elle began to cry.

Wait. Wait, no.

"Elle?"

"They know," she sobbed.

"How?"

"The letter. He said your major."

No. No.

"And." She paused. "And I guess Mary Jo's boyfriend told some people."

"How does *he* know?"

Elle stepped closer to Nick, her shoulders drooping. "I told Mary Jo. I'm so sorry. You were gone and you didn't answer my texts, I thought I could tell her. And she told him. I never would have told her if I knew he'd be so stupid."

His mind raced. If Chris knew . . . Chris didn't hang out with Mary Jo or her boyfriend. How many people had her boyfriend told for Chris to find out?

"How many people know? What are they saying?"

"I don't know," she said quietly. She was lying.

"Do they believe him?"

"Mary Jo's boyfriend?"

"*Ray*," Nick said.

Elle shrugged with a grimace. That looked like a yes.

"They do," he said.

"Just trash people who post in the comments on newspaper websites," she said as she sniffled against her hand. "People are commenting, that's all—it doesn't mean anything. It's too ridiculous to believe. Anyone who knows you believes you."

Nick looked down at his phone again. Pulled up the internet browser. Elle snatched the phone from his hands.

"Hold on, you're not reading it."

"Are you *fucking kidding* me? *Of course* I'm reading it. *Give* me my *fucking* phone, *Elle*." Nick forced the words out of himself in a voice he'd never heard before; pushing harder with each word felt good. He could let his anger out on Elle—she deserved it. That night hadn't been her fault, but this was. Her face was wet, but she had stopped crying. Her eyes were wide, like a sad baby deer. *Perfect, make me feel bad when I'm the one whose life is ruined, that's just classic Elle.*

"Please promise not to read the comments," she said quietly, handing the phone back.

"*Bye*" was all he said.

Elle turned and left quickly as Nick reached back into his hair and dug the scab off. It was smaller and drier from its days of respite, and it came off clean and fast. *There.* He quickly decided to check the local paper, *Seaside News*, though it sounded like it was in the larger papers, too. *Seaside* felt the most personal. There it was on the main page. MAN ARRESTED FOR SEXUAL ASSAULT SPEAKS OUT IN A LETTER TO THE EDITOR. As Nick clicked the link with his right hand, he felt the fingers of his left twirling a small section of hair next to the patch. *STOP*. He sat on his left hand and read.

It began with a paragraph in italics. The letter, it said, did not reflect the views of the newspaper. It was an opinion piece from a reader about the criminal justice system. He began to skim Ray's letter. Read the words without processing them: *brought the wrong man home, he had been drinking hard, rough play*. Rough play. Nick's stomach turned into a hot, solid mass, and adrenaline swept through him in a tidal wave. Rough play. Ray was saying Nick wanted it: the whole thing. Saying Nick pursued Ray, not the other way around. Nick asked to be hurt—asked for what Ray did to him. The slap, the punch, the hands on his neck—*stop it, stop it, don't think of that*.

Nick curled into a ball in his bed, barely able to breathe. Blood pounded in his ears. His mind was rushing, swirling, bursting, but he was too paralyzed to move. It had happened. Ray had hit back. Of course he had. He'd already proved he wasn't weak like Nick. And the prosecutor's motion to protect Nick's name hadn't mattered. Everyone knew it was Nick. His story to be weighed against Ray's. Nick would be proved one of two things: a victim or a liar. Finally, his hand began to reach for his head. *Stop. Too visible*. Nick reached below his sheets for his right thigh. He pinched a tuft of thin leg hair between his fingers and pulled slowly. His skin released the small bulbous hair roots with a collective *pop*.

21

TONY HALL, 2015

The view from the front porch had changed. The hay laid down on the field had lost its golden color, looked more gray-green after weeks in the dipping temperatures and occasional rain. On the horizon, the tree line had gone gray too: the colorful leaves had dropped to the ground, where they would eventually rot. Tony stood on the porch in his robe, the air cold on his bare ankles. Was the end of fall always this ugly?

He heard Chloe come down the stairs. He turned and watched through the door as she drifted by and down the hall. He'd closed the inner door behind him when he stepped out onto the porch. The bottom half was screen, the top half glass. Through the glass, he could see Seb down the hall, standing in the kitchen, watching Julia make pancake batter.

The furnace had kicked on, but the house was still warming up. The incident with Nick had thrown off their usual rhythm, and Julia hadn't yet renewed their annual debate about the ideal thermostat setting. For now, that left Tony in charge, and layers were much needed in the morning. Chloe's hair was in its usual after-sleep form—something like a rat's nest disasterpiece—and seeing it spilling from the blanket she was bundled in sent warmth through his bones.

Get out of the cold, he thought, *and go in to your family.*

Tony went down the porch steps and stooped to grab the newspaper on the front walkway. In truth, his subscription to the Sunday paper stretched their budget. But the tradition had grown too important to abandon; it was almost integral to his sense of self. He'd started reading the paper the summer he dropped out of law school—the same summer he started dating his former classmate, then Julia Clark. While Julia toiled on in school, Tony dropped out. He would never admit it out loud, but reading a physical paper made him feel like he was still an intellectual. Still able to match her in conversation, or at least keep up.

Tony slid the paper from its plastic sheath as he climbed the steps. The past few weeks, Tony had combed the paper for mention of Nick's assault. There had been short articles online following Walker's arrest, but the incident had not made the Sunday paper. He straightened the pages. There was no need to comb the paper today. It was on the front page.

In the bottom right-hand corner was a headline: MAN ARRESTED FOR SEXUAL ASSAULT SPEAKS OUT IN A LETTER TO THE EDITOR. Tony heard himself suck in air. *Something else*, he thought. *Another case, please.*

But it was not another case. Beneath the title was Raymond Walker's name. Tony began to read.

> I started writing this letter from the jail in Salisbury. One of the guards gave me paper and a dull pencil that I had to use in the common area. He didn't want me stabbing anyone or digging at my wrists, apparently. Overnight I was stripped of my humanity,

assumed I'd act like an animal in a cage, perhaps because I was put in one.

Take a moment, from the comfort of your home, and imagine yourself in my shoes.

So now you are in a cage. How did you end up there? Simple. You brought the wrong man home with you.

You met him at a bar. He sat beside you, offered you a shot, asked your name. He asked about your job, said he was in school for business, asked if you might teach him something. All you could see was that this young, dynamic man, to your lonely delight, was making a move on you. What you failed to see was that he had been drinking hard when you arrived, and he doubled your pace as you sat together talking.

You waited for him to grow tired of your graying hair and uncool style. Instead, to your delight and your destruction, he asked you to take him home.

He must have lived nearby for school, but you failed to think through why he didn't want you seen at his place. You were simply too eager, so you brought him to a hotel.

There, he surprised you again with an invitation you hadn't expected from the sweet-faced boy at the bar: one for rough play. It was an invitation you'd accepted with other partners, and you welcomed it that night. A conversation ensued in words and touches. A back-and-forth that climbed and crested.

Tony's vision blurred and doubled. With each line it grew harder to read. He cried out, a strange "gah" dragging from deep in his throat, and he ripped the front page off the paper, and the second, and third. He threw the paper down the steps and spun, trying to register something, anything he could strike. *Let it out. Let it out.* He turned to the house. *The door.* Tony lashed out with a tight fist and put his hand through the glass at chest-level. His foot went through the screen panel and he fell, scraping his arm down the broken glass.

"Jesus Christ!" Julia's voice echoed down the hall.

He staggered upright to see his wife rushing toward him, his children standing in the kitchen behind her.

22

Some smart-ass defense attorney had dropped off a couple dozen doughnuts at the station that morning, and Rice found O'Malley standing over them in the breakroom.

"I'm a goddamn cliché," she said with a mouthful of Boston cream.

"You're disgusting is what you are," Rice groaned. "Keep your mouth shut." He selected a plain, cakey doughnut.

O'Malley gulped to swallow her mouthful and pointed at Rice's selection. "You are also cliché."

A plain doughnut? "I'm classic!"

O'Malley rolled her eyes. "Just take your coffee and your plain doughnut and go play cop." She made a goofy, bug-eyed face at her own doughnut. "Leave us be."

"Gladly."

Rice made his way to his desk in the bullpen. For such a serious detective, O'Malley could get playful sometimes. Rice didn't mind, though. Unlike some, she could turn it off like she was flicking a switch. She was always professional when she needed to be. Her sense of humor was just her coping mechanism—humor, long-distance running, and apparently

Boston-cream doughnuts. Irene used to be Rice's favorite grounding force—sinking into her arms after a long day eased him like nothing else ever had. He still had mass and yardwork. Breakfast with his old friends. Visits from the grandkids; calls with his daughter.

Rice had spent a lot of his weekend thinking about the Hall family. It hadn't been the first time he'd struggled to leave the work at the office, so to speak, and it wouldn't be the last. In a small way, all the sadness that happened to the victims in these cases happened to him, too, and it had a way of building up in his mind. With decades of experience, Rice had learned to firmly tell unpleasant thoughts to leave him alone while he was off duty, but it didn't always work.

On Sunday, Rice opened his paper to see that Santa had dropped off his gift early this year. On the front page was a letter to the editor from Raymond Walker, admitting that he was, in fact, the man Nick met at the bar that night. Calling what had occurred at the motel "rough play." It was everything Rice had wanted, everything Walker wouldn't give him at the station two weeks ago: an admission and an unbelievable defense. Rice nearly kissed the paper.

But then it started to bother him. He'd even thought about calling Nick on Sunday, to check on him mostly, but also to talk to him. He prayed for the Halls at mass instead.

Now, he dragged his chair forward at his desk and pulled up the letter on the station computer. He scrolled to the words that had lodged in his brain.

> There, he surprised you with an invitation you hadn't expected from the sweet-faced boy at the bar: one for rough play. It was an invitation you'd accepted with other partners, and you welcomed it that night. A conversation ensued in words and touches. A back-and-forth that climbed and crested. You parted from him feeling understood, feeling like the luckiest man on earth.

A week later, the police call you at your work and ask you to come to the station. They show you a photo of the man you met at the bar. Your stomach flutters, and you wonder if he committed a crime. You say nothing, unsure if an acknowledgment would betray him.

Then the police say that this man has told them that you raped him.

To say you are shocked is an understatement.

They want your side of the story, they say. You almost give it to them, but you can feel the trick in it, and you hold back. They arrest you.

For the first time in your life, hard metal handcuffs are tightened around your wrists. You are sat down in a police car and driven to the jail. You are strip searched. You are given a uniform to wear, and you think, *Just like on television*. Because you were arrested on Friday and don't happen to have $100,000 in the bank, you spend the weekend in jail.

You have to wear the uniform when you go to court, and they add shackles, as if you'd be stupid enough to run. You meet with the free lawyer for the day, who looks about eighteen years old, in the holding cell with all the other prisoners. There's no privacy, not that the lawyer has time to talk about much with you. Still, she says enough to make your cellmates raise their eyebrows.

"They've charged you by complaint with gross sexual assault," she says. It's the beginning of a long morning of gibberish that will only occasionally be translated for you.

"They're going to indict you," she says, "so you don't have to enter a formal plea today. The only thing worth focusing on is getting your bail lowered."

In the courtroom awaiting you is the same judge who granted the arrest warrant. The same judge who told the police they could cuff you, swab your mouth for your DNA, and put you in a cage for the weekend. And why did she let them do all that? Because she read a story about you. A story the man from the bar told the police. This judge already hates you, has already chosen a side. She leaves the bail so high that you'll have to use your house as collateral.

"First you have to get it appraised," the free lawyer explains, "and you'll need to record the lien, there's a form; if you forget you can call the clerk's office."

Instead, you call your mother from the jail and tell her what's happened, because you need to ask her to arrange the appraisal. You need her to drive the papers around until the court is satisfied that it effectively owns your house if you violate your bail conditions.

In all, you spend twelve nights, thirteen days, in a cage, waiting to bail out. You are so obsessed with regaining your freedom that you don't realize the depth of what is happening until you walk out of the jail. You've tasted what it's like to lose your freedom. To sleep behind a locked door across from a toilet. To feel prisoners—and you're one of them—look at you sideways. You've heard your name on the news followed by the words *gross sexual assault*. You know that, if you cannot disprove a cry of rape, not only will you go to prison, but when you are out, you will never be free again. Your name will go on a list, and until you die, every person who sees that list will think that they know you. "Know" what you've done. "Know" that you are something less than human.

You will be reassured when you recall our experiment: this is my situation, not yours. My impossible battle to fight against a story. My life that will hinge upon who is more believable: me or the man from the bar. The man I found so charming, so trustworthy, that I went to bed with him.

His story might ruin my life. I don't understand it, this man's decision to lie. I can make educated guesses. Self-hatred. Shame. It's not easy for many of us to accept ourselves, as gay men. Add to that the taboo of what he likes in bed, and, well, I can say I hadn't planned on sharing my predilections with the public.

> I fear I will never know why this damaged young man has done
> this to me. My only hope is that the truth will come out in time,
> but my introduction to our system has left me with little faith.

A defendant dissatisfied with his arrest, Rice thought. *Newsworthy, indeed*. Another defendant who wanted to pretend the police were without physical evidence. They had the damage he'd done to Nick's body. Nick's blood left behind at the motel.

People wouldn't believe Nick had asked for that, would they? He dragged his chair closer to his desk and pecked at his keyboard to pull up the letter on the station computer. Rice scrolled to the comment section of the page. The top comment read:

> Shame on Seaside for publishing this vitriol.

Good, Rice thought.
Another read:

> It's probably true. Boy's crying wolf. Let's waste taxpayer money sorting this out.

Bad.
Someone had replied:

> God hates f*gs. Hope this sets that boy straight lol.

Disgusting. Rice copied and pasted the link into an email to the ADA, Linda Davis, and wrote:

> You see this?

At least Nick's identity was concealed. Still, it probably stung like hell, reading this. Someone should explain to Nick that this was a good thing. Rice pressed his finger into the doughnut crumbs on his desk, then scraped them from his fingertip with his teeth. Mostly a good thing.

His cell buzzed on the desk. It was Linda.

"I can't believe it," she said.

"Merry Christmas," Rice said.

She laughed. "Don't get cocky."

"I know."

"I got a call from Eva Barr yesterday." Linda's voice was tinged with anxiety Rice was certain she'd intended on hiding.

"Really."

"Yup. At least we know what we're dealing with."

Walker had hired Eva Barr, then. Better the devil you know, people often said, but Rice might have taken his chances elsewhere. Eva Barr was trouble in a rape case. It should have been an obvious tactic, but jurors always seemed to give Eva's clients extra credit just for having a pretty woman defending them. Eva was good at looking like she believed in her clients' innocence. She brazenly tried ugly, nasty cases that some attorneys would have bent over backward to settle, and she usually got an acquittal on the higher count or at least a mistrial. Rice had seen it in action himself: Eva had a charming, conspiratorial way about her that made the jurors lean toward her. In short, juries loved her and showed it with their verdicts. This also meant that her plea offers were better. Particularly from those few prosecutors afraid of a good fight. This was not Linda as a rule, but Linda didn't like to lose, and she'd lost hard to Eva around a year ago.

"Want me to forward her the letter, too?"

Linda laughed again. "I'm dying to know if she knew he was doing this."

"Giving us all these admissions? I doubt it."

"But it's well-written," Linda said.

And she was right. If he'd written it himself, the man could write a letter. Hopefully Walker wasn't as eloquent in person.

"Not believable," Rice said.

"No," she answered. "He was strangled."

"And the SANE report."

"Right, the trauma to his rectum."

In spite of himself, Rice's stomach clenched. So much of the horror he encountered went dull and flat with repetition. Hearing words like those ones always felt sharp.

"We knew this was coming," Linda went on. "I just wasn't expecting it this early."

"The gap in Nick's memory was always going to set him up. You worried?"

"No more than I already was," she said.

These cases were always troublesome in court. Nick Hall's was less than perfect. He'd been drinking. He didn't remember the assault itself. But they had his testimony that Walker attacked him, knocked him unconscious, and they had physical evidence to speak for him from there.

Walker's letter was bringing something else up for Rice, but he wasn't sure yet what it was. Walker sounded like a narcissist. But clearly intelligent. Well-spoken. He was holding down a job. And he'd been so controlled in their interview at the station, before the arrest. Neither of O'Malley's profiles seemed to fit him.

"You have time to do a quick follow-up today?" Linda asked.

"Sure."

"Can you get me more about Nick's boyfriend, or whatever he was?"

"The guy he was supposed to meet that night?"

"Yeah."

A blinking light started on Rice's phone.

"I've got someone on the other line. What do you want to know about the boyfriend?"

"Whatever you can get me."

"Easy enough."

Rice pressed the second line. "Britny Cressey," the receptionist said, "calling with information about Raymond Walker."

Who? "Put her through."

The receptionist did, and Rice introduced himself.

Her voice sounded young. "Hi, I'm calling about Ray Walker?"

"And you are?"

"Uh, an old girlfriend, kind of."

That was unexpected. "All right, and your name was Cressey?"

"Britny Cressey, sorry." She laughed cheerfully.

"That's okay."

"I just saw that Ray was arrested and charged with this thing, and I wanted to call and talk to someone."

Was this another report? Maybe Walker didn't stick to men when it came to assault. "How can I help?"

"I just wanted to tell you a little bit about him, since it seems like you're only getting one side of the story."

Ah. This was not a second report. "I don't know if you've seen the paper, but I do have his side of things."

"Ray was my best friend all through high school," Britny said. That made her Walker's age: thirty-eight or so. Her voice sounded about eighteen. "We dated for, like, a minute before he told me he was never gonna be into me."

She giggled. It was strange that she introduced herself as his ex.

"Well, I appreciate the historical information, but—"

"Ray was always such a nice guy. So smart and clever. Really mature. I wish we'd stayed close after graduation, but he went away to college, and that was kind of that."

"Okay."

"I reached out to him again when I saw what was happening on his mom's Facebook—that you guys arrested him. Ray and I have talked. He's really the same guy he used to be—he wouldn't have done this."

This was a waste of time. She didn't seem to know it, but who she really wanted to talk to was Walker's lawyer. Not Rice's job to help her figure that out. "I appreciate having your view, Ms. Cressey. Thanks for sharing."

"If I could just explain," she said.

"Explain what?"

"How well I know him, how I know he wouldn't have done what that guy says he did."

"I don't mean to be rude, but there's no way for you to know what happened in that motel room."

"No, but I was in his house every day for four years. I spent every second I could at Ray's house—they had cable, and he was an only child. My sister was so annoying then, I couldn't get a break from her if I was home. The only thing that sucked about Ray's house was his parents. His mom is crazy. Like smothering and kind of weird, I don't know how to explain it. She hated me. Thought I was trashy, and, like, I was, but I was sixteen." She laughed again. "She thought we were, *you know*, not like he was remotely interested in that. His parents didn't know then. His dad probably would have beat the shit out of him. His dad was a dick. And gross—he thought I was trashy, too, and he liked it, if you know what I mean?"

Rice's stomach tightened in disgust. "Help me see how this is related to the assault."

"Ray isn't violent," she said plainly. "He just isn't. There were a million times I'd have liked to punch his dad for being a creep, his mom for being *so* annoying. He never so much as yelled at them. I don't remember him having a single teenager meltdown *in four years*. I used to scream at my mom for no reason, didn't you?"

"I can't say I did, but I appreciate your point." Rice had never screamed at his mother, but he and his own daughter, Liz, had gone toe-to-toe on several occasions in her high school years. "I'll make a record of your call, Ms. Cressey. I've got a full plate today, so I need to sign off, all right?"

She repeated some of what she'd already said as Rice unpried her from their conversation and they hung up. He'd bet his house that Walker had put her up to that. Did Walker really think some old friend claiming Walker was a patient teenager would make one lick of difference to Rice? Even if she was credible, her observations were twenty years old. And she said it herself—they hadn't been sleeping together.

Rice grabbed his coat. There were more important questions to chase.

23

Julia had been meaning to reach out to Charlie Lee for months.

The main reason Julia left her law practice after they had the kids was to gain stability, which her trial work had never given her. When Chloe was born, Julia decided to get off the court-appointed roller coaster, at least temporarily, and find steadier money and shorter hours. It took her about a year to understand the stupidity in her decision to go into grant-funded policy work. She loved what she did, loved studying problems and recommending solutions. And just like when she was a defense attorney, she believed her job was important. Huge bonus points that working from home meant they didn't have to pay for day care. But a hallmark of grant work was recurring instability. Her job was always finite: when the money ran out, the job was over. She was always applying for a new grant, always thinking about what came next. Over the years, she became excellent at leaving a thought simmering on the back burner of her mind while she worked on something else in the foreground. It was the only way to do her job.

Her current project was to write a report about how juvenile records worked in Maine. What records were created when a kid was accused of a crime. What record was left behind, depending on the outcome of the case. Who could access the records. To what extent the records created would hold kids back later on in life.

In the spring, Julia had started in on her research. That summer, Julia began interviewing professionals in the system. Now, she would reach out to former juvenile defendants and ask them to anonymously answer questions about how their records had affected their lives. Some would be her own former clients. Some she would get from other attorneys. Months ago, when Julia laid out her plans, the institute she was working with approved a modest budget for a private investigator to help locate the former clients, who'd all grown up by now. There was only one PI she was interested in hiring, if she could have him: her favorite, Charlie Lee.

A day ago, while Tony was at urgent care, she'd thought of Charlie for another reason.

The sounds of that moment—the noise Tony made, like a dog roaring a warning before it attacked; the glass shattering; Seb's wail—she couldn't shut out the memory of it. But there was no use thinking about it any longer. She'd thought it to death throughout the night, and none of the obsessing had given her a better idea than asking Charlie Lee to do some digging on Raymond Walker. Tony wouldn't like it—when he was upset about something, he wanted to fix it himself. So she wouldn't tell him. Not unless Charlie found something that would be helpful to Nick's case, and then how could he be mad?

Now, her family gone, Julia stepped into her study and set her morning cup of tea on the windowsill. She normally chased her coffee with something herbal, but that morning she'd gone with Earl Grey; she needed the extra caffeine after her restless night. There was a door at the back right of her tiny office, and behind the door a narrow set of stairs stretched up to the attic. To the side of the door, Tony had hung shelves for her. She pulled down an accordion file where she kept articles and other scraps related to the report. From it, she retrieved her old client list. She sat on the stool at her desk and flipped through the pages, ticking with a pencil the names marked *JV*.

For the report, she wanted to interview people whose records ran the gamut, from essentially no record at all to a public felony record. She scanned the list, but she could only remember the precise outcome in three cases. Jin Chen: not competent, no record. Kasey Hartwell: hilarious case, driving record. And Mathis Lariviere—that was a name she'd never forget. He ended up with a private juvenile record, against all odds. The rest of the names bore some familiarity but the details were fuzzy, so she drained her tea, collected her things, and went up to the attic.

—◦—

Julia checked her phone—1:45. No wonder she was ravenous.

Even in late October, the air in the attic was thick and warm compared to the rest of the house. She wiped her brow but found no sweat. She simply *felt* clammy. She put Mathis's file back into the drawer marked *L–Q*. Closed the metal cabinet where she kept her old files. She had narrowed her list to fourteen names she wanted Charlie Lee to try to find. She'd written down each of their last-known contact information to give him a starting point.

She took the stairs back to her office, the cooler air kissing her forehead. She set down her things and pulled up Charlie's contact in her phone. He didn't answer, so she left a message.

She picked up her client list to put it away, but she paused. Her mind was snagged on the name at the center of the page: *Mathis Lariviere*. His name, and his mother's.

About a month into working on Mathis's case, Julia met with the seventeen-year-old at her office one evening. His license had been suspended because of his charges, and his mother, Elisa, had driven him to

Julia's office. When their meeting was over, Julia sent Mathis down the hallway. She assumed he and his mother were gone until she saw Elisa in the doorway.

"Do you have a moment, Julia?"

"Please, sit down."

Elisa closed the door behind her and sat across from Julia.

"You know Mathis is here under my visa."

"Yes. I've been working with an immigration attorney, doing everything we can to protect his status here."

"Mathis cannot return to France."

"Why not?"

"It should be enough that I tell you he can't."

Julia pulled a notepad out from under Mathis's file.

"No notes," Elisa said. Her posture was relaxed. She leaned back into her chair, her fingers interlaced in her lap.

"Is there something I can do for you?"

"I have a question. What happens to my son's case if the arresting officer doesn't testify?"

"Cops don't miss trials. That only happens in traffic court."

"Humor me."

Julia thought for a moment. "I don't know how the ADA could prove the drugs and gun were Mathis's without the first officer's testimony. But I don't know, I'd have to look into it. It's a weird hypothetical."

Julia smiled. Elisa didn't.

"Why are you asking?"

"Just curious. I don't know much about court, evidence."

That wasn't true, not according to Mathis. Mathis had told Julia that his mother was well-versed in criminal cases. That his whole family was.

Oh God. This woman was talking about . . . was she talking about paying this man off? Something worse?

"I don't like what you're implying."

"I'm not implying anything."

Julia's voice went shrill. "I think you are."

Elisa raised a hand. "Relax. We have the same goal here."

"I don't work with people who break the law."

Elisa narrowed her eyes a fraction. "Are you so sure of that?"

"Yes, I am."

Elisa shrugged and stood.

When she reached the doorway, Julia spoke again. "Elisa. I will drop your son's case if I even think you've done something."

"No need to grandstand," Elisa said. "You've made your point."

Julia heard the distant thud of the front door shutting, and she went to the window. She parted the curtain and watched Mathis and his mother cross the street to their car. Her hand shook against the lace.

As far as Julia could tell, Mathis's mother never meddled in his case. She came to every court date but never spoke to Julia like that again. And after more than a year of therapy, two hundred hours of volunteer work, and a clean report from his juvenile community corrections officer, Mathis earned an excellent outcome. Even some high praise from the judge on his last day in court.

In the hallway after the hearing, Elisa rested her manicured hand gently below Julia's elbow. They walked to a bank of windows away from the others outside the courtroom.

"Well done," Elisa said.

"It was a team effort."

"I like you, Julia." She smiled, the corners of her eyes crinkling under gray eyeshadow. "I am not so proud as to wish you ill. But if you had been in my place, with your own son, you would understand how I felt, that night we spoke at your office."

This woman, Julia realized, was bothered by the possibility that she had lost Julia's respect.

"I know it wasn't easy for you to trust me," Julia said.

"It is harder to play by the rules when it's your own family. And I hope with all my heart that you never, ever have to understand that."

That was true, Julia supposed. She didn't know what Elisa had felt, having her son face such serious charges. Even the possibility of deportation, back to a place where she believed he wasn't safe.

But Julia would never have been like Elisa, even if she had been standing in the woman's chic black shoes.

"I know you don't see it like I do," Elisa said, "but I feel like you've saved my son's life. If I can ever repay you—"

Julia cut her off. "Just pay your bill."

Elisa eyed Julia dryly, then let out a loud laugh.

Julia folded the client list closed. It would be nice, she thought, for Mathis's mother to see her now. See she'd been wrong about Julia. Just like there had been for Elisa, there was a young man Julia loved dearly whose life was, in a way, in the hands of the criminal court. And Julia was keeping her head down and trusting the system. Not hounding her old colleagues for gossip or favors.

But was Julia being as good as she thought, or was she simply not bothering to beat her head against a wall? Because in truth, there was nothing to do but wait for Nick's case to end, one way or another.

Below her office window, Julia could hear the telltale sound of the postman treading on the porch. She tidied up the desk, then went downstairs to the kitchen.

She put on the kettle for tea and got some bread out of the pantry. She heard the postman come back up on the porch. Now he was knocking on the door. Oh God, the door. Maybe he was going to ask about the broken window; she'd tell him Tony fell through it, like Tony had told the urgent care staff. Was that even believable? Julia opened the door and found she was out of time to assess the quality of her lie, because it wasn't the postman, after all. Standing on her porch was Detective Rice.

24

Rice parked on the road in front of the Hall house and checked his cell. It was just after two. He hadn't heard back from Nick yet, though he could have been in class. As the hours churned on he started to feel antsy. Walker's letter was so invasive. It wasn't uncommon for a victim in a domestic violence or sexual assault case to just drop away overnight, unwilling to prosecute. That letter—it would have made a lot of people think about giving up. He'd feel better if he could just talk to Nick. Assure him that the letter had helped his case. Make sure he was doing okay and knew this was just part of the process. And ask about Chris.

Someone was home: there was a red Subaru Baja—a distinctly hideous vehicle—in the driveway. But was Nick there? As Rice climbed the front steps to the porch, it occurred to him that he didn't know if Nick was still staying with his brother or if he'd moved back to his apartment. He could have tried Tony or Julia when Nick didn't call back. Instead, he'd driven to Orange without much thought at all.

Something was off about the outer front door . . . the glass was broken. And the bottom screen was ripped. Rice opened the door slowly, examining it. There was dried blood on the inside of the thin metal door. He knocked hard on the solid inner door. He heard muffled footfalls approaching.

The door creaked open to Julia's face. "Detective!"

"Good afternoon, miss. I was in your neighborhood and had a few minutes to spare, so I thought I'd swing by, 'case you were home."

"Sure, no problem, did you want to come in or . . ."

"I'll step in a minute, if you don't mind. Don't wanna cool off your house talking with the door open."

Julia smiled and stepped back from the doorway so that he could enter. "It's not that much warmer in here, I'm afraid."

Rice scuffed his shoes on the mat outside. "Say, what happened to your door here?"

"Oh, ah, accident," she said as she ushered him in. "We had an accident over the weekend, I just haven't had a chance to clean it up yet."

"What happened?" he asked again.

A kettle in the kitchen began to whistle, and Julia turned away from him. "Tony fell into the door yesterday, coming up onto the porch." She removed the kettle and switched off the burner with a snap. "He got to spend two hours of his Sunday at urgent care and now he's got this cast thing on."

Rice groaned. "Went clean through the glass? He all right?"

"Oh yeah, I'm sure it looks much more dramatic than it was. He did break a finger, but it sounds like it should heal fine." She turned to face him directly and asked, "Tea?"

"Ah, I'm not really one for tea, but thanks for offering."

"I could put on a pot of coffee for you, if you'd like?"

"No, dear, I don't want to trouble you. I'll just be here a minute."

Julia spooned what looked like loose tea leaves from a canister into a little clay teapot.

"How can I help, Detective?"

"Well, I'm assuming you saw the letter in the paper."

Julia nodded and breathed a sad yes.

"I'm so sorry for it. It's a terrible thing to have put out there like that."

She shook her head. "I just feel so sad for Nick. The . . . thing itself was already such an invasion, and now this."

"He doing okay?"

"I guess. We ended up going to see him last night. He wasn't answering us, so we just showed up." She paused. "He seemed kind of out of it, but he kept saying he was all right."

Rice felt some relief that it wasn't just his calls Nick was ignoring. And that Nick's family was on top of things, taking care of him.

"Well, I'm sure you know the letter's good for Nick's case."

Julia didn't speak; she looked like she was trying to work out how that could be.

"He's admitted we've got the right guy," Rice said, "and now we know the defense. It's all about consent."

"Huh," Julia said with surprise. "You're right. It's funny, I didn't even think of that. We were both so focused on how this would make Nick feel right now, we hadn't looked forward yet. But you're right."

Rice nodded.

"These are admissions," Julia said. "And he's screwed, don't you think? No one will believe someone would consent to what happened to Nick, right?"

Rice nodded. "Surely hope not. Do you know Nick's class schedule? I need to get in touch, but he hasn't gotten back to me, but clearly I shouldn't take it personal."

"No, I think he's just overwhelmed. It's not you. I don't know it off the top of my head but—"

Julia paused when her phone on the counter started to vibrate and ring.

Rice looked down at the screen, hoping it might say Nick's name. Instead, it read

Charlie Lee.

Charlie Lee? The PI?
"Oh, sorry, that's work. Do you mind if I take it quickly?"
"Be my guest."
Julia walked away down the hall as she answered the phone. "Hi, Charlie. I actually have company right now, maybe—yes—okay, let me just read you the list quick." Her voice grew quieter as she climbed the stairs.
Rice stood in the kitchen, listening to Julia's muffled voice above him, but he couldn't decipher a word. Why would she be working with a PI, if it was in fact *that* Charlie Lee? The Charlie that Rice knew had a pretty good reputation, at least for a PI who'd never been a cop. He came from insurance. They'd been on opposite sides of a couple cases; Charlie was usually hired by defendants.
Rice gave up trying to listen and leaned against the counter across from the stove. Checked his email until he heard a door shut somewhere above him and footfalls on the stairs.
"Sorry about that," Julia said as she reappeared at the end of the hall.
"That's fine, I've interrupted while you're on the clock."
She waved a hand.
"I have to ask, was that Charlie Lee the PI?"
"Yeah." Julia looked at him brightly and crossed her arms. "Yeah, I used to hire Charlie when I was a defense attorney, so I reached out to him on a project recently."
"I thought you worked more in policy now."
Julia set her phone back on the counter. "I do, I need him to track down some old clients for interviews."

"I see. Interesting."

She nodded.

"So, Nick's schedule," Julia said. "I think he's done with classes by three or four every day. I know he doesn't have any evening classes this semester." She picked up the teapot and swirled it gently, then tipped it into a mug on the counter.

The rush of liquid filling the cup sounded like music, and Rice regretted declining her offer for a drink.

"What do you need to talk to him about?"

"I just wanted to touch base after the letter. And, well." Rice adjusted himself against the counter. "Since I'm here, has Nick told you anything about the guy he was supposed to meet that night?"

Julia looked surprised. "Chris?"

"Yeah."

She considered his name. "I don't think I know anything about him, actually."

"Are he and Nick in a relationship?"

"No. Nick's liked him for a while, he mentioned him over the summer, I remember."

"Okay," Rice said.

She frowned. "What does this have to do with anything?"

"Probably nothing. I'm just making sure I've done my homework. Making sure we have all the information."

"I see," she said slowly. "You'll have to ask him."

⟶

Rice sat in his car for a minute before he drove on.

He had glazed over the issue with that vague due diligence talk. Maybe Julia sensed what he was getting at. She'd been a defense attorney.

Walker knew how to tell a good story. They knew that now, from the letter. He'd made admissions, but he'd also hit back against the charges. And as Linda had feared, the fact that Nick was a male victim seemed to make the media think this case was more newsworthy. Walker had hired Eva Barr, who would hire her own PI. It would only be a matter of time before the defense knew about Chris, and Chris was a problem. Chris gave Nick a reason to lie about the nature of his encounter with Walker. Chris was another thread for the defense to pull at.

25

Nick's stomach pitched at the sound of his phone. The short vibration meant a text message, not a phone call. He paused the show on his computer and rolled toward his bedside table.
Tony:

You doing okay?

Nick groaned. It was just the daily check in.
As he always did, he wrote back:

Yeah.

Thank God he wasn't staying with Tony anymore. At least Nick didn't have to deal with him in person. Tony was texting and sending Nick snaps all the time now, more in the last week than ever before. It was exhausting, reassuring Tony that he was fine. And every time Tony reached out, before Nick saw his name on the screen, Nick couldn't help but worry it was *another* classmate texting him because they'd heard about the case. Or worse: texting him because something new came out about that night. But that couldn't happen—only he and Ray knew what happened in that room, and they had both already talked.

There was a knock at the door, and Johnny stuck his head in.

"The detective is here. The guy."

"Why?"

"He didn't say."

Nick's phone buzzed in his hand.

Tony:

Need anything?

He typed quickly.

Yeah. Listen when I say I'm fine.

⟨⟩

Detective Rice was standing at the bottom of the stairs, in the messy entryway.

"Do you have somewhere private to talk?"

"Not really," Nick said. He didn't want this man seeing his bedroom.

"Go for a walk?"

Nick grabbed a jacket and beanie and followed him outside.

They went down Spring Street and toward campus. The detective brought up the letter first.

He was fine, Nick told him.

It was helpful to his team, the detective said. Now they know the defense, so they can prepare, he went on. And, they can use the letter against Walker in court.

Okay, Nick said.

Detective Rice moved along quickly.

"Hey, I meant to ask you, what's the situation with you and Chris?"

"Nothing," Nick said with a shrug.

"You're not together?"

"Nope." Nick had never responded to any of Chris's texts since the night it happened. He was probably the last person on the planet Nick wanted to talk to about this.

"Were you that night?"

"No," Nick said. "He stood me up."

The detective shook his head like Nick wasn't understanding him. "Were you in a relationship with each other that night?"

"No," Nick said. Did he have to spell it out? "He didn't want to date me."

The detective nodded. "Would it have mattered to him for any reason if you slept with someone else?"

But I didn't, Nick thought. His eyes must have betrayed his shock at the question, because the detective spoke again.

"I know you didn't *sleep with* Walker. What I mean is . . ." He paused. "The ADA just wanted to know more about your relationship, thinking it'll come up in court. You saw what Walker's saying. Him and his lawyer will probably try to make it look like you didn't want Chris to find out. Like you cheated on him."

"How would they know about Chris?"

"Well, he's part of your story. His name's in my report, your statement, other places. They'll get all that."

"Wait," Nick said. "Are people gonna talk to him?"

"I don't know," Detective Rice said. "Probably. They might interview him. I might need to."

"He has nothing to do with what happened."

"I know it's confusing from where you are. I just don't want to sugar-coat it. Court can end up reaching into all kinds of places you wouldn't expect."

Nick thought again of something his therapist said during their first session. Jeff was talking about confidentiality, almost going through a mental checklist, and he said something about how a court could order a therapist to turn over records.

"How can whether or not he raped me have anything to do with Chris?"

"Because if he can't come up with a good reason you'd lie, he's fucked."

Hearing Detective Rice speak so crassly was jarring. The man looked rough—he was big and old and wore a gun under his jacket. His face was pocked and wrinkled. But he'd never spoken to Nick like that.

"He's gonna do everything he can to make you look like a liar, Nick. He's facing years, decades even. And lifetime registration as a sex offender."

Nick's breathing had gone shallow. He felt like they were fighting, but over what he wasn't sure.

The detective was still talking. "He's gonna come for you, hard. Has anyone told you that?"

"You could have," Nick said.

Detective Rice's eyes opened in surprise. He lowered his voice. "You were hurting."

Meaning, I didn't want to hurt you more. The detective had been babying Nick. Just like Tony. Just like everyone who talked to him about this goddamn case. They were treating him like he was a child. And it was working. Every time he had to talk about the case, he felt himself sink backward, further away from the man he'd been before that night.

The detective was watching him as they walked on.

"We weren't dating. I wanted to; he didn't. He wouldn't have cared if I did sleep with someone else. That's it. There's nothing there."

Detective Rice's voice was calm. "Okay. If there's anything you're not telling me about you and Chris, you should do it now."

"Why?"

"Because it doesn't look good when you change your story later."

Something was happening. Deep under his eyes, he could feel tears threatening to well in the cool air.

"I don't get to keep your secrets," the detective said. "You tell me, the ADA tells him. Everything is fair game for him, that's how due process works."

But he can't have what the police don't have, Nick thought to himself. *You know this. Ray can't have it if you don't give it to anyone.*

The urge to cry faded.

"I don't know what you want from me," Nick said.

"Just the truth."

Nick shrugged. "You already have it."

26

Tony Hall, 2015

There was a hole in Tony's sneaker, where his big toe rubbed against the mesh. The shoes were gray with white detailing, originally, but now they were grass-stained and dingy with mud. He mostly wore them to play with the kids and mow the lawn. He couldn't remember the last time he'd gone running. He laced up and left the house. At the end of the driveway he went right, away from town center. He would turn around, he thought, at the small bridge around two miles down the road. The air was cold and dry in his nostrils, and a dull ache thrummed up his shins with each footfall.

The first time Tony went for a run outdoors was the summer after he graduated from college. It had been a summer of change, and he remembered it well. The last summer he threw a punch. With one exception, the last summer he had a drink. It was all connected.

Drinking was where he was weak: more than a couple and it was like the "restraint" switch in his brain flicked off. Tony's limbs got loose, and his laugh was too loud and he was funny and fun, usually, unafraid to sing or dance or hit on a beautiful girl. But sometimes he was not funny; his jokes got too sharp. And sometimes he was not fun. Sometimes a guy looked at him wrong, like he thought he was tough shit and he wanted

Tony to agree. There were a few drunken fights in college, always spurred on by that kind of thing, the posturing, a heavy-handed "What are you looking at?" Twice there were fistfights. His friends recounted these incidents with dramatic glee, like Tony was Rocky. Tony tried to see himself as they did: a take-no-shit badass. What he remembered of the fights, though, was the sensation that his arms were flailing, just barely within his control. Like he and the other guy were puppets thrashing against each other.

His last fight happened in the summer after college. That his then girlfriend called it a fight was barely accurate, actually, but his memory had logged it as one because of her. He and the guy went hands-on for seconds, really. The guy grabbed him by the shirt; he shoved the guy off. That was it.

The morning after, she was still mad. "You're too old for this."

"He grabbed me," Tony said in disbelief.

"You were yelling at him."

"If you think that was yelling—"

"You could see that he was a drunk asshole."

"He called that guy a fag."

"That guy didn't hear him."

"So?"

"You don't get to police everyone. What if you'd been arrested for fighting? What if he went crazy and hurt you, or me? You don't think about what you're risking, you just jump into some bullshit hero mode for people who aren't asking for your help. I don't like being out with you, wondering who might set you off. You're not like that when you don't drink."

"You don't think I would have said something to him if I'd heard that sober?"

"I don't think you would have gotten into a shoving match over it, no."

For the fight and other reasons, they broke up. She sent a goodbye email to his mother, apparently. Tony never got to read it, but in it she talked about his drinking. He knew because his mom brought it up the next time he saw her.

"You know your dad has quite a quick fuse when he drinks."

"Are you seriously comparing me to him?"

"No, honey. I know you're not just going around picking fights. Maybe you even have good reasons. But reasoning can get slippery when alcohol's involved."

Tony had spent his life watching his dad get worked up over something a sober person might not have noticed, let alone attached meaning to. Glances Ron perceived as disrespectful or unfaithful. With each popped tab came the potential for jealousy, anger, distrust.

Tony softened his voice. "I'm not an asshole like he is, Ma."

"I know you aren't." They were sitting at her kitchen table, eating the lasagna she'd made for his visit. "Sober, you're just about the best man I've ever known. Sometimes I can't believe you turned out like you did. Especially with your brother, my God you're good to him. I stayed with your dad as long as I did because I was worried that a divorce would ruin your life. I guess I was drinking the 'broken home' Kool-Aid. If I could have seen what an amazing man you'd become, I wouldn't have worried. I would have put you in the car and left years earlier. You are nothing like him." She paused. "You're nothing like him sober. But the drinking . . . nothing goes from zero to sixty. It's a slide. When I met your dad he was charming. Such a good dancer. He wasn't perfect, always a bit of a hothead, but he was different. There was a slide. And I think alcohol made it steeper and faster."

That month, Tony went to see a drug and alcohol counselor.

"Do you think you have a drinking problem?" she asked.

"No," he said. "But is it possible to be *pre*-drinking problem?"

"Like you're standing at the precipice of a problem, you mean?"

"Yeah."

"Absolutely." She said nothing. She wanted more from him.

"I think that's what my mom thinks. She's not, like, a dramatic mom. She doesn't helicopter. Or guilt trip. And she's seen it, serious alcoholism in my dad. So the fact that she thinks—" The words were too painful. He exhaled sharply, and the urge to cry passed. "The last thing I ever wanted was to turn out like him. She doesn't deserve that. And my little brother—he already looks up to me. And I want that, it makes me feel like I matter. I don't want him to think our dad is normal. I want to be that for him. And if I go over the ledge . . ."

She nodded. "So step back."

He decided to give up drinking, just for the rest of the summer, to see what he thought. The counselor gave him a list of local AA meetings, but he never went. She also told him to find a hobby that let him process what he was feeling. He started running that summer. It was his time to burn off nervous energy and useless thoughts. The summer ended, but he kept running. His runs got longer, and his highs got stronger.

He stopped a few months into dating Julia. He fell out of the habit so quickly—suddenly he hadn't gone out in a month. It wasn't that running had been bad; wasn't bad now. The stiffness in his ankles was loosening, and his strides grew longer. He remembered this, the kinks working out as his legs warmed up.

Maybe he stopped needing the run. By then he was used to not drinking. Happy with the person he was becoming. And who needs a runner's high when you've got a new girlfriend? He got higher off Julia than anything else. She made him feel blissed out and self-assured. Calm and strong. Not that he became flawless. He had, in fact, punched through a window in anger ten days ago. Broke his pinkie finger. It felt like a cosmic insult: *Think you're a tough guy, big man, punching glass? Now your wittle finger is broken.*

He passed a neighbor's house. They had a barn and an old grain silo that was falling to pieces, big hunks of metal missing from the sides and top. His lungs began to ache in the cold air. It was November now, thank God. October had been miserable all the way through. As much as he'd wanted Nick under his roof, the long visit had exhausted him, and then Walker's letter swept him off his feet. Tony had been doing so well for so long. Fifteen years—was that right? It was. Fifteen years since he'd made all those changes. And they had worked, he thought.

Once, on a run, he passed a fallen tree and it reminded him of a fable his mom used to read him as a kid, about an oak tree and a reed. The tree, with its thick trunk, looked indisputably stronger than the wispy reed on the riverbank, but when a fierce windstorm came, the tree was ripped out by the roots and fell, while the reed survived because it could bend. And suddenly he got it—the point his mom had been making. His father thought he was as tough as they came, and he wanted everyone to know it, but in truth he was the weakest person Tony knew. Ron Hall couldn't function in the morning without a fresh can of Bud. He broke things to scare his wife. He hit his sons. He was pathetic. Tony's mother, by comparison, was outwardly soft and gentle, but her inner strength was abundant. That day on the run, he'd gotten it. He'd learned the lesson. And he'd gone on for fifteen more years working at himself. Working at learning to bend.

But in spite of it all, the anger could rush him so easily. He'd read Walker's letter, read those sickening words, and he was blinded. Felt certain that hitting something, anything, would relieve the excruciating pain he was feeling. His father's method of coping was always going to be there, offering itself up to him. "Don't be a little pussy; be a man. Hit back. Don't take that." Fifteen years and it was still there. And what had it given him? A broken pinkie, damaged pride, and worst of all, two terrified children. Seb had wailed first, then Chloe. The shame he felt in that moment plagued him.

And yet, in spite of his shame, he had stayed angry. After all, Walker was the cause of his behavior. Tony was even a bit angry with Julia, for her shock. Yes, what he'd done was not rational. It was frightening. Violent. Fine, it was all the things he normally wasn't. But could she not forgive him, after reading what he had? Not only had this man assaulted Nick, but now he had reached them in their homes. Shoved his lies in their faces. Made up a bullshit story and twisted it all back around on Nick.

Tony ran faster, his feet beating the pavement. The ache in his lungs thickened, and his mouth began to water. Fuck Raymond Walker. Fuck him and his lies and his smug, self-important letter about truth and justice. Fuck him for doing this to Nick.

Nick.

A stitch began to stab the underside of his ribs, and he slowed to a walk, panting and grasping for the pain in his side. Nick told him to let it go. Nick was okay. He hadn't believed it at first; it didn't seem possible that Nick cared so little about the letter. But he said he was fine, and it seemed to be true. He answered Tony's texts. Sent Tony snaps on Snapchat. There was a bored selfie sent from class one day. Another day, a picture of the TV, his roommate off to the side watching with him. His life was going on like it had before. If anything, the only thing that seemed to be bothering him was Tony's constant checking on him.

Tony wasn't making anything better; he was only making himself sick. He turned and began to walk home. He hadn't reached the bridge, but he didn't care.

27

I n mid-November, when Charlie Lee's name lit up her phone screen, Julia hurried to her office to take the call away from Tony.

Charlie rattled through the list of her former clients' names, pausing long enough for Julia to record the address or phone number he'd confirmed. When they'd finished, Charlie lowered his voice playfully.

"So, the side project." The way he said it smacked of secrecy. And to be fair, it was a secret. She didn't want anyone knowing that she'd hired Charlie to look into Raymond Walker, to see if he could drum up anything to help secure a conviction. Not even Tony.

Charlie only told her two things that she hadn't already heard from either Nick or the detective.

The first was that Raymond Walker wasn't the one who rented the room at the motel where he took Nick. The man working the front desk told Charlie he booked the room to a woman who'd paid cash. Motel 4 didn't make patrons put down a credit card, so long as they paid for the room and had a driver's license staff could photocopy. Charlie hadn't located the woman who paid for Walker's room, but based on search results that came up for her name, she was probably transient. Walker had probably offered her cash to book the room. "Happens more often than you'd think," Charlie said.

Julia didn't know if the police knew Walker had paid someone to book the room under a different name, but she suspected they did. They must have checked at the desk when they were still trying to track him down. It was hard to think of an innocent reason to do something like that. The term *malice aforethought* floated up in her mind. It was a term lawyers didn't use much in Maine but she'd learned it in law school. It stood for something like internal recognition of the evil you would later perpetrate. Booking a room under someone else's name before you bring someone there . . . that sounded like Walker had planned to do this to someone. It was strange to think that Detective Rice knew about something like that without sharing it with them—or at least with Nick. But that was a silly way to see it. It wasn't his job to tell them things.

The second surprise Charlie delivered was that Raymond Walker had no criminal or PFA history come up in his database searches.

"Not what I expected," Charlie said, "but I do think we're dealing with a crime people are less apt to report. I'm gonna call around out of state, since he travels for work."

"There's no way I've paid you enough for any more of your time."

"Don't mention it, seriously. It's been slow. And I'm interested. No one's as clean as this guy seems right now." He chuckled. "Except maybe you."

28

NICK HALL, 2015

From his bedroom window, Nick saw Tony pull up on the street. Nick paused at his mirror one last time. Light blue button-down, Tony's tan trousers, scuffed brown dress shoes. He looked respectable and adult, albeit boring. All three seemed right for testifying at a grand jury.

Outside, it felt cold enough for snow, but the sky was clear.

Nick climbed into Tony's SUV. "Thanks for the ride."

"No problem," Tony said. "I wanted to bring you."

"I didn't give you much notice."

Tony looked away and began to drive. "It's fine. I know I've been a bit much."

"No," Nick said.

That was a lie—Tony *had* been a bit much. After Walker sent the letter to the paper, Tony started texting him almost daily.

How you holding up, Just checking in

just checking, checking, it was exhausting. So Nick had dealt with Tony as he had done before: Nick gave him quick, perfunctory answers.

Fine; Good; Can't talk, busy; In class.

Basically, he would say enough to reassure his brother, and he'd withhold enough to stifle conversation. It had worked, and eventually, Tony backed off. Now Nick felt guilty. Tony just wanted him to be okay. Was that so bad?

Back when he was tired of Tony's concern, he told Tony he wanted to go to the grand jury himself. Tony asked a few times, but Nick said no, and Tony gave up. Then that morning, Nick woke up gasping for air, clawing at his throat, and it had taken seconds, long seconds, for him to realize he was safe in his own bed. For the sound of laughter to fade from his head. He was safe. Safe, but alone. He texted Tony. Asked if he wanted to come after all.

When they got to the courthouse, Nick used the bathroom for the fourth time that morning. His stomach was killing him. He'd eaten some toast, but even that wasn't sitting well.

A marshal told them where to go, on the second floor of the courthouse. Linda came out into the hall and met Tony. Told them they could sit on the bench against the wall. Said it would be a while as she ducked back into the room down the hall.

They sat together talking about television, Nick's classes, a funny story about his niece, anything but why they were there. Tony was trying to distract him, and right now, Nick didn't mind.

The toast and acid in Nick's stomach were rioting, and the noise was getting obvious. A couple of times, he noticed Tony's eyes flick toward his stomach and back up again.

Finally, Tony said, "It sounds like a barrel of snakes in there."

Nick burst into laughter, shocked and delighted at the absurdity of it.

Tony laughed, too, clearly pleased with himself. "You must have been shitting your brains out earlier."

"I'm nervous," Nick groaned, still smiling. And he was nervous, but the laughter was settling his stomach.

The door opened. It was Linda again. "Ready?"

Suddenly, Nick felt Tony's hand close over his own. Three squeezes: *I love you*, like when Nick was little. Nick returned four squeezes. He did love Tony. He might have loved him more than any other person. His brother was a pain in the ass, but he took care of Nick like no one else did.

When he stepped into the room, first he noticed the people. Sherie, the advocate person for the case, had called him last week to talk about the grand jury, and she said there would probably be twenty-three of them. Twenty-three grand jurors who would vote on whether Linda had enough evidence to charge Ray with raping Nick. Twenty-three strangers who would decide what they thought of Nick.

There was wood paneling and Maine and American flags in the corner, but the room was a little unlike a courtroom, too. There was no judge, no seating for an audience. He sat down in a little booth, like he'd seen in court movies before. Linda stood to the side of him, and he faced the grand jurors.

Linda started off easy. His name, his age, where he lived, what he was studying.

"Now I have some questions about October second of this year."

The *thud-thud-thud* in Nick's chest quickened. He nodded.

Why did he go out? Who went with him? Did Chris show up? Was he dating Chris? What did he and Elle do at the bar? How many drinks did he have? How quickly? But over how much time? So he wasn't drunk, right? When did he notice the man who introduced himself as Josh?

"When I went up to the bar. Elle wanted another round."

"What time was that?"

He couldn't remember. Was that bad? Sweat broke out on his hairline. "I don't remember."

"Would you remember if you looked at your statement?"

Nick nodded.

Linda pulled a stapled set of pages from a folder on the table beside her. She folded over a page and underlined something with a pencil from the table. She handed it to Nick.

It was a police report. It read *DETECTIVE JOHN RICE* at the top. A sentence was underlined in pencil: *Nick told me it was sometime after 10:30 and before 11:00 that he met the man he would later identify as RAYMOND WALKER at Jimmy's Pub.*

"Do you remember now?" Linda asked.

"Yeah," he said. "It was sometime after ten thirty and before eleven."

"Okay. Was he at the bar when you went up?"

Nick's eyes drifted to the carpet. He pictured it. "No," he said. "He sat down beside me when I was already there."

"Who initiated the conversation?"

He didn't have to think about that one. "He did," Nick said quickly. Nick hadn't wanted to think back on that night—he wanted to let the memory of it wither and die in the dark. But Ray had written that letter, and he'd made it sound like Nick had been pursuing him. Nick couldn't help remembering, comparing his version to Walker's. That part just wasn't true.

Linda's questions went on. What name did the man give Nick? What did they talk about? How long did they talk? How many drinks did Nick have? How many did "Josh" have? Who invited whom to leave?

"He did," Nick said. He could hear it: "Wanna get out of here?" It should have been cheesy, but Josh—Ray—had the perfect voice for the line.

"How did you decide where to go?"

"He said he had a room, so we just went there."

"Where was the room?"

"Motel 4."

"How did you get there?"

"We took a cab?"

"What happened in the cab?"

Nick felt his face flushing.

He had liked Josh so much. He'd felt loose and pliable from the liquor, Chris's rejection. Josh was so handsome, mature, with crinkles by his light eyes. Josh had been so relaxed about himself. They'd gotten into the taxi, a male cabbie up front, Josh had said, "Motel 4," and he'd leaned into Nick. Josh didn't care what the cabbie thought, and in that moment, Nick didn't, either.

"We made out."

He was really getting into it now. Not just that he was gay—that alone was probably a problem for some of the people in the room—but that he'd been willing. *At first*, he reminded himself. *You were only willing at first.*

He looked out at the group of them, and he accidentally locked eyes with a man in the front row. The man looked away quickly.

"Just kissing?" Linda asked.

Nick's hands were in his lap, and he began to rub at his right forearm. It was dark in the cab, their breath had been fast, and Josh had brought a hand to Nick's groin. Nick hadn't told that detail to anyone yet.

"Yeah," Nick said.

He worked his thumb up under his sleeve.

⁓

When Nick came out of the double doors, Tony was standing at the end of the hallway.

"Hey," he said, and walked back to Nick quickly.

"Linda said I can leave if I want," Nick said.

"How did it go?"

"Okay." Slow and fast at the same time. Exhausting, stressful, but better than he'd worried it would be. He'd stuck to his story. Didn't fuck anything up. "I think I did okay," he said.

"Is he indicted?"

"She's not done."

Tony looked over Nick's shoulder, at the door behind him. "You don't want to wait, just in case?"

Nick shook his head. The adrenaline that had rushed him as he testified was draining. "I want to go home."

In the parking lot, Tony offered to take him to lunch first, but Nick was too tired.

He climbed into the front seat and sank back against it. He might fall asleep on the drive, he thought. As he brought his seat belt over his torso, the soft inner flesh of his forearm stung where it rubbed against the inside of his sleeve. He clicked the buckle into its lock, then turned his wrist upward. He looked down, as subtly as he could. A pinprick of blood had soaked through his sleeve.

29

Julia had said nothing in response. She just kept sipping at her tea. Even now, Rice couldn't help but be reminded of Irene when he looked at her. Irene had been solid as a rock. Julia used to look solid, too, but today her hands were shaking.

"You've never been to a grand jury," Rice said.

"No."

"Generally pretty boring, but Nick's was interesting."

"Why?"

"Well, for one, the victim doesn't always testify, but you know that. Linda wanted to give him a practice run, see how he did."

"Yeah," she said.

"Did you know he made a mistake?"

"No."

It was subtle enough that Linda Davis, the ADA, hadn't even noticed it, and she had pretty good attention to detail. Something about it, though, had bothered Rice. The boy had reached the part of his story where he and Raymond Walker entered the hotel room. He testified that he shut the door, and Walker hit him over the head. He said he fell to the floor, then Walker turned on the light, and that was where Nick's vision and memory faded out. Rice remembered looking at the boy's face as he said it. Nick was looking down, which was not abnormal; it wasn't easy stuff to talk about, let alone to a room full of strangers. But suddenly Rice felt itchy under his collar and like he needed to stand up. Rice had waited until the boy left and Linda began speaking to the jurors, then he leaned back in his chair as casually as he could and opened his folder. He pulled out his notes from his interview of Nick, but he would have to listen to the recording to be sure.

Back at the station, he sat at his desk, put on headphones, and pulled up his interview of Nick. Hunched forward, hands in his lap, he listened to the entire thing. Yes, it was small, but there it was. Nick had never mentioned Walker turning on the light before.

In the interview, Nick had said it was dark when Walker hit him, and that was the last thing he remembered. Now he said he fell to the floor and Walker turned on the light. Such a sensory detail. The kind of thing you couldn't help but picture: the black hole of a dark motel room flooding with yellow light. So why hadn't Nick mentioned it before?

"He changed something," Rice said.

"At the grand jury?"

"Yup. And as crazy as it sounds, that was the moment. That was when the case slipped away from me."

A case was never fully in the state's control start to finish—that was impossible. That wasn't what Rice meant. He walked into that grand jury feeling as good as he could about a case like Nick's. The story had been consistent. The physical evidence was on their side. Even Chris Gosling seemed to be less of a problem than they'd worried—Chris told O'Malley the same thing Nick told Rice: they weren't dating. As far as Rice knew, Nick didn't have a motive in the world to make up a sexual assault.

And then at the grand jury, Nick fumbled on the strangest point.

"What do you mean it slipped away from you?"

Rice shrugged. "I knew something was wrong, and I sat on it."

Julia stared at him, wide-eyed and miserable.

There was no way to atone for the sins he had committed. But at least he could confess.

"You know why I called you here, don't you?"

30

JULIA HALL, 2015

Last week, Raymond Walker was indicted. They hadn't gotten many details about the grand jury proceeding: just that it had been successful. This good news was followed swiftly by what felt like bad news: press coverage.

Linda had been smart to make Nick's name private, because the press seemed hooked on the rape case with the male victim. Even a paper up north had run an article on the case following the indictment. Julia couldn't remember any of her cases making the news like this, with statewide coverage or regular updates.

The articles discussed the procedure thus far—the arrest, Walker's bail, the indictment—and contained a couple quotes from Walker's lawyer, Eva Barr. The quotes were the same across the articles—she must have sent them by email. "We're unsurprised by the indictment, given that the grand jury only hears the prosecution's version of events. We're confident that when a jury has the chance to hear from Ray, he'll be acquitted." The article then recapped Walker's letter: according to him, "the alleged victim had been drinking, pursued Walker at the bar, and then the two consensually engaged in 'rough' sex."

That was hard enough to read, but Julia's primary anxiety, unfounded as it was, was that Nick's identity would somehow get linked to the case, destroying what little privacy he had in this mess. Julia wasn't a fan of reporters, per se, but she trusted them not to publish Nick's name, given that the judge had ruled it should be confidential in the court proceedings. It was the active comment sections of the articles that worried her. For whatever reason, people felt compelled to take to the internet and give their view of the case. The only people who knew "the victim" in these articles was Nick Hall were other Halls and a couple of Nick's best friends, save for the professionals. That someone might out him online seemed far-fetched, but even the possibility bothered her. The day after the indictment, she skimmed the comment sections of each article she could find. She tried to look only for capital *N*'s and *H*'s, but it was impossible to resist reading. Many of the comments were anti-Walker. Some were not.

There was the sexist:

> I might be able to swallow this if the "victim" were a smaller female, but a 20yo male gets knocked unconscious in a single blow? It's just very hard to buy.

And the bigot:

> Is this not how two dudes get down?

Mostly, the negative commenters questioned Nick's story.

> TBH this sounds like a kinky hookup?
>
> Do we really want judges, i.e., taxpayers, sorting out

levels of consent when this much alcohol was involved and two adults went to a hotel room?

So can we just get straight that this guy blacked out, wasn't hit on the head or whatever nonsense . . . just doesn't want to own that he drank himself dumb. If he doesn't remember what happened, that doesn't mean he wasn't consenting to it.

⟶

The comments bothered Julia for hours after she read them. They bothered Tony for days. He kept trying to show her new ones. Fresh grenades of hate lobbed at anyone who read them.

"I'm done with that stuff," she said.

"Why?"

"It's too painful. It's nothing new and it just—people suck. I don't need to keep reading all the ways that people suck."

"What if Nick is seeing this shit?"

They were in bed, Tony on his phone, Julia setting down the book he was distracting her from.

"He might be seeing it," she said.

Tony looked at her like, *exactly*. As if she could do something about *Seaside News*'s comment section. He was all revved up at the faceless users who'd left the comments, and the only person he could reach about it was Julia. She got that. But it was starting to piss her off.

"It is terrible," she said emphatically. "But I don't know what else to do."

"I wanna kill all these people."

She snuggled against him. "That is *super* reasonable."

He laughed softly.

She added, "We could fit some bodies out back."

Tony seemed to calm down about the whole thing for a couple of days, but apparently not enough to stop looking for news online. Julia was showering when Tony came in.

"He fucking did it again."

She pushed back the curtain. "Who did what?"

"Walker." Tony shoved his phone in her face.

It was a Facebook page. She read aloud. "'Confirmed: My son's accuser has a boyfriend.' Oh, Christ," she groaned. "Is this his mother?"

"Yup," Tony said. "Keep reading."

"I'm in the shower." The most self-evident statement she'd ever made. "Can it wait?"

Tony read on. "'Anyone think of a reason he doesn't want to admit to sex?'"

Julia turned off the water. "That's awful."

"He must have told her to post it."

"Can you pass me a towel?" Julia squeezed the water from her hair.

Tony handed her one through the curtain. "Can they use it against him in court?"

She wound the towel around her torso and secured it. "A statement by his mom? They can ask her about it, but I don't know what good it will do."

"Why don't you sound more upset?"

She pulled back the curtain. "I guess because we knew this was gonna happen. We knew they'd try to make something out of Chris."

"Can't the judge make him stop talking?"

"It's not his post."

"But isn't that a thing a judge can do?"

She sighed. "A gag order?"

Tony's mouth pulled into a tight line. "I'm annoying you."

"Kind of. I'm trying to get ready; I need to go to the store."

Thanksgiving was that coming Thursday. The grocery store would be a mob scene.

"I can go," Tony said.

"No," she said quickly. "I know this is hard. He's your brother. It sucks. I'll take care of the store."

In truth, she wanted the excuse to get out of the house and take a breather.

⟶

Julia's list was long, encompassing a normal week of meals and a dinner for ten, since Nick was bringing his roommate Elle. In a few days they would host Thanksgiving, as they had for years now. Julia considered their unit—herself, Tony, and the kids—to be the hub of the family. Her widowed mother, Tony's divorced parents and Jeannie, and Nick were the spokes they connected. One year Nick would have a serious boyfriend, and he might go to another family's dinner, but she hoped that once he was married, and if he had kids, he would continue to celebrate the holiday with them. She loved Nick. There had been moments that fall when Tony acted like he didn't believe she did. She had been heartbroken when he was assaulted. She felt miserable for him with each new invasion the process brought. Her feelings just didn't have the same staying power as Tony's. This was all much more personal for Tony. Maybe she would have understood if Nick were her brother, but it seemed to be more than that. Their relationship was different than most siblings she knew. Tony felt responsible for Nick.

Hopefully Tony would cool off in the hours she and Seb were at Shop 'n Save. Bless him, Seb was obsessed with the grocery store, and while Chloe would usually pass on the chaos of a weekend shopping trip, Seb would throw a fit before he'd be left at home. Though she was merely guessing, Julia assumed people who tripped on acid looked something like her son as he stepped through the automatic doors of their local Shop 'n Save. Every week, Seb was visibly in awe of the colors, smells, and busy sounds that inundated him on arrival.

The storefront of the Shop 'n Save in Orange hadn't actually worn that name in more than a decade. A big corporation bought it out and changed the name long before Julia even moved to Orange, but her neighbors still called it by the old name. The store's products and prices catered more to the inhabitants of the town center—mostly liberal, mostly wealthy, mostly that southern Maine mix of bougie and hippie. Sometimes Julia's neighbors in the country griped about what the store had become, and Julia felt like a fraud for feigning her agreement with them. With her creaky farmhouse and stay-at-home job, they didn't know she came from affluent stock by way of her parents in Yarmouth. They didn't know how much she liked to buy six-dollar loaves of rosemary bread, herbal face oils, and all organic everything, right down to the canned beans. "Shop 'n Overpay," her neighbor Willie called the store. Julia soothed her guilt by buying eggs from Willie every week. She always noted the irony that they were quite expensive.

This weekend the store was a madhouse, and Seb was in heaven. He cradled sweet potatoes in his arms, dropping one with a thud as Julia tried to intercept him on his way to the cart. He selected a purple onion and inspected it with a severe look on his face before holding it up to an older gentleman riffling through the pile to his left.

"Good choice," the man said with a nod, and Sebastian beamed. As they made their way through the store, her chatty son greeted neighbors and strangers alike. In the cereal aisle, Julia was crouching for a canister of oatmeal when she heard her son exclaim, "Detective!"

She turned to find Detective Rice standing over her. She must have looked startled, because he opened with an apology for sneaking up on her.

"It's fine," she said as she stood. "Hi."

"Hi," he said with a smile.

A woman came up next to the detective with her cart, and he moved out of her way in the cramped aisle.

"I didn't realize you lived over here, too," Julia offered.

"Oh, I don't, but my sister-in-law and her kids do. I'm due there for lunch, and I was stopping to grab bread." He held a single, fresh boule in his hand. It was from the bakery section across the store—had he followed her?

"Are you making sandwiches?" Sebastian asked brightly.

"I think so, little man."

"Is your wife here, too?" Julia asked.

"My wife passed away, actually, little over five years ago."

Julia winced; he continued before she could speak.

"It's all right, really."

"That's so sad," Sebastian said. "Do you miss her?"

Julia put a hand on Seb's shoulder; she felt an urge to shush him, but there was a sweetness to his innocent concern that didn't deserve to be silenced.

"Very much," the detective said.

"How did—" Seb began.

"Honey, Detective Rice needs to get to his family's house."

Detective Rice took the hint and nodded. "I just saw you and wanted to check on you quick. Lot of business in the news lately." He spoke in code for Seb's sake. "Hope you and your family are doing all right."

Fatigue crept over her shoulders. "We are." She let his eyes hold hers for a beat. What did he expect her to say? There was nothing to do but survive it. The wheels of justice were grinding along slowly, and there was no way for Detective Rice or anyone else to shut down the public chatter in the meantime.

Detective Rice departed with a quiet goodbye to Julia and a wave to

Sebastian, who had wandered to the end of the aisle, bored with the adults talking about the news. Julia watched the detective amble away, slightly hunched, looking older and maybe smaller now. Was it her new knowledge that he was a widower, and one who still wore his wedding band? Or was it the image of him, just a man on the weekend, off the clock, worried about what her family was going through? Julia had felt that way a thousand times before at her old job—like she couldn't do anything real for people who desperately needed help. She had assumed a man of Detective Rice's experience would be immune to such feelings of failure, but now she suspected she didn't know him as well as she had thought.

31

At least twenty minutes had passed since he heard the change in Julia's breath and knew she was asleep. Tony, on the other hand, could feel his mind revving up instead of settling for the night. Thanksgiving was a matter of hours away, and there was so much to do in the morning. Tony would handle the oven: the turkey, mashed potatoes, and pie; Julia would take the salad, hors d'oeuvres, and table. The kids would "help," meaning they'd double the time it took to do everything. People would start arriving at noon. Their mothers would be on time; Nick would not; Ron and Jeannie were a crapshoot. The first time Tony and Julia hosted the whole family for Thanksgiving, Ron showed up with a buzz on. Ron polished off a six-pack as they ate, and Tony ended up asking him to leave early. He and Jeannie left with less fuss than Tony had expected, but they didn't show up the next two years.

It was debatable whether Tony and Ron's relationship had improved or deteriorated with time. To Ron, he suspected, Tony had grown into a disrespectful man who'd adopted some soft-minded view that his father had been abusive. To Tony, he had finally grown too strong for his dad to control with his hands or his words. Over time, Ron had backed down, and eventually he became tolerable enough that Tony didn't mind him being around Chloe and Seb, so long as Tony or Julia was there. There was always a tension between the two of them, teeming under the surface of their uneasy truce. Neither respected, or even much liked, the other.

If Nick hadn't existed, Tony probably would have been long done with Ron Hall. But Nick did exist, and that kept Ron in the loop. As difficult a person as Jeannie was, Nick loved her, and she and Ron came as a set. Nick probably even loved Ron, too. He'd gotten a slightly modified version of him—he was still a shit dad, but he would have been worse if Tony hadn't stepped in.

It happened the same summer that Tony stopped drinking. The same summer he threw his last punch.

Nick was five then. Tony had just graduated from college. He moved back in with his mom while he figured out what to do next. He got a job waiting tables, usually working dinner shifts. Sometimes he went to see Nick during the day.

One day, he dropped by to find Nick playing outside by himself. Nick sat in front of the single-story house, smashing action figures together in the grass. When he saw Tony, Nick ran up to the car and yanked the door open. "Tony, Tony, Tony!"

He climbed out of his mom's car and swung Nick up, hooking an arm under his rear.

Simultaneously, Tony smelled a foul odor and felt something against his arm. Tony put him down. Nick had soiled himself.

Squatting down at his level, Tony asked quietly, "Did you have an accident?"

Nick smiled at Tony, placed a hand on his shoulder, and ignored the question.

"Can I look?" Tony spun Nick around and realized he had a diaper on. *What the fuck?*

Tony took his hand and brought him into the house.

Ron and Jeannie were on the couch, each holding a beer, a few empties at their feet. The TV was blaring.

"Nick needs a diaper change," Tony said.

"'Kay," Jeannie said.

Tony watched them for a beat. Obviously they knew Nick was wearing diapers, not like Nick had snuck that by them. Tony wasn't sure what he was expecting. An explanation.

He brought Nick to his room and changed him.

"Can you make cheese?" Nick asked. That meant mac and cheese.

It was late afternoon. "It's too early for dinner," Tony said.

Nick pouted.

"What did you have for lunch?"

"Um, nothing."

"Did you have lunch?"

Nick shook his head.

What was going on?

Tony walked out into the living room. "Has he had lunch?"

"Not yet," Jeannie said.

"It's almost three."

Jeannie looked up at Tony for the first time. "I tried at noon, but he wasn't hungry."

"So you just skip a meal?"

"He's old enough to decide when he's hungry, Tony."

Ron spoke. "Just feed him if he's hungry."

Tony wanted to lay into them both—*still in diapers but old enough to skip meals?*—but Nick was standing right next to him. He chewed the inside of his cheek and went into the kitchen to put on the water for pasta. He found a box of Kraft and a can of green beans.

Tony sat with Nick while he ate. Nick polished off the pasta but left the beans untouched.

"Can I have more?"

Ron got up to grab a beer from the fridge.

"Once you eat your veggies," Tony said.

Ron chuckled behind him. Popped the tab with a *crack*. "Not so easy, is it?"

"Much easier than you make it look," Tony said.

"What'd you say?"

"I don't like them," Nick said, pushing his plate away from him.

Ron stepped forward, saying, "Shut up and eat 'em," as he cuffed Nick's ear.

Tony didn't even feel himself stand up, he did it so fast. His hands were on Ron's shirt and *bam*, he walked Ron backward and slammed him into the fridge. Ron's beer can hit the floor, and cold liquid sprayed Tony's legs. The memory was blurry from there—Jeannie was yelling, "Stop it, stop it"; Ron was saying something; Ron's hands were up, and Tony punched him. It wasn't a clean hit, but he knew he made contact because Ron's teeth scraped his knuckles. More yelling, more noise, Tony stepped back, and Ron let him.

"The fuck out of my house."

At the table, Nick was wailing.

"It's okay," Jeannie said. "It's okay, it's okay."

Tony tried to move toward Nick.

Ron stepped toward him, his hand clutching where Tony had struck him. "Get. The fuck. Out."

Tony went back to his dad's the next day. He parked, and Ron came outside.

"You're done here," Ron said when Tony got out.

Tony walked partway up the walkway.

"Leave or I'll make you," Ron said.

"I just want to see him."

"Too bad."

"I don't need to see you or Jeannie. I just want to see Nick."

Ron shrugged. "Deal with it."

"I'll call DHS."

The words hung in the air between them.

"For what?"

"He's not potty-trained; he's fucking hungry; you *hit* him."

"You assaulted me; I could call the cops on you."

"Do it. I don't care. They'll still take him from you."

"Okay," Ron said with an ugly grin. "Call. Let them put him in foster care."

"You know what I learned?" Tony felt his face spread into the same smile. "They'll check for family first."

"They wouldn't give him to you."

"Maybe not, but they'd give him to my mom."

Ron's face went dark. "She ain't his family."

"She's the mother of his brother. And she'd take him." He hadn't discussed any of this with Cynthia, but Ron didn't know that.

"She knows better than to fuck with me."

"She *hates* you." He hissed the word between gritted teeth. "You know how *hard* I had to work to be able to see you after she left your ass?"

"You wanted to see me." Ron said it like it was an insult. A pathetic trait of Tony's, to want to be near his own father.

"I didn't know better. I do now."

"Then what do you keep coming back for?"

"Him." Tony pointed at the house. "I know how badly he needs me because I needed it, too. I was so desperate for it, I settled for a piece of shit like you."

"You're pissing me off," Ron said.

"You touch him again and I call. I show up and he's hungry or cold or sitting in his own shit, I call. You do right, I don't."

The change hadn't been night and day, but Ron must have known there was truth in the threat. Tony never saw Ron hit Nick again.

Tony checked the time on his phone. Almost midnight, and he was wired. He needed to turn off his brain and go to sleep or he'd be useless in the morning. Seeing Nick would make him feel better. They'd texted a bit since the grand jury last week, but it would be good to see him in person. Make sure he really was doing as well as Nick said he was. And then, Tony thought of Darlene Walker's Facebook post, and he decided to check her page on his phone.

Tony tilted the phone to keep the light from falling on Julia beside him. He pulled up Darlene's page. This was a mistake.

"Lesson to all," she had written on her wall on Tuesday of that week. "Have sex with a kink, make sure to film it, in case they call it rape later."

Tony's blood boiled. He crawled out of bed. Crossed the dark hall to the bathroom. Closed the door and read the words again.

There was no reason to think Nick had seen either of her posts, but it worried Tony. Nick would feel attacked if he did see them. And even if he didn't, Walker was poisoning people against him. Tony stood in the bathroom, staring at the sentence on his phone. Worst of all, it scratched at something problematic.

Walker's whole defense was unbelievable, but it was 2015, and there were still people out there who thought gay men were sex-crazed lunatics. There were people who believed that Nick had been complicit in what Walker did to him. People who believed it was more likely that Nick had wanted to be hit, choked, made to bleed, than it was that he'd been raped.

What if one of those people ended up on the jury? What if Walker stirred up people enough that the ADA got scared; what if it ended in a bullshit plea deal? Court couldn't change what had happened to Nick, Tony knew that, but Nick's name needed to come out of this clean. And Ray Walker deserved to suffer for what he'd done.

On his phone, he went to Google. He typed the words he'd thought of over a month ago—a search he hadn't bothered to run. He clicked through the link. There was another search bar. A drop-down menu. "Search by owner." There was a creak in the hallway, and Tony started. He stuck his head out of the bathroom. No one was there—just a house sound. He'd felt, for a second, like he was about to be caught doing something wrong. And maybe he was. He was getting himself all worked up again about something everyone else, Nick included, seemed to have accepted. Walker was going to blame Nick to try to save himself. Nick was going to have to wait, maybe a year, for the noise of the case to be over. And Nick's identity was private, at least for now. Tony closed the browser on his phone. He needed to get some sleep.

⁓

"Can I be excused?"

Blobs of mashed potatoes and gravy clung to the corners of Seb's mouth.

"Holy moly," Tony said, motioning for Seb to use his napkin.

Tony had woken up that morning with a nervous energy he'd only fueled by drinking two cups of coffee and fasting until they sat down to eat around one. As the massive meal settled into his stomach, he finally began to feel how tired he was. Tired and calmer. Everything was going well. The food had turned out great—his best turkey yet, Julia said—and everyone was getting along. Julia's mom, Marjorie, brought out his own mom's fun side, and the two of them had been laughing together all afternoon. Ron and Jeannie had shown up sober and friendly. Nick seemed to be doing okay. He brought his roommate Elle. The one who'd been there that night. Tony had felt anxious about seeing her for some reason, but when Nick asked if she could come, of course he'd said yes.

"Me too?" Chloe asked. They'd all been at the table for nearly an hour now.

"First," Tony's mother said, "could we go around and share what we're thankful for?" Cynthia was holding her handwritten name tag in one hand, clearly thankful for her grandchildren. Julia had had the kids make place cards for the guests. After Julia set up the folding card table against the dining room table and covered them with a long cloth, Tony noticed that she had set his parents' cards as far apart as possible.

He looked to Julia, who held up her glass. "Go for it."

"Well, I just wanted to say how thankful I am to have all of you in my life. I just love you all so much." She reached to her right and squeezed Chloe's cheek. Chloe grinned and squirmed away. "I have the best family in the world, and I'm so glad we're able to be together. All of us." She made a point to look at Ron and Jeannie at that moment. It was actually pretty sweet.

Julia's mom went next, and then Elle as they moved clockwise around the table. Tony couldn't help but notice that Nick looked a bit pained as his turn to speak drew nearer—he was wringing his hands together under the table.

Even more pained was Seb, who had already grown bored with being at the table. He began to slide, slow motion, out of his chair.

"Bud, stay in your seat," Tony whispered, but Seb kept sliding.

After Elle thanked the Halls for letting her join in their family event, she moved on to Nick. "I'm thankful for you, Nick. You're my best friend, and the best person I know. You've just been so brave."

"Seb, honey, come back up here," Tony said full volume.

A muffled voice under the table said, "What's that?"

Nick banged his hands against the underside of the table, making the silverware rattle over its surface. His face was white.

"Honey, come back to your seat," Julia said to Seb.

"What's what?" Elle asked, lifting the table cloth.

"What's on your arm, Uncle Nick?" Seb said.

Jeannie was looking at her son now—Nick was tugging at his sleeves.

"What *is* on your arm?" She reached over and yanked his left sleeve up.

From his seat, Tony could see a long, blotchy red wound running up Nick's forearm, continuing under his sleeve.

"The fuck is that?" Tony said involuntarily.

"*Tony.*" Instantly, Julia chastised him for swearing in front of the kids.

"Oh my God!" Jeannie pulled at Nick's sleeve, leaving the gashes on his arm visible.

Nick ripped his arm away and stood, knocking into the windowsill behind him. "Mom!" He pulled his sleeve back down and pushed past his parents' seats to run through the living room.

Tony shoved backward in his chair and followed.

"Tony!" he heard Julia call after him.

He made it up the stairs to the bathroom door just in time for it to slam in his face. The noise woke him up to what had just happened. He hesitated, then said, "Nick?"

"Go away, Tony." Nick's voice was sharp, punctuating each word.

Tony fought the urge to turn the knob—their old-house doors didn't lock. Instead, he leaned forward, resting his forehead on the door.

"Please," he said quietly. "Please let me in. I'm so scared." The relief that came from saying those words aloud nearly overwhelmed him.

After a pause, he felt Nick moving on the other side, and the door creaked open.

Nick's face dissolved into tears first, and Tony pulled him into a hug. Nick shuddered and sobbed wet, hot breath on Tony's neck.

What was that?

Tony clamped his teeth around the question. He knew what it was. He began to cry, and he held Nick tighter.

They stood, holding each other, until their surroundings came back. They were standing in the hall, excited voices downstairs in the dining room. Jeannie's voice was rising above the others.

Nick shifted to release himself from the embrace.

"Can we please talk?"

Nick nodded.

They sat on the bed in Tony and Julia's room, and Nick sighed a shaky breath. Tony didn't want to see the marks again. But did he have an obligation to look closer? "So that's— You— When did you . . . start doing that?"

Nick shrugged. "I guess not that long ago."

Was *Why?* a stupid question? Tony didn't know.

An obvious statement would be easier. "You're not doing okay."

Nick shrugged. His arms were crossed over his torso, and his legs were crossed, too. He looked like he was trying to shrink into a little ball. Tony realized he was unconsciously doing the same thing. He released his legs to sit wide.

"Does your counselor know?"

"Not yet."

"I need you to tell him."

"I will," Nick said quickly.

That was hard to trust, since Nick had been in counseling all this time. But how was he supposed to explain that to Nick?

"I don't want to say the wrong thing," Tony said.

Nick looked up at him. "Just say it."

"I'm afraid you won't tell him."

"I promise."

Tony looked down at Nick's covered arms. "I feel like you've been lying to me."

Nick frowned and looked away.

"You're cutting yourself?"

"No," Nick said. "Just . . . I'm not cutting."

"Then what is that?"

After a long pause, Nick said, "More like scratching."

"Nick," Tony whispered. Nick *was* in pain. Even more than Tony had worried.

In a quiet voice, Nick said, "I have been lying to you."

About hurting himself, or something else? Tony said nothing. Waited for him to speak.

"Everyone knows it's me."

Tony was confused. What did he mean? "That you're the victim? In the case?"

Nick nodded. Fresh tears began to run down his cheeks.

"How?"

"It doesn't matter."

"Who knows?"

"Everyone on campus."

"Fuck," Tony hissed.

"Yup," Nick said. He dragged his hands down his face and dropped them in his lap.

"What do I do? Fuck, Nick. What do I do for you?"

Nick stared at the floor in front of them. Tony reached for Nick's hand. Squeezed it three times.

Nick sighed. "Can you get me a tissue?"

"Okay. Can I get Julia, too?"

"Yeah."

⌐

Maybe an hour later, Tony, Nick, and Julia rejoined Marjorie and Elle, who were with the kids in the living room. Julia had told them upstairs that the rest were going home, to give them privacy. Tony had heard Jeannie earlier. She'd left angry. Julia had probably told her to stay downstairs, to not overwhelm Nick.

"Sorry about that," Nick said awkwardly to Julia's mom.

Marjorie shook her head and pulled Nick in for a hug. She whispered something inaudible to him.

Elle was on the couch, flanked by the kids, who were each just about sitting on her lap. She had turned to face the adults, her silhouette over *The Jungle Book* playing on the screen behind her. She said nothing, and Nick didn't look at her at all.

Upstairs, Julia had approached the situation with the calmness of an EMT. She knelt down low, below Nick's eyeline, and said that she needed him to call a crisis hotline with her. Nick had resisted at first, explaining that he wasn't suicidal, that he wasn't actually cutting himself, but Julia had worn away at him, and he eventually agreed to call. The woman at the hotline scheduled an emergency counseling session for Nick for the next morning, as his own counselor was on vacation until Monday.

Nick had declined their offer to stay over, and Tony was ashamed at the relief he felt when Nick said to Elle, "I'm ready when you are."

Tony stood in the window and watched the pair get into an unfamiliar car and pull away.

"Dad, you said the f-word," Chloe said behind him.

Tony turned. Seb's eyes were glued to the movie, but Chloe's were on him.

"I'm sorry, honey. I shouldn't have said that."

"Why did you say that?"

"I got scared."

"Scared how?"

A bone-tired fatigue washed over him. He didn't know what to say to her. Julia could take this one.

"Just scared," he said. "I need to go clean up, we can talk about it later."

He left her to find Julia and Marjorie in the kitchen, washing and drying dishes.

"You don't need to do that," he said to Julia's mom. "We can do all this."

"Nonsense," Marjorie said. "I stayed to help."

Julia stepped toward him. "Are you all right, honey?"

"Honestly, I think I could go to sleep."

"Oh, do," she said. "Really. We've got this. That was a lot."

"I'll just help for a minute," he said in spite of himself.

Tony walked across the kitchen and into the dining room, where the plates and silverware had all been cleared; cloth napkins were rumpled across the table and in chairs, and glasses of wine and water stood all about.

He stacked the water glasses into a tower, then started to grip two wineglasses with one hand. One of them—Julia's—was a third full. It would spill if he took it with another glass. Obscured by the French doors and the wall, Tony glanced around the room and drained the glass down his throat.

—

The room was dark.

"How long can we do this?" Tony said in a sleep-laden voice.

Julia was getting into bed next to him, and he felt her pause. "What?"

He felt himself wake up more, his eyes registering his bedside table, the clock, the lamp in the dark. "Hmm?"

"You said something."

"Sorry, was dreaming." He tried to hold on to his sleep, but it was slipping away from him. "What time is it?"

"After eleven. My mom finally left," she said with a laugh. "I tried to wake you earlier, but you were out."

He'd thudded upstairs and collapsed into bed sometime around four that afternoon. He couldn't even remember falling asleep.

Julia snuggled into the nape of his neck and kissed his ear. "You doing okay?"

No talk, not now. I'm so tired.

"I wanna keep sleeping," he said as he rolled away. "Love you."

She rubbed a hand over the back of his head. "Love you, too."

He tried to sink away, gently, not forcing the sleep to come.

Nick's scabbed, picked arm flashed in his mind.

Shh, go away.

Nick's tear-soaked face on his neck.

Stop. He tried to breathe deeply. The air he inhaled whistled down his throat, disturbing something like the taste of alcohol. He'd drank a glass of wine before he came to bed. Or was that a dream? Had he really done that?

This was all taking too long. Someone had to do something. A year of this? A year of articles and comments and letters and Facebook and everyone that mattered to Nick, everyone who saw him every day, knowing it's him? His body, his story, his reputation? A year of Nick trying to survive that? No. He couldn't. Something had to be done.

Nick was getting help in the morning. It would be fine.

But Nick *had* been getting help, and still he was digging his own skin off.

Soon Tony was pounding with adrenaline. He couldn't keep trying.

Slowly, he pushed his feet from the bed and found the floor. He slid from under the covers to stand. *Just walk, like you're going out to the bathroom.* Tony strode purposefully from the room, and Julia said nothing.

Down the stairs he crept, across the hall into the living room. It wasn't there. He circled the downstairs until he found it in the kitchen—his phone. He leaned against the counter and pulled up the browser. He would finish what he started a night ago. Town of Salisbury's Assessor's Office. Online Database. Search by Owner. Walker. And there it was. Raymond Walker's address.

32

Julia woke up to Chloe's face inches from her own.

"Oh, jeez!"

"Seb's in the cookies and he hasn't had breakfast yet." Chloe frowned at her bitterly.

Julia wiped the grit from her eyes. "What time is it?" She turned and saw that Tony was already out of bed. According to her phone, it was 8:23. How had she slept so late?

"Honey," she said. "We don't tattle. Only when someone's being unsafe."

"But you said it's not healthy to eat dessert before breakfast." Chloe raised her eyebrows and looked at Julia like they were standing on opposite sides of a courtroom.

Damn that clever child. She hadn't been awake long enough to enunciate a better definition of tattling. It was like SCOTUS on pornography: you just know it when you see it.

"Why are you blessing me with this information instead of Dad?"

"Dad's gone," Chloe said.

Another run, Julia thought, *finally*. Maybe he'd sweat off the emotional hangover he no doubt woke up with. Just remembering the day before made a fresh lump rise in Julia's throat. Poor Nick.

"Come snuggle me," she said.

Chloe climbed into bed, and Julia wrapped her arms around her, buried her face in her hair.

Chloe's voice was muffled. "Can I have a cookie, too, then?"

Julia squeezed Chloe tighter. "Yeah, let's go have cookies for breakfast."

They climbed from bed, and Julia followed Chloe from the room.

Down in the kitchen, her eyes skimmed over Tony's sneakers at their usual station, sitting in the corner by the door to the mudroom. Had she paused to register what she was seeing, that Tony was not on a run, it might have all been different.

33

TONY HALL, 2015

Tony had been sitting on the street in front of Raymond Walker's house for hours, waiting to see what would happen. At some point, he would make up his mind, or Walker would force a decision by emerging from the house.

Tony had checked the website again to be sure, but there was no question this was it. It was a gray bungalow on a quiet street in Salisbury, a way from Nick's apartment, across town from the bar where they met. The house looked wrong, not the way Tony would have pictured it. There were flowers out front: tall purple ones; white globes of petals on thin stems; bursts of orange and yellow. The driveway was empty and the door was down on the detached garage.

Tony knew what he wanted to say: his wife was a lawyer, and if Walker and his mother didn't stop posting stuff about Nick online, they'd sue him for invasion of privacy or libel. Julia had already said they probably couldn't sue him, but Walker didn't need to know that. Tony would stand tall, look him in the eye, and tell him he was done bullying Nick. Tell him he was lucky court was taking care of the situation instead of Tony.

But now that he was there, something was stopping him from getting out of the car. As soon as he knocked on the door to that house, there was no going back. As the morning sun climbed his windshield, the thought grew stronger that it was pointless to threaten a lawsuit. Walker was shameless. He took pleasure in hurting others—Tony would only be showing Walker that it was working. And what would happen if Tony pissed him off?

Then, the side door opened. Raymond Walker, clear as day, stepped from the doorway. Raymond Walker. The man who'd made Nick hurt so badly he'd gone on hurting himself. Walker turned to shut the door. Turned back to the driveway. Started to walk to the garage. Wait, he was leaving.

Tony fumbled his door open and stepped into the street. "Hey!" he yelled.

At the top of the driveway, the garage door was climbing upward; Walker was standing in front of the garage, waiting for the door to open. He turned toward Tony's voice.

"Raymond Walker," Tony said as he crossed the street. His voice was strong, commanding.

Raymond Walker tilted his head incrementally. "Yes?"

Tony was in the driveway now. His legs carried him faster than he could think. He was approaching Walker, who took a step back toward the truck in the garage.

"Hey—hey—*hey*," Walker yelped.

Tony grabbed him by the jacket and slammed him against the bed of the truck.

"You stay the *fuck* away from Nick Hall you piece of shit." His voice had gone shaky.

Walker raised his hands, squeezed his eyes shut. "Done," he said. "Done."

Spittle had flown from Tony's mouth, and it glistened on Walker's forehead. He could see the pores on his nose, he was so close to him.

Tony released the lapels of Walker's jacket and stepped back from him. He turned and strode down the driveway. What did he do? What did he just do?

He reached the street as Walker spoke.

"Hey, for future reference, are you the brother or the boyfriend?"

Walker was goading him; Tony needed to get in the car and leave. But his feet stopped. He swayed in the street. He didn't turn. *Just walk forward. Just get in the car.*

"He talked about his big brother." Walker's voice was edged with a strained cheeriness. "You certainly look big."

Just take a step forward and the other will follow. Get in the car.

"Maybe when all this blows over—"

"Open your mouth again and I will *kill* you." Tony turned to Walker. Gone was his strong voice or even the shaky one. Hot tears had sprung up as he spoke, and his voice went to a whisper. "I will *kill* you. You leave him alone."

Walker grinned, ugly and satisfied.

Tony turned back to the car, strode to it, climbed in, slammed the door, started it, pulled away, as Walker stood and watched.

34

Detective, call for you."

Rice had barely made it through the unit door when Officer Thompson called out to him.

"Take a message."

"Sorry, sir," Thompson said. He was new, painfully young, and a little clueless about station etiquette. Rice had been called in at four that morning for a burglary and aggravated assault and was just getting to the station; he didn't need to be jumped the second he walked in the door.

Rice continued across the bullpen, toward the breakroom, slow enough to hear Thompson say, "Sorry, Mr. Walker, I'll need to take a message for when th—"

"Hey!" Rice spun and waved his free hand at Thompson, coffee sloshing up onto the lid of his Styrofoam cup. "I'll take it," he mouthed.

"Oh," Thompson said as he watched Rice. "Why, there he is. I'll put you through to his line."

Rice set his coffee down on his desk at the edge of the bullpen and elected to press Speaker so he could stand. The unit was relatively quiet, and his back was aching—he'd forgotten to pop an Aleve before he left the house that morning.

"Detective Rice here."

"Good afternoon, Detective. So glad I was able to catch you." Raymond Walker's shit-weasel voice almost sounded sarcastic, he was trying so hard to sound charming.

Rice matched his tone. "What can I do for you, Ray?"

"I just wanted to make a report that Nick Hall's brother just came to my house and threatened to kill me."

Rice picked up the receiver. "He did, did he?"

"Yes, sir. I understand this must be hard for him, not knowing his baby brother is lying about the whole encounter."

Rice bit his tongue; Ray could easily be recording the call. In this day and age, never say anything on the phone you wouldn't want played back in court.

Ray continued. "I really do empathize with the family. But I can't have someone coming to my house, putting his hands on me, throwing me around."

Rice grimaced; was Tony Hall that stupid?

"I have to draw the line somewhere, don't I? Compassion must have its limits."

How much would Rice mind hearing "compassion my ass" played back in court? Instead, he said, "You sure this was Nick Hall's brother?"

"Oh, yes, so many of the same features. And I'm sure you know he drives a gray Ford Explorer."

Shit. What was Tony thinking? Tampering with a witness was a felony, not to mention assault and terrorizing charges. This would only complicate things. Julia would be a wreck. Rice felt almost dizzy, and he shook his head as though to scatter the thoughts.

"All right, Ray. Can you come in to give your statement?"

"Oh, I'm not pressing charges."

What?

Ray continued when Rice didn't speak. "I will if anything like this happens again, but for today I just wanted to make the report. He frightened me, Detective. He said he'd kill me. But I'm a reasonable man. I know he's grieving. And he doesn't have reason to believe me over his little brother . . . yet."

What was his game? Rice pulled a pen from his breast pocket and found a clean sheet on his desk. Wrote: *11-27-15 Call from RW. TH threatened to kill RW. RW not pressing, just reporting, knows he's grieving.* Rice paused then added quotation marks around *just reporting*.

"Well, I'll leave the choice with you, to press charges or not."

"And I'm choosing not."

"What time this happen?"

A pause. "This morning, around nine fifty."

"Well," Rice looked at his watch, "it's nearly two. Why'd you wait till now to call?"

"I went to brunch first. I was on my way out the door when he surprised me. He was waiting in the street."

"Mm. And where'd you go to brunch?"

"Why?"

"For your report. Better if I ask the details now so you don't have to remember them later if you change your mind." The whole thing reeked of ulterior motives. Rice scribbled down the times on his sheet.

"Fork and Napkin," Ray said quickly, then: "I need to get going." There was something to his voice. He just wanted Rice to write down exactly what he wanted . . . and he didn't want to linger on the restaurant.

"Over in Ogunquit? Great little diner. No problem, Ray, you go about your business today. I'll log your report and close it out."

"Thanks," Ray said flatly, and hung up.

Rice hung up the receiver slowly. What was he after?

When Rice called Fork & Napkin, a young voice told him that they'd had a pretty busy morning, the day after Thanksgiving usually was. She did remember a man coming in, though, whose name she did not know.

He was somewhere around thirty, maybe older, maybe younger, she was terrible with ages. But this man stood out to her.

"He said he was late for a ten o'clock, and he said a few different last names to check for, and I found the reservation but no one had shown up. Besides him, I mean." She told Rice the name the reservation was under—it was meaningless—and continued. "He seemed sad when I said no one else was there. I think he was stood up."

Rice thanked the girl and hung up. So at least some of Ray Walker's friends had the good sense to distance themselves. If only the idiots agreeing with him online had done the same.

Tony Hall needed to be set straight. If any part of Walker's story was true . . . how could he have been so foolish? Rice knew Tony and Nick were close. Tony was a father figure, in a way, to Nick. Clearly this was all driving Tony crazy. But he had simply given Walker ammunition: *See? The Halls are unstable.* He was hurting the very person he was trying to protect. Not to mention risking what could happen to Tony—how that would harm his children, his wife?

His mind paused on Tony's wife for a moment. Whenever Julia's face came into his mind he pushed it away, but today he let it linger. Her hair bathed in sunlight, like the first time he saw her at the kitchen sink. The longer he pictured her, the more her resemblance to his departed wife dawned on him. The hair was wrong, and the nose, and build, but the eyes, the smile, the warmth. That's what it was: just like Irene. They bore the markings of supremely *good* women. Good women who had married men who had to work to be good.

35

Tony's cell rang in the kitchen. Julia turned up the TV and left the kids on the couch, walking quickly to meet Tony as he answered the call. Tony had gotten home late that morning and told her what he'd done: found Walker's home address on Salisbury's registry, gone to Walker's house, pushed him, threatened him. Julia had laid into him, he'd cried, she'd holed up with the kids in the living room, ignoring him as she tried to process the insanity he had just confessed to.

Then nothing had happened for hours. She was certain the quiet wouldn't last.

And she was right. It was the detective on the phone.

"I just got a call from Ray Walker," Detective Rice said.

Julia's heart fell into her stomach. Tony was going to be arrested.

Tony opened his mouth to speak, and Julia held up a hand. Whatever Tony was going to say, she didn't want the police to hear it. No admissions.

After a beat, Detective Rice said, "You there?"

Julia nodded at him.

"Yup," Tony said.

"And Julia?"

"I'm here," Julia said.

"Okay," the detective said. "Tony, Ray Walker says you assaulted him at his house this morning."

Julia's gaze moved from the phone to her husband's face. His puffy eyelids were closed and his brow was furrowed with worry.

"Says you threatened to kill him."

A chill squirmed up her spine, and she shuddered.

"So it's assault, terrorizing, tampering with a witness."

Julia brought her hands to her face. The whole mess they were already living was going to start again, this time with Tony as the defendant. Her brain started listing potential outcomes: probation, jail time, a record. Tony's office would find out—lawyers were the biggest gossips. *The media* would find out. They were already all over Nick's case. Everyone would know.

After a long pause, Detective Rice said, "That's what you might have been charged with."

Julia lifted her face from her hands. Tony looked at her in confusion.

"He's not pressing charges," the detective said.

"What?" Julia asked.

"Yup. Not sure how you got so lucky."

Tony handed Julia the phone and laid down on the kitchen floor.

"So . . . that's it?" she asked.

"For now," he said. "Tony. I don't know what you were thinking. But this isn't going to help anyone. You hear me?"

On the floor, Tony nodded. His head lolled on the tiles, his arms down at his sides.

"I'm not a big fan of the *Boondock Saints*, you hear?" Rice said. "You let us take care of this."

"Thank you," Julia said.

"Don't thank me," he said. "This would have been a different conversation if Walker wanted to press charges."

They hung up.

"I don't know what I was thinking." Tony stared up at the ceiling. "I don't know."

Julia did.

Tony had always been a fixer. He liked to fix problems: mostly other people's.

It took Julia a while to notice it, but once she did, it bothered her. The porch light at her apartment burned out: he showed up with a bulb, screwdriver, and stepladder. She caught a cold: he brought take-out soup and encouraged her to nap. She was moody: he wanted to talk about it. Her best friend, Margot, told her it was romantic. Julia felt disrespected, like he thought she couldn't take care of herself. Julia may have had the perfect childhood, with all the financial and emotional security a kid could ask for, but she'd been dealt a tougher hand in college. Her dad withered and died in the span of a month. Her mother had to give up her business. Julia started bartending to help pay for school. By the time she met Tony, she'd grown confident in her self-sufficiency, and proud of it.

Then one night during their first winter dating, one of Julia's coworkers got mugged. The woman was walking to her car after she closed up the Ruby, the bar where she and Julia worked in Portland, when a white guy in a hat and scarf showed her a switchblade and demanded her purse. She wasn't hurt, she told Julia after, just shaken. Julia told Tony on her way to work. She regretted it instantly. In the span of their five minutes on the phone, he told her not to go in, asked her if she'd get a different job, grew angry, and told her she should quit. She hung up on him. She'd never even heard of a mugging in Portland before. The odds of it happening to her seemed low, her coworker was fine, and Julia didn't have much worth stealing. Near the end of her shift, Tony showed up at the bar. He started by apologizing for being so crazy on the phone. She almost believed him, until she realized he was there to walk her to her car.

When the last barflies buzzed off at closing time, she locked the door and turned to Tony. All the things she hadn't said came up at once, like she'd been keeping a list to lob at him. She could see what he was doing. He didn't trust her to take care of herself. He didn't respect her decisions. And then she upped the ante.

"You're possessive."

Tony shook his head in confusion. "*Possessive?*"

"Yes."

"You're being crazy. The girl who does the same job as you got mugged last night. He could have done a lot more than show her a knife."

"It's not just this, it's everything! You think I can't change a light bulb! You suffocate me! I'm not your child!"

"What the fuck, my *child*? You're my girlfriend, and I love you, why is that so hard for you?"

"Why is it so hard for *you* to let me take care of myself?"

"It's what I do!" Tony shoved the barstool back and stood. "I take care of the people I love." He was breathing heavily, like he'd just sprinted. "My love suffocates you?"

Julia crossed her arms, tried to collect herself. Instead, a sensation of terror washed over her. This might not be a fight. This might be the end.

"There is so much that I love about the ways you love me," she said. "But if you need to be saving someone all the time . . . that doesn't work for me. I don't need that, I don't want it. And I hope you don't, either—I hope you don't need to be with a weak woman to feel like a man."

He opened his mouth, and she held up her hand.

"I don't think you do," she said, "consciously at least, but you need to listen to what I'm saying. How you're acting right now, it's not how I want my boyfriend to be. I need you to change." She inhaled. Exhaled. Goddamn it, her tears had pooled and spilled anyway. "Or I need you to go."

She'd said what she had to, and she met his gaze now, defied him to call her wrong. His dark hair went black in low lighting like this, and he came toward her, sharp features on a pale face. He wound his arms around her middle, rested his face against her neck. He kissed the hollow of her collarbone and released her.

"Okay," he whispered.

He reached behind her, turned the dead bolt, stepped around her, pushed through the door and onto the street.

He was leaving. He was leaving her.

He turned back. "This isn't me leaving," he said, as if he could hear the voice in her head. He narrowed his eyes, angry but playful. "I'm letting you walk to your car." He shook his head, then he turned and left.

She'd been right to take a stand that night, but wrong, too. So much of love was contradiction. For Tony, loving Julia was letting her be her own hero, even though his self-worth seemed to be founded on what he could do for the people he loved most. For Julia, loving Tony was letting him take care of her, as much as it scared her to start needing what she could lose.

And right now, Tony wanted to take care of Nick. His little brother, the boy he'd saved again and again. He had nowhere to put all that anger and despair.

Julia laid down on the cool kitchen tile beside Tony and took his hand in hers.

⟶

The next afternoon, they found themselves playing a game that resembled football in the side yard. Chloe's version of the sport included throwing the Nerf ball at the participants and touchdowns by either team at the same apple tree. It was confusing to say the least, but each time Chloe announced a new rule as the game progressed, Julia found her too charming to reason with, and so they complied. The kids had Julia laughing so much that her mood had lightened, and Tony seemed to be trying his best. He ran the yard, bickered playfully over the rules, glanced at her with eyes that seemed to measure whether she was having fun. He was apologizing.

"Wait, Seb," Chloe said to her brother.

Seb paused midsprint for the apple tree, squeezing the ball between his two small hands.

"The tree is ghouls now."

Tony shook his head. "What?"

"Ghouls, Dad," Chloe said, like Tony was an idiot.

"Why would we have ghouls in football?" Julia laughed. Tony held his hand out toward her in a gesture that said *Thank you!* She smiled at Tony and held his eyes. Even when it was against their own children, it felt good to team up with each other.

"It's not football, it's tag-football-dodgeball," Chloe said.

"Dodgeball," Seb chortled as he threw the ball at his sister.

Julia's cell trilled in her pocket. There were only a handful of people she'd answer a call from right now—Charlie Lee was one of them.

"I've got to take this, but I'll be right back," Julia said as she jogged toward the house and out of earshot. She paused at the front step and sat beside the jack-o'-lanterns they'd left moldering there since Halloween.

Charlie apologized for calling over the weekend.

"Are you kidding? I've been dying to hear from you."

"Ah," he sighed.

And just like that, she wished she hadn't answered. "What? Nothing?"

"I'm sorry, Julia. If he did this to anyone else, I didn't find them."

Shit. "That's okay."

"I thought I was on to something at one point, but . . ." He paused.

"What do you mean?"

"Ah, it was a dead end. A bartender in Providence thought it was possible he saw Ray Walker one weekend at his bar, *two years* ago."

"Providence, Rhode Island?"

"Yeah, Walker's company sells all around New England. So I reached out to a bunch of gay bars in some of the bigger cities."

Julia's heart pounded in her ear against the phone. "And?"

"And nothing, really. He remembers a real handsome guy coming in two nights in a row, talking to a shy young regular. On the second night, the kid left with the guy. The bartender was planning to ask the regular about it the next weekend, but the kid never came back."

A yelp from Chloe drew Julia's eyes to the backyard. Tony was chasing her with the ball.

"Long time after that, the bartender saw the kid at a farmers market with a girl. He called her a 'beard'—I guess they were acting like boyfriend, girlfriend. Bartender thinks she got wise to things. He never thought anything bad had happened. Until he got my email."

"Does he remember the regular's name?"

"No, not his last name, anyway."

"So . . ." So it really was nothing.

Julia studied her boots. Rolled her ankles to see the bottoms. Her treads were filled with mud and strands of grass.

"I'm really disappointed," Charlie said. "What he did to your brother-in-law, there must be others out there. Just hard to find them."

"It was sweet of you to look for me, really."

"I still might hear back from some other bars. If I do—"

"Yeah, just give me a call, but don't spend any more of your time on this."

Charlie paused. "I know you're worried about court, but try not to be."

Julia pulled back her jacket sleeve to wipe her nose on her flannel beneath. She was starting to feel like crying.

"They have plenty to nail him," Charlie said. "If I had to put in my vote, I'd say Raymond Walker is a man whose lifetime of good luck has finally run out."

After they hung up, Julia sat by the pumpkins and turned her phone over in her hands. A lifetime of good luck, that could explain it. Charlie was good, but if no one had reported Walker, if no one had pictures of him, or DNA samples—she shuddered. A lifetime of good luck. She looked up across the lawn. Tony was swinging Chloe around by the waist while Seb leaped at her, trying to grab the Nerf ball from her hands. The kids were chattering and whooping. Tony laughed, set Chloe down, rolled his shoulders, dropped his smile. Watched the kids run for the tree, some kind of wistful look on his face. What about their long run of bliss? Had that run out, too?

36

It had snowed on the last day of November that year. They woke up one morning to find that the fall was over. The winter that followed buried them.

That was the winter where Julia learned that you could lose yourself in the snow. You could lose sight of where you were if you didn't keep your wits about you. You were closer to spring than you'd been in the fall, but the low light, the mounting snow, it blinded you to the promise of spring. Just like the plants outside, you had to strip yourself down and harden to survive.

She glanced sideways at Detective Rice.

If she'd never seen this man again, she might have died happy.

"You know why I called you here, don't you?"

Yes.

"No," she said.

Could he see the sweat at her hairline?

"I look back on Nick's case," the detective said, "and I see all the mistakes I made. What I sat on. And what I missed. When Walker called and told me what Tony had done . . . I look back on that day, and I wish I'd seen what was coming."

Detective Rice was taking his time, offering up his memories like they were apples he was plucking from the trees on a lazy stroll through an orchard. Like they were just occurring to him and she might like to see them. But he was moving chronologically—methodically. He'd walked her through the fall, and the winter would come next.

For a moment, Julia indulged the voice of her inner victim. *I shouldn't have to remember all of this. It's not fair.* Then she silenced the voice. The voice was a fake. In truth, she thought of that winter frequently, with or without detectives calling her to their apparent deathbeds. She had learned to control the strong feelings tied to that time—the memories still existed, but she viewed them with the cool detachment of a researcher, perhaps, observing the actions of unknown persons. That hadn't been them, Tony and Julia. That was some other couple. And when her mind drifted to that couple—on winter nights; or in the early moments of her waking from a nightmare; or, for some reason she could not recall, whenever Tony made BLTs—she would watch that strange couple for a moment and then release them.

Today, a long-sedated emotion had reawakened in the pit of her stomach as she sat facing the detective, the embodiment of the criminal justice process. His sagging skin and ill coloring were a distraction; a fortuitous ruse on his part, but she knew what he was. A cop was always a cop: retired or not, dying or not. And history always demanded justice, didn't it?

Because she knew why she was here. She knew what came next. The detective had taken his time, but they were approaching it now: the winter that Raymond Walker would go missing.

III.

DECEMBER

"We are nearer to Spring
Than we were in September,"
I heard a bird sing
In the dark of December.

OLIVER HERFORD, "I HEARD A BIRD SING"

37

Jeff's office was small and toasty. The wall behind Nick's seat on the couch was brick, and the window there cast the bright light of early winter onto the counselor's warm brown face. Per usual, Jeff was wearing a sweater and slacks. Every now and then, he hooked a finger under the band of his silver wristwatch and stretched it as he listened to Nick. Nick had taken off his boots at the door, and he rubbed his socks back and forth against the plush carpet as they talked.

"So it feels like a relief," Jeff said.

"Yeah." They were talking about what Nick had been doing to himself. The picking, or whatever.

He'd already talked about it in the emergency counseling session he had with some woman after Thanksgiving. Talking about the same stuff with Jeff wasn't going to help. He knew why he was doing it, picking at his skin. It was a distraction from the truth. He'd almost told Jeff once before. Almost told Tony, on Thanksgiving. He thought he could change the truth if he told himself the false story over and over, but it was only getting harder.

Jeff was saying something, and Nick cut him off.

"Can you explain again how it works with us, like with court?"

"What do you mean?"

"Like I know you can tell someone if I'm going to hurt myself or someone else, but you said something about court once."

"I did?"

Nick nodded. "The first time we met, you said a judge could make you give him my records."

"Oh. Well, that's possible. I guess it would depend—I like to tell clients up front that there are a few limits on confidentiality. As much as I want you to know I'll keep your secrets, I also want you to know that there are a few times when I can't. I think it's really important that I say so *before* something has happened."

Nick raised his hand to his head. The scab was still there. Drier and smaller, but he was still picking at it too often to let it heal all the way.

"Nick," Jeff said, and nodded in his direction.

Nick lowered his hand.

"I can't see a scenario where Ray gets your records, if that's what you're worried about." They called him Ray in Jeff's office. Nick didn't like to call him "Walker," like the prosecutor or Tony did. "What do you want to talk to me about?"

Nick's arm began to itch, and he rubbed at it.

"Nick."

Nick clasped his hands in his lap. He wasn't strong enough to keep the secret anymore. He'd tried to clamp down on it, shut it out, but he was too weak. If he didn't tell someone, he didn't know what he'd do.

"I want to tell you what really happened."

⟶

Nick heard Johnny's rusted-out Volvo before he saw it. Johnny had gotten there early and was waiting for him, just as he had been after each session since Nick left Tony's house.

Nick craned to see the car idling on the street behind the new snow-bank, courtesy of the storm a day before. His face was puffy from spending so much of the last hour crying; as he stepped onto the sidewalk, the cold air stung his eyes. There was a swelling of hope in his chest unlike anything he'd ever felt. Back in Jeff's office, he'd finally done what he had pretended to do so many times that fall. He gave someone the whole truth, and nothing but. When he was done, Jeff leaned forward in his chair and said Nick's name. Nick lifted his head and met Jeff's eye, and then, Jeff said the three most unexpected words.

"I forgive you."

Jeff said lots after that, but those three repeated in Nick's mind as he reached Johnny's car.

"I forgive you."

He could be forgiven for what he'd done.

Nick opened the door and slid in beside Johnny. The Volvo looked like shit from the outside and roared above forty miles an hour, but it was warm and clean and smelled like strawberries. Johnny was always swapping out air fresheners, and the latest was a pink jelly thing that clipped into the passenger heating vent. It always made Nick crave buttery toast with jam.

"How was it?"

"Fine. Good, actually." Nick pulled the seat belt over his lap and smiled at Johnny. "Thanks for picking me up."

Johnny smiled back as he drove. "You don't have to say that every time." Then the smile dropped from his face. "At least not as long as you're pitching me gas money."

Nick exhaled a soft laugh. As the only one with a car, Johnny was stuck chauffeuring his roommates on a regular basis. After the first two weeks of living together he'd started to get annoyed, but then they started paying him gas money and it became less of an issue. By now the system was simple: no payment, no Taxi Maserati—Nick had come up with that name back in September. He hadn't called the Volvo by that name in months.

At home, Nick handed Johnny a five and went straight up the musty stairs to his room, closing the door behind him.

He sat on his bed and pulled out his phone to look up the number for the DA's office. Jeff had said Nick should try to talk to the victim advocate person, Sherie. Sherie would probably be the best to deal with this. Nick pressed the number on the DA's webpage. If he didn't call now, while he was reeling with confidence that it was the right thing to do, he might never pick up the phone.

Nick pressed his way through a menu to reach a human.

"District attorney's office, this is Jodi speaking."

"Hi, um, I'm calling to talk to Sherie. The advocate, please."

"Sherie's out this week. Are you a victim in an open case?"

There was that word again. "Yeah, I— Yes I am, yes."

The voice softened. "Sherie's had a death in the family, she should be back next Monday. Would you like to speak to the attorney assigned to your case?"

Would he? No. She was intimidating. Sherie's whole job was to be there for Nick. She would be easier to talk to.

"Is the attorney the right person to talk to about your story, or your testimony? I mean, if I needed to . . . if . . ."

What am I doing?

"Never mind, I'll call back next week, thanks."

"Can I—"

Nick hung up. He needed to talk to Sherie. Not anyone else, not yet. He could make it a week. It wasn't his secret alone anymore—he'd told Jeff, and that counted for something.

Nick gently pushed his sleeves up one after another, careful not to scratch them down against the scabby wounds. They ran all over the undersides of his forearms, dry, brownish-red and pink rimmed. They itched to be picked at. Instead, he just observed them. They kind of looked like islands. He pictured Tony's face when he saw what he'd done to himself. Nick pulled his sleeves back down and stood up from the bed. *Enough of that*, he thought. *Redirect yourself, like Jeff said.*

Nick walked downstairs and popped an ice cube out of the tray in the freezer. He held it in his left hand, squeezing it tightly. The cold ached against his palm. He held out his throbbing hand and let the melt dribble into the sink. The pain in his hand was all he could feel, just like he wanted.

38

Julia could hear the kitchen from the bottom of the stairs. The sizzle of bacon, the sputtering of the coffeemaker, the familiar voices of local news personalities on the television. Channel eight's anchors hosted an inane show called *Saturdays with Michelle and Miguel*, which Tony sometimes turned on as he made breakfast. It was the cookie-cutter morning-show template of overcovered local news split up by segments on recipes and shelter pets. She'd never knock the show too much, though—any time she heard it, it meant breakfast was underway.

Julia paused at the doorway to the living room, where the kids were playing. Down the hall in the kitchen, a third voice chimed in between Michelle's and Miguel's. Julia didn't recognize the voice, but she knew immediately what they were discussing.

"What makes this case so interesting is that we have an adult male victim," the voice said. "I don't want to call it unheard of, but it practically is."

Julia hurried to the kitchen, where Tony stood motionless in his sweats. A heavy man in a suit was on the screen before him.

Julia moved to Tony's side. "What's this?"

"Shh!" Tony hissed.

On the screen, the man sat in a chair across from Michelle and Miguel. "It will be fascinating to see how a jury responds to the situation."

Julia stepped forward toward the TV. "Why are you watching this?" She reached out a hand to turn it off.

Tony pushed her hand down. "Leave it, I'm trying to watch."

"Why are you doing this to yourself?"

He widened his eyes in annoyance but kept them on the screen. "Can you stop talking?"

Julia settled back on her heels and crossed her arms.

Miguel leaned toward the man. "And what *is* the situation, as we know it?"

"The two men met at a bar, Jimmy's Pub, in Salisbury. Somehow they determined that they were mutually interested, and they left the bar together and went to Mr. Walker's hotel room. The State will be looking to prove that Mr. Walker essentially clobbered the victim at the hotel, and that the sexual assault followed while the man was unconscious."

"Now, why would it matter that the victim is male?" Michelle asked.

"It will really matter more in terms of the stories that the defense and the prosecution tell, and it may affect what the jurors believe happened. It could go either way. Will a jury believe that a strong, healthy man was essentially knocked out and has no memory of the event? There's a lot of speculation about how much alcohol the victim consumed, but as a male, his tolerance is higher, of course. And there probably won't be questions about what he was wearing," the man said with a gross little smile.

Julia shot out a hand and flicked off the TV. Tony stood motionless, staring at the black screen. She reached for him as he stepped away, and her hand passed through the air where he'd stood.

Without a word, he strode from the kitchen into the mudroom. After a pause, the door slammed. She heard the crunch of shoes on gravel, and Tony was gone.

⌐

Tony was sitting in bed with a book in his lap, staring at the window across from him. He'd been reading the same book for a month. Barely reading it, really—Julia kept seeing him like this, holding the book but off in his head somewhere. She climbed into the far side of the bed. She reached for the book at her bedside, but he spoke.

"That fucker needs to be put away."

He was talking about Walker. He was always talking about Walker. "He probably will be." She had more to say, but Tony cut her off.

"Probably?"

"You just never know. But even if he does go to prison, that's not going to make Nick stop hurting himself."

"It might."

"I think you're oversimplifying what Nick's going through."

"Meaning?"

"Walker going to prison isn't going to help Nick come to terms with whatever happened that night."

A small smile crept over Tony's face. It was an ugly smile—as though he'd thought to himself, "There it is." Like she'd just proved him right about something.

"What?"

Tony opened his book. "Nothing."

"That's not passive aggressive."

"Fine." He shut the book. "Sometimes I feel like you don't believe Nick."

"What? Where did you get that from?"

"I just feel it, the way you talk about him."

"How do I talk about him?"

"Just now, like he doesn't know what happened to him."

"I'm saying where he blacked out we don't know—"

"Stop." He flipped back the comforter and climbed from the bed.

"Whoa!" Clearly this had been a mistake.

He was at the dresser now. "Before you say what I think you're going to, I want you to remember what he looked like at the hospital. In our home. What the nurse said. You know what, I don't want to know what you think."

"Tony—"

"I won't be able to look at you if you think—"

"Tony—"

"No, just stop, I'm done with this."

They were talking over each other.

She didn't want to raise her voice with the kids down the hall. "Tony. *Tony*. Listen to me. I'm telling you I think Nick is telling the truth, but *he said* he doesn't know what happened. Don't you think it's weird there's no one else Walker's done this to?"

Tony eyed her meaningfully. "There's a first time for everything."

"What, us disagreeing?"

"We don't know there aren't other people out there."

"What if we do know that?"

"How would we? The police don't have time to look for others."

"Not the police."

"What are you talking about?"

Did she want to tell him about Charlie Lee? She'd thought she wanted to keep it private—keep him from being disappointed that Charlie hadn't found anything to help secure a conviction. But clearly she did want to tell him—she'd led him right to it.

"I asked Charlie Lee to look into things for us."

"Who's Charlie Lee?"

"That PI I used to work with."

Tony stared at her for a beat. "You hired a PI?"

It wasn't much money, but she'd leave that out entirely. "I was already using him for the juvenile records report."

"When did you talk to him?"

"Which time?"

"So you're *working with* a PI and you didn't tell me."

"I didn't think I *should* tell you—I called him right after you put your fist through a door in front of the kids."

Tony frowned and suddenly his face was all Sebastian, teetering on the brink of tears. That was harsh; she shouldn't have said that.

She softened her voice. "I'm sorry. But I think we need to be realistic about what court can give Nick. I know there's some other evidence, but it's really going to be Nick's word against Walker's, and Nick is going to say he doesn't remember what happened. That's not great. So I asked Charlie to see if he could find anyone else, and he couldn't, and he's really good at this."

"So what, he called *all the men in the world* and asked them, 'Hey, were you ever—'"

"Obviously not," Julia cut in. "But he tried a bunch of gay bars in New England, where Walker might have gone on work trips. Only one of them even thought it was possible he'd been there."

Tony's face lit. "Someone recognized him?"

"No, maybe, he wasn't sure. Just that he looked like a guy who went home with a younger regular once, but that was it. Charlie can't find who the regular was, so literally all we know is someone who looks like Walker went home with a young, shy guy, and the bartender never got to hear what happened."

"Are you listening to yourself? He has a type. He has an MO. This needs to go to the DA for court."

"God no, absolutely not! If I were Walker's attorney I'd have a field day with that. 'Where'd this information come from?' 'Nick Hall's family hired a private investigator.' 'And *all* he found is that someone who looks like my client went home with a guy at a bar two years ago?' It's worse than not having looked at all."

"Right there," Tony said as he pointed at her. "That's your problem."

"What?"

"'If you were his attorney.' You've been his attorney before, Julia. You've defended scumbags like him."

"So what?"

"You're looking at it from his point of view when you should be looking at it from Nick's."

"That is *so* insulting. That was work. This is personal—this is *family*. I just want you to be realistic about how this part of the whole thing might end. Walker might go to trial, and if he does, Nick will have to testify, and Walker could win."

Tony held up his hand. "I need a walk."

"Right now?" The window across the room was a black mirror. "It's dark; it's freezing."

"I'll wear a jacket."

It was too cold to go out on foot. And would he walk, or would he get in his car and drive? And where could a drive lead him but back to Walker's?

"Please don't go out right now." If she said what she was thinking, she would only entrench them further in *this*, this fight, whatever it was. But she had to know he wouldn't do something else he'd regret. "Please don't go again."

Maybe he feared the same thing she did, because he relented. "Fine." He snatched his pillow from beside her and retrieved the book from under the covers. He didn't look at her.

"Fine," she said.

He paused in the doorway. "Can I just point out, for all your talk about what you think I'm not saying, that was a pretty big secret you kept, hiring that guy."

She reached for an apology, but it wouldn't come. She wasn't sorry.

"Good night," she said, and she stretched her hand for the lamp at her bedside. She flicked it off, sending Tony into the darkness.

39

They'd finished the tea and time was getting on. It seemed strange to Rice that Julia had let him drag her through the fall into the winter—*that* winter—without complaint. Without asking where he was taking her. Her face looked about as pale as his did every time he caught his reflection in the bread box (he'd removed the mirrors weeks ago). Was it the standard civilian compliance he enjoyed when he asked questions on his home turf? Normally home turf meant the station—this was his first interrogation on Maple Street. It could be that. Or it could be that Julia didn't need to ask where he was taking her; perhaps she already knew.

"Here I am talking about what I was feeling, but I had no idea what your brother-in-law was going through."

Julia nodded. "I didn't either, really."

"Did you ever learn why he . . ." Rice paused.

Julia's voice was unapologetic. "Tried to overdose."

"That."

"I think it was a lot of things, all piling up on top of each other." She turned her head and thought. "I remember he had had a really hard week."

40

NICK HALL, 2015

The week went like this.

On Saturday night, Nick drank alone. He finished off Mary Jo's Stoli and an old jug of cranberry juice from the back of the fridge. He wondered if Mary Jo would ask him about it when she noticed the empty bottle, or if she'd avoid the topic like she had the assault, since her boyfriend broke the news to the whole campus. Nick still caught people staring at him, even fucking whispering, because Mary Jo hadn't been smart enough to see that her boyfriend was a douchebag.

Nick ended the night in the bathroom. He knelt on the floor and made himself vomit into the stained toilet bowl, hoping to stave off a hangover. Then he stood, rinsed his mouth out, and locked eyes with the reflection above the sink. Was that person really him? The lines of his face were harsh, his eyes wet and empty. The image was sharp, but his mind was melting, blurring. He wished he could dissolve into the cold water and wash down the drain.

On Sunday, he was hungover anyway.

Sherie called on Monday. At first he thought she knew, somehow, that he was the one who called looking for her the week before. But she immediately started talking about court, and Nick realized it was just a coincidence. She told Nick there would be a court date next Tuesday. She said she was reminding him of the date, but he didn't remember being given it.

"The dispositional conference," she said, "is what we call it when the prosecutor and the defense attorney meet at court, talk about the case, and try to come to an agreement to settle it."

"So it could all be over next Tuesday?"

"It could be, but please don't get your hopes up."

Right. Nick remembered the meeting at the DA's office. If the case did settle, it would probably happen closer to trial. Two months had seemed like a lifetime to Nick, but apparently they were still early on in the case.

"How does it work?"

"At court? The defendant goes, and there's a judge for part of it, but a lot of it is just the lawyers talking alone. Linda will tell Eva—that's the defense lawyer—Linda will tell her why she thinks she would win at trial, and what she thinks a fair sentence would be. Eva will tell Linda why she thinks Linda will lose, and what sentence they would accept to make the case go away."

"What kind of sentence would it be?"

"Linda wanted to know what you thought of him serving four years in prison, with a total of ten years he could serve if he violates probation."

Nick didn't know what to say. Four years in prison sounded like a long time. But maybe not. If they settled the case now, without Nick telling Sherie the truth, that would mean everyone would see the four years as Ray's payment for what Nick said Ray did: invited Nick to a hotel, knocked him out, and assaulted him while he was defenseless. Four years didn't sound so long, then.

"That's just an offer to get him to settle," Sherie went on. "If he won't settle, if Linda wins at trial, she would argue for way more time."

"So it would be four years if we skip the trial."

"Exactly," Sherie said.

If there was no trial, there was no reason to tell the prosecutor the story—the actual story. Was there? Would he be any freer, truly, just for having said it, if saying it would be pointless?

"That sounds good," Nick said to Sherie. And he didn't tell her.

—◦—

On Tuesday, he had therapy. He went into the session ready to tell Jeff what he'd decided as he spoke to Sherie: that he would wait until after the coming court date to tell anyone else what he'd told Jeff a week before. But when he saw Jeff in person, it hit him how much he liked Jeff. Jeff had shown him, over the last couple of months, what it looked like to be a man who had also been a victim. Proved to him that you could be a victim without it defining you. Jeff was married. He was funny, but also gentle. He was sure of himself. He was the kind of man Nick wanted to be. And this man might lose respect for him if he knew Nick wanted to wait and see if the case went away. Might find him cowardly—might even think, *I guess he's not as brave as I thought he was.* So Nick changed his mind and decided to lie.

"Have you talked to the advocate yet?"

"I called last week but she was gone for a family emergency." *Not even a lie*, he thought, but he still felt guilty.

"Oh. Did you talk to the prosecutor, then?"

"No. I'm just gonna wait and tell the advocate this week." *Definitely a lie*. "I'll try her again when I leave here."

Jeff hooked a finger under the band of his watch.

"You don't have to if you don't feel ready," he said. "You get to make the decisions. No one else."

Nick could hear the soft *tick-tick-tick* of the clock on the wall behind him.

"And as I said last week, I'm more than happy to be there when you call."

When he did tell Sherie—if he had to, if the case didn't settle next week—that would feel good. Familiar.

"Maybe," Nick said. Maybe it would feel good, or maybe it would feel like more of the same. Like he was a kid who'd spilled a glass of milk, and he was watching someone else clean it up.

Nick left Jeff's office feeling even worse than when he got there. As Johnny drove him home, he wished for an accident. He pictured a car slamming into theirs, hitting the passenger side of the Volvo and snapping him out of consciousness and into a coma. It would leave Johnny unscathed, somehow, and no one upset—everyone could know that the coma wouldn't last. His mom, Tony, Johnny, and Elle—none of them would have to worry. And Nick could sleep through it all. He could wake up after the case was done, after everyone had forgotten they were so interested in his life.

⌐

As it went sometimes after a bad day, Wednesday was okay.

On Thursday, he dreamed that Elle was knocking at his door, asking to come in, asking if he'd seen the news. She handed him a phone but the words were blurry.

"You lied," Elle was saying. "You lied. You let me believe you. You let me see what I wanted to see. Everyone knows now. Everyone knows what you are." She was sobbing. Nick was sobbing. And then he woke up.

He reached for his phone. Googled his name. Nothing new. Googled Walker's name. Nothing new. He should have stopped there, but he didn't. He was sick with guilt. He wouldn't pick at himself. Instead, he would read.

He scrolled to the bottom of the most recent article on *Seaside*. There were no new comments, so he reread what was there.

> I might be able to swallow this if the "victim" were a smaller female, but a 20yo male gets knocked unconscious in a single blow? It's just very hard to buy.
>
> So can we just get straight that this guy blacked out, wasn't hit on the head or whatever nonsense . . . just doesn't want to own that he drank himself dumb. If he doesn't remember what happened, that doesn't mean he wasn't consenting to it.

Nick was right not to tell Sherie. Not if he could help it. People already thought he was a liar. Already thought he was less of a man for the story he told. He didn't want to know what people would say, what they would think of him, if they knew the truth.

He could make it a week—less than a week—to hear if, by some miracle, the case would go away on its own. Only if it didn't would he need to make a decision. Would he tell the truth and watch the case fold and his reputation crumble? Or would he split himself in two: the real Nick only Jeff was allowed to see, and the fake Nick who'd appeared in the car on the way to the hospital and told the story no one seemed to believe?

⁓

Sherie called again on Friday. Court was pushed off, she said, until January 12.

Wait. January 12. That was a month away.

"Why?"

"His lawyer has a scheduling conflict next week."

So what? Why did that cost Nick another month of his life?

"So . . ." What could he say? What could she do?

"Right," she said. "So, there's really nothing to do at the moment. I'll call you after court in January to let you know where we landed. And now," she said like it was good news, "you can just focus on the holidays. Any special plans?"

The only thing Nick had thought about the holidays so far was that maybe, just maybe, all of this would be over by then.

⁓

On Saturday, he was drinking alone again when Elle knocked on his door.

His stomach rolled as he remembered his dream.

She opened the door and stuck her head in.

"Ooh!" she squealed. "We drinking?"

41

On December 13, Rice stepped out of mass feeling calm and centered. He sucked the cool air in through his nostrils and let it out his mouth, sending a white cloud of frozen breath out before him.

His Sunday morning ritual consisted of mass at eight sharp and breakfast with the boys downtown at ten fifteen. Bob Lucre and Jim Allen would be waiting for him in their usual booth at Dorothy's Diner in Cape. Hot coffee, a short stack, and a recap of the week. Most people seemed to feel filled up by their worship. Rice usually left feeling hollowed out, like all of the burdens he'd been carrying, all the negative thoughts, had been stripped from his head and given up to God. All his mistakes and bad choices, big and small, had been left behind in the rafters of the church. As freeing as it was to feel so light, his Sunday breakfast grounded him again.

Rice crunched down the cathedral's salted steps and made his way to his car. It had snowed earlier that week, enough that the lot had been plowed. Rice had parked right up against a low bank of snow, already dirty with grit.

He sat down into the car and reached for his phone. This morning he had two missed calls from the station, a voice mail, and a text message from Brendan Merlo.

Nick hall at YCMC. Suicide attempt. Heading there now

The message was time-stamped 8:03 a.m.

Rice read the message over again.

He shot off a text of his own—he wouldn't be making breakfast—then headed for the hospital.

—⌇

Brendan Merlo was just reaching his patrol vehicle when Rice pulled into the lot next to the emergency department, giving his horn two quick taps. Merlo stopped and waited for him to park.

He whistled as Rice shut his door. "Don't you look sharp."

"Mass," Rice said. "What's going on?"

Merlo moved leisurely to Rice's side. "Didn't mean for you to come over, we're all set."

"What happened?"

"Kid's roommate Ellen called it in, sometime around three this morning." Merlo fished a small notebook from his jacket as he spoke. "Elle, I mean. Said they were at their apartment, drinking last night into this morning, thought they were having a good time, blowing off steam. Elle said he told her he was going to the bathroom and he was gone long enough she went looking for him. Found him passed out on the floor with an empty bottle of his psych meds. Hard to say whether it was a genuine attempt or not."

"What does *that* mean?"

"Just my phrasing," Merlo said. "Nick says he can't remember doing it is all, and he doesn't feel suicidal now. Obviously swallowing a whole

223

bottle of pills looks like suicide, I just meant I don't know if he *really* wanted to die."

"What pills he use?"

"Fuck if I can pronounce it; it's the generic Zoloft. He says he doesn't want to hurt himself now." Merlo shrugged. "I believe him."

Rice didn't. Instead, he felt a panicked frustration rising up. "They're not letting him go home, are they?"

"Don't need to. His sister-in-law really worked him over on staying at a hospital-type program. He's going up to Goodspring in Belfast."

He needed to get inside. "Thanks, Brendan," Rice said, patting Merlo's shoulder as he passed him by.

"No problem," Merlo called after him.

Rice waved his hand in the air without turning back.

For the third time, Rice found himself walking down a sterile hallway in York County Medical Center headed for Nick Hall's room. This time his steps were propelled by an urgency not present for his first two visits.

Stepping into the ER was like waking up. He was at the ER. Off duty. To see a boy who'd tried to kill himself.

A nurse behind the large desk at the center of the unit looked up from the chart in his hands. "Can I help you?"

It was all wrong. The intrusiveness was clear: no one had called for his help. Nobody had invited him in.

"No," Rice said. "No, I—"

"Detective Rice?" Julia Hall was standing in the doorway of what must have been a bathroom on the far side of the unit.

Shit.

"Julia, hi."

She came toward him, not quite smiling. "Are you here for Nick?" She eyed his church clothes. "Or . . . something private?"

"Well, I was here for a personal matter, and I ran into Officer Merlo just now. Thought I'd stop over just in case . . ." He trailed off. *Just in case what? What could he do for them?*

For a second, Julia looked as though she was thinking the same. Then she half smiled and said, "That was sweet of you, but I think we're okay."

"Well, great. I'm glad. I heard he's going up to Goodspring?"

She frowned. "Uh, it's not set in stone yet, but it looks like that's gonna work out. Why?"

"Oh, no reason."

Julia crossed her arms over her chest and nodded. "If it affects the case, it affects the case, I guess is how I see it."

"Julia I—I wasn't even thinking of that. I want Nick to take care of himself, truly."

Her face softened, but her arms stayed crossed. "Me, too. Thanks for coming by, Detective."

"No problem," Rice said, and he turned away before she could beat him to it.

42

"*H*ouse *Hunters* is good," Tony said.

"Maybe when you're old," Nick answered.

Tony stood on his tiptoes, flicking through the channels on the TV mounted high in the corner of the room.

A woman in a wedding gown appeared on the screen.

"Pass."

"Oh, how about a dog show?" Tony asked with genuine enthusiasm.

Nick turned the dead remote control over in his hands and nodded. "That could work."

"We don't have to—"

"No, keep it here."

Tony rolled his shoulders as he came back to the chair next to Nick's bed.

Before that awful silence could creep in on them, Tony asked, "Should we get a dog?" It was a question he might have asked Chloe or Seb; it wasn't real. It was just a game.

Nick looked at him, then up at the screen. "Yeah," Nick said. "You should get . . . that one." Some kind of miniature Doberman–looking thing was being manhandled on a table.

"Christ. Probably more dangerous than the big version."

Nick chuckled softly. "Why *don't* you guys have a dog?"

"Julia's allergic."

"Oh yeah, I knew that." Nick turned the remote over and over. "Literally her only flaw."

That wasn't quite true. To most people, Julia looked perfect. She was pretty and kind and endlessly thoughtful. She never showed up empty-handed, always remembered birthdays and anniversaries, always asked how you were doing and meant it. But she could be headstrong and critical when she thought she knew better than someone else. Especially when it came to Tony. Sometimes she just didn't get him—didn't trust that he knew what he was doing. Until she was in college she'd been rich, at least compared to Tony's family, and then, abruptly, she wasn't. Her dad died and the floor fell out from under her and her mom. When Tony met Julia, it was only a few years after that, and she was *obsessed* with taking care of herself. Every time Tony tried to do something for her, she questioned and critiqued and pushed him away. It was equal parts enraging and arousing, figuring out how to get her to let him in. Even now, sometimes they'd have a standoff.

"Speak of the devil," Nick said with a faint smile as Julia appeared in the doorway.

"You boys talking about me?"

"Just your allergies," Nick said.

She squinted. "Scintillating. I'm gonna go down to the cafeteria—I just came back to take orders."

"Yes!" Nick said with the most enthusiasm he had mustered since they'd arrived earlier that morning to see him. "A coffee, with cream and sugar."

Julia winced. "You know, caffeine might be something to cut back on right now, it can kind of feed anxious feelings."

"Oh—"

"Christ, Julia. Let him have a coffee." Tony pressed his fingers into his temples. He could feel a splitting headache coming on.

Her voice was deflated. "Yeah, sorry, that was stupid."

"No, it wasn't," Nick said. "I could have tea instead."

"No, you can have a coffee." Tony pointed a hand at Nick.

"Well, if I should—"

"A coffee will make absolutely no difference," Julia said as she stepped farther into the room. "I don't even know why I said that. Do you want anything to snack on with it?"

Nick paused. "A cookie, if they have any. Or something else sweet."

"On it. Tony?"

"I might come with you," he said as he stood. "We can figure out what the plan is today, with the kids."

Julia backed out of Tony's way as he came through the door. She had this antsy energy around him, like she was afraid to stand too close to him. It was exhausting.

"We're running over to the cafeteria," she said to the nurse at the desk.

The man nodded. "You're good; I got eyes on him," he said quietly as they passed by.

They walked in silence most of the way down the hall. Tony wondered if Julia was preparing an apology. That would be just like her, to apologize when he had been snippy. She was too quick with her sorries, betraying that she didn't always mean them.

Instead, she said, "Detective Rice came by."

"Where, the house?"

"Here, in the ER."

"When?"

"Just now, I ran into him on my way back from the bathroom. It was kind of strange."

"Wait, was he in the ER for himself or—"

"No, to see Nick."

Tony considered this as they crossed the atrium, their boots crunching on the salt and dirt dragged in from outside. "But he didn't come in."

"I told him we were all set. I didn't think there was any use in Nick talking to *another* cop about it. And it's not like the two of them have a relationship outside of why he's here in the first place."

Tony nodded.

She went on. "I just couldn't tell if he was here out of concern or if it was more about, like, checking in on an important witness, you know?"

That was perfect. Just fucking perfect. He probably *was* here to check on his star witness, make sure he wasn't getting too *unstable* to testify. The ADA would probably drop by next.

"Fuck him if it was," Tony said.

Julia said nothing for a beat, and then: "I'm just so glad he agreed to go to Goodspring."

"Do you know anything about what it's like there?" Tony thought she may have, from her old job.

"Not Goodspring specifically, just enough to know he's better there than at home."

"Not even our home?"

Julia stopped walking and grabbed his arm. "Honey, we can't take care of this ourselves. We need real help. He needs to be . . . kept an eye on right now."

"We could do that. You're already home, and I could take a week off."

"No," she said. "I'm sorry, but no, I don't want to take this on, and with the kids."

"The kids? He would never do anything in front of them, he loves them."

"I know that, but clearly this is out of his control."

"He doesn't even want to hurt himself, it never would have happened if he hadn't been drinking on his meds! And he knows never to do that again."

Julia started walking again. "I'm not having this conversation right now."

Tony followed her. "He's gonna miss Christmas if he's stuck up there, did you even think of that?"

"Christmas?" She nearly shouted the word as she turned to face him, and he involuntarily took a step backward. "Tony, he almost missed *all* the Christmases! What do you even—he could have died last night."

"The doctor said—"

"That's not what I'm talking about. He could have done it differently. I don't care what he would have done sober. He wasn't sober. He was drunk out of his mind, and he tried to kill himself."

She was right, but she continued.

"I am *so* sick of you acting like you know better than everyone else. Christ! Nick needs to be with professionals, *wants* to be with them, and for some reason you can't stand that. You aren't the only one who can take care of him."

Tony's chest was tight, and he could feel his face flushing with heat. His eyes began to burn.

"I know that."

Julia's face softened, but she didn't move toward him. "Do you?"

A man passed by them in the hall and Julia fell silent and smiled at him. Can't have a stranger knowing they're fighting. Another thing about Julia: she was ashamed by the appearance of conflict.

When he was gone, she said, "I know you're terrified." She brought a hand to her chest and her voice choked. "*I* can barely stand it. I can't believe we could have lost him."

He was going to cry if she didn't stop talking. He wiped his eyes, stopping his tears before they started.

"I hate being powerless as much as you, but the only thing we can do for him is get him to Goodspring."

He didn't know what to say, so he said nothing.

They walked the rest of the way to the cafeteria in silence. Julia's words replayed in his mind like a sad song.

Nick had almost died. He'd almost lost him.

They were in a new place now: a place where Nick's life was at risk. Not just what people thought of him at school. Not just what would come of the court case. His life.

Julia didn't like to feel powerless, and neither did Tony. But Tony wondered if he was as powerless as she thought.

—

The drive to Goodspring was long and quiet. Tony tried to get Nick chatting a couple of times, but he couldn't keep him distracted from whatever it was that kept making him fall silent. Nick kept looking over at the GPS, like he was watching the minutes scrape off the time left in the car with Tony. Eventually, Tony stopped trying to make chitchat, and they drove in silence.

How did they get here? Two months ago, Nick had been like any other junior. Solid grades, living with his friends, too funny for his own good. He was born great, and Tony had managed to keep him that way. It sounded stupid, but it was true: it had been Tony. How else did you explain him being so functional after being raised by *two* alcoholics? Tony had been there from the beginning. When he was little. When he was suffering through the horror that is male puberty. Tony had been the one Nick came out to first. When Nick was sixteen, Tony and Julia took him into their home for weeks—with a three-year-old and a baby in the house!—after Ron caught Nick kissing a boy in the living room and threw Nick out. Later, Tony mediated between his dad and brother to get Nick back into the house so he could finish high school without transferring schools.

Had he really managed to ferry Nick out of their father's house and into well-adjusted adulthood, only to have him obliterated by someone else?

As they pulled off the highway and drove onto Route 3, a sign pointing them toward Belfast, Tony felt Nick grow tense. It was a shift in the air, like a swell of humidity. From the corner of his eye, he saw Nick fiddle with his sleeves, touch his hairline, and stop himself from doing more than that.

Goodspring was a flat, industrial-looking building at the end of a long driveway in the woods. There were walking trails around it, according to a nurse at the hospital. Nick would get to go on walks while he was there for the month. Tony thought about saying something about it, anything at all, as he pulled into a space in the lot.

"I need to tell you something," Nick said.

Tony put the car in park. "Okay."

Nick rubbed at his sleeves, then crammed his hands under his thighs.

"You can tell me anything," Tony said.

"I haven't . . ." Nick stopped. He breathed.

Tony's heart began thumping so hard it seemed to move his whole torso back and forth in his seat. "What is it?"

Nick breathed out of his mouth in a thin stream, like a kid learning to whistle. "I haven't been honest with you," he said. "About that night."

Chills spread down his spine as some part of Tony's brain warned him that something terrible was about to happen.

"And I know that's not the only reason I'm having a hard time. I know that." He sounded like he was trying to convince himself of something. "But the lie, the lie has made everything so much worse."

The lie. What did that mean?

God forgive him, Tony thought of Julia and what she said about Nick.

And just for a second, Tony wondered if Nick had made up the whole thing.

43

Tony was staring at him like he could see into Nick's head—like he could read the words Nick was about to say on a marquee behind Nick's forehead. So he said the words out loud.

"I remember everything."

Tony shook his head like he didn't understand.

"I made up the blackout."

Nick brought his hands up to his face and sobbed sharply. It was the same as when he told Jeff—the pain of it rushed him at once, overwhelming him. What Ray had done to him. What he'd done to himself. The shame he felt, and the anger that he felt any shame at all.

"I remember everything he did." His own voice was a wail in the cavern between his hands. "I thought I was going to die."

"Nick!" Tony was saying his name like Nick couldn't hear him, like Tony couldn't reach him. "Nick!"

Tony's hands were on his shoulders, pressing, squeezing, pulling him against Tony's chest.

"I'm so sorry," Nick sobbed. Snot poured from his nose onto Tony's shirt. "I'm so sorry, Tony."

"What are you sorry for?"

"Lying, fucking everything up."

Nick pulled himself back to look at Tony's face. "You didn't fuck anything up," Tony said.

"I did," Nick said. "I've lied so much. I lied *under oath*. When they find out—everyone will hate me. Even the prosecutor and the detectives. They'll all hate me."

Tony shook his head. "They'll understand. You were in shock."

"Yeah and it wore off. I kept lying. I kept pretending I didn't remember what happened in the middle. What happened in the room with him."

Tony frowned. Held something back. Nick knew what it was. Tony wanted to ask the obvious: Why *had* he lied? Nick decided not to make him say it.

"I decided on the way to the hospital," Nick said. "Everything was happening so fast, I got so upset, I couldn't breathe—I couldn't think. And then I got really calm, and I thought, I'll just tell them he knocked me out. He did hit me."

"I know," Tony said.

"It was such an easy lie. And telling it was easy—it was easy to say I didn't remember. I didn't want to."

"It's okay," Tony said.

"By the time you came . . ." Nick stopped to wipe his nose on his sleeve. "I'd already lied to the police. And I thought, *Okay, I won't tell anyone, ever, and eventually it won't feel like a lie.*"

Tony reached across the console and rubbed Nick's arm. "Why did you—you just didn't want to have to talk about . . . what he did?"

"No. I . . ." Nick paused. "I was bleeding."

Tears began to run down Tony's face.

"People were going to know he raped me. I didn't think I could hide that. I just didn't want anyone else to know what happened before that."

"What?"

"I was so ashamed," Nick said. "It was so confusing. With Ray. One

235

minute it was one thing and the next . . . I barely had time to think. I didn't want it."

"It's not your fault," Tony said quickly. "Whatever you did or didn't do. That doesn't mean—"

"That's not what I'm saying," Nick said. "I told him to stop. I tried to make him. But I didn't . . ." Nick paused. And he let himself remember.

They went into the room. He was nervous but eager, his hands trembling and restless. Josh—Ray—shut the door. Nick sat on the bed, and the springs bounced under him. Ray smiled, came toward him, stood him up. Kissed him. It was good, a little awkward, a rougher kiss than in the cab. Ray pulled his face back from Nick's. And then he hit Nick.

Not like Nick told the police. It was weird, there was no other word for it. It was open-palmed, slow-motion, not hard but jarring in its wrongness.

"You like that?" Ray asked.

Nick said something stupid, he couldn't remember what. Something like "I don't know."

Ray's eyes were playful. "Bad boy," he said.

Nick's stomach went hot.

Ray slapped him again, hard this time.

Nick's eye watered and his ears rang. It was awful, and horribly familiar. An old humiliation.

"Don't," Nick said. His voice was small, childish, and his breath hitched. He had made a mistake. This was a mistake.

"No?" Ray leaned forward and kissed his neck. "Sorry, baby."

Nick held still. He wanted to leave. He wanted to shove Ray back and walk out the door, but he held still. He didn't know why he had held still. But he did.

Ray started pushing him back toward the bed.

Nick planted his feet, slowly brought his hands up to Ray's shoulders. He started to say something. He couldn't remember what it was. Maybe

236

if he'd told the police right away, he would remember it now. He didn't know. All he knew was it happened quickly after that. Ray hit him again; Nick hit back. Ray forced him down; Nick scratched Ray's arms, cried out, tried to headbutt him, but Ray won. And Ray raped him.

"I didn't see it coming," he told Tony. "I mean I did, I felt it the second he hit me—that he wanted to hurt me, but my body, it was like I froze." Hot tears ran down Nick's face, soaking into his collar. "But then I fought, I did, I tried to stop him, but I couldn't get out from under him. I thought he was going to kill me." Nick brought a hand to his throat. Ray had pressed into his neck so hard, it felt like Nick's throat would collapse. "I wasn't strong enough. I fought back, and I lost."

When Tony spoke, his voice was hard. "I'm gonna kill him."

Nick shook his head. "When I tell the prosecutor what happened, she has to tell Ray and his lawyer. It'll change everything. He'll use that I lied against me. It'll be in the papers. Everyone will know."

"I'll kill him," Tony said again.

"Don't be stupid, Tony," Nick said. "Don't talk like that. I just need to decide whether to tell them at all."

Tony shifted a bit in his seat. "What else would you do?"

Nick shrugged. "Give up the case. I don't know if I ever cared to begin with."

"Don't do that. You told the police the part they needed to know— that he'd done it at all."

"I didn't tell them, though. Elle did. It was already done when they asked me what I wanted to do."

"Don't let him win," Tony said.

"You're not listening. No matter what, I lose."

They sat in silence for a minute. Through the windshield, Nick watched a woman come out of the building and get into a parked car.

"I wish you hadn't kept this from me."

Guilt cut through Nick's belly. "I'm sorry."

"No, I'm not blaming you. I mean I wish I'd been there for you."

"You have been," Nick said. "I just . . . I should have told you, but I didn't want to."

"Why?"

"I don't know." There were emotions tied to it, overwhelming feelings he could vaguely categorize. Pride, shame, fear, protection. He just didn't know how to talk about it yet.

"Why'd you tell me now?"

Nick shrugged. "Honestly, I'm just tired of keeping it from you."

"It's why you took all your meds, right?"

"I still don't know why I did that. I wasn't thinking straight."

"Nick." Tony's eyes were dry now. "You know there isn't a thing I wouldn't do if it meant saving your life, right?"

44

I was using that!" Sebastian shouted.

"Not so loud, Seb!" Chloe said even louder.

Julia stuck her head into the dining room. Chloe was holding the cereal box at arm's length from her little brother, who was stretching across the table.

"Nope," Julia said as she swiped the box from Chloe's grasp. "If you're still hungry, there's extra oatmeal in the kitchen. No seconds on the cereal." One of them must have grabbed it from the cupboard while Julia was occupied.

"Seb already got some," Chloe whined.

Julia leaned down to Chloe's eye level. "Honey, I don't like tattling." She kissed Chloe's forehead to show her that she was forgiven. "And, Seb, if you can't follow the rules, we won't do cereal for breakfast at all."

Seb's face burst with shock. "What!"

It was all she could do not to laugh in his adorable face. "Do either of you want oatmeal?"

Each grumbled a no.

"Backpacks," Julia prompted, and she cut through the living room for the stairs. She'd take the kids to the bus stop in a minute, but first she wanted to swap her pajama bottoms for warmer pants. Wind was pushing against the windows that morning, and it looked frigid outside.

At the top of the stairs, she heard Tony's voice in her study. He used the space every now and then, mostly for phone calls when he wanted to block out the background noise of the kids. He'd used it last night, too. Something for work, but Julia didn't know what.

"I just think you should wait until after that," he said. "Yeah."

She paused in the doorway of the bedroom, curious to know who he was talking to so early in the morning.

"Right," he said. "If you tell them before, it doesn't— Exactly. Okay. I just woke up thinking about it and wanted to ask. You're making the right decision."

She didn't have a clue who it could be until he signed off. "I love you too, bud."

It was Nick. That was odd. What were they talking about?

She opened the door to the bedroom closet and paused. The inside of the closet door was covered with pieces of the back-and-forth love letter they'd been writing for longer than they'd been married. There were notes from her to Tony, notes from Tony to her, the occasional note from the kids. A smattering of photos and concert tickets were scattered through the mix, and Tony's tie rack hung down the middle. Over the years the collage had nearly overtaken the door.

Her fleece-lined jeans were folded on the top shelf. Julia dropped her pajama bottoms and stepped into her pants. As she buttoned them closed— a little tighter every winter, it seemed—she took in the collage of her life with Tony.

Julia's girlfriend Margot had seen it one night after she came over for dinner. She'd asked what Julia would be wearing to a mutual friend's wedding, so Julia brought her upstairs and swung the closet door open.

Margot had stepped forward and sighed. "Are you kidding me? Could you two be any cuter?"

"Ignore that," Julia said with a grin as she dug for the dress.

"Impossible." Margot's eyes scanned the collection, and her voice went syrupy. "Aww, you're so romantic, Julia." Margot shoved her with a soft hand.

In truth, though, it was Tony's collection. She'd added the stray piece here and there, but he was the true curator. He was the one with a roll of tape in his sock drawer. Some mornings she'd find Tony standing in the closet, half dressed for work, staring at the door. She might watch him for a full minute before he turned to her, his eyes a little misty.

Tony's softness was one of his greatest qualities. He was so handsome, his body so strong, that even after more than a decade together, she could still be caught off guard by his tenderness. The way he'd touch her back so gently as he passed by her in the kitchen while they cooked. The way he pecked the kids on the head. The fatherly voice he used with his younger brother.

Tony was shutting the door to the study as she left the bedroom.

"Was that Nick?"

He looked surprised, like he'd been caught. "Yeah."

"What's going on?"

"Nothing," he said quickly. "Just—we were talking about court yesterday on the drive."

Tony had driven Nick to Goodspring a day ago. He said Nick had been quiet. They hadn't talked about the overdose or anything else.

"Oh, you were?"

"Just for a second. Barely. He's just nervous to testify. You know."

Julia nodded. It would be awful. The chance that it would settle in January seemed fleeting, but sometimes the possibility was the only thing that gave her any peace about what Nick would otherwise go through.

"Were you telling him not to tell the ADA that he's nervous? She'll understand."

"Not that he can't tell her, just that he doesn't need to think about it really." There was a defensive edge to his voice. "Until the next court date. Since it might settle. That's all."

Julia nodded. That made sense. Tony must have been so upset about all of this—Nick trying to overdose, going to the program. She replayed their fight—was it a fight?—at the hospital and regretted how harshly she'd spoken to Tony. But he needed to understand the severity of the situation with Nick's mental health. That they couldn't take on keeping him safe themselves.

And now both of them, Nick and Tony, were already back on court. Although they were premature, Nick's fears weren't misplaced. If there was a trial next fall, it would be awful. Eva Barr would try to make Nick look like he'd been drunk and willing. Photos of Nick's body would be shown in court. Eva would argue that the graph of Nick's actions only had one logical landing point: a consensual sexual encounter with her client.

And at the end of the trial, a jury of Mainers would decide what the situation looked like to them. The court would try to control for prejudice—would try to remove from the jury pool anyone who held a bias against gay people or male victims. But surely they would squeeze through: unspoken inclinations and unrealized beliefs. People who would watch the evidence for proof of their preheld beliefs about what a man like Nick or Walker would be like, and what must have happened between them.

It was too early to worry about that. She stepped forward and pecked Tony on the cheek. She was glad he thought so, too.

45

Tony was greeted by warmth as he opened the front door of the Portland Public Library. His face had gone stiff with cold on his walk from his office. His ears began to ache as he crossed the atrium with the bubbling fountain.

He took the stairs to the lower level and made his way to the nonfiction section, keeping his face turned away from the circulation desk. He remembered from the past two days that he was looking for the general range of 363–364. Eventually he would move into the pharmaceutical section, but he was going to take this one topic at a time.

It seemed the odds were higher that he'd run into someone he knew in Portland, but he was tired of using up most of his lunch break driving to and from libraries farther away. Besides, he had rehearsed for the possibility earlier in the week on those very drives.

"Oh, this?" (Sheepish laugh.) "I'm trying to write a murder mystery—how embarrassing is that?"

Maybe it was stupid to be using the library like this at all, but using his phone or a computer to plan anything seemed a dangerous idea. He'd deleted the history on Julia's computer earlier that week, but he couldn't shake the vague idea he had that for the police, everything electronic was traceable.

Tony walked around the edge of the room, reading the numbers on the sides of the shelves until he found the right range. With relief he quickly spotted the spine of a promising book he'd found on an earlier trip. *Now take it and go sit down.*

"Tony?"

Tony jerked his hand and sent the book pitching forward off the shelf. He caught it awkwardly, splaying the pages open between his hands.

"Whoa, sorry!" the voice said.

He turned to see it was Walt Abraham, a classmate from his first year in law school.

"Walt, hey!" They met mid-aisle and shook hands. "How've you been?" Tony folded his arms over the book against his chest.

Walt launched into the same chitchat Tony heard every time he ran into a former classmate. How long had it been? What was he up to? He was smart not to be a lawyer, what a slog. (As if human resources *at a law firm* was any better.) How about Julia? How old were the kids now? Tony squeezed the book to his chest and kept his answers short. In spite of Tony's decision to leave law school after the first year, his career and marital choices had left a foot firmly planted in the world of attorneys. He generally didn't mind running into a guy like Walt, but at the moment he wanted nothing to do with him.

"Well," Walt said at last. "I've gotta get moving, but I just had to stop when I saw you. I'm so glad to hear you and Julia are well. You know," he said, stepping closer to Tony and lowering his voice, "a lot of guys I run into after seven years, I might not expect they were still married to the same woman. But look at that—you even sound happy!"

Walt had gotten divorced the year after Tony left law school, then married again a few years after graduation, Tony had heard. Judging by his bare left hand, that one hadn't gone well, either.

"How do you two do it?"

"Oh, just lucky I guess," Tony said.

"Great running into you," Walt said as he walked away.

"You, too," Tony said. His heartbeat thudded against the book. Walt hadn't even noticed it. And why would he have?

He looked down at the book, nestled against his chest; there was a splash of coffee or tea spattered across the top edge of the pages. *Just go sit down and read. Standing here, staring at it is way more obvious than sitting down and reading it.* He strode across the collection room, sat in an overstuffed armchair, and read.

⌐

As he walked back to the office, Tony probably should have mulled over everything he'd read in the last forty minutes, but instead he couldn't distract himself from Walt's question. How had they stayed happy—save for the present blip—for so long?

His first and only year in law school, Tony had noticed Julia Clark, sure, but he noticed other pretty classmates, too. She was reserved in class, like a lot of them were that first year, and he hadn't thought too much at all about her. He was too busy bombing his classes. At the end of the first year, he dropped out. Then one night that summer, he walked into a bar with a friend and found Julia there, slinging drinks.

The bar was called the Ruby, and Julia looked different there. Her wild, curly hair was up in a ponytail. It swished against her neck as she wiped out the glasses with a cloth. She was wearing a tight tank top and high-waisted jean shorts that made her ass look ample—it wasn't, he'd snuck quick glances during the school year, but the illusion still excited him.

Struck by how *cool* she looked behind the bar, he worried what she would think of him ordering something nonalcoholic. When she greeted them and took their orders, Tony asked for something off the chalkboard behind her. It did not taste like alcohol—instead like vanilla and something spicy—and he drank it far too fast.

She stood behind the bar giggling and talking to him for an hour before his friend saw he'd become the third wheel and left. They'd covered their classmates, Tony's drop-out, and had started in on television when she asked if she could make Tony another.

What had felt like the warm fuzzies of infatuation suddenly went numb.

What number was that?

"Hold up," he said.

She turned to him, standing against a backdrop of liquor bottles—blue, green, amber. A loose curl had fallen to her collarbone, and in the dim lighting, her features were pronounced and beautiful.

"I don't drink."

"Oh." She looked down at the clean glass in her hand. "But you just drank."

"I mean, I do—no, I *can*." He felt his face flushing. "I just don't really like to." This was the part where she'd ask why—was he an alcoholic, or just afraid of becoming one?

"Okay," she said skeptically. "Can I get you a water?"

And just like that, everything changed. They stopped flirting and started talking. Over the next three hours, they laid themselves bare to each other, knowing that if either pulled away after this, it didn't count as real rejection, because it hadn't been a date to begin with. Tony told Julia, as best he could, why he didn't drink. About his father who did and the brother who still lived with him. How badly Tony wanted to fight whenever he drank, as stupid as that was.

"Are daddy issues sexy on a guy?" Tony asked.

Julia raised an eyebrow. "Wanna hear mine?"

Tony leaned forward. "Please."

She leaned down onto her elbows so her face was inches from his. "My dad was perfect."

Tony laughed and sat back.

She smiled. "Perfect for the first twenty years of my life. Then one day I went to my parents' for dinner, and my dad told me he had pancreatic cancer, stage four, and a month later my mom was giving his eulogy."

"Fuck."

"Yup. It sucked, big time. And the worst part?"

Tony shook his head.

"He refused treatment."

"Why?"

"He didn't want to spend all the money, didn't want to take medicine that would make him even sicker. I was never sure which reasons were real and which were bullshit, because none of them were good enough not to try to stay with us."

Tony didn't know what to say to that.

"For the record," Julia said, "I will never marry a man who isn't a fighter."

Tony leaned toward the bar again. "As you know, I fight too much to trust myself drinking."

She smiled and nodded. "I noticed."

As the memory played out in his mind, Tony felt a resolve swelling in his chest. He and Julia had compared their emotional baggage that night and found it compatible. He'd driven her crazy a few times over the years, and she him, but they worked together *because* of their pasts. Julia had always wanted a fighter.

And that, Tony was.

46

Rice and O'Malley were in the break room making their morning coffees when Merlo poked his head in and told Rice he had a visitor.

"Britny Cressey?" Merlo said.

Rice groaned.

"Britny who?" O'Malley asked.

"She called me a couple months ago—Ray Walker's old friend. Or girlfriend, but not." He shrugged.

"Right," O'Malley said as Rice followed Merlo out. "'He's not a violent guy, I just happen to want you to know that,' et cetera."

"Yep," Rice said. He had actual work to do today. She was just going to waste his time.

He set his coffee on his desk, then met the woman with the girlish voice in the lobby.

"To what do I owe the pleasure?"

"I don't even know where to begin," Britny said. In spite of her voice, she looked her age. Late thirties.

"Why don't you give it your best shot."

Her long hair was dyed an unnatural red, and she pulled a handful of it in front of her shoulder. "I told you Ray and I were friends in high school but we lost touch."

"Yes."

"I reached out to him when I heard about all this, and at first we just chatted a bit but not much, but we've started to get close again. I think he's losing friends because of everything, getting lonely." She pushed her hair off her shoulder and smoothed her part.

"All right," Rice said.

"We've had drinks a couple times and talked on the phone a lot, and at first I really did feel bad for him, but I've started to feel like he's hiding something."

"About this?"

Britny nodded and raised her eyebrows. She brought both her hands up and smoothed her hair again, then shook it over her shoulders. "Like, I think maybe he did hurt that boy."

Goose bumps spread over the back of Rice's neck. Had Walker confessed to his friend?

"Has he said anything to you about Nick or that night?"

"No, but I think he would if I asked the right way. He's talked about nearly everything else with me. He's so stressed about money and court. He tells me everything about his lawyer. She just wants him to take a plea deal and go on the sex-offender registry. He borrowed *so* much money to pay for her, and he fights with her constantly and can't afford to get someone new. I guess he wanted to testify that you wouldn't arrest someone who assaulted him?"

Of course. The call about Tony Hall, where Walker said he didn't want to press charges. "He's saying I wouldn't arrest someone?"

She nodded smugly. "He told me he *told* you *not* to arrest him, but he was going to testify different. He was gonna say it was just more proof you all decided he was guilty. To show you were wrong about the rape, too. But his lawyer won't let him lie in court. He's all pissed off about it.

I guess they're having huge problems, and she pushed court off because of it."

"Stop," Rice said, and held up a hand. "I—I'd be lying if I said I wasn't interested in all this, but I don't think you should be talking to me. I mean, I guess he's waived any privilege about these conversations by telling you, but—" His mind was racing. What Walker and his lawyer talked about was supposed to be privileged, confidential. But if Walker told Britny, Rice could let Britny talk, couldn't he? But why was she doing this? "Aren't you friends with him?"

Her gray eyes went wide. "Not if he's a rapist, which now I think he is."

"Okay, well—"

"I think I can help you."

"How?"

"He's telling me so much. He's so stressed. Even his mom is driving him nuts. I'm the only friend he has left. I think I can get him to tell me whatever you need to know."

"I don't want you to do anything for me."

She dropped her hands to her side. "What?"

"Hold up, let me be clear, Ms. Cressey—I've never asked you to do anything for me."

"I know that, I—"

"Let me explain something to you. He has a lawyer. He's asserted his rights. I cannot and would not try to get a statement from him by working around his lawyer, through you. You got that?"

Her lip trembled. "Yes."

"I know you're trying to be helpful. But don't be helpful for me." It was more than helpfulness—she was one of those people. The limelight people. She wanted to testify. It was probably why she reached out to Walker in the first place—to worm herself into the news or something.

And she didn't care whose side she was on, so long as some of the spotlight hit her.

"I think you should go." Rice waved toward the front doors. "I don't want any part of this."

Rice turned and strode for the stairs.

Her childish voice was a whimper behind him. "You don't want a confession?"

"Not like this." Rice let the door slam on the lobby without waiting to see if she was leaving, too.

His coffee was still warm at his desk. His mug read: "If you run, you'll just go to jail tired." It had been a parting gift from the last admin to retire from Salisbury. Something about filling that mug with coffee, holding it in his hand, drinking from it, even just seeing it at his workstation— it made him feel good. More competent, somehow. O'Malley was on the phone across the room, but as soon as she hung up she'd be asking about Britny Cressey. What a viper of a friend. Rice didn't need to be accused of making a civilian into his agent, trying to get a confession from Walker. They didn't need one.

But was that true? He sipped at his coffee and watched O'Malley absently. Her desk was much messier than Rice's, but she never seemed to lose things in the snowdrift of files and loose papers atop it. She laughed into the phone and crossed one leg over the other. Something was going on with Nick Hall. The suicide attempt. That could have to do with trauma, yes. But could it also speak to something else eating away at him? An attempt at escaping something besides a night he couldn't remember? An escape from something *he'd* done?

At this point, it wasn't his place to question whether he believed Nick Hall. The case was Linda Davis's, now. The system would have to do its best to sort it out.

47

T hat was another regret I had," Rice said. "I didn't make it easy for Nick to tell me the truth."

Julia looked surprised. "I don't think it was your fault."

"I do," he said. "A better detective would have done it differently. Would have known how to make him feel safe. I should have told him from the beginning that it was never too late to tell me new information."

"Doing a job like yours, you make mistakes with people. It's awful but there's nothing you can do."

"I could have done better. I shouldn't have been so concerned with getting everything up front and it staying the same."

Julia shook her head. "I don't know what happened between the two of you. What exactly you did or didn't say. But I know you're a good man, and he knew you were doing your best by him. And your job is to get the story up front. You do have to hope for consistent statements, because those statements get cross-examined. The press plays them on repeat. That's how our system works. It's not designed for sexual assault cases."

"We never got to find out, though."

"What?"

"In Nick's case. We never got to find out if the system would have done right by him."

He studied her face. She looked at her mug on the table between them.

"Because the defendant went missing," Rice said. "*Weird*, right?"

Her mouth twitched: a smile was threatening to break through.

It was wild how often people smiled while they were being interrogated. In his earlier years on the force he assumed it was an attempt at nonchalance—an oversimple idea that someone guilty wouldn't be smiling. Later he wondered if it was some kind of psychological hiccup— the brain smiling at the strangeness of being interrogated, like on TV. He eventually learned another possible explanation at a body language training: an evolutionary holdover where we smile out of fear.

"Yeah," Julia said, and she cleared her throat. "We just assumed from the beginning he skipped town."

He held her eye.

His voice was soft. "Did you."

48

Julia was in her office, trying to work on the records report. It had grown too complex to wrangle into a single readable narrative. Her bewilderment with the project was bleeding over, and she kept slipping sideways into other worries.

In the last few weeks, a low-level anxiety had kicked up in her chest, unrelated to the report. Tony had been off lately. The cause seemed obvious enough: Nick's overdose had rocked him. She didn't blame Tony for being upset, but something more than that was going on. For one, he had lied about going to visit Nick on Saturday.

At the end of Nick's first week at Goodspring, Nick was feeling lonely. Tony went up to see him for the day on Saturday. Tony told Julia all of this, and she believed it until a day ago. A day ago, she called Nick to find out how visiting hours were going to work on Christmas Day, which was fast-approaching.

Nick sounded anxious about them bringing the kids to see him at Goodspring.

"You don't want us to bring them?"

There was a long pause. "I guess I don't know. I don't want them to think I'm crazy."

"You aren't, honey. We could approach it so many ways, including just telling them you're there to feel better. We could even say it was a school you were at or something if you'd rather. But we'll do whatever sounds good to you. I guess I just want you to know that we don't have any thoughts about hiding you from them."

"Thanks," Nick said quietly. "It would be good to see you all."

"I want to see you, too. And the kids will be bonkers for you, you know that."

"But not Tony?"

Julia laughed. "Obviously he'll want to see you, but he just got to."

"Oh," Nick said. "I guess. This week has felt like a month."

"Will it blow your mind if I tell you it was yesterday?"

"What was?"

"That you saw Tony."

There was a pause. "I didn't see Tony yesterday."

That night, she tried to get the drop on Tony. She waited until he was undressing for bed, and she asked him, as casually as she could, if Nick mentioned anything he wanted for Christmas at their visit. No, Tony said, he didn't.

"Did you ask?"

Tony said nothing.

"Because he mentioned today that you weren't there at all yesterday."

Tony stammered a second, then told her she'd caught him.

"Christmas shopping," he said. A two-word explanation that was beyond cross-examination.

Even if she believed that he'd been occupied with some Christmas surprise for her all day Saturday, that didn't explain his behavior on the other days that had passed since Nick's attempted suicide. Every day, Tony had left early for the office and gotten home late. When he was home, he seemed absent, zoning out while the kids were talking to him. It wasn't like him at all.

There were other things that bothered her, too, harder things to name. The rehearsed quality of his voice, for example, when he answered a question about his day. It was the same voice she'd heard him use when he gave a toast at a friend's wedding. The tone of his voice was different when it was material he'd practiced.

She could barely focus on the work before her, and she was relieved when she felt her phone buzz on her desk. It was Charlie Lee.

She'd completely forgotten that Charlie was still looking at Walker for her.

She answered quickly, longing for some kind of good news about the case.

His greeting was defeat: "There's nothing I want to do more than tell you I found something."

"Oh, Charlie, that's okay. I didn't even remember you were still looking."

"I just wanted to circle back. Heard back from the last of the bars I'd contacted. Nothing helpful. He's been careful before, that's my guess. Careful and lucky. And now, he's on his best behavior, as far as I can tell."

She thought about telling Charlie what had happened with Nick—about the overdose and the hospitalization. But what was the point? It would probably only frustrate him to hear, since he hadn't found anything. "Thanks for trying, Charlie."

"I know he's been a real jackass in a public way, with the news and stuff, but at least he isn't confrontational. With your husband, I mean."

"Yeah," Julia said as she tried to process what he might mean.

"He isn't, is he? He wouldn't still be out on bail if he were being threatening or anything at the gym."

"What gym?"

"The gym they go to, him and your husband."

Tony didn't go to the gym. "The one in Orange?"

"No, the Weight Room in Salisbury."

"Tony doesn't go there."

Charlie paused. "I saw him in his car in the lot there. I drove by last week when I was over that way."

The hair on Julia's neck prickled.

"It certainly looked just like him," Charlie said. "I remember him from the photo at your old office. He was in a gray SUV in the gym's side lot."

"What day?"

"Would have been Thursday."

The chill in her neck went hot. "Must just be someone who looks like him," Julia said. "Tony doesn't really go to the gym, and Salisbury's too far a drive."

"Must be, that makes more sense. Figured you would have mentioned if they were running into each other."

"Thank you so much for trying, Charlie. You can stop looking now, really."

"Things're still slow, I'm happy to keep at it for a bit—"

"Please stop. Please just leave it."

"All right."

"Promise me you won't look into Walker anymore."

"Fine, I promise." There was silence, and Charlie said, "He'll get his justice, Julia. I know it's hard to wait, but it'll come in time."

Tony had been home late on Thursday. Said he had an emergency at work. What were the chances it was his lookalike in a gray SUV at Raymond Walker's gym all the way in Salisbury?

There was no way to tell Charlie how wrong he was—how sure she felt that the time for waiting was over.

—◦—

It wasn't until she saw the receptionist through the glass doors at Tony's office that Julia realized it might seem a bit nutty of her to drop in on him in the middle of the workday. She could give two shits what Tony thought about it, but there were other people at his office. Shirley, the receptionist, for one.

If she knew the thoughts running through Julia's head at that moment, Shirley would have fainted.

Shirley saw Julia and slapped the folder in her hand down on the desk. "Julia Hall," she singsonged. "What a surprise! What are you doing here?"

Julia felt called out immediately. She looked overbearing. She smiled but could feel it was a lame one. "I just need to see Tony quick."

Shirley frowned. "Did he come in today?"

"What?"

"He took the day off, or have I lost my marbles?" Shirley sat down and started clicking at the computer. "I always check everyone's calendar when I come in, and he's off today and all next week. Unless he popped in for something and I didn't see him. There he is, yes, he's out today."

Julia white-knuckled the lip of Shirley's desk. "Can you call down and make sure he isn't in?"

"Sure, hon." Shirley pecked out a number and let it ring on speakerphone. It rang and rang and rang until Tony's voice mail picked up.

"I must have misunderstood," Julia said quietly.

"Oh, shoot," Shirley hissed. "I probably just spoiled some kind of Christmas surprise."

"Maybe," Julia said. "I'm sorry to run, but I've got to go."

Shirley's face fell with friendly disappointment. "Oh, all right. We'll have to catch up next time!"

Julia nodded as she left. Shirley might not have even seen the nod, but Julia couldn't offer anything more polite—she couldn't speak.

She made it to the elevator. The air around her felt as though it was pressing in from all sides. She hit the button and it lit up. Heat rose up through her stomach, chest, neck, face. She kept walking down the hall, found the stairwell, and stepped in as she heard the elevator ding behind her. She walked halfway down to the next landing and sat on a step. Put her head between her legs. Breathed in through her nose. The smell of her jeans, like chemicals. Breathed out through her mouth. Another round, and another. The air thinned and her skin began to cool.

Julia pulled out her phone. Pressed Tony's cell number. On two rings he answered.

"What's up?" His voice was clipped. He sounded interrupted.

"Where are you?"

"At work?"

"Perfect, I'm out front. Meet me in the lobby."

She relished the pause.

"You're at my office?"

"Yup, I'm heading up."

"Wait."

There was silence. If he lied again—

"I'm going into a meeting, I can't see you now."

"Bullshit," she hissed. "*Bullshit*. I've already been up. You're not here."

"What are you doing at my office?"

"*Great* question. I show up to my husband's job expecting him to be there on a Tuesday after he kisses me goodbye in the morning and tells me he's going to work. Great question. *I'm* the one who owes an explanation? But I've got one, Tony, and since you're *not* at work, meet me at home in an hour and I'll tell you why I came looking for you."

Tony was silent for a bit. She'd really unleashed there.

"You want to do this at home?"

"We're out of time to do it anywhere else. I've gotta get Seb from the bus stop."

"What about Chloe?"

"My mom is picking her up for girl time, we talked about this last—"

"Right, right, I forgot. I'll get Seb."

"I can get him."

"Please. Let me get Seb, and we'll meet you at home."

She wanted to say no. Not until he told her where he'd been, what he was doing, what the fuck was going on. But this had nothing to do with Seb. This would not bleed over onto the kids.

"Fine."

She hung up without waiting to see if he'd say anything else. She'd given him time to prepare now. He was going to come up with some explanation for playing hooky, so she'd keep what she knew about the gym to herself until she had eyes on him. When had this happened? When had he started—whatever this was, scheming?—behind her back? And where was he now?

49

Julia had said he could pick up Seb. He needed to see his son. Tousle his hair, squeeze him tight. Because whatever was coming—a fight, a full-blown marital storm—was going to be a big one. Julia sounded ready to go up one side of him and down the other.

Tony did some quick math and determined he could, in fact, beat the bus home as long as he left now. He was glad—calling her back to admit otherwise would have been brutal.

He took one last look at Walker's house and put the car in drive.

—◡

Tony could see Julia through the living room window when he and Seb pulled into the driveway. He wondered, pointlessly, if she might have cooled off since she found he wasn't at work. Doubtful.

Seb went running into the house ahead of Tony. He was already chattering at Julia when Tony made it inside. He could hear them in the kitchen as he pulled off his boots in the mudroom.

"Dad said I could play with the Wii," Seb announced.

"Did he," Julia said.

Tony stepped into the kitchen. "Thought we could talk while he did."

Julia nodded, releasing the smile she'd put on for Seb.

"Just while we wrap some extra presents," Julia said to Seb. Christmas was in a matter of days. "That means you stay downstairs, got it?"

Seb nodded, wide-eyed and grinning like a maniac. The kids had all but forgotten about the Wii until a week ago when they saw an ad for a new game, and now they were obsessed with the stupid thing all over again.

Tony set Seb up with his game. He stooped to kiss the top of his head through his soft curls. When he straightened himself, Julia was staring at him from the stairs. She beckoned him with an impatient wave.

He knew what was coming, and they barely made it to the top of the stairs before she started.

"So, what's up with your day off?" She paused at the landing and turned to face him.

"Can't a man have some privacy around Christmastime?" He smiled as he moved past her and toward the bedroom. It could have been breezy, but he'd practiced it too much.

Julia shut the door to their room and took a deep breath. She looked tired. "Can you please, please not lie to me? Apparently I can't expect you to just offer me the truth yourself, but don't give me an outright lie. And don't look at me like that."

"Like what?"

"Like I'm hurting your feelings."

"How should I feel when you call me a liar?"

"What should I call you when you put on a tie and tell me you're going to work when you have the day off?"

Everything he hadn't said was welling up in his throat. He turned to their closet and fought to avoid looking at the door as he reached to pull down the last of the unwrapped gifts. Their notes from all their years together flooded his peripheral vision to his left, reminding him of all the things they'd said before. "Can we just do what we need to do before Seb gets restless and comes up here?"

"No, *this*"—she pointed at the two of them—"is what we need to do right now. You got dressed for work this morning. You carried your bag out. You went to his gym."

Tony started so violently that he dropped a plastic box to the floor. He dumped the rest of the presents onto their bed.

"Yeah," she said.

He turned to her. She didn't look angry. She looked like she hated him. For a second, he thought she knew the whole thing.

"Have you been following me?"

"Fuck off," she whispered. "How was I supposed to know following Walker meant following you?"

"You're following him?"

"No," she said. "Charlie was just giving him one last look."

Charlie Lee again. "When did he see me?"

"So you've been there more than once." She didn't sound angry. She sounded tired.

She stared at him with eyes that skimmed left and right, surveying the landscape of his face. Searching for something. Yes, he was guilty of that. But he was guilty of more, too, and that needed to stay his guilt alone. He said nothing.

"You're scaring me. You *need* to start talking to me. I can't—I'm losing my shit." Her voice cracked. "I don't know what to do with myself." Tears brimmed in her eyes and spilled. "I can't have *you* scaring me like this on top of everything else."

She wrapped her arms around herself and hung her head.

He was torturing her. Tony reached out to pull her into his chest. He kissed the top of her head and shushed her quietly. The urge to comfort her with the truth, all of it, was overwhelming. But it wouldn't comfort her, that was the problem. It would only put her at risk. If anything went wrong, it was better if she'd known nothing at all.

"I'm following him, too," he said finally.

She pulled her head back from his chest and looked up into his face. "Why?"

"I—" he started, and stopped. "I thought I could catch him doing something to get him in trouble. To make them send him back to jail."

Julia released from his embrace. "Swear."

"What?"

"Swear that's all this is."

"I do," Tony said quickly. He'd never lied to her like this before. Never sworn on a lie. He couldn't remember her ever asking him to swear he was being truthful. All of this was new. And he needed to sell it, to keep her innocent. "I swear," he said. "I'm just watching him."

"I want you to stop," she said. "I told Charlie to stop, and I want you to, too."

"Okay," he said.

"It can't get out that we were stalking him."

"It won't," Tony said. "We're done. We're done."

"Promise we won't keep secrets," she said.

"I promise," he said. What he was really promising was to keep her protected, but she had no way of knowing that. And to himself, he made a second promise: after this, he'd never keep a secret from her again.

50

R ice had struck a nerve, that much was obvious. Julia sat in her recliner, squeezing her hands together. Her mind probably going a mile a minute, trying to decide what to say next.

"I think I'm confused about where this is all going," Julia said. "Why wouldn't we think he had run away?"

Her question hung in the air.

Rice could say nothing, and his silence would compel her to say everything. She would talk against herself, trying to explain away whatever she thought he knew, and in doing so she would reveal everything to him.

"I feel like I'm missing something," she said.

It was already starting. The whole bit folded out in front of him now. He could see it, clear as he could see her. She was utterly terrified, and she would go wherever he might take her. It was all over, if he wanted.

He hummed quietly before he spoke. "Did you miss it then?"

Her voice was hoarse. "Miss what?"

Rice sighed. *Enough.*

"*I* know what happened," he said. "I've always wondered if you knew, too."

51

The visiting room at Goodspring was wide and bright. The hard walls were painted white and covered in patient artwork. It reminded Nick of a school cafeteria. There were groupings of tables and chairs all around the room, for patients to visit with whoever had come to see them. It was Christmas. The holiday seemed to lose more of its magic with each year as he aged, but this year was different. This year, Tony and Julia had packed up the kids on Christmas morning and driven two hours to come see Nick. This year it felt special again.

"I'm gonna hit the bathroom," Tony said as he stood up from their table.

Julia turned to Chloe. "Why don't you pick out a game for us to play?"

"I want to pick," Seb whined.

"There's no need for that," Julia said as she eyed him with a raised brow. "You can each pick one, but no whining. Especially on Christmas!" she added as the kids crossed to the far end of the room.

She smiled at Nick and leaned on a fist. "Are you hanging in there okay?"

He was a weekend shy of two weeks in the program now. "Yeah," he said. "At first, after I told Tony, I felt better than I had in months. It was like everything was going to be good again and I felt like my old self. But then it wore off, and it was awful—I'm so glad I was here."

266

Julia looked confused.

"My therapist here said I was probably just finally starting to process things. I told Jeff about the overall lie, you know, at the beginning of the month, but we still hadn't talked about what happened in detail. We were going to do it slowly over time, but it's all started to come up anyway. You know what I mean?"

She shook her head. "What lie?"

Did Tony not tell her? "What I told Tony."

"When?"

"When he drove me here."

"He didn't tell me anything."

Tony appeared in the doorway across the room.

Nick began to whisper. "Please don't ask him."

Julia whispered back. "What didn't he tell me?"

"Please, Julia—please not today."

They fell silent as Tony reached the table. "What's going on?"

Julia looked at Nick. He pleaded with his eyes.

Her voice was cautious. "The kids are picking games."

Tony sat down. "Cool."

Julia was staring at him. What was he thinking, not telling her?

Two game boxes slammed onto the table.

"Ea-sy," Tony cautioned with a frown.

"Connect Four," Nick read. "Love it."

Chloe beamed at his approval.

"One thousand— No, Seb, this is what you chose? A thousand-piece puzzle?"

Sebastian grinned at Tony so wide that Nick wondered whether he'd intended it as a joke.

"He liked the picture on the front," Chloe said with a shrug.

Nick kept looking back at Julia, whose eyes hadn't left Tony's face.

52

Tony Hall, 2015

I can't believe it." Julia was lying on her side in their bed, turned to face Tony. "He remembered everything."

Tony nodded.

"He's been so alone, all this time."

"I know."

Snow was falling outside the window across from the bed. Julia was doing what anyone would—she was processing what she'd just learned about Nick. Tony was just waiting for the other shoe to drop: why hadn't he told her?

"I don't know if I understand what he said about the fight," she said.

"He didn't want to tell anyone that he couldn't stop him."

"But isn't that . . . obvious? Even in the version he first told?"

"Yeah but . . . it was different. At first he told it, like, single cheap shot, he's out. What really happened made him feel powerless." Tears began to well. "He was awake for all of it—for the moment he was over-powered. Do you get it?"

Julia nodded. And maybe she did, to some extent. But Tony didn't know how to explain what it meant to Nick—what it would have meant to Tony—to be dominated by another man, in spite of being conscious when it happened. What it was like to spend your whole life hearing you were supposed to win fights, be strong. And if you couldn't do those things, you weren't a man.

"What are you going to do about it?"

There it was. Her eyes were steady on his face.

"Nothing."

"You always do something. You can't help yourself. What are you going to do about this?"

Tony rested a hand on her shoulder. "Nothing."

53

Two days after Christmas, Julia caught up with Margot. They'd become friends during law school and grown closer over the years. On paper they'd always looked quite different. Margot was engaged when school started; Julia was fiercely single. Margot was outspoken and confident; Julia usually had to be forced to give an answer in class. They had study carrels in the library near each other, and they bonded over their love of caffeine and TV shows that kept them up at night. Over a decade later, Margot was divorced and childless and Julia was married with kids, but the important stuff had stayed. They still met for coffee at least once a month, they still texted about *Criminal Minds* after every episode, and they still loved each other.

"Hey, I keep forgetting," Margot said, "send me that cauliflower rice recipe."

"Oh God, I haven't made that in so long."

"I tried to make it up myself and it was awful."

"I mean, it's cauliflower," Julia said.

"But it was so good the time I had it with you. Can you email me the one you used to make?"

Julia walked into the study and shook the mouse to wake up the computer. "Yeah, I'll find it for you."

"You're the best."

They hung up, and Julia opened Google. Typed *cauliflower rice*. There were so many results, and none of the hyperlinks were purple. She scrolled but couldn't tell which recipe was the one she'd been using in the spring.

She opened the internet history. Typed *cauliflower*. No results. That didn't make sense. She'd probably gone to that page ten times.

She clicked back to the main history page. Scrolled. The list of pages she'd visited ended on December 14. There were no results before that date.

There were searches and page titles from the fourteenth—the work she'd done that morning. Everything before that was gone. The history had been cleared on the thirteenth. The same day, she now knew, that Nick told Tony what Ray Walker really did to him.

She closed the history and returned to Google. Typed *How to restore history*. The page filled with links to articles. She clicked the first one. She could run a "system restore," apparently, and it should recover the lost history. She saved all her most recent work to a flash drive, just in case, and then followed the prompts in the article. She selected 12/13/2015 as the restore date and sat back on her stool to watch and wait.

She was being crazy. But why would Tony have deleted the history? He had come home from dropping Nick at Goodspring and gone into the study for a long time—at least an hour. He'd said that night he was working, but he wouldn't have deleted work stuff from the computer. She was probably just going to see where he'd bought her Christmas presents. Oh God, or pornography. She laughed softly. Her stomach was so upset with worry that she was sure she'd be glad to see he'd just been watching porn that night, even if she'd been reading in the next room.

After a few minutes, the computer rebooted. She opened the browser and clicked history. The most recent entry was a page titled "How to Delete Your Internet History."

Before that was a Google search: "Delete history."

Before that, a blog post titled "Ice Knives & Stone Fruit." What the hell did that mean?

Before that, a page that froze Julia in place.

A page called "Forum: How Would You Commit Your Perfect Murder?"

And before that one, "Forum: What Are the Main Causes of Unsolved Murders?"

And before that, a news article: "Why So Many Murders Go Unsolved."

And before that, a Google search: "Unsolved murder causes."

He was going to kill him.

Tony was going to kill Ray Walker.

54

H e found Julia in the bedroom. It was just after four, and she was under the covers.

"Honey?"

She didn't stir. What was going on? She took a call from Margot and went upstairs. Over an hour had passed before Tony noticed she hadn't come back down.

Something was wrong.

He sat down on the bed gently. "Honey?"

Without opening her eyes, she said, "I saw the computer."

"What?"

"I know what you're doing."

Dread spilled into his stomach. "What are you talking about?"

She sat up with her eyes clamped shut, a hand on her head like she was woozy. Then she opened her eyes, kept them on the bedspread. "Just tell me I'm wrong."

No. No, please, she doesn't know.

"About what?"

"What the fuck are you thinking?" she whispered violently as she shoved him.

"Hey!"

"I saw what you were looking at. Murder. *Murder?*" She pounded her palms against his chest again, and he brought his hands up to catch her wrists.

Fuck. Oh, fuck.

"How did you see it?"

"It was easy. Nothing you do on the computer is *ever* gone." She wrenched her hands from his grip.

"I'll get you a new one."

"So when you kill him and they take our computer, they won't be suspicious that it's brand-new?"

"Shh," he hissed. "Keep your voice down."

"Tell me what you're doing."

"I can't tell you."

"Why?"

"I don't want anyone knowing anything about it, not you or Nick or anyone."

"So you'll get me a new computer." She nodded, wide-eyed and tight-lipped. "And we'll be good."

"That was a one-off. I haven't done anything like that again."

"Everything is traceable, Tony."

"No, I've been careful."

"Besides this, besides using the computer in our house."

"Yes. I swear."

"So you're gonna do this."

Tony broke her gaze.

"Explain it to me. Explain why you think you're entitled to do this."

"Entitled?"

"Yeah. Nick's doing everything he's supposed to. He told the police, he's willing to testify, he's killing himself to get through court. Why do you think you get to—just—do this insane fucking thing?"

"He can't go on like this. You know that—he tried to kill himself."

"He's safe. He's getting help. You're pretending this is about him, but it's really about you."

"If you can't see how this would help Nick, I don't know what to say. He's our family."

"You want to talk about our *family*? You're talking about killing someone and our fucking kid is downstairs."

An awareness struck him, suddenly, of what Julia was missing. A simplicity to how he might help her see.

"One of our kids is downstairs," he said quietly. "But my first kid is in a hospital in Belfast."

She looked at him wide-eyed, then at the bed.

"If it were Seb or Chloe, maybe then you'd understand. He's like my kid."

Julia laid back down and rolled away from him.

"He's always been my kid to me." Tony walked around the bed and knelt before her. "Don't you see that?"

She didn't move. Her eyes looked strangely faraway, but her gaze rested somewhere near his back foot.

"He tried to kill himself." Tony's voice cracked and he shrugged at himself. "If he tells the rest of it . . . if the case doesn't settle, he's going to tell them what Walker did to him. When that comes out, it'll all get so much worse." He waited a while to go on. "We almost lost him. You said that; you know. He's part of your family, too."

She looked up at him then. "I know that."

"Then let me save him," Tony said.

Julia dropped her eyes back to the floor. Tony stood. Neither of them spoke. He walked around the bed and reached the door when he heard her voice.

"Promise me," she said quietly behind him.

He turned back.

"Promise me you'll wait to see if it settles in January."

He nodded. That was fine. January was a good month for it.

55

Depressingly, the week after Christmas was always a busy one at the station. Crime usually spiked around the December holidays: money problems, alcohol, too much time with family. Rice was just getting ready to leave on a domestic violence case when the receptionist paged his desk phone. Julia Hall was calling for him.

"I'm sorry to bother you," Julia said. "I'm sure you're busy."

"It's fine. Is everything all right?"

"Oh, yeah. I'm just calling to ask, ah." Her voice was all defeat. "Something I think I already know the answer to."

"Okay?"

"Is there any way that, um, Ray Walker's bail would be revoked because of anything that's happened?"

"What, with Nick?"

"Well, yeah. With him and his mom contacting the press so much, and all of it just having such a negative effect on Nick's mental health."

He was going to fail them again.

"No, I don't think so. He hasn't violated bail, he's had no contact with Nick. Nothing he's done has been criminal. It's terrible, what Nick's going through, but no judge would let us hold him just because Nick is

277

struggling. I talked to Linda, and she thinks we'll get into a pissing match, pardon my French, if we try to do anything to stop him or the press from running their mouths. Technically, they haven't released anything they weren't allowed to. Probably just end up drawing even more attention to the case."

Julia paused for long enough that Rice thought the call had dropped.

"Yeah, I figured. I just felt like I had to ask."

"You guys doing okay over there?"

It was a stupid question. He doubted she'd be calling if everything was coming up roses.

"Going a little crazy," she said softly.

"I'm so sorry, Julia. I wish there was something I could do, but unless he violates his bail, we're waiting out a plea or a trial."

"They told Nick they thought it could be a year. Was that just . . . you know, them managing his expectations? It could be sooner, right?"

"Anything's possible. But, I mean, I'm set for trial next month in a case I closed three years ago."

Julia was silent. Why was she so surprised? She'd been a defense attorney.

"You know how it is. Court's backed up, DA's backed up, and time hurts a case like Nick's, so Eva will push it out as far as she can."

"What if he can't wait that long?"

"Nick has to just live his life, try to forget about the case."

There was another long pause.

He started again. "Look, ah." She was a professional, in a way, even if she wasn't on this case. "Between us, Julia?"

"Yeah?"

"I'm not sure there'll be a trial."

"Really?"

"I just heard from a faux friend of Walker's that he knows his goose is cooked. I think he'll take a plea. Probably not until the eve of trial, you know how it goes, but then I bet he'll take it. I think some of his bravado is for show. He's scared shitless."

"Really? Did it sound like it would be soon?"

"Well, no, he seems the type not to roll over until it's really showtime. But Nick might not have to testify. Don't tell him that, don't get his hopes up, but I don't think you need to worry so much about the end result. I think it'll settle. It's the waiting we can't do anything about."

She paused. "Okay." Her voice was high and quiet. She sounded like she was trying not to cry. "Thanks for your time, Detective."

"I'm sorry I couldn't be more helpful, Julia." She'd already hung up, but he needed to say the words anyway.

56

JULIA HALL, 2015

Julia hadn't slept the past two nights. There were moments where it seemed she had fallen into a light sleep, but the whole time she was dreaming she was awake. Awake and obsessing over what her husband was going to do.

She asked him how he would do it. He wouldn't tell. When he would do it, and where. He wouldn't tell. How he would ensure he was free from suspicion. He would be sure, he said. He just kept repeating his mantra: "It's safer if you don't know."

Julia didn't feel safe. She felt frantic. He promised he would wait until the dispositional conference, when the case might settle. If Walker agreed to plead guilty, Nick wouldn't tell the prosecutor the truth, and maybe Tony would let this go. So she had until January 12. Two weeks. Two more weeks to try to figure something out.

She could go straight to Nick—try to get him to give up the case—but would that solve the problem? Or would Tony do it anyway, because giving up the case meant Walker went unpunished? And if something happened to Walker after Nick abandoned the case, would they be even more suspicious of Tony? Would it look like Nick had given up the case so that Tony could enact justice of his own?

She'd already tried calling Detective Rice the day before. It was pointless, just like she'd expected. Walker had done nothing to get himself thrown back in jail, out of Tony's reach.

She'd tried to reason with Tony: What about the kids? What about Nick? What about *her*? It was like he couldn't hear her. He thought he had the moral high ground—he was so far up there he had altitude sickness.

And morals—she was surprised by how little of her desperation to stop him came from the immorality of it.

So much of her identity, as a lawyer, as a mother, as a wife, friend, person, had been focused on *being good*. It was such a vague goal, but she never questioned it, maybe because it came easily to her. Do the right thing. Treat people well. What was *right* was usually easy for her to identify. The first time she met with Mathis Lariviere and his mother, she had to convince both of them, not just the boy, that he should have a substance abuse evaluation and start therapy immediately, long before he was sentenced.

"The better he is," Julia said, "the better his result in the case will be."

"You mean the better he *looks*, the better his result," his mother, Elisa, said coolly.

"No," Julia said. "He can't just sit through a year of therapy with his headphones in. He'll need to change. The judge will see through it, otherwise."

"I'm not so sure," Elisa replied. "Some of us are good at looking good."

At the time, Julia wrote off the woman's comment. They hadn't seen eye to eye on much, she and Elisa Lariviere, whose son had told Julia things about his family that gave her chills. For Elisa to insinuate that Julia's morality was an act had been laughable.

But now she wondered. Maybe Julia had just been good at *looking* like she was good. Acting like she believed in doing moral things. Because in this moment, she cared far more about looking good than being good.

Everything that kept her awake and squeezed sweat from her hairline had to do with Tony being caught. Not what he wanted to do in the first place.

If Tony was caught, she'd lose him. The *kids* would lose him. He was a good man. That sounded impossible, given what he was doing right now, but Tony Hall was a good man, and a great father, and her kids were going to lose him if he wasn't careful. And she'd told him from the start—from the first night they talked, she told him she would never marry a man who wasn't serious about what that meant to her. Who wouldn't fight like it was life or death to keep whatever they made together. She'd been so sure he was that man. How could he do this to her?

There was only one thing she'd thought of that might work.

She texted Charlie Lee.

I need one last thing

she wrote.

And Charlie responded,

Anything.

57

JULIA HALL, 2015

Julia leaned over her dresser as she worked mascara through the upper lashes of her left eye. Nina Simone crooned softly from her cell phone. She stepped back to survey her work—all that was left was lipstick. She selected a tube of brick red. It wasn't her favorite, but Tony loved it, and it would vamp up her plain black dress. She applied the color to her open mouth and took her hair back down. The grays at the crown of her head caught the low light of the lamp on her dresser; she was due for a touch-up. She scrunched her fingers into her roots and refocused on the music. Nina wouldn't worry about gray hairs—and she'd probably call them silver. Julia swayed a little to "Feeling Good" as the brass came in, letting the song seduce her. Sometime after they'd had babies, she'd come to feel that the act of *getting ready* for a date with her husband was the night's first opportunity for foreplay. She was forcing the magic tonight.

If they hadn't made a reservation months in advance, they probably would have stayed in. One of the side effects of their decision to get married on New Year's Eve nine years ago was that reservations were a necessity if they wanted to eat out on their anniversary. Julia had booked the table long before she knew she'd be spending all her free time wondering if her husband really was capable of killing a man.

Julia picked up the small purse she'd abandoned on the bed earlier. She snapped the clasp open, and the envelope of her card peeked out. The words inside were imperfect, and mostly stolen, but she was satisfied that she had captured what she was feeling at rock bottom, beneath all the other emotions. This card might go onto the collage in the closet, and it might not. Would either of them want to remember this time?

She knew what her notes meant to him, but this year she had been at a loss for what to put on paper. Earlier that evening, the card was still sitting blank in her office when she climbed into the shower. It was there that she'd thought of their first dance song: Barry White's "You're the First, the Last, My Everything." She'd slung a towel around herself and darted down the hall to write her favorite lines into the card. He was the sun and the moon, she wrote. "My first, my last, my everything."

Nine years ago today, they'd danced to this song. Everything had seemed so simple then. She had imagined their vows would be tested over a long life together, but not like this. She read the lines over again. The words seemed empty in the face of where they stood. But she had to say something, and there was still truth in the song. He was still everything to her. That's why it hurt so much.

Now, she pushed the tube of lipstick into her purse, next to the card.

"Wow," Tony said from the doorway. She caught a glimpse of him in the mirror as she turned—clean lines and dark hair.

"Wow yourself," she said. "I love that blazer."

"I know you do," he said, and he spun slowly for her to the music. "Notice anything . . . new?" he asked as he thrust his arm out in time with a trumpet's bleat. His new watch popped from his sleeve, and Julia laughed in spite of herself. She was holding on to something angry, sad; it was palpable. She would let it go. At least for tonight, she would let it go.

She bent to pull her heels on, and when she stood he had come to her. They were closer to eye level now with her added inches. He wrapped his hands around her waist and leaned in to kiss her gently; she sunk into him with a soft sigh. When her husband pulled away, his lips were smeared with melted red. She giggled and wiped them with her thumb, her fingers under his clean-shaven chin.

"Maybe when my mom comes for the kids we should skip dinner," he murmured, holding her close against his waist.

"She's watching them here—they'll be asleep when we get home." She pecked his cheek and stepped back.

"Stay a minute," he said with a wolfish grin, and pulled her back to him.

"No," she said flatly as she pushed his hands away and stepped back. He looked surprised, confused. She was, too. Something about him telling her to stay—holding her so firmly against him—had infuriated her, just for a split second. She crossed the room and paused at the door. She was being so cold to him lately; sometimes by choice, other times by impulse.

"Grandma's here!" Chloe shouted from the living room.

Julia took the stairs quickly, leaving Tony behind.

⟶

Julia scuffed her feet as she stepped into the warmth of Buona Cucina, grinding slush and salt into the welcome mat.

"Happy New Year," the hostess said as she collected menus from her post. "Coatrack's behind you."

Buona Cucina was a small, expensive Italian restaurant in downtown Orange where they'd celebrated a few anniversaries and birthdays over the years. With its exposed brick, hardwood floors, and decor, it reminded Julia of several places in Portland, including the Ruby, the bar she used to tend. Part of why she favored Buona Cucina for romantic nights was because it felt so much like the places she and Tony went on their first dates.

They crossed a landing into the smaller of two dining areas. As they walked, Julia reached out and squeezed Tony's hand: an unspoken apology for pushing him away earlier. Tony squeezed back.

They ordered a bottle of sparkling water for the table, and a glass of pinot noir for Julia.

"Will you at least tell me how you're going to do it?"

Tony looked surprised. "What?"

Julia lowered her voice. "You know what."

He sighed. "Why do you want to talk about this on our anniversary?"

"I can't get it out of my system because you won't tell me anything. Just tell me how."

"I want you to be safe. I need you to be, the kids—I think not telling you is what I have to do."

"But you can't plan something like this alone. You keep saying you're being careful, but how can I know that if you won't let me ask you questions—test your plan."

"They're not even going to know it was anything but an accident."

"Okay, so—" She shook her head. "Right there. That sounds like wishful thinking."

"It isn't." He adjusted the fork next to his plate.

"You're really going to do this?"

He looked surprised. "I thought you were okay with it."

"When have I *ever* said that?"

Tony frowned. "Well, I need you to *get* okay with it."

"Or what?"

"Or, nothing, I guess," he said as he straightened up in his chair. "I've told you what I'm doing."

"Where does that leave me?"

"Supporting me, I thought."

"Cornered," she said. "You've cornered me."

"I don't know how to make you understand."

She shook her head. "I do understand about you and Nick. I didn't grow up taking care of someone else. But I have you, and we have the kids. So what about us?"

His face went soft in the candlelight. "I promise you we'll be okay. I *know* it. Like I've known so much about you and me."

He put his hand over hers and went on. "I knew I'd marry you the day we went ice fishing with Margot and her ex, remember? And you dropped the flask in the hole, then snatched it out and took a sip?" He laughed softly. "I knew then, in a weirdly calm, almost psychic way, that we would be married, and everything would be okay. I feel the same now. I'll be careful, and we'll be fine."

Julia wanted to pull away from him, but she left her hand in his.

The waiter appeared in her peripheral vision, sidling up to the table like he knew he was interrupting something. He took their orders and left. They sat for a moment in silence, unsure of where to pick up.

Tony laid his napkin back on his plate. "I'm gonna hit the bathroom."

Julia was alone. She watched the flames flicker in the frosted glasses at the center of the table. Between the two candles was a single blossom in a thin glass. It was orange, with thin petals unfolding from the center.

She had lost. There was nothing more to do but admit that she was not, in fact, as good as she thought. All of Tony's talk about leaving her out of it was meaningless. When this was over, she would be complicit in what happened to Ray Walker.

Tony talked about the moment he knew he'd marry her. Hers hadn't been a moment so much as a day: a day they had a picnic with Nick. She'd met Nick before, but she'd been dating Tony for long enough on this day that they'd all dropped the pretenses of impressing each other. Instead, they were just being together. She watched how Tony talked to the boy. She listened to the strong warmth in his voice. Saw him put an arm around Nick at one point and squeeze him close. She saw all of this and thought, this is the man I want to make babies with. My children will have this man as their father. She had missed that he already was a father, in a way.

And as much as Tony had driven her crazy at times in the beginning, always trying to do things for her, she had liked how he was a fixer and a fighter. He wouldn't watch idly if their marriage grew stale. He would do anything for his family. And if he got sick one day, he would fight like hell to stay with them. As much as she loved Nick, loved him so much, she had missed how much a part of their family he was, by way of Tony. Tony was everything to her, but that didn't mean she didn't love the kids. Maybe even more than she loved him. The soul has room for competing loves. She had three. Tony had four.

She looked out the window beside their table. She could make out the shape of snow on the ground, but otherwise it was nothing but darkness. If they could just make it to spring, maybe everything would feel different. The sun and the crocuses would lighten up Tony's heart. He would see that the world had not, in fact, gone pitch black. But spring was months away, and between here and there, Nick would tell the ADA his story, and the ADA would be forced to tell Walker. There would be media again, more talk, more public opinion about things people knew nothing about. And that was the clock that Tony was racing against. It would all be over long before spring came. When the light came back, would they be able to face what they'd done in the dark?

Julia reached forward across the table and brushed her fingertips over the orange blossom's broad face. She tipped the bloom down into the flame and watched the petals singe.

58

Things got easier after their anniversary. After she found his stupid search on the computer, Julia kept surprising Tony with questions and arguments ad nauseum, every time they were away from the kids. He could feel her eyes on him when he looked at his phone or even just moved around the house. Tony wished she didn't know anything at all about Walker—he wanted her in the dark, just to be safe. If something ever went wrong, she would *not* be an accomplice to him. But still, she knew almost nothing. He had stood firm in the face of her questions, and finally, after their anniversary, she stopped asking.

At times he wondered if she was on his side, but the storm truly seemed to have passed. A day ago, Julia's phone rang and Charlie Lee's name lit up her screen. Tony locked eyes with her over the phone, then she answered on speaker and asked Charlie what was up. He said he had the contact information she needed for the records report. She gave Tony a withering look, and he put up his hands in surrender as she took the phone to the study. So it was true—she wasn't using Charlie Lee to investigate Raymond Walker anymore. Still, there was something in it all that Tony wanted to analyze. He took the first couple of days of January off, and the kids were on school break. He'd expected to spend the days hanging out with her and the kids, but instead she'd been working on her records report most of the time. It was like she was subtly punishing him for lying about going to work by working while they should have been together as a family.

At the moment, though, the four of them were together, sitting in the living room. Tony and Seb were lying in the recliner together, Seb's tiny body wedged against his. Julia sat on the couch; Chloe perched behind her on the couch's arm, her legs sticking out on either side of Julia. Tony was reading aloud from *Swallows and Amazons*, a gift that year from Julia's mother. The inscription showed it had been Julia's as a girl: *Dad used to read you this*, Julia's mother had written. *C & S will love it, too*. Tony wished, in moments like these, that he'd met Julia's father. He had been a wonderful parent, Julia told him. She desperately wished he'd made different choices at the end of his life, but until that moment, he had been perfect to her.

Chloe braided Julia's hair as Tony read the old adventure book, and he occasionally glanced up at their progress. First it was two braids, the left one thick and straight, the right one thin and wonky. Then the braids came out and Chloe started a single one down Julia's back. This time when he looked up, Julia was wiping her eyes. She held his gaze, then sighed and shook her head.

"I need to make a phone call," she said as she stood.

Tony stopped reading. "Right now?"

"Mom, your braid fell out!" Chloe groaned.

"Sorry, honey," she said to Chloe, then she turned in Tony's direction. "It won't take long, and I'll bring a hair tie back down when I'm done."

Chloe nodded with satisfaction and slid into Julia's spot on the couch.

Julia retrieved her cell phone from the coffee table and disappeared up the stairs.

Tony was making sandwiches when Julia came back downstairs.

"BLTs," he said in a dramatic voice, waving his hand over the spread as if it were a magic trick. The sandwiches were splayed open with lettuce and fat slices of ripe tomato; beside them was a container of bacon left-over from breakfast.

"They smell delicious," she said. "One for me?"

"Of course, my jewel," he whispered, wagging a strip of bacon at her.

She smiled absently. "Tea?" she asked.

"No, thanks." He felt an annoyance bubble up; she was still holding out on him, pushing off his playfulness. That was unfair of him, though. He'd had longer to process all of this. "Who were you calling?"

He heard the gas burner snap behind him and the rush of flame catching.

"Just people for the report."

"Today, though?"

"Just voice mails today." She came back into view and leaned on the counter next to him.

He handed her a plated sandwich. "You'll eat with us?"

"Yeah." She checked her phone, then pushed it into her sweatpants pocket. It immediately trilled. She dug it back out and looked at its face.

"I gotta take this," she said as she left the kitchen. "I'll come back for my tea," she called as she went down the hallway. "Take it off when it boils, please, but I'll come back for it!"

Her voice quieted as she said, "Hi, Elisa."

Tony heard the study door close, shutting out Julia's voice. The itch of an incomplete memory thrummed in his brain when he heard the name, but whoever Elisa was had faded into the recesses of his memory.

59

NICK HALL, 2016

"W"hat's this worth again?" Nick tipped his hand forward to reveal four spades to the man across the table.

"Four," David responded.

Nick laid his cards down. "Shit," he whispered. That was right. That was the hand that seemed like it was worth more. And he couldn't make fifteen from any of them. He pegged four on the cribbage board. "I think you're gonna smoke me again."

"Skunk," David said as he pegged twelve. He pushed his glasses up the bridge of his porous nose and grinned. "Probably."

David had only been there a week and a half. Nick was a day shy of a month. His counselor at Goodspring, Anne Marie, had written a letter to get permission for him to stay at the program for a little longer. She convinced insurance or whoever to give him extra time so he could be here for a while after the next court day, which, incidentally, was today.

Nick was glad to have David. He was fortysomething, dry and funny, and loved playing games like Nick did. Before David showed up, Nick hadn't really connected with anyone besides the staff. There was a guy there named Kedar who might be cute if he had a haircut and looked like he'd slept at all in the past year. But cute probably wouldn't do Nick any good right now. Cute had gotten Nick into this, in a way. He shouldn't blame himself, his counselors had been firm on that and they were right. But he'd gone home with a stranger. But he'd done that before. He wanted a boyfriend, but instead he was taking whatever he could get. He was a million miles from being ready for sex again, and yet if this cute program guy wanted to go there, he wasn't so sure he wouldn't follow. So he'd continue to give Kedar a wide berth.

Most of the people at Goodspring didn't want to be there. They either admitted so out loud or their actions said it for them. Some didn't think they needed the help; some hated the broken-in beds, the bright lights, the vegetable-heavy food, the windows in the bedroom doors for staff to do safety checks all night. But Nick liked being at Goodspring. It was so strange, so foreign to anything he'd experienced before that it made him forget his life outside the place. There was no DA in here. No criminal case. He was in a bubble.

At least, it normally felt like that. Today, even from the safety of the bubble, he felt the presence of the outside world pressing in on the walls. Out there, life was going on. Tony was stressing out over him. His parents were probably fighting. The winter semester had started. The ADA was at court, right now, with Walker and his lawyer. Real life would be waiting for him when he left Goodspring. He'd be right back where he started—standing in the middle of the mess he had made. His forearms started to itch under his sleeves.

"Nick?"

He looked up, and his counselor Anne Marie was standing in the doorway to the common room.

"You have a call."

It was Sherie.

"So there's no deal," she said. "I'm sorry."

It was what he expected, but his heart sank anyway. "Are you allowed to tell me what happened?"

"Oh, of course. The lawyers were just too far apart to come to a deal. I told you what she was going to offer him, right?"

"Yeah," Nick said. "Four years in jail but he could end up doing ten?"

"Right. It would be prison, not jail, but that's more of a technical thing. And Linda offered to change it from gross sexual assault to aggravated assault."

These were words he'd heard before, but it still felt like he was jogging to keep up with her.

"So the defendant and his lawyer didn't like that," Sherie said. "They wanted simple assault and six months in jail. His lawyer was acting like it was impossible to get him to even consider six months, but that's always how attorneys act when they negotiate. She and Linda couldn't get there. At least not today."

Simple assault, whatever that meant, and six months in jail. He wondered if that's where the case would end up, once he told them that he'd been lying. That it was worse than he'd said—but he'd lied about it. He would talk to Anne Marie and make a plan about telling them the truth.

"So now what?" Nick asked.

"Technically, jury selection is next."

"Already!" It wasn't going to take nearly as long as they made it sound.

"So, your case will get scheduled for jury selection in March. But the defendant will probably file a motion to push it out further than that. And when the next court date does happen, it's just a scheduling day where the judge tries to sort out what cases can have trials that month."

She paused. "Anything's possible, I guess, but you should still be prepared for the long haul. Okay?"

"Okay."

They hung up, and Nick sat for a moment. Anne Marie had left him alone in her office to take the phone call. He wanted to just skip this part—telling his family there was no deal. He wanted to go to bed. But they were all waiting for the news. And going to his room and sleeping wouldn't change the fact that the case still existed.

Nick stood and stuck his head into the hall. Anne Marie was nearby, talking to Kedar.

"Yeah?" she asked when she saw him.

"Can you get me my sister-in-law's cell number?" He wasn't allowed to have his cell phone for most of the day here, and he didn't have Julia's number memorized. He'd call her. She could pass on the news to Tony and his parents. It would be so much easier to talk to her than to Tony.

60

Julia and the kids were doing a Paw Patrol puzzle on the coffee table when her phone buzzed. It was Nick. She groaned as she stood from her seat on the floor.

"Hey, just give me a minute." She left the room and took the stairs quickly. "What happened at the hearing?"

"There's no deal."

"Shit," she hissed, and she meant it more than Nick knew. "That really sucks."

"Yup."

She closed the door to her office. Checked her notes. "Uh, you doing okay?"

"Yeah, just disappointed. Would you mind telling Tony?"

"Sure." No deal meant Tony went forward with his own plan. "Actually. This reminds me. He was saying he wants to come see you."

"He does?"

"Yeah. Friday. He wants to come Friday this week."

"Okay," Nick said. "Do you know why?"

She sighed and leaned against the closed door. "I think he misses you."

61

There was a large envelope jammed into the mailbox when Tony got home. It was addressed to Julia *Clark* and bore a Michigan return address. He would have guessed it was junk mail if it hadn't been handwritten.

He could hear Julia coming down the stairs as the kids mobbed him in the kitchen.

"Someone doesn't know you're married," Tony said as he handed her the package.

Julia looked at the envelope and smiled. "She knows I'm married. Just doesn't respect that I changed my name."

"Seriously?"

Julia rolled her eyes. "I'm positive."

"Who is she?"

"A lady I'm working with on the records report." She started to walk back to the staircase and stopped. "Before I forget: Nick wants you to go see him on Friday."

Tony frowned. "This Friday?"

"Yup. The hearing about a settlement got pushed out another week. He wants to see you before then."

Tony motioned, and they started to climb the stairs together.

"Did it sound important?"

"Important to him, yeah."

"Shit," Tony said quietly. They'd reached the landing. Julia held up a finger, walked down the hall, and put the envelope in her office. They moved into the bedroom.

"What's wrong?"

"Nothing," he said. "I was just hoping to go see him and have something . . . *good* to tell him, finally."

Julia's eyes widened. "That Walker is dead?"

"*Shh.*"

"Don't shush me, no one can hear me. You were hoping you'd have . . . taken care of Walker before you saw Nick again."

"Fine, yes."

"Nick wants to see you and court's in a week. You'll just have to go."

"I guess so."

Julia crossed her arms. "Once they have the hearing, if there's no deal, how soon are you going to do it?"

"Would you stop?"

"I will if you give me *something*. Anything. Tell me when. Not even a date—what time of day?"

62

RAYMOND WALKER, 2016

On January 15, 2016, at 6:00 p.m., clad in a bathrobe and scratching the stubble on his face, Raymond Walker came down his stairs and wondered, absently, why the lights were out in the living room below. He flicked the switch to his right as he stepped from the stairwell. The lamp in the living room snapped to life. In the same way one's peripheral vision might register the vague shape of a spider on the wall, out of place and threatening, Ray saw the figure of a man standing in the dark of his kitchen.

63

On January 16, 2016, Rice was pecking out a report at his computer when the receptionist paged him.

"Detective, there's a Darlene Walker calling about her son, Ray Walker, I thought you or Megan would want to take it."

"Yup," Rice said quickly.

"This is Detective John Rice."

"Yes, hello, Mr. Rice—Detective Rice—this is Darlene Walker. I'm calling regarding my son, Raymond." Her voice was full of nervous energy.

"Yes, ma'am."

"Well, something's happened to him, and somebody needs to get over here immediately."

Rice straightened. "What's happened to him?"

"I don't know, but I can't find him! I'm at his house, he gave me a key, and I let myself in when he didn't answer my calls or come to my house today—we were supposed to have lunch this afternoon, and he didn't show, didn't call, didn't answer when I called—"

"Ma'am, can you slow down a minute? You're—"

"No, *you* need to hurry up and get over here, you can't treat him any different just because you've made your mind up that he's a criminal, which

300

will be cleared in the courts, by the way, I'm confident of that. I tried calling the police where I live, but they said I had to call the police in Raymond's town, even though it seems like an obvious conflict of interest."

"All right, ma'am—*ma'am*." Rice paused until she finally stopped talking. "I'll be over shortly."

—⌐

Rice pulled up outside the small, gray house numbered *47*. So this was Raymond Walker's house. They'd never had probable cause to get a search warrant for anything besides Ray's DNA, which of course had been a match to the sexual assault kit. They'd also been able to do an inventory search of Ray's car, after towing it from the station lot after he was arrested. The search had yielded nothing of apparent value to the investigation involving Nick Hall.

Rice could see a light on inside as he walked up the short driveway to the back door—the front steps were unshoveled, and there was no discernable walkway to them. Ray's car was parked in the driveway.

Rice hadn't reached the door before it opened.

A woman around his age, give or take a few hard nights, leaned out toward him, immediately shivering in the cold. "Are you the detective I talked to?"

"Yeah." He offered his gloved hand to shake. "Should we go inside?"

"I'm not consenting to a search of the house." She pursed her lips and looked at him like a hundred people had before: like she thought she was a law professor.

"Understood. Just cold out." He smiled.

Darlene Walker turned back into the house, and Rice followed.

The mudroom was small but well organized. Tall shelves housed shoes and a box of scarves; heavy coats hung on a stand. Rice's boots squeaked on the floor as they moved into the kitchen.

"Ms. Walker, you said on the phone that you can't reach Ray and you expected to see him today."

"Yes, I was expecting—"

"I'm sorry to cut you off, but if I could ask a few specific questions. When did you last talk to Ray?"

"Friday morning, on the phone."

"Friday as in yesterday, or Friday as in a week ago?"

"Yesterday."

Rice noted *Friday, January 15*, on his pad.

"We made plans *yesterday* to have lunch *today*. He was supposed to pick me up."

"And he didn't."

"Nope."

"Do you have your phone with you?"

She narrowed her eyes in suspicion, like he might snatch it from her. "Why?"

"Some specific times would be helpful. Like what time you talked on the phone, what time you tried to reach him and couldn't."

She stood and pulled her cell phone from her purse on the counter. "We talked at ten sixteen yesterday."

"In the morning," Rice said as he wrote.

"Yes," she said like he was stupid. Sure it sounded like an obvious question, but people were always jumping around while they talked to him. Better to get it right and lock her in than wish later he'd been more thorough.

"Any contact since then?"

"No. I've tried, but he hasn't responded."

"When did you try?"

"Last night I texted him about something else, and then I texted him this morning about lunch."

"Times?"

She sighed. "Last night at eight twenty-seven I texted him. Nothing. Then this morning at eleven fifteen I texted him about what time he was getting to my house. Nothing. Then I started calling."

"Okay," Rice said. "He usually text you right back? My daughter isn't exactly reliable when it comes to answering my texts, is all."

"Same," Darlene said quietly.

"What time was he supposed to pick you up today?"

"Noon."

"How many times you call this morning?" This he asked more out of curiosity than anything.

She looked down at her phone. "Thirteen."

Seemed about right. "And what time you come here today?"

She continued to study her phone. "I can't drive right now, so I called a cab here at twelve thirty, and I must have been here before one."

"Why can't you drive?"

She looked up at him then and said tersely, "That's private."

"All right," Rice said with a shrug and smile. "Will you walk me through the house?"

Again, suspicion fell over her face. "I said I don't consent to a search of the house. There's nothing out of place."

"I don't need to open any drawers or touch his computer." *That will come later*, he thought with ugly satisfaction. "This is my job. I might see something you can't. If you really think something's happened to him."

Darlene stared at him. She looked like she was going to cry—for a moment he actually felt for her. She didn't know what to do, whether to trust him. Ray might have been her fault; her mistake unleashed on the world, on people like the Halls. But he was still her son, and Rice couldn't help pity her for that.

He used the pity to soften his face. "I give you my word," he said. "I'm not playing you."

Raymond Walker's mother walked Rice through the house. The first

303

floor was largely an open space that kept going back: the kitchen flowed into a living room with a small dining area, which stretched on into a room that looked like a sunroom that had been opened up and better insulated. There was a bathroom, a spare bedroom, and a couple closets on the first floor as well. All was clean and orderly; there were no signs of an altercation, or an abrupt departure.

Darlene took Rice up the stairs to the master bedroom and bathroom. The second floor was smaller than the first, but the suite was quite large. It occupied the whole floor. All appeared quiet here as well.

At Rice's request, Darlene opened the closet to show him her son's suitcase. Rice also noted what looked like a gym bag in the corner of the room, next to the hamper.

"He have any other bags?"

"No, I got him the suitcase for his birthday two years ago. He wanted to get rid of his old one—it had a broken wheel, or it was squeaky or something. I think it wouldn't roll. So this is the only one—it's the one I bought him." Not quite what he'd asked, and way more detail than he needed, but it was hard to say whether it was suspicious. It seemed to be how the woman talked in general.

She stood next to her son's bed with her arms crossed, rocking heel to toe. "So now do you believe me?" Her face was oddly smug. Was it because she thought she was pulling one over on him, or because she was the kind of person who would take some satisfaction in being proven right about anything, including her son's disappearance?

Rice stepped into the bathroom. Toothbrush on the sink. Darlene was in the doorway behind him with her eyebrows raised up, as though she were asking, *Well?*

"He say anything to you about going away?"

"He's followed all your little rules."

"Anyone else who might know where he is? His lawyer?"

Darlene expelled a laugh like a cough. "He wouldn't tell her."

"Why not?"

"She's part of the whole racket. She's in on it as much as you are. At least you don't pretend to be on his side."

He thought of Britny Cressey's phone call. Walker was fighting with his lawyer, unhappy with how she was handling things. Maybe he'd skipped town. If he had, Rice needed to move. He needed to freeze the house and have a crew come in—and Darlene needed to go. "Let's head downstairs, I need to call the station."

He motioned for Darlene to take the stairs first.

"What are you going to do?"

"Try to find your son." He motioned again.

"And you'll be looking into all the people who've been threatening him online and in the papers and on the radio, and all the real sex offenders who live around here, and that boy who lied about the rape in the first place?"

"Yes, we'll look into all those things. But you need to leave now."

"I'm going to wait here in case he comes home."

Rice took a step toward her, and he towered over her. She stunk of stale smoke. "No, Ms. Walker. You need to leave the house."

"Actually, Detective, you can go to hell." She'd inexplicably held up her fingers in air quotes as she'd said *Detective*. Her body jerked strangely as she pounded over to her son's bed and sat. "You're just using this as an excuse to search the house. It's illegal, and I *will* be calling your supervisor."

"You're more than welcome, but you need to get up from that bed and leave this house immediately, or I'll arrest you for obstructing." There was no time to do this gently. If Walker had run, every minute was going to count. And if he hadn't . . .

Darlene stared at him, her eyes brimming with hatred.

"You want to wait for Ray, that's fine. You pick: do it from your house or a jail cell."

She jerked up from the bed and blew past him with a flurry of threats of getting a lawyer and suing his department and taking his badge, her voice hoarse with tears.

Rice reached the ground floor just as Darlene was making her exit. She held her coat in one hand and her purse in the other. She waived the purse at Rice and shouted, "You're treating my son like a goddamn criminal!" She slammed the door behind her.

Rice strode to the door and locked it. From the kitchen window, he could see Darlene walking down the driveway, doing something with her hands. At the base of the driveway she turned, a fresh cigarette between her lips. She frowned at the house bitterly, said something, then began to peck at her phone as she walked up the road. He'd forgotten she needed to wait for a ride. Well, there was a gas station and a coffee place out on the main drag, she could wait there. He felt sick to his stomach. Was it Darlene? No. It was this house. Something had happened here. Ray could have made a run for it, but he was too arrogant to do that, wasn't he? Not to mention that he seemed to have left everything behind.

And of course, there was the trouble of the threat. Someone with every reason to hate Walker had been to this house and threatened to kill him. Tony Hall didn't seem the type, but when it really came down to it, no one ever did.

64

Detective Rice came unannounced this time. He'd done that before, Julia supposed as she welcomed him in, but this felt different. The police must have known Walker was missing. He didn't want to give them time to get their stories straight.

The detective arrived after breakfast on Sunday. Julia and Tony hadn't slept at all on Friday, and she'd spent Saturday obsessively watching her phone and starting violently each time it buzzed. Tony begged her to try to relax, but it was pointless. Then Sunday morning came, and their detective was at the door.

He rejected Julia's offer of coffee as he pulled off his heavy winter boots. Tony took his coat and sent the kids upstairs to read in their rooms. The three of them sat in the living room—Julia and Tony together on the couch, Detective Rice in a chair beside them.

He sat, apparently thinking for a moment, then reached into his pants pocket and produced his silver tape recorder.

"Ray Walker is missing."

The bluntness of his approach startled Julia, and she hoped it showed on her face. She looked at Tony, who looked back at her. "What?" she asked, as Tony said, "Missing how?"

"Missing like missing." He studied them overtly. "I need to ask you some questions, and I'd like to record it."

"All right," Tony said.

Detective Rice fingered the recorder and set it down on the coffee table.

"Like I said, Ray Walker is missing. I'd like you to account for your whereabouts Friday and Saturday of this week. Yesterday and the day before."

Julia looked to her husband. All three of them knew that Tony was the "you" he'd addressed.

"Um," Tony said with a shake of his head, "Friday I left work early and went to see Nick up at Goodspring, and yesterday we were home all day. Besides the library for a bit in the afternoon."

"What time were you at work Friday?"

"From about eight to two." Tony looked at Julia, and she nodded. A jolt of adrenaline rocketed through her—did he see her nod? Did they look rehearsed?

"And Goodspring?"

Her veins hummed as Tony answered. "Four to eight. A little after eight, actually. Maybe eight ten or something."

"And then?"

"Then home." Tony nodded at Julia. "I was here a little after ten, right?"

She cleared her throat. Her face was numb. "Yes, a little after ten."

Detective Rice looked her in the eye, and miraculously she held fast. He nodded and wrote on his pad.

"As for yesterday," Tony started, but the detective interrupted him.

"Make any stops on the way home?"

"No," Tony said. "No, I left a little after eight and came straight home. It's like a two-hour drive back from Belfast."

"Goodspring make you sign in for visits?"

Tony paused. "Yeah, they do."

"And work?"

Tony said nothing. He was staring at the coffee table.

Julia rested a hand on his thigh. "Honey?"

"Sorry," Tony said. "What?"

"You have a way to confirm when you were at work?"

"I don't, like, punch in or anything," Tony said, "but I'm sure the receptionist can vouch I was there until two. She tracks our calendars."

"And yesterday it was just you two and the kids all day?" The detective's eyes flicked up at the ceiling, and Julia wondered if he was going to ask to speak to them.

"They went to my mom's for a sleepover on Friday," Julia said. "She dropped them off Saturday morning, I can't remember when."

"Maybe nine or ten," Tony said.

They both knew it had been 9:17 a.m.—they'd been watching the clock obsessively that morning. But knowing anything too specific would sound bad.

"We can't get everything perfect," Julia had whispered in the hazy hours between Friday and Saturday. They laid in bed, Tony's head on her chest, her shirt wet with his tears. Her voice had been so calm then. "They'll have to question us because they know you threatened him. You have Goodspring, though."

Tony had nodded against her chest.

"It will take time for them to decide you must have been with Nick. Before that, they'll question us. We can't look like we knew this was coming. We need to act unsure of things, but only in the smallest ways."

Detective Rice was circling something on his notepad. Maybe he'd call Marjorie to confirm that Tony was home when she dropped off the kids Saturday morning. Maybe the police didn't know yet that Walker was long gone by morning. Julia straightened her posture to mask the shudder that had wormed up her spine.

It would be okay. It would be okay. The sign-in sheet at Goodspring would place Tony there from 2:00 p.m. to 8:00 p.m. The drive back down south was two hours. For now, that left Julia as the only witness to Tony's late Friday night and early Saturday morning hours. It was far from airtight—she'd lie for him, anyone had to assume that. But the police would figure it out eventually: that Tony had an alibi for the time that mattered.

"Julia." Detective Rice turned his body with his attention. "You were home when Tony got in Friday night?"

"Yes," she said. And she had been. She'd sat in the dining room, television blaring in the next room, and waited. Even now her stomach tightened, remembering how near she'd felt to vomiting as she waited for him to come home.

"And when do you remember him home?"

"Just a few minutes after ten." He held her eye for a beat. Should she say more? "I only know that because I was watching normal cable. And a new show had just started, so it was probably, like, ten oh three? I was waiting for him to come home. So I could hear about how it went with Nick." Tony took her hand and squeezed it. She was talking too much.

"And from when he got home to the kids getting in, did either of you leave the house at any point?"

"No," she said. "We just talked about his visit with Nick and went to bed."

Detective Rice retrieved the recorder from the coffee table and stopped it. He pocketed the silver bar, along with his little notebook and pen.

She walked him to the door, where he pulled on his boots and coat. As she watched him trudge down the front walk, it occurred to her that he hadn't separated them, like she would have expected. He'd asked his questions of both of them at once, allowing her to hear Tony's answers and simply confirm them. He hadn't asked questions about her at all.

He thought they were innocent. Or maybe he just wanted them to be.

65

Julia walked the detective to the door. From the couch, Tony could see Detective Rice pulling on his boots, tying the laces in silence.

Leave leave leave leave LEAVE—it was filling Tony's mouth, straining against his teeth he was so close to screaming it.

The door shut.

Tony stood. "Jesus Christ. Oh, Christ."

"Shh," Julia hissed from the hallway. "Keep your voice down."

"I don't think it matters. I don't think anything matters."

Now she was in the doorway to the living room. "What are you talking about?"

Tony's mouth was running, tripping over hot breath. "I fucked it all up."

"You didn't fuck anything up, you did fine. You're just upset. Take a breath."

"No, not today. I fucked up that day."

"How?"

Tony walked through the dining room, bumping against a chair. "If they think he's dead, that's it. I'm it. They'll be after me."

Julia followed him into the kitchen. "Take a breath, I can barely understand you."

He groaned, ran his hands through his hair. "What good is an alibi if there's no time attached to it?"

Someone was pounding down the stairs. The kids were yelling over each other about movies they wanted to watch.

Julia's voice was low but laser-focused. "What are you saying?"

"At Goodspring," Tony whispered as the kids rushed down the hall. "I forgot to fill in the sign-out time."

66

As Rice drove away from the Hall home late Sunday morning, he called the unit's head evidence technician, Tanya Smith, for an update on Walker's house.

Smith's voice betrayed her tendency to polish off a pack of Marlboro Lights over the course of a single shift. "We've got a cell phone," she said. "O'Malley's getting a warrant, but I doubt it'll matter. It's an iPhone. It'll have a passcode. Unless it's his mother's birthday I doubt we'll get in."

Rice grunted. With the advent of the smartphone came a whole universe of juicy evidence, but only if you could get to it. Nothing would convince Apple to let law enforcement past a passcode, warrant or not. You could probably have someone producing child porn with the phone itself and they wouldn't budge. The phone was a dead end.

"We've covered the ground floor of the house at this point. Williams collected some prints; so far I've come up dry on fluids." She chuckled at the joke he'd heard her make at least twice before.

Rice started to sign off. He wanted to call Goodspring. "Thanks, Tanya."

Down the line he heard the scrape of a lighter. Smith talked around a cigarette. "I say I was finished?"

"You smoking all over my crime scene?"

Smith laughed her witch's cackle. "Fuck the fuck off." He knew she'd be out in the street, far away from the scene.

"Might be nothing," she said, her tone cautious. "Basak canvassed the street, and the lady next door says she saw two men walking down the street on Friday night."

"Really," Rice breathed.

"Yeah, around seven thirty. Going down the street, away from the direction of her house and Walker's."

"She make out any details?"

"Average height and build, maybe one a bit bulkier. Couldn't make out skin tone or hair color or anything like that. It was already dark, and I don't think she paid them too much attention."

"But she thinks it was seven thirty?"

"That's what she said."

By the time they hung up, Rice had parked himself at a Dunkin' Donuts. He called O'Malley, and she forwarded him to voice mail. A minute later his phone buzzed: she'd texted,

Call you soon.

He pulled through the drive-through and ordered a small: two creams, two sugars.

A night ago, O'Malley meticulously sent out Walker's identifying information and mug shot to all the cab companies, bus depots, train stations, and airports in New England, and now she was following up by phone. That Walker had gotten antsy and skipped town was the simplest explanation, but Walker seemed incapable of seeing how guilty he looked. He'd spewed confidence everywhere he could—to the newspaper, the radio, social media. In the last article Rice read on the case, sometime in the last couple of weeks, his lawyer sounded like she was armed for bear. But then, Britny Cressey said Walker was panicking. Someone who did what Walker did to Nick Hall—that kind of person was good at hiding his true intentions, wasn't he? Come to think of it, Walker's incessant chatter about his innocence could have been a distraction. A long-term plan to take off could even explain why he'd reported the incident with Tony Hall but didn't press charges—to muddy the waters of his planned disappearance.

A lanky boy passed Rice his coffee through the window. He drove around the building, back into the lot and parked.

Two men, one a bit bigger and bulkier. That could be two brothers.

But the men were seen at seven thirty. Tony Hall couldn't have been walking down a street in Salisbury then if he really was at Goodspring from four to eight. Even if the neighbor was a bit off on the time, it was something like a two-hour drive from Nick's program back to Salisbury. Rice found the number for Goodspring Psychiatric Center online, and his stomach fluttered as he pressed to call.

The man who answered wasn't working on Friday night, but he was happy to check the sheet.

"I have a Tony Hall here on January fifteenth at four p.m. sharp."

"And the out time?"

"It's not filled in."

"It's *not* filled in," Rice repeated.

"Correct, sir."

"So no way to tell when he left." A neat little alibi evaporating on the spot.

"You could talk to whoever worked the desk. I think it's Ida but I'll make sure. Or you could speak to the patient he saw, if you know who it was, but I can't give—"

"Is it normal to see the out time left blank?"

"Yeah, or at least not *not* normal. I tell people when they come in to sign out when they leave. At the end of the shift I go down the list and make sure everybody's gone. But sometimes people forget. I remind people if I notice them forgetting as they're leaving. It's really just record keeping and security, knowing who's in the building."

"Can a visitor duck out without you seeing?"

"I guess anything's possible, but unless I'm in the can, I'm at the desk. And if he came in a car, he'd need his keys back."

"You hold the keys?"

"Yup."

Rice asked the man to find out who was working on Friday and have that person call his cell. He asked about security footage of the entrance, but the man said he should call back during the week to talk to the right person about that.

Rice hung up and sipped at his coffee. At first the convenience of Tony's alibi had bothered him, but it wasn't shaping up to be so convenient after all. If it turned out that Walker simply took off, all this signing-out business didn't much matter. But if Walker turned up dead in the woods, well, Tony Hall was an obvious suspect. Rice set his coffee down in the cupholder. It was giving him a stomachache. That this all might spell trouble for Tony's family—Julia, their kids, Nick—didn't make any difference. That was the judge's job: to decide how to sentence a family man who'd snapped, done something monstrous, but maybe understandable to on some level. That wasn't Rice's concern. First it was the judge's problem, and ultimately it was God's. Rice's job was easier. He didn't have to weigh right and wrong—didn't get to. He just had to find the truth.

67

JULIA HALL, 2016

The sound brought Julia to her feet before she recognized that her phone was ringing. With it came a rush of acid up the back of her throat. She slammed her hand down on the phone on the table in front of her. *Please*, she thought, *please be anyone but—*

It was Nick.

"Is Tony there?" he asked.

"No, he's not." Julia walked into the kitchen from the dining room where she'd been sitting. Tony was upstairs taking a cold shower, still trying to calm down after the detective's visit. She didn't want him hearing her on the phone when he got out. It would just stress him out more.

"Is everything okay?"

No, she thought as she stepped into the mudroom and shut the door behind her. Far from it. "Why, has someone called you?"

"I tried him first, but he didn't answer. Where is he?"

"Nick. Tell me why you're asking."

"The front desk guy said a detective called asking about Tony."

Julia kicked the kids' shoes out of her way as she began to pace the length of the mudroom. "Have you talked to them yet?"

"The police?"

"Yes," Julia breathed.

"No, are they gonna call me? What's going on?"

There was no reason not to tell him, was there? It would look strange of her not to, if the police *did* talk to Nick and they found out he'd talked to Julia but she hadn't mentioned it.

Nick spoke again. "Is something going on with *him*?" It was a "him" reserved only for Raymond Walker.

"Maybe." She nudged a shoe against the wall with her right foot. "He's missing."

Nick's voice was quiet. "Ray's missing?"

"Yeah. Detective Rice came to the house this morning and told us. They can't find him."

There was silence.

"Nick?"

"Yeah?"

Her stomach rolled. She took a deep breath; the mudroom smelled like wet rubber and stale feet. "Tell me Tony was with you on Friday."

"He was."

"Until eight."

Nick paused. "Did he tell you what we talked about?"

Yes. He told her everything. Too late for her to do a thing about it, but he told her everything.

"I don't know how much we should talk right now," she said. The possibility that the program monitored residents' phone calls seemed slim, but there was no way she was going to risk it. They couldn't talk details. But there was one thing she *had* to say. It wasn't fair to ask a single thing of Nick. Not after everything that had happened to him; after everything that had been taken from him. But she had to make sure he'd give the right answer if he was asked.

"They might call you," she said. "To ask if Tony was there until after eight on Friday. It looks like they're checking up on him, because, you know. But like he told them, he was with you until sometime after eight on Friday."

There was a beat. "Yeah, he was."

"I guess he didn't fill in the sign-out sheet. So they might ask you when he left."

"Okay. I'll tell them."

Julia slumped against the door to the kitchen; it was cool on her back. What she would have given to get off the phone now. To be able to run out into the back field and scream. To collapse on the floor with the dirty shoes. To cry. Why couldn't she cry? Her belly was full of salt water—all the tears she had swallowed that weekend. She and Tony had always been good at calibrating: when one went up, the other came down. Tony was a wreck right now, so she was the anchor. She didn't even have to work for it. It just happened; she just was. She didn't want to be. She wanted to scream and cry and run. She wanted to expel everything that was inside her.

"What a mess," she said.

"What do I do now?"

What *was* Nick supposed to do? How could they burden him with this? He was in a facility, for Christ's sake. He'd tried to overdose on his antidepressants. He'd been cutting himself. Keeping a secret had nearly killed him. What the fuck was he supposed to do with this?

And then she thought of what Tony told her, about his last conversation with Nick. The last things they said to each other before he got in the car and drove south. Nick was tired of being babied. Tired of everyone handling him with kid gloves, acting like the rape proved he was weak. And she knew, maybe, how he could survive one more secret.

"It's your turn to protect Tony."

68

Rice pulled up to Walker's house late Monday morning. The driveway was taped off, deterring anyone from adding to the footprints in the snow there. The crew had been using the front door to get in and out. Searching a potential crime scene always meant causing some amount of damage to that scene. Because the front walk had been totally print-free on the day Rice met Darlene Walker at the house, that was the path they chose to walk.

Earlier that morning, Rice and O'Malley had met at the station first thing, and they ran through their plans for the day. Rice was going to check in with the evidence team finishing up at the house. O'Malley was going to keep calling all the travel spots, trying to keep the pressure on them to check their surveillance systems and passenger lists.

Before he'd had a chance to call Tanya Smith for an update, Smith texted Rice and asked him to meet her at the house—there was something he needed to see. Smith enjoyed the drama of an in-person reveal, but she'd have told him if he called and asked her what she found. Rice hadn't wanted to call—he hadn't wanted to know whatever it was any sooner than he needed to. He also didn't want to admit to himself how poorly he'd slept the night before, worrying about what Tony Hall might have done to Walker.

By the time Rice got out of the car, officer Mike Basak was waiting for him in the front door of the house. He was the uniform who had talked to the neighbor about the two men she thought she saw in the area on Friday. Now, Basak waved Rice up the front walkway.

"I collected some shoe prints in the driveway and at the side door," Basak said, "so I'll need to get a print of your boots at some point, since you were here with the mother. He's got a lot of shoes inside, so they could all turn out to be his, but you never know till you know." He shrugged and handed Rice a pair of covers for his shoes so he could go into the house. "Starting to look like we could have a crime scene, though. Smith wants you in the upstairs bathroom."

From the top steps of the stairs to Walker's bedroom, Rice could see Tanya Smith in the dim bathroom on the far side of the room. Smith had blocked the window over the tub, casting the space into shadows.

"You rang," Rice said.

Smith stood up and stepped out of view to grab something. Her voice echoed off the high ceiling as she said, "You know where this is going."

Rice's stomach did a slow barrel roll, and he pictured a tub filled with the glow of a body's worth of luminol. He forced the usual chitchat. "Bad cleanup job?"

"Yep," Smith said as she stepped from the bathroom. She held her camera in her right hand, the strap swinging. They met in the center of the bedroom, a faint waft of stale cigarettes on her hair. On the LCD screen of her camera, she pressed Play on a video. It showed the darkened bathroom with a hint of luminol glowing on the lip of the bathtub and a larger smear on the floor beneath.

"Fatal?"

"No," Smith said. The video moved up to the inside of the tub to show it spotless. "We found a bloody towel in the waste bin, so I swept the bathroom but this was all that flared. The smear is only about the size of a hand towel, not a fatal amount of blood loss here. It's more the location that gets me—don't exactly look like a shaving injury."

"No," Rice agreed as he moved to the edge of the bathroom. The glow of the luminol was long gone, but he wanted to see the tub. It was an old-fashioned claw-foot bathtub standing alone in the middle of the room—there was a separate shower in the right corner of the bathroom. Sink in the left corner. So there had been blood on the outer lip of the tub and on the floor beneath. Standard bathroom injuries were cutting yourself shaving like Smith said, maybe slipping in the tub and hitting your head—but not the *outside* of the tub, leaving you bleeding on the floor.

"He's got a basement with a utility sink and a washer/dryer," Smith said. "I thought you'd want to join while I check the rest of the hot spots."

Rice's cell buzzed and rang in his coat pocket. "Yeah," he said absently as he pulled out the phone—Belfast area code. He waved the screen at Smith and said, "Goodspring."

He crossed the bedroom and went down to the kitchen as he took the call.

It was Ida, she said, from the front desk at Goodspring. Her voice was friendly, if a little anxious. "They said to call you?"

Rice introduced himself. "Were you working the desk this past Friday?"

"Yeah."

"Did a man named Tony Hall come in to see his brother?"

"I'm not supposed to reveal who's a patient here—"

"Well, I just meant—"

"But," she said, "Tony Hall did come on Friday."

"Okay. He show you an ID?"

"He didn't need to. I've seen him here before. Not a face you forget." The woman laughed nervously.

"He's not bad-looking," Rice said.

"Nope. Is he in trouble?"

"Do you remember when he left on Friday?"

"They said you were asking about the sign-out time. He was here so late I had packed up to leave; I think that's how I forgot to have him sign out."

"How late was it?"

"Visiting hours end at eight, it was probably a few minutes after that."

"A few minutes meaning?"

"Eight ten, maybe."

So Tony was at Goodspring until after eight. A two-hour drive away. *Maybe* he could shave off fifteen minutes with a lead foot.

Ida went on. "He and his, uh, the person he was visiting, they were having a serious conversation, I didn't want to rush them, but eventually I had to kick him out."

"What were they talking about?"

"I don't know. What's going on?"

"Why do you say it was a serious conversation?" Rice said.

She paused. "The way they looked, I guess. I could see them from the desk. It looked like they were fighting, at one point."

"Did you hold his car keys when he signed in?"

"Yeah, we have to."

"And could you see him the whole time he was there?"

She paused. "Well, the visits aren't, like, supervised. So I wasn't watching them the whole time."

"But are they happening near your desk?"

"Mostly the visits are in the visiting room, which I can see part of. But Tony Hall went back with a staff person first."

Rice thanked Ida and asked her to call back if she thought of anything else. Someone might be in touch with her about a written statement. She sounded disappointed to hang up with him. Maybe he'd misidentified the tone of her voice when she first called. Instead of nerves, maybe it was excitement in her voice. She wanted to have something important to say—wanted something to be going on, like she kept asking. But if Tony Hall was at Goodspring until after eight, he couldn't have been one of the men on Walker's street at seven thirty. They might have had nothing to do with this, but it felt like *something*. Whatever it was, did it involve the blood in the bathroom?

"Smith," he yelled up the stairs. "Ready for the basement when—"

His phone started up again and he laughed aloud. It never ends.

O'Malley's name was on the screen this time. "Hold on," he yelled up to Smith.

Rice turned back to the kitchen counter. He answered gravely. "I've got blood in Walker's bathroom and nothing but questions."

"They'll have to wait," O'Malley said. "I've got Walker."

69

JULIA HALL, 2016

I n the back seat, Seb's sweet voice was muffled by the cotton scarf
he'd been sucking on. "Could we play tag when we get home?"

Julia eyed him in the rearview as she drove. There was a wet patch
in the center of the scarf, where his mouth was.

"It's too snowy," Chloe said as she reached over and tugged his scarf
down.

"So?" Seb replied.

"I want to make a fort," Chloe said.

Seb squealed. "Will you help, Mumma?"

Julia grimaced at the mirror. "I'm not feeling very well, honey. I think
I need to stay in."

"What's wrong?" Chloe asked.

"I just have a headache. I'm going to put away the groceries and rest
for a bit." Julia twisted her hands back and forth on the steering wheel.
"You two can play outside, though." She wanted to give the kids some
semblance of normalcy while she and Tony were so upset, but there was
no way she could romp around in the snow today. She'd barely managed
to pull on real pants and go to the grocery store before she got the kids
from the bus stop.

Julia steered into the driveway and parked. The kids unbuckled themselves as she grabbed the two totes of groceries in the trunk.

Seb streaked by her, but Chloe paused at the gate. "Will you watch us?"

"For a minute," she said.

Chloe grinned and ran after her brother.

Julia paused at the fence and set the bags down in the snow. Chloe ran for the edge of the yard, to the spot where crocuses exploded from the earth every spring. They were buried now, sleeping deep under the snow. Julia felt, for a moment, that she had forgotten that the spring even existed. She had forgotten that everything, to some degree, was finite. Even the bleak winter that had, just days ago, seemed endless, would end.

Seb yelped as he ran after Chloe, trying to keep up. The two tracked their boot prints all over the backyard. Behind them, the rolling fields of Orange stretched until they touched the snowy tree line.

The earth would yawn and stretch in the spring, and everything would change again. Everything but one: what had happened would never change.

Complicit. It was such a persistent word. The sun came up that morning, white-yellow and cold, and they'd made it to Monday, and now she'd be complicit for the rest of her life. She'd never be *good* again. The kids dropped to their knees and buried their hands into the snow.

A dagger of a thought sliced down the center of Julia's brain, and *complicit* was a lie. *Complicit* was too soft, too quiet, for this. Her ears began to ring, an electronic hum that grew louder, the yard before her began to dim. Julia grabbed the fence post. Squeezed it as hard as she could. For a moment the sensation of wood against her palm was the only thing she could feel. Her knees buckled but she stayed on her feet. She hung onto the post, and the world came back in, slow and warm in her ears. When her head had steadied, she straightened up and looked back out at the yard. The kids hadn't noticed; they were scraping the snow into a mound.

Julia's heart pounded, but her stomach was settling, her vision was clear, and she loosened her grip on the fence. Her children were safe. Tony was safe. They were safe. They were whole. That was all that mattered. The rest would get easier. Spring would come, and she would forget who she'd become in the winter.

Julia turned to pick up her grocery totes. One of them had tipped over; she crouched to scoop the spilled oranges and bread back into the bag. As she stood, a dark car drove past the house and down the lane. She thought nothing of it and went into the house.

70

I know what happened," Rice had said. It felt like minutes had passed since he'd spoken, but it had probably been a matter of seconds. "I've always wondered if you knew, too." *Well, no longer*, he thought. The sheer shock on her face told him everything: for all these years, she'd never known that he'd figured it out. She had no idea that she'd made him an accomplice to her crime. She was responsible for the most colossal sin he'd committed in his days on earth, and she hadn't even known it. At least, not until this moment.

Julia sat beside him, bottom lip dropped open, revealing a trembling row of teeth.

What must she have been feeling? A small part of him wanted to punish her—to let her wither under his words. Compared to his years of burdensome knowledge, years of praying for forgiveness for a sin that was perpetual, Rice thought a moment of suffering was a short sentence indeed.

"Enough." The word was harsh, and she started. "I want to hear it."

"What?" she whispered.

"I want to hear it from you. Tell me what I already know. Tell me what happened on the day he went missing."

IV.

LUCKY

—∽

Don't try to make life a mathematics problem with yourself in the center and everything coming out equal. When you're good, bad things can still happen. And if you're bad, you can still be lucky.

BARBARA KINGSOLVER, *THE POISONWOOD BIBLE*

71

TONY HALL, 2016

At 4:00 p.m. on the day Raymond Walker would go missing, Tony Hall arrived at Goodspring. The pretty woman at the front desk perked up as he came through the door. She looked like she was in her forties, with stiff blond hair she'd had back in a clip each time he'd come in. There was always an air about her, as if she knew everything going on with Nick and she wanted Tony to know it.

"Mr. Hall, right?"

"Yeah," Tony said as he pounded his boots on the mat.

"Your brother's primary worker said to expect you. She's here today."

"Is she not normally?"

"Oh, no, she is. I just mean she's here for your meeting with Nick."

The woman's face begged him to ask why. Instead, he said, "Oh, okay," and he slid his car keys across the counter toward her.

She scooped up the keys and pushed the sign-in sheet toward him. It probably made her feel important, working there, getting to dip her toes into the drama of other people's lives.

She pulled the sheet back and said, "I'll let Anne Marie know you're here."

A couple had come in behind him, and Tony stepped away from the desk. He stood to the side, fixated on the double doors the woman had motioned toward a couple of times as they spoke.

After a minute, a woman appeared at those doors. She looked just about Nick's age; too young to be his therapist, or whatever she was.

"Mr. Hall?"

Tony went to her quickly.

"I'm Anne Marie." They shook hands, and the woman turned to start walking down the hallway. "I'm Nick's primary mental health worker here. Nick is looking forward to seeing you."

"Is something going on?" Tony still didn't know why Nick had asked him to come visit.

"Well, since you were coming up, Nick asked if we could do a little group session. He wants to talk to you about something." She pointed to a door they were fast approaching. "I'm really just here for support. We won't be too long, and then you two can move to the visiting area."

She opened the door without pause. Nick was sitting in a small chair on the opposite side of the room, his curly hair glowing in the low sun of late afternoon.

He stood to hug Tony. Tony had grown used to Nick's new, tense embrace, and he began to release his arms after a single squeeze. Nick held fast, though, and Tony looked to the side of his face, brought his arms back around his little brother, closed his eyes, and hugged him deeply for the first time in as long as he could remember. It was the kind of hug that sank into his chest.

When they released each other, Anne Marie was sitting behind a small desk near the door, and she motioned for Tony to sit beside Nick.

"What's going on?" Tony said to Nick.

Nick looked at Anne Marie.

"Nick?" she said.

"I guess I wanted to talk to you about some stuff."

"About that night?"

"No. About us."

"Oh." The knot in Tony's stomach loosened. He looked over at Anne Marie. "Oh, are we doing therapy?"

Anne Marie laughed, and Nick smiled nervously. "If that's okay?"

"Yeah," Tony said. "Sure."

"I just wanted to talk to you about something, and I feel like whenever I try to, I get all jumbled in my head. But when I'm with Anne Marie, or when I was with Jeff, I could talk about it better."

"It's really fine. What do you want to talk to me about?"

"I'm so scared to sound like I'm blaming you."

The knot returned. "For what?"

"I'm not, though. Please try to listen, please try to hear me, because I don't blame you for a single thing. You have done more for me than Dad or my mom ever has. More than I think they could—I don't think they're capable of love in a normal way. But this isn't about them or what's wrong with them. I'm so lucky I have you—I'd be fucked without you."

"Okay," Tony said.

Nick looked at Anne Marie, and she nodded at him.

"Sometimes, I feel like you baby me."

Oh. This was not news. Tony felt his hackles going up.

"I know you were young when you started taking care of me. You were younger than I am now. And I *was* a baby. I was helpless. All a baby can do is rely on the people around it. But I'm not a baby anymore."

"I know you aren't."

"Tony," Anne Marie said. "If you could let Nick finish what he needs to say, that would be really helpful."

"Sorry."

"It's okay." Nick's eyes welled. "Please don't apologize for anything you've ever done for me. I just need you to know that I need to feel like I'm taking care of myself now. When Ray raped me, that was the most powerless moment of my entire life. I felt like every fear I've ever had was

333

confirmed. I was weak. I wasn't a man. I couldn't stop whatever bad things people wanted to do to me—I could be used. I could even be killed, if he'd wanted to do that, and for part of that night, I thought he did. You remember how Dad was about me being gay. I felt like everything he'd ever said I was, Ray made me in that moment.

"And I'm never gonna get better if I can't start believing what Jeff and Anne Marie and all of you keep telling me. That it *wasn't* my fault. That it had nothing to do with who I am.

"And the more you say stuff to me like you wish you'd been there, you would have stopped him, you'll take care of me—the more you say that stuff, the more I feel like I'm still a victim. Like I can't save myself."

"Nick," Tony said quietly, and Nick nodded. Tony could speak now.

"I'm so sorry. I'm so sorry for how I've treated you. I swear, I know it doesn't change what I did, but I swear it doesn't match how I see you myself."

While Nick was talking, Anne Marie had gotten up to hand Tony a tissue. It was soaked through now, but he kept wiping his nose with it anyway.

"You are the best man I know. I am in awe of you." Tony hung his head. "I'm so stupid."

"No," Anne Marie said.

Tony looked at her in surprise. How could she not hate him after what she'd just heard?

"Nick and I have had a lot of time together," she said. "You want to know what I think?"

Tony looked at Nick. Nick nodded.

"I think you grew up in an unsafe home with a dad who was withholding, cruel, and unpredictably violent, until your mom took you away. And then, when you were a teenager, and you were figuring out who you were, you saw that same dad have another kid, and that kid didn't have a mom like yours. And you decided to be his hero."

Nick cleared his throat. "Jeff was talking about that one day with me. I asked him about, like, what would happen to me later. Like, would I become violent, because of what Ray did. And Jeff was saying that people who are hurt by other people, like abused, sometimes they have a hard time not getting hurt over and over after that. And sometimes they start hurting other people. But sometimes they get kind of obsessed with helping other people. And Jeff was talking about me and him, but I think that's what you did."

"I did think I was helping," Tony said to Nick. "I've only ever wanted to keep you safe."

"I love you for that. But you can't protect me from everything."

That was obvious. Look at what had happened.

"I want us to figure out a new way to be without me feeling . . . fragile every time I talk to you."

Tony blew his nose into the tissue. "Okay."

Nick reached for Tony's hand and squeezed it three times.

Tony squeezed back four.

72

At 5:30 p.m. on the day Raymond Walker would go missing, Tony and Nick entered the visiting room together. They went straight for the corner cabinet and selected a pile of games. Then they sat at a table and played checkers, then cribbage, then war, then Connect 4, then checkers again. Games had always been their favorite way to suspend reality when Ron and Jeannie were drunk or fighting, or when school felt like too much for one of them. Since that fall, *everything* had seemed too much, too heavy, too hard to do together. Nick hoped it would get easier.

"I've decided to go forward with it." Nick hopped Tony's checker piece and plucked it from the board. "At least for now."

"The case?"

Nick nodded.

"You're sure you want to do that?"

Nick eyed him.

Tony held up his hands. "Sorry, sorry. Your choice, and I trust you."

"If it gets too hard again, I can always tell them I'm done."

"But everyone will know."

That was true. Nick was sure his absence from the school had not erased everyone's memory that he was the one in the story. And the new story—the real story—would be in the news again. He would have to contend with what people thought of him. What they thought it said about him, as a man, to have failed to stop Ray. What they thought it said about him as a *person* to have hidden the truth. Whether they believed him at all.

"I know," Nick said. "But it's my fight to have, if I want it. And I do."

Tony rubbed a finger on a checker for a moment before he spoke. "You really want to go through it all? A whole year of this? A trial?"

"Yes," Nick said.

Tony moved the piece forward. "It's not what I would have chosen for you."

Nick laughed. "You're such a dad."

Tony's face lightened with surprise, and he laughed, too.

"It could settle," Tony said.

"I mean, it didn't, but it could later."

"I thought the court date got moved to next week."

"No, it was a few days ago. Julia didn't tell you?"

Across the board, Tony looked at Nick like this was news to him.

"Wow. You must have been being *insufferable* about my case."

Tony sighed. "You don't even know."

His brother didn't look angry, so Nick smiled. "I really meant for her to tell you." He'd called her the same day . . . wait a minute. The same day she told him that Tony wanted to come see him at Goodspring. "Why did you come visit today?"

"You wanted me to," Tony said.

Nick laughed. "Your wife is *sneaky*. I didn't ask you to come here. The second I told her the case didn't settle, she said *you* wanted to come see *me*."

"Really?"

"Guess she thought it would be good for me to tell you myself. That or she just didn't want to have to do it."

Tony sat back from the board and crossed his arms. "I don't blame either of you. I haven't exactly been . . . levelheaded about all of this. Did she say anything about me, or what we talked about today?"

"No," Nick said honestly. "I wanted to do this. We needed to talk."

Tony held Nick's eye for a minute then moved a piece forward on the board. "So there's no deal, and you *really* want to do this your own way, with court."

"Yep. Will you come with me the next time there's a hearing?"

"Of course. I'll do whatever you want me to."

"You sure you can take it? Is your head leveling out?"

"Yeah," Tony said. "You've set me straight."

"Thank God," Nick said as he jumped another piece of Tony's. "I was starting to worry you'd do something stupid."

73

JULIA HALL, 2016

A t 6:00 p.m. on the day Raymond Walker would go missing, Julia Hall was standing in the kitchen of a man she didn't know, a single sweaty palm gripping his counter, when she heard him descending the stairs.

He stepped from the stairwell, and a lamp went on in the corner of the living room.

She only saw him for a second, probably, before he saw her, but that second stretched like a warm taffy pull. There he was: Raymond Walker. Just like his mug shot, but alive and real. Wearing a robe like Tony wore. Regret crashed over her, and if she could have blinked and made herself disappear, she would have. Raymond Walker's eyes stuttered as he took her in, and he stepped back, knocking his heels against the bottom step of the staircase he had just come down. He wavered, then sat with a thud.

His voice was pure bewilderment. "Who are you?"

She hadn't disappeared. He could see her and she needed to speak. She could do this.

"I'm not here to hurt you," Julia said, holding her empty hands up at shoulder height. She'd thought about bringing a gun to scare him into listening to her, but she'd been worried she'd have shot him before either of them said a word. Given the tremor in her hands now, she was glad there wasn't a trigger under her finger.

"Who the fuck are you," he said. "Are you—" He tilted his head, like he was trying to see her face better. If her clothing was doing its job, he might have even thought she was a man. Her hair was slicked back tight under her hat, and she wore an oversize men's parka.

"I'm not gonna hurt you," she said again. "My name is Julia." She took an incremental step toward him. "Hall."

He shook his head. "Nick Hall's sister?"

"Sister-in-law," she said.

"Shit," he hissed as he turned. Before Julia could react, Walker had crawled himself to standing and was pounding up the stairs.

"Wait, wait, wait!" Julia called as she rushed across the kitchen.

She took the stairs two at a time; her baggy pants would have tripped her if she hadn't thought to wear a belt. She pictured Walker waiting at the top of the steps, ready to kick her back down, but when she rounded the bend in the narrow staircase he was gone.

She burst out onto the landing. Walker was across the room, next to the bed, his back to her.

Julia ran at him, and he started to move toward the bathroom door, but the phone he was clutching was plugged in next to the bed. She slammed into him arms first, driving him into the doorframe with a yelp. The phone released from its cord and clattered to the bathroom floor.

Walker stooped toward the phone, and Julia grabbed for his arms, but he wrenched them free. She clambered onto his back, a strange cry emerging from her throat.

"Get off!" he bellowed in confusion, jerking his body to the right.

She clamped her limbs around him. "I just want to talk!"

He moved toward the phone again, and she released a leg to drag her foot along the floor in front of him. She felt the phone underfoot, and with a miraculous yank she sent it skittering under the claw-foot tub.

Walker bucked her off and she fell to the floor.

"Stop," she groaned. Her ribs thrummed where she'd landed on the lump of papers folded in her coat pocket.

She picked herself up and saw him scrambling for the phone on his hands and knees.

She rushed toward him and shoved her hands against his shoulders, driving him squarely into the side of the tub. His head drove up into the lip of the tub and snapped back against his neck. A metallic *thong* rang out and he slumped to the floor.

Julia Hall stood in Raymond Walker's bathroom, swaying, her heart pounding in her ears.

And Raymond Walker did not move.

74

TONY HALL, 2016

A t 8:10 p.m. on the day Raymond Walker went missing, Tony called Julia as he crossed the parking lot outside of Goodspring. She'd been all over him about his calling her whenever he finished meeting with Nick. For some reason she'd gotten herself worked up about this visit. She didn't answer. It was a shame—she'd be happy to hear the news.

Nick, and the therapist to some extent, had convinced Tony. Tony had taken control of the hand Ron Hall dealt him by making himself a hero: Nick's hero first, then anyone who'd have him. That was fine when the person actually needed saving, but Nick didn't need or want to be saved. And Tony had been stifling him for a long, long time. It was a fine line, it seemed, between helping someone you love and hurting them. A line Tony hadn't even been looking for.

He got into the car and rattled off a text—"Heading home, call me"—then started the engine.

The whole drive home, Julia never called. The mile markers on 95, then 295 South ticked off in a blur, while Tony mourned the death of his plans to kill Ray Walker.

75

At 6:15 p.m. on the day Raymond Walker would go missing, Julia Hall reached her hand out of the stairwell on the ground floor of Raymond Walker's house, and she felt blindly up the wall to her right. There was the light switch under her shaking fingers, and she flipped it off with a heavy sigh. Once again, darkness flooded the living room.

"All right," she said. "Follow me."

She glanced behind her, then started for the kitchen. His footsteps were hesitant, but he followed.

She turned back. The opening to the staircase was black and vacant.

"Come on," she said firmly.

His voice resonated in the stairwell. "You aren't going to stab me with a kitchen knife?"

She exhaled a soft laugh. "You can hear me all the way across the room, right?"

Raymond Walker melted into the black square that was the stairwell. After a beat he stepped into the living room and made his way toward her. He still held the washcloth against his bloody hairline.

She had started in with her old routine up in the bathroom. When

343

she wanted to get her way with a client—earn their trust on something gravely important—she joked with them. It made her seem at ease, even when she was scared shitless, like now. She stood to the side of the refrigerator in Raymond Walker's kitchen, keeping her eye on him as she opened the freezer and grabbed a bag of mixed vegetables.

"You can really just relax now," she said as she shut the door. He was at the island, out of reach. "If I were here to kill you I'd have drowned you in that tub upstairs."

He looked at her incredulously. She stepped forward to hand him the bag. He snatched it and stepped back. "Who *are* you?" he asked as he swapped the cloth for the frozen bag.

"I've said I'm Tony's—"

"No, I—I got that." He waved the cloth in her direction. "Same style as him, you 'come over to talk' and I get beat up."

"I *am* here to talk, you just wouldn't—"

"You've said," he sighed, "as you cleaned my blood off the floor." He eyed her strangely, and she realized he was being funny. Was he just doing the same thing as her, or was her old trick working?

"I *am* sorry for your head."

"It would build trust if you'd give me my phone back."

She shook her head. His phone was wet in her sweaty palm. She was boiling with adrenaline. She wished she could take off the winter coat, but she didn't want to risk being seen without it. In the bathroom, Walker told her he thought she was a man when he first saw her in the kitchen. She knew the outfit was working to disguise her. It was just also cooking her to death.

"Let's go back upstairs," she said. "I'll explain everything."

"No, I'm staying right here."

She patted her pocket. "We'll need light to look at everything I brought."

"I'll turn on this light," he said as he leaned toward the wall at the end of the counter.

"No!" Julia lunged across the island and grabbed his wrist. "Someone will see."

"What?" he said as he shook his arm free. "What will they see?"

She took a deep breath and let it out. "I'm here to help you escape."

76

John Rice, 2019

Good, sweet Julia. God forgive him, he'd judged her the second he crossed the threshold of that house. Doing the dishes, watching the children, round-faced, a picture of femininity. He'd judged her as good on nothing but his own ideas of what a woman like her should be.

She sat beside him now, looking just like she did the day he came to question them about Walker's disappearance: wide-eyed, stiff as a board with fingers that trembled. That first time, he'd mistaken it as fear about Tony: fear about what her husband might have done. Well, she'd fooled him. It made him feel pathetic. Would she have fooled O'Malley? No. O'Malley would have seen it. Everyone got the same messaging about men and women—what they're like, what they aren't. But O'Malley was from a younger generation. A generation that saw the world differently.

They'd been frantic to find Walker, and O'Malley had been busy putting in calls, so Rice had gone to the Hall house alone. If he'd brought O'Malley, she would have seen what Rice couldn't. Julia hadn't been frightened of what her husband might have done. It was guilt in her eyes. Guilt and self-preserving terror, just like now.

Rice leaned toward her. "Is this your invocation?"

Julia said nothing.

"Which are you trying to invoke, Julia? God, or your right to remain silent?"

Her eyes flicked in his direction. She scratched at her sleeve. The wind whistled at the window behind her, and she held her tongue.

77

JULIA HALL, 2016

At 7:00 p.m. on the day Raymond Walker would go missing, Julia sat with him on the floor of the living room, shielded from the window by the couch. Walker had taken the small lamp and set it on the floor, and its orange glow fell over the pages Julia had brought.

Already, Julia had gone over each sheet and talked him through his journey. They'd start by walking several streets over, to where she'd parked her car. She'd keep her hood up and her head down, and hopefully, like Walker had, anyone who saw her would think she was a man. Then Julia would drop him at the bus in Portland, which he'd take to Boston using a ticket under the name Steven Sanford. There was a small sum of cab money for him to get himself to the train station there, and he'd get on the train west with a ticket to Chicago, also purchased for Steven Sanford. His eyebrows had raised, impressed, when she explained he'd get off the train early in Toledo, Ohio, and use a third ticket bought under a different name to take a bus to Columbus.

"And your friend will pick me up there," he said as they talked through it again.

"Yes." She glanced at her phone. Still nothing from Tony; that meant he hadn't left Nick yet, but he'd be in the car within the hour.

"And her name is?"

Julia looked up from the phone. "I hadn't said. Elisa."

"Elisa what?"

She shook her head. "I'm not giving you that. Or your phone back, at all."

Ray was looking at the bank statement again now. Even as he'd looked back through the other sheets, he'd kept a tight grip on that one.

"Afraid I'll change my mind halfway to Toledo?"

"So you're going?" she asked.

His eyes narrowed. "What will you do if I say no?"

Her stomach clenched, but she forced a smile. "Nothing."

"And when I call the police?"

"No one will believe your victim's family tried to help you get away with it."

He smiled. "You think I'm guilty."

"I know you are."

"No one but Nick or I can *know* that. Actually, even Nick doesn't know, what with his *blackout*. Very convenient."

Julia wasn't going to dignify that with a response.

"I'm just curious," he said. "You think I'm guilty. So how do you feel about this?" He paused. "Letting me get away with it?"

He was picking at it—the scab that had formed over the questions she kept asking herself. If everything went perfectly: If Walker went, if she was never caught, if Tony and the kids were safe when this was over, what would it mean? What would she have done, on a grander scale? Would she be hurting Nick even more than Walker had already? More than he'd be hurt by news coverage of the case, the opinions of strangers on the internet, the gossip of his classmates, the system?

"I'd rather do something than nothing," she said at last. "Wouldn't you?"

Now Walker was silent.

"Do you really want to see if a jury believes you? Because if they don't, your life is over. I know you know that, because you can't seem to shut up about it. Have you thought about what happens if you're acquitted? You're not proved innocent, and nobody thinks you are. They just think you got away with it. Did you know Nick could still sue you? That you could be fired for this? That every time someone googles your name, for the rest of your life, the word *rape* is gonna come up?"

He looked back at the sheet in his hands.

"You're not fooling me," she said. "You feel just as trapped as I do."

Walker sifted through the papers between them to pull out the photocopy of the passport. Elisa had mailed Julia the photocopy and retained the actual passport. It belonged, apparently, to a man named Avery King.

"So your friend *Elisa* will give me the actual passport when she picks me up in Columbus," he said.

He was talking like he was going to go. Like she was right. He just didn't want to say it. Julia decided not to push him. "Right," she said.

Walker studied the photo. "He does look a lot like me. How'd she get this?"

"Didn't ask; don't wanna know." This had always been her approach to Elisa, including when Julia was representing Elisa's son, Mathis. Julia felt, then and now, that she was on the tip of the iceberg with that family, and she was terrified to duck beneath the water and open her eyes.

"Your friend sounds shady as shit," Walker said. "How do you even know someone like this?"

Julia shifted the cross of her legs. "I helped out her son, a long time ago."

"Avery King. I could get used to that name."

Julia smiled. "It is a great name."

"Much better than *Steve Sanford*," he said with a grimace. He picked up the fake ID from the floor. The picture was actually Walker's mug

350

shot from his arrest. You'd never guess it without knowing: he looked calm, with the faintest crook of a smile. But Julia had recognized it from the paper instantly, when her package from Elisa arrived in the mail.

"When you meet Elisa, you become Avery. Steve's just a holdover until you get to her."

"Still," Walker said, and he smiled at her. She unpacked it in her mind: it was warm, teasing, genuine. He *was* starting to like her. Something deep inside her ached, and she spoke abruptly to break her train of thought.

"Are you with me?"

He looked back at the sheets in his hands. At the new life she was offering him.

He sighed. "Fuck it. Yeah."

The relief she felt at his words nearly overwhelmed her. "Okay," she breathed. "The last thing, then."

"Yeah?"

"Wait to call your mother."

His face went flat. He'd thought of it; why wouldn't he have? He could easily borrow a stranger's phone to make a call.

"It's in both of our best interests that your mother be genuinely unsure of what happened tonight," Julia said. "Whenever they figure out you're missing, they'll question her. Don't leave it to her acting skills—you need to make it to Elisa before they figure out that you left on your own."

Ray said nothing for a bit. Then he said, "That's actually a good point."

"I wouldn't want to leave my mom scared that something had happened to me," Julia said. "But I also wouldn't want to get her in trouble. And like I said, it'll help buy you time to get your money and get wherever you choose to go, before you tell her you're all right."

Ray nodded thoughtfully but said no more.

He looked around the living room. "Should we mess it up in here? Like a fight happened or something? So they go in the wrong direction, first?"

"No," Julia said quickly. "If we do a bad job of staging it, which I'm guessing we would, they'll suspect even faster that you're on the move."

Ray nodded slowly. "How long have you been planning this?"

In truth she wasn't sure—it had started subtly, like something she could see out of the corner of her eye that she didn't want to turn and look at too closely. The planning had been quick, but thinking about planning . . . that was harder to say. "I dunno. Long enough."

"You're a natural," he said.

She grimaced at him. "Really?"

"It's a compliment."

"Well, that makes me feel like a terrible person."

"I guess just get me to the bus, then, and you won't have to think of it again." He brought a hand to his chest. "I'll remember you fondly, though."

She grinned and pointed at the bank statement in his hand. "I'm sure you will!"

Terrible or not, Ray was right. She was good at this.

78

Tony Hall, 2016

At 10:00 p.m. on the day Raymond Walker went missing, Tony pulled into the driveway behind Julia's car. From outside, he could see the living room bathed in that flickering, blue-white light. Maybe she'd fallen asleep in front of the TV.

He pulled his boots off in the mudroom and wandered toward the living room, through the kitchen and into the dining room. He jumped when he found her sitting at the table there, facing him.

"Christ, you scared me."

The look in her eye was familiar but hard to place. Her face was drained of color, and she shivered, then crossed her arms. She looked frozen.

"Were you outside?"

She shook her head.

"Are you okay?"

She didn't speak, and kept her eyes on the table before her.

"Honey," he said as he crossed the room to her. "You're scaring me."

She shivered again as he knelt beside her. He placed a hand on her thigh and rubbed up and down her leg.

There was a palpable electricity between them, and he knew she would speak if he waited.

Finally, without turning her eyes from the table, she did.

"Before I tell you what I've done, promise you'll forgive me."

79

S till, Julia had not spoken. Rice would have given anything to see inside her head. Was she running over what she knew—what she thought safe to reveal? Was she planning a lie? Maybe. It would sting to hear her lie to him now, even if he knew she was doing so for understandable reasons. But she owed him the truth. She owed him after what he'd done.

The last time John Rice had seen Julia Hall, she was in her backyard, bundled in winter clothes, watching her children play.

Rice could remember January 18, 2016, more vividly than he could remember dinnertime yesterday, it seemed.

It was afternoon and bitterly cold. The sky was saturated with color—yellow sun on bright blue. He'd driven out to the pastures of Orange and found the Hall house deserted. He drove farther up the lane and parked the unmarked car. The Hall house was small in his rearview; he could have plucked it from the mirror and crumbled it between his fingers. Eventually he saw Julia's red Subaru Baja—unforgettably ugly—grow from a speck on the country lane in his rearview. The car pulled into the Hall driveway and parked.

How his heart had pounded as he watched that car. He'd recognized it on the grainy security footage from the Portland bus depot instantly. Two days after Raymond Walker disappeared, Megan O'Malley had called Rice to Portland to view a recording of Walker walking up to the depot at 8:11 p.m. on Friday, the day before his mother reported him missing. The video quality was poor, but he'd come right to the edge of the building, and his face was unmistakable. Then he boarded the eight fifteen bus to Boston, and he was gone.

O'Malley had directed the depot worker to pull up the footage of the parking lot. The first of his sins, Rice had shaken his head when O'Malley asked if he recognized "the truck" that dropped off Walker at the very edge of the screen. Only a hint of the car was visible, and the bed made it look like a small red truck. A ubiquitous vehicle in Maine. But Rice knew better. It wasn't a small truck—it was a Subaru Baja.

Guilty people were always trying to convince him that strange coincidences had caused their DNA to be at a crime scene, or stolen property to end up in their garage, or their make and model to happen to be the same as the getaway car. This was no coincidence: a Hall had driven Walker up to the bus station in Portland the night he disappeared, and Tony Hall was accounted for.

Watching her driveway three years ago, Rice had stared at that stupid car, waiting to see her face. He had been sure she'd done it to stop her husband from killing Walker. To keep her perfect life from collapsing with her husband's crime and inevitable arrest. Rice had craned in his seat, heart pounding in his neck, and strained to see her face. The face he had once compared to Irene's. She would look different to him now: selfish and vain, nothing like Irene. Nothing like who he made her out to be.

After a moment there was movement at the car, and the little girl climbed out on the passenger side. She ran ahead, and then Julia appeared in front of the car, walking toward the house. She was carrying two large totes of groceries, the little boy trailing after her. Rice had been too far away to be sure, but they looked like they were speaking. Her son had run past her, his smile wide enough to see from the street, and toward the yard behind the house. Julia had followed him, out of view. Slowly, Rice backed up until he was across from their driveway. Julia stood at the cedar fence, her back to the street. Her children ran in the yard, and she watched them. She'd put the groceries down at her feet, and one had tipped over, spilling groceries into the snow. She didn't care. She just wanted to watch her children.

In that moment, a realization washed over him slow and warm, like sinking into bathwater. He knew what she had done, but he had been wrong about why.

She'd saved her children from losing their father. She'd saved her husband from becoming a murderer. And she'd saved Ray Walker's life. Maybe she hadn't cared so much about that, but the purity of it all was overwhelming him. She had saved Walker's life. Not a good man, but a man nonetheless. Julia held the fence now and tilted her head down. Rice imagined what she might look like if he were facing her from the yard. A single tendril of her hair loose from her hat. Tears in her eyes, lips trembling in a smile. Overcome with joy, watching her children play and knowing they would be safe, knowing they would have their parents. Knowing she had committed a lesser sin only to halt a greater one.

Rice had watched her a moment longer, then put the car into drive. He'd driven down the country lane until it met an outlet, through the town center, onto the highway, and back to the station. And then he went inside, and he sat at his desk, and he said nothing.

Over the following months he and O'Malley had worked off of the 8:15 p.m. passenger list, trying to trace Walker's journey. The "truck's" license plate was only partially captured and totally indiscernible, so chasing Walker himself was the only option. The security footage confirmed that Walker had shown an ID to board the bus, and his real name was absent from the passenger list, so they meticulously moved through the names that had prepurchased tickets. They ran criminal and driving histories, searched social media, and compared pictures of the male passengers against the surveillance footage. It was slow going, and they were too bogged down with other work to make fast progress, but O'Malley was tenacious. She worked from a place of hell-bent rage that Walker had evaded justice and would move on to new victims. For his part, Rice worked alongside her, treating the horrific guilt he felt as penance for his sin. But he felt he, like Julia, had chosen the lesser of two evils.

They'd enlisted the help of the local FBI, in theory, but it was O'Malley who determined that Raymond Walker was the passenger listed as "Steven Sanford," and that "Steven Sanford" had also bought a train ticket from Boston to Chicago. The tickets were bought with stolen credit card information from the dark web, the federal agent told them. That was the sum total of his help.

As best they could tell, Walker never made it to Chicago. Where he'd gotten off early they never determined.

When the news broke that Walker had fled, Britny Cressey stepped into the light she'd been waiting for. She gave interviews to the local stations and papers, detailing what she'd learned from Walker before his flight. She was quick to qualify that she knew nothing about the escape itself or how he planned it. He'd never mentioned it to her, she said, but he had talked at length about the court process, the money he owed, the dread he felt that the game was rigged against him.

Eventually the story of the man who evaded his justice grew stale, and the news coverage stopped, and life moved on without Raymond Walker.

And then a month after Walker ran, Rice got a call from Linda Davis.

Nick Hall had called her and asked her to dismiss the case against Raymond Walker.

"He says he wants to just move on," she said. "He really didn't want to get into it. But he wanted us to know something: he was awake during Walker's assault."

Rice had been stunned.

"I know," Linda said. "He sounds like he wants to just move on from the whole thing. I can't say I blame him."

He'd been awake. Rice thought of O'Malley's work early on the case, about serial rapists. There was a second type of sadist that they'd ruled out initially: the type of person who didn't hurt their victims for the fun of it, but who fantasized about it. Maybe Walker was that type. Maybe he'd never had a victim fight back as hard as Nick, and it woke something up in him. Maybe that was why they never found anyone before Nick. He wasn't the first—he was just the first Walker had left unable to hide the violence that was done to him.

⟶

The silence had stretched on long enough.

"Julia," he said. "Say something."

80

He knew what happened. He'd always wondered if Julia real-ized it, too. He was saying he thought she might have known that *he* knew what she had done—of course not. She'd have lost her mind. He knew what she did. He knew? How? He'd always known. Why tell her now if not then? Why didn't he arrest her? What had she thought would happen? She would go to prison now. The kids—oh Christ, the kids. What did he want? What could she do? Julia's mind was barraged with thoughts, and she'd failed to piece together a coherent sentence when the dying detective spoke again.

"Julia. Say something." He sounded exhausted, like she was a child who wouldn't stop getting out of bed at night.

In all her years as a defender, she'd never met anyone guilty of a crime who was glad he spoke to the police, even to deny it or offer explanation. But then, a defense attorney wouldn't meet someone who successfully misled the police, would she? And her silence was damning. When she spoke her voice was miniscule.

"I don't know what you mean, about whatever happened."

She should have kept her mouth shut.

Detective Rice leaned back into his chair, and it squeaked under him.

He was calmer than she would have imagined, if this was a prelude to her arrest. If this wasn't a conversation but an interrogation. But then, what did she know of his self-control?

"You know," he said, "that depot's security cameras captured cars out by the road."

Shit. Her eyes went wider. *Oh, shit shit shit.* She'd thought of it just after, and a million times since, but no one had come asking questions. She should have called him a cab, or dropped him even farther away, but she had to see him get on that bus.

"I know it was you that dropped off Walker in Portland," the detective went on. "There weren't a lot of people driving those ugly Bajas." He laughed as he said the sentence, and when he finished, he was coughing hard. He reached for the mask at his side.

It gave her time to think. Why was he doing this? It had to be a trap. Without moving her head, her eyes scanned the room: no blinking light, no obvious recording devices. That recorder he used to use was so small, though; it could have been under her chair. Had he chosen her seat for her? Yes, he'd definitely told her to sit in this one . . . she'd gone for the other.

Julia drew a quiet, shaky breath and expelled it. If she didn't calm down she was going to have a panic attack. She breathed in. *Calm down.* She breathed out. *Calm down.* Detective Rice was reholstering his mask to the tank. He'd known for three years. Maybe this wasn't him coming after her, maybe it was something else. Because why now? Had something new happened?

Did they find Walker?

At the thought, the room began pressing in from all sides; an electronic hum rang in her ears. The light began to dim, and Julia felt the urge to tip forward to her knees. She did, and Detective Rice's voice was far away behind the hum.

She scooted backward against her chair and put her head between her knees. With each breath, the hum quieted and the rush of panic softened. When she opened her eyes, the room was light again.

"Julia." His warm hand was on her shoulder. "Julia."

She looked back at him then turned forward again. "Sorry."

"You all right?"

Julia nodded.

"Was that a panic attack?"

She nodded again. There was nothing to say. Her body had betrayed her guilt.

"Julia, I'm not—I didn't ask you here to arrest you or interrogate you. I've done this all wrong." He seemed to say the last bit more to himself than to her. "Please, sit so I can see you?"

On leaden legs, Julia pushed herself back up into the armchair.

"I'm not trying to scare you. Or, well . . ." He shook his head. "I dunno. Maybe I was."

She glanced at him sideways, then turned to him fully. His face was apologetic, and maybe something else.

"No one else knows," he said quietly.

"You said my car was on camera."

The detective smiled. "It looked like a truck. It was never identified as yours, not officially." He paused. "But I knew."

When Julia didn't speak, he went on. "I'm moving to hospice next week, and I didn't want to do this there. And, well, I don't want to die without having the conversation at all."

"Okay," she said quietly.

"I do think I get why you helped him run away. I didn't at first, and I meant to come out with it—expose what you'd done—but I wanted to talk to you before that. And then I went to see you, at your house. I saw you playing with the kids outside, and suddenly I understood."

"Understood?"

"That you did it for them. For your kids, and for him—for Tony. You thought he'd kill him."

She almost nodded.

"So you saved him instead."

Her eyes welled, and a heavy tear rolled down her cheek.

"You are so good," he said quietly. "It was always so clear about you. I was so angry when I saw your car on that tape. I felt like you'd betrayed *me*, isn't that strange? I wanted to scream at you, understand why you weren't who I thought you were. I drove to your house. Did you know that?"

She shook her head. She hadn't known. She couldn't even place the day.

"I was ready to rumble," he said with a laugh. "My mother would have called me *spittin' mad*. But then I saw you, in the yard with your kids. And it just hit me that I was wrong. I did know you. You *were* good. It was the only thing you knew to do."

The detective was looking at her with such tenderness that it seemed impossible he could be faking it.

"You sent him away," he said.

More tears slid down her cheeks. She still got upset sometimes, when she thought about what she did and how terrified she had been afterward.

Detective Rice had known all along. All the times she made herself sick wondering what would happen if he found out, he already knew.

"Was Tony angry with you?"

She was so tired.

Just a single word. It wasn't a confession.

"No," she said.

81

Sometime after 10:00 p.m. on the day Raymond Walker went missing, Tony held very still at Julia's side, his hand frozen on her thigh, while she told him what she had done.

When she was finished, Tony laid his head down on her lap. He only had a single thought: the only way forward was to tell her the truth.

"Jules."

"Do you hate me?"

"Jules, I changed my mind."

Her eyes went wide. "What?"

He told her everything that Nick had said. That Nick wanted to go through with the trial. That Nick needed him to stop trying to fix everything. That sitting in the visiting room at Goodspring, Tony changed his mind.

"Okay," Julia said. "Okay. Okay. Okay." Her mouth was a record, skipping on the word.

"We'll figure it out," Tony said quickly. He didn't have a clue how; he just wanted to take away whatever she was feeling.

"Okay," she said again. "I'll just call Elisa. I'll tell her to send him back."

"He's not gonna come back."

"She has everything he needs: the money, the passport. If she won't give it to him, he'll have to."

"Or he'll turn on you." Look what he'd done. Look what he'd fucking done.

"That was always a risk I was taking. We'll just have to deal with it."

"How?"

"I'll deny whatever he says. It'll get messy, but it already is. We have to get him back."

Tony stood. "Honey, the exact thing you were trying to protect the kids from could happen. You could get caught." His voice broke, and he finished in a whisper. "You could go to prison. Who knows how they'd punish this?"

Julia stood from the table and took his hands. "Take a breath. We'll figure it out."

"What if the police connect the tickets to the woman, Elisa," Tony said.

"They can't," Julia said. "And even if they did, she won't give them anything."

Tony spoke slowly. "Why blow it all up?"

"I've taken the one thing Nick had left."

"You didn't do that. I did."

"What if he doesn't forgive you? After everything he just told you."

She was right. Nick would have every reason to blame this on him—it was all his fault. But he would have to live with that.

"They'll figure out Walker got on a bus," Julia said. "It might take them a bit, but they'll have to figure that out."

"I think so," Tony said.

"So Nick will think he ran, too."

"Right," Tony said. "You're right."

"But what will he do? What will Nick do if he can't have a trial?"

"I don't know. But I don't think that's for us to figure out."

He walked around Julia and pulled out a chair. She sat back down beside him.

He leaned his elbows on the table and rested his chin in his hands. "I'm sorry I went so far away from you."

Julia pulled her chair closer to his. "It wasn't just you. I couldn't even see I was doing the same thing. If I'd just told you . . . we should have been doing it together."

They sat at the table talking it through. There was no way to unwind what was set in motion. The damage was already done. So they decided, together, to let Walker go.

82

Nick Hall, 2016

A month after Raymond Walker disappeared, Nick sat on a couch across from his counselor. Not at a hospital, not at a program, but at an office in Wells.

"So, how are you doing?"

Today Jeff's sweater was navy blue with a fisherman-style knit. He started the session with the same question he always did.

Nick sat forward on the couch. "I actually wanted to ask you that."

"I'm doing fine."

"No." Nick laughed. "I mean, how do you think I'm doing?"

"Mm," Jeff said. "I don't like this game."

"I know how I feel. I know I'm not gonna just be 'better' or 'fixed,' but what's my prognosis?"

Jeff raised a salt-and-pepper eyebrow. "Prognosis?"

"You must have it written down somewhere. Or you have one in your head."

Jeff fiddled with the band of his silver wristwatch.

"When will I sleep normal? I mean, am I ever gonna go home with a guy I like again?"

Jeff smiled. "Your prognosis is good, Nick."

Nick leaned back into the couch. Jeff might have been humoring him, but he didn't care.

"When we look at the data, you have some factors working in your favor toward a good outcome. But you know I'm not only about that. This right here is the most important piece, and it's also the only one you have in your control. Keep putting in the work, and your prognosis is real good."

It was like a knot in Nick's stomach untied itself. A feeling of comfort spread through his body as he listened to Jeff's voice.

"We can keep working through what happened with Ray, the stories you tell yourself about what the assault meant. How those stories have been scripted by your society, your father, even your brother. And we can work on integrating your identity—who you are as a man—with this one thing that happened to you. And eventually, it's going to get better. There isn't gonna be a last day you *ever* have any symptoms. I still have nightmares about my abuse, and I'm old as dirt. But it *will* get better. And how you see yourself, how you see other people, romantic relationships—all that looks good to me."

"Cool," Nick said. Sometimes he didn't have the words to match how he felt when he met with Jeff. The future Jeff had just imagined for him was everything he wanted. But what it would take to get there—reliving that night, saying out loud the worst things he thought about himself, airing every stupid thing he had ever heard about what it meant to be dominated by someone else—it would be brutal. But he would do whatever it took to get to the future Jeff thought he could have.

"Any updates on court?"

"Yeah, actually. I've decided to dismiss the case."

"Really? Why?"

It happened last week, after Nick had moved home from Goodspring. At first, when Ray went missing, Nick couldn't stop thinking that Tony had done something stupid. Worse than stupid. He knew from Julia that the police had gone to interview his brother, and she seemed worried. But then the ADA herself called Nick: Ray had gotten on a bus to Boston. The coward had run away. Their next court date was in March, Linda said. She wasn't sure if the judge would let her go forward with a trial if Ray hadn't been found by then, but she wanted to try. Nick decided not to tell her the truth about his testimony just yet. It sounded like he had some time to think about it.

Then last week Julia came to his apartment.

It was snowing softly, and the city hadn't plowed Spring Street. They trudged down it anyway.

Ray didn't jump bail alone, she told him. She, Nick's sister-in-law, had helped his rapist escape.

Nick was stunned. It sounded like a joke without a punchline.

"I need you to know," she said, "you changed his mind. It was just too late."

"Ray?"

Julia shook her head. "Tony." The realization dawned on Nick as she went on. She didn't even need to say it. "I thought he was going to kill him."

Tony had said so himself, when Nick told him that he'd been awake during the assault. Tony kept saying he was going to kill Ray.

"I swear, Nick, you changed his mind. He came to see you at Goodspring and he came home, and he told me he wasn't going to do it anymore." She looked at Nick miserably. "But it was too late. I sent Walker away while Tony was with you."

Another piece clicked into place. "I thought you sent him to Goodspring because you didn't want to deal with his reaction when he found out the case hadn't settled. But it wasn't that. I was his alibi."

Julia nodded. "Just in case something went wrong."

They had stopped walking at the end of Spring Street. They stood in the falling snow in silence for a moment.

"Why are you telling me?"

Julia wiped her nose with the backside of her mitten. "Because I have a favor to ask."

Julia told Nick what she feared might happen if Nick went forward with the case and a judge let him have a trial without Ray: in short, it would be a media circus. The press had been all over Nick's case to begin with—a fugitive rapist being tried by the man he assaulted? That could make national news. And national news might mean someone, even in another state, making a phone call about a man they saw. National coverage could mean Ray's discovery, and therefore Julia's.

Julia's eyes were tired, and the snow had collected on her cap. "I don't deserve to ask a single thing of you."

"That's not true."

"It is, after what I took from you." She shook her head. "But I'm still asking."

"Oh," Nick said quietly. She wanted him to dismiss the case. Of course he would, if the case could get Julia caught. It was just . . . Ray. "What if he hurts someone else?"

"Nick?" Jeff's voice pulled Nick out of the snowy memory.

"Sorry, yeah?"

"Why are you dismissing the case?"

Nick took a deep breath. "Can I be honest?"

"Of course."

No telling lies this time, or partial truths. "The truth is, I really don't feel like talking about it."

Jeff's face broke into a smile. "Okay. It's your session."

Nick breathed out hard. That felt good.

"So what do you want to work on today?"

Right. His session, his choice. Maybe one day, Nick would tell Jeff why he made up his mind to dismiss the case, what Julia told him. Maybe not. Nick got to decide.

83

Julia felt hollowed out. Her mind was limping along, trying to keep up with where he'd taken her. Detective Rice seemed so genuine; it all felt real. And besides, he already knew it was her. If he wanted to turn her in, what did it matter if she talked or not? She might as well tell him the kicker.

"When I told him Walker was gone, Tony was heartbroken. Not because he couldn't kill him, but because he'd changed his mind."

The detective shook his head. "No."

She nodded. "Nick really wanted to have the trial. And Tony didn't want to take that from him."

"Then why did Nick ask Linda to dismiss the case? We could have tried to push forward, without Walker. It's not unheard of. His trial hadn't started, the court might not have let us. But Nick told Linda he didn't want to try. He told her the truth about his statement, but he didn't want to go forward. I just don't understand. I know he would have suffered more press at a trial, but he might have earned a symbolic victory, at least."

"Yes," Julia said slowly. "He might have won that. But the whole thing looped back on itself."

"What do you mean?"

Julia smiled. "He dismissed it to keep me safe."

A month after Walker left, Julia told Nick everything. The *whole* truth.

"If the court actually held a trial, it probably would have become a national spectacle—a male victim, a trial in absentia, a fugitive. And that kind of coverage . . ."

"It could have hurt Nick even more."

"No. Well, yes, absolutely. But I was being selfish. I wanted Nick to dismiss the case for me. I didn't want someone to see the coverage and piece something together that would get me into trouble."

"Oh," Rice said.

"Or for Walker to see it," she added. "And decide to come back."

"So Nick did it for you."

"And Tony," she said. "I felt awful about everything, but it actually seemed to be just what he needed. It, like, reset a balance between him and Tony. Nick dismissed the case, the news died down, and I was safe."

Rice was quiet for a bit.

"You said there was something else?"

"I've never been a perfect Catholic," he said slowly. "I've sinned a lot in my life, and I've always confessed it. But this time, it took me a long time to confess what I did. That I let a defendant get away by sitting on the only lead: that my victim's sister-in-law had helped him." He shook his head. "I almost went down to Boston to make the confession, to a different church. I was so ashamed to tell my own priest. I knew he'd lose respect for me. He'd deny it if you asked him, but how could he not?

"But I decided, fuck my pride, I didn't deserve to be proud. I confessed in my church. At first I felt better, then one day I started to feel it again: an itch in my stomach, like something needing to be let out. So I confessed again. It went away, then came back.

"And then the cancer. And now I'm dying. This spring might be my last Easter, if the docs are right. And I keep feeling this need to confess a sin. And I finally realized, it's because my sin continues. My sin is my silence. I'm a Catholic, but I'm a cop, too. I swore an oath, and I broke it, and I break it every day that I don't turn myself in.

"I've confessed my sins to God but I don't know if he'll save me, because every time I step out of confession, I'm already sinning again. Unless I die in that booth, I'll die sinning."

Julia felt stunned. "You don't think God would punish you for a single thing you did, just one single thing, do you?"

"I dunno. A younger, more romantic me might agree with you, but it feels different once you see the X-rays, these impossible shapes in your body, once you're calling the lady who did your will twenty years ago." Rice shook his head. "I hope—in my heart, I believe he'll forgive me. God is just and merciful. He gets to choose. I was always just. That was my job: uphold the law, let God worry about mercy. I let people off every now and then, but not like this. Real crime, I always met with justice. Only once did I choose mercy."

This was why she was here.

"You're going to turn me in."

He looked at her with surprise. "I can't."

"Oh. Why not?"

"It would undo everything else I've ever done. It would be just like these DNA scandals. Something as big as this—letting a woman, the family of a victim, collude with a defendant to escape . . . every case I ever worked on would be in post-conviction review. Every imperfect justice I ever achieved for other victims would be threatened. Every family that found some little bit of peace would lose it."

"I'm so sorry. I had no idea what I did to you. I'm so sorry."

"Don't be. Just tell me it was worth it."

"What?"

"Tell me what good it did, so if I go to hell at least I'll have something to smile about."

"Oh." She laughed, a snotty burst of air, and she wiped her nose with her sleeves.

The detective's arms were crossed over his stomach, and his shoulders sank away from his neck. He'd never looked smaller, sicker, sadder. But hopeful, that's what it was—his eyes brimmed over with desperate hope. Hope for what she might give him. Hope for solace. Just like Tony had trapped her, she'd unwittingly done the same to this man. And they'd each made their choice. All these years, he'd been her silent partner in crime.

She told him what their crime had bought. Told him about Chloe, who was now ten and precocious as ever. In the last few months she'd become utterly dedicated to learning karate, and she was hoping to earn her yellow belt that spring. Told him that Seb, at eight, had discovered a phenomenon on YouTube where people would film themselves making and manipulating slime, and he watched these videos religiously. Tony had tried to channel this obsession of his into a broader interest in science, but he'd recently remarked with grave defeat that Seb truly only cared about slime. (The detective laughed at this and took another hit of his oxygen for it.) Speaking of Tony, Julia told Detective Rice, he and she had celebrated their twelfth wedding anniversary at the New Year. In the wake of what she'd done, they had turned toward each other, and their bond felt even stronger now than it had when they were young and stupidly in love. And finally, she told the detective about Nick. He was twenty-three now, and as funny as he'd ever been. He moved to Boston after graduation and was working in advertising. Last Christmas, he came home with a boyfriend they'd all liked very much.

"So you think we did the right thing?"

She shifted in her seat. "I don't know if we'll ever know that. Or I guess, maybe you'll know before me." She pointed at the ground, and he laughed. Suddenly it was hilarious, the idea of them going to hell together.

"I'd have done it differently," she said. "If I knew what would happen that day. But I didn't know."

He was silent. He wanted more from her. He'd never talked about it, it sounded, with anyone but his priest. She was tiring, but she could go a little longer.

"For a long time I felt—*wrecked* isn't the right word, it was worse than that. At first I held it together, because Tony was a mess, but eventually he kind of calmed down, and then I fell apart. I didn't know myself. I felt untethered from myself. And like a terrible, terrible person. At first it felt like what I'd done had changed me, and then I realized maybe I'd never even known myself, my whole life. And I felt stupid, so stupid. When all the stress of what had been happening was gone, I could see options I hadn't thought of. Maybe I could have had Tony hospitalized. It's not a crime to *want* to kill someone. If I'd acted quickly, ah. I don't know. I could have hobbled him like in *Misery*."

Rice choked on a laugh.

Julia felt herself smile. "Trapped him in the house." Then she grew serious again. "I could have told you. That was a big one. I could have stopped him by telling you. And that one I didn't miss. I'd thought of it before I . . . sent Walker away. But I didn't know what you'd do with it. Would you have arrested him? I thought if I told you, I'd lose him, and the kids would lose him, and Nick. So instead I sent Walker away. I got what I wanted—Tony couldn't get at him anymore, Tony couldn't get himself in trouble—but I didn't like what I'd done. So I was a mess for a bit. But Tony took care of me, and I think the kids missed most of it, or I tell myself they did, and eventually I started boxing it away again."

Their eye contact was unbroken. It was deeply intimate, almost uncomfortable, but it made it feel true, and she wanted to give him this truth, even if she couldn't give him all of it.

She went on. "I figured out that I'd never know if I did the right thing. I know I did a bad thing. But can't it be more complicated than that? I think so. And I started to accept that. And when . . . what I'd done would start to creep in, or more like just blast into my head, and I felt horrible, or I was just absolutely sick with fear I'd be caught and go to jail and put my kids through just what I was trying to, you know, avoid happening with Tony—"

She reached her hand across the space between them and rested it on his arm. He was thin under his sweater, and she squeezed his arm gently.

"I would take a breath, look at the kids, look at Tony, look at Nick. They were the best answer I was ever going to get—to the question, did I do the right thing."

Detective Rice's eyes had welled over. Was it relief or disappointment?

"That's kinda what I figured, too," he said.

He frowned. "Did you ever hear from . . . ?"

"No." She shook her head. "Never."

"I wonder if he left the country."

Julia's eyebrows began to rise on their own, and she pushed them higher to match her sensitive tone. "Maybe."

"He just didn't seem like the type to stop hurting people, or even just attention-seeking all the time, and for nothing to ever turn up. Someone who does something like that, I don't think they just do it once. I always figured he'd get caught somewhere else, or we'd hear about his DNA matching a new crime. He must have gotten himself out of the country."

Julia said nothing for a moment. Could she give him—did she owe him—solace here? She thought of the day Rice had called Tony and warned him off of threatening Ray Walker again. "I'm not a big fan of the *Boondock Saints*," the detective had said.

She wiggled the hand that was on his arm. "You're thinking about the wrong things if you want to make peace."

He nodded.

"For what it's worth," she said, "he did know how close he'd come to losing everything. He knew this was his chance for a fresh start."

"Do you really think someone like him is capable of change?"

And there it was. The question that had bothered her most over the years. "What he did to your brother-in-law," Charlie Lee had said to her, "there must be others out there. Just hard to find them." Charlie's inability to find other victims—maybe there was a boy in Providence. Maybe not. Julia would never know if Walker had hurt others. One day, she would grow old or sick like the detective, or she would meet her end some other way, and she would die never knowing if Raymond Walker was the monster her family thought he was. She could lull the question to sleep again, but it would always be there, ready to crack an eye and ask: Just how bad was he, Julia?

"I'd lose my mind if I thought about him," she said truthfully. "That's why I focus on my family until I can get my brain to move on to the next thing."

Detective Rice sighed heavily. "I feel like an elephant just got off my chest."

She laughed and gave his arm a final squeeze. "I owed you. I had no idea what I owed you."

He shrugged. "Well, it was nothing."

"No, it wasn't." She shook her head. "It was everything."

They sat in silence together as the wind hit the window again. She looked at her watch, not that the time mattered—she was ready to leave. "I'm so sorry, but I need to get going. I really don't like driving in the snow after it gets dark if I can help it."

"Of course," he said, and he began making the motions of standing up. Julia stood and gave him a hand.

Detective Rice walked her down the narrow hall, back to the entryway. Julia sat on the bench to pull on her boots.

"Do you garden?" She nodded to the bookshelf.

"Oh, yes," he said with a grin. "It was always a hobby, but after I retired it was really what got me up and going most days. Maybe, well, if by some miracle I'm still kicking this spring, I'd love you to come see me again, wherever I am, if I'm well enough to grow anything."

Julia gave him her warmest smile as she stood from the bench. "I'd love to." An overt lie. She didn't think she could stomach another meeting with the detective. But there was no good in telling him that, especially if he'd likely be dead before he'd have reason to know.

She *would* go to his funeral. She owed him that.

Julia embraced Detective Rice goodbye and stepped out onto the porch. She turned to shut the door, but he was already pushing it closed behind her. He waved through the small window beside the door, and she waved a mittened hand back.

Overt or not, to lie to a man on his deathbed seemed especially sinful. But it was kinder than telling him the truth.

84

It was half past midnight on the day after Raymond Walker disappeared, and Elisa Lariviere was early. She preferred it that way, especially when there was nothing noteworthy about a car waiting around a place like this. She backed into a spot at the far end of the lot with the front end of her Gran Coupe facing the building. She'd left her home in Michigan three hours ago to make her way there, to the bus terminal in Columbus.

The night was frigid, and she left the engine running. The brutal Ohio wind outside gave the impression of heavy snowfall, but in truth it was only a light flurry. Still, she'd have traded her weather at home for this without hesitation. After living in Boston for more than two decades, Elisa thought she would be comfortable with winters in Michigan, but she'd been mistaken. Winter on the lake was longer, darker, and wetter than in New England. For tonight's purposes, of course, Michigan's climate would have certain advantages.

A song began to play softly from the public radio station she had on low volume. She hadn't been listening to the disc jockey—perhaps he'd said something about this being a fitting song for a late Friday night?—but the tune was immediately familiar. Softly twanging, a guitar picked out the melody and Elisa's chest swelled with bittersweetness. A man began singing, and Elisa only had to wait a breath for the famous line: "Whack for the daddy-o / there's whiskey in the jar." The song aligned with the memory, and Elisa smiled at the coincidence.

She'd heard the old Irish song in a movie a year ago. The movie was *Conviction*; it was the true story of a woman who went to law school and dedicated her life to exonerating her brother. It had been a quiet movie—Elisa had watched it at home one night, years after its uneventful release. The story was a slow burner, and it had scorched her. Her son Mathis's own legal case came to mind early on as she watched, and although the comparisons between the two cases were few, the themes of justice, vigorous defense, and family rang true.

Helpless as she felt in the wake of her son's arrest in early 2005, Elisa had been obsessed with ensuring Mathis had a zealous advocate, and that was precisely what he had gotten, in the most unexpected package. Elisa had hired Clifton Cook—Maine's answer to the proverbial eight-hundred-pound gorilla—and her gorilla had gone and hired a capuchin named Julia Hall. Elisa had been deeply disappointed with frizzy-haired, baby-faced Julia on sight. She chuckled now when she thought back on her first interactions with Julia, who'd smiled too much, espoused the values of cooperation with the prosecution, and recommended numerous social services for Mathis.

"She's not a lawyer—she's a social worker," Elisa had guffawed into the phone from the stark white kitchen of her Boston high-rise.

Her boy's voice answered from the detention center. "Clifton says juvenile court is complicated and we need her. She's nice, Maman."

Elisa rolled her eyes at Mathis's words. "And *cute*."

"Not even," he lied.

The snow began to build up on Elisa's windshield, and she activated her wipers. She checked the time. Ten minutes.

Mathis had been a fool to have even such a small quantity of cocaine in the car with him, especially while he crossed state lines as he drove to see friends in Maine. And the gun—Elisa had nearly crumbled when she learned he'd been caught with a gun. Against all odds, though, it was clean. Elisa had gone to see him at the detention center. They'd sat at a long table in a sterile room and they'd whispered to each other as they played rounds of Old Maid, an insufferably simple card game available at the facility. She'd shredded him with her words, then given him the story he needed to tell the lawyers.

There had been quiet work done in other places, of course, but over the year that Mathis's case worked its way through Maine's juvenile court, Elisa had watched Julia put in late nights and long hours for Mathis. Each time they returned to court, Elisa listened to Clifton update the judge about how Mathis was participating in the services Julia had arranged. Julia would sit with Elisa, uninterested in credit for what she'd done.

"He's doing really well," Julia said quietly at their last court date. "He's earned such a good resolution to his case."

Elisa leaned toward her. "Don't discount your part in this." In the beginning, Elisa hadn't trusted Julia's insistence on playing by the rules. But Julia's method had worked.

"I'm not," Julia said, "but he's worked really hard. He deserves what he's getting today." Julia paused. "He feels a lot of pressure."

Elisa glanced at her sideways. Julia's eyes remained straight forward.

Then she said, "I hope he has the freedom to figure out who he is and what he wants in life."

Elisa said nothing.

In the hallway, Mathis had embraced Julia goodbye. Call with any questions, Julia told him. When Mathis turned to Clifton, Elisa took Julia lightly by the arm and walked her aside. She had a few things to say.

She'd thought about Julia a fair amount over the past year, after watching the story of the lawyer who exonerated her own brother. The night Elisa finished the movie, she'd had a near-overwhelming urge to try Julia's old number, but she refrained. The next morning she'd googled Julia, and Elisa was disappointed to see that she appeared not to be lawyering any longer. It had seemed strange, almost serendipitous, when Julia called such a brief time thereafter.

Earlier that month, Elisa had left the hairdresser to find a voice mail on her cell. It was Julia Hall, rambling and nervous, saying nothing of substance.

Elisa had returned the phone call the same day she received the message, but later from the comfort of her sunroom. It had been a dreary winter day on the lake; the rain ran slow down the large panel window behind her, and beyond that was only gray and mist. Elisa sat by the small woodstove and made the call.

Julia had seemed distracted when she answered. She reacted slowly to Elisa's greeting and seemed to be moving away from someone. Elisa heard a door shut, and the quality of Julia's voice changed—her speech was freer.

"Thanks for calling back," Julia said.

"It's no problem. I'm pleased to be calling you."

"You've moved quite far from Boston!"

"I am a lady of the lake now." Elisa waved her hand for the benefit of an audience that wasn't there.

"How are the winters in Michigan?"

"They're shit. Did you really call to ask about the weather?"

"No, and I see you're direct as ever."

Elisa could hear the smile in Julia's voice, but she knew she'd sent her squirming.

"Out with it, kid." Elisa smiled back.

The silence was too long.

"Is everything all right, Julia?"

Julia's voice was quiet. "No."

Julia told her about a man, Raymond Walker, and what he'd done to her brother-in-law. She told Elisa about the press, the boy's problems, the unprecedented tension in her marriage.

"I'm sorry to hear all that. Truly," Elisa said. Still, it was strange. She doubted a woman like Julia had some dearth of close, female confidants to air her problems to.

After a long pause, Julia said in a low voice, "I think my husband is going to do something."

"Something?"

"Something I'll never be able to undo."

Elisa weighed Julia's words. "I'm not sure I blame him. Did you think I would?" She passed her hand through the steady rush of steam escaping the cup of tea on her armrest. Remembered the conversation they had in Julia's office one night. Remembered Mathis's anxious confession about the family history he gave his pretty lawyer. "I know the things Mathis told you."

"I know," Julia said. "Tony can't do this."

Elisa dropped her hand away from her cup. So there it was.

"And I can, is that it?"

"I was thinking I could convince him—Walker—to leave. Even setting Tony aside, he has to know he'll go to prison for years, decades maybe. He must have thought of running, but he'd have no help, no money, but if I helped him, I think I could convince him to leave." Her voice dropped away, like words falling off a cliff. "Just go, forever."

"This man will just go away. Forever," Elisa repeated.

"Maybe, if I got it—"

"This man who is obsessed with the spotlight."

"If I—"

"This sadist, you'll set him free. And he'll fade into oblivion, permanently and willingly—never to come calling on you for more."

At that Julia said nothing. Good. She was too intelligent to play stupid like this, and with Elisa of all people.

"So, what, you'd like me to rent him a room on the lake? Help him find a job? Apply for a passport?"

Still nothing.

"I'm happy to keep patronizing you if it makes you feel better, but we both know why you called me."

At that, Julia spoke.

"If—" She said the word and stopped. An exhale against the mouthpiece. "If I wanted your help . . . that kind of help."

"I meant what I said, the day you left my life. You saved my son—my very favorite son, at that."

A breathy laugh, like relief.

"I assume you have children now, you always loved them so. You know. You saved my child, and I would do anything for you. I'm guessing you thought then that you would never want anything from someone like me."

The inhale that shook through the phone was distinctly marred by tears. Perhaps of resignation, perhaps of relief. "Yes."

Elisa brought her finger back to her mug and trailed it along the rim. "It's easy to be good when things are good."

Julia said nothing.

The woodstove was pleasant, but the cold was radiating in on Elisa's back from the window behind her. She shifted in her chair to pull her feet up to rest before her, so that she looked out over her knees. Her joints protested and she slid her heels forward an inch.

"How much time do we have?"

"You mean, before Tony . . ."

"Yes."

"Not a lot. There's a court date on January twelfth. He promised me it won't be until after that. And if the case settles, that's it."

"That's it?"

"I won't need you," Julia said.

Elisa doubted that Julia could be so sure, but there was no point in saying as much. Elisa could begin preparing either way.

"But, assuming it doesn't settle so early in the process, I think I need it done that week."

"That is soon," Elisa said. "Do you really think you could convince this man to run? Temporarily, of course."

Julia cleared her throat. "Maybe, yeah. As worried as we've been about court, I've heard that he is, too. He's facing serious time, the sex-offender registry, all the stigma and trouble that comes with an allegation like this. I've heard he's starting to freak out about it, so if I could make the right promises . . . but I would need your help to make it look like I was offering him everything he could need to live as someone else."

"Passport, money."

"Right. And tickets to get out of Maine, without using his name."

"Why involve him in the equation at all? He could be dealt with in Maine."

"If something happens to him here, they'll still suspect Tony. Even if he has an alibi at the right time, obviously he could have hired someone."

Elisa chuckled. "Obvious enough to me." She continued tracing the rim of her teacup. "You need it to look like this man left on his own."

"Right," Julia said.

"Then, if you want *my kind of help*, send him to me."

"Right to you?"

"Not to my doorstep. A city nearby, in Michigan or Ohio. Don't send me driving all night. Tell him I'll pick him up and take him somewhere to lie low, as they say."

"And then?"

"And then you won't have your problem anymore. And this man will get what he deserves."

"I don't agree with that."

Elisa closed her eyes and exhaled a harsh laugh. "Are you so sure of that?"

Julia was silent for a moment longer.

Elisa might have registered this as weakness in someone else, and an obvious reason to hang up the phone. It was not weakness in Julia, though. She was at war within herself. The naive little house cat who believed in rules and order was being toppled by the puma who knew that some days, the only law is kill or be killed.

And she was an attorney. Thinking was her religion. She thought she could solve this like a logic puzzle, leaving her family intact and her morals unscathed. Julia did not understand what Elisa did: that all the thinking and weighing is meaningless, because in the end we are only as good as we are. And there are more important things than goodness.

"I'm not going to talk you into this," Elisa said. "You don't need my permission—you need your own. I'm not certain you have it yet."

"No," was all Julia said.

They spoke for a long while about what Julia believed she would need to get Raymond Walker on a bus out of town. She wanted counterfeit identification papers, travel tickets bought from untraceable accounts, the false promise of money waiting for Walker at the end of his journey, and, of course, the reality of an end to it all upon his arrival. And she wanted all of this from Elisa. Apparently Mathis had told Julia even more about his family than he'd been willing to admit to his mother.

Elisa sipped around the dregs of her tea as they sorted out the details of what Julia would need, and what Julia would do to get Raymond to Elisa. Julia occasionally interjected something like "if I even decide to do this," and Elisa would respond with a gentle "of course, of course." But she could feel her deciding.

Before they hung up, they agreed not to speak again by phone unless absolutely necessary—Julia had a clever explanation for their phone call, something to do with research for work related to her old cases, but it wouldn't explain multiple calls to the Midwest if her family fell under suspicion. Instead, Julia would send a postcard with the specifics Elisa needed to book the tickets, and only if Walker did not depart would Julia call Elisa again, to tell her that it was off.

In the days following their conversation, Elisa had put out calls in anticipation, collecting some of the pieces Julia would need. She only had to wait a week before the card came in the mail. It was postmarked Portland, Maine.

> *Dear Auntie Elisa,*
>
> *I'm excited to visit you this winter! I have quite a journey ahead of me. On Friday January 15 I'll be taking the 8:15 p.m. Concord Coach bus from Portland to Boston, then the 10:55 p.m. Amtrak train from the South Station to Toledo, though I think I might buy a ticket that could bring me all the way to Chicago, I've heard it's a lovely city. I'll arrive in Toledo on Saturday January 16 at 3:25 p.m., and from there I'll take the 3:55 Greyhound bus to Columbus, where I was hoping you'd pick me up. It would be around 12:25 a.m. on Sunday—I hope that is not too late.*
>
> *Looking forward to our visit. If there are any problems, you know how to reach me!*
>
> *Love,*
> *Your niece*

A couple of days later, Elisa overnighted a package to Julia: it held a fake driver's license; a photocopy of a dead man's passport; bank statements in the dead man's name, holding cash from one of Elisa's slush funds; and the bus and train tickets Julia had requested.

The baton passed back to Julia, Elisa had reviewed the postcard a final time before she flicked it into the woodstove.

Now, somewhere in the space between January 16 and 17, Elisa sat in her car and waited. Her foot drummed rhythmically against the floor in front of the pedals, sending reverberations through her body. She checked the time again.

The bus was two minutes late when it lurched into the station.

She thought back on the postcard. *If there are any problems, you know how to reach me!*

Julia did not want to know when it was done. She only wanted to know if it was not.

A young man stepped into view from behind the bus. The tall lights above the station cast shadows over his brow, pitting his eyes into holes as he scanned the parking lot.

Elisa flashed her lights, and Raymond Walker started toward the car.

She never did have occasion to contact Julia.

Acknowledgments

There are so many people who have had an impact on this story and its path to publication, and I'm afraid it's an impossible task to properly acknowledge each one of them. Fear of failure is a terrible reason not to do something, though, so here are the people I want to thank:

Helen Heller, the agent who blew up my life in the span of a week. Deciding to partner with you has been the best professional decision I've ever made.

My editorial team, Pamela Dorman, Jeramie Orton, Clio Cornish, Jill Taylor, and Marie Michels. You turned this novel into the story I was trying to tell. Erica Ferguson, copyeditor extraordinaire, who caught more mistakes than I will ever admit to making. Everyone at Pamela Dorman Books and Michael Joseph who touched this project and made me feel at home.

Editor and writer Clarence Haynes, whose notes on Nick's character and experience were invaluable.

Saliann St-Clair, Jemma McDonough, and Camilla Ferrier, who worked so hard to earn foreign deals for this book and then gamely answered my most inane questions about all of the weird tax forms. Ari

Solotoff, my former classmate who talked me through each contract because I cannot turn off the lawyer anxiety.

My early readers, including Melissa Martin, Anna Polko Clark, authors Maureen Milliken and Jeneva Rose, and my friends at the South Portland Public Library Writers' Group.

Taylor Sampson, Amanda Bombard, and James, who answered very different questions for me.

My aunt Cindy and uncle John Mina at Curry Printing in Portland, who printed many drafts of this novel over the last three years and cheered me on with each one.

Chloe, my best writing friend who let me steal her name, and who batted around query letters with me until I was brave enough to send them. Susan Dennard and Pitch Wars, for teaching me how to query agents in the first place.

My sister, Hannah, who told me to breathe deep and chase my crazy dream of publishing a novel. Mum and Dad, who encouraged reading and writing all my life. Mr. Ramsey, who told my dad I should stop worrying so much about what major I picked in college because I was just going to end up being an author.

And finally, Ben. You are the steady Julia to my spiraling Tony. Thank you for every single thing.

He just wanted a decent book to read ...

Not too much to ask, is it? It was in 1935 when Allen Lane, Managing Director of Bodley Head Publishers, stood on a platform at Exeter railway station looking for something good to read on his journey back to London. His choice was limited to popular magazines and poor-quality paperbacks – the same choice faced every day by the vast majority of readers, few of whom could afford hardbacks. Lane's disappointment and subsequent anger at the range of books generally available led him to found a company – and change the world.

'We believed in the existence in this country of a vast reading public for intelligent books at a low price, and staked everything on it'
Sir Allen Lane, 1902–1970, founder of Penguin Books

The quality paperback had arrived – and not just in bookshops. Lane was adamant that his Penguins should appear in chain stores and tobacconists, and should cost no more than a packet of cigarettes.

Reading habits (and cigarette prices) have changed since 1935, but Penguin still believes in publishing the best books for everybody to enjoy. We still believe that good design costs no more than bad design, and we still believe that quality books published passionately and responsibly make the world a better place.

So wherever you see the little bird – whether it's on a piece of prize-winning literary fiction or a celebrity autobiography, political tour de force or historical masterpiece, a serial-killer thriller, reference book, world classic or a piece of pure escapism – you can bet that it represents the very best that the genre has to offer.

Whatever you like to read – trust Penguin.

Maisie ...

Jacqueline Winspear was born and [...]
lives in California. The Maisie Dob[...]
acclaim and have been nominated [...]
Feather, *Pardonable Lies* and *Messeng[...]*
Maisie Dobbs mysteries, are all now available.

Praise for Maisie Dobbs

Winner of the Agatha Award
Shortlisted for the Edgar Award for Best Novel
Winner of the Macavity Award for Best First Novel

'A wry and immensely readable beginning to what promises to be a vivid new addition to crime fiction' *Mail on Sunday*

'Readers sensing a story-within-a-story won't be disappointed. But first, they must prepare to be astonished at the sensitivity and wisdom with which Maisie resolves her first professional assignment' *New York Times*

'Compelling . . . A gem' *Houston Chronicle*

'It's a long time since I've read a crime novel that begins as well as Jacqueline Winspear's *Maisie Dobbs* . . . [Winspear has] a very bright future as a crime novelist' *Daily Mail*

'Jacqueline Winspear's Maisie Dobbs is a welcome addition to the sleuthing scene. Simultaneously self-reliant and vulnerable, Maisie isn't a character I'll easily forget' *Elizabeth George*

'Surprisingly fresh . . . Compelling' *San Francisco Chronicle*

'Maisie Dobbs is a welcome and unusual addition to the crowded world of literary d[...] whodunnit' *Sai[...]*

'Even if detective stories a[...] *Maisie Dobbs'*

Maisie Dobbs

A Novel

JACQUELINE WINSPEAR

John Murray

© Jacqueline Winspear 2003

First published by Soho Press, Inc. in the United States of America

First published in Great Britain in 2004 by John Murray (Publishers)
A division of Hodder Headline

Paperback edition 2005

The right of Jacqueline Winspear to be identified as the
Author of the Work has been asserted by her in accordance
with the Copyright, Designs and Patents Act 1988.

17

A CIP catalogue record for this title is
available from the British Library

ISBN 978-0-7195-6622-6

Typeset in Bembo
Printed and bound by Clays Ltd, St Ives plc

Hodder Headline policy is to use papers that are natural, renewable
and recyclable products and made from wood grown in sustainable
forests. The logging and manufacturing processes are expected to
conform to the environmental regulations of the country of origin.

John Murray (Publishers)
338 Euston Road
London NW1 3BH

$\mathcal{T}$his book is dedicated to the memory of
my paternal grandfather and my maternal grandmother

JOHN "JACK" WINSPEAR sustained serious leg wounds during the Battle of the Somme in July 1916. Following convalescence, he returned to his work as a costermonger in southeast London.

CLARA FRANCES CLARK, née Atterbury, was a munitions worker at the Woolwich Arsenal during the First World War. She was partially blinded in an explosion that killed several girls working in the same section alongside her. Clara later married and became the mother of ten children.

Now, he will spend a few sick years in institutes,
And do what things the rules consider wise,
And take whatever pity they may dole.
Tonight he noticed how the women's eyes
Passed from him to the strong men that were whole.
How cold and late it is! Why don't they come
And put him to bed? Why don't they come?

Final verse "Disabled," by Wilfred Owen. It was drafted at Craiglockhart, a hospital for shell-shocked officers, in October 1917. Owen was killed on November 4, 1918, just one week before the armistice.

SPRING 1929

CHAPTER ONE

Even if she hadn't been the last person to walk through the turnstile at Warren Street tube station, Jack Barker would have noticed the tall, slender woman in the navy blue thigh-length jacket with a matching pleated skirt short enough to reveal a well-turned ankle. She had what his old mother would have called "bearing." A way of walking, with her shoulders back and head held high, as she pulled on her black gloves while managing to hold on to a somewhat battered black document case.

"Old money," muttered Jack to himself. "Stuck-up piece of nonsense."

Jack expected the woman to pass him by, so he stamped his feet in a vain attempt to banish the sharp needles of cold creeping up through his hobnailed boots. He fanned a half dozen copies of the *Daily Express* over one arm, anticipating a taxi-cab screeching to a halt and a hand reaching out with the requisite coins.

"Oh, wait! – May I have an *Express* please?" appealed a voice as smooth as spooned treacle.

The newspaper vendor looked up slowly, straight into eyes the colour of midnight in summer, an intense shade that seemed to him to be darker than blue. She held out her money.

"'Course, Miss, 'ere you are. Bit nippy this morning!"

She smiled, and as she took the paper from him before turning to walk away, she replied, "Not half! Better get yourself a nice hot cuppa."

Jack couldn't have told you why he watched the woman walk all the way down Warren Street toward Fitzroy Square. But he did know one thing: She might have bearing, but from the familiar way she spoke to him, she certainly wasn't from old money.

At the end of Warren Street, Maisie Dobbs stopped in front of the black front door of a somewhat rundown Georgian terraced house, tucked the *Daily Express* under her left arm, carefully opened her document case, and took out an envelope containing a letter from her landlord and two keys. The letter instructed her to give the outside door a good shove after turning the key in the lock, to light the gas lamp at the base of the stairs carefully, to mind the top step of the first flight of stairs – which needed to be looked at – and to remember to lock her own door before leaving in the evening. The letter also told her that Billy Beale, the caretaker, would put up her nameplate on the outside door if she liked or, it suggested, perhaps she would prefer to remain anonymous.

Maisie grinned. I need the business, she said to herself. I'm not here to remain anonymous.

Maisie suspected that Mr Sharp, the landlord, was unlikely to live up to his name, and that he would pose questions with obvious answers each time they met. However, his directions were apt: the door did indeed need a shove, but the gas lamp, once lit, hardly dented the musky darkness of the stairwell. Clearly there were some things that needed to be changed, but all in good time. For the moment Maisie had work to do, even if she had no actual cases to work on.

Minding the top step, Maisie turned right on the landing and headed straight for the brown painted door on the left, the one with a frosted glass window and a To Let sign hanging from the doorknob. She removed the sign, put the key into the lock, opened the door and took a deep breath before stepping into her new office. It was a single room with a gas fire, a gas lamp on each wall, and one sash window with a view of the building across the street and the rooftops beyond. There was an oak desk with a matching chair of dubious stability, and an old filing cabinet to the right of the window.

Lady Rowan Compton, her patron and former employer, had been correct: Warren Street wasn't a particularly salubrious area. But if she played her cards right, Maisie could afford the rent and have some money left over from the sum she had allowed herself to take from her savings. She didn't want a fancy office, but she didn't want an out-and-out dump either. No, she wanted something in the middle, something for everyone, something central, but then again not in the thick of things. Maisie felt a certain comfort in this small corner of Bloomsbury. They said that you could sit down to tea with just about anyone around Fitzroy Square, and dine with a countess and a carpenter at the same table, with both of them at ease in the company. Yes, Warren Street would be good for now. The tricky thing was going to be the nameplate. She still hadn't solved the problem of the nameplate.

As Lady Rowan had asked, "So, my dear, what will you call yourself? I mean, we all know what you do, but what will be your trade name? You can hardly state the obvious. 'Finds missing people, dead or alive, even when it's themselves they are looking for' really doesn't cut the mustard. We have to think of something succinct, something that draws upon your unique talents."

"I was thinking of 'Discreet Investigations,' Lady Rowan. What do you think?"

"But that doesn't tell anyone about how you use your mind, my dear – what you actually do."

"It's not really my mind I'm using, it's other people's. I just ask the questions."

"Poppycock! What about 'Discreet Cerebral Investigations'?"

Maisie smiled at Lady Rowan, raising an eyebrow in mock dismay at the older woman's suggestion. She was at ease, seated in front of the fireplace in her former employer's library, a fireplace she had once cleaned with the raw, housework-roughened hands of a maid in service.

"No, I'm not a brain surgeon. I'm going to think about it for a bit, Lady Rowan. I want to get it right."

The grey-haired aristocrat leaned over and patted Maisie on the knee. "I'm sure that whatever you choose, you will do very well, my dear. Very well indeed."

So it was that when Billy Beale, the caretaker, knocked on the door one week after Maisie moved into the Warren Street office, asking if there was a nameplate to put up at the front door, Maisie handed him a brass plate bearing the words "M. Dobbs. Trade and Personal Investigations."

"Where do you want it, Miss? Left of the door or right of the door?"

He turned his head very slightly to one side as he addressed her. Billy was about thirty years old, just under six feet tall, muscular and strong, with hair the colour of sun-burnished wheat. He seemed agile, but worked hard to disguise a limp that Maisie had noticed immediately.

"Where have they put the other names?"

"On the left, Miss, but I wouldn't put it there if I was you."

"Oh, and why not, Mr Beale?"

"Billy. You can call me Billy. Well, people don't really look to the left, do they? Not when they're using the doorknob, which is on the right. That's where the eyes go straightaway when they walk up them steps, first to that lion's 'ead door knocker, then to the knob, on the right. Best 'ave the plate on the right. That's if you want their business."

"Well Mr Beale, let's have the plate on the right. Thank you."

"Billy, Miss. You can call me Billy."

Billy Beale went to fit the brass nameplate. Maisie sighed deeply and rubbed her neck at the place where worry always sat when it was making itself at home.

"Miss . . . ."

Billy poked his head around the door, tentatively knocking at the glass as he removed his flat cap.

"What is it, Mr Beale?"

"Billy, Miss. Miss, can I have a quick word?"

"Yes, come in. What is it?"

"Miss, might I ask a question? Personal, like." Billy continued without waiting for an answer. "Was you a nurse? At a casualty clearing station? Outside of Bailleul?"

Maisie felt a strong stab of emotion, and instinctively put her right hand to her chest, but her demeanour and words were calm.

"Yes. Yes, I was."

"I knew it!" said Billy, slapping his cap across his knee. "I just knew it the minute I saw those eyes. That's all I remember, after they brought me in. Them eyes of yours, Miss. Doctor said to concentrate on looking at something while 'e worked on me leg. So I looked at your eyes, Miss. You and 'im saved my leg. Full of shrapnel, but you did it, didn't you? What was 'is name?"

For a moment, Maisie's throat was paralyzed. Then she swallowed hard. "Simon Lynch. Captain Simon Lynch. That must be who you mean."

"I never forgot you, Miss. Never. Saved my life, you did."

Maisie nodded, endeavouring to keep her memories relegated to the place she had assigned them in her heart, to be taken out only when she allowed.

"Well, Miss. Anything you ever want doing, you just 'oller. I'm your man. Stroke of luck, meeting up with you again. Wait till I tell the missus! You want anything done, you call me. Anything."

"Thank you. Thank you very much. I'll holler if I need anything. Oh, and Mr . . . Billy, thank you for taking care of the sign."

Billy Beale blushed and nodded, covered his burnished hair with his cap, and left the office.

Lucky, thought Maisie. Except for the war, I've had a lucky life so far. She sat down on the dubious oak chair, slipped off her shoes and rubbed her feet. Feet that still felt the cold and wet and filth and blood of France. Feet that hadn't felt warm in twelve years, since 1917.

She remembered Simon, in another life it seemed now, sitting under a tree on the South Downs in Sussex. They had been on leave at the same time – not a miracle of course, but difficult to arrange, unless you had connections where connections counted. It was a warm day, but not one that took them entirely away from the fighting, for they could still hear the deep echo of battlefield cannonade from the other side of the English Channel, a menacing sound not diminished by the intervening expanse of land and sea. Maisie had complained then that the damp of France would never leave her, and Simon, smiling, had pulled off her walking shoes to rub warmth into her feet.

"Goodness, woman, how can anyone be that cold and not be dead?"

They both laughed, and then fell silent. Death, in such times, was not a laughing matter.

CHAPTER TWO

The small office had changed in the thirty days since Maisie had taken up occupancy. The desk had been moved and was now positioned at an angle to the broad sash window, so that from her chair Maisie could look up and out over the rooftops as she worked. A very sophisticated black telephone sat on top of the desk, at the insistence of Lady Rowan, who maintained that "No one, simply no one, can expect to do business without a telephone. It is essential, positively essential." As far as Maisie was concerned, what was essential was that the trilling of its authoritative ring be heard a bit more often. Billy Beale had also taken to suggesting improvements lately.

"Can't have folk up 'ere for business without offering 'em a cuppa, can you, Miss? Let me open up that cupboard, put in a burner, and away you go. Bob's yer uncle, all you need for brewing up. What d'you think, Miss? I can nip down the road to my mate's carpentry shop for the extra wood, and run the gas along 'ere for you. No trouble."

"Lovely, Billy. That would be lovely."

Maisie sighed. It seemed that everyone else knew what would be best for her. Of course their hearts were in the right place, but what she needed most now was some clients.

"Shall I advance you the money for supplies, Billy?"

"No money needed," said Billy, winking and tapping the side of his nose with his forefinger. "Nod's as good as a wink to a blind 'orse, if you know what I mean, Miss."

Maisie raised an eyebrow and allowed herself a grin. "I know exactly what that saying means, Billy: what I don't see, I shouldn't worry about."

"You got it, Miss. Leave it to me. A couple o' ticks, and you'll be ready to receive your visitors in style."

Billy replaced his cap, put a forefinger to the peak to gesture his departure, and closed the door behind him. Leaning back in her chair, Maisie rubbed at tired eyes and looked over the late afternoon rooftops. She watched as the sun drifted away to warm the shores of another continent, leaving behind a rose tint to bathe London at the end of a long day.

Looking again at her handwritten notes, Maisie continued rereading a draft of the report she was in the midst of preparing. The case in question was minor, but Maisie had learned the value of detailed note-taking from Maurice Blanche. During her apprenticeship with him, he had been insistent that nothing was to be left to memory, no stone to remain unturned, and no small observation uncatalogued. Everything, absolutely *everything*, right down to the colour of the shoes the subject wore on the day in question, must be noted. The weather must be described, the direction of the wind, the flowers in bloom, the food eaten. Everything must be described and preserved. "You must write it down, absolutely and in its entirety, write it down," instructed her mentor. Maisie thought that if she had a shilling for every time she heard the words, "absolutely, and in its entirety," she would never have to work again.

Maisie rubbed her neck once more, closed the folder on her desk, and stretched her arms above her head. The doorbell's deep clattering ring broke the silence. At first Maisie thought that someone had pulled the bell handle in error. There had been few rings since Billy installed the new device, which sounded in Maisie's office. Despite the fact that Maisie had worked with Maurice Blanche and had taken over his practice when he retired at the age of seventy-six, establishing her name independent of Maurice was proving to be a challenge indeed. The bell rang again.

Maisie pressed her skirt with her hands, patted her head to tame any stray tendrils of hair, and hurried downstairs to the door.

"Good. . . ." The man hesitated, then consulted a watch that he drew from his waistcoat pocket, as if to ascertain the accurate greeting for the time of day. "Good evening. My name is Davenham, Christopher Davenham. I'm here to see Mr Dobbs. I have no appointment, but was assured that he would see me."

He was tall, about six feet two inches by Maisie's estimate. Fine tweed suit, hat taken off to greet her at just the right moment, but repositioned quickly. Good leather shoes, probably buffed to a shine by his manservant. *The Times* was rolled up under one arm, but with a sheet or two of writing paper coiled inside and just visible. His own notes, thought Maisie. His jet black hair was swept back and oiled, and his moustache neatly trimmed. Christopher Davenham was about forty-two or forty-three. Only seconds had passed since his introduction, but Maisie had him sized up. This one had not been a soldier. In a protected profession, she suspected.

"Come this way, Mr Davenham. There are no appointments set for this evening, so you are in luck."

Maisie led the way up to her office, and invited Christopher Davenham to sit in the new guest chair opposite her own, the chair that had been delivered just last week by Lady Rowan's chauffeur. Another gift to help her business along.

Davenham looked around for a moment, expecting someone else to step out to meet him, but instead the young woman introduced herself.

"Maisie Dobbs. At your service, Mr Davenham." She waved her hand toward the chair again. "Do please take a seat, Mr Davenham. Now then, first tell me how you came to have my name."

Christopher Davenham hid his surprise well, taking a linen

handkerchief from his inside pocket and coughing lightly into it. The handkerchief was so freshly laundered and ironed that the folds were still knife sharp. Davenham refolded the handkerchief along the exact lines pressed by the iron, and replaced it in his pocket.

"Miss, er, Dobbs. Well, um, well . . . you have been highly recommended by my solicitor."

"Who is?"

Maisie leaned her head to one side to accentuate the question, and to move the conversation onto more fertile ground.

"Oh, um, Blackstone & Robinson. Joseph Robinson."

Maisie nodded. Lady Rowan again. Joseph Robinson had been her personal legal adviser for forty-odd years. And he didn't suffer fools gladly unless they were paying him – and paying him well.

"Been the family solicitor for years. I'll be frank with you, Miss Dobbs. I'm surprised to see you. Thought you'd be a chap. But Robinson knows his stuff, so let's continue."

"Yes, let's, Mr Davenham. Perhaps you would tell me why you are here."

"My wife."

Maisie's stomach churned. Oh, Lord, after all her training, her education, her successes with Maurice Blanche, had it come to this? A love triangle? But she sat up to listen carefully, remembering Blanche's advice: "The extraordinary hides behind the camouflage of the ordinary. Assume nothing, Maisie."

"And what about your wife, Mr Davenham?"

"I believe . . . I believe her affections are engaged elsewhere. I have suspected it for some time and now, Miss Dobbs, I must know if what I suspect is true."

Maisie leaned back in her chair and regarded Christopher Davenham squarely. "Mr Davenham, first of all, I must tell you that I shall have to ask you some questions. They may not be questions that are easy or comfortable for you to answer. I will have questions about your responses, and even questions about your questions. That is my job. I am unique in what I do. I am also unique in what I charge for my service."

"Money is not a problem, Miss Dobbs."

"Good. The questions may be, though."

"Do continue."

"Mr Davenham, please tell me what personal evidence you have to suspect that your wife is betraying your marriage in any way?"

"Tuesdays and Thursdays, every week, without fail, she leaves the house immediately after I have departed for my office, and returns just in time to welcome me home."

"Mr Davenham, time away from the house is no reason for you to suspect that you are being deceived."

"The lies are, though."

"Go on." Maisie wrote in her notebook without taking her eyes off Davenham, a skill that unnerved him.

"She has told me that she has been shopping, visiting friends or her mother – and upon investigation I find that if she has made such visits, they have taken only an hour or so. Clearly they are a smoke-screen."

"There are other possibilities, Mr Davenham. Could your wife, perhaps, be visiting her physician? Is she undertaking a course of study? What other reasons for her absences have you explored in your investigations, Mr Davenham? Such absences may have a completely innocent explanation."

"Miss Dobbs. Surely that is for you to find out? Follow her, and you will see that I am right."

"Mr Davenham. To follow a person is an invasion of the right of that individual to privacy. If I take on this case – and I do have a choice in the matter – I am taking on more than the question of who did what and when. I am taking on a responsibility for both you and your wife in a way that you may not have considered. Tell me, what will you do with the information I provide?"

"Well, I . . . I'll use it. It will be a matter for my solicitor."

Maisie placed her hands together in front of her face, just touching her nose, as if in prayer. "Let me ask you another question. What value do you place on your marriage?"

"What sort of question is that?"

"A question to be answered, if I am to take on this investigation."

"A high value. Vows are meant to be honoured."

"And what value do you place on understanding, compassion, forgiveness?"

Davenham was silent. He crossed his legs, smoothed the tweed trousers, and leaned down to rub away a nonexistent scuff on his polished leather shoes before responding. "Damn and blast!"

"Mr Davenham —"

"Miss Dobbs, I am not without compassion, but I have my pride. My wife will not divulge the nature of her business on those days when she is absent. I have come here in order to learn the truth."

"Oh yes. The truth. Mr Davenham, I will ascertain the truth for you, but I must have an agreement from you — that when you have my report, and you know the truth, then we will discuss the future together."

"What do you mean?"

"The information I gather will be presented in a context. It is in light of that context that we must continue our discussion, in order for you and your wife to build a future."

"I'm sure I don't know what you mean."

Maisie stood up, walked to the window, then turned to face her potential client. The bluff of the stiff upper lip, thought Maisie, who keenly felt the man's discomfort, and was immediately attuned to his emotions. Intuition spoke to her. *He talks about pride when it's his heart that's aching.*

"My job is rather more complex than you might have imagined, Mr Davenham. I am responsible for the safety of all parties. And this is so even when I am dealing with society's more criminal elements."

Davenham did not respond immediately. Maisie, too, was silent, allowing him time to gather his resolve. After some minutes the stillness of the room was broken.

"I trust Robinson, so I will go ahead," said Davenham.

Maisie moved back to the desk, and looked down at her notes, then to the rooftops where pigeons were busy returning to newly built nests, before she brought her attention back to the man in the leather chair before her.

"Yes, Mr Davenham. I will, too." Maisie allowed her acceptance of the case to be underlined by another moment of silence.

"Now then, let's start with your address, shall we?"

CHAPTER THREE

*M*aisie rose early on Tuesday, April 9. She dressed carefully in the blue skirt and jacket, pulled a navy blue wool overcoat across her shoulders, placed a cloche hat on her head, and left her rented room in a large three-story Victorian terraced house in Lambeth, just south of the Thames. It was cold again. Blimey, would spring ever spring up? she wondered, pulling gloves onto already chilled fingers.

As usual Maisie began her morning with a brisk walk, which allowed her time to consider the day ahead and enjoy what her father always called "the best of the morning." She entered Palace Road from Royal Street, and turned right to walk toward Westminster Bridge. She loved to watch the Thames first thing in the morning. Those Londoners who lived just south of the river always said they were "going over the water" when they crossed the Thames, never referring to the river by name unless they were speaking to a stranger. It had been the lifeblood of the city since the Middle Ages, and no people felt the legacy more keenly than those who lived with it and by it. Her maternal grandfather had been a lighterman on the water, and like all of his kind, knew the river's tides, her every twist and turn.

Londoners knew she was a moody creature. Human beings possessed no dominion over the Thames, but care, attention and respect would see any vessel safely along her meandering way. Maisie's grandfather had all but disowned her mother when she had taken up with Maisie's father, for he was of the land, not that Frankie Dobbs would have called the streets of London "the land." Frankie was a costermonger who sold vegetables from a horse-drawn cart that he drove from Lambeth to Covent Garden market every weekday morning. To Frankie Dobbs the water was a means to an end, bringing fruit and vegetables to market for him to buy in the early hours of the morning, then sell on his rounds and be home by teatime, if he was lucky.

Maisie stopped at the centre of the bridge, waved at the crew of a pilot boat, and went on her way. She was off to see Celia Davenham, but Celia Davenham would not see her.

Once across the bridge, Maisie descended into Westminster underground station and took the District Line to Charing Cross. The station had changed names back and forth so many times, she wondered what it would be called next. First it was Embankment, then Charing Cross Embankment, and now just Charing Cross, depending upon which line you were travelling. At Charing Cross she changed trains, and took the Northern Line to Goodge Street, where she left the underground, coming back up into the sharp morning air at Tottenham Court Road. She crossed the road, then set off along Chenies Street toward Russell Square. Once across the square, she entered Guilford Street, where she stopped to look at the mess the powers that be had made of Coram's Fields. The old foundling hospital, built by Sir Thomas Coram almost two hundred years before, had been demolished in 1926, and now it was just an empty space with nothing to speak of happening to it. "Shame," whispered Maisie, as she walked another few yards and entered Mecklenburg Square.

Named in honour of Charlotte of Mecklenburg-Strelitz, who became queen consort upon her marriage to George III, the gracious Georgian houses of the square were set around a garden protected by a wrought-iron railing and a locked gate. Doubtless a key to the lock was on a designated hook downstairs at the Davenham residence, in the butler's safekeeping, for only residents had access to the garden.

Maisie jotted a few more lines in her notebook, taking care to note that she had been to the square once before, accompanying Maurice Blanche during a visit to his colleague, Richard Tawney, the political writer who spoke of social equality in a way that both excited and embarrassed Maisie. At the time it seemed just as well that he and Maurice were deep in lively conversation, so that Maisie's lack of ease could go unnoticed.

While waiting at the corner and surveying the square, Maisie wondered if Davenham had inherited his property. He seemed quite out of place in Mecklenburg Square, where social reformers lived alongside university professors, poets, and scholars from overseas. She considered his possible discomfort, not only in his marriage but in his home environment. As Maisie set her gaze on one house in particular, a man emerged from a neighbouring house and walked in her direction. She quickly feigned interest in a window box filled with crocus buds peeking through moist soil. Their purple shoots seemed to test the air to see if it was conducive to a full-fledged flowering. The man passed. Maisie still had her head inclined toward the flowers when she heard another door close with a thud, and looked up.

A woman had emerged from the house Maisie had been observing, and was now depositing a set of keys in her handbag. She adjusted her hat and made her way down the steps and onto the pavement. Christopher Davenham had provided Maisie with an excellent description of his wife Celia, a petite, fair-complexioned woman with fine features, no taller than five feet two. Celia Davenham had silky blonde hair that tended to unsettle a hat that already required more than one hatpin to render it secure, and hands that seemed constantly to fiddle with bag, gloves, hat and hair as she walked to the main road.

Even from a distance of several paces, Maisie noted the quality of the woman's deep burgundy gabardine suit, and the soft leather gloves and felt hat chosen to complement the expensive ensemble precisely. Her shoes had clearly been chosen with care as well, for they were of fine burgundy leather with half straps at each side that met in the center and were secured with a grosgrain ribbon tied in a small bow. Maisie was intrigued by the bow for it suggested a certain girlishness, as if the woman could not quite accommodate the maturity her age suggested.

Celia Davenham made her way toward Heathcote Street and turned into Grays Inn Road, where she hailed a taxi-cab outside the Royal Free Hospital. Fortunately Maisie managed to secure a taxi-cab at once, so that she could travel immediately behind Mrs Davenham. As she sat in the rear seat of the heavy black motorcar, she hoped that the journey would be a short one. For Maisie travel by any means other than her own two feet was nothing but an indulgence. The journey by underground to Warren Street was a treat she allowed herself in the morning only if she considered that she had worked hard enough to warrant the additional expenditure.

At Charing Cross station Celia Davenham climbed out of the cab, paid the driver, and proceeded to the ticket counter. Maisie followed closely. She stood behind Mrs Davenham at the ticket counter, and pretended to fumble in her bag for her purse, listening keenly as the childlike woman with the soft blonde hair stated her destination.

"Nether Green, please. First-class return, thank you."

What on earth could this woman want at Nether Green, a small town just south of London, on the borders of Kent? Apple orchards giving way to terraced houses, an old station, a few good homes. Now if she had asked for Chislehurst, with its new-money grandeur, Maisie thought she might have understood. But Nether Green? Maisie requested a second-class ticket for the same destination, then proceeded to the correct platform to await the train. She stopped only to buy a newspaper, which she carried under her arm.

The train pulled in with a loud hiss, pumping clouds of smoky steam as the engine reached the buffers and the screeching brakes were applied. The olive green livery of Southern Railways, painted on each carriage, was tarnished by coal dust and wear. Celia Davenham immediately walked toward the first-class compartments, whereupon a guard hurriedly stepped forward to open the sturdy, iron-framed door, and to extend a steadying hand as she stepped up into the carriage. Maisie passed on the way to the second-class carriages, and just before the door closed, noticed that the collar and cuffs of Mrs Davenham's burgundy suit were edged with the same ribbon used to form a bow on her shoes. She quickly re-estimated the cost of the clothes the woman was wearing that day.

Having ensured that the object of her investigation was aboard the train, Maisie claimed a seat in a second-class carriage, pulled down the window to observe the platform, and waited for the whistle to blow and the train to chug out of one of London's busiest stations. Eventually the guard walked down the platform, instructing Maisie as he passed that it would be better for "yer 'ead, Miss," if she sat down. He checked that the train was clear of all platform onlookers, blew his whistle, and waved his green flag to the engine driver.

As the train chugged and puffed its way through south London and out into the borders of Kent, Maisie pondered the changes she had seen in the city in her lifetime. London was creeping outwards. Where there had been fields, houses now stood. Rows of shops were doing brisk business, and a new commuter class was working to improve itself. By the time the train reached Grove Park, Maisie had brought her notes up to date again, ensuring that each small detail of her journey, from the time she left her rented flat in south London that morning until the present moment, was recorded – along with every penny she had spent along the way.

The next stop was Nether Green. Maisie stood, inspected her reflection in a mirror strategically placed between two dim lights above her seat, adjusted her hat, and sat down again to wait for the train to slow down, for the hissing of brakes. As the carriages rolled into the station, Maisie stood once more, pulled down the window and poked her head out to keep an eye on the first-class compartments. When the train came to a halt Maisie put her arm out of the window so she could open the heavy carriage door from the outside and, keeping the first-class compartments in view, she jumped smartly from the train and walked at a brisk pace toward the ticket collector. Celia Davenham was ahead by only a few yards, obscured slightly by other passengers, including a very slow old lady who would not be rushed.

"Now just you wait, young man," said the old woman to the ticket collector. "It's a poor state of affairs if you can't give your elders and betters a minute or two to find the ticket."

The ticket collector stepped back a pace, as if anticipating a blow to the head from the doughty woman's black umbrella. Maisie waited impatiently, for Celia Davenham had passed through the barrier and was leaving the station. Finally she reached the ticket collector, handed over her ticket, and walked as quickly as she could to the station gate. Glancing both ways, Maisie saw that Celia had paused by a flower stall. Luck indeed. She walked toward the stall, rearranging the newspaper under her arm and consulting her watch, even though she knew the time to the second. She approached it just as Celia Davenham was walking away.

Maisie looked over the bunches of fragrant blooms while addressing the stallholder. "Lovely flowers, the ones you wrapped for that lady."

"Yes, Ma'am, very nice. Always has the irises."

"Always?"

"Yes, twice a week. Never fails."

"Oh well, she must like them," said Maisie, picking up a small bunch of Jersey daffodils. "I think I'll have something a bit different, though."

"Colour of mourning, those irises," observed the man. "These daffs are a lot more cheerful!"

Maisie looked at her watch and made sure that Celia Davenham was still in sight. She walked slowly, but was not distracted by goods displayed in shopwindows. Keeping her eyes focused on the ground, she seemed to be avoiding any contact with people passing by.

"Well, I think so, too. I'll take the daffs, thank you very much."

"We sell a lot of irises, what with the cemetery up the road. That and chrysanths, always popular."

Maisie took the bunch of daffodils and handed over the exact change in pennies.

"Thank you. Very nice indeed."

She set forth at a steady pace, and was soon just a few steps behind Celia Davenham. They had passed the shops now, and although there were still passersby, the number of pedestrians heading in the same direction was thinning out. Celia Davenham turned right, then left onto the main road. She waited for some motorcars and a horse-drawn cart to pass, looking ahead to the green-painted iron gates of Nether Green Cemetery. Maisie followed, careful to maintain her distance yet still keep the other woman in view.

Celia Davenham walked with purpose, her head lowered but her step firm. Maisie watched her, mentally noting every detail of the other woman's demeanour. Her shoulders were held too square, hunched upward as if on a coat hanger. Maisie copied the woman's posture as she walked, and immediately felt her stomach clench and a shiver go though her. Then sadness descended, like a dark veil across her eyes. Maisie knew that Celia Davenham was weeping as she walked, and that in her sadness she was searching for strength. With a sense of relief, as she walked along Maisie shook off the other woman's way of holding herself.

She followed Celia Davenham through the open gates, and along a path for about fifty yards. Then, without changing her pace, the object of Maisie's investigation turned in from the path and walked across the grass, pausing by a relatively fresh grave. The large marble angel towering above a neighbouring grave caught Maisie's eye, and she made a mental note of this landmark. She knew she'd have to be careful. One grave can seem much like the next one when you are in a cemetery.

The cold seemed to close in around Maisie as she walked past Celia Davenham. A train chugged along the tracks nearby, its sooty vapour lingering for a moment over the headstones before being carried away by a chill breeze.

Maisie stopped by a grave that had clearly received no attention for years. She bowed her head and, carefully, looked sideways between the marble memorials towards Celia Davenham. The woman was on her knees now, replacing dead flowers with the fresh irises, and talking. Talking to the dead.

Maisie, in turn, looked at the headstone she had unwittingly chosen as her cover. It bore the words: "Donald Holden. Born 1900. Died 1919. Beloved only son of Ernest and Hilda Holden. 'Memory Is A Golden Chain That Binds Us 'Til We Meet Again.'" Maisie looked at the weeds underfoot. They may have met already, she thought, while keeping a keen but inconspicuous watch on Celia Davenham, who remained at the immaculate neighbouring grave, her head bowed, still speaking quietly. Maisie began to clear the weeds on Donald Holden's grave.

"Might as well look after you while I'm here," she said quietly, placing daffodils in the vase, which was mercifully full of rainwater. She couldn't afford to trudge all the way across the cemetery to the water tap: Celia might depart while she was gone.

As Maisie stepped to the side of the path to deposit a pile of weeds, she saw Celia Davenham move toward the headstone where she had held her vigil. She kissed the cold, grey marble, brushed away a tear, then turned quickly and walked away. Maisie was in no hurry to follow. Instead she nodded at Donald Holden's headstone, then walked over to the grave that the Davenham woman had just left. It said "Vincent." Just "Vincent." No other name, no date of birth. Then the words, "Taken from all who love you dearly."

❋

$\mathcal{T}$he day had warmed by the time Maisie reached the station for the return journey to London. Celia Davenham, already on the platform, glanced at her watch repeatedly. Maisie went into the ladies' toilets, walked across chilly floor tiles that radiated more moisture into the damp air, and ran icy water into the porcelain sink to rinse the dirt from her hands. She looked up into the mirror and regarded the face that looked directly back at her. Yes, the dark blue eyes still held a sparkle, but the small lines around her lips and across her brow betrayed her, told something about her past.

She knew that she would follow Celia Davenham this afternoon until the woman returned to her home in Mecklenburg Square, and believed that nothing else of note would occur that day. Maisie knew that she had found the lover, the man who had caused Christopher Davenham to pay a princely sum for her services. The problem was that the man Christopher Davenham thought was cuckolding him was dead.

CHAPTER FOUR

*M*aisie sat in the early morning half-light of her office considering her subject. Only one small lamp illuminated the room, but it was angled downward toward Maisie's notes and a clutch of small index cards. Maurice maintained that the mind was at its sharpest before dawn.

In the early days of her pupilage with Maurice, he had told Maisie of his teachers, the wise men who spoke of the veil that was lifted in the early hours, of the all-seeing eye that was open before the day was awake. The hours before dawn were the sacred time, before the intellect rose from slumber. At this time one's inner voice could be heard. Maisie had strained to hear that inner voice for days, since the single word "Vincent" had piqued her curiosity, since the apparent ordinariness of Celia Davenham's grief had given rise to more questions than answers.

Slipping off her shoes and pulling her wool cardigan around her shoulders, Maisie took a cushion from her chair and placed it on the floor. Lifting her skirt above her knees to allow freedom of movement, she sat on the cushion, crossed her legs and placed her hands together on her lap. Maurice had taught her that silencing the mind was a greater task than stilling the body, but it was in those still waters that truth could be mirrored. Now, in the darkness, Maisie sought the guidance of intuition and formed the questions that, in time, would give her answers.

Why only one name? Why no dates etched into the headstone? What was keeping the relationship between Celia and Vincent alive? Was it simply grief, perpetuated by disbelief that a dear one has departed? Or another emotion? Maisie saw the grave in her mind's eye, allowed her eyes to regard all aspects of the place where Vincent was laid to rest. But if he was at rest, why did she feel compelled to seek a path that was not as yet marked?

What is this question I cannot voice? Maisie asked herself. Donald Holden died just a year after the war. His grave bore signs of age. Vincent's seemed fresher, as if the ground had been disturbed only in recent months.

Maisie sat for a while longer, allowing the stillness to calm her natural busyness, until the brighter, grainy light of the waking hours signalled her to move. She stood, stretching her arms high while standing on tiptoe. Today she would follow Celia Davenham to the cemetery again.

Celia was a creature of habit. This day she left the house promptly at nine o'clock in the morning, immaculately dressed in a suit of shamrock green wool, the broad collar of a cream silk blouse flat against her jacket, and pinned with a jade brooch, clearly part of a set that included her jade earrings. Matching shoes and bag with a carefully coordinated hat and umbrella completed the ensemble. This time the shoes were plain in design, but each shoe bore a fashionable clip in the shape of a leaf pressed onto the front. Maisie wore her navy skirt and jacket. Her serious business clothes. The journey to Nether Green was uneventful. Once again Celia Davenham travelled first class, while Maisie sat in the prickly discomfort of a second-class carriage. Celia bought her customary bouquet of irises, while Maisie decided upon something different for Donald – and for her purse – this morning.

"I'll have a nice bunch of daisies, please," said Maisie to the flower seller.

"Right you are, Miss. Always look cheerful, daisies, don't they, Miss? Last a while too. Newspaper all right, or do you need them wrapped special?"

"Yes, they are cheerful, aren't they? Newspaper will be fine, thank you," she said, holding out the correct change for a bunch of daisies.

Then Maisie quickly walked on, trailing Celia Davenham toward the cemetery. She entered through the green gates, and by the time she walked past Vincent's grave toward Donald Holden's resting place, Celia was standing in front of the marble headstone, tracing Vincent's name with the shamrock-green-gloved fingers of her right hand. Maisie walked past, her head lowered, and stopped in front of Donald's grave. After a respectful silent prayer, she busied herself, emptying water from the vase and pulling a few weeds. Picking up the now-dead daffodils from her previous visit, she walked over to the tap, threw the dead flowers onto the compost heap and filled the vase with fresh water. Maisie returned to Donald's grave, replaced the vase, and arranged the daisies. As she worked, she looked sideways at Celia, who had removed her gloves and was arranging her bouquet of irises at the base of Vincent's headstone. Having placed them to her satisfaction, she continued to kneel by the stone, staring at the name.

Maisie observed Celia Davenham, and once again moved her body to mirror the woman's position. Her head seemed to sink lower on her long neck, her shoulders rounded, her hands tightened with pain. Such melancholy. Such an unending yearning. Maisie instinctively knew that Celia was dying inside, that each yesterday was being lived anew and that there could be no place for her husband until Vincent was allowed to rest in peace.

Suddenly the woman shuddered and looked straight at Maisie. She did not smile; it was as if she were looking beyond Maisie to another place. Regaining her own natural posture, Maisie nodded acknowledgment, a small movement that brought Celia Davenham back to the present. She nodded in return, brushed at her skirt, stood up, replaced her gloves, and quickly left Vincent's grave.

Maisie was in no hurry. She knew that Celia Davenham would go home now. Home to play the loving wife, the role she would assume as soon as she walked through the door. It was a role that her husband had seen through easily, although his conclusions had been erroneous. Maisie also knew that the second's glance and the deliberate acknowledgment she had initiated between herself and Celia ensured that the other woman would recognize her when they met again.

Maisie lingered for a while at Donald's grave. There was something healing in this ritual of making a comfortable place for the dead. Her thoughts took her back to France, to the dead and dying, to the devastating wounds that were so often beyond her skill, beyond everyone's. But it was the wounds of the mind that touched her, those who still fought their battles again and again each day, though the country was at peace. If only she could make the living as comfortable, thought Maisie, as she tidied a few more stubborn weeds in the shadow of Don's headstone.

"Making a nice job of that one."

Maisie swung around, to see one of the cemetery workers standing behind her, an older man with red, bony hands firmly grasping the handles of a wooden wheelbarrow. His ruddy complexion told of years working outdoors, but his kind eyes spoke of compassion, of respect.

"Why yes. It's sad to see them so uncared for, isn't it?" replied Maisie.

"I'll say, after what those boys gave for us. Poor bastards. Oh, Miss, I am sorry, I forgot —"

"Don't worry. It's as well to voice one's feelings," replied Maisie.

"That's the truth. Too much not said by 'alf."

The man pointed to Donald's grave.

"Haven't seen this one being tended for a few years. His old Mum and Dad used to come over. Only son. Killed them, too, it did, I reckon."

"Did you know them? I would have thought it would be difficult to know all the relatives, with so many graves," said Maisie.

"I'm 'ere every day 'cept Sundays, that is. Been 'ere since just after

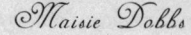

the war. I get to know people. 'Course, you don't 'ave long talks, no time for that, and folk don't always want to talk, but, there again, there's those that want to 'ave a bit of conversation."

"Yes, yes, I'm sure."

"Not seen you before, not 'ere." The man looked at Maisie.

"No, that's true. I'm a cousin. Just moved to the city," said Maisie, looking at the man directly.

"Nice to see it being taken care of." The man firmed his grip on the wheelbarrow handles, as if to move on.

"Wait a minute. I wonder, could you tell me, are all the graves here, in this part, war graves?" asked Maisie.

"Yes and no. Most of these are our boys, but some lived a long time after their injuries. Your Don, well, you'd know this, but 'e 'ad septicaemia. Horrible way to go, 'specially as 'e was brought home. Lot of folk like to bury 'em 'ere because of the railway."

The man set the wheelbarrow down, and pointed to the railway lines running alongside the cemetery.

"You can see the trains from 'ere. Not that these boys can see the trains, but the relatives like it. They're on a journey, you see, it's a – you know, what do they call it, you know – when it means something to them."

"Metaphor?"

"Yeah, well, like I said, it's a journey, ain't it? And the relatives, if they've come by train, which most of them do, can see the graves as the train pulls out the station. They can say another good-bye that way."

"So, what about that one there? Strange, isn't it? Just one word, the Christian name?" asked Maisie.

"I'll say. The whole bleedin' thing was strange. Two years ago 'e came, that one. Small family burial. 'e was a captain. Injured at Passchendaele. Terrible show that was, terrible. Wonder 'e came 'ome at all. 'e'd lived away from the family, apparently, after bein' 'ome for a bit. Wanted to be known just by 'is Christian name. Said it wasn't important anymore, seein' as they were all nobodies who could just be written off like leftovers. Shame to 'is family, accordin' to a couple of 'is mates that came up 'ere for a while after. Now only that woman comes. Think she was 'is mate's sister, known 'er for years, 'e 'ad. Keeps the grave nice, you'd think 'e only went down yesterday."

"Hmm. Very sad indeed. What was his surname, do you know?"

By now the man was well into the telling of stories and seemed glad of the opportunity, and importance, that a question brought him.

"Weathershaw. Vincent Weathershaw. Came from Chislehurst. Good family, by the looks of them. Mind you, 'e passed away where 'e was living. A farm, I think it was. Yes, 'e lived on a farm, not that far from 'ere – though more in the country like. Far as I know, quite a few of 'em lived there."

Maisie felt a chill as the stillness of the cemetery seeped through her clothing and touched her skin. Yet the shiver was familiar to Maisie, who had felt that sensation even in warm weather when there was no cooling breeze. She had come to recognize this spark of energy passing across her skin as a warning.

"Quite a few of them?"

"Well, you know." The man rubbed his stubbled jawbone with the flat of his thick, earth-stained hand. "Them who got it in the face. Remember, we're not far from Sidcup 'ere – you know. Queen Mary's, the 'ospital where they did all that special work on faces, trying to 'elp the poor sods. Amazin' when you think about it, what they tried to do there – and what they did do. Miracle workers, they were. Mind you, I wouldn't mind bettin' a few of them boys still weren't fancy-looking enough for their sweethearts, and ended up at that farm."

The old gardener picked up the handles of the wheelbarrow. Maisie saw that he was ready to move on, away from recollections of war.

"Well, I had better be getting on, Mr . . ."

"Smith. Tom Smith."

"Yes, I have to catch the two o'clock, Tom. And thank you."

Tom Smith watched as Maisie picked her way past the graves to the path, and as he turned to leave he called to her. "I daresay I won't see you 'ere again . . . but you know, Miss, the funny thing about this 'ere Vincent is that 'e wasn't the only one."

"The only one what?"

"The only one buried with just a Christian name."

Maisie held her head to one side, encouraging Tom to continue.

"There was a few of them, and you know what?

"What?" said Maisie.

"All lost touch with their families. Tragic it was, just tragic. Seeing their parents. They should never 'ave 'ad to go through that, never. Bad enough seeing those boys go off to war, let alone losing them when they come back."

"Yes, that is tragic."

Maisie looked at Tom, then asked the question that had been with her since the man had first spoken to her. "Tom . . . where is your boy resting?"

Tom Smith looked at Maisie, and tears rimmed his eyes. The lines etched in his face grew deeper, and his shoulders dropped. "Down there." He pointed to the row of headstones nearest the railway line. "Loved trains as a boy. Loved 'em. Came back from France not quite right up 'ere." He tapped the side of his head. "You'd 'ear 'im scream in the middle of the night, but it was all you could do to get a sound out of the boy in the daytime. One mornin' the missus goes up to take 'im up a cup of tea and there 'e was. Done 'imself in. She was never the same. Never. Broke 'er spirit, it did. Passed away three years ago come December."

Maisie nodded, held out her hand, and laid it upon his arm. They stood in silence.

"Well, this will never do," said Tom Smith. "Must be getting along. Got to look after them, 'aven't I? Good day to you, Miss."

Maisie Dobbs bade the man good-bye but didn't leave the cemetery immediately. Later, while waiting on the platform for the train back to London, she took a small notebook from her handbag and recorded the events of the day. Each detail was noted, including the colour of Celia Davenham's shamrock-green gloves.

She had found two more graves whose headstones bore Christian names only, not very far from the final resting place of Vincent Weathershaw. Three young "old soldiers" who had withdrawn from their families. Maisie sat back on the bench and started to compose her questions, the questions to herself that would come as a result of her observations. She would not struggle to answer the questions but would let them do their work.

"Truth walks toward us on the paths of our questions." Maurice's voice once again echoed in her mind. "As soon as you think you have the answer, you have closed the path and may miss vital new information. Wait awhile in the stillness, and do not rush to conclusions, no matter how uncomfortable the unknowing."

And as she allowed her curiosity full rein, Maisie knew what her next move should be.

CHAPTER FIVE

he Celia Davenham file comprised several pages by now, and included details beyond excursions to Nether Green Cemetery. Celia's birthdate (September 16, 1897), parentage (Algernon and Anne Whipton), place of birth (Sevenoaks, Kent), school (St. Mary's), and miscellaneous other details were recorded. Her husband was ten years older, not such a division in years at thirty-two, but it would have been something of a chasm at the age of nineteen or twenty, especially when the past offered more in the way of excitement than the day-to-day round of life in a maturing marriage.

Maisie knew where Celia shopped for clothes, where she took afternoon tea, even of her interest in needlework. Maisie also observed her comfort in solitude, and wondered how such a solitary soul could build a bridge to another. Did the Davenham marriage endure behind a veil of courtesy? The mundane communication that one would accord an acquaintance met on the street, but the formality of which could stifle the bond of affection between man and wife? It was evident that only one person could answer certain questions, and that was Celia Davenham herself. Maisie carefully replaced the pages in the file, placed it in her desk drawer, pushed back her chair and made ready to leave her office.

A sharp knock at the door was followed by Billy Beale's freckled face and shock of wheat-gold hair, topped by a flat cap, poked around the dark wood doorjamb.

"Good afternoon to you, Miss Dobbs. 'Ow's business? Don't seem to 'ave seen much of you lately, though I 'eard that you'd 'elped old Mrs Scott get something out of that thieving son of 'ers. Thought I'd pop me 'ead in to see if you need anything done in the way of 'andiwork in the office 'ere."

"Billy, yes, Mrs Scott is a client. But you know better than to expect a comment from me, don't you?"

"You're spot-on there, Miss Dobbs. But you can't stop folk talking about your business, 'specially when you've 'elped them. People round 'ere don't miss a trick, and we've got memories like elephants into the bargain!"

"Have you now, Billy? In that case, perhaps you can tell me if you know someone I think you might have heard of."

"Fire away!"

"Confidential, Billy."

"Nod's as good as a wink . . ." Billy tapped the side of his nose to emphasize the integrity of any information he might receive – he could keep a secret.

"Vincent Weathershaw. Captain. Know him?" asked Maisie.

"Weathershaw. Weathershaw. Now that name rings a bell. Let me think."

Billy took off his cap and scratched at his golden hair.

"You know, 'ere's what it is – I've 'eard about 'im. Never actually took an order from the man, but 'eard about 'im. By reputation, like."

"What sort of reputation?" quizzed Maisie.

"If I remember rightly, a bit devil-may-care. Mind you, you saw it a lot. Some of them got so as they couldn't care less about their own lives. Like they were in it so long that the shelling didn't scare 'em any more. Poor sods. Some of them officers came out of their fancy schools and straight into the trenches."

"Was he reckless?"

"If it's the feller I'm thinking of, not reckless with 'is men. No, 'e was reckless with 'imself. Got so as 'e would just climb out of the bunker, no 'elmet, to go up and look around for the Kaiser's boys. Reckon they were more surprised than us when they copped sight of 'im walking around without a care in the world."

"Ever hear about him again, Billy?"

"Miss Dobbs, it's not like I talk about it much. Best left behind. But you know that, don't you? You saw enough, must've done."

"Yes, I saw enough for a lifetime, Billy."

Maisie buttoned her coat, secured her hat in place, and pulled on her gloves.

"But tell you what, Miss. I'll ask around down the Prince of Wales, some of the lads might know something. This Weathershaw, he a client like?"

"No, Billy. No, he's not. He's dead. Two years ago. See what you can find out, Billy."

"Right you are, Miss," replied Billy. Maisie ushered Billy out of the office and locked the door behind her as she left with him.

"It's confidential, Billy. Just bring it into the conversation," instructed Maisie.

"Yes, Miss. Don't worry. Like I said when you moved in. Anything you want, you just ask Billy Beale."

Maisie decided that a brisk walk to Piccadilly Circus would be just what she needed to clear her head for the next part of her task: information gathering, as Maurice would say.

Fortunately there had been several new clients since she had moved into the office in Warren Street. Christopher Davenham's appearance had represented the beginning of a respectable stream of visitors. There were a couple of referrals from Lady Rowan's solicitors, along with three of Maurice's former clients who finally overcame any reticence they might have had about completely confiding in his former assistant, who happened to be a woman.

The work ranged from simple analysis of correspondence to reveal anomalies in funds paid to a company to a report on a "missing" daughter. As Maisie expected, there had not yet been the requests for assistance from government or from the legal or judicial services that Maurice had enjoyed, but she knew that such business would come in due course. She was qualified to consult on matters far beyond those that had come to her. Maurice had seen to that.

Maisie was now busy, and more to the point, had the money to research matters that presented themselves for investigation without initiation by an actual client. Unless you could call Vincent Weathershaw a client.

The restaurant at Fortnum & Mason's was busy, but as she walked in and feigned interest in the menu, Maisie quickly scanned the room and immediately saw Celia Davenham sitting by a window. She was looking out at the rooftops as if in a dream, with her hands clasped around a cup of tea.

"May I have a seat by the window?" requested Maisie of the tall waiter with slicked-back, brilliantined hair who greeted her.

Taking the table next to Celia, Maisie deliberately sat facing the woman, although she did not look at her as she removed her gloves, placed them on top of her bag, and set the bag on the chair next to her. Maisie opened the menu and read down the list of dishes until she felt the woman's eyes upon her, then she looked up, meeting Celia's gaze. Maisie smiled. Her "planetary" smile, as Simon had once said. She quickly banished all thought of Simon; her concentration had to be on the job in hand.

"Hello," said Maisie in greeting. "Such a lovely day today, isn't it?"

"Yes. Yes it is," responded Celia. She smiled at Maisie. "Forgive me . . . but, have we met?"

"You know, you look very familiar, but I . . . I can't think where." Maisie smiled again.

"Nether Green. I've seen you at Nether Green." Colour flushed Celia Davenham's cheeks as she recognized Maisie.

"Why, yes, yes. Look, would you like to join me?" Maisie moved her bag and gloves from the seat next to her, an invitation to Celia Davenham.

A waiter quickly came to assist Celia, and placed her teacup, saucer, and place mat on Maisie's table. The perfectly-dressed woman sat down opposite Maisie, who held out her hand.

"Blanche. Maisie Blanche. How do you do."

"Celia Davenham. I'm very well, thank you."

For a while the two women talked of small matters. The price of flowers at the stall, the late arrival of trains this past winter. Before Celia could ask, Maisie offered the story of her visits to the cemetery.

"Donald was a cousin. Not close, but family all the same. I thought that now I'm here in town, it would be easy to go out to Nether Green. One doesn't like to forget, does one?"

"No. Absolutely. No. Not that I could," replied Celia.

"Did you lose your brother?" asked Maisie.

"Yes, one of them. In the Dardanelles. The other was wounded. Seriously wounded."

"I'm sorry. You were lucky to have your brother come home from the Dardanelles," said Maisie, knowing that often brother fought alongside brother, which led to many a mother grieving the loss of not one child but two or three.

"Oh, no. No. My brother's body was never found. He was listed missing. I visit the grave of my other brother's friend. Vincent." Celia fussed with her handkerchief.

"I see. Is your brother, your other brother, recovered?"

"Um. Yes, yes, in a way."

Maisie held her head to one side in question but added, "Oh, this is such a difficult subject –"

"No, I mean, yes. Yes. But . . . well, he has scars. Vincent had scars too."

"Oh. I see."

"Yes. George, my brother who survived, is like Vincent. His face –"

Celia slowly moved her finely manicured hands and touched her cheek with delicate fingers. She flinched and tears filled her eyes. At that moment Maisie saw her chance for connection. A connection that was deeper than she would admit. She reached out and touched

Celia lightly on the arm until the other woman's eyes met hers. Maisie nodded her understanding.

"I was a nurse," said Maisie, her voice lowered, not to avoid being heard but to draw Celia toward her. "In France. When I returned from France I nursed again in a secure mental hospital. I understand the wounds, Mrs Davenham. Those of the body – and of the soul."

Celia Davenham took Maisie's hand. And at that moment Maisie knew she was in the woman's confidence, that she was trusted. Maisie had anticipated that it would take no longer than the twenty minutes that the women had sat together at the same table. Such was Celia's hunger for connection to someone who understood. And the depth of Maisie Dobbs's understanding of her situation was greater than Celia Davenham could possibly imagine.

Celia Davenham sat for a moment before speaking again. Wave upon wave of grief seemed to break across her heart with such force that she made a fist with one hand, and gripped Maisie's offered hand of understanding with the other. A waiter coming toward the table to inquire if more tea was required stopped suddenly and moved away, as if repelled by the force of her emotion.

Maisie closed her eyes, concentrating her calming energy on the woman who sat opposite her. The moment passed, and Maisie opened her eyes to observe Celia relax her shoulders, arms, and the tight grasp on her hand. But she did not let go.

"I'm sorry."

"Don't be, Mrs Davenham. Don't be. Take some tea."

Keeping Maisie's hand in hers, the woman took the cup in her other hand and, shaking, lifted it to her lips to sip the still-hot tea. The two women sat in silence for several more minutes until Maisie spoke again.

"Tell me about Vincent, Mrs Davenham."

Celia Davenham placed the fine bone china cup in its saucer, took a deep breath, and began to tell her story.

"I fell in love with Vincent – oh, dear me – it must have been when I was about twelve. I was just a girl. He came to the house with my brother George. It was my brother Malcolm who died. George was the oldest. Vincent was one of those people who could make anyone laugh – even my parents, who were very stiff indeed. It was as if the sun shone upon Vincent and everyone felt compelled to look at him, just to warm themselves."

"Yes, I have known such people. I expect he was quite the charmer," said Maisie.

"Oh yes, quite the charmer. But he didn't realize it. He just went through his life bringing out the best in people. So, he was definitely officer calibre. His men would have followed him to death's door."

"And beyond, no doubt."

"Yes. And beyond. Apparently when he wrote to the parents or wives of men who had fallen, he always mentioned some small detail about them – a joke they had told, an act of courage, a special effort made. He didn't just say, 'I'm sorry to tell you this, but . . .' He cared."

Celia took up her cup again, keeping one hand on Maisie's. Maisie, for her part, made no move to withdraw, realizing the strength her touch gave the other woman. She moved only to pour more tea and to bring her own cup to her lips.

Occasionally she would look out of the window, and as dusk drew in saw the reflection of Celia Davenham in the windowpane as she told her story. In this way Maisie observed her as an onlooker might, rather than as a confidante. As Celia spoke, releasing the weight of hoarded memory, she seemed to gain strength. She sat straighter. Celia was an attractive woman, and in the reflected scene, Maisie saw the faces of other people in the tearoom occasionally looking toward them, drawn to a conversation they could not overhear but could not help observing.

Maisie knew well, more than the onlookers, that they were drawn by the power of revelation. They were witnesses to the unfolding of Celia Davenham's story, to the unburdening of her soul, though they might not be aware of it. And she knew that once outside, wrapping a scarf around a neck to shield it from the biting wind, or holding on to a hat, a woman might say to her companion, "Did you see that woman, by the window, the well-dressed one?" and her companion would nod and they would speak for a while of what might have been said by the woman near the window to the woman who allowed her hand to be held so tightly. And the picture of Celia Davenham squaring her shoulders to tell her story would come back to them on occasion, especially when they were sad and looking for the answer to a question of the heart.

Celia Davenham paused, as if to summon the fortitude to continue. Maisie waited, then asked, "Tell me what happened to Vincent."

"It was at Passchendaele."

"Ah yes. I know . . ."

"Yes, I think we all know now. So many –"

" – and Vincent?"

"Yes, although some might believe him to be lucky. He came home."

Celia stopped again, closed her eyes, then continued. "I try, sometimes, to remember his face before. When it was complete. But I can't. I feel awful, that I can only remember the scars. I try at night to close my eyes and see him, but I can't. I can see George, of course; his injuries weren't so bad. But I can't think of *exactly* how he was before the war either."

"Yes, it must be very hard."

"There was something about Vincent, his enthusiasm for life, that turned into something else, as if it had another side. His company came under intense enemy fire. Vincent was hit in the face by shrapnel. It is a miracle he lived. George lost an ear and has scars on the side of his face, which you would think were unbearable but seem light compared to Vincent's."

Maisie looked at the woman, whose grip had relaxed as she told Vincent's story. Celia was exhausted. Maurice had counselled her, in the early days of her apprenticeship, when she was the silent observer as he listened to a story, gently prodding with a question, a comment, a sigh, or a smile, "The story takes up space like a knot in a piece of wood. If the knot is removed, a hole remains. We must ask ourselves, how will this hole that we have opened be filled? The hole, Maisie, is our responsibility."

"Mrs Davenham, you must be tired. Shall we meet again another day?" she asked.

"Yes, Miss Blanche, do let's meet."

"Perhaps we might walk in Hyde Park, or St. James's; the lake is so lovely at this time of year."

The women made arrangements to meet the following week, for tea at the Ritz, then a stroll through Green Park to St. James's. But before they parted, Maisie suggested, "Mrs Davenham, you probably have to rush home soon, but I wonder. Liberty has some lovely new fabrics, just arrived from India. Would you come with me to look at them?"

"Why, I'd love to."

Later, when Celia Davenham reflected upon her day, she was surprised. For though she still felt sadness, the memory she reflected upon most was that of huge bolts of fabric being moved around at her behest by willing assistants who could sense in her the interest that led to a purchase. With an enthusiastic flourish, yards of vibrant purples, yellows, pinks, and reds of Indian silk were pulled out, to be rubbed between finger and thumb, and held against her face in front of the mirror. And she thought of the person she knew as Maisie Blanche, who suddenly but quietly had to take her leave, allowing her to indulge her love of texture and colour for far longer than she had intended. Thus a day that had seen so many tears ended in the midst of a rainbow.

CHAPTER SIX

aisie made her way back to her office. It was dark by now, and although she was gasping for a cup of tea much stronger than the light Darjeeling served at Fortnum & Mason's, she needed to work. She reflected upon the Davenham story, knowing only too well that there was a lot more to elicit. But by leaving much of the story untold, Maisie allowed the door to remain open. Instead of being exhausted by her own revelations and memories, Celia Davenham was being helped to shed her burden gradually, and Maisie was her guide.

Jack Barker greeted Maisie outside Warren Street station, doffed his cap and bid her good evening.

"Evening Miss Dobbs. My, you are a sight for sore eyes at the end of the day."

"Thank you Mr Barker. I'll be even better when I get a cup of tea inside me."

"You should get that Billy to make you one. Does too much talking, he does. I 'ave to tell him sometimes that I'm busy and can't keep puttin' the world to rights with him."

Maisie grinned, knowing by now that Jack Barker could talk the hind leg off a donkey, and that the same complaint about Jack was likely to come from Billy Beale.

"Billy's a good sort, though, isn't he Mr Barker?"

"'E is that. Amazing how fast 'e can move with that leg. You should see 'im sometimes, running 'ere and there, dot and carry one with that leg. Poor sod. But at least he came back, didn't he?"

Maisie agreed. "Indeed, Mr Barker, at least he came home. I'd best be on my way, so I'll say good evening. Any reason to buy the latest edition before I rush off?"

"All bloomin' bad if you ask me. They're talkin' about a slump down in the City."

"I'll leave it then, Mr Barker. Goodnight."

Maisie turned into Warren Street, walking behind two women students from the Slade School of Art who were making their way back to lodgings nearby. Each carried an artist's portfolio under one arm, and giggled as the other recounted her part of a story about another woman. They stopped to speak to a group of young men who were just about to enter the Prince of Wales pub, then decided to join them. They pushed past a woman dressed in black who had been standing outside the pub smoking a cigarette. She shouted at them to look out, but her warning was met with more giggles from the students. She was soon joined by a man, who Maisie suspected already had a wife at home, for he betrayed himself by quickly looking up and down the street before taking the woman by the arm and hurrying her inside the pub.

"It takes all sorts," said Maisie in a low voice as she passed, and continued on down Warren Street to her office.

Maisie opened the door that led to the dark stairwell, and as she went to turn on the dim light to see her way up the stairs, the light over the upper stairwell went on and Billy Beale called out.

"'S only me, Miss. See yer way up?"

"Billy, you should be knocking off work by now, surely."

"Yeah, but I've got some more news for you. 'Bout that feller you was askin' about. Weathershaw. Thought I'd 'ang about in case I don't see you tomorrow."

"That's kind, Billy. Let's put the kettle on."

Maisie led the way into her office, turned on the light, and went to put the kettle on the small stove.

"And that telephone has been ring, ring all day. What you need is someone to 'elp you out, Miss, to write down messages, like."

"My telephone was ringing?"

"Well, ain't that what it's there for?"

"Yes, of course. But it doesn't ring very often. I tend to receive messages via the postman or personal messenger. I wonder who it was?"

"Someone with an 'ead of steam, the way it was ringing. I was working on the boiler, making a fair bit of noise meself, and every now and again, there it went again. I come up a couple of times, t'see if I could answer it for you, but it stopped just as I got outside the door – I c'n use me master key in an emergency, like. I tell yer, I nearly got me kit and put in a line so I could answer it downstairs meself."

"Pardon?"

"Remember Miss, I was a sapper. Let me tell you, if I could run a line in the pourin' rain and on me 'ands and knees in the mud – and get the brass talkin' to each other while the 'un's trying to knock me block off as I was about it – I can do a thing or two with your line."

"Is that so, Billy? I'll have to remember that. In the meantime, whoever wants to speak to me will find a way. Now then, what do you have to tell me?"

"Well, I was askin' round some of me old mates, about that Vincent Weathershaw. Turns out one of them knew someone, who knew someone else – you know – who told them that 'e wasn't quite all there after one of the big shows."

Billy Beale tapped the side of his forehead, and Maisie inclined her head for him to continue.

"Lost a lot of men, 'e did. Never forgave 'imself. Took it all on 'imself, as if 'e was the one that killed them. But what I also 'eard was that some funny stuff went on between 'im and the top brass. Now I don't know about that, but . . ."

"Go on, Billy," Maisie urged.

"Well, Miss, you know, if truth be told, we were all plain scared 'alf the bleedin' time."

"Yes, I know, Billy."

"O' course you do, Miss. You know, don't you? Blimey, when I think of what you nurses must've seen . . . anyway, truth was, we was all scared. You didn't know when you was going to catch it. But some of 'em . . ."

Billy stopped, turned away from Maisie, and took the red kerchief from his neck and wiped his eyes.

"Gawd – sorry, Miss."

"Billy. It can wait. Whatever you have to tell me. It can wait. Let me pour that tea."

Maisie went to the stove, poured boiling water from the kettle onto the tea leaves in the brown earthenware teapot, and allowed it to steep. She took two large tin mugs from the shelf above the stove, stirred the tea in the pot, then poured tea for them both, with plenty of sugar and a splash of milk. Since her time in France, Maisie had preferred an army-issue tin mug for her private teatimes, for the warmth that radiated from the mug to her hands and to the rest of her body.

"There you are, Billy. Now then . . ."

"Well, as you know, Miss, a lot of the lads that enlisted were too young. Boys tryin' to be men, and blimey, the rest of us weren't much more than boys ourselves. And you'd see 'em, white as sheets when that whistle blew to go over the top. Mind you, we was all as white as sheets. I was barely eighteen meself."

Billy sipped his tea and wiped his mouth with the back of his hand.

"We'd 'ave to get 'em under the arms, shove 'em over, and 'ope that the push would get 'em through. And sometimes one of 'em didn't make it over."

Billy's eyes misted over again, and he wiped them with the red kerchief.

"And when that 'appened, when a boy was, like, paralyzed with fear, 'e could be reported for cowardice. If 'e 'adn't gone over with the rest of his mates, the brass didn't ask too many questions, did they? No, the poor sod's on a charge and that's it! So we 'ad to look out for each other, didn't we?"

Drawing the red cloth across his brow, the young man continued his story for Maisie.

"Court-martialled, they were. And you know what 'appened to a lot of 'em? Shot. Even if some of 'em weren't quite so innocent, getting up to no good when they should've been on the line, it ain't the way to go, is it? Not shot by their own. Bloody marvellous, ain't it? You pray your 'ead off that the Kaiser's boys don't get you, then it's your own that do!"

Maisie allowed silence to envelop them and held the steaming mug to her lips. This was no new story. Only the storyteller was new to her. Happy-go-lucky Billy Beale.

"Well, this Vincent Weathershaw, as far as the brass were concerned, was too soft with 'is men. Said it was enough with the trenches and shells killing 'em without their own 'avin' it in for 'em. Apparently they wanted to 'arden 'im up a bit. I don't know the 'ole story, but from what I've been told, 'e was commanded to do a few things 'e didn't want to. Refused. There was talk of strippin' 'im of 'is commission. No one quite knows what 'appened, but it was after that 'e sort of lost 'is 'ead and started to do daft things, walkin' around without 'is 'elmet on in front of the other lot. Then, o' course, they got 'im – at Wipers – Passchendaele. Not far from where I copped it really, but it seemed like 'undreds of miles at the time."

Maisie smiled, but it was a sad, reflective smile as she remembered how men made easy work of pronouncing "Ypres," referring to it as "Wipers."

"Mind you, they didn't get me coming out of a trench and over the top. No, it was all that business at Messines, not knowing whether the other lot were in the trench next door, or below us, and not knowin' whether the buggers – pardon the language, Miss – but not knowin' where they'd laid mines. Us sappers 'ad our work cut out for us there."

Billy lowered his head, swirled dregs of tea to soak up sugar at the bottom of his mug, and closed his eyes as memories pushed through into the present.

Maisie and Billy Beale sat in silence. Maisie, as she so often did nowadays, remembered Maurice and his teaching:

"Never follow a story with a question, Maisie, not immediately. And remember to acknowledge the storyteller, for in some way even the messenger is affected by the story he brings."

She waited a few more minutes, watching Billy sip his tea, lost in his memories as he looked out over the rooftops.

"Billy, thank you for finding this out for me. You must have worked hard to track the details down."

Billy lifted the mug of tea to his lips.

"Like I said, Miss – you need anything doing, Billy Beale's your man."

Maisie allowed more time to pass, and even wrote some notes in her file in front of Billy, to underline the importance of his report.

"Well, Billy," said Maisie, closing the file and placing it back on the desk, "I hope you don't mind me changing the subject, but there is one thing. No rush, in your own time."

"You name it, Miss."

"Billy, I really need to have this room painted or wallpapered. It's so drab, it needs a bit of cheering up. I noticed that on the ground floor you did such a nice job with Miss Finch's room – the door was open as I came through one day and I looked in – it was so bright and cheerful. What do you think?"

"I'll see to it right away, Miss. I'll put my mind to the colours on the way 'ome, and tomorrow I'll go by me mate's place – painter and decorator, 'e is – and see what 'e's got in the way of paints."

"That'll be lovely, Billy. And, Billy – thank you very much."

And so another storyteller fell asleep that night thinking not of the telling of the story but of the possibilities inherent in colour and texture. But for Maisie, there was a different end to the day. She made notes in her file, simply named "Vincent," and started to sketch a diagram, with names and places linked.

Maisie Dobbs was even more convinced that her instinct had not betrayed her, that Vincent's death was simply one thread in an intricate web that led to no good. She knew that it would not be long before she discovered what connected the bright thread that was Vincent to the other boys who were buried with only one name at Nether Green Cemetery. And it was her intention that the next meeting with Celia Davenham would reveal how Vincent had spent the time since the war, and his exact location at his death.

More important, Maisie wanted an explanation as to why he was simply "Vincent."

CHAPTER SEVEN

aisie sat back in the wooden office chair and brought her knees up to her chest so that her heels rested on the edge of the seat. She had slipped off her shoes an hour or so ago, to put on the thick bed socks that she kept in her desk drawer. Maisie leafed through her report to Christopher Davenham and wondered how she might best advise him. It was at times like this that she missed the counsel of Maurice Blanche. The relationship between teacher and pupil was an easy one. She had opened her mind to learning his craft, and he had passed on to her the knowledge gleaned in a lifetime of work in what he referred to as "the forensic science of the whole person." Although he could still be consulted, Maisie knew that now that he had retired it was his intention for her to make her way in the world alone.

She could hear his voice now: "Remember basics, Maisie, dear. Whenever you are stuck, go back to our earliest conversations. And remember connections, that there are always connections."

Now Maisie had to decide how far she should go in her report to Christopher Davenham. The man simply wanted to know where his wife was going and if another man was involved. Any information over and above what he had requested would not be necessary. Maisie thought for one more moment, put her feet back on the floor, placed the file on the table in front of her, and stood up.

"No, that's enough." She said to the empty room.

✦

"*D*o sit down, Mr Davenham." Maisie's chilled feet were now smartly clad in leather shoes.

"You have a report for me, Miss Dobbs?"

"Yes, of course. But first, Mr Davenham, I must ask you some questions."

"Haven't you already asked enough? I would have thought my purpose in coming here was clear. I seek information, Miss Dobbs, and if you are half as good as your reputation, you will have that information."

"Yes, I do. But I would like us to discuss openly how you might use this information once you have it."

"I'm not sure I understand, Miss Dobbs."

Maisie opened the file, took out a blank sheet of paper that had previously covered her extensive notes, closed the file, and placed the paper on top. It was a technique learned from Maurice, which had proved to be most useful: The blank sheet of paper represented the future, an empty page that could be filled as the observer chose. Pages of notes brought out during conversation were a distraction, so a written report was given only at the end of meeting. "Mr Davenham, if there were no other man, no reason for you to suspect that your wife's affections lay elsewhere, what would you do?"

"Well, nothing. If there's no reason for my suspicions, then she's in the clear. There would be no problem to do anything about."

"I see. Mr Davenham, this is a delicate situation. Before I proceed, I must ask you to make a commitment to me —"

"Whatever do you mean?"

"A commitment to your marriage, actually. A commitment, perhaps, to your wife's wellbeing and to your future."

Christopher Davenham stirred uneasily in his chair and folded his arms.

"Mr Davenham," said Maisie, looking out of the window, "it's a very fine day now, don't you think? Let's walk around Fitzroy Square. We will be at liberty to speak freely and also enjoy something of the day."

Without waiting for an answer Maisie rose from her chair, took her coat from the stand, and passed it to Christopher Davenham who, being a gentleman, stifled his annoyance, took the coat, and held it out for Maisie. Placing her hat upon her head and securing it with a pearl hatpin, Maisie smiled up at him. "A walk will be lovely."

She strolled with Davenham along Warren Street, then turned left at Conway Street into Fitzroy Square. The sun had broken through the morning's grey clouds, and there was a promise of warmer weather to come. The walk was by no means an idle suggestion. Maisie had learned from Maurice Blanche the importance of keeping the client open to whatever was being reported or suggested. "Sitting in a chair gives too much opportunity to retreat into the self," Blanche had said. "Keep the person moving, in the way that an artist keeps the oil moving when he is painting. Don't give them a chance to dry up; don't allow the client to shut you out."

"Mr Davenham, I have decided to give you my report and my recommendations. I say 'recommendations' because I believe you are a man of compassion."

Davenham maintained an even pace. Good, thought Maisie. She matched his stride, keenly observing the position of his arms, the way he held his head forward and tilted back slightly, as if sniffing the air for a predator. He's terrified, thought Maisie, feeling fear rise up as she began to imitate his manner of walking and carriage. She closed her eyes for just a few seconds to be clear about the feelings now seeping through her body, and thought: he's afraid to give, for fear of losing.

She had to be quick to banish the fear.

"Mr Davenham, you are not being deceived. Your wife is faithful."

The tall man breathed an audible sigh of relief.

"But she does need your help."

"In what way, Miss Dobbs?" The tension that ebbed with her revelation had no chance to reclaim him before Maisie spoke again.

"Like many young women, your wife lost someone she loved. In the war. The man was her first love, a puppy love. Had he lived, no doubt such an affection would have died with the onset of maturity. However –"

"Who?"

"A friend of her brother. His name was Vincent. It's in my report. Mr Davenham, may we slow down just a little, you see, my feet . . ."

"Of course, yes, I'm sorry."

Christopher Davenham settled into a more relaxed gait, to match Maisie, who had reduced her stride to allow him to consider her words.

"Mr Davenham, have you ever spoken with your wife about the war, about her brother, about her losses?"

"No, never. I mean, I know the facts. But one just has to get on with it. After all, you can't just give in, can you?"

"And what about you, Mr Davenham?"

"I didn't serve. I have a printing company, Miss Dobbs. I was required by the government to keep the people informed."

"Did you want to serve?'

"Does that matter?"

"Perhaps it does, to your wife. Perhaps it matters to your wife to be able to discuss her past with you, for you to know –"

"Your report will give me the facts, Miss Dobbs."

"Mr Davenham, you may know the facts, but it isn't a catalogue of facts that is causing your wife's melancholy. It is the storage of memories and of feelings. Do you understand?"

The man was silent, as was Maisie. She knew she was out of bounds. But this was not new for her. She had spent much of her life out of bounds, living and speaking where, according to some, she had no business.

"Allow the past to have a voice," Maisie continued. "Then it will be stilled. It's only then that your marriage will have a future, Mr Davenham. And Mr Davenham . . ."

"Yes."

"Just in case you were considering such a move, your wife does not need medicines, and she does not need a doctor. Your wife needs *you*. When she has you, Vincent will be allowed to rest in peace."

The man took a few more steps in silence, then nodded.

"Shall we go back to the office?" Maisie asked, her head on one side.

Davenham nodded again. Maisie allowed him his thoughts, allowed him the room that he needed in which to take her words to heart. If she persisted, he might become defensive. And this was a door that needed to remain open. For there was something about the experience with Celia Davenham that nagged at Maisie. She didn't yet know what it was, but she was confident that it would speak to her. Maurice Blanche maintained that amid the tales, the smokescreens, and the deceptive mirrors of life's unsolved mysteries, truth resides, waiting for someone to enter its sanctum, then leave, without quite closing the door behind them. That is when truth may make its escape. And Maisie had ensured that the door was left open when she last saw Celia.

It was Maisie's intention that Thursday's meeting would reveal what she needed to know about Vincent's passing, about the mystery of the single name on his headstone, and what had occupied his time between the end of the war and his death. She wanted her next meeting with Celia to reveal Vincent's whereabouts just prior to, and at the time of, his death.

Maisie felt that she understood much about the relationship between Celia and Vincent. Their love had been more of a youthful infatuation – Celia had admitted as much herself – and in going forward with marriage to Christopher Davenham she had tried to bury her feelings for Vincent at a time when emotions were running high throughout the country. But the ordinary rituals of marriage to the seemingly bland Christopher Davenham could not erase the memory of Vincent, the hero of her imagination, the handsome, fearless knight she might have married. Maisie believed that, to Vincent, Celia had remained simply the younger sister of a dear friend. Yet it was among the friends of one's brothers that so many young women found suitable partners.

Maisie met Celia Davenham at the Ritz for afternoon tea on Thursday, as arranged. As she made her way from the main doors of the Piccadilly entrance to join Celia, Maisie caught her breath when she saw the heavy marble columns at either side of the Winter Garden ahead. She walked toward the steps leading up into the tearoom, and felt soothed by the warm shafts of light that entered through the windows at either end of the room. For a minute she allowed herself not to consider the expense of the expedition. The opulent grandeur of the Winter Garden, designed to resemble a French pavilion, with decorated cornices and a skylight that allowed soft natural light to bathe the room, almost took Maisie's breath away. With perfect white damask tablecloths, shining silver cutlery, and voluminous swags of fabric hung around the windows, the Winter Garden might not have encouraged intimate conversation between the two women, but the surrounding mirrored panels, and calming presence of water in the golden mermaid sculpture, brought a certan serenity to the room. Instead, with the delicate sound of Royal Doulton china clinking in the background, as cups were replaced on saucers, talk between the two women was light, skimming over the surface of confidence like a fly buzzing over a tranquil millpond.

Maisie touched each side of her lips with her table napkin, and placed it at the side of her plate. "I think it's time for that walk, Mrs Davenham. Such a lovely day, one feels as if summer is almost here." She reached for her handbag and gloves.

"Oh yes, indeed. Let's walk . . . and please, do call me 'Celia.' I feel as if we know each other so very well now." Celia Cavendish inclined her head in invitation.

"Thank you, Celia. It does seem as if the time for such formality has passed, so I expect you, in turn, to use my Christian name."

With the bill settled, waiters hurried to pull back chairs for the women, their deep bows signalling the exit of a well-satisfied customer, and that the table must be cleared and prepared for the next duo of well-heeled ladies. Maisie and Celia left the Ritz and entered Green Park.

"It's so lovely here – the daffodils are pretty, but they're late this year, aren't they?"

"Indeed they are."

"Maisie, the fabrics at Liberty were simply gorgeous, almost overwhelming, as always. I have to confess, I bought three yards of the most exquisite sheer lilac silk."

"Good for you. How very clever of you to be able to sew."

"I learned from one of our maids who was an absolute whiz with a needle. Mummy insisted upon such drab colours and styles – it was the only way for me to avoid looking like a dowdy schoolmistress. Of course, during the war it wasn't as easy to get fabric, but remember there *was* the passion for all things Indian, wasn't there?"

Maisie nodded, remembering the demand for goods from the Indian subcontinent after the Gurkha regiments joined British forces in France. She remembered Khan, laughing as he told her about the invitations he was suddenly receiving from the very best houses, simply to have the presence of one who seemed, in the eyes of hostesses of the day who were not always clear about the geography of the Indian subcontinent, to be an ambassador for the legion of small, hearty, fearless Nepalese men fighting alongside the regular British soldiers.

There was a comfortable silence as Maisie and Celia made their way along Queen's Walk toward St. James's Park. Strolling alongside St. James's Park lake, they commented that it would have been a good idea to save some pieces of bread to feed the swans, and laughed together at an anxious nanny running in pursuit of a pair of mischievous children toddling on chubby legs toward a pair of mallards. Yet as she brought her step into line with that of her companion, and held her shoulders, arms, and hands as if she were her shadow, Maisie felt once again the melancholy that gripped Celia. But Maisie also knew that Celia would soon confide in her as she had when they last met, for her feelings for Vincent had been dammed up inside her, and having been once unleashed, demanded to be heard.

"It was 1917 when Vincent came back to England. He was admitted immediately to hospital, for his wounds were so, so . . ."

Celia put her hand to her face again, searching for a word to describe Vincent's wounds that would reflect her newfound bravery in telling the tale.

"Utterly devastating, Maisie. I could hardly recognize him when I visited. I had to beg my brother to take me with him – George had arrived home some time before Vincent as his injuries were not as severe. Vincent wore a linen mask and only removed it when I assured him that I would not flinch."

"Go on," encouraged Maisie.

"But I couldn't contain myself. I burst into tears and rushed from the room. My brother was furious. Yet Vincent wasn't angry with me. But he was angry at everything else."

"Many men were angry when they returned, Celia. Vincent had a right to his anger."

Celia stopped in her walk, shielded her eyes from the sun, which was now late-afternoon low in the sky, then looked again at Maisie.

"That was when he said that he wanted to be just 'Vincent.' He said that as far as Britain was concerned he was just a piece of meat anyway, he might as well buck the whole system. He said he'd lost his face, so he could be whomever he wanted to be. Except he wasn't quite as polite as that."

"Indeed. Do you know what happened in France? To Vincent?"

"I know, mainly from my brother, that something happened – more than being wounded. I believe there was some . . . discord. With his commanding officers."

"What happened when Vincent was discharged from hospital?"

"Convalescence. By the sea, in Whitstable. The army took over one of the large hotels. Vincent wanted to write about his experiences in France. He was very upset. But each time we sent him a quantity of paper, it was taken away from him. The doctors said that writing distressed him. My brother was furious. He gave Vincent a typewriter, which was confiscated and returned. Vincent maintained he was being silenced, but said he was determined to speak before the war was long gone and no one wanted to know any more."

"The poor man."

"Then I met Christopher. A very solid man. Of course, he hadn't gone to France. I have to admit I never really found out why. I believe his business protected him from conscription. I seemed to go forward into marriage with a numbness in my mind. But I'd lost one brother, and of course Vincent was deeply, deeply injured. Christopher was a port in the storm. And he is, of course, so very good to me."

"What happened to your friend Vincent after the war, Celia? It seemed that he died some time later."

"Yes, he died only a few years ago. He returned to his parents' home, but as he was terribly disfigured he became a recluse. Oh, people tried to get him out of the house socially, but he would sit in the drawing room, looking out of the window, or reading, or writing in his diary. He worked from home after a while – for a small publishing house, somewhere not far from here I think."

Celia rubbed her forehead as if pressure would squeeze memories into the present moment.

"He read manuscripts, wrote reports. He had obtained the connection through his uncle's business contacts. Very occasionally he would have someone drive him to the office to discuss something. He'd had a mask made, of sorts, out of that very fine tin. It was painted in a glaze that matched the color of his skin. And he wore a scarf which he bundled around his neck and lower jaw – well, where his lower jaw used to be. Oh, poor, poor Vincent!"

Celia began to cry. Maisie stopped walking and simply stood next to her, but made no move to console by placing a hand on Celia's shoulder or a comforting arm around her.

"Allow grief room to air itself," Maurice had taught her. "Be judicious in using the body to comfort another, for you may extinguish the freedom that the person feels to be able to share a sadness."

She had learned, with Maurice Blanche as a teacher, respect for the telling of a person's history.

Maisie allowed some time to pass, then took Celia's elbow and gently led her to a park bench, set among a golden display of daffodils nodding sunny heads in the late-afternoon breeze.

"Thank you. Thank you for listening."

"I understand, Celia," replied Maisie.

As Maisie imagined Vincent's brutal disfigurement, she shuddered, recollecting the time she had spent in France, and the images that would remain with her for ever of men who had fought so bravely. She thought, too, of those men who had cheated death, only to struggle with the legacy of their injuries. And, in that moment, she remembered Simon, the gifted doctor who was himself a soldier in the struggle to tear lives free from the bloody clutches of war.

Maisie was brought back from the depths of her own memories by Celia, who was ready to continue her story.

"It was a bit of luck, really, that one of the patients he had been in hospital with remembered him. I wish I could recall his name. He had returned to France for a time after the war and saw that men with facial disfigurement were looked after in a different way. They were brought together for holidays, taken to the country to camps where they could live together for a while without having to worry about people drawing away – after all, they all had wounds. And I suppose, more importantly, the public didn't have to look at them. Terrible, isn't it? Anyway, this man came back to England and wanted to get the same sort of thing going here."

Celia Davenham looked around her and briefly closed her eyes in the warmth of the waning spring sunshine.

"He bought a farm that was on the market, then got in touch with the men he had met while recovering from his own wounds. According to Vincent, he – heavens, what was his name? Anyway, this man had been deeply affected by the war in a way that made him want to do something for those with disfiguring wounds. Vincent was a strong supporter of the idea. It gave him an energy I certainly hadn't seen since before the war. In fact, the man was rather taken with Vincent's stubborn refusal to be known by anything but his first name. So Vincent went to live at The Retreat."

"Was that what it was called? The Retreat?"

"Yes. I think it was Vincent's idea. The name. There was a connection to 'Beating the Retreat,' I think, in that they were withdrawing from society, which for many of them had become the enemy. Vincent said that it commemorated each man who died in France, and every man brought home to live with injuries. He said that it was for all those who suffered and should have had a place to go back to, when there never was one."

"Did he remain there, at The Retreat?"

"Yes, he did. He became very reclusive. My brother would visit occasionally. Of course, by then I was married to Christopher, so I did not visit. I wanted to, though. In fact, I have considered making the journey, since Vincent died. Just to see where –"

"He died at The Retreat?"

"Yes. I'm not really sure what happened. My brother was told by Vincent's people that he slipped and fell by the stream. Breathing was difficult for him anyway due to his injuries, but perhaps he hit his head. His parents have passed on now. I think they didn't really ask questions. Everyone agreed that it was a terrible accident, but it might have been a release for him."

"Did The Retreat close?"

"Oh no. It's still very much open. The farmhouse has been converted so that the residents each have a room, and specialist craftsmen were employed to work on the outbuildings, so that they could also be used for accommodation. I understand that new residents are welcomed. They are all men who have suffered injury of some kind during the war, and need a place to go."

"How does this man who set up The Retreat pay for everyone?"

"Oh, *they* pay. Resources are pooled. Christopher thought it was all very odd in that respect. But, you understand, Christopher would think that. He's very careful with money. Vincent gave Adam – that's it, Adam Jenkins, his name is Adam Jenkins – Vincent gave Adam Jenkins control of his finances when he decided to become a resident rather than a short-term visitor. The residents work on the farm as well, so it's still a going concern."

"Well, well, well. Vincent must have had tremendous respect for this man Adam Jenkins."

The two women had started walking back towards the north entrance of St. James's Park. Celia looked at her watch.

"Oh my goodness! I must hurry. Christopher is taking me to the theatre this evening. It's quite amazing, you know. He's always been such a stick-in-the-mud, but now he's planning all sorts of outings. I love the theatre. I thought I would never go again when I married Christopher, but he's suddenly become quite agreeable to an evening out."

"How lovely! I must dash too, Celia. But before you go, could you tell me where The Retreat is? I have a friend who may be interested to know about it."

"It's in Kent. Near Sevenoaks, that area. In fact, it's not too far from Nether Green. Good-bye, Maisie – and here's my card. Do call me again for tea. It was so lovely. I feel so very light after spending time with you, you know. Perhaps it's being out here in the fresh air of the park today."

"Yes, perhaps it is. Have a lovely time at the theatre, Celia."

The two women parted, but before making her way to the St.

James's Park underground station, Maisie walked back into the park to reconsider their conversation. She would probably not see Celia again.

Vincent had died while living in a community of ex-soldiers, all of whom, initially, were facially disfigured in some way, although it seemed that the doors were now open to those who had other injuries. There was nothing untoward about the motives of Adam Jenkins, who seemed to want to help these men. It must cost a pretty penny to arrange care for the residents, but then again, resources were pooled, and they were self-sufficient and working on the farm. A farm called, ambiguously, The Retreat. Maisie considered the meanings of "retreat", and wondered if the soldiers were, in fact, relinquishing their position, seeking a place of shelter from the enemy. For such men perhaps life itself was now the enemy.

Maisie picked up the heavy black telephone and began to dial BEL 4746, the Belgravia home of Lord Julian Compton and his wife, Lady Rowan. There was a short delay, then Maisie heard the telephone ring three times before being answered by Carter, the Compton's long-serving butler. She checked her watch immediately the call was answered.

"Compton residence."

"Hello, Mr Carter. How are you?"

"Maisie, what a pleasure. We are all well here, thank you, but not looking forward to Cook's retirement, though it's long overdue."

"And what about you, Mr Carter?"

"Now then, Maisie, as long as I can manage these stairs, I will be here. Her ladyship has been very anxious to speak to you, Maisie."

"Yes, I know. That's why I've telephoned."

"Oh, well . . . I should know better than to ask how you know, Maisie."

"Mr Carter, it really isn't difficult, is it? Lady Rowan is a terrier in disguise."

Carter laughed and connected the call to Lady Rowan, who was in the library reading the late-edition newspapers.

"Maisie, dear girl. Where have you been? I thought you'd gone off somewhere."

"No, Lady Rowan. I've been busy."

"Excellent news. But you really must not become a stranger here. Are you sure that you wouldn't like to move into the rooms upstairs? I know I keep asking, but this is such a big house now. It never used to seem this big. Perhaps I'm getting smaller. They say that about age."

"No, Lady Rowan. Not you. Shall I come to see you this week?"

"Yes. Definitely. Come tomorrow. And I insist that you have dinner with me, and that you stay. I simply cannot have you travelling on your own after dark, and I know that you will refuse to let us drive you home."

"Yes, Lady Rowan. I'll stay – but just for one night. Is everything all right?"

There was a silence on the line.

"Lady Rowan, is everything all right?"

"I want to talk to you about James. I thought you might have some advice for a poor misunderstood mother."

"Lady Rowan –"

"Yes, I'm laying it on a bit thick. But I'm worried about him. He's talking about going off to live on a farm in Kent. Sounds very strange to me. In fact, it sounds more than strange. Maisie, I confess, I'm frightened for James. He has been in the depths of melancholy since the war, it seems, and now this!"

"Of course. I'll do anything I can to help," replied Maisie.

"Thank you so much, my dear. What time will you be here?"

"Will six o'clock be all right?"

"Perfect. I'll tell Carter. Mrs Crawford will be delighted to see you."

"Until then, Lady Rowan."

"Take care, Maisie. And remember, I want to know everything about what you are doing."

"I will leave no story untold, Lady Rowan."

The two women laughed, bade each other good-bye, and replaced their respective telephone receivers. Without a second's delay Maisie checked her watch. She reached into the top drawer of her desk and took out a small ledger with "Telephone" marked on the cover. Inside she made a note that the call to Lady Rowan Compton had taken four minutes. Maisie replaced the ledger and closed the drawer before walking to the window.

Of course she would offer Lady Rowan any assistance in her power, for she was indebted to her for so much. And Maisie knew, too, how difficult the aftermath of the war had been for James – but not, perhaps, as hard as it had been for the likes of Vincent. Yet Maisie was sympathetic to his melancholy, which was as much due to a loss still mourned as to his injuries. Maisie wondered whether Lord Julian had concerns regarding the ability of his only son to take on the family's business interests, and she was aware that Lady Rowan had often been the peacekeeper between the two. Tall, blond, blue-eyed James had always been the apple of his mother's eye. Years ago, when his son was no longer a child, Lord Julian had been heard to say on many an occasion, "You're spoiling that boy, Rowan." And now the once mischievously energetic James seemed hollow and drawn. Lady Rowan had been secretly relieved when James, a flying ace, was injured – not in the air but during an explosion on the ground. She knew his wounds would heal, and that she would have him safe at home at a time when so many of her contemporaries were receiving word that their sons had been lost to war.

Maisie turned from the window, and walked toward the door. Taking her coat and hat from the stand, she looked around the room, extinguished the light and left her office. As she locked the door behind her, she reflected upon how strange it was that a man who had significant financial resources, time, and a beautiful house in the country would seek the peace and quiet that might dispel his dark mood by going to live on a stranger's farm. Making her way downstairs in the half-light shed by the flickering gas lamp, Maisie felt a chill move through her body. And she knew that the sensation was not caused by the cold or the damp, but by a threat – a threat to the family of the woman she held most dear, the woman who had helped her achieve accomplishments that might otherwise have remained an unrealized dream.

SPRING 1910–SPRING 1917

CHAPTER EIGHT

*B*orn in 1863, and growing up in the middle years of Queen Victoria's reign, Lady Rowan had delighted her father, the fourth Earl of Westavon, but had been the source of much frustration for her mother, Lady Westavon, who was known to comment that her daughter was "a lady in name only!" It was clear that, far from being content with pursuits more becoming her position and upbringing, she was happiest with her horses and with her brother, Edwin, when he came home from school in the holidays. From an early age she had questioned her father, disagreed with her mother, and by the time she was on the cusp of womanhood, caused her parents to wonder if a suitable match would ever be found.

Maurice Blanche was ten years Lady Rowan's senior, a school friend of her brother. At first Rowan was fascinated by Maurice during those weekends when Edwin brought Maurice home from Marlborough.

"His people are in France, so I thought he might like to get out for a bit of a break," said Edwin, introducing the short, stocky boy who seemed to have little to say.

But when Maurice spoke, the young Rowan hung on his every word. His accent, a hybrid that came as a result of his French father and Scottish mother, intrigued her. As she grew older, Lady Rowan realized that Maurice moved with ease among people of any background, often changing his accent slightly to echo the nuances and rhythm of the other person's speech. The listener only vaguely appreciated the distinction, but nevertheless leaned in closer, smiled more easily, and probably shared a confidence to which no other person had been privy. Gradually his influence on the life of Lady Rowan challenged and inspired her, and in turn, his trust in her honest opinion was unfailing.

In the course of his life's work, Maurice Blanche could count among his friends and colleagues philosophers, scientists, doctors, psychologists, and members of the judiciary. It was a self-designed career that had rendered him invaluable to an extraordinary range of people, whether government ministers, those investigating crime, or simply people who needed information.

In 1898, the year in which Lady Rowan celebrated the tenth anniversary of her marriage to Lord Julian Compton, it was clear to Maurice that Rowan needed to be engaged in more than simply London's social calendar. Her only son, James, had just been sent away to a preparatory school, an inevitable event Lady Rowan had dreaded. During a heated political discussion Maurice dared the very vocal and opinionated Lady Rowan to follow her own challenging words with actions.

"It's not enough to say that you want equality, Ro. What do you intend to do about it?

Lady Rowan swallowed hard. Soon after, she became a fully fledged and active suffragette.

Eleven years later Lady Rowan Compton shocked Belgravia by marching on Westminster, demanding the vote and equality for women, rich and poor. Lord Julian was long-suffering, but the truth of the matter was that he adored Rowan and would walk on hot coals rather than cross her. Questioned about his wife's involvement,

Lord Julian would simply reply, "Oh, you know Ro, once she's got the bit between her teeth . . ." and people would nod sympathetically and leave the subject alone, which was exactly what Lord Julian wanted them to do. However, it was Maurice Blanche who challenged Rowan once again on the depth of her commitment.

"So you march on Westminster, and you have these meetings with your sister suffragettes, but what are you actually doing?"

"Maurice, what do you mean, what am I *doing?* This house is full of women meeting together three times a week – and we're forging ahead, make no mistake!"

Lady Rowan had barely taken a sip from her glass of sherry when Maurice issued an instruction. "We're off. Got something to show you. Go and change. Plain walking skirt and a jacket will do. And good sturdy shoes, Rowan."

Blanche stood up and walked toward the window, a move that suggested she should be quick.

"Maurice, you had better have good reason –"

"Hurry up, Rowan, or I shall leave without you."

Lady Rowan went immediately to her room and when Nora, her personal maid, came to ask if she was needed, she was turned away.

"No. That's quite all right, Nora. I can help myself, you know."

Lady Rowan dressed quickly, with only a cursory glance in the mirror. She cut a handsome figure, and she knew it. Not that she was quintessentially pretty, but with her height and aquiline profile she was striking. She was an athletic woman, a keen and competitive tennis player, an accomplished equestrienne, and a notoriously reckless skier on the slopes of Wengen until she was well into her forties. Her once rich chestnut hair had dulled slightly and was peppered with grey, but mercifully her weight had changed little since the day of her marriage. On the day Maurice Blanche demanded she accompany him, Lady Rowan Compton was forty-seven.

Rowan was excited. Maurice was prodding her at a time when life had lost some of the edge it had had in her youth. Yes, she was involved in the suffragette movement, she had her horses in the country, and of course there was the London social calendar, engagements and reciprocal entertainment making up an important part of her life in town during the season. James had just finished school. She had looked forward to his company at home when his school years were over, but she rarely had it, for no sooner had he returned from the city than he seemed to vanish again. James was a man now, if still a very young one.

As she dressed, Lady Rowan tingled with anticipation. Maurice might provide her with a diversion to fill a gap that seemed to be widening with the passing years. She returned to the drawing room, and they left the house quickly. The two old friends walked along the tree-lined street, conversation unnecessary, although Lady Rowan was aching to know where they were going.

❋

"I'm not saying that you are not busy, Rowan," Maurice broke their silence. "Not at all. And the cause is a worthy one. For women to have a place of account in this society, they must have a political voice. And having had one queen on the throne in the modern age does not constitute such a voice. But Rowan, with you the voice always comes from a safe place, does it not?"

"You should have been on the march, Maurice. That wasn't safe at all."

"I'm sure. But we both know that I'm not talking about marches. I'm talking about the safe place that we remain in, within the world we were born to. Swimming forever in the confines of our own pond. Socially, intellectually −"

"Maurice −"

"Rowan, we will speak again of equality later, for it is equality that you claim to want. Now then, we must wait here for an omnibus."

"A *what?* Now, I told you, Maurice − we should have called for the motor."

"No, Rowan. We are stepping out of your pond today. I have the fare for us both."

✦

$\mathcal{I}$t was dark when they returned to Belgravia in silence. Rowan was deep in thought. She had seen much that troubled her. But nothing troubled her more than her own emotions.

"You'll come in . . ."

"No, Rowan. You are tired from swimming in another pond today. A pond that, though discussed in your meetings and debates, you could not truly imagine. Poverty is something we think we understand from description. It is only when it is close to hand that we have a grasp of what it means to be unequal."

"But what can I do?"

"No need to wear a hair shirt, Rowan. But perhaps opportunities will present themselves. One only has to ask, 'How might I serve?' Goodnight, my dear."

Maurice bowed slightly, then left Rowan in the entrance hall of her grand home.

He had taken her to the East End. First to the noisy markets, which thrilled her, although she could not look directly at some of the street urchins. Then into the depths of London's poorest areas. And it seemed that always someone knew him.

"Evenin', Doc, alright then?"

"Well, very well. And how is the youngest?"

"Comin' on a treat, Doc. Thanks to you."

Rowan didn't ask about his relationship to the people who greeted him so readily. Maurice was certainly a doctor, but after attending King's College Medical School, he had studied at the University of Edinburgh's Department of Legal Medicine. Rowan was under the impression that he no longer practised. At least not upon people who were still alive.

"To answer the question that is written all over your face, Rowan – once or twice a week I attend women and children at a small clinic. There is precious little set aside for the poor, there is a constant need for help, for . . . everything. And, of course, bringing children safely into the world and providing care when they are sick is a refreshing change for me."

Rowan rang the bell in the drawing room. She had dismissed Carter, the butler, as soon as she arrived home, but now she craved inner warmth.

How may I serve? What can I do? What would be sensible? What would Julian say? Well, that was something she would not have to think about. If Maurice was her challenger, Julian was her rock.

"Yes, Your Ladyship?"

"Carter, I'd like some hot soup, please – something simple, nothing too clever, you understand. And a sherry please, Carter."

"Very good, Ma'am. Cook prepared a tasty vegetable soup this afternoon, as soon as the delivery arrived."

"Perfect. Perfect, Carter."

Carter poured sherry into a crystal glass and held it out on a silver salver.

"Oh – and Carter. Before I forget. I would like to speak to you about the dinner next week and our guests. Lord Julian's business colleagues. Tomorrow morning after breakfast, tell Cook to come to my study as well. Ten o'clock."

"Very good, Your Ladyship. Will that be all?"

Later, as Lady Rowan finished the hot soup that had been brought on a tray to the drawing room, she leaned back in her chair and contemplated what she had seen that day, and her conversation with Maurice. It is so easy, she thought. All I have to do is snap my fingers and someone runs. Equality. Maurice is right, I can do more.

While Lady Rowan readied herself for bed in her grand house in Belgravia on that night in the spring of 1910, a thirteen-year-old girl cried herself to sleep in the small back room of a soot-blackened terraced house in southeast London. Her jet black hair, released from a neat braid and purple ribbon, cascaded over the pillow, and the deep blue eyes that so easily reflected joy were rimmed with dark circles and red with tears. She cried for her loss and cried, too, for her father, whose dreadful, deep breathless sobs echoed from the kitchen below.

Maisie had held her tears back for days, believing that if her father did not see or hear her crying he would not worry about her, and his burden would be lighter. And each day, his heart breaking, he rose in the early hours of the morning, harnessed his horse to the cart, and made his way to Covent Garden.

At first, after her mother died, Maisie would pinch herself three times on the right arm before sleeping, assured that this one action would make her rise at three o'clock in the morning, in time to make his tea and spread a thick slice of bread with beef dripping for him to eat in front of the coal stove before he set off for the market.

"You don't 'ave to do that, love. I can watch out for meself, Maisie. You go on back to bed. And mind you lock that door after I leave."

"I'm all right, Dad. You'll see. We'll be all right."

But Frankie Dobbs was at a loss. A widower with a thirteen-year-old daughter. She needed more, and Lord knows that the girl and her mother had been close, thought Frankie. No, he had to find something better for the girl than for her to be little woman of the house.

Oh, there was so much that they had wanted for Maisie, the child that had come to them in later life and who was, they said, the answer to many prayers. She was a bright one, they knew that almost from the beginning. In fact, people would remark that even as a newborn it seemed that Maisie could focus on a person and follow them with her eyes. "That girl can look right through you," people would say, when she was still a babe in arms.

The Dobbses had been putting money away for Maisie's education, so that she could stay on at school, perhaps even go on to be a teacher. They were so proud of their girl. But the money was gone, long gone to pay for doctors, medicine, and a holiday at the seaside, just in case the fresh salty air worked a miracle. But nothing had worked. Frankie was alone with his girl now, and he was afraid. Afraid that he couldn't do well by her, that he had nothing left to give her. No, it was settled. He had to find a place for Maisie.

It seemed to Frankie that even Persephone, his old mare, had lost pride in her step. Frankie always made sure his horse and cart were well turned out; it made a difference to business. He might be a costermonger, but there was no excuse for looking shabby. With trousers pressed under the mattress each night, a clean white collarless shirt, fresh brightly coloured neckerchief, his best woollen waistcoat, and a cloth cap set jauntily on the side of his head, Frankie himself was always well turned out. "Just because I use me 'ands to make a livin' doesn't mean to say I can't do with a bit of spit and polish," Frankie had been heard to say.

And as he climbed up onto the driver's seat of his cart, Frankie was more than proud of his shining horse and the gleaming leather and brass traces. Persephone, a Welsh cob, trotted proudly down the street, lifting her hooves high as if she knew how good she looked. But since the death of Maisie's mother, Frankie's inner malaise was felt keenly by Persephone, who now trotted in a desultory manner, as if the family's grief had added several hundredweight to her load.

In the kitchen of the house in Belgravia, Carter and Lady Rowan's cook, Mrs Crawford, were deep in conversation about the morning's meeting to discuss the week's dinner plans.

"What time will Mr Dobbs be here, Cook? You'll need to have a complete list of fresh vegetables for Lady Rowan, and your menu planned for the week."

Cook rolled her eyes. Just what she loved, being told how to do her job.

"Mr Carter, menu suggestions are in hand. I asked Mr Dobbs to stop by again today to give me a list of what is best at market this week. He's going out of the way to be at our service, poor man."

"Yes indeed, Cook. Mr Dobbs certainly has his hands full, I quite agree."

Outside the rear entrance of the house a horse and cart came to a halt. They could hear Frankie Dobbs talking to Persephone, putting on her nosebag of oats, telling her he wouldn't be long, then setting off down the stairs that led to the back door.

"That'll be him now." Cook wiped her hands on a cloth and went to answer the door.

"Mr Dobbs," she said, standing aside so that Frankie Dobbs could enter the large warm room. As he removed his cloth cap, Mrs Crawford cast a glance at Carter, frowned, and shook her head. Frankie Dobbs looked pale and drawn.

"Good morning, Mr Dobbs. How are you?"

"Very well, all things considered, Mr Carter. And you?" It was a thin response, and both Cook and Carter glanced at each other again. This was not the jovial, robust Frankie Dobbs they were used to doing business with. "I've brought a list of the best vegetables and fruit this week. If I take the order today, I can deliver tomorrow morning. The broccoli and sprouts are looking very nice, and of course there's some hearty cabbage at the market. I know Her Ladyship is partial to a nice bit of cabbage."

"She certainly is, Mr Dobbs." Cook took the rough piece of paper from Frankie and ran a finger down the list of vegetables. "I think we'll need something of everything this week. Full house, you know."

"Right you are." Standing uneasily in the kitchen, Frankie fingered his cap. "I was wondering, Mr Carter, if there was something I might discuss. With both yourself and Mrs Crawford here."

"Of course, Mr Dobbs, sit down at the table. Cook, a cup of tea for Mr Dobbs. What can we do for you?"

Carter faced Frankie across the heavy pine table.

"Well, it's about my girl. She's a bright lass, very bright . . ." Frankie faltered, looked at his shining boots and twisted his cap. "Since 'er

mother died, well, we was going to send 'er on to the big school . . .
and she got a scholarship and all . . . but there's the money for the special clothes and books, and what with the doctor's bills . . ."

Cook placed a cup of tea in front of Frankie, leaned toward him,
and covered his hand with hers. "You're a good man, Mr Dobbs. You'll
do right by young Maisie."

Frankie shrank at his daughter's name, afraid of what he was about
to ask. "I was wonderin' if you had a place for my Maisie 'ere, like. In
service. She's a good girl. 'ard worker. Very bright. You won't need to
tell 'er anythin' twice. She's well mannered and speaks nicely – 'er
mother, God rest her soul, saw to that. I thought that after a while, she
could go back to night school, you see. Take up where she left off.
Loves learnin', does Maisie."

Carter and Cook glanced at each other once again, and Carter
spoke quickly. "Mr Dobbs, you have come at the right time and in
answer to a prayer, hasn't he, Mrs Crawford?"

Cook looked at Carter and nodded her head in agreement. She
had absolutely no idea what he was talking about.

"One of our more junior maids recently left service. We need help.
Have your girl come to the house at five today – she can pick up the
order for tomorrow's delivery. I think you have to check quantities,
don't you, Mrs Crawford?"

Cook nodded agreement and looked at the list of vegetables again.
They both knew that Frankie Dobbs never had to be told quantities,
and always delivered exactly what was needed. Carter continued, "I'll
interview her, just to make sure that she is right for the position."

Frankie breathed a sigh of relief.

"Thank you Mr Carter, Mrs Crawford. I'll be getting on now.
Maisie will be here at five sharp."

The grieving man left quickly, and before leading his horse away,
put his head against the Persephone's soft nose and wept. "It's for the
best," he whispered. "It's for the best."

It was the nearest he had come to having "words" with his daughter. As Frankie broke the news to Maisie – that times were difficult,

that he was only thinking of her, that he wanted her to be safe, and that the Compton household was a fine place to work – he watched the tears well up in her eyes, her jaw tighten with the effort of not giving in to the pressure to cry, and her fine, long-fingered hands clench into fists held firmly by her sides.

"But Dad, you know you need me here. I can help. I helped when Mum was ill. I can get another job, I can even do this job and come home at night, Dad."

"Maisie love, we'll still see each other, you know that. Sunday afternoons we can go to the park, take a turn, have a cup of tea. We can go to see yer Nan and Granddad. But at least you'll have a place, a good job. And later on, we can get you into night school, to catch up. I'm all out, love. There's no money, and there's bills to pay. I don't even know if I can keep renting this house. Yer mother going . . ."

Maisie drew away as he reached out to her, turned her back to him, and looked out the window. They hadn't been well off, not by any means, but there used to be enough for a few extras. Now there was nothing, and there was ground to be made up. Then they would be all right. She sighed deeply in resignation.

"Dad, if I work at Lady Rowan's, and if I send you my money and we make up the bills, then can I come back?"

"Oh, love. Then what would you do? I was thinking you might go on from there. Maybe get out of the Smoke. She's got a place in the country you know. Down in Kent. She's got contacts, woman like that. You do yer classes at night, you might get yerself a private teaching job at one of them big 'ouses. You don't want to be back 'ere. Yer mother and me wanted so much for you, love."

Her father was tired beyond reckoning. They were both tired beyond reckoning. Too tired for this talk. But she would go to Lady Rowan's to see this Mr Carter. And so help me, I'll work my way out of that place, thought Maisie. And on my own. I'll work so hard I'll take care of Dad. He won't have to get up at three in the morning by the time I've finished. Maisie bit her lip and looked up at nothing in particular on the wall. You'll see, I'll show him who can take care of herself. Maisie sighed, then reached out and put her arms around her father's waist.

"Dad, I'll go. You're right. Annie Clark down the road is in service now. So's Doreen Watts. Lot of girls are. It'll be all right. I'll see Mr Carter. I won't let you down, Dad."

"Oh love. You could never let me down."

Frankie Dobbs hugged his daughter close for a moment longer, then pushed her back. "Now then, this is where you go."

Maisie Dobbs watched her father as he took a short pencil from his waistcoat pocket, licked the lead, and began to scribble directions on the back of a scrap of paper.

CHAPTER NINE

*D*ays after securing the position of in-between maid, Maisie returned to the white four-storey mansion in Belgravia, at the southern end of Ebury Place. Before reporting for work, Maisie stood in front of the building and looked up, wondering what it might be like to enter such a house through the front door. Transferring the canvas bag containing her clothes, hairbrushes and several books from her right hand to her left, Maisie took a handkerchief from her coat pocket and wiped her eyes, hoping that no tell-tale marks were left of the tears shed on the bus from Lambeth. She sighed and, making her way to the left of the house, braced her shoulders and held on to the wrought iron banister to steady herself as she walked down the stone steps that led to the kitchen.

Once welcomed by Carter and Mrs Crawford, Maisie took her belongings to the top floor of the house. The very top floor, the attic reached by "back stairs" from the kitchen. She shared the room with Enid.

Enid was a worldly sixteen-year-old, with pressed rouge on her cheeks and a hint of colour on her lips, who had now reached such a high position of authority that she would be called upon to serve in the breakfast room come tomorrow morning. A thin, gangly girl, Enid was friendly enough to Maisie, who felt that circumstances would never give her cause to laugh again.

"That's your bed over there," was Enid's welcome to the shared bedroom. "Make yourself at home. We're up early in the morning. Half past four, five at the latest, so I hope you don't snore and keep me awake."

She grinned at Maisie, her freckled nose crinkling over the teasing remark. Enid was concentrating on her pronunciation, convinced that if she was to get anywhere in the world, she had to work quickly to introduce aitches into her speech. Thus every word beginning with the letter *h* was overpronounced, with a breathy start and a rapid completion. *Huh-ome, huh-ouse, huh-ope.* In fact, Enid's rather zealous pursuit of something better resulted in the occasional *h* where *h* had no place.

"H-ave you bin in s-h-ervice before, or is this your first pos-hishun?" asked Enid.

"No, this is my first. My mother passed on and my father thought it better . . ."

Enid nodded. She never did know what to say when confronted by loss.

"Well, I reckon you'll do all right. You're tall, not as tall as me, mind, but taller than some of them short girls. They reckon the tall ones always do all right, get promoted quickly to serving, being as we look better in the uniform, more, you know, suited to the h-occasion. And you won't find them upstairs doin' any little tests to see if you're an h-onest sort — like puttin' a farthin' under the carpet to see if you take it or leave it on the side. Anyway, come on Dobbsie, I'll show you where the facilities are. Come along with me."

Enid put her hand on Maisie's shoulder and led her along a dimly lit hallway to the "fac-hilities."

Carter had chosen to introduce her at breakfast. Maisie knew that in some houses the staff weren't introduced until they had reached a higher position, if at all. The practice changed at the Compton residence when Lord Julian had asked a maid to inform Lady Rowan that he would take tea with her in the drawing room, to which the maid had answered, "Yes, Sir. And who shall I say is calling?" Lady Rowan was appalled, and since that time had insisted upon meeting whoever was under her roof, even if the meeting was a short one.

"Your Lordship, Your Ladyship, may I introduce our new downstairs member of staff, Miss Maisie Dobbs." Carter held his hand out toward Maisie who took one step forward, curtsied, and stepped back to her place alongside Carter.

Lord and Lady Compton were cordial, welcoming Maisie to the household, saying they were absolutely sure that she would be happy there. After a brief encounter, she left the dining room with Carter to go down to the kitchens and receive her instructions for the day.

"My word, Julian, what a striking girl."

Lord Compton looked over a folded edge of *The Times* toward his wife. "Striking? Yes. Yes, I suppose so. Very young."

"Yes, very young. Very . . . there was something about her, wasn't there?"

"Mmm? About whom?" Lord Julian continued to read the newspaper.

"About Maisie Dobbs. Something quite different about her, don't you think? Julian, are you listening?"

"Hmm? Oh, Rowan. Yes. Maisie Dobb, Dobbins . . . what was her name? Dobbs?" Lord Julian looked out of the window to recall the conversation. "You know, Rowan, I think you are right. Could be those eyes. Very deep blue. Don't see that very often."

"Julian, I don't think it was the colour of her eyes. It was nothing I could put my finger on."

Lady Rowan spread a thin slice of toast with butter and marmalade as Lord Julian turned to the next page of the morning paper. "Yes, Darling, probably nothing."

Within a few days, most people agreed that Maisie Dobbs had indeed settled in well to life in the Compton household. Her day started at half past four, when she rose and poured cold water from the pitcher on the washstand into a large china bowl. She splashed her face and moistened a cloth to wash her body before hurriedly dressing, then tiptoeing down to the lowest level of the house to fill the coal-scuttles.

Her first job was to take heavy coal-scuttles to the breakfast room, the drawing room, His Lordship's study, the morning room, and to the hall. Kneeling by each fireplace she pulled back the black iron grate cover, swept out yesterday's ashes, and placed them in an old empty scuttle. She rolled sheets of yesterday's newspaper, placed them in the grate, then carefully positioned dry kindling on top and lit the newspaper with a match.

As flames licked up and caught the kindling, Maisie leaned forward and balanced bricks of coal, one by one, on the spitting wood. Sitting back, she watched for just a few seconds as the fire crackled and flared into life. Satisfied that the wood and coal had taken the flames, she brushed splinters, coal dust and ash under the grate, replaced the cover, and put a few more pieces of coal onto the mound before giving the fireplace a quick dust. She was ready to move on to another room.

When she had finished lighting fires in each of the rooms, it was time to fill the scuttles again and feed the fires so that the rooms were ready to warm those who had time to sit by a fire – people who had the time to be warmed by something other than hard work.

Throughout the day Maisie cleaned, ran errands for Cook, and generally served at the bidding of anyone above her in the pecking order, which was almost everyone in the household. But the duties of her waking hours brought a calm to Maisie's life that she had not known since before her mother became ill. She had only to follow the direction of others, and in the rhythm of her daily round, whether blacking the fireplaces, sweeping the stairs, or polishing furniture, there was room for thought – thought of what might be.

Maisie's "day off" was Sunday afternoon. As soon as the heavy clock on the mantelpiece over the kitchen stove struck a single chime at half past eleven, Maisie waited for Cook to look up at her and nod toward the door.

"All right lass, off you go. And mind you're back by a decent hour!"

It was a feigned warning, because Maisie had nowhere to be at an indecent hour.

Untying her pinafore as she hurried from the kitchen and up the back stairs toward the servants' quarters, Maisie thought that her legs would never carry her as fast as her mind wanted to travel. She quickly changed into a long black skirt that had belonged to her mother and a clean cotton blouse. She checked her reflection in the mirror just once, pushed her hat onto her head, and reached for her coat and coin purse before rushing through the bedroom door again. She was off to see her father, knowing that at twelve noon he would pull the fob watch from his waistcoat pocket and smile to himself. Frankie Dobbs couldn't wait for his girl to come home so they could spend a few hours together, a precious respite from a work-weary week.

On Sundays, Frankie was always to be found at the stable where he kept his mare, under the dry arches that were part of the southern construction of Waterloo Bridge. Sunday was the day to clean the horse from head to hoof, to oil the leather traces, polish the brasses, and make sure the cart was ready for another week's work. It was an easy morning, a morning made sweeter by the knowledge that soon Maisie's footsteps would clatter on the cobblestones leading to the stables.

"Love, you are a sight for sore eyes. How are you, my girl?"

"Well enough, Dad. I'm well enough."

"Let me just finish this, then we'll go home for a cuppa."

Together they worked in the stable, finally leaving the horse to the remainder of her day at rest. After a cup of tea, Frankie would dress in his Sunday best, and father and daughter would catch a bus to Brockwell Park, where they walked together before stopping to eat a packed lunch.

"You should see the library, Dad! I've never seen so many books. Walls of them. About everything."

"You and your books, girl. You keeping up with your reading?"

"Yes, Dad. I go to the public library every week on a Wednesday afternoon. Mrs Crawford sends me with a list for her and Mr Carter, and I get books for myself as well. Mind you, Enid says she can't sleep with the light on, so I can't read for long."

"You watch your eyes, my girl, you only get one pair, you know."

"Dad!"

"I know, I'm naggin'. So, what about the other folk downstairs, what're they like then?"

Father and daughter sat down on a wooden bench overlooking a flowerbed. "Well, you know Mr Carter and Mrs Crawford."

"That I do. Good people, both of them."

"Well, anyway, Mrs Crawford is called 'Cook' and 'Mrs Crawford' without any — well, without any method to it."

"What do you mean, love?"

"I mean sometimes she's called 'Cook' and sometimes 'Mrs Crawford' and there's no rule — sometimes it's both names in one sentence."

Frankie chewed on a sandwich and nodded his head for Maisie to continue.

"There's two footmen, Arthur and Cedric, and there's Her Ladyship's maid, Nora — she's a bit quiet. Apparently at the big house, in Kent, there's more staff and a housekeeper, Mrs Johnson. There's some scullery maids — Dossie, Emily, and Sadie — who help Mrs Crawford in the kitchen, and of course there's Enid."

"What's she like, then?"

"She's got hair the colour of a blazing fire, Dad. Really red, it is. And when she brushes it out at night, it goes right up like this."

Maisie held out her hands to indicate a distance away from the sides of her head, which made Frankie laugh. Something he couldn't understand — how she could look like a child one minute, and like a mature woman the next.

"She nice to you, love?"

"She's all right Dad. Blows hot and cold, though. One minute she seems full of the joys of spring, and the next, well, I just keep out of her way."

"I might've guessed. Yer carrottops are always the same. Remember, love, the more you're yerself, the more it's like you've put iron shoes on yer feet – they'll 'old you to the ground when that 'ot and cold air comes at you from 'er direction. That's the way with that sort."

Maisie nodded, as if to take in this important advice, and continued with her story. "The other thing about Enid is that I think she's sweet on Master James."

Frankie laughed again. "Oh! I see it didn't take you long to get wind of the goings-on! What's 'e like, then, this James? Bit old to be called 'Master,' in' 'e?"

"Well I heard Cook saying His Lordship gave instructions that Master James was to be called Master until he 'proved his worth'. Or something like that. He comes into the kitchen sometimes, you know, of an evening, after dinner. I've watched him. He comes in to see Cook, and as he walks by Enid he always winks at her. She goes all red in the face and looks the other way, but I know she likes him. And Cook pretends to tell him off for coming into her kitchen, like he was still a little boy, but then she brings out a big plate of ginger biscuits and he gets stuck into them standing right there in the kitchen! Drives Mr Carter mad, it does."

"I should think it does! Likes order, does Mr Carter. Now then, tell me about the 'ouse itself."

And Maisie smiled, glad to be in the easy company of her father, a man who was given to remark that a person could take him as they found him; there were no airs to Frankie Dobbs. And Frankie was more at peace now. Life itself was easier – easier now that he knew his daughter to be in good hands. Easier now that the bills were being paid. Yes, thought Frankie Dobbs as he walked with his daughter in the park, it was all getting easier.

✦

Maisie was fascinated by the library. It was well used, for both Lord and Lady Compton enjoyed literature, politics, and keeping up with the fancies of intellectual London. But when Maisie opened the door and brought in the coal-scuttle at five in the morning, it was a quiet room. The lush velvet curtains kept draughts at bay and allowed warmth to seep into every corner after Maisie had lit the fire ready for whoever would use the room that morning.

Each day she lingered just a little longer before kneeling down to the fireplace, before her hands were blackened by the lighting of fires. Each day she learned a little more about the depth and breadth of knowledge housed in the Comptons' library, and each day her hunger grew. Gradually she became braver, first tentatively touching the leather binding as she read the title on the spine of a book, then taking the book from its place on the shelf and opening the fine onionskin pages at the front.

The library seized Maisie's imagination, rendering the small public library with which she was familiar a very poor runner-up in her estimation. Of all the rooms in the house, she loved this the most. One morning, as she replaced a book to attend to the fireplace, a thought occurred to Maisie.

After her mother's death, she had been used to rising at three in the morning to make her father his tea. It had never hurt her then. In fact, she considered getting up at half past four to be "lying in." So, what if she got up at three in the morning and came down to the library? No one would know. Enid could sleep through the roof falling in over her head, and she had started coming up to bed late over the past week anyway. Lord knows where she had been, but it certainly wasn't out, because Carter locked up the house as if it were the Bank of England every night. She dreaded that Enid might be with Master James. Just two weeks ago, as she was leaving Lady Rowan's sitting room, where she had been sent to collect a tray one

evening, Maisie saw Enid and James together on the first-floor landing. Without being observed by them, she watched as James ran his
fingers through his fair hair and continued speaking with Enid, his
grey eyes intent upon her response to his question. Was it a question?
Surely it was, because she saw Enid shake her head and look at the
carpet, while brushing her right shoe back and forth across the fibres.

And now Enid was never in bed before midnight – which meant
that, thankfully, she would be deep in slumber by three o'clock.
Maisie resolved to come to the library when the house was asleep.
That night, before pulling up the covers and extinguishing the small
lamp beside her bed, Maisie pinched the skin on her right arm
sharply three times to ensure that she would awake in time to put her
plan into action.

The next morning Maisie awakened easily by three o'clock. A chill
in the attic room tempted her to forget her plan, but she sat up, determined to go through with it. She washed and dressed with hardly a
sound, crept out of the room carrying her shoes and a cardigan, and
felt her way downstairs in the dark. In the silent distance, the kitchen
clock struck the single chime of a quarter past the hour. She had
almost two hours before the coal-scuttles had to be filled.

The library was silent and pitch black as Maisie entered. Quickly
closing the door behind her, she lit the lamps and made her way to
the section that held philosophy books. This was where she would
start. She wasn't quite sure which book to start with, but felt that if
she just started somewhere, a plan would develop as she went along.
The feeling inside that she experienced when she saw the books was
akin to the hunger she felt as food was put on the table at the end of
the working day. And she knew that she needed this sustenance as
surely as her body needed its fuel.

Maisie's fingers tapped along the spines of books until she could
bear the electric tingle of excitement no longer. Within minutes she
was seated at the table, opening *The Philosophical Works of David Hume,*
and drawing the desk lamp closer to illuminate the pages. Maisie took
a small notebook and pencil from her apron pocket, set it down on

the desk and wrote the title of the book and the author's name. And she read. For an hour and a half, Maisie read. She read with understanding on a subject she had barely even heard of.

As the library clock chimed a quarter to five, Maisie turned to her notebook and wrote a precis of what she had read, what she understood, and her questions. The clock struck five, Maisie put the notebook and pencil away in her apron pocket, closed the book, replaced it ever so carefully on the shelf, extinguished the desk light, and left the room. She closed the door quietly behind her and went quickly downstairs to fill the coal-scuttles. Just a short while later she opened the library door again. Without looking at the shelves, as if eye contact with the spines of the beloved books would give her game away, she set the coal-scuttle down and knelt by the grate to build and light the fire.

Each weekday morning Maisie rose at three to visit the library. Sometimes a party at the house would keep the Comptons up until the small hours, and the change in routine made the library expeditions a risk she could not afford. She was liked in the house, though she had been spoken to by Lord and Lady Compton only once, when she had first arrived.

Half past two. Maisie crept out of bed. It was earlier than usual, but she couldn't sleep. She had gone to bed early, so it would be just as well to get up now. Enid slept soundly, which hardly surprised Maisie as the girl hadn't been in bed long. She was becoming a late one, that Enid. As late as Maisie was early. One of these days we'll meet in the doorway, thought Maisie. Then we'll have to do some talking.

The house was silent; only the ticking of clocks accompanied her to the library. Now when she entered the room it was as if she were falling into the arms of an old friend. Even the tentacles of cold receded as she turned on the light, placed her notebook and pencil on the desk, and went to the bookshelves. She took down the book she had been reading for the past three days, sat at the desk, found her place, and commenced.

Frankie Dobbs always said that when she was reading Maisie had "cloth ears." She always seemed instinctively to know the time and when she would need to stop reading to run an errand or complete a chore, but as far as Frankie was concerned, "Those ears don't even work when you've yer nose in a book!" And he loved her all the more for it.

Lord and Lady Compton were caught up in the midst of the London season, which Lady Rowan loved for its energy, even if she did have to tolerate some people she considered to be "light." Fortunately late nights usually fell on weekends, but this invitation, in the middle of the week, was not to be missed: an intimate yet sumptuous dinner with one of society's most outspoken hostesses.

"Thank God there's someone with a bigger mouth than mine," Lady Rowan confided to her husband.

Guests were to include some of the leading literary lights of Europe. It was an opportunity for sparkling conversation; definitely not to be missed. Maurice Blanche would accompany them, a rare event as he was known to shun society gatherings.

After-dinner conversation drifted past midnight. It was only as Maisie Dobbs crept downstairs to the library that Lord and Lady Compton, along with Maurice Blanche, bade their hostess adieu, thanking her profusely for a wonderful evening. They arrived home at three in the morning. Carter had been instructed not to wait up, but an evening supper tray had been left for them in the drawing room. Lady Rowan was still in fine argumentative fettle as Lord Julian led the way.

"I tell you, Maurice, this time you are mistaken. Only last week I was reading – where was I reading – oh yes, that new book. You know, Julian, what was it called? Anyway, I was reading about a new hypothesis that utterly controverts your position."

"Rowan, could we please –" interrupted Lord Julian.

"Julian, no, we couldn't. Pour Maurice a drink. I'll find the book, then you'll see!"

"As you please, Rowan. I am very much looking forward to seeing what you have read. One always welcomes the opportunity to learn," said Maurice Blanche.

While the men settled by the embers of the drawing room fire, Lady Rowan stormed upstairs to the library. Maisie Dobbs was deep in her book. She heard neither footsteps on the stairs nor the approach of Lady Rowan. She heard nothing until Lady Rowan spoke. And she did not speak until she had watched Maisie for some minutes, watched as the girl sucked on the end of her single braid of thick black hair, deep in concentration. Occasionally she would turn a page back, reread a sentence, nod her head, then read on.

"Excuse me. Maisie."

Maisie sat up and closed her eyes tightly, not quite believing that a voice had addressed her.

"Maisie!"

Maisie shot up from the chair, turned to face Lady Rowan, and quickly bobbed a curtsy. "Sorry, Your Ladyship. Begging your pardon, Ma'am. I've not harmed anything."

"What are you doing, girl?" asked Lady Rowan.

"Reading, Ma'am."

"Well, I can see that. Let me see that book."

Maisie turned, took the book she had been reading, and handed it to Lady Rowan. She stepped back, feet together, hands at her sides. Bloody hell, she was in trouble now.

"Latin? Latin! What on earth are you reading Latin for?"

Lady Rowan's surprise stemmed questions that another employer might have put to the young maid.

"Um . . . well. Um . . . I needed to learn it," replied Maisie.

"You needed to learn it? Why do you need to learn Latin?"

"The other books had Latin in them, so I needed to understand it. To understand the other books, that is."

Maisie shifted her weight from one foot to the other. Now she needed to pee. For her part Lady Rowan was regarding Maisie sternly, yet she felt a strange curiosity to know more about the girl she had already thought unusual.

"Which other books? Show me," demanded Lady Rowan.

One by one Maisie took down the books, her hands shaking, her legs turning to jelly as she moved the library steps from one shelf to another. Whatever happened next, it was sure to be bad. Very bad. And she had let down her dad. How would she tell him she had been sacked? What would she say?

Maisie was so scared that she did not notice that, in her curiosity, Lady Rowan had forgotten the formality with which she would ordinarily address a servant. She asked Maisie about her choice of books, and Maisie, taking up her notebook, recounted what she had learned in her reading, and what questions had led her to each text in turn.

"My, my, young lady. You *have* been busy. All I can remember of Latin is the end of that verse: 'First it killed the Romans, and now it's killing me!' "

Maisie looked at Lady Rowan and smiled. She wasn't sure if it was a joke, but she couldn't stop the grin from forming. It was the first time she had truly smiled since coming to the house. The expression was not lost on Lady Rowan, who felt herself torn between regard for the girl and the appropriate response in such a situation.

"Maisie, there is still time for you to enjoy a short rest before you begin your duties. Go back to your room now. I shall need to discuss this incident. In the meantime, do not use the library until you hear from Carter, who will instruct you as to how we will deal with this . . . situation." Lady Rowan felt the requirements of her position pressing upon her, just as it had when she had been taken by Maurice to the East End. How could she do what was right without compromising – how had Maurice described it? Yes, without compromising "the safety of her own pond"?

"Yes, Your Ladyship." Maisie put her notebook into her pocket, and with tears of fear visibly pricking the inner corners of her eyes, bobbed another curtsy.

Lady Rowan waited until Maisie had left the room before extinguishing the lights. It was only as she walked slowly down the staircase that she remembered that she had gone to the library for a book.

"Bloody fool," she said to herself, and walked toward the drawing room to speak with her husband and Maurice Blanche on a new topic of conversation.

CHAPTER TEN

*M*aisie had hardly been able to concentrate on anything since being discovered. She felt sure that notice to leave the employ of Lord and Lady Compton would soon follow, and was surprised that one week had gone by without any word. Then Carter summoned Maisie to his "office," the term he sometimes used – especially in grave situations where a reprimand was to be meted out – to describe the butler's pantry, a small room adjacent to the kitchen where he kept meticulous records regarding the running of the house.

Maisie was in a miserable state. The embarrassment of being caught, together with the pain of anticipating her father's dismay at her behaviour, was almost too much to bear. And of course, she no longer had access to the Comptons' library. Wringing her already work-reddened hands, Maisie knocked on the door of Mr Carter's office. Her nails were bitten down to the quick, and she had picked at her cuticles until her fingers were raw. It had been a nerve-racking week.

"Enter," said Carter, with a tone that was neither soft and welcoming nor overtly displeased. It was a tone that gave nothing away.

"Good morning, Mr Carter." Maisie bobbed a curtsy as she walked into the small room. "You wanted to see me, Sir?"

"Yes, Maisie. You know why I have sent for you. Lady Compton wishes to meet with you at twelve noon today. Sharp. In the library. I shall myself be in attendance, as will a colleague of both Lord and Lady Compton.

"Yes, Mr Carter."

Maisie could bear the wait no longer, and although fear was nipping at her throat and chest, she had to know her fate.

"Mr Carter, Sir?"

"Yes, Maisie?" Carter regarded her over half-moon spectacles.

"Mr Carter. Can't you just get on with it? Give me the sack now, so that I don't have to –"

"Maisie. No one has said anything about the sack. I am instructed only to accompany you to a meeting with Lady Rowan and Dr Blanche. I have also been requested to take your notebooks to the library this morning at half past ten. Please bring them to me directly so that I can take them to Lady Rowan."

"But . . ." Maisie did not understand, and although she thought that Carter did not understand either, she suspected he might have an inkling. "Mr Carter, Sir. What's this all about?"

Carter adjusted his tie and swept an imaginary hair from the cuff of his crisp white shirt. "Maisie, it is most unusual. However, I do not believe your employment here is at an end. In fact, rather the contrary. Now then. The notebooks. Then I believe the sideboard in the dining room is to be waxed and polished this morning, so you had better get on."

Maisie bobbed another curtsy and turned to leave the office.

"And Maisie," said Carter, sweeping back his well-combed grey-at-the-temples hair. "Although respect should always be accorded our employers and their guests, there's no need to keep bobbing up and down like a sewing-machine needle when you are downstairs."

Maisie absentmindedly bobbed again and quickly left the office. She returned fifteen minutes later with her collection of small notebooks for Carter. She was terrified of the meeting that was to take place at twelve noon, and was sure that she would spend half the time until then in the lavatory.

Carter was waiting at the foot of the first-floor stairs at five minutes to twelve when Maisie walked toward him from the landing that led to the lower stairs and the kitchen. He drew his pocket watch from his waistcoat pocket, determined to be not a moment too soon or a second too late.

"Ah, Maisie," he said as she approached, hands clasped together in front of her white pinafore.

Carter looked the girl up and down to check for marks on the pinafore and scuffs on her shoes, for stray tendrils of hair escaping from her white cap.

"Nicely turned out. Good. Let us proceed."

Carter checked his watch once more, turned, and led the way to the library. Maisie had a horrible taste in her mouth. What would her father say when she came home with her small canvas bag and no job? Well, perhaps it was for the best. She missed him something rotten, so perhaps it would be a very good thing. Carter knocked briskly at the door. A voice could be heard within.

"Come in."

Maisie closed her eyes for a second, put her hands behind her back, and crossed her fingers.

"Ah, Carter. Maisie. Do come in."

"Thank you, Ma'am," said Carter. Maisie bobbed her curtsy and looked sideways at Carter. Lady Rowan beckoned Maisie to her.

"Maurice, this is the girl of whom we have been speaking." Then, inclining her head slightly toward Maisie, she said, "I would like to introduce Dr Maurice Blanche. He knows of our meeting in the library, and I have consulted with him regarding the situation."

Maisie was now utterly confused. What situation? And who was this man? What was going on? Maisie nodded and curtsied to the man standing alongside Lady Rowan.

"Sir," she said in acknowledgment.

She didn't know what to make of this small man. He wasn't as tall as Lady Rowan, and while he looked well fed, there was a wiriness to him. Solid, as her dad would have said. Solid. She couldn't even guess his age, but thought he was older than her dad, but not as old as Grandad. Over fifty, perhaps sixty. He had blue-grey eyes that looked as if they were floating in water, they were that clear. And his hands – they had long fingers with wide nails. Hands that could play the piano, very exact hands that made precise movements. She saw that when he took up her notebooks from a walnut side table and flicked over a page or two.

He was a plain dresser, not done up like two penn'orth of hambone like some of them that she'd seen at the house. No, this was a plain man. And he looked right through her. And because she thought that she had nothing to lose and because her dad had told her always to "stand tall," Maisie stiffened her spine, pulled her shoulders back, and looked him straight in the eye as he had looked at her. Then he smiled.

"Miss Dobbs, Maisie. Lady Rowan has spoken with me about your encounter in the library last week."

Here it comes, thought Maisie. She clenched her teeth.

"Now then, come with me."

Maurice Blanche walked to the library table and sat down, then invited Maisie to sit next to him with her notebooks in front of them.

Lady Rowan nodded at Carter, who remained by the door, as she walked to stand by the window. They watched as Blanche spoke with Maisie.

Gradually he broke down Maisie's shyness and the formalities that separated housemaid and houseguest. Within fifteen minutes the two were in animated conversation. Maurice Blanche asked questions, Maisie answered, often with another question. Clever, thought Carter, very clever. The way that Dr Blanche drew Maisie out, with his voice, his eyes, a finger tapped upon the page, a question punctuated by a hand placed on the chin to listen. Lady Rowan was equally riveted by the discourse, but her interest was of a more personal nature. Maisie

Dobbs's future was part of her own quest to challenge herself, and what was considered correct in a household such as hers and for a woman of her titled position.

An hour passed. An hour during which Carter was sent to bring tea for Dr Blanche. Nothing was requested for Maisie. It would never do for a man of Carter's position to be at the service of a maid. Yet Carter sensed that something important was happening, that this was an hour during which the established structure of life in the house was changing. And he foresaw that changes that came as a result of whatever came to pass in this room this morning would affect them all. And these were strange-enough times already, what with old King Edward just dead and King George V's coronation around the corner.

Finally Maurice Blanche asked Maisie to close and collect her books. She did as instructed and drew away from the table to stand next to Carter, while Lady Rowan joined Maurice Blanche at the table.

"Rowan, I am more than satisfied," said Dr Blanche. "You may reveal our plan to Miss Dobbs and Mr Carter. Then we shall see if Mr Carter agrees and how we may begin."

Lady Rowan spoke, first looking at Carter, then at Maisie. "Last week when I came upon Maisie in the library, I was struck by the breadth of her reading. We know that anyone can take down a book and read, but when I briefly looked at her notebooks I realized that there was also a depth of understanding. You are a very bright girl, Maisie."

Lady Rowan glanced at Maurice Blanche, who nodded to her to continue.

"I know that this is most unusual. Carter has already been given an indication of my thoughts, and has concurred with my decision. Now I can be more specific. Lord Compton and I are believers in education and opportunity. However, opportunities to contribute directly are rare. Maisie, we have a proposal for you."

Maisie blushed and looked at her shoes as Lady Rowan continued.

"Under the direction of Dr Blanche you will continue your

studies here. Dr Blanche is a busy man, but he will meet you once a fortnight in the library. Your studies, and the tutorials with Dr Blanche must, however, be in your own time and must not interfere in any way with your work in the house. What do you say to that, Maisie?"

Maisie was shocked, but after taking a moment to consider, she flashed the smile that seemed to be working its way back into her life. "Thank you, Ma'am. Sir – Dr Blanche – thank you."

"Miss Dobbs," said Maurice Blanche, "hold your thanks for the time being. You may not take kindly to me when you have seen my plans for your education."

That night, when Maisie was in bed, she was hardly able to sleep for wondering about the events of the day. Carter had been accommodating, but then he was kind. And the other staff, when they had learned about it later – because that Mrs Crawford was a right old chatterbox – seemed to be all right with it all, as long as she pulled her weight in the house. There hadn't been any snide comments, or jealousy. But when Enid finally came to bed in the early hours, she wasted no time in voicing a thought that had been at the back of Maisie's mind.

"You'd've thought they would've just sent you to one of those fancy schools, on the QT, like. Or even paid for your uniform and all that, for the school where you won the scholarship. They're not short of a few bob, are they?"

Maisie nodded.

"But you know what I reckon, Mais? To be perf-hectly honest with you. I reckon they knew you would 'ave a rotten time there. What with all them toffs. It would get you down, it would. Reckon that's what it is."

Without waiting for a response, and using her hairbrush as a pointer for emphasis, Enid continued. "And what you've got to remember, Dobbsie, is that there's them upstairs, and there's us downstairs. There's no middle, never was. So the likes of you and me can't just move up a bit, if that's what you think. We've got to jump, Dobbsie, and bloody 'igh too!"

Maisie knew that there was more than a grain of truth in her words. But if Her Ladyship wanted a cause, someone with whom to play Lady Bountiful, she didn't mind being on the receiving end if it meant getting on with her education.

Maisie changed the subject. "So, where were you tonight, Enid?" she asked.

"Never you mind. You keep that there clever mind of yours on your own business now, and don't you be thinking about mine."

Maisie closed her eyes, then quickly fell asleep. She dreamt of long corridors of books, of Dr Blanche at the library table, and of Enid. And even with the excitement of her lessons with Dr Blanche, it was the dream about Enid that remained with her throughout the next day and for some days to come. And she tried not to think about the dream and Enid, because every time she did, she shivered along the full length of her spine.

CHAPTER ELEVEN

ord Julian Compton knew of his wife's "project" and gave the education of Maisie Dobbs his blessing, although secretly he believed that the exercise would soon falter and any ambitions shown by young Miss Dobbs would be extinguished under the strain of trying to be two very different people, to say nothing of being a girl on the cusp of womanhood. He was intrigued by Maurice Blanche and his interest in Maisie's education, and it was this involvement, rather than his wife's philanthropic gestures, that led him to allow that the project might, in fact, have some merit. He held Maurice Blanche in high esteem, and was even in some awe of the man.

Maisie, for her part, felt no fatigue at the end of a long day. She began her chores in the household at her usual early hour, starting with the lighting of fires, the cleaning of rooms, and the polishing of heavy mahogany furniture. The job of cleaning cutlery fell to the junior footman, though when she handled the solid silver knives and forks, perhaps when cleaning the dining room after dinner guests had departed to the drawing room, she looked with care at the inscription. Each piece of fine cutlery bore the Compton crest, a great hunting dog and a stag together with the words "Let There Be No Ill Will." Maisie pondered the crest as she collected the used silverware. The hunter and the hunted, the suggestion of forgiveness between the victor and the victim, and the fact that both stood tall and proud. In fact, Maisie had taken to pondering just about everything that happened in the course of a day, seeing coincidences and patterns in the life around her.

Mrs Crawford put Maisie's behaviour down to her work with Maurice Blanche, an assumption that was, of course, correct.

"I dunno, when I was a girl learning meant your reading, your writing, and your 'rithmetic. None of this lark, this philosophy nonsense."

Mrs Crawford pointed a floury finger at Maisie, who had just returned from the weekly visit to the library. She was placing books, those for Mrs Crawford and Mr Carter, as well as her own, carefully in a kitchen cupboard, so they would not become soiled by the business of the kitchen. Later she would take her selection to her room for more late-night reading. Cook had immediately noted the girth of Maisie's books, and could not resist comment – to which Carter felt bound to respond.

"I am sure that Mr Blanche knows more about the education of a young person for today's world than either you or I, Cook. But I must say, Maisie, that is rather a large tome, is it not?"

Carter, decanting a fine port, did not interrupt his task to wait for an answer, but cast his eyes over his spectacles in Maisie's direction.

"Maisie – are you listening to Mr Carter?"

Carter exchanged glances with Mrs Crawford, and both rolled their eyes in a compact that hid their true feelings. They were very proud of Maisie Dobbs, and laid some claim in their hearts to the discovery of her intellectual gifts.

"Sorry, Mr Carter. Were you speaking to me?" She had to remove her little finger from her mouth to speak. Maisie had hurried back from the library to allow an extra few moments to dip into one of her books.

"Yes, Mr Carter was speaking to you, Maisie – and if I see that finger in your mouth again, I swear I'll paint your nails with carbolic. It's a wonder you've got hands left, they way you chew on those fingers."

"Sorry Mrs Crawford. Begging your pardon, Mr Carter. I'll get going again now. I just thought I'd take a quick peek."

Carter studied the kitchen clock. "You can have five minutes. Cook and I were commenting on the width of that book. It's a fair size. Is Dr Blanche working you too hard, Maisie?"

"It's Kierkegaard. Mr Blanche says I should read this because he – Kierkegaard – has had a considerable influence on modern thought. And no, don't worry, I can keep up with everything."

Cook and Carter exchanged glances once again, neither wanting to show ignorance about some newfangled thing that sounded to both of them like "kick the guard."

In the meantime Maisie took a notebook from her apron pocket and began to write down her questions and observations for Maurice Blanche. As Carter had suspected, she had already started reading the book on her way back from the library, and was sufficiently into it to be completely absorbed. Once finished, she replaced the notebook in her pocket, glanced at the heavy oak clock with the pearl white face and bold black numbers that was visible from any angle in the kitchen, and rose from the table.

"I just need to put my book away, then I'll get on with making up the stove before I do the polishing."

Maisie moved quickly from the room, remembering the house rule that those from "below stairs" never ever ran, though when speed was of the essence, a brisk walk was permissible.

"I don't know how she still manages to see her poor father, what with her work down here, and all that book learning. I will say this for her, she's got some spirit, has that girl." Mrs Crawford swept her forearm across her brow and continued with the pastry-making. Carter had completed the task of decanting the port and was now uncorking brandy, to be carefully poured into a fine cut-glass decanter. He made no reply to Mrs Crawford's comments, which rather annoyed the woman, as she was given to strong opinions and the need to defend and discuss them.

"I wonder, Mr Carter, what will happen when Maisie has a young man. I wonder, you know, what will happen to her. Fish can't survive long out of water, you know."

Mrs Crawford stopped rolling the pastry and looked at Carter, who remained silent. "I said, Mr Carter —"

"Cook — Mrs Crawford — I know what you said. I would suggest that the education of Miss Dobbs is in good hands. I would also suggest that Miss Dobbs is a very determined young woman who will be more successful than most when it comes to surviving outside her established boundaries. Now then, it is not for us to question the decisions of those upstairs. We can do only what is required of us in the circumstances, don't you think?"

Mrs Crawford, who had been filling a pastry-lined dish with fresh-sliced apple, added cinnamon and clove with rather more than her usual flourish and replied with a certain asperity, "Right you are, Mr Carter," before turning her back on him to check the oven.

Maisie's education was indeed going well. Maurice Blanche had encouraged an easy camaraderie while maintaining the certain distance required by his position, and by Maisie's. Within eighteen months of embarking upon the demanding timetable set by Blanche, Maisie was studying at a level of which a master at one of the more prestigious public schools would have been proud.

For her part Maisie knew only that the work challenged and excited her. When Maurice handed her a new text, she felt a thrill of anticipation. Would the book be brand new, unread, with pages untouched by another? If so, then Maurice would request a précis of the content, and her assessment of the text.

"Four pages of quarto, if you please. And a word of advice. This man has opinions. Opinions, as we have discussed, are not fact. But of course, as we know Maisie, they may be the source of truth. I will be speaking with you about the truth demonstrated in this thesis, Maisie, so be prepared!"

Of course, the volume might have already been read, and in that case each page would bear pencilled notation in Maurice Blanche's small, fine handwriting with its slight slant to the right. A single page of questions would be tucked inside, between the back page and the cover. Maisie knew that each question must be answered.

"I never want to learn that you 'don't know,' Maisie, I want to know what you *think* the answer is to the question. And once more, a word of advice: stay with the question. The more it troubles you, the more it has to teach you. In time, Maisie, you will find that the larger questions in life share such behaviour."

❖

It had been almost two years since Maisie's mother passed away, and still Frankie Dobbs grieved. He swore that it was Maisie who kept him going, for Frankie Dobbs lived for Sundays, and always the ritual was the same.

Although it was not a market day, Frankie would be at the stable with Persephone from an early hour, not as early as on a weekday, but early all the same. He talked softly to his mare, brushing her coat until she shone, caring for mane and tail, and checking hooves that had to pull a heavy load over a considerable distance each day. There was a warm, oaty sweetness to the stable, and here Frankie, often so ungainly when walking down the street or in company, was completely at case. It was usually as Frankie was halfway through the Sunday morning round of chores that Maisie could be heard walking along the cobble-stones toward the stable.

"Dad, I'm here," Maisie called out to him before looking over the half-door and waving. Always she brought something for Frankie from Mrs Crawford, perhaps a pork pie wrapped in fine white muslin and brown paper, freshly baked bread still warm to the touch, or a steamed apple pudding that needed only "a bit o' warming up over the stove," according to the cook.

Maisie quickly pulled off her coat and rolled up her sleeves. Father and daughter worked together to finish the morning's labour, their talk made easier by their movement. They shared confidences easily as their hands were busy with the job of work.

"So, your learning's coming along, is it, girl?"

"Yes, Dad. Dr Blanche is looking ahead, he says. Reckons I could be ready for scholarship and entrance exams next year."

"Entrance for what?" asked Frankie, as he moved toward the pump to refill his bucket with water to rinse Persephone's leather reins and traces, which he had just lathered with saddle soap.

"Well, um, university. Dr Blanche says I can do it. Her ladyship is very keen for me to apply to Cambridge, to Girton College. Says it's the place for an individualist."

"Did she now? Cambridge. Well, there's posh for you, my girl!" Frankie laughed but then looked seriously at Maisie. "As long as you don't push yourself, love. And Cambridge is a long way off, isn't it? Where would you live? And what about mixing with the type of folk at a place like that"

"I dunno, Dad. I have to live at the college, I think. There are all sorts of rules about that, you know. And I will meet people. I'll be just fine, Dad. Girton is a women's college away in a village, after all."

"Yes, but those other young women have more money than you do, and they've got more, you know, connections like."

Maisie looked up from brushing Persephone. Even though Frankie had already brushed the horse from head to tail, Maisie loved to feel the warm animal close to her, and knew the horse appreciated her efforts.

"Dad, I'm not a child any more. I'm fifteen now. And I've seen more than a lot of girls my age. Dr Blanche knows what he's doing."

"Yes, love, I'm sure he does. Clever man, that one. I just worry about you."

Frankie rubbed the cleaned leather with a dry cloth, and hung reins and traces from a hook on the low ceiling. Later, after Maisie's return to Belgravia, Frankie would come back to the stable to feed Persephone, then take down the dry reins, bridle and traces, and rub warmed neatsfoot oil into the leather.

"Don't worry about me, Dad. I'm doing very well, you know. Now then, where shall we go for our walk? I've got some nice sandwiches and a couple of bottles of ginger beer for us."

Three days after her visit with Frankie, Maisie walked briskly toward the library for her early-evening lesson. She saw Maurice Blanche on alternate Wednesday evenings, meeting promptly at half past five in the library for three hours, until Dr Blanche left to join the Comptons for an informal supper in the dining room. She studied alone until he had finished supper, when both he and Lady Rowan joined Maisie in the library to review her work. Lady Rowan was well pleased with the education of Maisie Dobbs, asking questions and suggesting new areas of study. But this evening a new possibility was discussed.

"Maisie, I think it is time for us to embark on some fieldwork."

Maisie looked first at Blanche, then at Lady Rowan. Botany. It had to be botany.

"Lady Rowan has spoken with Mr Carter, and next week, on Wednesday, we will be taking an excursion. In fact, I have several such outings planned, and on those afternoons we must meet a little earlier than usual."

"What sort of outings? Where are we going?"

"Various places," said Blanche, "Of historical, social, or economic interest."

Little more was said, but in the following weeks Maisie was taken by Blanche to meet people with whom she would spend time alone in conversation. At first Maurice would remain with her, but as time went on, he would quietly leave the room to allow for conversation between Maisie and his friend, for each person who met with Maisie was considered a "friend" by Maurice Blanche. As far as Maisie was concerned, some of them were a strange lot, and she wasn't sure what Frankie Dobbs would have to say about it all.

"Today we will be meeting with my dear friend Dr Basil Khan," Maurice Blanche informed Maisie as they journeyed to Hampstead by taxi-cab. "An extraordinary scholar, born in Ceylon, into a very-high-caste family. His first name was given as a mark of respect to one of his father's former colleagues, an Englishman. Khan, as he prefers to be known, is completely blind. He lost his sight in an unfortunate accident, but as these things do, it became the foundation for his life's work."

"What's his life's work?"

"Khan, as you will see, is a man of great wisdom, of insight. His work uses that insight. He grants audiences to politicians, people of commerce, men of the cloth. He came to England as a young man, sent by his parents to see ophthalmic specialists, to no avail. While in England he gained his doctorate in philosophy at Oxford. Then he returned to Ceylon, and later travelled throughout the Indian sub-continent, himself seeking the counsel of wise men. To do this he had to give up the life he had once enjoyed in London and Oxford, which he had ceased to enjoy. Now he resides in Hampstead."

"So why am I to see him?"

"Maisie, we are visiting for him to see *you*. And for you to learn that seeing is not necessarily something one does with the eyes."

The visit to Khan was illuminating for Maisie. His rooms in a grand house were furnished in a simple manner: plain wooden furniture, curtains without pattern or texture, candlelight, and a strange smell that made her cough at first.

"You will get used to it, Maisie. Khan uses incense to bring a fragrant atmosphere to the house."

At first Maisie was timid when led into a large room with only cushions on the floor and an old man sitting with legs crossed. He was positioned by the long French window as if contemplating the view, so that as Maisie and Maurice Blanche walked towards him, Khan was framed by shafts of light, and appeared to have been borne into the room by some mystical means of transportation. Without turning, Khan gestured toward Maisie with his hand.

"Come, child, come sit with me. We have much to speak of."

To her surprise Maurice Blanche motioned Maisie to step forward, and moved towards Khan himself. He leaned down towards Khan, took the old man's bony brown hands in his own, and kissed his lined and furrowed forehead. Khan smiled and nodded, then turned to Maisie.

"Tell me what it is you know, child."

"Um . . ."

Both Khan and Maurice laughed, and the old man with long grey hair and almost colourless eyes smiled kindly at Maisie.

"Yes, a good start. A very good start. Let us talk of knowing."

So Maisie Dobbs – daughter of a costermonger from Lambeth, just south of the water that divided London's rich and poor – began to learn in the way that Maurice had intended, from the centuries of wisdom accumulated by Khan.

With Khan she learned to sit in deliberate silence, and learned too that the stilled mind would give insight beyond the teaching of books and hours of instruction, and that such counsel would support all other learning. When she first sat with Khan, she asked what it was she was to do as she sat with legs crossed on the cushion in front of him. The old man lifted his face to the window, then turned his clear white eyes toward her and said simply, "Pay attention."

Maisie took the practice of sitting with Khan seriously and to heart, with an instinctive knowledge that this work would serve her well. In just a few short years, the lessons learned in the hours with Khan would bring her calm amid the shellfire, the terrible injuries, and the cries of wounded men. But for now, Maurice Blanche told Maisie, it was no small coincidence that she often knew what a person was going to say before he or she spoke, or that she seemed to intuit an event before it had occurred.

CHAPTER TWELVE

*"M*aisie, you'll ruin your eyes if you read by that
good-for-nothing light in the corner – and look
at the time, you've to be up in three hours!"

"So have you, Enid, and you aren't anywhere near asleep yet."

"Don't you be worrying about me. I've told you."

Maisie slipped a page of notes into the book to mark the place,
closed the book, and placed it to one side on her small table. She
looked directly at Enid.

"And don't you look at me with those eyes either, Maisie Dobbs.
Gives me the willies, it does."

"You are being careful, aren't you, Enid?"

"'Course I am. I told you not to worry."

Khan might be teaching her many things about the human mind,
but as far as Maisie was concerned, it didn't take much in the way of
foresight to see that Enid was going to get into some trouble before
long. In truth it was a surprise that the older girl was not only still as
slim as a whip but was still employed at the house in Belgravia at all.
But Enid, who was now almost eighteen, was loved by everyone
downstairs. Her efforts at correct enunciation still fell short, and

sometimes Maisie thought she sounded more like a music hall act than a maid in service. But she, too, had come to love Enid, for her laughter, for the unsought advice she gave so freely, and most of all for her unselfish support of Maisie.

Enid slipped a thick cotton nightdress over her head, pulled on woollen socks, and proceeded carefully to fold her clothes into the chest of drawers by the wall. Shadows cast by the oil lamp flickered on the sloping ceiling of the top-floor bedroom as Enid brushed out her thick hair with a hard bristle brush.

"One hundred strokes for a good thick head of hair – have I told you that, Mais?"

"Yes, many a time."

Maisie ensured that her books and papers were carefully put away, and clambered into bed.

"Brrrr. It's cold in here."

Enid took an old silk scarf that had been hanging over the cast-iron bedpost, wrapped it around the head of her brush, and began brushing the silk over her hair to bring it to a lustrous shine.

"No, and it ain't getting any warmer. I tell you, Maisie, a chill wind blows through 'ere sometimes, a chill wind."

Maisie turned to face Enid.

"Enid, why don't you like it here?"

Enid stopped brushing, held the brush in her lap, and fingered the scarf. Her shoulders drooped, and when she looked up at Maisie, it was with tears in her eyes.

"Enid, what is it? Is it James? Or that Arthur?"

Maisie had guessed that the reason for Enid's absences over the past year resided in rooms on the third floor. Though it might have been Arthur, the young footman who had come to work at the house a month before Maisie. His position had been elevated since then. He had been given the task of ensuring the good health of the Comptons' Lanchester motorcar, keeping it polished, oiled, and spick and span. She thought that he had taken a shine to Enid, too.

"No, it's not 'im. That one's full of the old bluster, all mouth and no trousers, that's Arthur. No, it's not 'im." Enid picked at the hair-brush, taking out long hairs and rolling them between her fingers.

"Come on, Enid. Something makes you sad."

The older girl sighed, the familiar defiance ebbing as Maisie's eyes sought her confidence.

"You know, Maisie, they're all very nice here until you overstep the line. Now you, you'll land on your feet; after all, 'avin' brains is like 'avin' money, even I know that. But me, all I've got is 'oo I am, and 'oo I am i'n't good enough."

"What do you mean?"

"Oh, come on, Maisie, you must've heard talk – they love to talk down in the kitchen, 'specially that old Mrs Crawford." Enid put down the brush, pulled back the bedclothes and climbed into bed. She turned to face Maisie. "I don't know what it is about them eyes of yours, Mais, but I tell you, the way you look at me makes me want to spill my insides out to you."

Maisie inclined her head for Enid to continue.

"It's James. Master James. That's why His Lordship is talking about sending him away. To Canada. As far away from the likes of me as they can get 'im. It's a wonder they don't send me off too, to look for another job, but 'er Ladyship isn't a bad old bird, really. At least she can keep an eye on me if I'm 'ere – otherwise, who knows? I might just go to Canada meself!"

"Do you love James, Enid?"

Enid rolled to face the ceiling, and in the half-light Maisie saw a single tear run from the corner of her eye onto the pillow.

"Love 'im? Gawd, Maisie, what business 'ave I got, going in for all that nonsense?"

Enid paused, dabbing at her eyes with a corner of the sheet. "Love don't put food on the table, does it?" She looked at her crumpled handkerchief, dabbed her eyes, and nodded. "I suppose I do, love him that is. I do love James, but –"

"But what? If you love him, Enid, you can –"

"Can what, Maisie? Can what? No, theres no 'buts' in the matter.

He's going, and when he's gone, I've got my life to get on with. And in some way or another, I've got to get out of this 'ere job. I've got to get on, like you're getting on. But I've not got your cleverness."

"Dr Blanche says that having a mental picture works. He said once that it's good to have a vision of what the future may hold. He says it's important to keep that in mind."

"Oh, he does, does he? Well, then, I'll start seeing myself all dolled up like a lady, with a nice husband, and a nice house. How about that for a picture?"

"I'll picture that for you too, Enid!"

Enid laughed and rolled over. "I tell you, Maisie Dobbs, you're one of a kind! Now then, you just turn off that thinking and imagining mind of yours, and let's get some kip."

Maisie did as she was told, but as she settled into the quiet of the night, she was sorry that the conversation had ended. It was always like that with Enid, as soon as you got a little closer to her she moved away. Yet Maisie knew that at this very moment Enid was thinking of James Compton, hoping that if she held on to a picture of them together, it would come to pass. And Maisie thought of them together, too. Of seeing them on the landing, not long after she had come to work at 15 Ebury Place. She had seen them since, once in Brockwell Park when she was walking with her father. They must have thought that no one would recognize James south of the river – his sort rarely ventured across the water. Enid was in her Sunday best: her long deep-lavender coat, which she kept hanging in the wardrobe covered in a white sheet and protected by mothballs. Her black woollen skirt poked out underneath, and you could just about see her laced-up boots, polished to a shine. She wore a white blouse with a high neck and a little sprig of lavender pinned to the front of the collar, right where a brooch might have been if Enid had owned one. She wore black gloves and an old black hat that Maisie had seen her hold over a steaming pot of water in the kitchen, then work with her hands to mould it into shape, before making it look just like new with a band of purple velvet ribbon. Oh, she did look lovely, with her red hair tied in a loose knot so that you could see it beneath her hat. And James, she remembered him laughing when he was with Enid, and just before she managed to steer her father in another direction, so that Enid and James wouldn't see her, she watched as he took the glove off Enid's right hand and lean over to press his lips to her thin knuckles, then turn it over to the palm and kiss it again. And as he stood up, Enid reached up and flicked back his fair hair, which had flopped into his eyes.

And though she was now snuggled down into the bedclothes and blankets, a hot-water bottle at her feet, Maisie shivered and was frightened. Perhaps she should speak to Dr Blanche about it, this strange feeling she had at times, as if the future had flashed a picture into her mind, like being at the picture house and seeing only a few seconds' worth of the show.

Just one week after Enid had taken Maisie into her confidence, James Compton departed on a ship bound for Canada. As a result Enid had become less than affable.

"I do wish you would turn out that bloomin' light so that I can get some shut-eye. I'm sick of it, I am. 'Alfway through the night and all I can hear is you turnin' those bloomin' pages over and over."

Maisie looked up from her book, over to the lump that was Enid in the adjoining bed. She could not see Enid's face, for she was curled sideways with her back to Maisie and the blankets over her head.

"I'm sorry, Enid, I didn't realize —"

Suddenly one arm came over the blankets as Enid pulled herself up into a sitting position, her face furiously red. "Well, you *wouldn't* bloomin' realize, *would* you, Miss Brainy? Always got yer 'ead in a book when everyone else is workin'."

"But Enid, I pull my weight. No one else has to do my work for me. I can manage my jobs."

"Oh yes? You can manage your jobs, can you? Well, next time you go over to that mirror to do yer 'air, take a look at the sacks of coal under yer eyes. Your idea of pullin' weight is just a bit different from mine. And what with all that other stuff you 'ave to think about, it's a wonder you can get up in the morning. Now then. I'm off t'sleep, and it'd be a good idea if you did the same thing."

Maisie quickly marked her place in the book Maurice had given her earlier in the week, and extinguished the lamp at her bedside. Pulling the covers up to her shoulders and pressing her hands to her sore, watering eyes, she sought refuge from Enid's words. It seemed to Maisie that since Enid confided in her, she had become standoffish and unpleasant, as if her frustrated aspirations to become a lady had caused an unbearable resentment to grow. Maisie had begun to avoid her when Enid lost her temper at being asked to replenish coal in one of the upstairs rooms, and was reprimanded by Carter. But something must have clicked with Carter, for he called Maisie into the butler's pantry next to the kitchen.

"Maisie, I am worried about your ability to manage both your routine in the house and the schedule set by Dr Blanche."

"Oh Mr Carter, I am managing."

"I want you to know that I will be watching, Maisie. I must obviously support Her Ladyship's wishes, but I must also bring it to her attention if changes need to be made."

"No, you don't have to do that. I'll manage, sir. I promise."

"Right you are, Maisie. You may continue with your duties. But do make sure, doubly sure, that your work is complete at the end of the day."

"Yes, Mr Carter."

* * *

It was with a heavy heart that Maisie visited Frankie Dobbs on the following Sunday. More than at any other time since she had started lessons with Dr Blanche, Maisie couldn't wait to leave the house and immerse herself in the warmth of the stable and her father's love.

"There you are. Bit late today, young Maisie, aren't you?"

"Yes, Dad. I was late getting up, then had to stay to finish some jobs and missed the bus. I had to wait for the next one."

"Oh, so you couldn't get up in time on the one day you come to see your poor old dad?"

"That's not it, honestly Dad," responded Maisie defensively.

She took off her hat and coat, folded them and put them on top of her basket, which she left just outside the stable door. She walked over to Persephone and rubbed the soft spot behind her ears.

"I was just a bit late, that's all Dad."

"You doin' too much of that readin'?"

"No, Dad. No, I'm not."

"So how about your week then, love? What've you been doing?"

"Oh, we had a to-do in the kitchen this week. Mrs Crawford was experimenting with pouring brandy over the cooked meat and then adding a flame to it. Some new French idea of Lady Compton's. The whole kitchen nearly caught alight. You should have seen it, Dad. It was hilarious!"

Frankie Dobbs stopped work and looked at Maisie.

"What is it, Dad?" The smile seemed to evaporate from her face.

"'Ilarious, was it? I like that. 'ilarious. Can't use ordinary words any more. Got to use big ones now, 'aven't you?"

"But Dad . . . I thought . . ."

"That's the trouble with you. Too much of that thinking. I dunno . . ."

Frankie turned his back on Maisie, the set of his shoulders revealing a seldom-seen anger. "I dunno. I thought this was all very well and all, you gettin' an education. Now I dunno. Next thing you know, you won't want to talk to the likes of me."

"Now that's silly, Dad."

"Silly, am I?" Frankie looked up again, his eyes blazing.

"I didn't mean it like that. What I meant was . . ." Maisie was exhausted. She let her arm drop to her side. Persephone nuzzled her to continue the ear rubbing, but there was no response. Father and daughter stood in stony silence.

How had this happened? How was it that one minute it seemed that everyone was on her side, and the next everyone was against her? What had she done wrong? Maisie went over to an upended box in the corner and slumped down. Her furrowed brow belied her youth as she tried to come to terms with the discord between her beloved father and herself.

"I'm sorry Dad."

"I'm sorry too. Sorry that I ever talked to that Mr Carter in the first place."

"You did right, Dad. I would never have had this opportunity . . ."

Frankie was also tired. Tired of worrying about Maisie, tired of fearing that she would move into circles above her station and never come back. Tired of feeling not good enough for his daughter. "I know, love. I know. Let's 'ave an end to the words. Just make sure you come back and see your old dad of a Sunday."

Maisie leaned over to Frankie, who had upended another wooden box to sit next to her, put her arms around his neck, and sobbed.

"Come on, love. Let's put the words behind us."

"I miss you, Dad."

"And I miss you, love."

Father and daughter held on to each other a moment longer, before Frankie announced that they should be getting along to the park if they were to enjoy the best of the day. They worked together to finish jobs in the stable and, leaving Persephone to her day of rest, went to the park for a walk and to eat the sandwiches that Mrs Crawford had made for Maisie.

As she travelled back to Belgravia that evening, Maisie couldn't help but remember Frankie's outburst, and wondered how she would ever balance her responsibilities. As if that were not enough, Enid's tongue was as sharp as a knife again when Maisie entered the room they shared on the top floor of the house.

"It's a wonder you can bring yourself to see that costermonger father of yours. Isn't he a bit lower class for you now, Maisie?"

Maisie was stunned and hurt by Enid's words. Slights against herself she could handle, but those against her father she would not tolerate. "My father, Enid, is one of the best."

"Hmmph. Thought he wouldn't be good enough, what with you bein' 'er Ladyship's pet."

"Enid, I'm not anyone's pet or favorite. I'm still here, and working hard."

Enid was lying on her back on the bed, pillows plumped up behind her head. She was reading an old copy of *The Lady* while speaking to Maisie.

"Hmmph. Maisie Dobbs, all you've done is give 'er Ladyship a cause. They like causes, do these toffs. Makes 'er feel like she's doin' something for the lower classes. Right old do-gooder she is, too. And as for that funny old geezer, Blanche, I'd worry about 'im if I was you. D'you really think you can become a lady with all this book lark?"

"I've told you before, Enid – I don't want to be a lady."

Maisie folded her day clothes and put them away in the heavy chest of drawers, then took up her hairbrush and began to unbraid her glossy black hair.

"Then you're as stupid as you are silly lookin'."

Maisie swung around to look directly at Enid.

"What is *wrong* with you? I can't do a thing right!"

"Let me tell you what's wrong with me, young Maisie. What's wrong with me is that I might not be able to do the learning from books that you can, but mark my words, I'll be out of here before you, 'er Ladyship or not."

"But I'm not stopping you –"

In frustration Enid flounced to her feet, pulled back the bedclothes, and threw herself into bed. Without saying goodnight she turned her back on Maisie, as had become her habit.

Maisie said nothing more, but climbed into her heavy brass bed to lie upon the hard horsehair mattress between the coarse cold white sheets. Without attempting to read her book or work on the assignment Maurice Blanche had given her, she turned out the light.

Jealousy. Now she was beginning to understand jealousy. Together with the exchanges of the past few weeks, and the heated conversation with her father, Maisie was also beginning to feel fully the challenge of following her dream. And she was disturbed, not for the first time, by Enid's words about Lady Rowan. Was she just a temporary diversion for Lady Rowan, a sop to her conscience so she could feel as if she was doing something for society? Maisie couldn't believe this, for time and time again she had seen genuine interest and concern on her employer's face.

"So, Maisie. Let me see your work. How are you progressing with Jung?"

Maisie walked into the library for her meeting with Maurice Blanche and stood before him.

"Sit down, sit down. Let us begin. We have much work to do."

Maisie silently placed her books in front of him.

"What is it, Maisie?"

"I don't think, Dr Blanche, that I can have lessons with you any more."

Maurice Blanche said nothing but nodded his head and studied Maisie's countenance. Silence seeped into the space between them, and Maurice immediately noticed the single tear that emerged from Maisie's right eye and drizzled down her face.

"Ah, yes, the challenge of position and place, I think."

Maisie sniffed and met Blanche's look. She nodded.

"Yes. It has been long overdue. We have been fortunate thus far, have we not, Maisie?"

Once again Maisie nodded She expected to be dismissed, as she would in turn dismiss her ambitions and the dream she had nurtured since first planning to visit the Comptons' library at three o'clock in the morning so long ago.

Instead Maurice took up the book he had assigned at their last meeting, along with her notes, and the lessons she had completed in the subjects of English, mathematics and geography.

Looking through her work, Maurice inclined his head here, and raised his eyebrows there. Maisie said nothing, but inspected her hands and pulled at a loose thread in her white pinafore.

"Maisie. Please complete these two final chapters while I speak to Lady Rowan."

Once again Maisie was left, if only for a short time, to wonder at her fate, and whether all would be well. As Maurice Blanche left the room, Maisie took up the book and turned to the chapters he had indicated. But try as she might, she could not read past the first paragraph of her assignment and retain what she had read. Instead she put her right hand to her mouth and with her teeth worried a hangnail on her little finger. By the time Maurice Blanche returned with Lady Rowan and Carter, Maisie had to plunge her right hand into her pinafore pocket so that the blood now oozing from the cuticle would not be seen.

Clearly much discussion had taken place in the interim. It fell to Carter, as head of the domestic staff, to stand at Lady Rowan's side as she told Maisie of a plan that had been incubating and had just hatched, inspired by her genuine need. It was a plan that would in turn help Maisie. And not a moment too soon.

"Maisie, the Dowager Lady Compton lives in the dower house at Chelstone Manor, in Kent. My mother-in-law is in command of her faculties but has some difficulty in movement, and she does sleep long hours now that she is of advanced age. Her personal maid gave notice some weeks ago, due to impending marriage."

Lady Rowan glanced at Maurice Blanche and at Carter before continuing. "Maisie, I would like to offer you the position."

Maisie said nothing, but looked intently at Lady Rowan, then at

Carter, who simply nodded, then raised an eyebrow, and focused his gaze quickly on her hand in the pinafore pocket.

Maisie stood up straighter, twisted a handkerchief around the sore finger, and brought her hand to her side.

"The Dowager Lady Compton has only a small staff," said Lady Rowan, "as befits her needs. Aside from her personal maid and a nurse, household staff do not live at the dower house but at the manor. When we are in residence, as you know, Carter and Mrs Crawford travel to Chelstone to join the staff. However, Mrs Johnson, the housekeeper, is in sole charge of the household at Chelstone while we are in London."

Lady Rowan paused for a moment, walked to the window and crossed her arms. She took a moment to look out at the garden before turning back into the room to continue.

"Employment with my mother-in-law will allow you some – let us say 'leeway' – to continue your work with Dr Blanche. In addition you will not be subject to some of the scrutiny that you have experienced in recent weeks, although you *will* report to Mrs Johnson."

Maisie looked at her feet, then at Carter, Lady Rowan, and Dr Blanche, all of whom seemed to have grown several inches while Lady Rowan was speaking.

Maisie felt very small. And she was worried about her father.

As she remained silent, Carter raised an eyebrow, indicating that she should speak.

"Is there a bus so I can get back to London to see my father on Sundays?"

"There is a train service from the village, on the branch line via Tonbridge. But you may wish to make the visits to Mr Dobbs farther apart, since the distance requires several hours of travel," replied Maurice Blanche.

Then he suggested that Maisie be given a day to consider the offer.

"You will see Mr Carter with your decision tomorrow at five o'clock Maisie?"

"Yes, sir. Thank you, sir – and thank you, Your Ladyship, Mr Carter."

"Right you are. I will bid you goodnight."

Carter bowed to Lady Rowan, as did Dr Blanche, while Maisie bobbed a curtsy, and put her hand back in her pocket lest the company see her handkerchief bloodied from the bitten hangnail.

"I think, Mr Carter, that Maisie should continue with her household responsibilities this evening, rather than her assignments from me. Such endeavours will be a useful accompaniment to the process of coming to a decision.'

"Right you are, sir. Maisie?"

Maisie curtsied again, then left the room to return to her duties.

Blanche walked over to the window and looked out at the gardens. He had anticipated young Maisie's challenges, which had come later than he might have expected. How he despised wasted talent! He knew that the move to Kent would be a good one for her, but the decision to pursue her opportunity was one Maisie alone would have to make. He left the house, wending his way to familiar streets south of the Thames.

* * *

It surprised the staff when Frankie Dobbs came unsummoned to the back door of the kitchen the next morning to report that some very nice lettuces and tomatoes had just been brought in from Jersey, and would Mrs Crawford be needing some for the dinner party on Friday night?

Usually Frankie would not see Maisie when he came to the house to deliver fruit and vegetables each week, but on this occasion Mrs Crawford took no time at all to summon Maisie to see her father, for she knew that the motive for Frankie Dobbs's appearance extended beyond urgent notification of what was best at Covent Garden market.

"Dad . . . Dad!" cried Maisie as she went to her father, put her arms around his waist, and held him to her.

"Now then, now then. What's all this? What will Mr Carter say?"

"Oh Dad, I'm *so* glad you came to the house. What a coincidence!"

Maisie looked at her father inquisitively, then followed him up the outside stairs to the street, where Persephone waited, contentedly eating from the nosebag of oats attached to her bridle. Maisie told Frankie about the new position she had been offered with the Dowager Lady Compton.

"Just as well I 'appened by then, innit love? Sounds like just what you need. Your mother and me always wanted to live in the country, thought it would be better for you than the Smoke. Go on. You go, love. You'll still see me."

"So you don't mind then, Dad?"

"No, I don't mind at all. I reckon bein' down there in the country will be a real treat for you. Hard work, mind, but a treat all the same."

Maisie gave Carter her answer that evening. It was agreed with Lady Rowan that she should leave at the end of the month. Yet even though he wanted her to see and learn all there was to see and learn, Frankie often felt as if fine sand were slipping through his fingers whenever he thought of his girl, Maisie.

CHAPTER THIRTEEN

aisie first came to Chelstone Manor in the autumn of 1913. She had travelled by train to Tonbridge, where she changed for Chelstone onto a small branch line. She'd brought one bag with her containing clothes and personal belongings, and a small trunk in which she carried books, paper, and a clutch of assignments written in Maurice Blanche's compact almost indecipherable hand. And in her mind's eye Maisie carried a vision. During their last lesson before she left for Chelstone he had asked Maisie what she might do with this education, this opportunity.

"Um, I don't really know, Dr Blanche. I always thought I could teach. My mum wanted me to be a teacher. It's a good job for me, teaching."

"But?"

Maisie looked at Maurice Blanche, at the bright eyes that looked into the soul of a person so that they naturally revealed to him in words what he could silently observe.

"But. But I think I want to do something like what you do, Dr Blanche."

Maurice Blanche made a church and steeple with his hands, and rested his upper lip on his forefingers. Two minutes passed before he looked up at Maisie.

"And what do I do, Maisie?"

"You heal people. That is, I *think* you heal people. In all sorts of ways. That's what I think."

Blanche nodded, leaned back in his chair, and looked out of the library window to the walled gardens of 15 Ebury Place.

"Yes, I think you could say that, Maisie."

"And I think you find out the truth. I think you look at what is right and wrong. And I think you have had lots of different . . . educations."

"Yes Maisie, that is all correct. But what about that vision?"

"I want to go to Cambridge. To Girton College. Like you said, it's possible for an ordinary person like me to go, you know, as long as I can work and pass the exams."

"I don't think I ever used the word 'ordinary' to describe you, Maisie."

Maisie blushed, and Maurice continued with his questions. "And what will you study, Maisie?"

"I'm not sure. I'm interested in the moral sciences, sir. When you told me about the different subjects – psychology, ethics, philosophy, logic – that's what I most wanted to study. I've already done lots of assignments in those subjects, and I like the work. It's not so – well – definite, is it? Sometimes it's like a maze, with no answers, only more questions. I like that, you know. I like the search. And it's what you want, isn't it, Dr Blanche?"

Maisie looked at Maurice, and waited for his response.

"It is not what I want that is pertinent here, Maisie, but what you are drawn to. I will, however, concur that you have a certain gift for understanding and appreciating the constituent subjects of the moral sciences curriculum. Now then, you are young yet, Maisie. We have plenty of time for more discussion of this subject. Perhaps we should look at your assignments – but remember to keep those hallowed halls of Girton College uppermost in your mind."

✦

$\mathcal{T}$he old lady was not too demanding, and there was the nurse to take a good deal of the responsibility for her care. Maisie ensured that the dowager's rooms were always warm, that her clothes were freshly laundered and laid out each day. She brushed her fine gray hair and twisted it into a bun which the dowager wore under a lace cap. She read to the dowager, and brought meals to her from the main house. For much of the time the old lady slept in her rooms, or sat by the window with her eyes closed. Occasionally, on a fine day, Maisie would take her outside in a wheelchair, or support her as she stood in the garden, insisting that she was quite well enough to attend to a dead rose, or reach up to inhale the scent of fresh apple blossom. Then she tired and leaned on Maisie as she was assisted to her chair once again. But for much of the time Maisie was lonely.

There was little conversation with staff up at the manor, and despite everything Maisie missed Enid and her wicked sense of humour. The other members of staff at Chelstone would not speak with her readily, or joke with her, or treat her as one of their own. Yet though she missed the people she had come to love, she did enjoy having solitude for her studies. Each Saturday Maisie walked into the village to post a brown-paper-wrapped package to Dr Blanche, and each Saturday she picked up a new envelope with her latest assignment, and his comments on her work of the week before. In January 1914 Maurice decided that Maisie was ready to take the Girton College entrance examinations.

✦

$\mathcal{I}$n March, Maurice accompanied Maisie to Cambridge for the examinations, meeting her early at Liverpool Street Station for the journey to Cambridge, then on to the small village of Girton, home of the famous ladies' college of Cambridge University. She remembered watching from the train window as the streets of London gave way to farmland that was soft in the way that Kent was soft, but instead of the green undulating hills of the Weald of Kent, with hedges dividing a patchwork quilt of farms, woodland, and small villages, the Cambridgeshire fens were flat, so that a person could see for miles and miles into the distance.

The grand buildings of Cambridge, the wonderful gardens of Girton College two miles north of the town, the large lecture hall, being taken to a desk, the papers put in front of her, the hours and hours of questions and answers, the nib of her pen cutting into the joint at the top of the second finger of her right hand as she quickly filled page after page with her fine, bold script, were unforgettable. Thirst had suddenly gripped at her throat until she felt faint for lack of breath as she left the hall, whose ceiling now seemed to be moving down towards her. Her head was spinning as she leaned on Maurice, who had been waiting for her. He steadied her, instructing her to breathe deeply, as they walked slowly to the village teashop.

While hot tea was poured and fresh scones placed in front of them, Maurice allowed Maisie to rest before asking for her account of each question on the examination papers, and her responses to them. He nodded as she described her answers, occasionally sipping tea or wiping a crumb from the corner of his mouth.

"I believe, Maisie, that you have done very well."

"I don't know, Dr Blanche sir. But I did my best."

"Of course. Of course."

"Dr Blanche. You went to Oxford, didn't you?"

"Yes, indeed, Maisie – and I was only a little younger than you at the time. Of course, as I am male, a degree could be conferred upon me. But there will be a time, I hope before too long, when women will also earn degrees for their advanced academic studies."

Maisie flicked the long braid of jet black hair from her shoulder and felt its weight along her spine as she sat back in her chair to listen to Maurice.

"And I was also fortunate to study in Paris at the Sorbonne, and in Edinburgh."

"Scotland."

"I'm glad to see that you have a grasp of geography, Maisie." Maurice looked over his spectacles at Maisie and smiled at her. "Yes, the Department of Legal Medicine."

"What did you do there, Dr Blanche?"

"Learned to read the story told by a dead body. Especially when the person did not die of natural causes."

"Oh . . ." said Maisie, temporarily bereft of speech. She pushed away the crumbly scone and took a long sip of the soothing tea. Maisie slowly regained energy after the ordeal of the past few hours, which she had endured along with several dozen other hopeful students. "Dr Blanche. May I ask you a question?"

"Of course."

"Why did you want to learn about the dead?"

"Ah. A good question, Maisie. Suffice it to say that sometimes one's calling finds one first. When I first came to Oxford it was to study economics and politics; then I went to the Sorbonne to study philosophy – so you see we have similar interests there – but it was as I travelled, seeing so much suffering, that medicine found me."

"And legal medicine? The dead bodies?"

Maurice looked at his watch. "That is a story for another time. Let us now walk over to the college again, where no doubt you will be studying later this very year. The gardens really are quite lovely."

The Comptons had gathered a coterie of important and influential guests, not only to sample the delights of a July weekend in the country but for animated discussion and conjecture upon the discord that had been festering in Europe since June, when the Austrian archduke was assassinated in Serbia. It was predicted that the conflict, which had started two years earlier, in 1912, in the Balkans, would become general war, and as the Kaiser's armies reportedly moved into position along the Belgian border fear of its escalation grew. Dread stalked Europe, snaking its way from the corridors of government to the households of ordinary people.

Carter was in full battle mode for the onslaught of visitors, while Mrs Crawford held her territory in the kitchen, blasting out orders to any maid or footman who came within range of her verbal fire. Lady Rowan swore she could hear Cook's voice reverberating through every beam in the medieval manor house, though even she declined to intervene at such a time.

"Rowan, we have the very best cook in London and Kent, but I fear we also have the one with the loudest voice."

"Don't worry, Julian, you know she'll pipe down when everything's in its place and the guests start to arrive."

"Indeed, indeed. In the meantime, I wonder if I should tell the War Office about her in advance. She could put a seasoned general to shame – have you seen how she marshals her troops? I should have every new subaltern serve in Cook Crawford's battalion for a month. We could overcome the Hun by launching meat pies clear across France and into the Kaiser's palace!"

"Julian, don't be absurd – and don't be so full of certainty that Britain will be at war," said Lady Rowan. "By the way, I understand that our Miss Dobbs received a letter from Girton this morning."

"Did she, by Jove? Well, not before time, my dear. I don't think I could bear to look at those nail-bitten fingers holding onto the tea tray any longer."

"She's had a hard life, Julian." Lady Rowan looked out of the windows and over the land surrounding Chelstone Manor. "We can't presume to imagine how difficult it has been for her. She's such a bright girl."

"And for each Maisie Dobbs there are probably ten more that you can't save. Remember, we may not have done her any favours, Rowan. Life can be very difficult for someone of her class at Cambridge."

"Yes, I know, Julian. But times are changing. I am glad that we were able to contribute in some way."

She turned from the window to look at her husband. "Now then, shall we go downstairs to see what news the letter from Girton has brought? I don't know if you've noticed, but it has gone awfully quiet in the house."

Lord and Lady Compton went together to the large drawing room, where Lord Julian rang the bell for Carter. The impeccably turned-out and always punctual butler answered the call within a minute.

"Your Lordship, Your Ladyship."

"Carter, what news does Miss Dobbs have from Cambridge?"

"Very, very good news, M'Lord. Miss Dobbs has been accepted. We are all terribly proud of her."

"Oh, that's wonderful, wonderful!" Lady Rowan clapped her hands. "We must get word to Maurice, Julian. Carter, send Miss Dobbs to see us immediately."

CHAPTER FOURTEEN

*M*aisie could not wait to tell Frankie Dobbs her news in person, and as soon as she could, travelled by train to Charing Cross, and from there to the small soot-blackened terraced house that had once been her home.

"Well, what do you know? Our little Maisie all grown up and going away to the university. Blow me, your mum would have been chuffed."

Frankie Dobbs held his daughter by the shoulders and looked into her eyes, his own smarting with tears of pride – and of concern.

"Do you think you're ready for this, love?"

Frankie pulled out a chair and beckoned Maisie to sit with him by the coal stove in the small kitchen. "It's a big step, isn't it?"

"I'll do all right, Dad. I've won a place, and next year if I do well, I might get a college scholarship. That's what I'm aiming for. Lord and Lady Compton will be my sponsors, for the first year anyway, and I've been putting a bit by as well. Lady Rowan is going to give me some of her day clothes that she doesn't want, and Mrs

Crawford said she'll help me with tailoring them to fit me, although there are strict rules about what I can wear. Not much different from a maid's uniform, but without the pinny, from what I can make out."

Maisie rubbed her father's hands, which seemed strangely cold.

"I told you, I'll be all right Dad. And at Christmas, Easter, and summer I can come back to the house to earn some more money."

Frankie Dobbs could barely meet his daughter's eyes, knowing only too well that it would be nigh on impossible for Maisie to return to the Comptons' employ once she had left. He knew how it was in those houses, and once she had moved beyond her station she could never go back. She'd been lucky so far, but after she left she wouldn't be so easily accepted. The gap between Maisie and the other staff would become a chasm. And what worried Frankie more than anything was that Maisie might not ever fit into *any* station, that she would forever be betwixt and between.

"So when will you be leaving?"

"I'll start in the autumn. They call it the Michaelmas term, you know, like those mauve Michaelmas daisies that bloom in September, the ones Mum used to love. I had to get special permission because I'm not quite eighteen."

Frankie got up from his seat and rubbed his back. He wanted to get the conversation back to a point at which he could voice his offer.

"Well, talking about 'avin' a bit more, like we were before we started talking about the daisies, I've got something for you love." Frankie reached up and took down a large earthenware flour jar from the shelf above the stove.

"Here you are, love. After I paid off the debts, you know after your mother . . . I started putting a bit by each week meself. For you. Knowing that you'd be doing something important one day, where a bit extra might come in 'andy."

Maisie took the jar, her hands shaking. She lifted the lid and looked into the earthenware depths. There were pound notes, some brand new ten-shilling notes, florins, half-crowns, and shillings. The jar was full of Frankie Dobbs's savings for Maisie.

"Oh, Dad . . ." Maisie stood up and, clutching the jar of money with one hand and her father with the other, held him to her.

In August 1914 people still went about their business, and war seemed to be something that had nothing to do with ordinary life. But then a boy she knew in the village was in uniform, and certain foods were just a little more difficult to find. A footman at the Belgravia house enlisted, and so did the grooms and young gardeners at Chelstone. Then one weekend Maisie was called to Lady Rowan's sitting room at Chelstone.

"Maisie, I am beside myself. The grooms have all enlisted and I am fearfully worried about my hunters. I have spoken to all sorts of people, but the young men are going into the services. Look, I know this is unusual, but I wonder, do you think your father might consider the position?"

"Well, M'Lady, I don't really know. There's Persephone, and his business."

"There is a cottage in the grounds for him if he wants it. You'll be able to see him when you are not at Girton of course, and his mare can be stabled here. They will both be well looked after."

The next day Maisie travelled by train to London to see her father. To her complete surprise, Frankie Dobbs said he would "think about it" when she told him of the offer from Lady Rowan. "After all, I'm not getting any younger, and neither is Persephone. She could do with a bit o' the old fresh country air. And 'er Ladyship's been very good to you, so come to think of it, if I 'elped 'er out it'd be only right. It's not as if I'm a stranger to Kent, 'aving been down there picking the old 'ops every year when I was a bit of a nipper meself."

Frankie Dobbs and Persephone moved from Lambeth on a misty, unseasonably cold morning in late August 1914, to take up residence in the groom's cottage and stables, respectively, at Chelstone Manor. Instead of rising at three o'clock to take Persephone to Covent Garden market and then setting out on his rounds, Frankie now enjoyed a lie-in before rising at five o'clock to feed Lady Rowan's hunters and Persephone, who seemed to be relishing her own retirement. In a short time Frankie Dobbs was being feted by Lady Rowan as the man who knew everything there was to know about the grooming, feeding and well-being of horses. But it was a deeper knowledge that would endear him to her for the rest of her life.

*O*nly days remained before Maisie was to leave for Cambridge, so time spent in each other's company was of prime importance to Maisie and her father. They had resumed the ritual of working together in making a fuss of Persephone as often as possible. It was on such an occasion, while they were working and talking about the latest war news, that Lady Rowan paid a surprise visit.

"I say, anybody there?"

Maisie snapped to attention but Frankie Dobbs, while respectful, simply replied, "In 'ere with Persephone, Your Ladyship."

"Mr Dobbs. Thank goodness. I am beside myself."

Maisie immediately went to Lady Rowan, who always claimed to be "beside herself" in a crisis despite a demeanour that suggested otherwise.

"Mr Dobbs, they are coming to take my hunters – and possibly even your mare. Lord Compton has received word from the War Office that our horses are to be inspected for service this week. They are coming on Tuesday to take them. I *cannot* let them go. I don't want to be unpatriotic, but they are my hunters."

"And they ain't taking my Persephone either, Your Ladyship."

Frankie Dobbs walked toward his faithful old horse, who nuzzled at his jacket for the treat she knew would be forthcoming. He took sweet apple pieces from his pocket and held them out to Persephone, feeling the comforting warmth of her velvety nose in his hand, before turning back to Lady Rowan.

"Tuesday, eh? You leave it to me."

"Oh, Mr Dobbs – everything depends upon you. What will you do? Take them somewhere and hide them?"

Frankie laughed. "Oh no. I think I might be seen running away with this little lot, Your Ladyship. No, I won't have to run anywhere. But here's one thing –" Frankie Dobbs looked at Maisie and at Lady Rowan. "I don't want anyone coming in these stables until I say so. And Your Ladyship, I'll come to the 'ouse on Tuesday mornin' and tell you what to say. But the main thing is, whatever you see or 'ear, you're not to mind or say anything else other than what I tell you. You've got to trust me."

Lady Rowan stood taller, regained her composure, and looked directly at Frankie Dobbs. "I trust you implicitly."

Maisie's father nodded, tipped his cap towards Lady Rowan, and then smiled at Maisie. The stately woman walked towards the stable door, then turned round. "Mr Dobbs. One thing we spoke about only briefly when you first came to Chelstone. I seem to remember that you were at a racing yard as a boy."

"Newmarket, Your Ladyship. From the time I was twelve to the time I came back to 'elp my father with the business at nineteen. Bit big for a jockey, I was."

"I expect you learned a thing or two about horses, didn't you?"

"Oh yes, Your Ladyship. A thing or two. Saw a lot, good and bad."

The men from the War Office came to Chelstone at lunchtime on Tuesday. Lady Rowan led them to the stables apologizing profusely and explaining, as she had been instructed by Frankie Dobbs, that she feared her horses might not be suitable for service as they had contracted a sickness that even her groom could not cure. They were met by Frankie Dobbs, who stood in tears by Sultan, her jet black hunter.

The once-noble horse hung his head low as foam dropped from his open mouth. His eyes rolled back in his head as he struggled for breath. Lady Rowan gasped and looked at Frankie, who would not meet her alarmed eyes with his own.

"By God, what's wrong with the beast?" asked the tall man in uniform, who held a baton under his arm. He stepped carefully towards Sultan, avoiding any soiled straw that might compromise the shine on his highly polished boots.

"Not anything I've seen for years. Caused by worm. Bacteria," Frankie Dobbs replied, and spoke to Lady Rowan directly. "I'm sorry, Your Ladyship. We'll probably lose them all by tomorrow. That old cart 'orse will be first. On account of 'er age."

The men stopped briefly to glance into Persephone's stall, where Frankie Dobbs's faithful horse lay on the ground.

"Lady Compton. Our sympathies. The country needs one hundred and sixty-five thousand horses, but we need them to be fit, strong and able to be of service on the battlefield."

Lady Rowan's tears were genuine. She had been primed by Frankie as to what she should say, but had not been prepared for what she would see. "Yes . . . yes . . . indeed. I wish you luck, gentlemen."

The two men were soon gone. After seeing them off, Lady Rowan ran immediately to the stables once again, where Frankie Dobbs was working furiously to pour a chalky liquid down Sultan's throat. Maisie was in another stall, feeding the liquid to Ralph. Persephone and Hamlet were on their feet.

Lady Rowan said nothing, but walked over to Hamlet and touched the pale, drawn skin around his eyes. As she brought her hand away she noticed the white powder on her gloves and smiled.

"Mr Dobbs, I shall never ask what you did today. But I will remember this for ever. I know what I asked of you was wrong, but I just couldn't bear to lose them."

"And I couldn't bear to lose Persephone, Your Ladyship. But I 'ave to warn you. This war is far from over. You keep these 'ere horses on your land. Don't let anyone outside see 'em, just them as works 'ere. Times like these changes folk. Keep the animals close to 'ome."

Lady Rowan nodded and gave a carrot to each horse in turn.

"Oh, and by the way Your Ladyship. I wonder if Mrs Crawford could use two and a half dozen egg yolks? Terrible waste if she can't."

⊞

𝒯en household staff sat down to dinner at the big table in the kitchen at Chelstone Manor on Maisie's last night before leaving for Cambridge. She was on the cusp of her new life. The Comptons were in residence, so the servants whom Maisie loved from the Belgravia house were there to see her off.

Carter sat at the head of the table in the carver's chair, and Mrs Crawford sat at the opposite end within easy striking distance of the big cast-iron coal-fired stove. Maisie sat next to her father and opposite Enid. Even Enid, who had been summoned from the London house to assist with late-summer entertaining at Chelstone, joined in the fun and looked happy: She had brightened up considerably since Mr James had returned from Canada.

"Lummy, I think the world's spinnin' even faster these days. What with the war, Master James coming home, Maisie goin' to Cambridge – Cambridge, our Maisie Dobbs! Then there's all the important people coming tomorrow to see Lord Compton," said Cook, as she took her seat after a final check on the apple pie.

"All arrangements are in order Mrs Crawford. We will make a final round of inspection after our little celebration here. Now then . . ."

Standing up, Carter cleared his throat and smiled. "I'll ask you to join me in a toast."

Chairs scraped backward, people coughed as they stood up and nudged one another. The entire complement of household staff turned to face Maisie, who blushed as all eyes were upon her.

"To our own Maisie Dobbs! Congratulations, Maisie. We've all seen you work hard and we know you will be a credit to Lord and Lady Compton, to your father – and to us all. So we've got a small token of our affection. For you to use at the university."

Mrs Crawford reached under the table and took out a large flat box which she passed down the table to Carter with one hand, while the other rubbed at her now tearful eyes with a large white hand-kerchief.

"From all the staff at Chelstone Manor and the Compton residence in London – Maisie, we're proud of you."

Maisie blushed and reached for the plain brown cardboard box. "Oh, my goodness. Oh, dear. Oh –"

"Just open it, Mais, for Gawd's sake!" said Enid, eliciting a scowl from Mrs Crawford.

Maisie pulled at the string, took off the lid and drew back the fine tissue paper to reveal a butter-soft yet sturdy black leather document case with a silver clasp.

"Oh . . . oh . . . it's . . . it's . . . beautiful! Thank you, thank you. All of you."

Carter wasted no time in taking his glass and continuing with the toast. "To our own Maisie Dobbs . . ."

Voices echoed around the table.

"To Maisie Dobbs."

"Well done, Mais."

"You show 'em for us, Maisie!"

"Maisie Dobbs!"

Maisie nodded, whispering, "Thank you . . . thank you . . . thank you."

"And before we sit down," said Carter, as the assembled group were halfway down to their seats again. "To our country, to our boys who are going over to France. Godspeed and God save the King!"

"God save the King."

*T*he following day Maisie stood on the station platform, this time with an even larger trunk of books that far outweighed her case of personal belongings. She clutched her black document case tightly, afraid that she would lose this most wonderful gift. Carter and Mrs Crawford had chosen it, maintaining that Maisie Dobbs should not have to go to university without a smart case for her papers.

On her journey up to Cambridge, when Maisie changed trains at Tonbridge for the main service to London, she was taken aback by the multitude of uniformed men lining up on the platform. Freshly posted handbills gave a hint of things to come:

LONDON, BRIGHTON & SOUTH COAST RAILWAYS
MOBILIZATION OF TROOPS
PASSENGERS ARE HEREBY NOTIFIED THAT IT MAY BE NECESSARY
TO SUSPEND OR ALTER TRAINS WITHOUT PREVIOUS NOTICE

It was clear that the journey to Cambridge would be a long one. Sweethearts and the newly married held tightly to each other amid the crush of bodies on the platform. Mothers cried into sodden handkerchiefs; sons assured them "I'll be back before you know it," and fathers stood stoically silent.

Maisie passed a father and son standing uncomfortably together in the grip of unspoken emotion. As she brushed by, she saw the older man clap his son on the shoulder. He pursed his lips together, firmly clamping his grief in place, while the son looked down at his feet. A small Border collie sat still between them, secure on a leash held by the son. The panting dog looked between father and son as they began to speak quietly.

"You mind and do your best, son. Your mother would have been proud of you."

"I know Dad," said the son, moving his gaze to his father's lapels.

"And you mind you keep your head out of the way of the Kaiser's boys, lad. We don't want you messing up that uniform, do we?"

The boy laughed, for he was a boy and not yet a man.

"All right, Dad, I'll keep my boots shined, and you look after Patch."

"Safe as houses, me and Patch. We'll be waiting for you when you come home, son."

Maisie watched as the man pressed his hand down even harder on the young man's shoulder. "Listen to that. Your train is coming in. This is it, time to be off. You mind and do your best."

The son nodded, bent down to stroke the dog who playfully wagged her tail and jumped up to lick the boy's face. He met his father's eyes only briefly, and after passing the leash to the older man, was suddenly swallowed up in a sea of moving khaki. A guard with a megaphone ordered, "Civilians to keep back from the train" as the older man stood on tiptoe, trying to catch one last glimpse of his departing son.

Maisie moved away to allow the soldiers to board their train and watched the man bend down, pick up the dog, and bury his face in the animal's thick coat. And as his shoulders shook with the grief he dared not show, the dog twisted her head to lick comfort into his neck.

CHAPTER FIFTEEN

*U*pon arrival at Girton, Maisie registered with the Porter's
Lodge and was directed to the room that had been assigned
to her for the academic year. Assured that the trunk of
books would be brought up to her room in due course, clutching her
bag, she began to leave the lodge, following the directions given by the
porter, who suddenly called her back. "Oh, Miss! A parcel arrived today
for you. Urgent delivery, to be given to you immediately."

Maisie took the brown paper parcel and immediately recognized
the small slanted writing. It was from Maurice Blanche.

Few women were already in residence when Maisie arrived, and the
hallways were quiet as she made her way to her room. She was anxious to unwrap the parcel, and paid hardly any attention to her new
surroundings after opening the door to her room. Instead she quickly
put her belongings down by the wardrobe and, taking a seat in the
small armchair, began to open the package. Under the brown paper, a
layer of tissue covered a letter from Maurice, and a leather-bound book
with blank pages. Inside the cover of the book, Maurice had copied
the words of Søren Kierkegaard, words that he had quoted to her from
memory at their last meeting before her journey to Cambridge. It was

as if Maurice were in the room with her, so strong was his voice in her mind as she read the words: "There is nothing of which every man is so afraid, as getting to know how enormously much he is capable of doing and becoming." She closed the book, continuing to hold it as she read the letter in which Maurice spoke of the gift:

> In seeking to fill your mind, I omitted to instruct you in the opposite exercise. This small book is for your daily writings, when the day is newborn and before you embark upon the richness of study and intellectual encounter. My instruction, Maisie, is to simply write a page each day. There is no set subject, save that which the waking mind has held close in sleep.

Suddenly the loud crash of a door swinging back on its hinges, followed by the double thump of two large leather suitcases landing one after the other on the floor of the room next door, heralded the arrival of her neighbor. Amplified by the empty corridor, she heard a deep sigh followed by the sound of a foot kicking one of the cases.

"What I wouldn't give for a gin and tonic!"

A second later, with wrapping paper still between her fingers and her head raised to follow the audible wake of her neighbour, Maisie heard footsteps coming toward her room. In her hurry to open the parcel from Maurice, she had left her door ajar, allowing the young woman immediate access.

A fashionably dressed girl with dark chestnut hair stood in front of her, and held out her finely manicured hand. "Priscilla Evernden. Delighted to meet you – Maisie Dobbs, isn't it? Wouldn't happen to have a cigarette, would you?"

***

It seemed to Maisie that she lived two lives at Cambridge. There were her days of study and learning, which began in her room before dawn, and ended after her lectures and tutorials with more study in the evening. She spent Saturday afternoons and Sunday mornings in the college chapel, rolling bandages and knitting socks, gloves, and scarves for men at the front. It was a cold winter in the trenches, and no sooner had word gone out that men needed warm clothes than every woman suddenly seemed to be knitting.

At least Maisie felt that she was doing something for the war, but it was her studies that were always at the forefront of her mind. If anything, the endless talk of war seemed to her a distraction, something that she just wanted to be over, so that she could get on with her life at Cambridge – and whatever might come after.

There were times when Maisie was thankful that a very bright spark was resident in the next room. Priscilla seemed to gravitate toward Maisie and, surprising Maisie herself, appeared to enjoy her company.

"My dear girl, how many pairs of these infernal socks must one knit? I am sure I have kitted out an entire battalion."

Another sharp observation from Priscilla Evernden. In truth Maisie loved Priscilla's theatrical tone as much as she had loved Enid's down-to-earth wit, and she was only too aware that, though miles apart in their upbringing, the two girls shared a ready exuberance that Maisie envied. Despite her early fumblings with the language of the aristocracy, Enid was sure of who she was and sure of what she wanted to be. Priscilla was equally sure of herself, and Maisie loved the sweep and flourish of her language, punctuated as it was by exaggerated movements of her hands and arms.

"You seem to be doing quite well, really," said Maisie.

"Oh, sod it!" said Priscilla as she fumbled with her knitting needles, "I fear, dear Maisie, that you are clearly born of knitting stock, one only has to look at that plait hanging down your back. Good Lord, girl, that plait could be a loaf at Harvest Festival! Obviously you have been bred for knitting."

Maisie blushed. Over the years the edges had been chipped away from her London accent. She might not pass for the aristocracy, but she could certainly be taken for a clergyman's daughter. And not one bred for knitting.

"I hardly think so, Pris."

"Well, I suppose not. One only has to look at your academic work, and those books that you read. Anyone who can read those turgid tomes can make short work of a sock. Dear God, give me a drink that bites back and good tale of love and lust any day of the week."

Maisie dropped a stitch and looked up at Priscilla. "Now, don't tell me that, Pris. Why did you come up to Cambridge?"

Priscilla was tall, giving the impression of strength, though she carried no extra weight. Her chestnut hair hung loose around her shoulders, and she wore a man's shirt with a pair of man's trousers, "borrowed" from her brother before he left for France. She claimed that they wouldn't be in fashion by the time he returned anyway, and swore that she would only wear them indoors.

"Dear girl, I came to Cambridge because I could, and because my dear mother and father were ready to fling themselves burning into the lake rather than have me roll in through the window at two in the morning again. Out of sight, out of mind, darling . . . Oh my dear Lord, look at this sock! I don't know what I am doing wrong here, but it's like knitting into a funnel."

Maisie looked up from her work.

"Let me see."

"Whoopee! M. Dobbs to the rescue."

Priscilla got up from her place on the old armchair, where she had been sitting sideways with her legs dangling over the arm, while Maisie sat on the floor on a cushion.

"I'm going out now, and to hell with Miss What's-Her-Name downstairs' curfew."

"Priscilla, what if you get caught? You're not supposed to be out late. You could be sent down for this."

"Dear Maisie, I will not get caught, because I will not be coming in late. If anyone asks, I know you will say that I've taken to my bed. And of course, when I come in at the crack of dawn tomorrow – well

– I needed the early morning fresh air to clear the mind after my indisposition."

Minutes later Priscilla reappeared, dressed from head to toe in evening wear and carrying a small bag.

"One thing you have to admit about war, darling – there's nothing quite like a man in uniform. See you at breakfast – and for heaven's sake do stop fretting!"

"*G*ood Lord, Maisie Dobbs, where do you think you're going with those books?"

Priscilla Evernden was leaning out of the window of Maisie's room, and turned back to draw upon the cigarette she gamely smoked through a long ivory holder. It was the end of her second term at Girton, and Maisie was packing to go back to Chelstone for Easter.

"Well, Pris, I don't want to fall behind in my work, so I thought it wouldn't hurt –"

"Tell me, Maisie, when do you ever have fun, girl?"

Maisie reddened and began to fold a cotton blouse. The intensity of her movements as she ran the side of her hand along the creases and patted down the collar revealed her discomfort.

"I enjoy reading, Priscilla. I enjoy my studies here."

"Hmmm. You'd probably enjoy it a lot more if you went out a bit. You were only away for a few days at Christmas."

Maisie smarted, remembering her return to a depressed household at the end of her first term. The war had not ended by Christmas – as predicted – and though nothing was said, Maisie felt that others found her studies frivolous at a time when so many women were volunteering for jobs previously held by men who had enlisted to serve their country.

Holding a woollen cardigan by the shoulders, Maisie folded it and placed it in her case before looking up at Priscilla. "You know,

Priscilla, life is different for some people. I don't go back to my horses, cars and parties. You know that."

Priscilla walked towards the armchair and sat down, folding her legs to one side. Once again she drew heavily on the cigarette, leaned her head back, and blew smoke rings towards the ceiling. Then, holding her cigarette to one side, she looked at Maisie directly. "For all my strange, peculiar privileged ways, Maisie, I am quite acute. You wear your sackcloth and ashes a little too proudly at times. We both know that you will do terribly well here. Academically. But I tell you this, Maisie – we are all a long time dead when we go, if you know what I mean. This is our only ride on the merry-go-round."

She drew again on the cigarette and continued. "I have three brothers in France now. Do you think I'm going to sit here and mourn? Hell, no! I'm going to have fun enough for all of us. Enough fun for this time on earth. And just because it took a tremendous leap for you to be here doesn't mean that you can't enjoy life along with all this – this – studying." She waved a hand toward the books.

Maisie looked up from her packing. "You don't understand."

"Well, perhaps I don't. But here's what I do know. You don't have to rush back to wherever it is you are rushing back to. Not this evening, anyway. Why not go tomorrow? Come out with me tonight. We may not have a chance again."

"What do you mean?"

"Oh, look at me, Maisie. I really am not cut out for all this. I received a severe reprimand when I arrived back here after my last evening out, and was reminded that when I took up my place I had denied another, more deserving young woman the opportunity to study. Which is true, no getting away from it. So, I'm leaving – and quite frankly, I'm sick of sitting on the sidelines either listening to crusty old dons or knitting socks when I can do something far more useful. And who knows, I might even have an adventure!"

"What are you going to do?"

Maisie walked over to the chair and sat on the arm, next to Priscilla.

"Got to find yourself a new person to share rooms with, Maisie. I'm off to France."

Maisie drew breath sharply. Priscilla was the last person she thought would enlist for service. "Will you nurse?"

"Good Lord, no! Did you see my church hall bandages? If there's one thing I cannot do, it's walk around playing Florence Nightingale in a long frock – although I will have to get a First Aid Nursing Certificate. No, I have other strings to my bow."

Maisie laughed. The thought of the dilettante Priscilla having skills that could be used in France was worthy of mirth.

"You may laugh, Maisie. But you've never seen me drive. I'm off to be a Fannie!"

"A what?"

"Fannie. F-A-N-Y. First Aid Nursing Yeomanry. An all-women ambulance corps. Actually they are not in France yet – although from what I understand, it might not be long, as Mrs McDougal – she's the head of FANY – is planning to ask the War Office to consider using women drivers for motor ambulances. Apparently you have to be twenty-three to go to France, so I am extending the truth a little – and don't ask me how, Maisie, please."

"When did you learn to drive?"

"Three brothers, Maisie." Priscilla leaned forward to take the ciga-rette stub from the holder and to press in a fresh cigarette, which she took from an engraved silver case drawn from her pocket. "When you grow up with three brothers you forget your cuts, scrapes, and bruises and concentrate on your bowling arm, on coming back in one piece from the hunting field, and on not being run over by the lugworms when they come to the table. And unless you show that you are as good at everything as they are, you find that you spend virtually all your time running behind them screaming like a banshee, 'Me too, me too!'"

Priscilla looked over her shoulder to the gardens beyond the window and bit her bottom lip. She turned and continued telling her story.

"The chauffeur taught us all to drive. At first it was only going to be the boys, but I threatened to tell all if I was not included. And now the fact is, my dear, I simply cannot have them in France without me. It's 'Me too, me too!'"

Priscilla wiped the hint of a tear from the inner corner of her left eye and smiled.

"So, what do you say to a party this evening? Despite my dismal record, I have permission to go out – probably because they will soon see the back of me, and also the hostess this evening is a benefactor. How about it, Maisie? You can go back to wherever it is you go to wash the ashes from your sackcloth tomorrow."

Maisie smiled and looked at Priscilla, sparkling in defiance of what was considered good behaviour for young women at Girton. There was something about her friend that reminded her of Lady Rowan.

"Whose party?"

Priscilla blew another smoke ring.

"Given by family friends, the Lynches, for their son, Simon. Royal Army Medical Corps. Brilliant doctor. Always the one who remained at the bottom of the tree just in case anyone fell from the top branches when we were children. He leaves for France in a day or two."

"Will they mind?"

"Maisie, I could turn up with a tribe and no one would turn a hair. The Lynch family are like that. Oh, do come. Simon will adore it. The more the merrier for his send-off."

Maisie smiled at Priscilla. Perhaps it *would* do her good. And Priscilla was leaving.

"What about permission?"

"Don't worry, I'll take care of that – and I promise, all above board. I'll telephone Margaret Lynch to make the necessary arrangements."

Maisie bit her lip for just a second longer.

"Yes. I'll come. Though I've nothing to wear, Pris."

"No excuse, Maisie darling, absolutely no excuse. Come with me!"

Priscilla took Maisie by the arm and led her to her own adjacent room. Pointing to the chair for Maisie to take a seat, she pulled at least a dozen gowns of various colours, fabrics and styles from her wardrobe and threw them on the bed, determined to find the perfect dress for Maisie.

"I think this midnight blue is really you, Maisie. Here, let's just pull the belt – oh gosh, you are a skinny thing aren't you? Now let me just pin this here . . ."

"Pris, I look like two penn'orth of hambone trussed up for the butcher's window."

"There. That's just perfect," replied Priscilla, "Now step back, step back. Lovely. Very nice. You shall have that dress. Have your Mrs Whatever-Her-Name-Is at Chelstone hem it properly for you."

"But Priscilla –"

"Nonsense. It's yours. And make the most of it – I saw a bill posted yesterday that I memorized just to remind myself to have some fun while I can."

Priscilla stood to attention, mimicked a salute, and affected an authoritarian mode of speech: TO DRESS EXTRAVAGANTLY IN WARTIME IS WORSE THAN BAD FORM. IT IS UNPATRIOTIC!

She began to laugh as she continued adjusting the blue silk dress on Maisie's slender frame.

"I'll have no need of evening dresses in France, and besides, there will be new styles to choose from when I get back."

Maisie nodded and looked down at the dress. "There's another thing, Pris."

Priscilla took up her cigarette, placed her hand on her hip, and raised an eyebrow. "Now what's your excuse, Maisie?"

"Priscilla, I can't dance."

"Oh, good Lord, girl!"

Priscilla stubbed out the cigarette in the overflowing ashtray, walked over to her gramophone near the window, selected a record from the cabinet below, placed it on the turntable, wound it up using the small handle at the side of the machine, and set the arm across the record. As the needle caught the first spiral ridge in the thick black disc, Priscilla danced toward Maisie.

"Keep the dress on. You'll need to practice in what you'll be wearing tonight. Right. Now then, start by watching me."

Priscilla positioned her hands on imaginary shoulders in front of her, as if held in the arms of a young man, and as the music began she continued.

"Feet like so, and forward, side, together; back, side, together; watch me, Maisie. And forward, side, together . . ."

❖

A car had been sent to collect Priscilla and Maisie, and as they climbed aboard for the journey to the Lynches' large house in Grantchester, Maisie felt butterflies in her stomach. It was the first time she had ever been to a party that had not been held in a kitchen. There were special Christmas and Easter dinners downstairs at the Belgravia house and at Chelstone, and of course she had been given a wonderful send-off by the staff. But this was a real party.

Margaret Lynch came to greet Priscilla as soon as her arrival was announced. "Priscilla, darling. So good of you to come. Simon is dying for news of the boys. He can't wait to get over there, you know."

"I have a lot to tell, Margaret. But let me introduce my friend, Maisie Dobbs."

"How lovely to meet you, my dear. Any friend of Priscilla's is welcome here."

"Thank you, Mrs Lynch." Maisie started to bob, only to feel a sharp kick from Priscilla.

"Now then, you girls, let's see if we can get a couple of these young gentlemen to escort you into the dining room. Oh, there's Simon now. Simon!"

Simon. Captain Simon Lynch, RAMC. He had greeted Priscilla as one would greet a tomboy sister, asking for news of her brothers, his childhood friends. And as he turned to Maisie, she felt a shiver that began in her ankles and seemed to end in the pit of her stomach.

"A pleasure to meet you, Miss Dobbs. And will the British Army be at your mercy as you sit behind the wheel of a baker's lorry, converted and pressed into service as an ambulance?"

Priscilla gave Simon a playful thump on the arm as Maisie met his green eyes. She blushed and quickly looked at the ground. "No. I think I would be a terrible driver, Captain Lynch."

"Simon. Oh, do call me Simon. Now then, I think I'd like a Girton lass on each arm. After all, this is my last evening before I leave."

As a string quartet began to play, Simon Lynch crooked an elbow toward each girl and led them into the dining room.

Simon had completely drawn Maisie from her shell of shyness and embarrassment and had made her laugh until her sides ached. And she had danced. Oh, how Maisie Dobbs had danced that evening, so that when it was time to leave, to return to Girton, Captain Simon Lynch made a gracious sweeping bow before her and kissed her hand.

"Miss Dobbs, you have put my feet to shame this evening. No wonder Priscilla kept you locked up at Girton."

"Don't take my name in vain, Lynchie – you brute! And it's a book of rules that keeps us all locked up, remember."

"Until we meet again, fair maiden."

Simon stepped back and turned towards Priscilla. "And I'll bet my boots that any wounded in your ambulance will go running back to the trenches rather than put up with your driving!"

Simon, Priscilla and Maisie laughed together. The evening had sparkled.

CHAPTER SIXTEEN

he young women arrived back at the college in the nick
of time before their extended curfew – arranged at the
request of The Honourable Mrs Margaret Lynch –
expired. Just six hours later, standing on the station platform waiting
for the early train that would take her to London for her connection
to Chelstone, Maisie replayed, yet again, the events of the evening. In
her excitement she had not slept a wink, and now that same excitement rendered her almost oblivious to the chilly air around her.
Maisie held her coat closer to her body and up to her neck, feeling
only the memory of sheer silk next to her skin.

As Maisie reflected upon the three of them laughing just before
they left the party, she realized that it was laughter that held within it
the sadness of a bigger departure. The gaiety of Simon's party had an
undercurrent of fear. She had twice looked at Margaret Lynch, only
to see the woman watching her son, hand to her mouth, as if any
minute she would rush to him and encircle his body in her protec-
tive arms.

Her fear was not without cause, for the people of Britain were only
just receiving news of the tens of thousands of casualties from the

spring offensive of 1915. Once a land of quiet farms in the French countryside, the Somme Valley was now a place writ large in newspaper headlines, inspiring angry and opinionated debate. The Somme was indelibly inscribed on the hearts of those who had lost a son, a father, brother, or friend. And for those bidding farewell, there was only fearful anticipation until the son, father, brother, or friend was home once again.

From Liverpool Street, Maisie travelled to Charing Cross for the journey to Kent. The station was a melee of khaki, ambulances, red crosses, and pain. Trains brought wounded to be taken to the London hospitals, nurses scurried back and forth, orderlies led walking wounded to waiting ambulances, and young, new spit-and-polished soldiers looked white-faced at those disembarking.

As she glanced at her ticket and began to walk toward her platform, Maisie was suddenly distracted by a splash of vibrant red hair in the distance. She knew only one person with hair so striking, and that was Enid. Maisie stopped and looked again.

Enid. It was definitely Enid. Enid with her hand on the arm of an officer of the Royal Flying Corps. And the officer in question was the young man who loved ginger biscuits: James Compton. Maisie watched as they stopped in the crowd and stood closer together, whispering. James would be on his way down to Kent, most probably on the same train as Maisie, except that she would not be travelling first class. From there Maisie knew that James would be joining his squadron. He was saying good-bye to Enid, who no longer worked for the Comptons. Mrs Crawford had informed Maisie in a letter that Enid had left their employ. She was now working in a munitions factory, earning more money than she could ever have dreamed of earning in service.

Though she knew it was intrusive, Maisie felt compelled to stare as the two said good-bye. As she watched, she knew in her heart that Enid and James were truly in love, that this was not infatuation or social climbing on Enid's part. She lowered her head and walked away so that she would not be seen by either of them. Yet even as she walked, Maisie could not help turning to watch the couple once again, magnetized by two young people clearly speaking of love amid the teeming emotion around them. And while she looked, as if bidden by the strength of her gaze, Enid turned her head and met Maisie's eyes.

Enid held her head up defiantly, the vibrant red hair even brighter against her skin tone, which was slightly yellow, a result of exposure to cordite in the munitions factory. Maisie inclined her head and was acknowledged by Enid, who then turned back to James and pressed her lips to his.

Maisie was sitting at a cramped table in the station tea shop when Enid found her.

"You've missed the train to Chelstone, Mais."

"Hello Enid. Yes, I know, I'll just wait until the next one."

Enid sat down in front of Maisie.

"So you know."

"Yes. But it doesn't make any difference."

"I should bloody 'ope not! I'm away from them all now, and what James does is 'is business."

"Yes. Yes, it is."

"And I'm earning real money now." Enid brushed her hair back from her shoulders. "So, how are you my very clever little friend? Cambridge University treating you well?"

"Enid, please. Let me be." Maisie lifted the cup to her lips. The strong tea was bitter, but its heat was soothing. The sweet joy of meeting Simon Lynch seemed half a world away as she looked once again at Enid.

Suddenly Enid's eyes smarted as if stung, and she began to weep. "I'm sorry. I'm sorry, Mais. I've been so rotten to you. To everyone. I'm just so worried. I lost him once. When 'e went to Canada. When they sent him away because of me. And now 'e's goin' to France. Up in one of them things – I've 'eard they only last three weeks over there before they cop it, them flyin' boys – and if God 'ad wanted us to leave the ground, I reckon we'd 'ave wings growin' out of our backs by now, don't you?"

"Now then, now then." Maisie moved around to sit next to Enid and put her arms around her. Enid pulled out a handkerchief, wiped her eyes, and blew her nose.

"Least I feel as if I'm doing somethin'. Making shells, like. Least I'm not just sittin' on my bum while them boys get shot to bits over there. Oh, James . . ."

"Come on, Enid. He'll be all right. Remember what Mrs Crawford says about James – he's got nine lives."

Enid sniffed again. "I'm sorry, Maisie. Really I am. But it just gets me 'ere sometimes." Enid punched at her middle. "They look down their noses at me, think I'm not good enough. And 'ere I am working like a trooper."

Maisie sat with Enid until she became calm, as the ache of farewell gave way to anger, tears, and eventually calm and fatigue.

"Maisie, I never meant anything. Really, I didn't. James will come back, I know he will. And this war is changin' everything. 'ave you noticed that? When the likes of me can earn a good livin' even in wartime, the likes of the better-offs will have to change, won't they?"

"You could be right there, Enid."

"Gaw, lummy . . . look at that time. I've got to get back to the arsenal. I'm not even s'posed to leave the 'ostel without permission. I'm workin' in a special section now, handlin' the more volatile – that's what they call it – the more volatile explosives, and we earn more money, specially as we're 'avin' to do double shifts. All the girls get tired, so it gets a bit tricky, tapping the ends of the shells to check 'em, and all that. But I'm careful, like, so they promoted me. Must'a bin workin' for that Carter for all them years. I learned to be careful."

"Good for you, Enid."

The two women left the tea shop and walked together toward the bus stop just outside the station, where Enid would catch a bus to work. As they were bidding farewell, a man shouted behind them. "Make way, move along, make way please."

A train carrying wounded soldiers had arrived, and the orderlies were hurriedly trying to bring stretchers through to the waiting ambulances. Maisie and Enid stood aside and looked on as the wounded passed by, still in mud-caked and bloody uniforms, often crying out as scurrying stretcher-bearers accidentally jarred shell-blasted arms and legs. Maisie gasped and leaned against Enid when she looked into the eyes of a man who had lost most of the dressings from his face.

After the wounded had passed Enid turned to Maisie to say good-bye. The young women embraced, and as they did so Maisie felt a shiver of fear that made her tighten her hold on Enid.

"Come on, come on, let's not get maudlin, Mais." Enid loosened her grasp.

"You mind how you go, Enid," said Maisie.

"Like I always said, Maisie Dobbs, don't you worry about me."

"But I do."

"You want to worry about something, Maisie? Let me give you a bit of advice. You worry about what you can do for these boys." She pointed toward the ambulances waiting outside the station entrance. "You worry about whatever it is you can *do*. Must be off now. Give my love to Lady Bountiful for me!"

It seemed to Maisie that one second she was with Enid, and then she was alone. She walked towards the platform for the penultimate part of her journey home to her father's cottage next to the stables at Chelstone. With trains delayed and cancelled due to troop movements, it would once again be many hours before she reached her destination.

The journey to Kent was long and arduous. Blackout blinds were pulled down in compliance with government orders issued in anticipation of Zeppelin raids, and the train moved slowly in the darkness. Several times the train pulled into a siding to allow a troop train to go by, and each time Maisie closed her eyes and remembered the injured men rushed into waiting ambulances at Charing Cross.

Time and again she fell into a deep yet brief slumber, and in her half waking saw Enid at work in the munitions factory, at the toil that caused her skin to turn yellow and her hair to spark when she brushed it back. Maisie remembered Enid's face in the distance, reflecting the love she felt as she looked at James Compton.

She wondered about love, and how it must feel, and thought back to last night, which seemed so many nights ago, and touched the place on her right hand where Simon Lynch had placed his lips in a farewell kiss.

As the train drew in to Chelstone station late at night, Maisie saw Frankie standing by his horse and cart. Persephone stood proudly, her coat's gloss equaled only by the shine of the leather traces that Maisie could see even in the half-light. Maisie ran to Frankie and was swept up into his arms.

"My Maisie, home from the university. My word, you're a sight for your dad."

"It's grand to be back with you, Dad."

"Come on, let me have that case and let's get going."

As they drove back to the house in darkness, dim lanterns set at the front of the cart swinging to and fro with each of Persephone's heavy footfalls, Maisie told Frankie her news and answered his many questions. Of course she mentioned the meeting with Enid, although Maisie left out all mention of James Compton.

"The arsenal, eh? Blimey, let's 'ope she wasn't there this afternoon."

"What do you mean, Dad?"

"Well, you know 'is Lordship's with the War Office and all that. Well, 'e gets news before even the papers, you know, special messenger, like. He's very well —"

"Dad, what's happened?"

"'is Lordship 'ad a telegram late this afternoon. The special part of the factory went up this afternoon, where they 'andle the 'eavy explosives. Just as the new shift come on. Twenty-two of them munitions girls killed outright."

Maisie knew that Enid was dead. She did not need the confirmation that came next morning, when Lord Compton told Carter that Enid had been among the young women killed and that he should inform the staff in whatever way he saw fit. Not for the first time,

Maisie considered how so much in life could change in such a short time. Priscilla enlisting for service, the wonderful evening, meeting Simon Lynch – and Enid. But of the events that had passed in just three days, the picture that remained with Maisie Dobbs was of Enid, swishing back her long red hair and looking straight at Maisie with a challenge. A haunting challenge.

"You worry what you can do for these boys, Maisie. You worry about whatever it is you can *do*."

CHAPTER SEVENTEEN

aisie caught sight of the London Hospital in the distance and did not take her eyes off its austere eighteenth-century buildings until the bus had shuddered to a halt, allowing her to clamber down the steps from the upper deck to the street below. She looked up at the buildings, then at the visitors filing in, people leaving, many in tears, and the ambulances drawing alongside to allow their wounded and bloody cargo to be taken to the safety of the wards.

Maisie closed her eyes and took a deep breath, as if about to jump from a precipice into the unknown.

"'scuse me, Miss, comin' through. You'll get run over if you stand there, young lady."

Maisie opened her eyes and moved quickly to allow a hospital porter through carrying two large boxes.

"Can I 'elp you, Miss? Look a bit lost to me."

"Yes. Where do I enlist for nursing service?"

"You bloomin' angel, you. You'll be just the medicine some of these poor lads need, and that's a fact!"

Positioning his left foot awkwardly against the inside of his opposite shin, the porter held the boxes steady on his knee with one hand, pushed back his flat cap, and used his free hand to direct Maisie.

"You go through that door there, turn left down the long green-tiled corridor, turn right at the end to the stairs. Up the stairs, to the right, and you'll see the enlisting office. And don't mind them in there, love – they pay them extra to wear a face as long as a week, as if a smile would crack 'em open!"

Maisie thanked the man, who doffed his cap quickly before grabbing the boxes, which were about to fall to the ground, and then went on his way.

The long corridor was busy with people lost in the huge building, and others pointing fingers and waving arms to show them the way to reach a certain ward. Taking her identification papers and letters of recommendation out of her bag, Maisie walked quickly up the disin-fectant-cleaned tiled staircase and across the landing to the enlisting office for nurses. The woman who took Maisie's papers glanced at her over her wire-rimmed spectacles.

"Age?"

"Twenty-two."

She looked up at Maisie again and peered over the top of her spectacles.

"Young-looking twenty-two, aren't you?"

"Yes, that's what they said when I went to university."

"Well, if you're old enough for university, you're old enough for this. And doing more good while you're about it."

The woman leafed through the papers again, looking quickly at the letter with the Compton crest that attested to Maisie's compe-tence and age. There would be no questions regarding the authentic-ity of documents that bore not only an impressive crest but the name of a well-known figure at the War Office, a man quoted in newspapers from the *Daily Sketch* to *The Times* commenting on dispatches from France.

Maisie had taken the sheets of fine linen paper from the bureau in the library at Chelstone and written what was needed. Emboldened by Enid's challenge, she had felt only the shallowest wave of guilt. She was going to do her part for the boys, for those who had given of themselves on the fields of France.

❊

"*Y*ou've done *what?* Are you mad, Maisie? What about your university learning? After all that work, all that . . ."

Frankie turned his back on Maisie and shook his head. He was silent, staring out of the scullery window of the groom's cottage, out toward the paddocks where three very healthy horses were grazing. Maisie knew better than to interrupt until he had finished.

"After all that fuss and bother . . ."

"It's only a postponement, Dad. I can go back. I will go back. As soon as the war is over."

Frankie swung around, tears of fear and frustration welling in his eyes.

"That's all very well, but what if you get sent over there? To France. Blimey, if you wanted to do something useful, my girl, I'm sure 'is Lordship could've got a job for a bright one like you. I've a mind to go up to that hospital and shop you for your tales – you must've said you were older than you are. I tell you, I never thought I'd see the day when my daughter told a lie."

"Dad, please understand –"

"Oh, I understand all right. Just like your mother, and I've lost her. I can't lose you, Maisie."

Maisie walked over to her father and put her hand on his shoulder. "You won't lose me Dad. You watch. You'll be proud of me."

Frankie Dobbs dropped his head and leaned into his daughter's embrace. "I've always been proud of you, Maisie. That's not the point."

❊

As a member of the Voluntary Aid Detachment, Maisie's duties seemed to consist of a daily round of mopping floors, lining up beds so that not one was out of place, and being at the beck and call of the senior nurses. She had obtained a deferment from Girton, and no sooner had the letter been posted, along with another to Priscilla, than Maisie put her dream behind her and with the same resolve that had taken her to university, vowed to bring comfort to the men coming home from France.

Maisie became a VAD nurse at the London Hospital in May, amid the never-ending influx of casualties from the spring offensive of 1915. It was a hot summer, and one in which Maisie saw little rest and spent only a few hours at her lodgings in Whitechapel.

Sweeping a stray tendril of hair under her white cap, Maisie immersed her hands in a sinkful of scalding hot water and scrubbed at an assortment of glass bottles, bowls and measuring jugs with a bristle brush. It was not the first time in her life that her hands were raw or her legs and back ached. But it could be worse, she thought, as she drained the suds and began to rinse the glassware. For a moment she allowed her hands to remain in the water as it began to cool, and looked straight ahead through the window to the dusk-dusted rooftops beyond.

"Dobbs, don't think you've got all day to rinse a few bottles, not when there are a dozen other jobs for you to do before you go off duty."

Maisie jumped as her name was spoken, quickly rushing to apologize for her tardiness.

"Don't waste time, Dobbs. Finish this job quickly. Sister wants to see you now."

The nurse who spoke to her was one of the regulars, not a volunteer, and Maisie immediately reverted to the bobbed curtsy of her days in service. The seniority of the regular nurses demanded respect, immediate attention, and complete deference.

Maisie finished her task, made sure that not a bottle or cloth was out of place, then went quickly to see Sister, checking her hair, cap, and apron as she trotted along the green-and-cream-tiled corridor.

"Nurses never run, Dobbs. They walk briskly."

Maisie stopped, bit her bottom lip and turned around, hands by her sides and balled into fists. Sister, the most senior nurse on the ward. And the most feared, even by the men who joked that she should be sent out to France – that would send the Hun running.

"I'm sorry, Sister."

"My office, Dobbs."

"Yes, Sister."

Sister led the way into her office, with its green-tiled walls, dark wood floor and equally dark wooden furniture, and walked around to the opposite side of her desk, sweeping her long blue dress and bright white apron aside to avoid their catching on the corner. A silver buckle shone at the front of her apron, and her scarf-like cap was starched. Not a hair was out of place.

"I'll get quickly to the point. As you know we are losing many of our staff to join detachments in France. We therefore need to move our nurses and volunteers up through the ranks – and of course we need to keep many of our regular nurses here to keep up standards and direct care of the wounded. Your promotion today to Special Military Probationer means more responsibility in the ward, Dobbs. Along with Rigson, Dornhill and White, you must be prepared to serve in military hospitals overseas if needed. That will be in one year, at the end of your training. Let me see . . ."

The austere woman shuffled papers in a file on the desk in front of her.

"Yes, you'll be twenty-three at the end of the year, according to your records. Eligible for duty abroad. Good."

Sister looked up at Maisie again, then checked the time on the small watch pinned to her apron. "I have already spoken to the other VADs in question during their duty earlier today. Now then, from tomorrow you will join doctors' rounds each day to observe and assist, in addition to your other duties. Is that understood?"

"Yes, Sister."

"Then you are dismissed, Dobbs."

Maisie left the office and walked slowly toward the kitchen.

Yes, sooner than she had thought she would be in France. Possibly this time next year. How she longed to see Maurice, how she ached to speak with him. For here was time again, the trickster, changing the circumstances of her life in an instant. Yet she knew that Maurice would ask her if she was not herself the trickster. She had lied about her age unashamedly to do this work, and now she was burdened by doubt. Could she do what was required of her? Could she live up to Enid's memory?

CHAPTER EIGHTEEN

*M*aisie pulled herself away from the side rail of the ship. She had never dreamed that seasickness could be this bad. A salty wind blew around her head and nipped at her ears as she struggled to keep the heavy woollen cape drawn across her aching body. Nothing in the world could top this. Nothing could be this unbearable.

"Here, miss, old merchant navy trick for the sickness . . ."

She looked sideways from the place she had claimed, holding on to a handrail that led to a cabin door, then rushed to the side of the boat again. She felt a strong hand between her shoulder blades and pushed against the guard rail to bring herself to a standing position. A member of the crew, sensibly wearing foul-weather clothing, with his cap miraculously still on his head, held out a tin mug of hot cocoa and a lump of Madeira cake. Maisie put her hand to her mouth in terror.

"What you do is, when you think you're going to lose your insides again, you takes a bite o' this and a quick swig of cocoa. And you do it every time you feel queasy. Then it'll go away; you'll see."

Maisie looked at the man, shook her head and leaned over the side rail. Exhausted to the core, she stood up again and held out her hands for the cake and cocoa. It had to be worth a go.

Iris Rigson, Dottie Dornhill, Bess White and Maisie Dobbs had set sail with a small contingent of nurses on July 20, 1916, bound for service in France. Iris, Dottie and Bess had not suffered unduly on the requisitioned freighter, now in the service of king and country, ferrying supplies – and in this case nurses, too – between England and France. But Maisie Dobbs, granddaughter of a lighterman on the Thames, was embarrassingly seasick. Whatever the battlefield had to offer, it could not possibly make her feel worse than this, though she had in her pocket a letter from Priscilla, who had been sent to France in January with the first FANY convoy. The censors might be able to take out words, but they could not delete the emotion poured from inkwell to paper. Priscilla was exhausted, if not in body then in mind. Her words seemed to bite through the edges of Maisie's thoughts and expectations. For just a moment, as she fingered the letter in her pocket, she felt as if she were a ghostly presence watching over Priscilla as she worked. Priscilla had written:

My back is killing me, Maisie. Florrie the Lorry did not want to go to work this morning, so I did double duty with the starting handle. I had only two hours rest last night, after a twenty-hour shift. Maisie, I can only barely remember the last time I slept for more than just a few hours. My clothes are becoming one with my body, and I dread to imagine how I must reek! Mind you, one simply cannot go on about one's aching back and stinging eyes when faced with the good humour of these boys, even as they are suffering the pain of torn limbs and the terror of seeing comrades die. Despite rain that seems to come down in buckets here, there are some days that suddenly get very hot and humid indeed, especially if you are lugging around the added weight of a heavy uniform glued to your body. Many of the boys have taken a knife to their woollen trousers to get some relief from the chafing of army issue cloth. I suppose it's less for the doctors to cut away, but loaded on to Florrie they look like schoolboys who've taken a wrong turning into hell. I had a boy die on me yesterday. Maisie, his eyes were as deep a blue as that dress you wore to Simon's party, and he could not have been more than seventeen. Poor lad hadn't even begun to shave, just a bit of fluff on his chin. I wanted to just sit there and weep. But you know, you just have to go on. If I stood around in mourning for them, another poor boy would die for want of an ambulance. I don't know what the papers are saying, but here's

Priscilla's letter was abruptly halted by the heavy black ink of the censor's pen.

"Here she is. Maisie o' the high seas!" Iris announced as Maisie returned to the cabin.

"Blimey, Maisie, how're you now, then?" Dottie came over to Maisie and put an arm around her shoulder. "Come and sit down. We'll soon be there. Le Havre can't be much longer – can it?" She looked at the other nurses, their heavy capes drawn around them, and settled Maisie into a seat. "You poor little mite, Dobbs. There's nothing of you to start with. Never you mind, we'll soon be in Le Havre. Get us a nice cuppa. That's if the French can make tea."

Iris felt Maisie's forehead and looked at her watch. "You do seem a bit better, though."

Maisie looked at the other girls and leaned against Iris. "Cocoa and cake," she muttered, and promptly fell into a deep sleep.

❖

*F*rom Le Havre the train journey to Rouen passed uneventfully. The young women were tired from the journey but managed to keep awake long enough to watch their first few minutes of foreign soil speed past. Arriving at the port of Rouen the nurses were met by a medical officer and taken to the Hotel St. Georges, where they expected to stay for two nights while they waited for orders.

"Let's get ourselves a nice wash and have a cup of tea downstairs," suggested Iris as they settled into the room all four women were to share.

Iris was a tall, big-boned girl, whose uniform always looked rather too small for her. She considered this a blessing. The unfashionably long and impractical woollen dress of the uniform was shorter on her than on the other nurses. Not only could she move with greater ease, but soon she would avoid having her hemline drag in the never-ending mud, the bane of a nurse's life in France.

"How are you feeling, Dobbs?" asked the soft-spoken Bess, maintaining the discipline of hospital address.

"Much better, thank you. And a cup of tea would be just lovely."

The women each unpacked their few belongings, washed faces and hands at the large white enamelled stone sink, and brushed hair back into place. As usual Maisie struggled to fasten the stray tendrils of jet black hair that crept out from under her hat. When they left the room the women looked almost as fresh as they had in the early hours of the morning, when they had joined their train at Charing Cross for the journey to Folkestone, their port of departure for France.

"Look at those cakes. My word, never seen a pastry like that before; it's a wonder they can do that in wartime," said Dottie.

"No, and you've never tasted a cup of tea like this before either."

Iris winced at the weak tea and reached out to take one of the delicate pastries from the china plate placed in the centre of the table.

Maisie was quiet, looking around her at the rather aged grandeur of the dining room at the Hotel St. Georges. Large mirrors were positioned on each wall, and ornate archways led into the lounge on one side and the marble-floored lobby on the other. Waiters ran back and forth, elegant in black trousers that shone with too much pressing, white shirts, black ties, and long white aprons. They were all older men, for the younger men had gone to war.

The clientele was mainly military personnel, and the hotel was packed with officers going on leave or passing through on their way back to join their regiments. Some were with sweethearts or wives, still others with parents, the fortunate ones whose people could make a journey across the Channel to bid them farewell in France.

Maisie sipped her tea, feeling the warmth, if not the flavour, reach the core of her tired body. She was aware of the conversation at their table, a familiar to-ing and fro-ing of observations and opinions, a giggle here, a raised voice there. But for the most part, as the journey to France ebbed away behind her, Maisie was lost in her own thoughts.

"Excuse me, it's Miss Dobbs, isn't it?"

Maisie was jolted from her daydream back into the dining room. She jumped up and turned to face the person who had spoken to her.

"Oh my goodness!" said Maisie, spilling tea onto the white cloth.

Captain Simon Lynch quickly took her elbow to steady Maisie and greeted her with a broad smile, which he then extended to her table companions, who had immediately stopped all conversation, indeed all movement, to look at the man who had come to the table to see Maisie.

"Captain Lynch. Well, what a surprise this is!"

Maisie regained her composure and took Simon's proffered hand. A waiter quickly and efficiently replaced the tablecloth and offered to bring a chair for Simon who declined, commenting to her companions that he had just been leaving when he had seen his friend, Miss Dobbs.

Simon turned again to Maisie, and as he did so she noticed that he seemed older. Not just in years, for it was just over a year since they had first met. No, he was older in his soul. His eyes were ringed with grey skin, lines had formed on his fresh young man's face, and already grey hair was showing at his temples. Yet he could be no more than twenty-six.

"Just here for two days' leave. Not enough time for Blighty, I'm afraid. I'd heard from Pris that you'd joined up."

"How is she? Have you seen her?"

"Our paths crossed only once. She brought wounded men to my hospital but, well, we didn't have time to stand and chat." Simon looked at his hands, then back at Maisie. "So, do you know where you are going yet?"

"No, we get our orders tomorrow morning, perhaps even this evening. Seems a bit chaotic, really."

Simon laughed.

"Chaotic? You haven't seen chaotic until you've been out there."

"I'm sorry." Maisie rubbed her hands together. "What I meant was —"

"No, *I'm* sorry. That was horrible of me. And, yes, it *is* chaotic. The right arm of the British army hardly seems to know what the left arm's doing. Look, I have to dash off now, but I wonder, is there any chance that you could have dinner with me tomorrow evening? Or do you have to be chaperoned?"

Simon grinned and looked into Maisie's eyes.

"Well, um, well . . ."

Maisie looked sideways at her companions, who were continuing with their tea quietly in order to listen to the conversation. She caught Iris's eye and saw the other woman smile, nod her head and mouth the word "Go." Maisie turned back to Simon.

"Yes, Captain Lynch. Dinner would be lovely. And, yes, actually I do have to be chaperoned, so my friends will be dining nearby."

"Right you are. Let's make it an early one then, I'll meet you in the lobby at six o'clock. In fact, I'll meet you all in the lobby at six o'clock!"

Simon bowed, bade good-bye to the nurses, smiled at Maisie, and moved to go.

"Oh, and by the way – that uniform – it's almost as stunning as the blue silk dress."

And then he was gone.

Maisie took her place once again, amid the giggles of Iris, Dottie, and Bess.

"And what silk dress might that be, Dobbs?"

"You kept that one quiet, didn't you?"

"Sure you want a chaperone?"

Maisie blushed at the teasing, which she knew would continue for some time. She was about to explain that Simon was only a friend of a friend when an RAMC officer approached their table.

"Dobbs, White, Dornhill, and Rigson? Good. Orders are here, and travel warrants. Sorry. You won't be going to the same place. White and Dornhill together at the base hospital. Dobbs and Rigson, you're going to the Fourteenth Casualty Clearing Station – enjoy it here while you can."

And with that he was gone, clutching several large manila envelopes under his arm while negotiating his way through the busy dining room in search of other nurses on his list.

The four women sat in silence for a few minutes, looking at the brown manila envelopes.

"Well, he's a bundle of joy, isn't he?" said Iris, taking a knife from the table and slicing open the envelope.

"Dobbsie, my girl, we are indeed off to the Fourteenth Casualty Clearing Station near Bailleul, like Cheerful Charlie over there said. A CCS, that's as near to the battlefield as nurses are allowed, isn't it?"

"And we're at the base hospital here in Rouen, so we won't be going far, will we, Bess?"

"Well, there we are, then. Let's make the most of it, that's what I say. And let's get some sleep."

Iris dabbed at her mouth with her table napkin, and a waiter scurried over to pull out her chair.

"Yes, good idea. At least one of us needs her sleep if she's to be walking out with an officer!"

"Oh, Dottie, he's just —"

Maisie rushed to defend herself as the women left the table, but her protestations were lost amid the teasing and banter.

※

*R*emembering the events of her dinner with Simon Lynch took Maisie's mind off the journey. First by train, then by field ambulance along mud-filled and rutted roads, Maisie and Iris travelled to the casualty clearing station where they would be based until due for leave in four months' time.

As the train moved slowly along, though it was still light, Maisie had a sense of darkness descending. Gunmetal grey clouds loomed overhead, splashes of rain streaked across the windows, and when the train stopped at a station the sound of heavy artillery in the distance seemed to echo and reverberate along the tracks. Even the birds had been silenced by the mighty orchestra of battle. With the sights and sounds of war around them, people in the landscape loomed with a stark intensity.

Maisie watched from the train window as lines of people trudged along, and more lines of battered humanity appeared to be strung out into the distance. Whole families were leaving communities close to the battlefields, seeking a place of safety with relatives in other towns and villages. Yet the river of civilian evacuation was a stream compared to the long column of marching soldiers, battle weary in weathered uniforms. Young men with faces prematurely aged, showing fatigue and fear as well as a determined levity.

> What's the use of worrying?
> It never was worthwhile, so
> Pack all your troubles in your old kit-bag,
> And smile, smile, smile.

The marching songs rang out, and as their train passed by, Iris and

Maisie leaned out of the slow-moving carriages, waved to the soldiers and joined in their songs.

It's a long way to Tipperary, it's a long way to go;
It's a long way to Tipperary, to the sweetest girl I know;
Good-bye Piccadilly, farewell Leicester Square,
It's a long, long way to Tipperary, but my heart's right there.

With a final wave, Iris and Maisie pulled up the window and tried to make themselves comfortable again on the prickly wool train seating.

"Funny that your young man's not that many miles from us, isn't it Dobbs?" Iris looked inquiringly at Maisie when they were settled.

"Oh, for goodness sake, he's not my young man. He's just an old friend of a very good friend of mine. It really is a coincidence that I saw him at all."

"That's as may be, Dobbsie, but I saw the way you two were look-ing at each other, and I'd say that you were a-courting. Right pair of turtle doves if you ask me."

"Nonsense. And don't you go repeating this silliness either, Iris. Please. I hardly know him – and I could get into trouble!"

"Blue silk dress eh?"

Iris continued to tease Maisie.

Iris, Dottie, and Bess had taken a table next to Maisie and Simon at dinner, lest it be thought that she was dining completely without a chaperone. But surprising even herself, Maisie hardly noticed other people in the hotel dining room. From the time he had greeted her in the lobby, at six o'clock as arranged, and held out his arm to her, Maisie and Simon Lynch had eyes only for each other.

Now Maisie lowered her eyelids and feigned sleep, which effec-tively silenced Iris. Left in peace, she was able to envision the dining room again, the waiters running to and fro, and the busyness of peo-ple enjoying last farewells or a few days' respite from the business of war. And there, at the table with her, was Simon.

Simon who made her laugh with his jokes, putting her at ease.

Simon who asked her why she had become a nurse, and when she told the story of Enid, leaned across and took her hand. "She must have meant a lot to you, your friend."

"Yes, yes, she did . . . she made me think about all sorts of things. While I was busy with my head in a book, she would bring me down to earth with a thud. Yes . . . she made me reconsider my opinions on more than one occasion."

Simon did not release Maisie's hand, and for a moment their eyes met again and they were silent. Abashed, Maisie pulled her hand away and took up her fork. She poked at her food.

"I hope I didn't embarrass you. I, I didn't think —"

"Oh no. That's all right." Maisie blushed.

"It's a strange thing, war. Maisie, you must prepare yourself for what you are going to see. This past year . . . the Somme . . . I cannot tell you what injuries the men suffer. As a doctor I was trained to deal with one surgical case at a time: I operated on a leg, or a chest, or an arm. But these men are brought in with multiple gaping wounds, I —"

Simon stopped speaking and reached for his glass of claret, which he gripped but did not pick up. He stared into the wine, at the deep red liquid, and then closed his eyes. As he did so, Maisie saw again the lines that crept from the edges of his eyelids to his temples, the creases on his forehead and the dark circles above his cheekbones.

"I came here thinking I could save every one of them, but half the time —" Simon hesitated, swallowed deeply, and looked directly at Maisie.

"It's so very good to see you, Maisie. It reminds me of how it was before I left England. How I felt about being a doctor. And how very much I hoped that I would see you again."

Maisie blushed again but smiled at Simon.

"Yes, Simon. I am glad too."

Without thinking she reached out her hand, which he took and gripped tightly. Suddenly aware of the proximity of other diners, Maisie released her hold and they took up their knives and forks.

"Now then, tell me all about Lady Rowan. I've heard of her, of course. She has quite a reputation as a staunch supporter of the suffragettes. And I've heard that Lord Julian is an absolute saint – although I doubt he has much time to worry about what she's up to, now that he's at the War Office."

Conversation slipped into the exchanging of stories, of opinions and observations, and by the time dinner was over Maisie noticed that they had spoken of their dreams, of what they would do "when the war's over."

In that moment she remembered Maurice, walking with her in the orchard one day while at Chelstone, as she broke the news that she had requested a deferment of her place at Cambridge, that she had enlisted at the London Hospital.

She remembered him looking into the distance and speaking, very quietly, almost to himself. "Such is the legacy of war . . . the discarded dreams of children . . . the waste. The tragedy."

Simon looked at his watch. "Well, sadly, Maisie, I must go. I have meetings while I'm here, I'm afraid. So much for leave, eh?"

"Yes, I have to go too. We set off early tomorrow morning."

As Maisie placed her white linen table napkin alongside her plate, Simon watched her intently. "Would you mind very much if I wrote to you? It may take a while, but letters can be sent up the line. I'll work out something."

"Yes, that would be lovely. Please write."

Simon rose to pull out Maisie's chair, and as he did so Maisie noticed her three friends at an adjoining table, all holding coffee cups to their lips and looking at her over the rims of the cups. She had forgotten they were there.

In the lobby Simon once again made a sweeping bow. "You may be clad in that wonderfully practical nursing attire, Miss Dobbs, but in my eyes you will forever be wearing a stunning blue silk dress."

Maisie shook hands with Simon and bade him good-bye, before joining the three nurses standing directly behind her and doubtless waiting to begin teasing her once again.

✦

*M*aisie and Iris saw the tents in the distance, a musty afternoon cordite-laden fog lingered overhead, and a heavy ground mist was moving up and around them.

"I'm freezing just looking at that lot, and it's nowhere near winter yet," said Iris.

"I know what you mean. Looks bleak, doesn't it?"

Maisie pulled her cape around her body, though the day was not that cold.

The main tents had giant red crosses painted on top, and beyond were bell tents that were home to the nursing contingent of the casualty clearing station. The ambulance moved slowly along the rutted road, and as they came closer to the encampment, it was clear that they were in the midst of receiving wounded.

The ambulance pulled alongside the officers' tent, where records were kept and orders given. All around them people moved quickly, some shouting, others carrying fresh supplies. Iris and Maisie stepped down and had barely taken up their bags when a sister rushed up to them.

"No time to dawdle. We need you now – time for the paperwork and receiving line later! Get your capes off, your aprons on, and report immediately to the main tent. It's the deep end for you two."

Two hours later, as Maisie stood over a young man, cutting heavy uniform cloth away from an arm partially severed by shellfire, Maisie remembered Simon's words: "You must prepare yourself for what you are going to see."

Quickly pushing the still-fresh words to the back of her mind, and brushing the sweat from her forehead with the back of her bloodied hand, Maisie felt as if she were in the eye of the storm. The young soldier lying in front of her was conscious, watching her face all the time, searching for the glimmer of expression that would give away her assessment of his wounds. But the sisters of the London Hospital had taught their nurses well: Never, never ever change your expression at the sight of a wound – they'll be looking into your eyes to see their future. Look straight back at them.

As Maisie worked quickly, taking up disinfectant and swabs, a surgeon accompanied by nurses and medical orderlies moved from one soldier to the next, cutting away skin, bone and muscle, pulling shrapnel from the bodies of boys who had taken on the toil of men.

The soldier continued to stare into Maisie's eyes as she prepared his wounds for the surgeon's knife. Following the trail of blood and flesh, Maisie cut away more uniform, taking her scissors to his trousers, pulling at the bindings around his lower leg. And as she felt her hand sink into the terrible injuries to his thigh, the soldier cleared his throat to speak.

"Rugby player's legs, those."

"I thought so," said Maisie as she continued to work on his leg, "You can always tell the rugby players."

"Nurse, nurse," the soldier reached out towards her with his uninjured hand, "Nurse, could you hold my hand?"

And as Maisie took his hand in hers, the young man smiled.

"Thank you, nurse."

Suddenly Maisie was aware that someone was bending back the soldier's fingers and moving his arm to his side, and she looked up at the nursing sister in charge. An army chaplain placed his hand on her shoulder for barely a second before lifting it to perform last rites over the young soldier's not-yet-cold body, while two stretcher-bearers waited to remove him to allow room for more wounded.

"Oh, I'm sorry –"

"No time for sorry," said the sister. "He's been gone less than a minute anyway. You did all you could. Now then, there's work to do here. No time to stop and think about it. Just got to get on with it. There's plenty more waiting outside that need your helping hand."

Brushing back a stray hair with the back of her hand once again, Maisie prepared the table as best she could for the next soldier.

"'Allo, Nurse. Going to make me all better, are you?" said the man as the stretcher bearers quickly but carefully placed him on the table.

Maisie looked straight into the man's eyes and saw intense pain masked by the attempt at humour. Taking up scissors and swabs, along with the pungent garlic juice used to disinfect wounds, she breathed deeply and smiled.

"Yes. I'm going to make you all better, young man. Now then, hold still."

CHAPTER NINETEEN

*M*aisie awoke in the tent she shared with Iris. Snuggling under her blankets, she looked over at her friend and, in the half sleep of early morning, thought for a moment that it was Enid, but realized that it was the bump of Iris's behind forming a mound in the bed as she, too, curled herself against the early morning chill.

She took a deep breath. The chill air notwithstanding, Maisie suddenly sat up, pulling the blanket around her shoulders as she did so. She must do everything in her power to keep a calm head, to brace herself for the day, and to prepare herself for the elements. Rain had started to fall again. Rain that soaked into the ground to form a stew of mud and filthy water that seeped up into the cloth of her long woollen dress, making it hang heavily against her ankles as she worked again and again to clean and bandage wounds. By the end of each day the mud had worked its way up to her knees, and time and time again she told herself that she was warm, really, that her feet felt dry, really. Then at night, she and Iris would hang up their dresses to allow the moisture to evaporate, and check each other's bodies for the battlefield lice that seemed to know no defeat.

"You first, Maisie," said Iris, still clutching the bedcovers around her body.

"You just don't want to be the one to crack the ice."

"What ice?"

"I told you, Iris, there was a layer of ice on the top of that water yesterday."

"No!"

Iris turned over in her cot to look at Maisie, who sat cross-legged on her bed.

"I don't know how you can sit like that, Dobbs. Now then, are you telling me there was ice on the water? It's not even proper winter yet."

"Yes. Even though it's not proper winter."

Maisie took another deep breath, which, when exhaled, turned to steamy fog in front of her face. She cast the blanket aside and nimbly ran over to the water pitcher and bowl that stood on top of a wooden chest.

"And the sitting in the morning – it's what helps to keep me from freezing solid all day, Iris. It clears my head. You should try it!"

"Hmmmph!"

Iris turned over in bed and tried to ignore her cold feet.

Maisie poked her finger into the water pitcher. She cracked the thin layer of ice as if tentatively testing a piecrust, then gripped the handle of the pitcher with both hands and poured freezing cold water into the bowl. Reaching over to the side of the chest, Maisie unhooked a flannel, which she steeped in the water. After wringing it out, Maisie unbuttoned the front of her nightgown and washed first her face, then under her arms and up to her neck. Oh, what she would give for a bath! To sit in a deep bathtub filled with piping hot water and soap bubbles coming up to her ears.

Again she plunged the flannel into the cold water, squeezed the excess water back into the bowl, and this time lifted her nightgown and washed between her legs and down to her knees. A nice hot bath. For hours. She wouldn't come out for hours. She'd keep twiddling that hot tap with her big toe, and she wouldn't come out until every last molecule of mud, blood, sweat and tears had been washed away.

Taking down her still-damp dress, which had been hanging from a wire she and Iris had rigged up inside the tent, Maisie checked every seam and in the hem for lice. It was the morning drill: check for lice everywhere, and when you've finished checking, check some more, because lice are crafty little beggars. She dressed quickly, finally slipping a white armband with a red cross just above the elbow of her right sleeve, and taking out a fresh apron and attaching a silver watch pin to the left side of the bib. Along with the black leather document case, which now held her writing paper and letters received, the nurse's watch was her talisman from home, a gift from Lady Rowan.

Finally Maisie placed a towel on her bed and leaned over it to brush her hair, looking carefully for lice falling out. She and Iris checked each other's hair every night or, if they were on duty at night, whenever they were both in the tent and awake at the same time. But Maisie always checked again in the morning, brushing her hair over a towel until her head spun. Then she quickly pinned her hair up into a bun and placed her cap on her head.

"I'm all finished, Iris."

"Right you are, Dobbsie." Iris shivered under her bedclothes. "Lord knows what this will be like in the real winter."

"At least we're not up to our waists in mud in the trenches, Iris. Least we're not piling up bodies to make a wall to protect us. Not like the boys."

"You're right there, as always," said Iris as she leaped from bed and began the morning ritual that Maisie had just finished. "Brrrr . . . I 'spect you're going over to see if there's a letter from your young man."

Maisie rolled her eyes. "I've told you, Iris. He's not —"

"Yes, I know, I know. He's not your young man. Well then, go and get your letter from your special friend of a friend then, and leave me to my delousing, if you don't mind!"

The young women laughed, as Maisie pulled back the tent flap, leaving Iris to her morning ablutions. Picking her way across wooden boards covering mud and puddles, Maisie made her way to the cooks' tent to get tea and bread for breakfast.

"There you are, Sister, get this down you." The orderly on duty held out a large enamel mug along with a slice of bread and dripping for Maisie, addressing her as "sister" in the way that soldiers called all nurses, regardless of rank.

"And a little something else for you, passed on to me this morning." He reached into his pocket and brought out a simple brown envelope that clearly contained a long letter, such was the thickness of the packet. The envelope was crumpled and bore stains of the four sets of dirty hands it had passed through before reaching its destination.

The letters from Simon Lynch to Maisie Dobbs would never travel through the censor's office, passed as they were from orderly to ambulance driver to stretcher bearer to cook. Her letters in return were passed in the same way, from person to person. And each time a letter changed hands, there would be a comment exchanged, a remark about young love, or that it was all very well for him, Captain Romantic over there.

The writers said nothing of love when the first letter, from Simon to Maisie, was sent and received. But in the way that two people who are of one mind on any subject move closer, as if their heads were drawn together by thoughts that ran parallel toward a future destination, so the letters of Simon and Maisie became more frequent, one hardly waiting for the other to reply before setting pen to paper again. Bearing up under exhaustion that weighed on their backs and pushed like a fist between their shoulder blades, Simon and Maisie, each in a tent several miles apart, and each by the strained light of an oil lamp, would write quickly and urgently of days amid the detritus of war. And though both knew that war, and the ever-present breath of despair might have added urgency to their need to be together again, they began unashamedly to declare their feelings in the letters that were passed from hand to hand. Feelings that, with each shared experience and story, grew deeper. Then Simon wrote:

My Dearest Maisie of the Blue Silk Dress,

I have been on duty for 30 hours without so much as sitting down for five minutes. Wounded started coming in again at eleven yesterday morning. I have bent over so many bodies, so many wounds that I fear I have lost count. I seem to remember only the eyes, and I remember the eyes because in them I see the same shock, the same disbelief, and the same resignation. Today I saw, in quick succession, a man and his son. They had joined up together, I suspect one or both lying about their age. And they had the same eyes. The very same. Perhaps what I see in each man is that no matter what their age (and by golly, some of them shouldn't be out of school), they seem so very old.

I am due for a short leave in three weeks. I will receive orders soon. I plan to go back to Rouen for two days. I remember you said that you would be due for leave soon, too. Would it be too presumptuous for me to ask if we might possibly meet in Rouen? I so long to see you, Maisie, and to be taken from this misery by your wonderful smile and inspiring good sense. Do write to let me know.

Iris had leave at the same time as Maisie, providing Maisie with a female companion. The journey to Rouen seemed long and drawn out, until finally they reached the Hotel St. Georges.

"I swear I cannot wait to get into that bath, Maisie Dobbs."

"Me too, Iris. I wonder if we can get our dresses cleaned. I've another day dress with me that I haven't worn. How about you?"

"Yes, me too. Not supposed to be out of uniform, but for goodness sake, this dress will walk to the laundry if I don't take it."

Maisie and Iris hurried immediately to their assigned room. The ceilings seemed extraordinarily high and there was chipped paint on the walls and doorframe. The room itself was small and simple, containing two single beds and a washstand, but after several months of living with the roof of a leaking tent barely six inches above their heads, they saw only grandeur. Two bathrooms were situated along the red-carpeted corridor, and the ever vigilant Iris immediately checked to see whether either was already occupied.

"One already gone, I'm afraid, and he's singing at the top of his voice."

"Golly, I am just aching for a nice hot bath," said Maisie.

"Tell you what. I'll put on my day dress and see if I can get our laundry done while you draw a bath. We can top and tail it – check for the dreaded lice at the same time. It'll save waiting. Did you see the officers coming in after us? Bet they'll be bagging the bathrooms a bit sharpish."

"Don't some officers get rooms with bathrooms?"

"Oh, yes. Forgot that. Privilege and all that."

Iris and Maisie had discarded their uniform dresses quickly, and Iris gathered the laundry and walked toward the door.

"Never know, Maisie, p'raps your Captain Lynch will let you use *his* bathroom."

"Iris!"

"Only joking, Dobbsie. Now then, go bag us a bathroom."

The bathtub easily accommodated the two women, who lay back in the steaming water and audibly allowed the tension of the past few months to drain away.

"Bit more hot water, Maisie. Another five minutes and we'll swap ends."

"And about time!"

Maisie turned on the hot tap and pulled the plug to allow some of the cooler water out at the same time. After wallowing for another five minutes they swapped ends, giggling as they moved, and continued to linger in the soothing steamy heat.

"Maisie," said Iris, as she leaned back, trying to comfortably position her head between the heavy taps, "Maisie, do you think your Captain Lynch will ask you to marry him, then?"

"Iris —"

"No, I'm not joking. I'm serious. What with the war and all. Makes you a bit more serious, doesn't it? Look at Bess White — gets a letter from her sweetheart, says he's going home on leave, she goes on leave, and bang! There they are — married, and him back at the front."

Maisie leaned forward, dipped her head in the water and sat up, sweeping back the long dark tresses.

"Here's what I do know, Iris. I know that when this is over, when the war is done with, I'm going back to university. That's what I know. Besides, when the war's over, I don't know if I'll be . . . well, Simon comes from a good family."

Iris looked at Maisie, then, sat up and took hold of her hand.

"I know exactly what you're just about to say, Maisie, and let me tell you this, in case you haven't noticed. We're living in different times now. This war has made everything different. I've seen the letters from your dad, and from that Carter and Mrs Whatsername with the pies. Those people, Maisie, are your family, and they are every bit as good as Simon's. And you are every bit as good as anyone Captain Simon Lynch will ever meet."

Maisie held on to Iris's hand, bit her bottom lip and nodded. "It's just that — I can't explain it, but I have a feeling here," she held her hand to her chest, "that things will change. I know, I know, Iris, what you're going to say, 'It's the war. . .' But I know this feeling. I know it to be true. And I know that everything will change."

"Come on. This water's going to your head, Maisie Dobbs. You're a grand nurse, Dobbsie, but I tell you, sometimes I wonder about all your wondering."

Iris put her hands on either side of the bath and levered herself up. She stepped out onto the tiled floor, grabbed one of the sturdy white towels and began to dry herself. Maisie continued to sit in the rapidly cooling water while Iris dressed.

"Come on, dreamer. We'd better get a move on. That's if you want to see young Captain Lynch for dinner this evening. What time did he say to meet him?"

"The note said seven o'clock. By the desk in the main corridor as you come into the hotel."

✦

Wearing a plain grey day dress, her hair up in a bun, and accompanied by Iris, Maisie walked down the wide sweeping staircase of the hotel. She had tried not to anticipate meeting Simon again in case she imagined too much, in case the expectation of excited conversation, of hands held, of feelings expressed, were to clash with reality.

Iris was accompanying Maisie, but had already made up her mind to retire early. Not that she should, really. Fraternizing between men and women in uniform was frowned upon. But with a bit of luck, Maisie's young man would have a nice friend for company. Chaperone, my eye! thought Iris. Nothing like being the piggy in the middle.

Maisie and Simon Lynch saw each other at exactly the same time, and moved quickly through the throng of visitors. The thumping of Maisie's heart seemed to radiate to her throat, and stopped the words of greeting she had so carefully planned. Simon simply stood in front of her, took both her hands in his and looked into her eyes.

"I thought I would never see you again, Maisie."

Maisie nodded and looked down at their hands held together.

A deep, throaty "Ahem!" brought Simon and Maisie's attention back into the room. Iris was looking at her feet, inspecting the soles of her shoes, when the man accompanying Simon spoke.

"Think you could introduce us, Lynch? Don't know how you folks do things, but where I'm from, we try to get acquainted."

"Oh, I'm sorry. Please forgive me. Maisie, Iris, may I introduce Captain Charles Hayden. Currently sporting a British uniform, but as you can hear, he's an American. Good man came over here with the Massachusetts General Hospital contingent to do his bit. God bless them all. We've been exchanging notes about dealing with gas poisoning. Charles – Miss Maisie Dobbs and Miss Iris Rigson."

"And delighted to meet you. It was worth coming all this way. And Lynch was becoming a bit of a bore, as you might say. Well, are we going to eat, or stand here all evening? Personally I'm for eating."

"Me too," said Iris.

Charles Hayden provided the group with a much-needed dose of humour at dinner, and as time passed the waves of conversation shifted so that the voices of Hayden and Iris could be heard above all others, laughing loudly, teasing, and generally exchanging good cheer. Instinctively they had assumed the task of allowing their friends the intimacy that can be had, even in a crowded room, when two people want only to be with each other.

"I have longed to see you, Maisie, and yet now that you're here, I hardly know what to say."

"Yes, I know."

Simon turned his body toward Maisie and reached for her hand.

"Talk to me about anything, Maisie. I want to know everything about you. Even if you've already told me in a letter. I want to hear your voice. Start anywhere, but not with the war. Tell me about London, Kent, about your father, your mother – and what about that funny little man Maurice Blanche? Tell me about it all, Maisie."

Maisie smiled, looked briefly across the table at Iris laughing with her head back.

"I'll tell you about my father. Francis. Known to just about everyone as Frankie. He has three loves in his life. My mother, who died when I was a child, me, and Persephone, his horse."

Maisie and Simon each unfolded tales of their lives that transported them from the memory of more recent experiences. Even after dinner had ended, the two walked close together along a cobbled street that led to nowhere in particular and back again. For two days Simon and Maisie were almost exclusively with each other, apart only when Simon kissed her hand at the end of each day and watched as she climbed the stairs to the room she shared with Iris.

"Well, we're off tomorrow, Maisie. Back to the delightful Maison Tent."

"Have you enjoyed yourself, Iris?"

"Thank God for Chuck – that's what he calls himself – Hayden. Nice man, good company. We swapped sweetheart stories while you collected stars in your eyes."

"Iris, I'm sorry. I can't thank you enough."

"Oh, Maisie, don't get me wrong. It was a very nice time I had. Seriously, like I said, he was good company. Left his wife and young son behind to come over here with other American doctors and nurses. Misses his family something rotten. I told him all about my Sid. Blimey, I dunno if I would've come over here if I didn't have to."

"You didn't have to come here, Iris."

"I know. But there again I did, because it's my country that's here in this war. They're our boys and I'm a nurse. But they didn't; the Americans didn't have to come here. Though Charles seems to think it won't be long before they're in."

Iris began packing her small bag ready for the journey back to the casualty clearing station. "Made a nice job of the uniforms they did, here in the hotel laundry. And in double-quick time. Enjoy the clean dress, my girl; we'll be in mud up to our knees before long. And fighting off the lice again."

"Oh don't, Iris . . ."

Simon accompanied Maisie and Iris to the station, and while Iris walked along to the platform for their train, Simon and Maisie stood together. Maisie shivered.

"I'll write as usual."

"That would be lovely, Simon. Gosh, it's cold."

Simon looked at her and without thinking put his arms around her.

"Please," Maisie protested weakly.

"Don't worry. No nasty sisters around to report you for dawdling with an unscrupulous RAMC captain."

Maisie laughed and shivered at the same time, moving her body closer to Simon. He held her to him and kissed her first on her forehead, then, as she looked up at him, Simon leaned down and kissed Maisie again on her cheek, then her lips.

"Simon, I –"

"Oh dear, will I get you into terrible trouble?"

She looked up at him, then around at the other travellers, none of whom seemed to notice the pair, and giggled nervously.

"Well, you might if someone sees us, Simon."

The guard signalled a loud whistle to alert passengers that the train would soon be leaving. Steam from the heavy engine was pushed up and out onto the platform. It was time for Simon and Maisie to part.

"Maisie. Look, I have a leave coming up again in a few months. Back to England. When's your leave? Perhaps it will be at the same time."

"I'll let you know Simon. I'll let you know. I must run. I'll miss the train."

Simon held Maisie to him, and as the guard signalled the "all aboard," she pulled herself away and ran along the platform. Iris was leaning out of the window of their carriage waving to her. She clambered aboard and sat down heavily on the seat just as the train began to move.

"I thought I'd be leaving without you, Dobbs."

"Not to worry, Iris. I'm here."

"Yes. You're here, Dobbsie. But I think you've left your heart behind with a certain young man."

Catching her breath as the train pulled out of the station, Maisie closed her eyes and thought of Simon. And as she saw his face in her mind's eye, the pressure returned to her chest. Rain slanted down across the windows as the fields of France seemed to rumble past with the movement of the train. Maisie looked out at this country she had willingly come to, so close to home, yet so far away from all that she loved. Almost. Simon was near.

CHAPTER TWENTY

On a cold, wintry morning in February 1917, with the sun barely visible through the morning fog, Maisie pulled the wool cape around her shoulders and walked back to the tent she shared with Iris. Burning a hole in her pocket were two letters. One was from Simon. The other contained her leave papers. Her fingers were crossed.

"So, did you get it?" asked Iris, as Maisie tore at the small buff-coloured envelope.

"Wait a minute, wait a minute. Yes! Yes! Yes!"

Maisie jumped up and down. She was going on leave. A real leave. Allowing two days for travel, she would have three days at home. Three days! One whole day more than her last leave, which was – she couldn't even remember. She immediately opened Simon's letter, scanned the lines of fine, right-slanted handwriting and jumped up and down again.

"Yes, Yes! He's got it, he's got leave!"

And the dates, April 15 to 20, were almost the same as hers. They would have two days together. Two whole days.

Iris smiled and shook her head. Oh, how that girl had changed.

Not in her work. No, the skill and compassion she brought to her work were as unquestionable as ever. But this joy, this excitement, was something new.

"Dobbsie, I do believe you're becoming a normal young woman!"

"Nonsense. I've always been normal," said Maisie, continuing to read Simon's letter.

"No, you haven't. I can tell. Taken life far too seriously, you have."

Iris reached for her cape and shivered. "And you can't do that in these times, Maisie. Take your work seriously, yes. But the rest of it, it'll drive you mad."

Iris carefully positioned her cap so that the red cross was in the centre of her crown and the point of the linen square was centred at the back of her head, just grazing the area between her shoulder blades.

"Ready, then?"

"Yes, I'm ready."

"Good. Let's get to work."

The weeks seemed to drag on, yet when Maisie looked back at the time between the arrival of her leave papers and the moment when she walked onto the boat for the crossing back to Folkestone, it seemed that time had flown. As she stowed her bags, sought out hot cocoa and cake, Maisie almost dreaded the start of her leave, for by this time next week she would be back in France. It would be over.

The crossing was calmer than last time, and though the sea was not quite like a millpond, the boat did not seem to pitch and toss as violently as before, and the tops of waves did not suddenly rear up and cover the deck. The nausea of her previous journey was not repeated to the same extent, yet a band of pressure around her forehead caused her to lean against the rail, counting off the quarter hours until land came in sight. She breathed in, waiting for sea saltiness to give way to the clear air of Kent.

Oh, how she ached to see her father, to be drawn into the warm, steamy atmosphere of Mrs Crawford's kitchen. In France she had dreamed of Kent, of apple orchards in full blossom, primroses and bluebells carpeting the woodland, and the soft countryside stretching out before her.

She longed to be home. She could hardly wait to see Simon.

Maisie disembarked, walking down the gangway and towards the port buildings. As she came through into the main waiting area she saw her father, cap in hand, anxiously searching the sea of faces for her. Pushing her way through people jostling for extra height to see over the heads of others to the line of weary passengers, Maisie pulled at her father's arm.

"Dad! What are you doing here?"

"Darlin' girl. Couldn't wait for you to get to Chelstone, could I? So, I took the day off and come down to meet you off the boat. Gawd, this ain't 'alf a busy old place! Come on, let me get that bag of yours, and let's get out of this lot. Never could stand a crowd, even at the market."

Maisie laughed and, still holding tightly to his arm, followed as he pushed his way through the surging throng making their way to the station.

The journey to Chelstone took another two hours, first by train to Tonbridge, then by the small branch line down to Chelstone. In a field across from the station Persephone was grazing, her cart resting just inside the gate.

"Just a minute, love. Won't take me long to get old Persephone ready. Stationmaster let me leave the old girl here. I know it's not a fancy motorcar, but I thought you'd enjoy a ride home on the old cart."

"That I do, Dad."

They rode in silence for a while, Frankie Dobbs with his arm around his daughter's shoulder.

"'Ard to know what to say to you, love. Daresay you don't really want to talk about it, do you?"

"No. Not now, Dad. I'm not home for long. I'll be back there soon enough."

"And how long will I see you for?"

Frankie looked sideways at Maisie.

"Well, I'll be seeing a friend while I'm on leave. But we've got all day tomorrow."

"Is that all I get? Blimey, this Captain Lynch must be an interestin' bloke."

Maisie swung round to her father.

"How do you know – ?"

"Now then, now then. Just you 'old your 'orses, young lady. You're still my girl, and that's a fact."

Frankie grinned at Maisie. "There's a letter waiting indoors for you. Just sent to Miss Dobbs at Chelstone Manor. Got 'is name printed on the back of the envelope. Very posh. Knows your old Dad's the groom, does 'e?"

"Yes. He does Dad. He knows who you are and who I am."

"Good. That's all right then. Look forward to meeting the man."

"Well, I don't know . . ."

Frankie put his arm around Maisie again, and in the security of her father's embrace and his love for her, she slept as she had not been able to sleep since she left for France.

❖

"Well, I never. Look at you. All skin and bone Maisie, all skin and bone."

Mrs Crawford drew Maisie to her, then pushed away to inspect her from head to toe.

"A good dinner, that's what you need my girl. Thank heavens we're all down here now, have been ever since her ladyship said it was too dangerous in London, what with the Zeppelin raids. Anyway, at least I can get a good dinner down you. That's what you need – a good dinner."

Maisie had hardly stepped from Frankie Dobbs's cart before the "welcome homes" began. And it seemed that one welcome was followed by another. She had been immediately summoned to the drawing room to see Lady Rowan. Already the short leave was turning into a whirlwind, but the next day Maisie spent time only with her father, alone.

Frankie Dobbs and Maisie groomed the horses together, walked across farmland, and speculated on the apple crop that would surely be the result of such fine hearty white blossom. And sitting alone in the gardens at Chelstone, Maisie wondered about the war, and how it was that such blooms could give joy to the soul, when one only had to stand on cliffs overlooking the Channel to hear the boom of cannon on the battlefields of France.

On the second day of her leave Maisie was to see Simon in London, a meeting arranged in letters passed between their respective medical stations in France. She would meet his parents at the family's London home during their first day together. They both knew better than to have Simon suggest she stay at the house, as an overnight invitation would come only after a more formal luncheon meeting, the invitation for which had arrived from Mrs Lynch, and along with Simon's letter, had awaited Maisie's return to Chelstone. Simon wrote that he couldn't wait to see her.

Frankie Dobbs took Maisie to the station and they stood awkwardly on the platform to wait for the local train, which would connect with the London train at Tonbridge.

"Now, you make sure you don't overdo it. That Crawford woman was right. Skin and bone you are. You're like your mother, a long streak of nothing in a dress."

"I'll eat them out of house and home, Dad."

"And you mind yourself, Maisie. I've not met this young man, but seeing as you've been invited by his people, I'm sure he's a fine person. And a doctor. But you mind yourself, Maisie."

"Dad, I'll be back on the train this evening –"

"Maisie. It's in 'ere that I'm talking about."

Frankie Dobbs pressed his hand to the place that still held grief for his departed wife.

"I'm talking about your 'eart, Maisie. Mind out for your 'eart."

❖

The sun was shining by the time the engine met the end-of-the-line buffers at Charing Cross station. Maisie checked her face in the compartment mirror. She had never been one to fuss over her appearance, but this was different. This was important.

Once again butterflies were holding court in her stomach, and once again she was filled with the joyous anticipation of seeing Simon Lynch. She opened the heavy carriage door and stepped down onto the platform.

"Maisie!"

"Simon!"

The young officer swept Maisie up into his arms and unashamedly kissed her, much to the delight of people rushing to catch trains or anxiously waiting for loved ones on the platform. There was usually little cause for humour or delight at a wartime railway station, filled as they often were with war wounded, anxious farewells and the bittersweet greetings of those who would have such a short time together.

"I have missed you so much. I can hardly believe we are here."

Maisie laughed, laughed until the tears rolled down her cheeks. How she would hate to say good-bye.

The time spent at the Lynches' London house could not have been more perfect. Simon's parents welcomed Maisie into their home with great affection, as if she were part of the family. Mrs Lynch personally showed Maisie to a guest room to "repair after the long journey."

Maisie's fears that she might have to field questions about her father's line of business proved to be unfounded, and she was asked only about her time at Cambridge and whether she might return when the war was over. Simon's parents understood that talk of "intentions" was almost futile at such a time, and the joy of having a dear son home was not to be sullied by questions that might give rise to discord. Time was too short.

Simon and Maisie had one more day together, then Maisie would leave early on Sunday morning for France. After lunch Simon escorted Maisie to Charing Cross again, and spoke of what they would do next day.

"So, I've managed to get the car, lucky, eh? I'll leave early for Chelstone, then we can have a nice day out together – perhaps go on to the Downs."

"That would be lovely."

"What is it, Maisie?"

Maisie looked at her watch, and at the many men and women in uniform at the station.

"Remember to come to the groom's cottage, Simon. Not to the main house."

"Oh, I see. You're worried about me coming to Chelstone, aren't you?"

Maisie looked at her hands, and at Simon. "A little."

"It doesn't matter to me, Maisie. We both know that there are bigger things to worry about. Besides, it's me that has to worry about Chelstone, what with the formidable Mrs Crawford waiting to render judgment!"

Maisie laughed. "Yes, Simon, you may have a good point there!"

Simon held her hand and escorted her to the platform. The arrival of her train had just been announced.

"Tomorrow will be our last day together." said Simon. "I wish I understood time, Maisie. It vanishes through one's fingers."

He held her hands together in front of his chest, and touched each of her fingertips in turn.

"Maurice says that only when we have a respect for time will we have learned something of the art of living."

"Ah, yes, the wise man Maurice. Perhaps I'll meet him one day."

Maisie looked into Simon's eyes and shivered. "Yes, perhaps. One day."

Simon arrived at Chelstone at half past nine the next morning. Maisie had been up since half past five, first helping Frankie with the horses, then going for a walk, mentally preparing for Simon's arrival. She strolled through the apple orchards, heavy with blossom, then to the paddock beyond.

Half of what was, before the war, grazing for horses, was now a large vegetable garden providing fresh produce not only for Chelstone Manor but also for a wider community. In a time of war, flowers and shrubs were seen as an extravagance, so every cottage garden in the village was almost bereft of blooms. Even the smallest postage stamp of land was needed for growing vegetables.

Maisie made her way back to the cottage and waited for Simon. Eventually the crackle of tyres on gravel heralded his arrival. Frankie drew the curtains aside to look out the window in the small parlour.

"Looks like your young man is here."

Maisie rushed from the room while Frankie stood in front of the mirror, adjusted his neckerchief and pulled down the hem of his best waistcoat. He rubbed his chin, just to make sure, and took off the flat cap that almost never left his head. Before going to the door to meet Captain Simon Lynch, Frankie took up the cherished sepia photograph of a woman who looked so much like the girl who had run joyously to the door. She was tall and slender, dressed in a dark skirt and a cotton blouse with wide leg-o'-mutton sleeves. Though she had fussed with her hair in anticipation of having the photo-graph taken with her two-year-old daughter, there were still stray curls creeping onto her forehead.

Frankie ran his finger across the glass, tracing the line of the woman's face. He spoke to the image tenderly, as if she were in the room with him, for Frankie Dobbs had prayed for her spirit to be at his side today.

"I know, I know . . . go easy on 'im. I wish you was 'ere now, love. I could do with a bit of 'elp with this."

Frankie replaced the photograph, and with one last look in the mirror, just to make sure that he wouldn't let Maisie down, he walked from the cottage to greet the man to whom his daughter had run so eagerly.

⁂

For hours Simon and Maisie talked, first on the journey by motor car across to Sussex, then throughout lunch at a small inn. It was only after they had parked the car by a clump of trees and walked high up on the South Downs, seagulls whooping overhead, that they spent time in silence. Their pace aligned as they walked along the rough path on the crest of the hills overlooking the Channel. They moved closer together, hands brushing but not quite touching.

The day was warm, but Maisie still felt cold. It was a cold that had seeped into her bones in France and now seemed never to leave her. Simon sat down on the grass under a tree and beckoned her to sit next to him. As she sat down he took her hand and grimaced, then playfully reached for one of her walking shoes, untied the laces and held her foot in his hand.

"Goodness, woman, how can anyone be that cold and not be dead!"

Maisie laughed along with Simon.

"It's that French mud that does it, gets right into your bones."

The laughter subsided, and seconds later they were both silent.

"Will you definitely return to Cambridge after the war?"

"Yes. And you, Simon?"

"Oh, I think I'll be for the quiet life, you know. Country doctor. Delivering babies, dealing with measles, mumps, hunters' accidents, farmworkers' ailments, that sort of thing. I'll grow old in corduroy and tweed, smoke a pipe, and swat my grandchildren on their little behinds when they wake me from my afternoon snooze."

Simon leaned forward, plucked a blade of grass and twisted it between his long fingers. "What about after Cambridge, Maisie?"

"I'm not sure."

Conversation ebbed as Simon and Maisie looked out over the sea, both daring their imagination to wander tentatively into the future. Maisie sighed deeply and Simon held her to him. As if reading her thoughts, he spoke.

"It's hard to think about the future when you've seen so many passing through who don't have tomorrow, let alone next year. No future at all."

"Yes."

It was all she could say.

"Maisie. Maisie, I know this is rather soon, possibly even presumptuous, but Maisie, when this is all over, this war, when we are back here in England . . . would you marry me?"

Maisie inhaled sharply, her skin prickly with emotion. What was that emotion? She wanted to say "Yes" but something stopped her.

"I know, I know, you don't have to say anything. It's the thought of corduroy trousers and tweeds isn't it?"

"No, Simon. No. It was just a surprise."

"Maisie, I love you."

He took her hand and looked deeply into her eyes.

"Yes. And I love you too, Simon. I love you too."

Simon drove Maisie back to Chelstone, and brought the car to a halt on the road at the end of the driveway that led to the manor. He leaned over and took Maisie's left hand.

"You never gave me an answer, Maisie."

"I know. It's just me, Simon. And doing what we have to do. In France. I want to wait until it's over. Until there's no more . . . no more . . . death. I can't say yes to something so important until we're home again. Until we're safe."

Simon nodded, his compassion for her feelings at war with his disappointment.

"But Simon. I do love you. Very much."

Simon did not speak, but cupped Maisie's face in his hands and kissed her deeply. At first, Maisie began to pull away, afraid that someone from the manor might see, but as Simon's arms enfolded her she returned his kiss, reaching for his neck to pull him closer. Suddenly Maisie was aware of moisture on her face and, pulling away, she looked into Simon's eyes and touched her cheek where their tears had met.

"God, I wish this war would end," Simon wiped the back of his hand across his eyes before facing her once again. He kissed her gently on the lips. "I love you Maisie, and I want you to be my wife. I promise that as soon as this war is over I will walk across miles of trenches to find you, and I will stand there in my muddy clothes until you say 'Yes!'"

They kissed once more. Then, taking up her bag, Maisie asked Simon to let her walk back to the house alone. She did not want to suffer a difficult farewell, possibly in front of her father and whoever else might be in the gardens to witness their parting. Simon objected, on the grounds that no gentleman would allow a lady to walk unaccompanied to her home, but Maisie was adamant, reminding Simon that she had walked along that lane many a time, and often with a heavy basket.

Simon did not argue. Instead of more words, they held each other close and kissed. She went swiftly from the motorcar and along the driveway, eventually hearing Simon start the engine in the distance and pull away onto the road.

Maisie insisted that she travel alone back to Folkestone, and Frankie, seeing a new maturity and independence in his daughter, agreed to allow Lady Rowan's new chauffeur, an older man passed over for military service, to take her to the station. Maisie said goodbye to her father at home. She had no stomach for more platform farewells.

It was on her journey to Folkestone, and then to France, that she thought back over the events of the days she had spent on leave. She remembered Simon's easy camaraderie with her father, his smile upon introduction, and how he immediately began asking about the horses and allowed himself to be led to the stables so that Frankie Dobbs was relaxed in the domain over which he was the obvious master.

Time and again Maisie replayed Simon's proposal in her head and, though she would no doubt receive a letter from him soon, considered how she avoided making a commitment. She knew only too well the source of such reticence.

As the train moved through the early morning mist of a Kentish springtime, Maisie breathed deeply, as if to remember the aroma of freedom. Though there had yet to be a victor in this great war that had begun almost three years ago, Maurice had written to her that they had, all of them, on all sides, lost their freedom. The freedom to think hopefully of the future.

It was later, much later, more than ten years after the war, that Maisie remembered every thought that had entered her mind on the journey back to the battlefield hospital.

She remembered praying to see Simon just one more time.

SUMMER 1929

CHAPTER TWENTY-ONE

*M*aisie took the underground from Warren Street to Charing Cross, then changed to the District Line for Victoria. As the train rocked from side to side, Maisie wondered what the evening's conversation with Lady Rowan might reveal. She suspected that the farm where James intended to take up residence was the same place that Celia had described over tea.

Leaving the train at Victoria, Maisie made her way out of the underground station and walked along Lower Belgrave Street towards Ebury Place. And as she walked, she thought of Maurice, who had told her so many times that coincidence could simply be what it appeared to be: two events connected to each other by the thoughts and experience of a person. But he also told Maisie to pay attention to coincidence.

Coincidence was a messenger sent by truth.

Carter took Maisie's cloche and jacket and welcomed her into the entrance hall. "So lovely to see you, Maisie. How are you? Her lady-ship is waiting for you in the drawing room – and very anxious to see you she is, too."

"I'm well, thank you, Mr Carter. I'll just nip down to see Mrs Crawford first. I don't want her giving me an earful for not coming straight down to see her."

"A very wise decision, Maisie. You know the way."

Carter left to hang Maisie's outer garments in the cloakroom as Maisie made her way through the door to the right of the entrance hall and downstairs into the kitchen. The stone stairwell was as chilly as she remembered, but as soon as she walked through the door to the kitchen she was enveloped in the welcoming warmth and mingling aromas that sent her back to her girlhood.

Mrs Crawford had become hard of hearing, and continued to work as Maisie stood at the threshold of her domain. Maisie wondered if she had ever seen the old cook's hands clear of either flour or water. They were rough and work-worn hands, but Maisie knew that before touching any food Mrs Crawford would have stood at the big square earthenware sink and scrubbed her hands with a coarse bristle brush and a bar of coal tar soap. And by the time she plunged her hands into pastry dough, her red, sausage-like fingers would be in stark relief to the white flour. Maisie loved Mrs Crawford's apple pie, and if she was visiting there would be a pie for the sweet course *and* a pie for her to take home.

"Mrs Crawford," said Maisie in a raised voice, "I'm here!"

Mrs Crawford turned quickly, her purposeful frown transformed into a beaming smile.

"Well, look at you now! Don't you go getting those nice clothes all covered with flour."

Mrs Crawford rubbed her hands on her pinafore and came towards Maisie with her arms open wide. Maisie was only too pleased to relinquish her body to a hug that was warm and close, even though the old woman was careful to keep her hands away from Maisie's clothes, instead embracing Maisie with pressure from her elbows.

"Are you eating, Maisie? There's nothing of you! I always said that a puff of wind would blow you clear away to Clacton!"

"I promise I'm eating Mrs Crawford. In fact, what's for dinner?"

"A nice vegetable soup, followed by roast beef with all the trimmings – and it's not even Sunday. Then there's apple pie and the cheese board."

"Oh my goodness. I'll pop!"

"Not all for you, but mind you eat a good bit of it. His Lordship will be home late again this evening and will have dinner in his study. And if that James comes in with his face as long as a week, they'll probably eat together. Otherwise Master James will eat in his rooms, with his misery for company."

"I thought he had his own flat – I didn't know he was back at home."

"When he likes. I know, I know, you feel sorry for the boy and all that, and you know we all love him – have done since he was but a streak of lightning running around. But the fact is, he's not a boy any more, is he? And there's plenty of men out there what saw everything over there in France that he did, and they did what we all have to do – they just got on with it instead of moping around like a lost, wet gun dog, all soppy eyes and sodden coat."

Maisie knew that it was no good reasoning with Mrs Crawford, who had firm ideas when it came to coping with life's ups and downs.

"That's the trouble with these privileged boys. Not that I'm criticizing, far from it, I've been treated very well by them upstairs, very well. But that James has had too much time to think about it all. Too much going on up here." Mrs Crawford had gone back to her pastry but tapped the side of her head to emphasize the point. Realizing that she had touched her hair, she went over to the sink to scrub her hands again but lost no time in continuing to make her point.

"Look at the boys who came back and had to get straight out in the farms and the factories – they had wives and families to look out for. You don't see them dragging their heels along, do you? No, that James should be at His Lordship's side, taking some of the weight so that His Lordship isn't in the City at all hours. Not right for a man of his age. After all, look at James, he's thirty-eight this year."

Mrs Crawford came back to her pastry, rolling out the dough with more than a little thumping of the rolling pin on the table. "Have you heard from your father lately?" Mrs Crawford looked up at Maisie, yet continued flouring the pastry and sizing it to the pie dish.

"Yes. Mind you it's difficult, Mrs Crawford. It's not as if he ever liked to put pen to paper. But he's still busy at the house. Master James goes down quite a lot to ride, so there's always work with the horses. And Her Ladyship likes to know that her own horses are cared for, even though she can't ride any more."

"And that's another thing. All that going down there to 'think,' if you please. It's like I said, too much money and too much time on his hands."

Suddenly one of the bells over the door rang.

"That'll be Her Ladyship now. She probably reckons I've had long enough with you. Now then, don't forget to come down for your pie to take home when you leave in the morning."

Maisie kissed Mrs Crawford on the cheek and went upstairs to the drawing room.

"Maisie, how lovely to see you. I had to ring or Mrs Crawford would have hogged you for the whole evening! Come here and sit by the fire. I expect you know what's for dinner already. I told Julian that you would be dining with me and he said 'Oh, good, we'll get some apple pie.' Come on, over here."

Lady Rowan tapped the place next to her on the sofa. The two women spoke of Maisie's business and her new clients. For Rowan Compton Maisie was a breath of fresh air, and she lived vicariously through Maisie's stories.

"And Maurice is keen to see you again soon, you know."

"I thought he would be glad to have a break from me, to tell you the truth."

"Now then, Maisie. You are like a daughter to him. You are his protégée. You are carrying his torch and shining your own light too. But I know he made a promise to himself to give you a little room for you to make your own way. He said to me, 'Rowan, it is high time to let our Maisie Dobbs fly free.'"

"I'll bet he said a bit more than that. I know Maurice too, Lady Rowan."

"Well, yes. He said that you would always look down as you were flying overhead, and if the ground was good for a landing, in you would come – or something like that. You know, that man talks in parables. I swear that sometimes I think he is the most profound person I know, and at others he infuriates me with his obscurity." Lady Rowan shook her head. "Will you visit him soon, Maisie?"

"Yes, I mean to. In fact, I need to consult him."

"Anything interesting?"

Maisie smiled at Lady Rowan without speaking.

"I know, you can't divulge a secret."

"Tell me about James," asked Maisie.

Lady Rowan rolled her eyes, took up her glass from the side table, and sipped her sherry. "James. Oh, that James. I am at a loss Maisie. I knew it when that boy was a child, too sensitive by half. Have you noticed how we always call him a boy? Even now. It wouldn't be so bad if he were gadding about town wining and dining and getting into mischief. But this malaise . . . I wish he would speak to Maurice. But he won't go to see Maurice, and you know that Maurice won't go to him. One of his riddles, that James must open the door and walk along the path to him."

"Maurice is right, Lady Rowan."

"Well, you would say that, wouldn't you? You're a chip off the old block. By the way, he and your father are like two old peas in a pod down there, ever since Maurice bought the dower house."

"Tell me about James," Maisie prodded her.

Lady Rowan took another sip of her sherry. "Frankly, I'm worried. Julian is also worried, but he expresses it in a different way. He seems to think that if we are all patient, then James will come round, and that he won't be so incredibly depressed any more."

Maisie did not speak, allowing Lady Rowan to gather her thoughts. Sitting still and allowing the silence to grow, Maisie felt the frustration, misunderstanding and anger that had built up in the house, permeating every room – along with an expectation that James would one day bound in as the happy-go-lucky young man he had once been.

Carter came in to announce that dinner would be served in the dining room, and led the way. Maisie held out her arm to steady Lady Rowan, who now walked with the aid of a silver-topped cane, as they moved into the dining room.

"Wonderful, Carter, wonderful. Compliments to Mrs Crawford, as always."

The conversation continued lightly as each dish was served, moving once again to the subject of James only after Carter had left the room.

"Some weeks ago James met a wartime colleague who had heard of a farm, coincidentally in Kent, where ex-soldiers could go to live with others who 'understood.' That was the term they used, 'understood.' As if no one else is able to understand. It seems that this farm is quite a revolutionary idea. It was originally set up for those suffering facial wounds, but now it is open – obviously when a room becomes available – to those with other wounds."

Lady Rowan set her knife and fork down on the plate, reached for her wine, and took a sip before continuing. "Of course, James still suffers pain in his leg and arm from the shrapnel, but Maurice has said that his discomfort is a result of melancholy. Yet James has become most interested in this community of wounded. He has visited, met the founder, and has decided to go to live at this . . . this farm for the foreseeable future!"

"You seem distressed by his decision, Lady Rowan. Is there anything else?"

"Yes. A lot more. The founder, a man called Adam Jenkins, maintains that because everyone on the battlefield should have been equal, officers and enlisted men, because they all faced the same enemy, then there should be no advantage while in residence at this farm. Which is fair enough, but James said something about giving up his surname and title. Whatever next?" Lady Rowan shook her head.

At once Maisie thought of Vincent Weathershaw. Vincent.

Lady Rowan went on, "I wish to heaven James would go back to Canada. He seemed happy there, before the war, and at least he would be working and useful. Certainly his father would be delighted; it would be a weight off his mind. I know Julian wants to slow up a bit and wishes James would begin to take up the reins. And now he's signing over his money . . ."

Lady Rowan had hardly touched her food. Instead she ran the fingers of her right hand up and down the stem of her wine glass.

"What do you mean?" Maisie asked.

"Apparently it's one of the stipulations for entering this Retreat or whatever it's called. You come with nothing, to be part of the group. So James has transferred his personal funds to this Jenkins fellow – and it's not just him, others have done the same thing. Thank God his father is still alive and there are limits to what James can actually relinquish financially. Julian is taking steps to protect the estate – and James's future – until he gets over this horrible idea. Of course Julian had already done a lot to shore up the estate when he saw the General Strike coming a few years ago. I married a sensible man, Maisie."

"What does Jenkins do with the money?"

"Well, it's a sizable property to run, and I'm sure the upkeep isn't insignificant. Of course, when one leaves one is refunded any monies remaining and given a statement of account. James said that he saw samples of the statements and refund documents, and he was happy with the arrangements. Mind you, he seemed eager to isolate himself on this farm. He said that people would understand him there. As if I don't!"

Lady Rowan reached over and clasped Maisie's hand. Maisie had never seen the usually stoic Lady Rowan so vulnerable.

"Where is James now?"

"Out. Possibly at his club, but he doesn't go there much now. Quite honestly, I don't know where he is. He could be wandering the streets for all I know. Most probably he's spending time with some old

comrades. He visits them you know, those that are still institutional-
ized. He'll probably be back later. Much later. I told him he could
remain at Chelstone; after all, it's in the country, there's peace and
quiet, and he could do what he likes and come back when he's ready
for the City. Lord knows Julian needs his help. But he's determined to
go to this farm. I have never felt so . . . so . . . cut off from my son."

Maisie pushed the food around on her plate. There was a time when
mother and son had been almost inseparable, sharing a dry wit and a
mischievous sense of humour. She remembered being at the London
house soon after she received news that she had been accepted by
Girton. James had just returned from Canada, hoping to join the Royal
Flying Corps. There was much joy in the household, and as she walked
down the outside stairs toward the kitchen, Maisie saw the tall, fair
young man through the window, creeping up behind Mrs Crawford
and putting his arms around her ample waist. And as Maisie watched
through the condensation that had built up inside the pane of glass, Mrs
Crawford swung around, clipped the young man around the ear and,
laughing, pretended to admonish him. "You, young James, why no
sooner you're back than you'll be the death of me. Look at you, you
young lout – and if you're after fresh ginger biscuits, I've baked up a
batch 'specially for you, though I'm not sure you deserve them now!"

Maisie had walked in through the back door of the kitchen just as
James was taking his first bite of a fresh ginger biscuit.

"And look who else is here," said Mrs Crawford. "Maisie Dobbs, I
do believe you're even thinner! My back only has to be turned for
one minute, and you're not eating properly."

With crumbs around his mouth, James swallowed the biscuit and
struggled to greet Maisie politely. "Ah, the clever Miss Maisie Dobbs,
passing exams that the rest of us mere mortals have nightmares
about!"

Then as Mrs Crawford turned to the stove, James whispered to
Maisie, "Tell Enid I'm home."

Later, as she walked past the drawing room on her way to Lord
Julian's study to serve afternoon tea, which he had elected to take

alone, she saw James and Lady Rowan through the open door. Lady Rowan was laughing heartily, having been whisked by her son into an impromptu dance, accompanied only by the sound of his own booming voice:

> Oh, he floats through the air with the greatest of ease
> The daring young man on the flying trapeze
> His actions are graceful, all girls he does please
> And my love he has stolen away.

"I won't ask you to see James, Maisie," continued Lady Rowan, bringing Maisie back into the present, "I know your opinion will be the same as Maurice's, so I know better than to ask. But I wonder. Would you find out something about this farm, or whatever it is? I have to say that I do feel he would be better in the world rather than trying to escape from it."

"I will certainly look into it, Lady Rowan. I'll go down to Kent next week. I have to go anyway as I need to talk to Maurice, and I must see my father. I'll find out about James's retreat as well."

"Maisie. Take the MG. I know very well that you can drive, so do please take the car. It's not as if I've used it much since Julian bought it for me to run around in – and George drives Julian to the City in the Lanchester."

"Yes, all right, Lady Rowan. It's very kind of you to offer, and I may need to be flexible, so the car will be handy."

"It's almost new, so it should get you there and back with no trouble at all. And Maisie – don't forget to send me your bill!"

Maisie directed conversation to other matters and soon Lady Rowan was laughing in her old infectious manner. Carter watched as two maids cleared the table and brought in the delicious apple pie, to be served with a generous helping of fresh clotted cream. After dinner Maisie and Lady Rowan returned to the drawing room, to sit beside the fire until Lady Rowan announced that it was past time for her to be in bed.

Maisie made her way to the guest room that had been prepared for her visit. Nora had already unpacked Maisie's small bag and laid out her nightclothes on the bed. Later, as she snuggled closer to the hot water bottle that warmed the sheets, Maisie remembered, as she always did when she slept at the Compton's, the nights she'd spent in the servants' quarters at the top of the house.

She left before breakfast the next morning, stopping quickly to drink tea with Carter and Mrs Crawford and to collect the apple pie. Billy Beale would love that apple pie, thought Maisie. She might need it when she asked him if he would take on a very delicate task for her. In fact, as the plans began to take shape in her mind, she might need more than apple pie for Billy Beale.

CHAPTER TWENTY-TWO

"**R**ight then. Watch carefully, miss. 'Ere's how you start 'er up."

The young chauffeur walked round to the front of the 1927 MG 14/40 two-seater and put his hand on the bonnet.

"You've basically got your five steps to starting this little motor, very straightforward when you know what you're about, so watch carefully."

George enjoyed the attention that came as a result of his expertise in the maintenance and operation of the Compton's stable of very fine motor-cars.

"First you lift your bonnet, like so."

George waited for Maisie to nod her head in understanding before continuing with his instructions, and as he turned his attention once again to the MG, she grinned with amusement at his preening tutorial.

"Right. See this – you turn on your fuel. Got it?"

"Yes, George."

George closed the bonnet and indicated that Maisie should move away from the side of the car so he could sit in the driver's seat.

"You set your ignition, you set your throttle, set your choke – three moves, got it?"

"Got it, George."

"You push the starter button – on the floor, Miss – with your foot and –"

The engine roared into life, perhaps somewhat more aggressively than usual, given the enthusiasm of George's lesson.

"There she goes."

George clambered from the seat, held open the door and, with a sweep of his hand, invited Maisie to take his place.

"Think you've got all that, Miss?"

"Oh yes, George. You explained everything very clearly. As you say, it's very straightforward. A lovely motor."

"Oh, nice little runner, to be sure. 'Cording to them up at Morris, this one can do sixty-five miles an hour – up to fifty in the first twenty-five seconds! 'Er ladyship goes out of 'ere like a shot out of a gun, doesn't know where she's going but goes like a shot anyway. Comes back all red in the face. Worries me with them gears though. Talk about crunch! Makes me cringe when I 'ear it. Thank 'eavens for us all that she don't get out in it much any more. Now, then, sure of your way?"

"I'm sure, George. Down the Old Kent Road and just keep on from there, more or less. I've done that journey many a time when I was younger."

"'Course, you was at Chelstone, wasn't you? Mind you, if I were you, I'd go out onto Grosvenor Place, then along Victoria Street, over Westminster Bridge, St. George's Road, and just the other side of the Elephant and Castle . . ."

"I think I can remember the way George, and thank you for the advice."

George walked around to the back of the MG and dropped Maisie's bag into the car's rear luggage compartment, while she made herself comfortable in the rich claret leather seat. He checked once again that her door was closed securely before standing back and giving her a mock salute.

Maisie returned the wave as she eased the smart crimson car out into the mews. It wasn't until she was across the Thames and past the Elephant and Castle that Maisie felt she could breathe again. At every turn she sat up straight and peered over the steering wheel, making sure that each part of the vehicle was clear of any possible obstruction. She had learned to drive before returning to Cambridge in 1919, but took extra care as it had been quite some time since she'd had an opportunity – although she did not want to admit as much to George. In fact, she did not change out of first gear until she was well out of George's hearing, fearing a dreadful roaring as she reacquainted herself with the intricacies of double-declutching.

It was a fine day in early June, a day that seemed to predict a long hot summer for 1929. Maisie drove conservatively, partly to minimize chances of damage to the MG and partly to savour the journey. She felt that she only had to smell the air and, blindfolded, she would know she had arrived in Kent. And no matter how many times she came back to Chelstone, every journey reminded her of her early days and months at the house. As Maisie drove she relaxed and allowed her mind to wander. Memories of that first journey from the house in Belgravia came flooding back. So much had happened so quickly. So much that was unexpected yet, looking back, seemed so very predictable. Ah, as Maurice would say, the wisdom of hind-sight!

Drawing to a halt at the side of the road to pull back the roadster's heavy cloth roof, Maisie stood for a moment to look at the medley of wildflowers that lined the grass verge. Arrowheads of sunny yellow charlock were growing alongside clumps of white field-mouse-ear, which in turn were busily taking up space and becoming tangled in honeysuckle growing over the hedge. She leaned down to touch the delicate blue flower of the common speedwell, and remembered how she had loved this county from the moment she first came to work for the dowager. It was a soft patchwork-quilt land in which she found solace from missing her father and the Belgravia house.

Maisie had decided already that the day in Kent should become a two or three day excursion. Lady Rowan had given her permission to keep the car for as long as it was needed, and Maisie had packed a small bag in case she chose to stay. The hedgerows, small villages and apple orchards still full of blossom were working their magic upon her. She stopped briefly at the post office in Sevenoaks.

"I'm looking for a farm, I think it's called The Retreat. I wonder if you might be able to direct me?"

"Certainly, Miss."

The postmaster took a sheet of paper and began to write down an address with some directions.

"You want to be careful, Miss."

Maisie put her head to one side to indicate that she was listening to any forthcoming advice. "Yes, Miss. Our postman who does the round says it's run like a cross between a monastery and a barracks. You'd've thought that the blokes in there had seen enough of barracks, wouldn't you? There's a gate and a man on duty − you'll have to tell him your business before he'll let you in. They're nice enough, by all accounts, but I've heard that they don't want just anyone wandering about because of the residents."

"Yes, yes indeed," said Maisie, taking the sheet of paper. "Thank you for your advice."

The sun was high in the sky by the time Maisie came out of the post office, and as she touched the door handle of the MG it was warm enough to cause her to flinch. Pay attention, Maurice had always cautioned her. Pay attention to the reactions of your body. It is the wisdom of the self speaking to you. Be aware of concern, of anticipation, of all the feelings that come from the self. They manifest in the body. What is their counsel?

If those from the outside were questioned, albeit in a nonthreatening manner, when they entered, how might it be for the residents, the men who had been ravaged by war, in their coming and going? Maisie decided to drive on toward Chelstone. The Retreat could wait until she had seen Maurice.

Frankie Dobbs put the MG away in the garage and helped Maisie with her bags. She would stay in the small boxroom at the groom's cottage, which had once been her bedroom and was now always made up ready for her to visit, even though such visits were few and far between.

"We don't see enough of you, love."

"I know Dad. But I've been occupied with the business. It's been hard work since Maurice retired."

"It was 'ard work before 'e retired, wasn't it? Mind you, the old boy looks as if 'e's enjoyin' 'avin' a bit of time to 'imself. He comes in 'ere to 'ave a cup of tea with me now'n again, or I'll go over to see 'is roses. It surprised me, what 'e knows about roses. Clever man, that Maurice."

Maisie laughed.

"I have to go over to see him, Dad. It's important."

"Now then, I'm not stupid. I know that I'm not the only reason for you comin' all this way. Mind you, I 'ope I'm the main reason."

"'Course you are, Dad."

Frankie Dobbs finished brewing tea and placed an old enamel mug in front of Maisie, then winked and went to the cupboard for his own large china cup and saucer. As he brought some apple pie out of the larder, Maisie poured tea for them both.

"Maisie. You are lookin' after yourself, aren't you?"

"Yes, Dad. I can take care of myself."

"Well, I know that this work you do is sometimes, well, tricky like. And you're on your own now. Just as long as you're careful."

"Yes, Dad."

Frankie Dobbs sat down at the table with Maisie, reached into his pocket and pulled out a small package wrapped in brown paper and secured with string. "Anyway, I was in the 'ardware shop last week, talking to old Joe Cooke – you know 'ow that man can jaw – and, well, I saw this little thing. Thought it might come in 'andy, like, for you. Natty, ain't it?"

Maisie raised an eyebrow at her father, wondering if he was teasing her. With nimble fingers she pulled away the string and opened the paper to reveal a shining new stainless-steel Victorinox pocket knife.

"Old Joe said it was a bit odd, buying a thing like this for me daughter, but I said, 'Joe, let me tell you, a daughter on 'er own can make more use of a thing like this, with them little tools, than any of them lads of yours.' In any case, y'never know when it might be just the thing you need, 'specially if you're runnin' all over in that motor."

"Oh, Dad, you shouldn't go spending money on me." Maisie pulled out each tool in turn, then looked at the closed knife in the palm of her hand. "I'll keep it with me all the time, just in case." Maisie slipped the knife into her bag, leaned across the table to kiss her father on the cheek, then reached for her tea.

Father and daughter laughed together, then sat in companionable silence drinking tea and eating apple pie, comfortable with only the heavy tick-tock of the grandfather clock for company. Maisie was thinking about The Retreat, and how she would present the story to Maurice.

Years of working with Maurice had helped Maisie prepare her answers to some of his questions, like a chess player anticipating the moves in a game. But she knew that the ones likely to be most difficult were those that pertained to her own past.

Frankie Dobbs interrupted Maisie's thoughts.

"So, that MG. Nice little motor, is it? What's she like on the corners?"

After tea Maisie walked though the gardens and down to the dower house. Maurice had been invited to use the house after the dowager's death in 1916, and he had purchased the black-and-white beamed home in 1919. After the war, like many landowners of the day, the Comptons decided to sell parts of the estate and were delighted when the much-loved house became the property of a friend. The gardens had suffered during the war as groundsmen left to enlist in the army, and land that had lain fallow was requisitioned to grow more produce. At one time it was feared that Chelstone Manor itself would be requisitioned to house army officers, but thankfully, given Lord Julian's work with the War Office together with the fact that the fifteenth-century ceilings and winding staircases rendered the building unsuitable for such use, the manor itself was spared.

Though Maurice officially became resident at the dower house in 1916, he was hardly seen throughout the war years, and came to Chelstone for short periods, usually only to rest. The staff speculated that he had been overseas, which led to even more gossip about what, exactly, he was doing "over there." Maurice Blanche had become something of an enigma. Yet anyone watching him tend his roses during the scorching summer of 1929, as Maisie did before opening the latched gate leading to the dower house garden, would think that this old man wielding a pair of secateurs and wearing a white shirt, light khaki trousers, brown sandals and a Panama hat, was not one for whom the word "enigma" was appropriate.

Maisie hardly made a sound, yet Maurice looked up and stared directly at her immediately she walked through the gate. For a minute his expression was unchanged, then his face softened. He smiled broadly, dropped the secateurs into a trug and held both hands out to Maisie as he walked toward her.

"Ah, Maisie. It has taken you a long time to come to me, yes?"

"Yes, Maurice. I need to talk to you."

"I know, my dear. I know. Shall we walk? I'll not offer you tea, as your dear father will have had you swimming in the liquid by now."

"Yes. Yes, let's walk."

Together they passed through the second latched gate at the far end of the garden, and then walked toward the apple orchards. Maisie unfolded the story of Christopher Davenham, of his wife Celia, the poor departed Vincent, and how she had first heard about The Retreat.

"So, you have followed your nose, Maisie. And the only 'client' in the case is this Christopher Davenham?"

"Yes. Well, Lady Rowan is a sort of client now, because of James. But we always took on other cases, didn't we? Where we felt truth was asking for our help."

"Indeed. Yes, indeed. But remember, Maisie, remember, truth also came to us as individuals so that we might have a more intimate encounter with the self. Remember the Frenchwoman, Mireille – we both know that my interest in the case came from the fact that she reminded me of my grandmother. There was something there for me to discover about myself, not simply the task of solving a case that the authorities could not begin to comprehend. Now you, Maisie, what is there here for you?" Maurice pointed a finger and touched the place where Maisie's heart began to beat quickly. "What is there in your heart that needs to be given light and understanding?"

"I've come to terms with the war, Maurice. I'm a different person now," Maisie protested.

The two walked on through the apple trees. Maisie was dressed for the heat and wore a cream linen skirt with a long, sailor-collared linen blouse and a cream hat to shield her sensitive skin from the beating sun, yet she was still far too warm.

When they had walked for more than an hour, Maurice led them back to the dower house and into the cool drawing room. The room was furnished tastefully, with chairs covered in soft green floral fabrics of summer weight. Matching curtains seemed to reflect the abundant garden with foxgloves, hollyhocks, and delphiniums framing the exterior of the dower house windows. As the winter months drew in, the light materials would be changed, with heavy green velvet curtains and chair covers bringing a welcome warmth to the room. For now the room was light and airy, and bore the faint aroma of potpourri.

Some indication of Maurice's travels was present in the form of artworks and ornaments. And if one went into Maurice's study, adjacent to the drawing room, there were two framed letters on the wall from the governments of France and Britain, thanking Dr Maurice Blanche for his special services during the Great War of 1914–18.

"I am expecting a visitor this evening, for sherry and some reminiscences. The Chief Constable of Kent, an old friend. I will ask him about this Retreat, Maisie. I believe and trust your instincts. Go there tomorrow, proceed with the plan you have outlined to me, and let us speak again tomorrow evening after dinner – no doubt you will dine with your dear father – and let us also look again at your notes, to see what else speaks to us from the pages."

Maisie nodded agreement. A feeling of anticipation and joy welled up inside her as she realized how very lonely it had been working without Maurice. Before she left the house, Maurice insisted that Maisie wait for one minute.

"A new book. I thought you might be interested. *All Quiet on the Western Front*. It has just been published. You have no doubt read reviews and commentary about it."

Maisie raised an eyebrow, though she would never ignore a recommendation from Maurice Blanche.

"Remember, Maisie, while there is always a victor and a vanquished, on both sides there are innocents. Few are truly evil and they do not need a war to be at work among us, although war provides them with a timely mask."

"Yes, I suppose you are right there, Maurice. I'll read it. Thank you. And I'll see you tomorrow when I get back from The Retreat."

As Maisie turned to walk down the path and across the garden to the stables and groom's cottage, Maurice stopped her.

"And Maisie, when you visit The Retreat, consider the nature of a mask. We all have our masks, Maisie."

Maisie Dobbs held the book tightly in her hand, nodded, and waved to Maurice Blanche.

CHAPTER TWENTY-THREE

*O*n a bright sunny day The Retreat seemed truly to live up
to its name, a place that would afford one sweet respite
from the cares of the world. As she drew up at the Gothic
cast-iron gate with a pillar of rough stone at either side, Maisie could
see through the railings to the sun-drenched farm beyond. The road
leading from the entrance to the front of the house was dusty, causing a rippled haze of heat to work its way up toward a blue sky dot-
ted with only a few cotton wool clouds.

In the distance she could see a large medieval country farmhouse
fronted by apple orchards. A high brick wall restricted further inspection of The Retreat, but as she regarded the subject of her investigation and imagination, she noticed in front of her the pink and red
blooms of roses that had grown furiously upward on the other side of
the wall and now seemed to be clambering toward her, to freedom.
Each bloom nodded up and down in the breeze, and in that moment
the wave of roses reminded Maisie of the men who scrambled from a
mud-soaked hell of trenches over the top and into battle. Bleeding
from their wounds, millions of young men had died on the sodden
ground and barbed wire of no-man's land.

Maisie closed and opened her eyes again quickly to extinguish the images that presented themselves so readily in her mind's eye and had been haunting her since she had torn at the weeds on Don's grave at Nether Green Cemetery. She reminded herself that she could not afford to be distracted or influenced by her memories.

Maisie was leaning back against the MG's door, looking up at the gates, when a man walked through a smaller pedestrian entrance built into the wall. "Can I help you, Ma'am?"

"Oh yes indeed. Is this The Retreat?"

"Yes it is. And what might your business be here today?"

Maisie smiled at the man and approached him. He was tall and thin, with hair that seemed to be grey before its time. She was about to reply when she saw the long, livid scar running from his forehead across his nose and down to his jaw. There was no left eye where the left eye should have been, not even a glass one. The socket was laid bare, defiantly. And as Maisie looked into the right eye of the disfigured man she saw that he dared her to turn away. She met the man's gaze directly.

"I have written but have received no reply, so I decided to visit without an appointment. It's about my brother. I understand that he might stay here, at The Retreat, until he is healed."

And remembering how Celia Davenham so delicately touched her own face when speaking of Vincent's wounds, Maisie brought her fingers to her left cheek, mirroring the unseen pain of the wounded man before her. He visibly took a deep breath, and waited a second before replying. "You've come to the right place, Ma'am. Wait here and I'll be back in ten minutes. Mr . . . er . . . Major Jenkins is who you need to see, and I'll have to get permission."

Maisie nodded, smiled, and said she would be glad to wait. He hurried back through the pedestrian entrance and, taking a bicycle that had been leaning on the other side of the wall, raced along the driveway toward the house. Maisie squinted to watch as the man, now a speck in the distance, stood the bicycle by a door at the side of the house, then ran inside. Five minutes later the speck came running out of the door, took up the bicycle, and grew larger in her vision as he neared the front gate once more.

"You can come in and meet Major Jenkins, Ma'am. I'll open the gate for you. Drive slowly to the front of the house and park your motor by the big fallen tree on the gravel there. Major Jenkins is waiting for you."

"Thank you, Mr . . ."

Maisie held her head to one side, seeking a name.

"Archie, Ma'am."

"Thank you, Mr Archie. Thank you."

"Actually, it's just Archie Ma'am. We don't use surnames here."

"Oh, I see. Thank you, Archie. Is 'Jenkins' the major's Christian name?"

The man's face reddened, except for the scar, which became pale as the surrounding skin heated.

"No. 'Jenkins' is the major's surname."

"Ah," said Maisie, "I see."

Maisie started the MG and drove to the gravel by the fallen tree as instructed. As she applied the handbrake the door of the car was opened by a man who wore beige jodhpurs, a white shirt and tall leather riding boots, and carried a baton.

"Miss Dobbs, I understand. I'm Major Jenkins."

Maisie took the hand offered to balance her as she got out of the car. Jenkins was of average height and build, with dark brown hair, brown eyes and pale skin that did not seem to match his hair and eye colouring. His hair was so neatly swept back that ridges left by his comb reminded Maisie of a freshly ploughed field. She quickly regarded his face, looking for the scars of war, but there were none. None that were visible.

"Thank you, Major Jenkins. No doubt Archie told you why I am here. Perhaps you could tell me more about The Retreat."

"Indeed. Do come to my office, and we'll have tea and a talk about what we are trying to do here."

Jenkins sat in the Queen Anne chair opposite Maisie, who was seated in an identical chair. Tea had been brought earlier by Richard, another man who seemed not yet to be thirty, who had worked hard to mouth words of greeting to Maisie, his shell-blasted jawbone moving awkwardly as he made an enormous effort to physically frame the sounds that came forth from his throat.

For her part Maisie did not draw back from the men at The Retreat, although she was sure she was not seeing those with the more devastating wounds. She had seen such wounds when freshly shattered bone and skin still clung to the men's faces, and scars were the best outcome to be hoped for.

"I read about it, in fact," said Jenkins, "then went over to France to have a look for myself. It seemed that these French chappies had a cracking good idea – provide a place of refuge for the men whose faces were altered, or taken, by war. It was certainly not the easiest thing to get going especially as, just after the war, many of the men here had such terrible injuries."

"What happened to them?"

"Frankly, for some it was just too much – bad enough having the wounds in the first place, but being young and having the girls turn away, not being able to go out without people staring, that sort of thing. To tell you the truth, we lost some – but of course we were their last chance of a bearable life anyway."

Jenkins leaned forward to offer Maisie a biscuit, which she declined with a wave of her hand. He nodded and set the plate down on the tray again.

"Of course, for most of our guests, being here helps. The men have no fear of sitting out in the sun, enjoying life outside. The physical work is good for them. Makes them feel better about themselves. No sitting around in bath chairs and blankets here. We go into Sevenoaks to the pictures occasionally – it's dark in the picture house, no one can see."

"And how long does a patient stay here?"

"Not 'patient,' Miss Dobbs. 'Guest.' We call them guests."

"What about the first names only, Major Jenkins?"

"Ah yes. Reminds them of better times, before they became pawns in the game of war. Millions of khaki ants clambering over the hill and into oblivion. The familiarity of using Christian names only is in stark contrast to the discipline of the battlefield, of this terrible experience. Relinquishing the surname reminds them of what's really important. Which is who they are inside, here." He held his hand to the place just below his rib cage to indicate the centre of his body. "Inside. Who they are inside. The war took so much away."

Maisie nodded accord and sipped her tea. Maurice had always encouraged judicious use of both words and silence.

"Now then. Your brother?"

"Yes, Billy. He wasn't injured facially, Major Jenkins. But he walks with some difficulty and has been so very . . . very . . . unwell. Yes, unwell, since the war."

"Commission?"

"Commission, Major Jenkins?"

"Yes, is he a captain, a second lieutenant?"

"Oh. Actually, Billy was a soldier, a corporal when he was injured."

"Where?"

"The Battle of Messines."

"Oh God. Poor man."

"Yes. Billy saw more than enough. But then they all saw more than enough, didn't they Major Jenkins? Major Jenkins, why is Billy's rank important?"

"Oh, it's not important really. Just enables me get a sense of what he might have experienced."

"And how might that have been different for Billy than for, let's say yourself, Major?"

"It's just that we have found that men have different experiences of recovery."

"Are you a doctor?"

"No, Miss Dobbs. Simply a man who wanted to do some good for the men who gave their identity for the good of the country and returned to a people who would rather see their heroes walking tall, or at best limping, than bearing the scars caused by our leaders' ill-conceived decisions."

Maisie took another sip of tea and nodded. It was a fair comment.

She left The Retreat thirty minutes later after a tour of the premises. She had been escorted to her car by Jenkins, who watched as she made her way to the gate at a very sedate five miles per hour, the gravel crackling under the tyres like sporadic gunfire.

Archie waited for her, touched his forehead in a partial salute as she approached, and leaned down toward her open window as she drew alongside him.

"So, what do you think? Will your brother be joining us, Ma'am?"

"Yes. Yes I think so, Archie. I believe it would do him a power of good."

"Righty-o. We'll look forward to seeing him then. Hold on while I open the gate."

Maisie waved as she pulled out onto the road, the roses once again nodding in the breeze as Archie waved her on her way.

While she hadn't flinched or drawn back from his wounds, Maisie felt the discomfort of Archie's injury. The sun shone through the windscreen of the MG, its heat and brightness causing her eyes to smart and a sharp pain to move from the socket of her left eye to a place on her forehead. The body empathizing with another's pain, thought Maisie. The subconscious mind alerting her to Archie's agony, though she had been successful in appearing to ignore the scar and empty eye socket.

Maisie didn't go far. Stopping once again in Westerham, she sat on a bench in the old churchyard, took the notebook out of her handbag and began to write an account of her visit.

A walk through the grounds of The Retreat accompanied by Major Jenkins had revealed very little to her that she did not already know, only now she was familiar with the extent of the house, where the "guest" rooms were and how the farm worked.

There were twenty-five guests living in the main house and an old oasthouse, no longer used for drying hops. Though converted to living quarters years before, the oasthouse still bore the strong peppery aroma of warm hops.

The youngest man she met must have been thirty, which meant that he had been shipped to France at about the age of seventeen. The eldest was no more than forty. Questioning Jenkins, Maisie had learned that although the guests were free to come and go at will, most remained, comfortable in the freedom from stares The Retreat afforded them.

Though the farm was to a large extent self-sufficient, each guest entrusted his personal savings to The Retreat, to draw upon for expenses beyond those of day-to-day living, and to contribute to the cost of helpers. If the farm's produce was bringing in a tidy sum, and providing much of the food, the pooled savings must have earned interest and amounted to a pretty penny in someone's bank account. The thought troubled Maisie.

The needs of the guests seemed to be few. There was no doctor on the staff to provide for the physical care of those living with such terrible wounds, and no seasoned professional used to dealing with the emotional needs of those traumatized by war. Some of the men still wore the tin masks that had been provided for them when first recovering from their wounds. But the fine glaze used on tin moulded to fit a face ten years younger now provided little respite from the mirror's reflection.

Maisie questioned Jenkins's approach. True, it seemed a benevolent idea, and she knew how successful the "holiday camps" had been in France, providing a resting place for wounded men struggling to return to peacetime life. But if The Retreat had been inspired initially by the success of an idea born of compassion, what fuel drove the engine now? The war was almost eleven years past. Then again, those who lived with its memory were still very much alive.

What about Jenkins? How and where had he served? Clearly the men at The Retreat were troubled as a result of their wounds and their memories. But Jenkins's soul was troubled in a way that was different. Maisie suspected that his wounds lay deep within.

James would soon be going to The Retreat so she had to act quickly. It was time to go back to London. Archie thought that The Retreat would do her "brother" a world of good. She wondered how Billy Beale would feel about his newfound siblinghood and if, in a month, he would feel as if time in the country had done him a power of good.

CHAPTER TWENTY-FOUR

"So what you think is that this Jenkins feller is getting up to no good down there at this Retreat 'e's set up?"

Billy Beale sat in the chair in front of Maisie Dobbs, his hands working around and around the fabric on the perimeter of his cap, which he had taken off when he came to answer Maisie's call. Maisie had lost no time in telling Billy Beale why he had been summoned, and how she needed him to help her.

"Yes I do, Billy. I would only need you to be there for a week, no, let's say two weeks. To let me know what is happening, what you see."

"Well, you've come to the right person if you want someone what's willing. But I'm not sure I'm your man. Not as if I'm a toff, to mix with the likes of them."

"Billy. You don't need to be a toff. You just need to have some money —"

"And that's even bloomin' funnier. Money — the likes of me!"

"It's taken care of, Billy. As soon as you are accepted as a guest at The Retreat, a sum will be moved from your bank account to Major Adam Jenkins's account."

Billy Beale looked at Maisie and winked. "And I bet I know who's got me a bank account I never 'ad before in me life."

"Yes. It was arranged today."

Suddenly Billy was quiet. He looked again at his cloth cap, and sat with obvious discomfort in the too-small chair opposite Maisie's desk. It was the end of another humid day in London: the summer of 1929 was breaking records for lack of rain and for heat.

"I'd do anything for you, Miss. I said that when you moved in 'ere to run yer business. I've seen you work all hours 'ere. And I've seen 'ow you 'elp people."

Billy tapped the side of his nose in his usual conspiratorial fashion.

"What you do isn't what you'd call regular. I can see that. And if this 'elps someone, then I'm your man. Like I said before. You 'elped me Miss, when you weren't more than a girl. I remember."

"It could be risky, Billy. I believe this Jenkins is a troubled man, and possibly a dangerous one."

"No. Don't you worry about me. You've explained it all very well. I understand what's involved, Miss. And it won't take me long to set up a line for us, soon as I get the lay of the land. Now then. Let's look at that map again. Mind you —"

Billy rose to look down at the map that Maisie had spread out on the table.

"Just as well the missus is taking the nippers down to 'er sister's in 'astings. You reckon we leave tomorrow?"

"The sooner the better, Billy. Let's go over the plan again, and the story. We'll leave for Chelstone tomorrow. We'll be seeing Maurice Blanche in the afternoon. He has been seeking some additional information for us from one of his contacts."

"And who might that be, if I may ask?"

"The Chief Constable of Kent."

"Bloody 'ell . . ."

"Quite, Billy. Now then William Dobbs, we expect a letter from The Retreat to arrive at Chelstone by Friday, so we can drive over on

Saturday. The other gentleman I told you about, who must not see me or know that I am involved in anything to do with The Retreat, will be taking up residence in just a few weeks. I hope to have this . . . this . . . investigation concluded by that time."

"Right you are, Miss. I'd better be getting 'ome then. Got to pack me ol' kit bag again, for the good of me country."

"Dr Blanche has arranged for your clothes, Billy."

"It wasn't clothes I was going to pack, Sis," said Billy, with an impish smile, "You don't mind if I call you Sis, get used to it like? I need to pack the other bits and pieces of kit I'll be needing for this job."

Maisie looked up at Billy Beale and smiled.

"This is good of you Billy. You were the only person I could ask. I can't tell you how much I appreciate it. Your help will not go unrewarded."

"It already 'as been rewarded. Been getting a bit bored around 'ere anyway. I need a change."

Maisie lingered for a while in the office before leaving, closing the door behind her and making her way along the hallway to another unmarked door. Here she took a key from her pocket and entered the room. Home. She had moved a few weeks before, when it was clear that she needed to be closer to her work. The bed-sitting-room was small, but all that she required was within the walls of this room. And when she needed some respite from the dour familiarity of such spartan accommodation, there was usually an invitation to stay at Ebury Place, or she would go down to Chelstone, to spend time in the calm and comforting company of her father.

"There. Reckon I've got everything."

Billy Beale placed one more bag in the luggage compartment of Lady Rowan's car and stood to watch Maisie, who was securing her navy blue beret with a long pearl-headed pin. Her corduroy jacket had been thrown around the back of the driver's seat, giving the impression of a rather stout old man who had just sat down. An observer might have considered the young woman "fast," for today Maisie was wearing a pair of long beige cuffed trousers, with a linen blouse and brown walking shoes.

Maisie looked at her watch and took her place in the driver's seat of the MG.

"Good. Not too late. We'd better get a move on. We need to be at Chelstone by noon."

Billy Beale hesitated.

"What is it, Billy?"

"Nothing really, Miss . . . it's just that . . ." He took the cap from his head and looked up at the sky. "It's just that this is the first time I've left London since I got back from the war. Couldn't face it. O' course the missus 'as been away with the nippers. Been down to Kent with 'er people 'op-picking, and o' course to 'er sister's in 'astings. But not me, Miss."

Maisie said nothing, made no response. She understood the power of reflection well, and as she had done with Celia Davenham just a few short weeks before, she made no move to soothe Billy Beale, allowing him the time he needed to step into the car.

"But you never know, at least I might get a good night's sleep down there in the country." Still he hesitated.

"What do you mean, Billy?"

Maisie shielded her eyes from the morning sun as she looked up at him.

Billy sighed deeply, took a breath, opened the car door and sat down on the passenger seat. The claret leather of the hardly used seat creaked as Billy moved to make himself comfortable.

"Just can't sleep, Miss. Not for long anyway. 's'bin like that since I got 'ome from France. That many years ago. Soon as I close my eyes, it all comes back."

He looked into the distance as if into the past.

"Blimey, I can almost smell the gas, can 'ardly breathe at times. If I fall asleep straight away I only wake up fighting for breath. And the pounding in my 'ead. You never forget that pounding, the shells. Mind you, you know that, don't you Miss?"

And as he spoke Maisie remembered her homecoming, remembered Maurice taking her again to see Khan, who seemed never to age. In her mind's eye she saw herself sitting with Khan and telling her story, and Maurice sitting with her.

Khan spoke of bearing witness to the pain of another's memories, a ritual as old as time itself, then asked her to tell her story again. And again. And again. She told her story until, exhausted, she had no more story to tell. And Maisie remembered Khan's words, that this nightmare was a dragon that would remain alive, but dormant, waiting insidiously to wake and breathe its fire until she squarely faced the truth of what had happened to Simon.

"You all right, Miss?"

Billy Beale placed a hand on Maisie's shoulder for just a second.

"Yes, yes, I was just thinking about what you said, Billy. So what do you do when you cannot sleep?"

Billy looked down at his hands and began pulling at the lining of his cap, running the seam between the forefinger and thumb of each hand.

"I get up, so's not to wake the missus. Then I go out. Walking the streets. For hours sometimes. And you know what, Miss? It's not only me, Miss. There's a lot of men I see, 'bout my age, walking the streets. And we all know, Miss, we all know who we are. Old soldiers what keep seeing the battle. That's what we are, Miss. I tell you, sometimes I think we're like the waking dead. Livin' our lives during the day, normal like, then trying to forget something what 'appened years ago. It's like going to the picture 'ouse, only the picture's all in me 'ead."

Maisie inclined her head to show understanding, her silence respectful of Billy's terrible memories, and of this confidence shared. And once again she was drawn back, to that year in the wards after her return from France, working to comfort the men whose minds were ravaged by war. Small comfort indeed. Yet for every one who could not bring his mind back from the last vision of a smoke-filled hell there were probably dozens like Billy, living now as good father, good husband, good son, good man, but who feared the curtains drawn against darkness, and the light extinguished at the end of the day.

"Ready, Billy?" Maisie asked when Billy put the cap firmly back on his head.

"Reckon I am, Miss. Yes, I reckon I am. Do me the world of good will this, Miss. Bein' useful like."

They spoke little on the journey to Kent. Occasionally Maisie asked Billy questions as they drove along the winding country roads. She wanted to make doubly sure that he understood everything that was required of him. Information. She needed more information. A feel for the place. How did it work when you were on the inside? Was anything amiss?

She spoke to him of intuition, abbreviating the teaching she had received from Maurice and Khan many years before.

"You must listen to the voice inside, Billy," said Maisie, placing her hand on her middle. "Remember even the smallest sensation of unease, for it could well be significant."

Billy had been quick to learn, quick to understand that his impressions were important, just as relevant as facts on a page. As Maisie knew from their first meeting, Billy Beale was sharp, an acute observer of circumstances and people. He was just what she needed. And he was willing.

But was it fair to draw Billy into her work? If she thought that Vincent's death was questionable, was it right to involve Billy? Then again, he would not be at The Retreat for long. And they would be in daily contact. She had promised Maurice that as soon as she had gathered enough information she would refer her findings to the authorities – if what she found required it.

Maisie knew that her curiosity was drawing both Billy and herself deeper into the mystery of Vincent. And even as she drove she closed her eyes briefly and prayed for the confidence and courage to face whatever was hidden in the darkness.

CHAPTER TWENTY-FIVE

*M*aisie parked the car outside the dower house and led Billy into Maurice Blanche's home, to introduce her old teacher to her new assistant, and to have lunch together before she and Billy proceeded to The Retreat.

They talked about The Retreat, and Billy added weight to Maisie's earlier deliberations about the naming of this place where the wounded of a war over ten years past still sought refuge.

"O' course, it might not be just The Retreat, you know, as in gettin' away from it all into shelter. There's 'The Retreat,' in't there? You know, the bugle call at sunset. S'pose you'd 'ave to be an army man to know that, eh? Like 'retreating from a position' as well. That's what we should've done many a time – would've saved a few lives, and that's a fact."

Maisie set down her knife and fork and nodded thoughtfully.

The Retreat, the ultimate play on words to describe a place for the wounded. But what happened if someone wanted to retreat, as it were, from The Retreat?

"Maisie, while you are visiting your father, before you and

Mr Beale – or perhaps I should say 'Dobbs' to get him used to the name – anyway, before you depart for The Retreat I will walk with Mr Beale in the meadow, just beyond the orchard."

Maisie knew that this was not a chance suggestion and watched the two men walk toward the meadow, heads together in conversation, the younger man ever so slightly ready to steady the older man lest he falter. If only he knew, she thought, how much the old man feared the faltering of the younger.

As soon as they returned, Maisie took Billy to The Retreat, but before entering she drove around the perimeter of the estate and parked under the shade of a beech tree.

"It's a retreat all right, ain't it, Miss? Pity they don't allow visitors for the first month. Wonder what they'll say when I tell them I'm out after two weeks? Prob'ly be a bit upset with me, eh Miss?"

Billy surveyed the landscape, the fencing, the road, and the distances between landmarks.

"Look, 'ere's what I think. No point trying to get all fancy here, rigging up lines to, y'know, communicate. Why don't I just meet you at the same time every evening by that bit of fence there, and tell you what I know."

"Well, Billy, it seemed as if we had a good plan, for your safety that is."

"Don't you worry about me. From what you've said, I don't think I'm that important to the likes of them. I'm just your average bread and butter, aren't I? No big legacies being signed over or anything."

Billy smiled at Maisie and pointed towards the fields between the large house in the distance, and the road.

"Tell you the truth, looking at this landscape now, it's best if we don't mess around with telephone lines coming too near the 'ouse. Draw more attention. No one's goin' to question an old soldier what wants to go off by 'imself for a jaunt of an evenin'. But they might question an old sapper fiddling around with a telephone line in the dark. And you know Miss, I might be good at that sort of thing, but I never did say I was invisible. And I can't run like I used to, not with the leg 'ere." Billy slapped the side of his leg for emphasis. "But 'ere's what I can do now. I can rig up a line to that telephone box we just passed back there, on the corner as you leave the 'amlet. I 'ad a quick look as we drove by – not that I 'ad much time, what with the speed and all –"

Maisie grimaced at Billy, who continued. "It's one of them new ones, a Kiosk Number Four, I think. They 'ave em in places where there ain't no post office – did y'see? It's got a stamp machine on the back, and a pillar box for letters. Sort of all purpose – mind you, me mate what works on the things says that the stamps get soggy when it rains, and then they all stick together and make a right old mess. So, anyway, getting' back to me and the old lines 'ere, if I need to get 'old of you urgent like, or if I'm in an 'urry to get out of 'ere, I can always jump through this fence – well, sort of jump, what wiv the leg and all – and use the box and line what I rig up to connect with the outside line at that box up the road. D'you see what I mean, Miss? Then I'll run like a nutter, bad leg an' all!"

Maisie laughed nervously. "Right you are, Billy, I think I follow you. It sounds like a good idea."

Billy opened the car door, pulled himself out of the low seat, and walked around to the luggage compartment. He carefully took out two large old canvas kit bags and placed them on the ground. Taking out spools of cable, "small, so's I can work with them on me own," Billy walked over to the ditch at the base of the perimeter fence.

Moving aside grasses and wildflowers growing innocently at the side of the road, Billy began to unwind the cable into the ditch, moving away from Maisie who remained in the car. It was a quiet thoroughfare, so they had little to fear from passing traffic, but nevertheless, country folk were apt to be inquisitive about two strangers lingering on the road. Especially if one were seen unravelling cable.

Maisie got out of the car and walked over to the fence, looking out over the land belonging to The Retreat. The perimeter fence, six feet high and topped with barbed wire, would merge into a stone wall just half a mile along in the opposite direction to the line being laid out by

Billy. The main gate was situated another half mile away from the beginning of the wall. Eventually Billy returned.

"Nicely done, and quick too. Managed to save meself some work by using the bottom wire of this 'ere fence." Billy pulled back the grass to point to the wire in question. "I hear that's what they've done over there in America, y'know – used the fences on farms to make connections between places, like." Billy pushed back his cap, and wiped the back of his hand across his forehead. "Stroke of luck it bein' there – the telephone – see more of them in the towns, don't you? S'pose it's used by them what live in the terraced cottages in the 'amlet. I tell you, no one will see that line, believe you me."

Billy caught his breath, and for the first time Maisie heard the wheezing that revealed gas-damaged lungs. "You shouldn't be running like that, Billy."

"I'm alright, Miss. Now to this end." Billy held up a telephone receiver. "The old 'dog and bone,' Miss. We used to say in the trenches that them as is on the end of the line only bloomin' 'ear 'alf of what's said – and then only what they want to 'ear anyway. Personally, meself, I reckon it's a poor old situation when you 'ave to make out a person's intentions from their voice in a tin cup."

Billy worked on as he spoke, wiring the receiver to a metal box he placed in the ditch before leaning in and connecting lines. He picked up the receiver, turned the dial and listened. The operator answered his request for a connection, charges to go to the recipient of the call, and put him through to Maurice's telephone number. They spoke briefly before Billy replaced the receiver on its cradle.

"I know it's not perfect, and it takes a bit o' time, but it might come in 'andy, you never know."

After ensuring that their makeshift telephone was hidden and secure, Billy then cut into the wire of the perimeter fence, forming a "door" through which he could escape, should escape become necessary. He secured the door with spare wire to camouflage the fact that the fence had been tampered with.

The first part of their task finished, Maisie and Billy loaded up the car again and drove slowly toward the main entrance to The Retreat. They said little, only speaking to confirm the time at which they would meet each evening.

Billy would take a solitary stroll at seven o'clock, which would bring him to the fence by the large beech tree at half past seven. Maisie would be waiting to meet with him for just a few moments, then he would make his way back to the main house. In all other dealings with the residents of The Retreat there was to be nothing about him that could be remarked upon. He was to be invisible but for the bed he slept in and the food he consumed. But he was to watch, and listen and report back to Maisie.

"Welcome back to The Retreat, Miss Dobbs," said Archie as he opened the gate.

He walked toward the car, leaned down so that his face was alongside the passenger window, and addressed Billy.

"William, isn't it? The major is waiting to welcome you personally to The Retreat."

Billy Beale took the proffered hand and seemed not to see the terrible scars that had changed Archie's countenance for ever. Maisie nodded to Archie and moved the car slowly along the driveway.

"Poor bleedin' bugger – oh, I am sorry, Miss – I forget meself at times. Least I can get about and no one worries about a bit of a limp. Blimey, that poor feller, with that face. Not that I 'aven't seen worse. Just not seen it for a long time, not close up. That's all."

Maisie slowed the car even more. "Billy, if you have any doubts –"

"Not likely," said Billy, straightening his shoulders. "If there's any funny business going on here that can cause any more damage to these poor blighters, then I want to do my bit to stop it." He paused to look at Maisie. "Can't blame them for wanting to get away, can you?"

"No, you can't. But there's a lot that can be done for them now."

"Not when you've been through what they've been through. Just want to be left alone 'alf the time, I should think, never mind being messed around with by newfangled ideas of skin medicine and what 'ave you."

The car drew alongside the main building as Adam Jenkins, the major, came through the front door and down the steps towards them.

"Ah, William. Welcome to The Retreat. I am sure you will be comfortable here. Come into my study for tea, then we can get you settled later."

Adam Jenkins led the way, his white shirt once again crisply laundered, leather riding boots polished to a blinding shine, and not a hair out of place. He invited Maisie and Billy to take a seat, standing behind Maisie's chair to hold it for her, then indicating, with a nonchalant sweep of his hand, the seat by the window for Billy.

How strange, thought Maisie, that he should direct Billy to a seat that took the full strength of the late-afternoon sun, rays that would cause Billy to become hot and uncomfortable, and to have to shield his eyes with the hand that he would need to reach out for the teacup as it was offered to him. Strange to unsettle a person so.

Billy met Maisie's look and raised an eyebrow. He knows, thought Maisie. He knows that Jenkins has placed him by the window on purpose.

Ten minutes of seemingly purposeless conversation had been exchanged between Jenkins and Maisie. As befitting his character – the tired veteran of a war over ten years past – Billy was silent. And hot. Maisie looked at Billy again. She saw the perspiration on his brow, his discomfort as he ran the forefinger of his right hand along the edge of his shirt collar.

Jenkins suddenly directed his attention away from Maisie towards Billy. "My dear man. How remiss of me. How utterly stupid. Move over to this other chair and into the cool of the room immediately."

Jenkins put down his cup and used one hand to beckon Billy away from the window seat, and the other to indicate another seat.

Interesting, thought Maisie. A small gesture, but a subtle and significant one. Was it a ploy to begin to inspire Billy's trust? Placing himself immediately in the role of saviour, and of one prepared to acknowledge a mistake. Or was Adam Jenkins genuinely admitting an error of judgment? Was this opening of his outstretched arms a move to render Billy more comfortable in another seat, an act of genuine concern? Or was it perhaps a deliberate action to draw Billy into his circle of admirers? Arms spread wide to bring him within the force of his influence.

Maisie watched Jenkins carefully while attending to the business of afternoon tea. In her work with Maurice, Maisie had learned much about the charm and charisma of the natural leader which, taken to an extreme, can become dictatorial and vindictive. Was Adam Jenkins such a man? Or an enlightened and concerned soul?

"Well, it's time to get some pawprints on the page, don't you think?" said Jenkins. He glanced at his watch, stood up and walked over to a large heavily carved desk. The top was covered in rich brown leather, and only one plain manila file sat waiting for attention on top of a wooden board. He opened the file, checked the papers within, took a fountain pen from the inside pocket of his light linen jacket and returned to the chair next to Maisie.

"We have received the necessary documents – thank you, Miss Dobbs – pertaining to the financial arrangements." He turned to Billy. "And I know you completely understand the commitment we request upon taking up residence at The Retreat, William. Now, perhaps you would be so kind as to sign here."

He placed the papers on the wooden board to provide a stable writing surface and passed them to Billy, tapping the place for signature with his forefinger.

After Billy carefully wrote "William Dobbs" in the space indicated, Jenkins rang the bell for an assistant to escort Billy to his quarters, and as he did so Billy winked at Maisie. Yet when Jenkins turned back to the two supposed siblings, he saw only the blank resignation of the man, and the worry etched in the face of his sister. But Maisie's concern was no act. She *was* worried for Billy. She had to ensure that he was at The Retreat not a moment longer than necessary.

CHAPTER TWENTY-SIX

*M*aisie waited anxiously at Maurice Blanche's cottage. Billy had been at The Retreat for three days, and each evening at seven o'clock Maisie set off in Lady Rowan's MG, along country lanes filled with the lingering aroma of Queen Anne's Lace and privet, to meet Billy Beale by the perimeter fence, across the road from the ancient beech tree.

Each evening, with summer midges buzzing around her head, she watched as Billy approached. First she would see his head bobbing up and down in the distance, as he walked across the fallow fields of tall grass. Then as he came closer, his wheaten hair reflected the setting sun, and Maisie wondered why no one noticed Billy Beale taking a walk each evening.

"Evenin', Miss," said Billy as he curled back the fence wire and clambered through.

"Billy, how are you?" As always, Maisie was both relieved and delighted to see Billy. "You've caught the sun, Billy," she remarked.

"Reckon I 'ave at that, Miss." Billy rubbed at his cheeks. "All this workin' on the land, that's what's done it."

"And how is it, the working on the land?"

"'Not bad at all, Miss. And it seems to do these lads good. You should see some of them. Seems they were right down in the dumps when they came 'ere. Then slowly like, the work and the fact that no one looks twice at 'em starts to give 'em the, you know, the sort of confidence they need."

"Nothing unusual, Billy?"

"Can't say as there is, Miss. Not that I can go around asking questions, but I keep me eyes open, and it seems like it's all on the up and up. The major is a funny bloke, but 'e's doing 'is bit, i'n'e? And now that there's space 'ere, what with some fellers gone, they're taking other blokes with other injuries, not just to the face and 'ead, like. But you know that, don't you, otherwise I wouldn't be 'ere, not with this fine lookin' physog."

Billy grinned at Maisie and rubbed his chin.

"Quite, Billy. So is everyone happy there?"

"I should say so, Miss. Not much to dislike, is there? Mind you, there is one bloke, has some terrible scars on his face, just 'ere."

Billy turned his head to the right and with the forefinger of his left hand indicated a line going from his ear to his jaw, then to his chest. He grimaced, then continued.

"I think 'e's 'ad enough of being out 'ere – says he feels good and well enough to get back to the real world."

"And what does the major say to that?"

"I don't know that 'e's said anything, Miss. I think they like 'em to give it some thought, you know, them as wants to leave."

"What makes you say that? What would stop someone from just leaving? It's in the contract that you can leave when you want."

"Well, what I've 'eard is that some blokes get back their confidence and next thing you know, they want to go back out, face the world. Then when they gets back out they find that it ain't all that rosy, that they get the stares an' all. Apparently that's 'appened a few times, and the blokes topped themselves."

"Is that what you've heard, Billy?"

"'ere and there. You 'ear talk. They think that this feller, who's wanting to get back to what 'e calls the 'real world,' is worrying the major. Seems the major has said 'e's . . . what was it 'e was supposed to 'ave said?"

Billy closed his eyes and scratched the back of his head. As he did so, Maisie saw the red sunburn on his neck, the farm labourer's "collar."

"That's it. The major said 'e's suspectible."

"Do you mean susceptible, Billy?"

Billy smiled again. "Yes, reckon that's it Miss."

"Anything else, Billy?"

"Not really Miss. The major seems a really good bloke, Miss. I don't know what 'appened to those fellers you found out about. P'raps they left and then was the type what couldn't stand up to bein' on the out-side. But I will say this. There's blokes 'ere what love the major, you know. Think 'e's a lifesaver. And I s'pose 'e is really, when you think about it. Given some boys a way of life since the war, boys who thought they didn't 'ave none."

Maisie noted Billy's comments on index cards and nodded her head. Slipping the cards and the pencil into her work-worn black document case with the silver clasp, she looked directly at Billy.

"Same time tomorrow evening, Billy?"

"Yes Miss. Although, Miss . . . can we make it a bit earlier? 'bout 'alf past six? Some of the boys are 'aving a snooker tournament. Like to give it a go if I can. Join in with a bit of fun."

Maisie was silent for some seconds before replying. "Right you are, Billy. But keep your eyes open, won't you?"

"Don't worry, Miss. If there's anything funny goin' on 'ere I'll find out all about it."

Maisie watched as Billy turned and walked through the field again. She walked back across the road, opened the car door and sat down in the driver's seat, leaving the door ajar to watch Billy become but a speck in the distance.

Had she made a mistake? Had her gift, her intuition, played tricks on her? Were the deaths of Vincent – and the other boys who used only one name – suicide? Or simply coincidence? She sighed as she started up the MG again.

Maisie spent her days at Chelstone close to the telephone. She would pass a precious hour or two with her father each day, but quickly returned to the dower house in case she was needed. Together she and Maurice went over old cases for clues and inspiration, and speculated over the details of life at The Retreat.

"I would very much have liked to see the postmortem findings on our friend Vincent and his colleagues."

"I located the inquest proceedings, and it seems that they were all attributed to 'accidental death' in some form or another."

"Indeed, Maisie. But I would like to inspect the details, to observe through the eyes of the pathologist, so that hopefully I might see what he did not. Let's go back over the notes. Who conducted Vincent's postmortem?"

Maisie passed Maurice the report.

"Hmmm. Signed by the coroner, and not the attending pathologist."

Maurice stood up and walked around the room.

"To solve a problem, walk around," he said, noticing her smile.

How often in the past had they worked together in this way, Maisie sitting on the floor, legs crossed in front of her, Maurice in his leather chair. He would get up, pace the floor with his hands together as if in prayer, while Maisie closed her eyes in meditation and breathed deeply, as she had been instructed years ago by Khan.

Suddenly Maurice stopped walking and at almost the same moment, so close that neither would have been able to say who was first, Maisie came to her feet.

"What is it that you find so interesting about the reports, Maisie?"

She looked at Maurice. "It is not the actual contents of the report, Maurice. It is the lack of detail. There's nothing to go on, no loose threads. There's not the slightest particle of information for us to work with."

"Correct. It is too clean. Far too clean. Let me see . . ." Maurice flipped the pages back. "Ah, yes. Let me telephone my friend the chief inspector. He should be able to help me." He looked at the time, it was half past nine in the evening. "Indeed, he should be delighted to help me – his interior will have been warmed by his second single malt of the evening."

Maisie took her place on the cushion again and waited for Maurice. She heard his muffled voice coming from the room next door, the rhythm of his speech not quite English yet not quite Continental. The telephone receiver was replaced on the cradle with an audible thump, and Maurice returned.

"Interesting. Extremely interesting. It seems that the attending pathologist in the case of Vincent, and probably also in the other cases, was on call in the early hours of the morning, with his duty ending at half past eight – and so was able to go to The Retreat immediately after he was summoned. He returned home after completing his cursory examination and writing a brief report. His name, Maisie, is Jenkins. Armstrong Jenkins. Something of a coincidence, I think. And the examination lists time of death at . . . let me see . . . yes, it was at five o'clock in the morning."

"Dawn," said Maisie.

Maisie leafed through the papers that she had spread across Maurice's desk. Her mentor came to her side.

"Maurice. They died at dawn. The time of death for each of the men buried at Nether Green is dawn."

"An almost mystical hour, don't you think Maisie?"

Maurice clasped his hands behind his back and walked to the window.

"A time when the light is most likely to deceive the eye, a time between sleep and waking. A time when a man is likely to be at his weakest. Dawn is a time when soft veils are draped across reality, creating illusion and cheating truth. It is said, Maisie, it is darkest just before dawn."

"So there's still nothing much to tell you, Miss."

Billy Beale stood with his hands in the pockets of his light sailcloth summer trousers and kicked at the dry ground between his feet. He had been at The Retreat for only a week.

"Don't worry, Billy. It wasn't definite that you would find something. You're only going to be here a short time anyway. I just thought that some inside observations might be helpful."

Maisie moved to stand next to Billy, and without his noticing, adopted the same stance. She was wearing trousers again, and a light cotton blouse, so it was easy for her to place her hands in her pockets, emulating Billy's pose exactly.

He's embarrassed about something, thought Maisie. There's something he doesn't want to tell me. As Billy moved in discomfort, so did Maisie. She closed her eyes and felt Billy's dilemma.

"And you think this Adam Jenkins is a good man, do you Billy?"

Billy kicked at the ground again, and though his face was tanned from working on the land, she saw a deep blush move from his chin to his cheeks.

"Well, yes, reckon I do, Miss. And I feel awful, at times. After what 'e's done for them, 'ere I am sniffin' around for something nasty."

"I can see how that might be difficult for you, Billy. You admire Adam Jenkins."

"Yes. Yes, I admire the man."

"That's good, Billy."

Maisie turned to face Billy and with the intensity of her gaze compelled him to look back at her.

"That's good. That you admire the man. It'll make your time here easier, and what I ask you to do easier."

"'ow do you mean?"

"Just go about your business, Billy. Just go about doing what you have to do here. You don't have to do anything other than be yourself. Although I do request two things: that we keep to our evening meetings, that's one. The other is that you take care to maintain your assumed name. Do not give anything away. Is that clear?"

Billy relaxed as Maisie spoke to him and nodded his head.

"I just want to know about your days. That's all, Billy. Then next week I'll come and collect you. In fact, I'll come tomorrow if you want."

"No. No, miss. I'll stay on as we agreed. Don't expect I'll find anything, though. These 'ere meetings might get a bit boring."

Maisie nodded her head and continued to mirror Billy's movements with her own.

"Just one more thing, Billy. About the man who wanted to leave. Remember, you told me about him? What's happened to him?"

"Can't say as I've seen 'im for a day or so. Mind you, that's not unusual, if one of the fellers wants to 'ave a bit of time alone. Like they do."

Billy stopped speaking, kicked his feet at the ground, then looked up at Maisie.

"What is it, Billy?"

"Just a thought, though. So keen to leave, 'e was. End of the month, 'e said. Wouldn't think 'e wanted any time to 'imself, now I come to think about it."

Maisie made no move to agree or disagree. "Like I said, Billy. You don't need to go snooping around. Just meet me here every day."

"Right you are, Miss. Now then. Best be going, before I'm missed."

Maisie waited a second before responding to Billy's movement toward the fence.

"Billy . . ."

"Yes, Miss?"

With his good knee bent, ready to go through the hole in the fence, Billy turned to meet Maisie's direct stare.

"Billy. Don't you think that someone would understand that you just needed some time to yourself – if you're back a bit late, that is?"

"Oh, they might do, Miss," Billy replied thoughtfully. Then with a wink added, "But not when I'm due to defend my snooker title in 'alf an hour."

Maisie smiled as Billy climbed through on to the other side of the fence and secured the wire. But instead of going back to the car, she remained in the same place to watch Billy Beale once again walk across the fields, back to his temporary life at The Retreat.

"Oh, please don't worry about the car, my dear. Heavens above, I can't even drive the thing, not with my hip at the moment. Besides, I think your need is greater than mine, and you are working in my interests."

Maisie had been holding the telephone receiver away from her ear while Lady Rowan spoke, but brought the receiver closer to reply.

"Thank you. I was worried. But I should have it back to you by the middle of next week."

"Right you are. Now, tell me. What's happening? James is due to leave for The Retreat in ten days. And heaven knows he won't be spoken to about anything. Not even by his father. I swear he hasn't been the same since that girl —"

"Yes, Lady Rowan. I know."

"And if it weren't for you, I would be absolutely frantic."

"Lady Rowan, may I speak to Lord Julian please?"

"Yes, yes . . . I know, I am just about to become tedious. He's in his study. I'll just nip next door to get him. Won't wait for Carter, it would take all day."

Maisie smiled. It would probably take a while for Lady Rowan to walk next door to the study to get Lord Julian. She hadn't been able to "nip" anywhere for some time.

Eventually, she heard Lord Julian Compton's voice. "Maisie, what can I do for you?"

"Lord Julian. In confidence."

"Of course."

"I wonder if you could help me with some information that I believe you may be able to obtain for me from your former contacts at the War Office."

"I'll do what I can – what do you need, Maisie?"

"Jenkins. Major Adam Jenkins. I need to see his service record, if at all possible."

"I've already obtained it, m'dear. Didn't like the sound of this Retreat business when I heard about it from James. Got the service record in my office now. Didn't know he called himself Major, though. I only heard him called Jenkins by James."

"The men at The Retreat call him Major."

"That's interesting. Jenkins was just a lieutenant."

"Is there anything else there, Lord Julian? Any other anomalies?"

"Of course a service record is limited. He was discharged though, medical discharge."

"Where to?"

"Craiglockhart."

"Oh."

"Yes. Right up your alley I'd say, Maisie. Mind you, he was a mild case, apparently. Of course I don't have a record of his treatment. Just the notes of his commanding officer. Says that he went gaga after a couple of chaps in his command deserted. Seems to have been an innocuous fellow, quite frankly. Got a commission based on need rather than any military talent, I would say from the record. Officers were dropping like flies, if you remember. Well, of course you remember. Mind you, the chap's obviously got a business head on him, setting up this Retreat."

"The men seem to adore him for what he's done there. Providing a place for them to go," said Maisie.

"Yes, I've got to hand it to him. Now he's opened the doors to those who sustained other injuries. Like James. Bit like a monastery though if you ask me, wanting people to sign over their assets. Mind you, if the idea is a place of refuge for ever . . ."

"Yes."

"Shame, isn't it? That we only like our heroes out in the street when they are looking their best and their uniforms are 'spit and polished,' and not when they're showing us the wounds they suffered on our behalf. Well, anything else m'dear?"

"No. I think that's all. Is there any chance that I might see – ?"

"I'll have it sent down to Chelstone in the morning."

"Thank you, Lord Julian. You've been most helpful."

Maisie had spent most of that day at the dower house with Maurice, taking only a short break to visit Frankie Dobbs. She declined to sleep in the small bedroom that had always been hers at the groom's cottage, instead electing to remain by Maurice's telephone, just in case Billy needed her. Time and again she ran through the details of events and research information she had accumulated.

Adam Jenkins had lied about his status. But was it a lie, or had a man simply called him "major" and it stuck? She remembered her grandfather, working on the Thames boats. People called him The Commander but he had never been in the navy, never commanded anything. It was just a nickname, the source of which had been lost over the years. But how did Jenkins, "an innocuous little man," assume such power? Billy had become a believer, and the men seemed to adore him. Was fear a factor? Was there a deeper connection between Vincent and Jenkins? And what about Armstrong Jenkins? Family member, or coincidence?

She had missed something. Something very significant. And as she re-examined, in her mind's eye, each piece of collected evidence that had led her to this place, she considered Maurice's words and felt as if each day, all day, she was living in the moment before dawn broke. Maisie thought back, to that earlier dawn, more than ten years earlier. The beginning of the end, that was what it had been.

CHAPTER TWENTY-SEVEN

"*T*he time is drawing closer, is it not my dear?" Maurice asked her now. He looked at the grandfather clock, patiently tick-tocking the seconds away.

"Yes it is. Maurice, I want to take Billy out of The Retreat."

"Indeed. Yes. Away from Jenkins. It is interesting, Maisie, how a time of war can give a human being purpose. Especially when that purpose, that power so to speak, is derived from something so essentially evil."

Maurice reached forward from his chair towards the wooden pipe stand that hung on the chimney breast. He selected a pipe, took tobacco and matches from the same place and leaned back, glancing again at the clock. He watched Maisie as he took a finger-and-thumb's worth of tobacco from the pouch and pressed it into the bowl of the pipe.

"Your thoughts, Maisie?"

Maurice struck a match on the raw brick of the fireplace, and drawing on the pipe, held the flame to the tobacco. Maisie found the sweet aroma pungent, yet this ritual of lighting and smoking a pipe soothed her. She knew Maurice to indulge in a pipe only when the crux of a matter was at hand. And having the truth revealed, no matter how harsh, was always a relief.

"I was thinking of evil. Of war. Of the loss of innocence, really. And innocents."

"Yes. Indeed. Yes. The loss of that which is innocent. One could argue that if it were not for war, then Jenkins —"

The clock struck the half hour. It was time for Maisie to leave to meet Billy Beale. Maurice stood, reaching out to the mantelpiece to steady himself with his right hand.

"You will be back at what time?"

"By half past eight."

"I will see you then."

Maisie left the cottage quickly, and Maurice moved to the window to watch her leave. They needed to say little to each other. He had been her mentor since she was a young girl, and she had learned well. Yes, he had been right to retire. And right to be ready to support her as she took on the practice in her own name.

"*B*illy. Good timing. How are you?"

"Doin' alright, Miss. Yourself?"

Without responding to his question, Maisie continued with her own.

"Any news?"

"Well, I've been thinking a bit and keeping my eyes open."

"Yes."

"And I've noticed that the feller who wanted to leave ain't around."

"Perhaps he's left, gone home."

"No, no. Not in the book."

"What book?"

"I found out there's a book. By the gatehouse. Records the ins and outs, if you know what I mean. Took a walk over to 'ave a word with old Archie the other day, and it looks like the bread delivery is all that's gone on in a week."

"And Jenkins?"

"Chummy as ever."

"Billy, I think it's time for you to leave."

"No – no, Miss. I'm safe as 'houses. Sort of like it 'ere, really. And no one's looking twice at me."

"You don't know that, Billy."

"One more night, then, anyway. I want to find out where this feller's gone. I tell you, I keep my eyes peeled, like I said, and one minute 'e's there and the next 'e's not. Mind you, there is someone in the sick bay."

"And who tends the sick bay?"

"Well, there's a feller who was a medic in the war, 'e does all your basic stuff, like. Then this other feller come up today. In a car, doctor's bag and all. I was working in the front garden at the time. Dead ringer for Jenkins actually. Bit bigger, mind. But you could see it round 'ere." Billy rubbed his chin and jaw. "'round the chops."

"Yes. I know who that is," Maisie whispered as she wrote notes on an index card.

"What, Miss?"

"No. Nothing. Billy, listen, I know you think that Jenkins is essentially a good man, but I fear that you may now be in some danger. You are an innocent person brought into my work because I needed information. That must change. It's time for you to leave."

Billy Beale turned to Maisie and looked deeply into her eyes. "You know Miss, when we first met, when I said I'd seen you before, after that shell got me leg. Did you recognize me?"

Maisie closed her eyes briefly, looked at the ground to compose herself and then directly at Billy. "Yes. I recognized you, Billy. Some people you never forget."

"I know. I told you, I would never forget you and that doctor. Could've 'ad my leg off, 'e could. Anyone else would've just chopped the leg and got me out of there. But 'im, that doctor, even in those conditions, like, 'e tried to do more."

Billy gazed out across the land to The Retreat.

"And I know what 'appened. I know what 'appened after I left. 'eard about it. Amazing you weren't killed."

Maisie did not speak but instead slowly began to remove the pins that held her long black hair in a neat chignon. She turned her head to one side and lifted her hair. And as she drew back the tresses, she revealed a purple scar weaving a path from just above her hairline at the nape of her neck, through her hair and into her scalp.

"Long hair, Billy, hides a multitude of sins."

His eyes beginning to smart, Billy looked towards The Retreat again, as if checking to see that everything was still in its place. He said nothing about the scar, but pressed his lips together and shook his head.

"I'll stay 'ere until tomorrow, Miss. I know you need me to be at this place at least another day. I'll meet you 'ere at half past seven tomorrow, and I'll 'ave me kit bag with me. No one will see me, don't you worry."

Billy did not wait for Maisie to respond, but clambered back through the fence. And as she had each evening for more than a week now, Maisie watched Billy limp across the field to The Retreat.

"I'll be here," whispered Maisie. "I'll be here."

Maisie did not go to bed, and was not encouraged to do so by Maurice. She knew that the time of reckoning could come soon. Yes, if Jenkins was to make his move, it would be now. If not, then the investigation would lie dormant; the file would remain open.

She sat on the floor, legs crossed, watching first the night grow darker, then the early hours of the morning edge slowly towards dawn. The clock struck the half hour. Half past four. She breathed in deeply and closed her eyes. Suddenly the telephone rang, its shrill bell piercing the quiet of the night. Maisie opened her eyes and rose to her feet quickly. Before it could ring a second time, she answered the call.

"Billy."

"Yes. Miss, something's goin' on down 'ere."

"First, Billy – are you safe?"

"No one's seen me leave. I crept out, kept close to the wall, came straight across the field and through the fence to the old dog 'n' bone 'ere."

"Good. Now – what's happening?"

Billy caught his breath. "I couldn't sleep last night, Miss. Kept thinking about, y'know, what we'd talked about."

"Yes, Billy."

Maisie turned to the door as she spoke and nodded her head to Maurice, who had entered the room dressed as he had been when he had bidden her goodnight. He had not slept either.

"Anyway. 'bout – well, blimey, must 've been over 'alf an hour ago now – I 'eard a bit of a racket outside, sounded like a sack bein' dragged around. So, I goes to the window to see what's what."

"Go on, Billy. And keep looking around you."

"Don't you worry, Miss, I'm keepin' me eyes peeled. Anyway, it was 'im, bein' dragged away down the dirt road."

"Who?"

"The feller that wanted to leave. Could see 'im plain as day, in the light coming from the door."

"Where does the dirt road lead to – the quarry?"

"Yes, Miss. That's right."

Maisie took a deep breath.

"Billy, here's what you are to do. Go into the hamlet. Keep very close to the side of the road. Do not be seen. There may be someone else coming from that direction heading for The Retreat. Do not let him see you. Meet me by the oak tree on the green. Go now."

Maisie replaced the receiver. There was no time to allow Billy Beale another question before ending the call.

Maurice handed Maisie her jacket and hat and took up his own. She opened her mouth to protest but was silenced by Maurice's raised hand.

"Maisie, I never, ever said that you were too young for the many risks you have taken. Do not now tell me to stay at home because I am too old!"

⊹

$\mathcal{B}$illy clambered out of the ditch and stretched his wounded leg. Kneeling had made him sore, and he rubbed at his cramped muscles. The sound of a breaking twig in the silence of the early morning hours, as leaves rustled in a cool breeze, made him snap to attention. He remained perfectly still.

"Now I'm bleedin' 'earin' things," whispered Billy into the dawn chill that caught his chest and forced his heart to beat faster, so fast he could hear it echo in his ears.

"Like waitin' for that bleedin' whistle to go off for the charge, it is."

Billy took his bag by the handle and slung it over his shoulder. Looking both ways, he began to cross the road to take advantage of the overhanging branches that would shield him as he made his way along the lane into the hamlet. But as he moved, his leg cramped again.

"Blimey, come on, come on leg! Don't bleedin' let me down now."

Billy tried to straighten his body, but as he moved his war wounds came to life, shooting pain through him as he tried to take a step.

"I'm afraid you've let yourself down, William," a man's voice intoned.

"Who's that? Who's there?" Billy fell backwards, his arms flailing as he tried to regain balance.

Adam Jenkins stepped out of the half-light in front of Billy. Archie stood with him, together with two other longtime residents of The Retreat.

"Desertion is what we call it. When you leave before your time."

"I just, well, I just wanted to 'ave a bit of a walk, Sir," said Billy, nervously running his fingers through his hair.

"Well, a fine time to be walking, William. Or perhaps you prefer 'Billy?' A fine time for a stroll."

Jenkins signalled to Archie and the other men, who pinioned Billy's hands behind his back and tightly secured a black cloth across his eyes.

"Desertion, Billy. Terrible thing. Nothing worse in a soldier. Nothing worse."

Maisie drew up alongside the oak tree in the hamlet of Hart's Lea. There was no sign of Billy.

"Maurice, he's not here," said Maisie, as she swung the car in the direction of The Retreat and accelerated. "We've got to find him."

Maisie drove at high speed along the lane to The Retreat, scanning the side of the road as she manoeuvred the car. Beside her Maurice was silent. Abruptly she swung the car onto the verge by the beech tree and got out. Kneeling on the verge, she ran her fingers over the rough ground. In the early light of morning she could see signs of a scuffle.

Yes, they had Billy.

Maurice climbed out of the car with some difficulty, and joined Maisie.

"I must find him, Maurice. His life is in danger."

"Yes, go, Maisie. But I would advise that this is the time –"

Maisie sighed, "Of course, you're right, Maurice. Over here I think we might be in luck."

Lowering herself into the ditch on the other side of the road, near the perimeter fence of The Retreat, Maisie reached down, and pulled up Billy's makeshift telephone.

"Thank God! They didn't find it – they must have arrived just after he replaced the receiver. I'm not really sure how you –"

"Go now, Maisie. I will see to it. I may be old, but such things are not beyond the scope of my intelligence."

Maisie rushed over to the MG, opened the door and took out the black jacket that Maurice had handed her when they left the house. Pulling on the jacket, Maisie was about to close the door of the car when she stopped and instead reached behind the driver's seat for her bag. She hurriedly took out the new Victorinox knife, slipped it into the pocket of her trousers and closed the car door. Maisie crossed the road, pausing only to touch Maurice's shoulder with her hand, before pulling back the wire and squeezing through the hole in the fence. She ran quickly across the field, aided by the grainy light of sunrise.

At first Maisie took care to step quietly past the farm buildings, but soon realized that they were deserted, a fact that did not surprise her. "He will probably want to set an example to the residents," Maisie had said to Maurice as they left the dower house. "He'll have an audience. An 'innocuous' little man would love an audience."

Maisie squinted at the silver watch pinned to the left breast pocket of her jacket. The watch that to this day was her talisman. Time had survived with her, but now time was marching on. Billy was in grave danger. She must be quick

Within minutes she reached the quarry, and as she ran the memories cascaded into her mind. She must get to him. Simon had saved him, and so must she. She must get to Billy.

She slowed to a walk and quietly crept into the mouth of the quarry, keeping close to the rough sandstone entrance so that she would not be seen. Maisie gasped as she scanned the tableau before her. A sea of men were seated on chairs, facing a raised platform with a wooden structure placed upon it. With their damaged faces, once so very dear to a mother, father or sweetheart, they were now reduced to gargoyles by a war that, for them, had never ended. There were men without noses or jaws, men who searched for light with empty eye sockets, men with only half a face where once a full-formed smile had beamed. She choked back tears, her blue eyes searching for Billy Beale.

As the rising sun struggled against the remains of night, Maisie realized that the wooden structure was a rough gallows. Suddenly, the men's faces moved. Maisie followed their gaze. Jenkins walked towards the platform from another direction. He took centre stage, and raised his hand. At his signal Archie and another man came towards the platform, half guiding, half dragging a blindfolded man between them. It was Billy. As she watched, Billy – jovial, willing Billy Beale – who surely would have given his life for her, was placed on his knees in front of the gallows and held captive in the taut hangman's noose. It would need only one sharp tug from the two men working in unison to do its terrible work.

The audience stood unmoved, yet in fear; their eyes, behind the terrible deformities war had dealt them, showing terror. And in that dreadful moment when she thought that the strong, fast legs that had borne her to this place had become paralyzed, Maisie was haunted by the past and present coming together as one. She knew that she must take action, but what could stop this madness immediately, without the men rising up against her – such was Jenkins's control over them – and without risking Billy's immediate death? "Fight like with like," she whispered, remembering one of Maurice's lessons, and as she uttered the words a picture flashed into her mind, a memory, of being on the train with Iris, of watching the soldiers as they marched off to battle, singing as they beat a path to death's door. There was no secret route along which she could stealthily make her way to Billy's side. She had only one option. For just a second Maisie closed her eyes, pulled her shoulders back and stood as tall as she could. She breathed deeply, cleared her throat, and began to walk slowly toward the platform. For Billy she must be a fearless warrior. And as the men became aware of her presence, she looked at their faces, smiled kindly, and began to sing.

> There's a rose that grows
> In No-Man's Land
> And it's wonderful to see

Though it's sprayed with tears
It will live for years
In my garden of memory . . .

As she approached the platform, now keeping her eyes focused on Jenkins, Maisie heard a deep resonant voice join her own. Then another voice echoed alongside her, and another, until her lone voice had become one with a choir of men singing in unison, their low voices a dawn chorus that echoed around the quarry.

It's the one red rose
The soldier knows
It's the work of the Master's hand
'Mid the war's great curse,
Stands the Red Cross Nurse
She's the Rose of No-Man's Land . . .

Maisie banished all fear as she stood on the ground below Jenkins. Dressed in the uniform of an officer who had served in the Great War, he stood with eyes blazing. She avoided looking at Billy, instead meeting Jenkins's glare while ascending the steps to the platform. The men continued to sing softly behind her, finding solace in the gentle rhythm of a much-loved song. Standing in front of Jenkins, she maintained eye contact. Her action had silenced him, but in mirroring his posture she knew of his inner confusion, his torment, and his pain. And in looking into his eyes, she knew that he was mad.

"Major Jenkins . . ." She addressed the officer in front of her, who seemed to regain a sense of place and time.

"You can't stop this, you know. This man is a disgrace to his country," he pointed his baton towards Billy. "A deserter."

"By what authority, Major Jenkins? Where are your orders?"

Jenkins's eyes flashed in confusion. Maisie heard Billy groan as the rope cut into his neck.

"Has this man received a court-martial? A fair trial?"

Voices murmured behind her as Jenkins's audience, the wounded "guests" of The Retreat, began to voice dissent. She had to be in control of each moment, for if one word were out of place the men could easily become an angry mob – dangerous not only to this mind-injured man in front of her but to Billy and herself.

"A trial? Haven't got time for trials, you know. Got to get on with it! Got a job to do, without having to tolerate time-wasters like this one." He pointed his baton at Billy again, then brought it to his side and tapped it against his shining leather boots.

"We *do* have time, Major." Maisie held her breath as she took her chance. Billy had begun to choke. She had to make her bravest move.

Though Maurice had cautioned Maisie in the use of touch, he had also stressed the power inherent in physical connection: "When we reach to place a hand on a sore knee or an aching back, we are really reaching into our primordial healing resources. Judicious use of the energy of touch can transform, as the power of our aura soothes the place that is injured."

"Major Jenkins," said Maisie, in a low voice. "It's over. . . the war is over. You can rest now . . . you can rest . . ." And as she whispered the words she raised a hand, stepped closer to him, and instinctively held her palm against the place where she felt his heart to be. For a moment there was no movement as Jenkins closed his eyes. He began to tremble, and with her fingertips Maisie could feel him struggle to regain control of his body – and his mind.

The onlookers gasped as Jenkins began to weep. Falling to his knees, he pulled his Webley Mk IV service revolver from its holster and held the barrel to his head.

"No," said Maisie firmly but softly, and with a move so gentle that Jenkins barely felt the revolver leave his grasp, she took the weapon from his hand.

At that moment, as the audience watched in a stunned silence that paralyzed all movement, she saw lights beginning to illuminate the entrance to the quarry. Uniformed men ran toward the platform shouting, "Stop, police!" She abandoned Jenkins, who was rocking back and forth, clasping his arms about his body and moaning with a rasping, guttural cry.

Maisie pushed the revolver into her pocket and moved quickly toward the lifeless body of Billy Beale. Archie and his assistant were nowhere to be seen. Maisie quickly took out her pocket knife and, holding back the flesh on Billy's neck with the fingers of her left hand, she slipped the blade against the rope and freed Billy from the hangman's noose. As Billy fell towards her, Maisie tried to take his weight and stumbled. She was aware that Jenkins was now flanked by two policemen, and that all around her the frozen moment had thawed into frenzied activity.

"Billy, look at me, Billy," said Maisie, regaining balance.

She slapped his face on both sides, and felt his wrist for a pulse.

Billy choked, and his eyes rolled up into their sockets as his hands instinctively clamoured to free his neck from the constriction that he could still feel at his throat.

"Steady on, Miss, steady on, for Gawd's sake."

Billy choked, his gas-damaged lungs wheezing with the enormous effort of fighting for breath. As he tried to sit up, Maisie supported him with her arms around his shoulders.

"It's alright, Miss. I'm not a goner. Let me get some air. Some air."

"Can you see me, Billy?"

Billy Beale looked at Maisie, who was now on her knees beside him.

"I'm alright now that you're 'ere, even if you are a bit 'eavy 'anded. Mind you . . ." he coughed, wiping away the blood and spittle that came up from his throat, "I thought you'd never get over chattin' wiv that bleedin' lunatic there." Billy pointed toward Jenkins, then brought his hand back to his mouth as he coughed another deep, rasping cough.

"May I have a word, Miss Dobbs?" The man looking down at her beckoned the police doctor to attend to Billy, then held out a hand to Maisie. Grasping his outstretched hand, she drew herself up to a standing position and brushed back the locks of black hair that were hanging around her face. The man held out his right hand again. "Detective Inspector Stratton. Murder Squad. Your colleague is in good hands. Now, if I may have a word."

Maisie quickly appraised the man who was standing in front of her. Stratton was more than six feet tall, well-built, and confident, without the posturing that she had seen before in men of high rank. His hair, almost as black as her own except for wisps of grey at the temples, was swept back. He wore corduroy trousers and a tweed jacket with leather at the elbows. He held a brown felt hat with a black grosgrain band in his left hand. Like a country doctor, observed Maisie. "Yes. Yes, of course, Detective Inspector Stratton. I . . ."

". . . Should have known better, Miss Dobbs? Yes, probably, you should have known better. However, I have been briefed by Dr Blanche, and I realize that you were in a situation where not a moment could be lost. Suffice it to say that this is not the time for discussion or reprimand. I must ask you, though, to make yourself available for questioning in connection with this case, perhaps tomorrow?"

"Yes, but —"

"Miss Dobbs, I have to attend to the suspect now, but in the meantime —"

"Yes?" Maisie was flushed, tired and indignant.

"Good work, Miss Dobbs. A calm head — very good work." Detective Inspector Stratton shook hands with Maisie once again, and was just about to walk away when she called him back.

"Oh, Inspector, just a moment . . ." Maisie held out the service revolver she had taken from Jenkins. "I think you'll need this for your evidence bag."

Stratton took the revolver, checked the barrel and removed the ammunition before placing the weapon safely in his own pocket. He inclined his head toward Maisie and smiled, then turned towards Jenkins, who was now flanked by two members of the Kent Constabulary. Maisie watched as Stratton commenced the official caution: "You are not obliged to say anything unless you wish to do so, but what you say may be put into writing and given in evidence."

Maisie looked around at Billy to satisfy herself that he was safe – he was now on his feet and speaking to the doctor – then surveyed the scene in front of her. She watched as Maurice Blanche walked among the terrified audience of "old soldiers" who still seemed so very young, his calming presence infectious as he stood with the men, placing a hand on a shoulder for support, or holding a weeping man to him unashamedly. The men seemed to understand his strength, and clustered around to listen to his soothing words. She saw him motion to Stratton, who sent policemen to lead the residents of The Retreat away one by one. They were men for whom the terror of war had been replayed and whose trust had been shattered. First by their country, and now by a single man. They were men who would have to face the world in which there was no retreat. Maurice was right, they were all innocents. Perhaps even Jenkins.

Jenkins was now in handcuffs and being led to a waiting police car that had been brought into the mouth of the quarry, his unsoiled polished boots and Sam Browne belt shining against a pressed uniform. Not a hair on his head was out of place. He was still the perfectly turned-out officer.

CHAPTER TWENTY-EIGHT

"So, what I want to know," said Billy, sitting in Maurice Blanche's favourite wing chair, next to the fireplace in the dower house, "Is 'ow did you get on to Adam Jenkins in the end. And I tell you, 'e certainly 'ad me there. I was beginnin' t'think 'e was a crackin' bloke."

Maisie sat on a large cushion on the floor sipping tea, while Maurice was comfortable on the sofa opposite Billy. She set down her cup and saucer on the floor and rubbed at her cold feet.

"I had a feeling, here." Maisie touched the place between her ribs at the base of her breastbone. "There was something wrong from the beginning. Of course you know about Vincent. And the others. That was a mistake on Jenkins's part, suggesting to Vincent's family that he be interred at Nether Green because it's a big cemetery, with lots of soldiers' graves. It was a mistake because he used it several times."

Maisie took a sip of her tea and continued. "I questioned the coincidence of several men buried with only their Christian names to identify them. Then I found out that they were all from the same place. The Retreat."

"And what else?" asked Billy, waving a hand to disperse the smoke from Maurice's pipe.

"A mistrust – on my part – of someone who wields so much power. The inspiration for The Retreat was admirable. Such places have worked well in France. But, for the most part, those places were set up for soldiers with disfiguring wounds to go to on holiday, not to be there for ever. And using only Christian names was Jenkins's innovation. Stripping away a person's name is a very basic manner of control. It's done in all sorts of institutions, such as the army – for example, they called you 'corporal,' not 'Billy,' or possibly – rarely – even 'Beale.'"

Billy nodded.

"The irony is, that it was one of the first men to live at The Retreat, Vincent Weathershaw, who gave him the idea for the Christian-names-only mode of address."

Maisie caught her breath and continued.

"More evidence came to hand after you went to The Retreat. Each cause of death was different – there was even a drowning listed – yet each could be attributed to asphyxiation of some sort. To the untrained eye, an accident. The word of the pathologist would not be questioned. No police were involved, they were considered to be deaths from 'accidental' or 'natural' causes – and as the men were all seeking relief from torment by coming to The Retreat, the families had no lingering questions. In fact, there was often relief that the loved one would not have to suffer any more," said Maisie.

"Indeed." Maurice looked at Maisie, who did not return his gaze. He took up the story. "Then there was Jenkins's own history. How could someone who had given his superiors cause to refer to him as "innocuous" have gained such power? Maisie telephoned the doctor who had supervised his care at Craiglockhart – the hospital in Scotland where shell-shocked officers were sent during the war. The poet Siegfried Sassoon was there."

"Well, sir, I ain't never bin much of a one for poetry." Billy waved smoke away from his face once more.

"The doctor, who is now at the Maudsley psychiatric hospital in

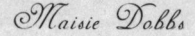

London, informed me that Jenkins's mental state was not as serious as some," said Maisie. "But there was cause for concern."

"I'll bet there was." Billy rubbed at the red weal left by the rope on his neck.

"You know what happened to deserters, Billy?"

Billy looked at his hands and turned them back and forth, inspecting first the palms, then his knuckles. "Yes. Yes I do, Miss."

"They were taken and shot. At dawn. We talked about it. Some of them just young boys of seventeen or eighteen – they were scared out of their wits. It's been rumoured that there was even a case of two being shot for accidentally falling asleep while on duty." Tears came to Maisie's eyes and she pursed her lips together. "Jenkins was the commanding officer instructed to deal with a desertion. 'Innocuous' Jenkins. Much against his will – and apparently he did question his orders – he was instructed to preside over such an execution."

"And . . ."

Billy sat forward in the leather chair.

"He carried out orders. Had he not, then he might well have been subject to the same fate. To disobey would have been insubordination."

Maisie got up from the floor and walked to the window. Maurice's eyes followed her, then turned to Billy. "The mind can do strange things, Billy. Just as we can become used to pain, so we can become used to experience, and in some cases a distasteful experience is made more palatable if we embrace it."

"Like putting sugar in the castor oil."

"Something of that order. Jenkins's sugar was the power he claimed. One might argue that it was the only way for him to stomach the situation. He was not a man strong in spirit. So close was he to the act of desertion that it made him detest the actual deserter, and in meting out this terrible, terrible punishment, he maintained control over the part of him that would have run away. He became very good at dealing with battlefield deserters. Indeed, he enjoyed a level of success, we understand, that he did not enjoy in other areas of responsibility."

Maurice looked again at Maisie, who turned to face Billy. "Jenkins's idea of founding The Retreat was formed in good faith. But once again the need for control emerged. The chain of murders began when one of the men wanted to leave. Jenkins felt the man's decision keenly. He was, in effect, deserting The Retreat. For Jenkins, his mind deeply affected by the war, there was only one course of action. And then one death made the others easier."

"Blimey," whispered Billy.

"Had you been at The Retreat longer, you too would have heard it said that it was difficult to depart with one's life. Obviously he could not shoot a man – it would not be easy for the pathologist to disguise the truth of such a wound – but he could use a more dramatic method. This gallows in the quarry would not break a man's neck, but would deprive the body of oxygen for just about long enough to take a life. A death that it would be easy to attribute to suicide or accident. And he must have been in a hurry with you, Billy, because with the others a heavy cloth was wrapped around the noose. The rope marks were not as livid as the necklace you're now wearing."

Billy once again rubbed at his neck. "I reckon it's all bleedin' wrong, this 'ere business of shootin' deserters. I tell you, 'alf of us didn't know what the bloody 'ell we were supposed to be doin' over there anyway. I know the officers, specially the young ones, didn't."

Maurice pointed the stem of his pipe at Billy, ready to comment. "Interesting point, Billy. You may be interested to know that Ernest Thurtle, an American by birth, now the MP for Whitechapel, has worked hard in Parliament to have the practice banned – it wouldn't surprise me if a new law were passed in the next year or so."

"About bloody time, too! And talkin' about deserters, what's the connection with Vincent Weathershaw? Remember me finding out that there was something that went on with 'im?"

"Yes," continued Maisie. "From what we know, Weathershaw was disciplined because he complained about the practice of military execution. He was vocal about it too, upsetting higher-ups. He was

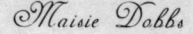

injured before he could be stripped of his commission and court-martialed for insubordination."

Billy whistled between his teeth. "This gets worse."

"It did for Weathershaw. He came to The Retreat in good faith, a terribly disfigured man. He had known something of Jenkins while in convalescence, but at The Retreat he found out about his reputation as a battlefield executioner. Vincent had put two and two together, so Jenkins decided he had to go. He'd suffered terrible depression, poor man, so accident or suicide was entirely believable."

"Poor sod. What about this other Jenkins?"

"Cousin. We thought Armstrong Jenkins was a brother, but he's not, he's a cousin. Surprisingly, Adam Jenkins was not in it for the money. His reward was the sensation of control. King of all he surveyed, and with a legion of serfs who listened to his every word and despite what they heard, adored him. And that is the part of the puzzle that is most intriguing."

"Indeed," said Maurice. "Most intriguing."

"That despite the rumours, such as they were, and the demise of those who 'left' The Retreat, Jenkins was held in very high regard by the men."

Billy blushed.

"An interesting phenomenon," said Maurice. "Such control over a group of people. It is, I fear, something that we shall see again, especially in times such as this, when people are seeking answers to unfathomable questions, for leadership in their uncertainty, and for a connection with others of like experience. Indeed, there is a word to describe such a group, gathered under one all-powerful leader, taken from the practice of seeking answers in the occult. What Jenkins founded could be described as a cult."

"This is givin' me the shivers," said Billy, rubbing his arms.

Maisie took up the story again. "Armstrong Jenkins was the one who persuaded his cousin to have the men sign over their assets. And for a man coming into The Retreat, so desperately unhappy that he would willingly cloister himself, it was not such a huge step.

Armstrong held the purse strings. He came to this area to work as pathologist when The Retreat opened. Like his cousin, his is a case of power laced with evil."

"I'll say. Gaw blimey, that was close."

"I made three telephone calls before our last meeting in the lane, and what I learned alerted me to the level of your danger. One was to the Maudsley, to speak to Adam Jenkins's doctor; one was to the county coroner, to confirm Armstrong Jenkins's history, and finally one to Maurice's friend, the Chief Constable, to inform him of my suspicions. It was his intention to begin an investigation of The Retreat the following day – but of course events overtook him. Billy, I wanted you to relinquish your task as soon as you told me that another man wished to leave The Retreat. But you were adamant."

Billy met Maisie's eyes with his own. "I told you, Miss, I didn't want to let you down. I wanted to do something for you. Like you and that doctor did for me. You never did it 'alf-'earted because you was all tired out. You had men linin' up all over the place, but you saved my leg. When I got 'ome, the doc said it was the best bit of battlefield leg saving 'e'd ever seen."

Tears smarted in Maisie's eyes. She thought the pain had ceased. She hated this tide of tears that came in, bidden by truth.

"And I know it's a bit off the subject, like, but I wanted to ask you somethin', and I . . . I dunno . . . I just felt you didn't want to talk about it, and who can blame you? But . . . what 'appened to 'im? What 'appened to that doctor?"

A strained silence fell upon the room. The excited explanation of events at The Retreat gave way to embarrassment. Maurice sighed, his brow furrowed, as he watched Maisie, who sat with her head in her hands.

"Look, I 'ope I ain't said nothin' wrong . . . I'm sorry if it was out of turn. It ain't none of my business, is it? I thought you were a bit sweet on each other, that's all. I remember thinking that. So I thought you'd know. The man saved my leg, probably saved my life. But I'm sorry. Shouldn't 'ave said nothin'." Billy picked up his jacket as if to leave the room.

"Billy. Wait. Yes. Yes, I should have told you. About Captain Lynch. It's only fair that you should know. After what you've done for me, it's only fair."

Maurice moved to Maisie's side and took her hand in his. She answered Billy's question.

CHAPTER TWENTY-NINE

*I*t seemed to Maisie that no sooner had she returned to the casualty clearing station from her leave at home with Simon than droves of injured were brought in. As day stretched into night, the few hours' sleep that Maisie managed to claim each night offered only a brief respite from the war.

"Did you remember to tie the scarf, Maisie?" asked Iris, referring to the cloth tied to the tent pole, which would indicate to the orderlies that the nurses inside were on the first shift to be called if wounded came in at night.

"Yes. It's there, Iris. 'Night."

"'Night, Maisie."

Often Maisie would fall into a deep sleep immediately upon climbing into her camp bed. Time and again her dreaming mind took her back to Chelstone, walking towards her father in the orchard. Yet as she came closer to him he moved away, reaching up to pick rosy red apples before moving on. She would call out to him, and he would turn and wave, but he did not stop, he did not wait for her. This Frankie Dobbs simply picked the deep red apples, placed them in his wicker basket and moved through the long grass of late summer. Such was the weight he carried that rich red juice ran from the bottom of the basket, leaving a trail for her to follow. She tried to run faster, yet her long, heavy woollen dress soaked up the red juice, clung to her legs and caught in the grass, and as the distance between them extended, Maisie cried out to him. "Dad, Dad, Dad!"

"Bloody hell, whatever is the matter with you?"

Iris sat up in bed and looked across at Maisie who, in her sudden wakefulness, lay on her back staring straight towards the top of the main tent pole, her violet eyes following drops of rainwater as they squeezed through the canvas and ran down to the ground.

"Are you all right?"

Iris leaned over and nudged Maisie.

"Yes. Yes, thanks. Bad dream. It was a bad dream."

"Not even time to get up yet. Brrr. Why doesn't it ever seem to get warm here? Here we are in the third week of May and I'm freezing!"

Maisie did not answer, but drew the blankets closer to her jaw.

"We've got another half an hour. Then let's get up and go and get ourselves a mug of that strong tea," said Iris, making an attempt to reclaim the comfort of deep sleep.

❖

"*L*ooks like we've got some 'elp coming in today, ladies."

One of the medical officers sat down with Iris and Maisie, ready to gossip as he sipped scalding tea and took a bite out of the thick crust of bread.

"Lord, do we need it! There's never enough doctors, let alone nurses," said Iris, taking her mug and sitting down on a bench next to Maisie.

"What's happened?" asked Maisie.

"Think they're coming in from the hospital up the line. We've been getting so many in each day 'ere, and someone pushing a pencil at a desk finally got wind of it. Some docs are being moved. Down 'ere first."

Maisie and Iris looked at each other. She had written to Simon only yesterday. He had said nothing to her about being moved. Was it possible that he was one of the doctors being sent to the casualty clearing station?

"Mind you, they might not like it much, what with them shells coming in a bit closer lately," added the medical officer.

"I thought the red cross meant that we were safe from the shelling," said Iris, cupping her hands around her mug.

"Well, it's supposed to be safe. Red crosses mark neutral territory."

"When will they arrive . . . from the hospital?" asked Maisie, barely disguising her excitement. Excitement laced with trepidation.

"End of the week, by all accounts."

It was late afternoon when new medical personnel began to appear. Maisie was walking through the ward, with men in various stages of recovery waiting for transportation to a military hospital in beds on either side of her, when she saw the silhouette she knew so well on the other side of the canvas flap that formed a wall between the ward and the medicines area. It was the place where nurses prepared dressings, measured powders, made notes, and stood to weep, just for a moment, when another patient was lost.

He was here. In the same place. They were together.

Without rushing, and continuing to check her patients as she made her way toward Simon, Maisie struggled to control her beating heart. Just before she drew back the flap of canvas she took a deep breath, closed her eyes, then walked through into the medicines area.

He was on his own, looking through the pile of records and familiarizing himself with the stocks of medicines and dressings. As Maisie entered, Simon looked up. For a moment neither moved.

Simon broke the silence, holding out his hand and taking hers.

"Why didn't you tell me in your letter?" whispered Maisie, looking around, fearful that someone might see her talking to Simon.

"I didn't know I'd be sent. Not until yesterday." He smiled. "But now we're together. Couldn't believe my luck, Maisie."

She held his hand tighter. "I am so glad. So glad that you are here. And safe."

"Good omen, don't you think? That we're here in the same place."

In the distance Maisie heard a wounded soldier calling for her, "Sister. In 'ere. Quick."

Simon held onto Maisie's hand for a second before she rushed to attend to her patient.

"I love you, Maisie," he said, and brought her hand to his lips.

She nodded, smiled, and ran to her duties.

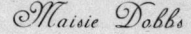

Working side by side was easier than either had thought it might be. For three days, wounded were brought in to the hospital and, time and time again, Maisie saw another side of the Simon she loved, the Simon who had stolen her heart as she danced in a blue silk dress. He was a brilliant doctor.

Even under the most intense pressure, Simon Lynch worked not just to save a life but to make that soldier's life bearable when the soldiering was done. With Maisie at his side, ready to pass instruments to him even before he asked – to clear the blood from wounds as he brought shattered bones together and stitched vicious lacerations – Simon used every ounce of knowledge garnered in hospitals back home in England and in the operating tents of the battlefield.

"Right, on to the next one," said Simon, as one patient was moved and orderlies pushed forward with another soldier on a stretcher.

"What's waiting for us in the line?"

"Sir, we've got about a dozen legs, four very nasty heads, three chests, three arms, and five feet – and that's only as far as the corner. Ambulances coming in all the time, sir."

"Make sure we get the ones who can travel on the road as soon as possible. We need the room, and they need to be at the base hospital."

"Yes sir."

The orderlies hurried away to bring in the next soldier, while Simon looked down at the wounded man now dependent upon his judgment and skill, a young man with hair the colour of sun-drenched wheat and a leg torn apart by shrapnel. A young man who watched his every move so intently.

"Will you be able to save me leg, sir? Don't want to be an ol' peg-leg, do I?"

"Don't worry. I'll do my best. Can't have you not able to chase the ladies, can we, Corporal?" Simon smiled at the man, despite his exhaustion.

Maisie looked up at Simon, then down at the corporal, and as Simon removed the shrapnel, she cleaned the bleeding wounds so that he could see the extent of the injury. To keep the soldier's spirits up – this man so conscious of everything happening around him – Maisie would look up for a second from her work and smile at him. And as Simon cut skin and brought together flesh, muscle and bone that had been torn apart, the soldier took heart. For though he could not see Maisie's smile through the white linen mask that shielded part of her face, her warm blue eyes told the soldier what he wanted to hear. That all would be well.

"Right. On your way to Blighty you are, my man. Done the best for you here, and God knows you've done your best for Blighty. The sooner you get home, the sooner they'll get you moving again. Rest assured, Corporal, the leg is staying with its owner."

"Thank you, Captain, sir. Thank you, Sister. Never forget you, ever."

The soldier looked intently at Simon and Maisie, fighting the morphine to remember their faces. A "Blighty," a wound sufficiently severe to warrant being sent back to England – and he would keep his leg. He was a lucky man.

"This one's ready for transport. We're ready for the next one."

Simon called out to the orderlies, and Maisie prepared the table as Corporal William Beale was taken to an ambulance for transfer to a base hospital closer to the port. He would be home within two days.

"*I* feel sorry for the ones who are left," said Maisie.

She and Simon were walking by moonlight along a corridor of ground between the tents, quiet and ready to part quickly should they be seen together. Distant sporadic gunfire punctured their conversation.

"Me too. Though the ones I ache for are the ones who are injured so terribly, so visibly to the face or limbs. And the ones whose injuries can't be seen."

"In the London Hospital, there were many times when a woman cried with relief at the passing of her husband or son. They had wounds that the family couldn't cope with – that people on the street couldn't bear to see."

She moved closer to Simon, who took her hand.

"It'll be over soon. It has to be, Maisie. The war just can't go on like this. Sometimes I feel as if I'm doctoring in a slaughterhouse. One body of raw flesh after another."

Simon stopped and drew Maisie to him and kissed her. "My Maisie of the blue silk dress. I'm still waiting for an answer."

Maisie drew back and looked into Simon's eyes. "Simon, I said to ask again when this is over. When I can see a future."

"That's the trouble," said Simon, beginning to tease her. "Sometimes I think you *can* see the future – and it gives me chills!"

He held her to him again. "I tell you what, Maisie. I promise that I won't ask you again until the war is over. We'll walk together on the South Downs and you can give me your answer then. How about it?"

Maisie smiled and looked into his eyes, bright in the moonlight. Simon, Simon, my love, she thought, how I fear this question. "Yes. Yes, Simon. Ask me again on the South Downs. When the war is over."

And Simon threw back his head and laughed, without thought for who might hear him.

⬚

"God . . ."

Simon's lips were drawn across his teeth as he looked at the wound to the soldier's chest, and uttered his plea to the heavens. Maisie immediately began cleaning the hole created by shrapnel, while Simon staunched the flow of blood. Nurses, doctors, anaesthetists, orderlies and stretcher-bearers were everywhere, rushing, running, working to save lives.

Maisie wiped the sweat from Simon's brow and continued to work on the wound. Simon inspected the extent of the injury. Lights flickered, and the tent shuddered.

"God, I can hardly even see in here."

Suddenly it seemed as if the battlefield had come to the hospital. As they worked to save the lives of men being brought in by the dozen, the tent shook again with the impact of a shell at close quarters.

"What the bloody hell . . .?"

"Sir, sir, I think we're coming under fire," an orderly shouted across to Simon. The operating tent was becoming part of the battlefield itself. Maisie swallowed the sour liquid that had come up from her stomach and into her mouth. She looked at Simon, and to combat her fear she smiled at him. For one second he returned her smile broadly, then turned again to his patient. They could not stop.

"Well, then. Let's get on with it!"

Let's get on with it.

Those were the last words she heard Simon speak.

Let's get on with it.

CHAPTER THIRTY

*I*t was on a warm afternoon in late September that Maisie stepped out of the MG and looked up at the front of an imposing Georgian building in Richmond. Two Grecian-style columns stood at either side of the steps, which in turn led to the heavy oak doors of the main entrance. The house had once been a grand home with gardens that extended down towards the Thames, where the great river grew broader on its meandering journey from the village of Thame in Oxfordshire, after it emerged as a small stream. From Richmond it would rush on toward London, through the city and into the sea, fresh and salt water meeting in a swirling mass. Maisie loved to look at the river. There was calm to be found in viewing water. And Maisie wanted to remain calm. She would walk to the water and back, to get her bearings.

The Retreat affair had been brought to its conclusion. Jenkins was now in Broadmoor, incarcerated with those who were considered mentally ill and dangerous. Archie and others involved in Jenkins's wrongdoing at The Retreat were also in institutions where they would find a measure of compassion and solace. They were not being held "at His Majesty's Pleasure" but would be released in time. Other men had returned to families or to their solitary lives, some finding renewed understanding.

Billy Beale found that he did not really enjoy publicity, that it was enough for him to go about his business each day, though if a person needed help, then he, Billy Beale, was the man.

"Of course, the missus don't mind gettin' a bit extra when she goes into that skinflint butcher for a nice bit of lamb, and the attention's brought a bit of a smile to 'er face. But me, I dunno. I'm not a big one for bein' noticed on the street."

Maisie laughed at Billy, who daily told of the latest encounter that came as a result of being the hero of events at The Retreat. He was supervising the placement of her new office furniture, which had just been moved to a larger room on the first floor of a grand building in Fitzroy Square, just around the corner from the Warren Street premises. Finally giving in to Lady Rowan's insistent nagging, Maisie would now be living in her own rooms at the Belgravia house.

"Look, my dear, Julian and I have decided to spend most of our dotage at Chelstone. Of course we'll come up for the Season, and for the theatre and so on. But it is so much calmer in Kent, don't you think?"

"Well, Lady Rowan . . ."

"Oh, no, I suppose it wasn't that calm for you, was it?" Lady Rowan laughed and continued. "Anyway, with James on his way to Canada to take care of our business interests again – thank heavens – the house will be all but empty. We'll have a skeleton staff here, naturally. Maisie, I must insist you take over the third-floor. In fact, I need you to."

Eventually Maisie concurred. Despite the fact that business was coming in at a respectable clip, Billy was now working for her, and money saved on her own rent would contribute to his wages.

As was Maurice's habit at the closure of a case, Maisie had visited the places of significance in The Retreat affair. During her apprenticeship she had learned the importance of such a ritual, not only to ensure the integrity of notes that would be kept for reference, but for what Maurice referred to as a "personal accounting," to allow her to begin to work with new energy on the next case.

Maisie had walked once more in Mecklenburg Square, though she did not seek a meeting with Celia Davenham. She had received a letter from Celia after events at The Retreat became headline news. Celia had not referred to the inconsistency with the surname Maisie had given, but instead thanked her for helping to put Vincent's memory to rest.

She took tea at Fortnum & Mason, and at Nether Green Cemetery she placed fresh daisies on the graves of Vincent and his neighbour Donald, and stopped to speak to the groundsman whose son rested in a place overlooked by passing trains.

Maisie drove down to Kent in early September, when the spicy fragrance of dry hops still hung in the warm air of an Indian summer. She passed lorries and open-top buses carrying families back to the East End after their annual pilgrimage to harvest the hops, and smiled when she heard the sound of old songs lingering on the breeze. There was nothing like singing together to make a long journey pass quickly.

She drew the car alongside menacing heavy iron gates and looked up, not at blooms, but this time at blood red rosehips hanging over the wall. The Retreat was closed. Heavy chains held the gates and a sign with the insignia of the Kent Constabulary instructed trespassers to keep out.

Because memories had been given new life by her investigation, they too were part of her personal accounting. Maisie wrote letters to Priscilla, now living with her husband and three young sons in the South of France, each boy bearing the middle name of an uncle he would never know; to the famous American surgeon Charles Hayden and his family; and to Iris, who lived in Devon with her mother. Like many young women who came of age in the years 1914–18, Iris had no husband, for her sweetheart had been lost in the war. Maisie's letters did not tell the story of The Retreat, but only reminded the recipients that she thought of them often, and was well.

Now, as Maisie stood in the gardens of the great house, looking out over the river and reflecting once again upon how much had happened in such a short time, she knew that for her future to spread out in front of her, she must face the past.

She was ready.

The conversation demanded by Billy had untied a knot in her past, one that bound her to the war in France over ten years ago.

Yes, it was time. It was more than time.

❖

"Miss Dobbs, isn't it?"

The woman at the reception desk smiled up at Maisie, her red lipstick accentuating a broad smile that eased the way for visitors to the house. She crossed Maisie's name off the register of expected guests and leaned forward, pointing with her pen.

"Go along the corridor to your left, just over there, then down to the nurses' office. On the right. Can't miss it. They're expecting you. Staff Nurse will take you on from there."

"Thank you."

Maisie followed the directions, walking slowly. Massive flower arrangements on each side of the marble corridor gave forth a fragrance that soothed her, just as the sight of water had calmed her before she entered. Yes, she was glad she had made this decision. For some reason it was not so hard now. She was stronger. The final part of her healing was near.

She tapped on the door of the nurses' office, which was slightly ajar, and looked in.

"I'm Maisie Dobbs, visiting . . ."

The staff nurse came to her.

"Yes. Good morning. Lovely to have a visitor. We don't see many here."

"Oh?"

"No. Difficult for the families. But you'd be surprised what a difference it makes."

"Yes. I was a nurse."

The staff nurse smiled. "Yes. I know. His mother told us you would be coming. Very pleased, she was. Very happy about it. Told us all . . . well, never mind. Come with me. It's a lovely day, isn't it?"

"Where is he?"

"The conservatory. Lovely and warm in there. The sun shines in. They love the conservatory."

The staff nurse led the way down the corridor, turned left again and opened a door into the large glass extension to the main building, a huge room filled with exotic plants and trees. Staff Nurse had not stopped talking since they left the nurses' office; they do that to put the new visitors at ease, thought Maisie.

"This was originally called the Winter Garden, built by the owner so the ladies of the house could take a turn in the winter without going outside into the cold. You can have quite the walk in here. It's a bit too big to call it a conservatory, I suppose. But that's what we call it."

She motioned to Maisie once again. "This way, over to the fountain. Loves the water, he does."

The staff nurse pointed to an open window. "And though it's warm, it doesn't get too warm, if you know what I mean. We open the windows to let the breeze blow through in summer, and it still feels like summer, doesn't it? Ah. Here he is."

Maisie looked in the direction of her outstretched hand, at the man in a wheelchair with his back to them. He was facing the fountain, his head inclined to one side. The staff nurse walked over to the man, stood in front of him, and leaned over to speak. As she did so she gently tapped his hand. Maisie remained still.

"Captain Lynch. Got a visitor, you have. Come to see you. A very beautiful lady."

The man did not move. He remained facing the fountain. The staff nurse smiled at him, tucked in the blanket covering his knees, and then gave Maisie a broad smile before joining her.

"Would you like me to stay for a while?"

"No, no. I'll be fine." Maisie bit her lip.

"Right you are. About twenty minutes? I'll come back for you then. Never find your way out of the jungle alone!"

"Thank you, Staff Nurse."

The woman nodded, checked the time on the watch pinned to her apron and walked away along the brick path overhung with branches. Maisie went to Simon and sat down in front of him, on the low wall surrounding the fountain. She looked up at this man she had loved so deeply, with all the intensity of a first love, a love forged in the desperate heat of wartime. Maisie looked at the face she had not seen since 1917, a face now so changed.

"Hello, my love," said Maisie.

There was no response. The eyes stared at a place in the distance beyond Maisie, a place that only he could see. The face was scarred, the hair growing in a shock of grey along scars that lay livid across the top of his skull.

Maisie put her hand to his face and, running her fingers along the jagged lines, wondered how it could be that the outcome of wounds was so different. That scars so similar on the outside concealed a different, far deeper injury. In comparison, her own wounds from the same exploding shell had been superficial. Yet Simon's impairment freed him from all sensation of the deeper wound: that of a broken heart.

Simon still did not move. She took his hands in hers and began to speak. "Forgive me, my love. Forgive me for not coming to you. I was so afraid. So afraid of not remembering you as we were together, as you were . . ."

She rubbed his hands. They were warm to the touch, so warm she could feel the cold in her own.

"At first people asked me why I didn't come, and I said I didn't feel well enough to see you. Then as each month, each year passed, it was as if the memory of you – of us . . . the explosion – were encased in fine tissue-paper."

Maisie bit her lip, constantly kneading Simon's still hands as she spoke her confession. "I felt as if I were looking through a window to my own past, and instead of being transparent, my view was becoming more and more opaque, until eventually the time had passed. The time for coming to see you had passed."

Breathing deeply, Maisie closed her eyes and gathered her thoughts, then continued, her voice less strained as the weight of formerly unspoken words was lightened.

"Dad, Lady Rowan, Priscilla – they all stopped asking after a while. I kept them at arm's length. All except Maurice. Maurice sees through everything. He said that even if people couldn't see my tissue-paper armour, they could feel it, and would not ask again. But he knew, Maurice knew, that I would have to come one day. He said that the truth grows even more powerful when it is suppressed, and that often it takes only one small crack to bring down the wall, to release it. And that's what happened, Simon. The wall I built fell down. And I have been so filled with shame for being unable to face the truth of what happened to you."

Simon sat still in his wheelchair, his hands unmoving, though blood coloured his skin.

"Simon, my love. I never did tell you my answer. You see, I knew that something dreadful was going to happen. I couldn't promise you marriage, a future, when I could see no future. Forgive me, dear Simon, forgive me."

Maisie looked around, trying to see what Simon's stare focused upon, and was surprised to see that it was the window, where they were reflected together. She, wearing her blue suit and a blue cloche, her hair in a chignon at the base of her neck. A few tendrils of hair, always the same few tendrils of black hair, had flown free and fallen down around her forehead and cheeks. She could barely see his facial wounds in the reflection. The glass was playing tricks, showing her the old Simon, the young doctor she had fallen in love with so long ago.

Maisie turned to face Simon again. A thin line of saliva had emerged from the side of his mouth and had begun to run down his chin. She took a fresh linen handkerchief from her handbag, wiped the moisture away and held his hand once again, in silence, until the staff nurse returned.

"How are we, then?" She leaned forward to look at Simon, then turned to smile at Maisie. "And how about you?" she asked.

"Fine. Yes, I'm fine," she swallowed and returned the nurse's smile.

"Good. Bet you've done him the world of good." Staff Nurse looked at Simon again and patted his hand. "Hasn't she, Captain Lynch? Done you a power of good!"

Simon remained perfectly still.

"Let me lead you out of the maze here, Miss Dobbs."

As she walked away, Maisie stopped to look back at Simon, then at his reflection in the windowpane. There he was. Forever the young, dashing Simon Lynch who had stolen her heart.

"Will you come again?"

They had reached the main door of the house. A grand house that was now a home for men stranded in time by the Great War, men trapped in the caverns of their own minds, never to return.

"Yes. Yes I will come again. Thank you."

"Right you are then. Just let us know. Loves a visitor, does Captain Lynch."

$\mathcal{M}$aisie drove back into London, waving to Jack Barker as the MG screeched around the corner into Warren Street before stopping at her new office in Fitzroy Square. She parked the car in front of the building and watched as Billy positioned a new brass nameplate with tacks, then stood back to appraise the suitability of his placement before securing the plate with screws. He rubbed his chin and moved the plate twice more. Finally he nodded his head, satisfied that he had found exactly the right place for her name, a place that would let callers know that M. Dobbs, Psychologist and Investigator, was open for business.

Maisie continued to watch as Billy worked, polishing the brass to a glowing shine. Then Billy looked up and saw Maisie in the MG. He waved and, rubbing his hands on a cloth, walked down the steps and opened the car door for her to get out.

"Better get weaving, Miss."

"Why, what's happened?"

"That Detective Inspector Stratton from Scotland Yard, the Murder Squad feller. Been on the dog and bone four times already. Urgent, like. Needs to be 'in conference' with you about a case."

"Golly!" said Maisie, grabbing the old black document case from the passenger seat.

"I know. 'ow about that? We'd better get to work, 'adn't we, Miss?"

Maisie raised an eyebrow and walked with Billy to the door. She ran her fingers along the engraving on the brass plate, and turned to her new assistant.

It was time to go to work.

"Well then, Billy – let's get on with it!"

ACKNOWLEDGMENTS

First and foremost, I am indebted to Holly Rose, my friend and writing pal who read the initial tentative pages of *Maisie Dobbs* and pressed me to continue. Adair Lara, my writing mentor, was the first to suggest I consider writing fiction, and later, after my "accident horribilis," when *Maisie Dobbs* was barely half written, insisted that convalescence was an ideal time to finish the book – broken arm notwithstanding.

I have been truly blessed in my association with Amy Rennert and Randi Murray of the Amy Rennert Agency, for their wise counsel, wonderful humour, hard work, and most of all, their enthusiastic belief in *Maisie Dobbs.* I am equally blessed in my editor, Laura Hruska, who has the qualities that make her one of the best – including, I believe, psychic powers that enable her to see into my mind.

My godmother, Dorothy Lindqvist, first took me to London's Imperial War Museum when I was a child, an experience that brought a new reality to my grandfather's stories of the Great War of 1914–18. Now, years later, many thanks must go to the museum for its amazing resources, and to the staff who were most helpful during my research visits.

The following people kindly responded to emails and phone calls, providing me with detail that has brought color and texture to the life and experience of Maisie Dobbs: Kate Perry, Senior Archivist at Girton College; Sarah Manser, Director of Press and Public Relations at The Ritz, London; Barbara Griffiths at BT Group Archives, London; John Day, Chairman of the MG Car Club Vintage Register; and Alison Driver of the Press & PR Department of Fortnum & Mason, London. For his dry wit and dogged investigative skills, my utmost gratitude goes to Victor – who knows who he is.

On a personal level thanks must go to my parents, Albert and Joyce Winspear, for their great memories of "old London," and their recollections of my grandfather's postwar experiences; my brother, John, for his encouragement; my friend Kas Salazar, who constantly reminds me of my creative priorities; and last – but certainly not least – my husband and cheerleader, John Morell, for his unfailing support, and for sharing our home with a woman called Maisie Dobbs.

Available now in hardback

Birds of a Feather

A Maisie Dobbs Mystery

JACQUELINE WINSPEAR

Maisie Dobbs returns in a second brilliant case

Joseph Waite is a man who knows what he wants. With his Havana cigars and Savile Row suits, he is one of Britain's wealthiest men. But behind the gates of his Dulwich mansion, trouble is brewing, and the last thing he needs is a scandal. So he summons a woman known for her uniquely intuitive approach to criminal investigation, and for her discretion – the one and only Maisie Dobbs.

The first pages of Maisie's new investigation follow here.

Maisie parked outside the main gates leading to a red-brick neo-Georgian mansion that stood majestically in the landscaped grounds beyond an ornate wrought iron gate.

"D'you reckon someone'll come to open the gate?" asked Billy.

"Someone's coming now." Maisie pointed to a young man wearing plus fours, a tweed hacking jacket, wool shirt and spruce green tie. He hurriedly opened an umbrella as he ran toward the entrance, and nodded to Maisie as he unlatched the gates and opened them. Maisie drove forward, stopping alongside the man.

"You must be Miss Dobbs, to see Mr Waite at three o'clock."

"Yes, that's me."

"And this is . . .?" The man bent forward to look at Billy in the passenger seat.

"My assistant, Mr William Beale."

Billy was still dabbing his nose with Maisie's handkerchief.

"Right you are, Ma'am. Park in front of the main door please, and make sure you reverse into place, Ma'am, with the nose of your motor pointing toward the gate."

Maisie raised an eyebrow at the young man, who shrugged.

"It's how Mr Waite likes it done, Ma'am."

"Bit picky, if you ask me," said Billy as Maisie drove toward the house. " 'Reverse in wiv the nose pointing out'. Perhaps that's 'ow I should walk in there, backwards, wiv me nose turned away! I wonder who 'e thinks 'e is?"

"One of the richest men in Britain, if not Europe." Maisie manoeuvered the car as instructed. "And as we know, he needs something from us, otherwise we wouldn't be here. Come on."

They strode quickly from the car toward the main door where a woman waited to greet them. She was about fifty-five, in Maisie's estimation, and wore a plain slate grey mid-calf length dress with white cuffs and a white Peter Pan collar. A cameo was pinned to the centre of her collar and her only other adornment was a silver wristwatch on a black leather strap. Her grey hair was drawn back so tightly that it pulled at her temples. Despite her austere appearance, when Maisie and Billy reached the top step she smiled warmly with a welcoming sparkle in her pale blue eyes.

"Come in quickly before you catch your death! What a morning! Mr Harris, the butler, has been taken poorly with a nasty cold. I'm Mrs Willis, the housekeeper. Let me take your coats." Mrs Willis took Maisie's mackintosh and Billy's overcoat, and passed them to a maid. "Hang them on the drier over the fireplace in the laundry room. Mr Waite's guests will be leaving in –" she looked at her watch "– approximately thirty-five minutes, so get the coats as dry as possible by then."

"Thank you very much, Mrs Willis," said Maisie.

"Mr Waite will join you in the library shortly."

Maisie sensed a mood of tension pervading the house. Mrs Willis's pace was hurried, urging them forward. At the library door she checked her watch as she reached for the brass door handle. A door opened behind them and another woman hurried to join the trio.

"Mrs Willis! Mrs Willis, I will take over from here and show Mr Waite's guests in to the library," she panted.

Mrs Willis relinquished them, frowning with annoyance, "Certainly, Miss Arthur. Please continue." She turned to Maisie and Billy. "Good morning," she said as she stepped away without looking at Miss Arthur again. Unfortunately she was prevented from making a dignified exit as the door opened once more and a rotund man strode towards them, consulting his watch as he approached.

"Right then, it's three o'clock. We'd better get on with it." Barely looking at Maisie and Billy, he strode into the library.

Billy leaned towards Maisie and whispered, "It's like a three-ring-circus in 'ere!"

She responded with a brief nod.

"Sit down, sit down," Joseph Waite pointed to two chairs on the long side of a rectangular polished mahogany table and immediately seated himself in a larger chair at its head. His girth made him seem short, though he was almost six feet tall and moved deceptively quickly. According to Maurice's notes, Waite had been born in 1865, which meant he was now sixty-five. His navy blue pinstripe suit was doubtless constructed at great expense by a Savile Row tailor. It was complemented by a white shirt, light grey silk tie, highly polished black shoes, and light grey silk socks that Maisie could just see as she glanced down at the floor. Expensive, very expensive, but then Joseph Waite reeked of new money and of the large Havana cigar that he moved from his right hand to his left in order to reach out first to Maisie, then to Billy.

"Joseph Waite."

Maisie took a breath and opened her mouth to reply but was prevented from doing so.

"I'll get directly to the point, Miss Dobbs. My daughter, Charlotte, is missing from home. I'm a busy man, so I will tell you straight, I do not want to involve the police because I don't for one minute think that this is a police matter. And I don't want them turning this place upside down while they waste time speculating about this and that, and drawing every bored press man to my gates while they're about it."

Maisie once again drew breath and opened her mouth to speak, but Waite held his hand up, his palm facing her. She noticed a large gold ring on his little finger, and as he replaced his hand on the table, she saw that it was encrusted with diamonds. She stole a sideways look at Billy, who raised an eyebrow.

"It's not a police matter because this is not the first time she's left my house. You are to find her, Miss Dobbs, and bring her back before word gets out. A man in my position can't have a daughter running around and turning up in the newspapers. I don't 'ave to tell you that these are difficult times for a man of commerce, but Waite's is trimming its sails accordingly and doing very nicely, thank you. It's got to stay that way. Now then." Waite consulted his watch yet again. "You've got twenty minutes of my time, so ask any questions you want. I won't 'old back."

Maisie perceived that although Waite had worked hard to eliminate a strong Yorkshire accent, the occasional revealing long vowel and the odd Northern dropped *h* broke through.

"I'd like some details about your daughter." Maisie reached for the blank index cards that Billy handed her. "First of all, how old is Charlotte?"

"Thirty-two. About your age."

"Quite."

"And with about half the gumption!"

"I beg your pardon, Mr Waite?"

"I'll make no bones about it; Charlotte is her mother's daughter. A wilting lily, I call 'er. A good day's work wouldn't do her any harm at all, but of course the daughter of a man in my position has no need. More's the pity."

"Indeed. Perhaps you could tell us something about what happened on the day Charlotte disappeared. When was she last seen?"

"Two days ago. Saturday. Morning. At breakfast. I was down in the dining room, and Charlotte came in, full of the joys of spring, and sat down at the other end of the table. One minute she seemed as right as rain, eating a bit of toast, drinking a cup of tea, then all of a sudden she starts with the tears, sobs a bit, and runs from the room."

"Did you go after her?"

The man sighed and reached for an ashtray, into which he tapped the smouldering end of his cigar, leaving a circle of pungent ash. He drew deeply on the cigar again and exhaled.

"No, I didn't. I finished my breakfast. Charlotte is a bit of a Sarah Bernhardt, Miss Dobbs. An actress – should've been on the stage, like her mother. Nothing is ever good enough for her. I thought she'd've made a suitable marriage by now, but no, in fact – you should write it down there –" He waved his cigar toward Maisie's index card. "She was jilted by her fiancé a couple of months ago. Even with my money she can't get a husband!"

"Mr Waite, the behaviour you describe suggests that your daughter may have been in a state of despair."

"Despair? *Despair*? She's always had fine food in her belly, clothes – and very good clothes, I might add – on her back. I've given her a good education, in Switzerland, if you please. And she had a proper coming out ball. You could've fed a family for a year with what I spent on the frock alone. That girl's had the very best, so don't tell me about despair, Miss Dobbs. That girl's got no right to despair."

Maisie met his gaze firmly. *Here it comes*, she thought, *now he's going to tell me about his hard life.*

"Despair, Miss Dobbs, is when your father dies in a pit accident when you're ten years old and you're the eldest of six. That's what despair is. Despair is what gives you a right good kick in the rump and sets you off to provide for your family when you're nobbut a child."

Waite, who had slipped into broad Yorkshire, went on. "Despair, Miss Dobbs, is when you lose your mother and her youngest to consumption when you're fourteen. That, Miss Dobbs, is despair. Despair is just when you think you've got everyone taken care of, because you're working night and day to make something of yourself, and you lose another brother down the same pit that killed your father, because he took any job he could get to help out. That, Miss Dobbs, is despair. But you know about that yourself, don't you?" Waite leaned forward and ground his cigar into the ashtray.

Maisie realized that somewhere in his office Joseph Waite had a dossier on her that held as much information as she had acquired about him, if not more.

"Mr Waite, I am well aware of life's challenges, but if I am to take on this case – and the choice is mine – I have a responsibility for the welfare of all parties. If this type of departure is something of a habit for your daughter and discord in the house is at the heart of her unsettled disposition, then clearly something must be done to alleviate the, let us say, *pressure* on all parties. I must have your commitment to further conversation with respect to the problem when we have found Charlotte."

Joseph Waite's lips became taut. He was not a man used to being challenged. Yet, as Maisie now knew, it was the similarity in their backgrounds that had led him to choose her for this task, and he would not draw back. He was a very intelligent as well as belligerent man and would appreciate that not a moment more could be lost.

"Mr Waite, even if Charlotte has disappeared of her own volition, news of her disappearance will soon attract the attention of the press, just as you fear. Given your financial situation and these difficult times, there is a risk that you may be subjected to attempts at extortion. And though you seem sure that Charlotte is safe and merely hiding from you, of that we cannot be certain until she is found. You speak of prior disappearances. May I have the details?"

Waite leaned back in his chair shaking his head. "She runs away, to my mind, anytime she can't get what she wants. The first time was after I refused to allow her a motor car." He looked across the lawns and waved the cigar in the direction of what Maisie expected were the garages. "She can be chauffeured anywhere she wants. I don't hold with women driving."

Maisie exchanged glances with Billy.

"So she ran to her mother's house, no doubt to complain about her terrible father. I tell you, where I come from, there's women who'd give their eye teeth to have someone to drive them instead of walking five miles to the shops pushing a pram with a baby inside, a couple of nippers on top, and the shopping bags hanging off the handle!"

"And the second time?"

"Oh, she was engaged to be married and wanted to get out of it. The one before this last one. Just upped and moved into the Ritz, if you please. Nice home here, and she wants to live at the Ritz. I went and got her back myself."

"I see." Maisie imagined the embarrassment of a woman being frog-marched out of the Ritz by her angry father. "So in your opinion Charlotte has a tendency to run away when she is faced with a confrontation."

"Aye, that's about the measure of it," replied Waite. "So what do you think now about your little 'further conversation' when Charlotte returns, eh, Miss Dobbs, considering the girl can't even look her own father in the eye?"

Maisie was quick to respond. "My terms remain, sir. Part of my work in bringing Charlotte home will be to listen to her and to *hear* what she has to say."

Waite scraped back his chair, pushed his hands into his trouser pockets, and walked to the window. He looked up at the sky for just a moment and took out a pocket-watch. "I agree to your terms. Send your contract to me by nine tomorrow morning. Miss Arthur will take care of any deposit required, and will settle your account and expenses upon receipt. If you need me to answer more questions, Miss Arthur will schedule an appointment. Otherwise I expect your progress report by Friday. In person and at this same time – that is, should you fail to have found her by then. I'm a busy man, as I've said, Miss Dobbs." He turned to leave.

"Mr Waite?"

"Yes?"

"May we see Charlotte's rooms, please?"

"Miss Arthur will call Mrs Willis to show you the rooms. Good afternoon."

Mrs Willis was instructed to show Maisie and Billy to Charlotte's suite. They were escorted up the wide staircase to the second floor, where they turned right along a spacious landing. Mrs Willis lifted her hand to knock at the door and then, remembering that there was no need, took a bunch of keys from her pocket, selected one, and unlocked the door to reveal a large sitting room with additional doors on either side that Maisie thought would lead to a bathroom and bedroom respectively. The sash windows were open to a broad view of the perfect lawns at the front of the house, with stripes of light and dark green where gardeners had worked with mowers and rollers to give an immaculate finish.

Mrs Willis beckoned them into the rooms, which were aired by a light breeze that seemed to dance with the cabbage-rose-printed curtains, flicking them back and forth. Though appointed with the most expensive furniture and linens, the rooms felt cold and spartan to Maisie. There was none of the ornamentation she had expected: no photographs in frames, no mementos, no books on the bedside table, no exotic perfume bottles set on top of the dressing table. Maisie walked through into the bedroom, and back into the sitting room. Like the Queen Anne chairs beside the fireplace, the rose-printed curtains were traditional, but the dressing table and wardrobe were modern, constructed of solid dark wood with geometric lines. The dressing table mirrors were triangular, a jagged icy triptych that unsettled Maisie. Her skin prickled as if pierced by tiny needles. The design of the dressing table itself was matched by that of the wardrobe, with its centre mirror set into the wood. It seemed to Maisie that no rest was to be had in this room, unless one stared out of the window or at the curtains.

"Lovely rooms, aren't they? We only changed the curtains last week – she has pale green velvets in winter. Lined with a special combed cotton, they are, to keep the rooms warmer. The dressing table suite was made 'specially to Mr Waite's specifications."

Maisie smiled and nodded. "Thank you, Mrs Willis. We may need to ask you some more questions in a while. At the moment we just need to look around."

Mrs Willis pursed her lips, hesitating. "Of course. I'll come back in about twenty minutes, but if you need me in the meantime, just press this button." She indicated one of three brass buttons on a panel beside the door.

Sensing that Waite had given instructions that they were to be escorted at all times, Maisie smiled and nodded. She suspected that Mrs Willis had enough on her plate to worry about in the house without chaperoning private investigators.

As the door closed, Billy turned to Maisie. "It looks as if nobody ever set foot in these rooms, dunnit?"

Maisie made no reply, but set her document case down on a chair with a cover that matched the curtains and, in the bedroom, even the counterpane on Charlotte's bed. Maisie's work with Maurice Blanche had taught her that a person speaks not only with the voice but with those objects she chooses to surround herself. That photographs tell a story is well accepted, but the way furniture is positioned in a room tells something about its occupant; the contents of a larder reveal desire and restraint, as most surely does the level of liquid in a decanter.

"What are we lookin' for, Miss?"

"I don't know, Billy, but I will when we find it."

They worked together, carefully and systematically searching through drawers, in the wardrobe, and in every nook and cranny of the room. Maisie asked Billy to search carefully under the bed and behind furniture, to pull out cushions from the chair, and to list all items in the medicine cabinet in the white-tiled bathroom. She, in turn, would investigate the contents of the dressing table, wardrobe and writing desk.

Though she was troubled by the design of the furniture, Maisie was even more intrigued by Charlotte's clothing. Instead of suits, dresses and gowns from the houses of Worth, Schiaparelli or Molyneux, as would befit a woman of Charlotte's station, there were just a few plain grey and brown skirts and jackets bought from Debenham & Freebody. A long black gown protected by a sheet of fine muslin was Charlotte's one concession to evening wear, and there was also a black afternoon dress in a style fashionable several years earlier, with a low waistband and below-the-knee hemline. Charlotte's blouses were equally plain and it seemed as if she had bought several of similar design at the same time. Had she taken more colourful and frivolous clothing with her, leaving behind a life that lacked colour in search of something more vibrant?

It was in the writing desk, to the right of the window, that Maisie found an address book. At first, she thought that she would find no other personal papers, no letters, nothing that gave away anything of

Charlotte Waite's character or hinted at the cause of her distress, but as she opened the second drawer, underneath a collection of pens and stationery, Maisie found a prayer book along with a copy of *The Monastic Rule of Saint Benedict*, and several pamphlets on the life of a contemplative. Taking up the books, Maisie walked again to the wardrobe and touched the dark, drab fabrics of the clothes Charlotte had left behind.

"Miss, look what I've found." Billy came towards Maisie with a piece of paper in his hand.

"What is it, Billy?"

"Found it shoved down the side of that chair cushion. Could've been put there deliberately or fallen out of a pocket." Billy handed Maisie the small slip of paper.

"Looks like someone's jotted down train departures. See here –" Maisie pointed to the letters and read: " 'Ch. X to App. Chg Ash'. Then there's a list of times. Hmmm. I'll keep it with these other things for now and we'll look at them later." She folded the paper and placed it inside the prayer book, then turned to Billy.

"Billy, I'd like to spend some time in here alone."

He was now used to Maisie's way of working and showed no surprise at her request. "Right you are, Miss. Shall I interview Mrs Willis?"

"Yes, do that. Here's what we need to know: first, Charlotte – her behaviour over the past two or three months. Was there any change in her manner or appearance? Ask about even the slightest change in habits of dress, diet, recreation." Maisie looked around the room. "She doesn't have her own telephone, so find out who has called; the staff always know when a new name comes along. Speak to Miss Arthur about her allowance; how much, when it's paid and how it's paid. Does she have her own accounts – heaven knows, I hope the poor woman has some privacy – and are statements kept by Miss Arthur?"

Maisie paced back and forth, as Billy licked his pencil, ready to continue taking notes.

"Most important: find out about Charlotte's former fiancé, his name, profession – if he has one – and where he works. I'll need to see him. Speak to the chauffeur, Billy, and find out where she goes, whom she sees. You know the ropes. Oh, and a recent photograph, one that really looks like Charlotte; ask different staff if it's a good resemblance. See what you can get hold of. I want about fifteen minutes here, then I'd like to speak to Charlotte Waite's personal maid. Find out who she is and have her come up to this room."

"Awright, Miss, consider it all done."

"Oh, and Billy, tread very carefully on this one. We don't know where loyalties lie yet, though I must say, I can feel a certain chill when there's any mention of Charlotte."

"You know, I reckon I felt that meself."

"Well, keep it in mind. Leave no stone unturned."

Billy quietly shut the door behind him. Maisie sat in Charlotte's chair and closed her eyes. She took four deep breaths through her nose, as she had been taught so many years ago by Khan, the blind Ceylonese mystic to whom Maurice had introduced her, to learn that seeing is not necessarily a function of the eyes alone. From her days of sitting with Khan, and her instruction in deep meditation, Maisie was attuned to the risks inherent in using such a tool in her work, and knew that even her strong spirit was vulnerable to the auras of the troubled soul. Maisie concentrated on her breathing, stilling both her body and her mind, and she began to feel the strength of emotion that resided in the room. This was Charlotte's refuge while in the house and had become a receptacle for her every thought, feeling, inspiration, reflection and wish. And as she sat in meditation, Maisie felt that Charlotte had been deeply troubled and that her departure had had little to do with a broken engagement. Charlotte Waite had run away, but what was she running from? Or to? What had caused such an intense ache in her heart that even now in her room, Maisie felt Charlotte's lingering sorrow?

Maisie opened her eyes and continued to sit in silence for some moments. Then she began to inspect the books and pamphlets that Charlotte had collected. *The Monastic Rule of Saint Benedict* opened immediately at the place marked with a haphazardly torn envelope fragment. She inspected the scrap of vellum closely, for it seemed heavy, then turned it over. On the reverse side was a thick smudge of red sealing wax, about three-quarters of an inch in diameter, pressed into a rose-shaped seal with a cross in the centre. Maisie squinted to see the words etched into the seal above and below the cross. She shook her head, reached down into her document case and took out what initially looked like a powder compact but that, when opened, revealed a magnifying glass. Maisie leaned closer to the seal and, using the glass, read the words "Camden Abbey." *Camden Abbey*. The name sounded familiar.

There was a knock at the door. Maisie quickly placed the books, pamphlets and other items in her case, ensured they were secure, then rose, breathed deeply again, and opened the door. A young woman of about nineteen bobbed a half-curtsey in front of her. Her black dress was shorter than the one Maisie had worn when she was a servant at the home of Lord and Lady Compton; a small bibbed apron to protect her dress and a delicate white lace band on top of her tightly curled hair completed the maid's uniform.

"Miss Dobbs? I was told you wanted to see me, Ma'am. I'm Perkins, Miss Waite's personal maid."

"Oh, come in, Miss Perkins." Maisie stood to one side to allow the woman to enter the room.

"Would you like to sit down?"

The maid shook her head. "No, Ma'am."

"Well then, let's stand by the window. It's a blustery day now, but I do like to look out upon gardens." Maisie knew that an enclosed area encouraged an enclosed mind. Maurice had taught her: always take the person to be questioned to a place where there's space, or where they can see few boundaries. Space broadens the mind and gives the voice room to be heard.

Maisie sat on the low, wide windowsill, the toe of one shoe touching the floor for balance. Perkins stood at the opposite end of the windowsill, facing Maisie.

"Tell me, Miss Perkins, how long have you worked for Miss Waite?"

"Mr Waite. I work for Mr Waite. Mr Waite pays my wages, so it's him I work for. Looking after Miss Waite is what I do in his house, and I've been her maid for a year."

"I see." Maisie noticed the speed with which she had been corrected, and thought that with just one question, she had discovered where Perkins' loyalties lay.

"And who was Miss Waite's maid before you?"

"Well, there were lots of them, Ma'am. Isabel Wright left last year, then six months before her there was Ethel Day – I remember them because I've worked for Mr Waite since I was twelve, Ma'am."

"And do you like working here, Miss Perkins?"

"I like working for Mr Waite. He's very good to us here, Ma'am."

Maisie nodded, and looked out of the window. She was aware that the maid had leaned forward to see the gardens.

"I'll bet you are too busy to look out of the windows, aren't you?"

"Oh yes, 'specially with the way Miss Waite keeps me running . . . Oh, begging your pardon, Ma'am."

Maisie smiled, encouraging Perkins into her confidence. "Tell me – what is it like working for Miss Waite? And I should add that everything you tell me will remain between the two of us." She leaned forward, and though the maid did not consciously discern any alteration in Maisie's speech, she had allowed her accent to change slightly so that she sounded just a little like the young woman in front of her. "I need to ask questions to get a sense of what has been happening in Miss Waite's life in the past two or three months, and especially in more recent weeks."

The young woman gazed into the distance again, chewed her inner lip, then moved closer to Maisie. She began to speak, at first tentatively, then with greater strength. "To tell you the truth, she's not the easiest person to work for. She'd have me running up and downstairs all day. Wash this, press that, cup of tea, not too hot, not too cold, lemon – oh no, changed my mind, cream instead. First she's going out, then she's staying in; then suddenly, just as I'm laying my head on the pillow, the bell rings, and I have to go down and dress her for a late dinner. No thank-you's or anything, no little something extra left on the sideboard for me, and I'm the one that has to clean up when she has a tantrum!"

"Oh dear."

"It's like being outside, you know: no climate but all weather. Hot and cold she is, never seems to know her own mind. One minute she's all happy, the next, you'd've thought the moon had crashed into the stars and set light to the sky outside her window." Perkins shrugged. "Well, that's what Miss Harding, the cook, says."

"And what about the past few weeks or so? More of the same behaviour?"

Perkins watched the clouds for a moment before answering. "I'd say she was quieter. More . . . more *distant*, I think you'd say. I mean, she always went through times like that. Miss Harding said she ought to be taken to see somebody about her moods. But this was different. It sort of went on and on, and she didn't go out much. Didn't seem to dress up as much either. In fact, she got rid of some lovely clothes, you know, from Paris and Bond Street. Very strange for a lady, to want to walk around in them drab clothes all day, and only have one evening dress, 'specially as she used to go to the collections, you know, and have mannequins walk up and down the room for her to pick and choose what she wanted. You should have seen it in here when the boxes arrived!"

"Have you any idea what might have caused her to withdraw?"

"Not really. None of my business. I was just glad there were no bells ringing at midnight."

"Do you think Mr Waite noticed?"

"Mr Waite works hard. We all know that. Far as I know, they don't see much of each other."

"Are you aware of discord between Miss Waite and her father?"

Perkins looked at her shoes and stepped away from the window just a little. Maisie noticed immediately. *She's closing her mind. Deliberately.*

"Not my business to pry, Ma'am. I just do my job. What they think of each other upstairs isn't any of my concern."

"Hmmm. Yes. Your work is demanding enough, Miss Perkins. No reason for you to keep tabs on people. One more question, though: do you know whom Miss Waite saw, or where she went, in the weeks preceding her departure from this house? Did you notice anything out of the ordinary?"

The maid sighed in a way that indicated that she had said all she wanted to say, but that she would try to answer the question. "She did go up to Town a few times. I'm not sure where she went, but she mainly sees a woman called Lydia Fisher, I think. She lives in Chelsea, somewhere around there. And I reckon she was going somewhere else as well, because she took a pair of walking shoes with her on a couple of occasions. But a lot of her time was spent just sitting up here."

"Doing what?"

"Not sure I know, Miss. Sort of in a daydream, looking out of the window."

"I see." The younger woman began to fidget with her hair, her lace headband, her apron, indicating to Maisie that no more valuable information would be forthcoming. As they moved toward the door, Maisie reached into her bag and took out a calling card.

"Miss Perkins, I am familiar with the workings of a house of this size, and also appreciate that the staff are usually the first to know when something is amiss. Please feel free to telephone me if you think of anything that might be useful. It's clear that you have had some difficulties with Miss Waite, but despite everything, her father – your employer – wants her home."

Read more . . .

Jacqueline Winspear

BIRDS OF A FEATHER

The extraordinary Maisie Dobbs returns in her second case

London, 1929. Joseph Waite is a man who knows what he wants.
With his Havana cigars and Savile Row suits, he is one of Britain's
wealthiest men. And the last thing he needs is a scandal. When his
daughter runs away from home, he is determined to keep the case
away from the public eye. So he turns to a woman renowned for her
discretion and investigative powers – the extraordinary Maisie Dobbs.

Maisie soon discovers that there are reasons why Charlotte might have
left home. Instinctively she feels that Charlotte is safe. Yet, suddenly,
she finds herself confronting a murder scene.

'In Maisie Dobbs, Jacqueline Winspear has given us a real gift. Maisie
Dobbs has not been created – she has been discovered. Such people
are always there amongst us, waiting for somebody like Ms Winspear
to come along and reveal them. And what a revelation it
is!' Alexander McCall Smith

'A terrific mystery . . . Both intriguing and full of suspense, it makes
for an absorbing read' *Observer*

Order your copy now by calling Bookpoint on 01235 827716 or
visit your local bookshop quoting ISBN 978-0-7195-6624-0
www.johnmurray.co.uk